I0739727

6

a novellanthology

Coeur de Lion

First published in Australia in 2009
by coeur de lion publishing
www.coeurdelion.com.au
Please direct all enquiries to the publisher at:
coeurdelion@optusnet.com.au

Cover design by Kirby Jones
Internal design by Keith Stevenson
Printed and bound in Australia by Griffin Press

National Library of Australia Cataloguing-in-Publication entry:

X6 : a novellanthology / Margo Lanagan … [et al.] ;
edited by Keith Stevenson.
1st ed.

ISBN 9780646510354 (pbk.)

Short stories, Australian--21st century--Collections.

Other Authors/Contributors:
Lanagan, Margo.
Stevenson, Keith,

A823.4

contents

Introduction

> [The novella] is one of the richest and most rewarding of literary forms... it allows for more extended development of theme and character than does the short story, without making the elaborate structural demands of the full-length book. Thus it provides an intense, detailed exploration of its subject, providing to some degree both the concentrated focus of the short story and the broad scope of the novel.
>
> Introduction to *Sailing to Byzantium*, Robert Silverberg

I couldn't say it any better than Robert Silverberg. But despite the novella's perfect form, writers often find them hard to sell. Magazines and anthologies generally choose works under 10,000 words to maximise the number of writers and stories they can pack between their covers. It's understandable, but the upshot is that readers have generally missed out on enjoying the relatively fast but immersive read that a novella can provide.

When the X^6 idea came up a couple of years back, we didn't know we were tapping into a zeitgeist. But looking at what's happening in a number of independent presses recently, it seems the speculative fiction novella is finally leaving what Stephen King called its 'ill-defined and disreputable banana republic' far behind. The novella is back.

X^6 grew out of discussions with a number of authors who had good, strong novellas but nowhere to publish them. Some had been working on these ideas for years, honing them with little hope of finding a home. Of course not everyone can write convincingly at novella length. It's relatively easy to create an effective vignette in a short piece but it's quite another thing to sustain a story over 20,000 words plus. Success demands what Jack Dann describes as 'the writing chops', which is why the X^6 authors were all hand-picked and are well known in the Australian speculative fiction scene and, in some cases, well beyond.

We didn't have a theme for our novella anthology nor did we want one. Speculative fiction grants writers permission to create the non-existent in whatever form they wish. Nor did X^6 contain any borders, no rules other than a minimum length. All we asked was that our writers let their imaginations loose. As you might expect, the results are eclectic: the settings here and now, the future, the alternative past, the space in-between space, the furthest corners of the galaxy; the voices strongly diverse. And yet even in such different works, there's a common thread. It's a familiar conversation within the speculative fiction field and one of the genre's chief strengths. It's informed our work for over a century, that discourse on the nature of humanity, how it is tested or altered or co-opted by extraordinary circumstances and events, and what that reveals about us as a species. It's why many of us are drawn to speculative fiction in the first place, and why we keep coming back.

You are about to embark on six journeys into the very heart of what makes us. Prepare to be challenged.

Keith Stevenson

Sea-Hearts

Margo Lanagan

There's never silence, is there? There's always the sea, sucking and sighing. However many doors you like to close between yourself and it, when all other bustlings and conversations cease or pause, always it whispers: Still I am here. Hear me?

'That oul witch Messkeletha is down there again,' said Raditch.

''t's all right. We're plenty,' said Grinny.

'We're plenty and we have business,' James said with some bluster — he was as scared of her as anyone. He shook his empty sack. 'We have been sent by our mams. We're to provide for our famblies.'

'Yer.'

'Hear.'

And down the cliff we went. It was a poisonous day. Every now and again the naughty wind would take a rest from pressing us to the wall and try to pull us off it instead. We would grab together and sit then, making a bigger person's weight that it could not remove. The sea was grey with white bits of temper all over it; the sky sailed full of different clouds, torn into strips, very ragged.

We spilled out onto the sand. There are two ways you can fetch sea-hearts. You can go up the tide-wrack; you will find more there, but they will be harder, drier for lying there, and many of them dead. You can still eat them, but they will take more cooking, and unless you bile them through the night more chewing. They are altogether more difficult.

Those of us whose mams had sighed or dads had smacked their heads for bringing them went down the water. Grinny ran ahead and picked up the first heart, but nobody raced him; we could see them all along the sea-shined sand there, plenty for all our families. They do not keep, once collected. They can lie drying in the wrack for days and still be tolerable eating, but put them in a house and they'll do any number of awful things: collapse in a smell, sprout white fur, explode themselves all over your pantry-shelf. So there is no point grabbing up more than you need.

Along we went, in a bunch because of the witch. She sat halfway along the distance we needed to go, and exactly halfway between tideline and water, as if she meant to catch the lot of us. She had a grand pile of weed that she was knitting up beside her, and another of blanket she had already made, and the knobs of her iron needles jittered and danced as she made more, and the rest of her was immovable as rocks, except her swivelling head, which watched us, watched the sea, swung to face us again.

'Oh,' breathed James. 'Maybe we can come back later.'

'Come now, look at this catch,' I said. 'We will just gather all up and run home and it will be done. Think how pleased your mam will be! Look at this!' I lifted one; it was a doubler, one sea-heart clammed upon another like hedgehogs in the spring.

'She spelled Duster Kimes dotty,' he whimpered.

'Kimeses are all dotty,' I said. How like my dad I sounded, so sensible, knowing everything. 'Duster is just more frightenable than the rest. Come, look.' And I thrust a good big heart into his hands, sharp with barnacles to wake him up.

The ones as still floats is the best, most tender, though the ones that's landed, leaning in the wet with sea-spit still around them, is still good, and so even are those that have sat only a little, up there along the drying rime, beginning to dry themselves.

The others were dancing along the wrack, gathering too much, especially lad Cawdron. He was too little; why hadn't Raditch told him? We would have to tip most that sack out, or he'd stink up half the town with the waste.

'They'll not need to go as far as us,' said Grinny at my elbow.

I dropped a nice wet-heavy heart in my sack. 'We can call them down here, make us up some numbers…'

No more had I said it than Grinny was off up the beach fetching them. He must have been scareder than he looked.

I preoccupied myself catching floating ones without sogging my trouser-edges. Some people eat the best ones raw, particularly mams; they drink up the liquor inside, and if there is more than one mam there they will exclaim how delicious, and if not they will go quiet and stare away from everyone. If it is only dads, they will say to each other, 'I cannot see the traction, myself,' and smack their lips and toss the heartskin in the pot for biling with the rest. If you bile the heart up whole, that clear liquor goes curdish; we were all brung up on that, spooned and spooned into us, and some kids never lose the taste. I quite like it myself, but only when I am ailing. It is bab-food, and a growing lad needs bread and meat, mostly.

Anyway, the wrack-hunters came down and made a big crowd with us. Harper picked up a wet heart and weighed and turned it, and emptied his sack of dry ones to start again. Cawdron watched him, in great doubt now.

'Why'n't you take a few o' these, Cawdron?' I said. ''Stead of all them jaw-breakers. Your mam will think you a champion.'

He stared at the heart glistening by his foot, and then

came alive and upended his sack. Oh, he had some dross in there; they bounced down the shore dry as pompons.

I picked up a few good hearts, if small, to encourage him. 'See how all the shells is closed on it? And the thready weed still has some juice in it, see? Those is the signs, if you want to make mams happy.'

'Do they want small or big?' he says, taking one.

'Depends on her taste. Does she want small and quicker to cook, or fat and full of juice? My mam likes both, so I take a variety.'

And now we were quite close to the witch, in the back of the bunch, which was closer, quieter, and not half so dancey as before, oh no. And she was fixed on us, the face of our night-horrors, white and creased and greedy.

'Move along past,' I muttered. 'Plenty on further.'

'Oh, plenty!' says Messkeletha, making me jump and stiffen. 'Naught want to pause by oul Messkel and be knitted up, eh? Naught want to become piglets in a blanket!' Her eyes bulged in their cavities like glisteny rockpool creatures; I'd have wet myself had I had any in me to wet with.

'We is only c'lecting sea-hearts, Messkeletha,' says Grinny politely, and I was grateful to him for dragging her sights off me.

'Only!' she says, and her voice would tear tinplate. 'Only collecting!'

'That's right, for our mams' dinners.'

She snorted, and matter flew out one of her nostrils and into the blanket. She knitted on savagely, the iron needles noising as would send your boy-sacks up inside you like started mice to their hole. 'That's right. Keep 'em sweet, keep 'em sweet, those pretty mams.'

There was a pause, she sounded so nasty, but Grinny

took his life in his hands and went on. 'That's what we aim to do, ma'am.'

'Don't "ma'am" me, sprogget!'

We all jumped.

'Move along, all ye, and stop your gawking,' spat the witch. 'So I'm ugly and unmanned! So's I make my own living! What's the fascination? Staring there like folk at a hanging. Get out my sight, 'fore I emblanket youse and tangle you up to drown!'

Well, we didn't need her to tell us twice.

'You can never tell which way she'll go,' muttered Grinny.

'You did grand, Grin,' said Raditch. 'I don't know how you found a voice.' And Cawdron, I saw, was making sure to keep big Batton Baker between himself and the old crow.

'Sometimes she's all sly and coaxy? Sometimes she loses her temper like now.'

'Sometimes all she does is sit and cry and not say a word or be frightening at all,' says Raditch. 'Granted, that's when she's had a pot or two.'

We collected most efficiently after that, and when we were done we described a wide circle way round the back of her on our way to the foot of the path. 'From behind she ain't nearly so bad,' I said, for she was a dark lump almost like a third mound of weed, only smoother-edged, and with her needle-knobs bobbing beyond her elbows.

It was wintertime when we ruined everything. It was Cawdron, really, but he would not have said it had we not put a coat on him and got him overexcited.

The weather was all over the place: that was why we were back of the pub. The first snow had fallen, but that was days ago, and it lay only little rotten bits in the shade of walls, nothing useful. We had made a man of what was available in the yard at back, but he was more of a snow-blob, it had gone to such slop — although he had a fine rod on him made of the brace of a broken bar stool Raditch's dad had put back for mending, so you knew at least he was a man-blob.

Anyway, it was beastly cold and the wind had begun to nip and numb us, so we came in the back, and it felt like heaven just the little heat that had leaked out into the hall from the snug, and there was no-one to tell us to hie on out again before our ears turned blue from the language we might hear, so we milled there thawing out and being quiet.

And then Jakes Trumbell found the coatroom door unlocked.

'How is that?' he said, the door a crack open in his hand. He looked up and down it as if it must be broken somewhere.

We were all standing just as shocked. The sea-smell came spilling out the crack, sour and cold.

'Wholeman must have left it,' said Raditch. 'Wholeman must store other stuff in there.'

'What other?' said Baker. 'Would there be food, mebbe? Would they notice a little gone? Crisps or summink?'

At the word 'crisps' the door went wider and our fright dissolved into hope and naughtiness. And as none of us had ever seen in there we went in, several at a time because there was not much room; the coats crowded it up pretty thorough.

'Ain't they strange?' said Angast ahead of me. 'Like people theirselves.'

'They're thick,' said Raditch. 'Have a feel. And

smooth.'

'Just like a mam,' said Jakes from the door, and some giggled and some jumped on him and started quietly fighting.

'I wish I could see,' said Raditch, because it was afternoon and the most we could make out was glooming shapes, and hung up very tall. 'I want to know how the heads go.'

'Bring one out,' suggested Angast, 'to the better light.'

I was glad to go out ahead of him; that room was too much for me, the heavy things pressing at us, hung so closely they pushed out wide at the bottom. And the smell was the smell my mam got when she lay abed unhappy. It was like being suffocated.

We managed to get one of the smaller ones out, and each tried it on awhile, except Cawdron, who would not.

'How do they swim in these things?' said Raditch, lifting his sealie arm.

'It is all bonded to them, proper,' said Angast. 'And the water holds them up, you know.'

Jakes was the only one put the hood over, and we made him stop when he looked out the eyes and lurched at us — he has dark mam-type eyes, and it was too eerie.

'It smells,' he said, taking it off. I sniffed the arm of my woolly to see if the smell had stuck. I was worried Mam would smell it on me later, and go into a mood. It was hard to tell. The whole air, the whole hall there, was greenish with that sad smell.

'Cawn, Kit,' said Jakes to Cawdron, 'let us see you in it; you will make a great little mam, you're so pretty.'

'Not on your nelly,' Cawdron said. 'It'll flatten me, that will.'

'We will hold up the weight of it, from the shoulders, so you can stand. Come on; it will suit you so well.'

And seeing as there was nothing else to do but persuade him, we set to it, and Jakes hauled out another bigger coat and put it on, and urged some more, and before too long we had weakened the poor lad sufficient to drape the thing dark and gleaming and — I cannot describe to you the feeling of putting it on. It was as if you found yourself suddenly swimming right down the bottom of the sea, a weight of black water above you.

The snug door opened and there was a scramble. Somehow the coatroom door got pulled and the coats got hid behind legs and we were all lounging idle and innocent when Batton Baker's dad passed us on his way out the back pisser.

'What you lads brewing?' he says, swaying back when he sees all our eyes.

But none of us need answer, 'cause he opens the yard door then, and the wind hits him to staggering.

'It's perishin' out there, Mister Baker,' says Grinny in just the right voice, dour and respectful.

'I'll freeze my man off, pissing in that.' He squints into the darkening yard. 'I see a chap who's frozen out there already,' he adds jocular. 'A fine upstanding chap, if I'm not mistaken.'

And he laughs and out he goes, leaving the door banging.

'He sees so much of a sleeve-edge, we are beaten,' says Grinny, into the quiet of our relief. 'Beaten and put in our rooms and no suppers for ever — and our mams so disappointed.'

We had time to hide them better before Baker came back. He swayed and looked at us, all in our same places.

'Don't do anything I wouldn't do,' he finally said, and tapped his nose and went off.

And that might have ended it there and then, and all been tip-top and usual.

Except, 'Come, Kit,' whispers Jakes. 'You looked the perfect mam.'

So we lumped the coat on Cawdron again, and Jakes put the other one on, and then they made us laugh, trying to walk about like mams, trying to move their hands all delicate and their heads all thoughtful. Cawdron was the best at it, of course, being so delicate anyway, and with the colouring. Jakes was funnier, though, being more dad-like, all freckles and orange hair and hands like sausage-bunches.

'I of been abed for days, so mis'rable, Missis Cawdron,' he said, and the way he leaned and rolled his eyes, and his voice trying and failing to trill and sing — we were holding each other up, it was so funny.

And then Kit Cawdron joined in and, my, he was good, because his voice was not yet begun to go, and he could really sound the part. 'Because I'm to have another bair-beh,' he says, and we were all just about rolling on the slates there, but as quiet as we could.

'I thought you just had one, missis?' says Jakes, through laughing.

'Oh'm, I did. But 'twas only a girl, so I took her down and drowned her.'

'Grand!' says Jakes. 'Another sea-wife for our lads to net, come sixteen summers.'

'Oh no,' says Cawdron proudly — proudly because he was doing such a fine job of imitating, proudly because he was playing a proud mam. 'I tied the cross on her breast just like you done, so she cannot be caught,' he said, and gave Jakes a stage-wink, whose face was already falling. 'She'll never suffer like we've had to, Missis Trumbell.'

And he was just overacting a suffering mam, staggering, with the back of his hand to his forehead, when he realised how still we all were, how puzzled our faces.

He looked beyond us, and up. His hand snatched to his side and he tripped at his coat-edge and banged up against the wall. His face was not mammish no more, and not at all playful; he was the littlest of us, and the most frightened. He had the most to lose, after all, with Baker's dad there at the back of us, and Mister Grinny too, come soundless from the snug to catch us at whatever.

We all of us shrank together and back, all around Cawdron and Jakes against the wall there, staring at those men. They were red already in their natural colouring, but the drinking had enflamed them, and now the rage tided up across their faces and they scarcely looked human. Baker's dad — jolly Mister Baker, who would toss a flour-roll out his shop door at a quiet time, to any boy, and mustle your hair as soon as look at you — honest, I thought his head were going to burst, it swelled and trembled so, and stared.

'What did you say, lad?' he hissed into the utter silence. Someone gave a little peeping fart at the sound of such rage, and nobody even snickered, we were all so close to shitting ourselves, every lad of us.

Cawdron didn't whimper or sniff; I could hear behind me how he was applied, how glued, to the wall, trying to melt away into it.

I expected Baker to wade in. Everyone expected it. I saw Grinny's dad expect it, and decide it must not happen, and put a hand on Baker's arm.

'Take that off, lad,' he said to Kit Cawdron, gentle as gentle.

The crowd of us loosened, but only a little, at the immediate danger's easing. 'Here,' Raditch muttered, helping Cawdron behind. Silence except for the fumbling, Cawdron's unsteady breathing, the clop and slide of the coat.

'Come,' said Mister Grinny, holding out his hand. I could not tell what he might be thinking — how does anyone else's dad think, and what might he want? — but he was not so red now and I was relieved. I thought, Good, they'll not thrash Cawdron then. It is too bad even for that. 'Hang them coats up, lads,' he says, and he stands there, one freckly hand ensausaging Kit's little white slip of a paw, and the other on Baker's sleeve who was steaming and readying to roar and punch something, as we hauled the flemming things into the coatroom and managed to re-hang them. Everybody was shaking like the leaves of the poplars on Watch-Out Hill; everyone was clumsy and needed each other's help.

When it was done and the door closed, whisper-quiet, Mister Grinny was still there holding Cawdron, but Baker was gone, the snug door slamming and beyond it his hard voice spreading a silence through the snug.

'You'll not touch them things again, all right?' says Mister Grinny, still gently.

'No, sir.'

'No, Mister Grinny.'

'We won't. Promise.'

'Even if you find it unlocked,' he says. 'Even if the door is swinging wide open, you will not go in. You will not lay a finger on your mams' coats.'

'Not a finger, sir.' We all shook our heads.

'Shan,' he says to his boy, 'you go on home to your mam. All you boys, go on home. Look to your mams and see if they need aught. Bring in some coal. Make them a tea. Rub their poor feet. Or just sit and talk to them the way they like, about nice things, the spring, mebbe, or the fishing. Go home and do something nice for your mams, each lad of you, because things will go not-so-nice for them for a while. And Shan? On your way? Fetch up Jod Cawdron. The lad should have his father by him, for this.'

Out into the cold street we scattered.

'What will they do to Kit?' said Raditch shiveringly to me as we ran. 'They will kill him!'

'They will kill his mam,' I said. 'They will kill all the mams — all those who's had girl-babies, anyhow.'

'Oh gawd, you think?'

'Not kill,' I said. 'But I don't know what they will do to them.'

'Still, I would not be Kit, for all the tea in China.'

'I would not be Jakes,' I said. 'It is all his fault and he will feel it. I know I will knuckle him, for one.'

'I don't know,' said Raditch. 'I don't think a knuckling is going to set this right.'

'No,' I said over my shoulder, leaving him on his house-step, 'but I must hurt something.'

And I ran on home.

For a while Mam paced back and forth, muttering, the shaggy blanket dragging out behind her like a king's cloak. From one window, past the door, to the other window, and muttering as I say, no words that I could hear.

My dad had gone, the door banged behind him, and the bang seeming still to ring on and on throughout our house. All the swish and scratch of her blanket could not still it, all her hissing whispering, or the pad of her foot soles on the grey boards.

Then she paused by one of the windows, fenced off from me by the chair backs, a seaweedy hummock of her shoulders and then her head, against the glary cloudlight, her hair pushed and pulled a little, a few strands waving in the wind of her warmth. She stood there applying herself to the view and silent, and I stood at the kitchen door silent, listening to the distress.

I went to her, stood at the sill as if I were interested, innocently interested, also in the view. The same lanes slanted away: the one up, the one down. The same front steps shone whitewashed like lamps up and down the lane. The same tedious cat sat in Sacks's window, now blinking out at us, now dozing again. And through the gaps and over some of the roofs, the sea rode charcoal to the horizon, flat-coloured as a piece of slate, with neither sail nor dragon nor dinghy to relieve the emptiness.

She was turning and turning her silver wedding ring, which she did when she was upset sometimes, to the point of reddening the spare flesh around it. She pressed and turned, as if to work free the stuck lid of a jar.

I laid my hands on hers, paler than hers. She looked down from the view.

'What is it, Daniel?'

I took her hands one from the other. I turned to the window again, and draped the ring hand over my shoulder, down to my chest, and I held it and took from her the task of turning the warm silver, moving it much more gently upon her finger than she had been doing. It was loose; let it go and it would slide down to the first joint. If you held it higher and quite careful it need not touch her finger-skin at all. But I did not play so with it, only continued the turning of it for her.

She laughed very softly, deep in her throat. 'Sweetest

boy,' she said. She kissed the top of my head and then laid her other hand there. And so we stood, she in her cloak blanket and me wearing her like a cloak, turning the ring on her finger while outside the steps glowed and the cat dozed and the sea sat flat behind it all, nothing of anything changing.

My mam had never had daughters — only me, and a couple of those seal-things that did not live more than a few minutes outside of her. So after that first unpleasantness — which was all about did she know, and why had she not said, and how could they do this to the men who loved them so — our peaceful life went on. But Lonna Trumbell, across the lane, she had drowned six — 'Daughters-in-law for all of ye,' Marcus Trumbell had boasted up at Wholeman's. Trumbell woke us up every night now, rolling down the hill when Wholeman turned him out, bellowing foulness. He would force into his house, and sometimes in his rage and hurry to hit her he would forget closing the door, and the whole dire scene would pour straight into our woken ears. Sometimes it was surprising when morning came up and the house there looked quite the same as always, after the smashings and roarings that had come from it in the night.

I would get up and go to my dad in the front room, at the moonsilver lace at the window, his face and front patterned with its flowers. We would stand and flinch there together awhile — we had had the conversation about how Dad could do nothing, having lost no daughters himself. I have lost as many wives for my boy as has anyone, he had said to them, but still he had not the same rights to misery. He would stand there, his great hand on my shoulder and arm, his thumb at my hair and ear, and I would hold to his leg as to a big warm tree, while Trumbell's shouts, and the wife's, and sometimes Jakes's and Kerry's as well, made a kind of awful weather over there, that might yet blow across the lane, and break something of ours.

When Dad patted and sent me off I would go in to Mam, curled tight as a hedgehog in their bed, sometimes sea-blanketed and sometimes wool. There! If you want to be held tight, clamber up next to your sea-mam when she is alarmed; she will pull you into the knot of herself where nothing can get at you. Her breath will change from uneven and muttering to slow, steady, sea-like as your presence consoles her, and behind the rushing of it and the beat-beat of her pulse's calming, Trumbell's rage is nothing, Trumbell's blows, Jakes's pleas; it is all happening in another house, another world, as separate from us as a birds' duel among the clouds, as fish-monsters' battling away down in the sea.

They spoiled their wives' faces, some of them. Some men made the women stay home and not show anyone, until they were not so swollen; others took them out on their arms, and very gentlemanly escorted them about the streets and in the lanes around. If you came upon the men they would greet you gruesome heartily, and say how they and their lady-wife were out for a stroll and weren't it lovely weather?

And you would not be able to not glance just a little at the wife. You needed to know — although what good did it do, to know a tooth was gone, to marvel how tight and shiny and bright purple eye-skin could swell up?

And then you were caught; somehow you felt again as if you were abandoning the woman to her bully man by walking on. But my, the most thing you wanted to do was run from this awful game, from the two faces, one so wrong-coloured and -shaped, the other a skin of mawkish friendliness over a red-biling rage.

They used all to go down together, the mams, and wash their blankets in the sea. They would sit about on the rocks at the start of the south mole, with their feet hooked in the seaweed, and the water would rush up, and fizz and shush in the blankets, and rush away again. It seemed to soothe them, and we liked to be with them then, clambering about at our own play among them while they joked to one another. 'I've a mind to let it go,' Grinny's mam might say, 'the way he's been treating me. I've a mind to lift my feet and let it float away, free as a summer cloud.' Or my own mam: 'Not many sea-hearts down the washing-beach this year, anyone find? Usually there is a good lot coming up by now.' They sat so solid there, and watched the crowding sea so attentive, you could imagine them not getting up from there ever, sitting like sea-rocks all night even, searching the black waves as the water and knitted weed bobbed and sucked around them.

Messkeletha would walk along the mole above; the mams always ignored her. She would climb down now and again muttering, and wade out to one woman's blanket and another's. From her belt-string she took a length of weed for mending, and worked there scowling a while. Then she knotted and bit off the shining weed, and waded back, climbed back, and paced and stared again above.

When the washing was done and the mending, she would loose one of her two-finger whistles up to Wholeman's Inn — which would set us boys to practising our own whistles, none of us achieving anything like the witch's piercingness except sometimes by luck. Dads would file out of Wholeman's — not all the dads, maybe six or seven — and gather along the rail there and watch while the mams dragged their blankets up, and spread them on the mole-top, some of them, or carried the great wet bundles in their arms or on their heads, up to their own clotheslines to dry.

'Bye, Sal, then.'

'Bye, Peachy. Don't you take no nonsense now.'

That was how it was done, before Titch Cawdron let slip. Now Messkeletha came to your door and took out your mam individual — which was terrifying, that she knew where you lived and might come back of a night and snatch you out through your dreams. It was horrible; everyone seemed blamed.

Some mams went tall and proud ahead of her, pretending their weed was not such a burden; others, particularly ones whose dads had beaten them, walked as if smacked low, or expecting to be, bobbed along, gathering up corners and turning their faces from all the windows as they went.

'My dad watches them go by,' I heard Grinny say to Asham. 'Every one, and he's not a good word to say of any of them. My mam will be scrubbing and scrubbing over the sound of him, but he'll just talk louder — the sly look of that one, the three girls that one stole away, how Martyr walloped the smile off that one's face. It's shocking, and he will not let me go, not out into the yard, even. He makes me stay and listen.'

We were none of us let out at that time, even the sons of the mam called to washing. We were a distraction, the town said, and it would grow from there: a lad would have his friend, and then his friend's friend would tag along, and before you knew it the lot of them would all be down there, arrayed on rocks and scheming again.

We lived high enough in the town that not many women were brought by. But when they were, Mam or Dad would hurry to close the door, and open the lace so as to show no-one was looking from behind it, and find works to do in yard and scullery, and ways for me to help them. When the knock came for my mam, Dad would always have some job ready. 'Here, take the other end of this, Dan'l; save your old man's back.' Or, 'Is that ash-bin still out the back lane, I'm wondering?' So that I should never see her go, never see Messkeletha take her. Or maybe that he shouldn't see. Perhaps he was as frightened of the oul witch as I was.

They used — and it seemed so foolish to me now, but it wasn't then, in those accepting days when we all ran about among our mams' skirts — they used to be allowed to gather, in this house and that, the mams and children, by themselves without men or Messkeletha. At first there would be talk and tea and sitting upright and eyes everywhere. They would talk of their men and their men's tempers; they would talk of us, and how we were coming on, how we ate and grew.

Then one of them would sigh and cross from table to armchair, or settee or fireside stool. All their movements would suddenly change, slowing and swaying, and their voices would lower from so bright and brittle, and someone might laugh low, too. As we ran in and out we would see more of them gather at the seated one, leaning to her or pulling her to lean on them. Hairs would be unpinned and fall, and combs brought out and combing begin, and there is nothing happier than the sight of a mam's face when her hair is being combed. When we were littler we would run in from our play and lie among them, patted and tutted over and our own hairs combed and compared, the differences in wave and redness. Sometimes we were allowed the combing, but our arms were never long enough to do it as well as they did for each other, long slow silky sweeps from scalp to tips, the combed mam dreamy, the comber thoughtful above.

But of course that came to an end once the daughter-matter were out. Mam combed her own hair now, and if Dad or I saw her at it we would take it on too, and it was always a pleasant time, but it was not the same, though I didn't like to say, as a room full of warm mams murmurous by the fire, and several hairs to plait and play with as you would, and any number of bosoms to lay your head upon and doze away an afternoon.

Nobody expected Aggie Bannister, after all her time hid away from us, so no-one stopped her. They were too astounded seeing this white creature in midst of the clouds and grey, among coats and wool hats and clumpy boots this naked thing, all that bared skin in the cold air, the wobbling nipple-eyes mad below her determined face, and then the wobbling bottom behind, the feet that we remembered from summer, toenails and bunions and cracked heels freed of the shoes that so pained them, the slap of cobbles against foot soles. Wrong, so wrong, for this season, for this place.

Down she ran, Aran's mam, through the dark grey town like a running flare, through the streets like an animal gone wild, like someone's stock got out and not knowing about towns and hard surfaces and cold. Or about real people, and their eyes and their laughter and their cruel words. Oh, gracious who was that! Aggie Bannister! It's Aggie! Her name, which was not her name at all but

Bannister's chosen name for her, his own name with a girl's name that he liked, tied on before like the front end of a horse costume — her name got passed all down the streets and back over shoulders into the houses, and from being on so many lips it became soiled so badly that the woman might never be able to lift her head in Potshead streets again, nor Bannister pass by without laughter breaking out behind him, nor Aran nor Timmy nor Cornelius neither.

It was clear where she was headed, and while she was not thinking straight, we were. Or at least, she was after a different aim: to reach the sea, whereas we only needed the view of it, so we all headed down Totting Lane and Fishhead Lane straight down, while she ran the full ramp length of the main street and across to the mole and then she clambered, all white bottom and — you could see every fold of her if your eyes were good as mine, while the young men whooped and whistled and the women and the married men turned their faces away behind their hands, and glanced again and groaned and laughed. She clambered, slipped, clambered down and then turned and, with one bloodied knee ran limping, ran clumsy as if she were transforming back right there, down the pebbly grey sand towards the water.

And then she was in it, a naked back and bottom in the middle of a white fan of water. And then the green-white froth passed over her and her hair wasn't wild any more but pasted flat to her head. Thank goodness! I thought. The seals will come and fetch her and she never will have to flounder ashore and face our kindness and our ridicule. And she was embracing the waves, and swimming there so strongly, you could tell they were her home; she was not clumsy there.

'She want to stay within the lee of the mole,' said

Prentice Meehan above me. 'It's dirty farther out.'

A howl of the wind turned to the howl of a man, the howl of Bannister running out the house ends. 'Aggie!'

'Look at him! He has her coat!' Which made him look somewhat octopus-ish, all its arms and flaps a-flapping.

'Don't you expect me to do that for you,' muttered Arthur Sack to his missus. He was standing his hand locked around hers, glaring at her, while she gazed now towards lumbering woeful Bannister, now out to the water, where Aggie was a dot of black, a momentary shining white haunch, a white foot splashing, and now hidden behind the green glass upshelving of a wave.

Along the mole ran Bannister. All our men is taciturn, when not angry; I cannot describe to you the uncomfortableness of seeing him so come out of himself, his mouth wide in his face like a bawling bab's, his arms reaching. His bellows were torn up by the wind and waves and thrown at us in shreds, some strange animal's cry, not a man's, not a grown man's.

Right out to the end he got, and still he yearned farther. He made to clamber down the end point.

'Don't be daft, man!' said some man.

'He will be swept away!' a woman said dreamily.

But the sea jumped up and smacked the mole-end, a great fanfare of spray, and Bannister staggered back in it, soaked with it. And there he stood a moment, clutching her coat and staring out to where she came and went, came and went, bobbing and struggling now among the wilder, dirtier waves.

A spot of sun came then, poked a hole in the clouds and cut a bar through the spume and lighted on them both as he flung the coat, as it flew — not far, it was so heavy — as it lumped out into the air and splatted on the water and was gone there, then was there again, struggling, just as she was, to stay above water.

And the laugh-and-chattering here against the rail stopped, because coat and Aggie were so far apart, and neither of them were swimming towards the other. We saw the coat edge at the surface, the shadow of the coat within a big sunlit wave; we saw her face, her mouth, her arm and breast, and a different wave crash down, folding her down into the sea. Bannister knew not to dive in; even mad with grief he knew. He stood instead a little way down from the mole-top, stood with legs bent and red hands claws upon his knees, bellowing out to Aggie not to die.

She did not obey him. She lay slumped in the water when next we saw her, only her back, and then the sun went away and the sea brought her in behind the mole again. Through the grey rain-beginning, through the green-grey waters, the rows and curling rows of them, up and down it brought her slow — mams ushered some of the littler boys away. It deposited her not three yards from where it had thrown up the empty coat, a welter of black flesh and stirred pebbles, onto Potshead beach.

'It is all our faults,' shivered little Thomas Davven, left behind with me on the rail while the men ran, while the woman pushed children away, while here came Messkeletha with one of her blankets for a shroud. 'If we had not faddle-arsed around in that coat room…'

'It is all their faults,' I said and savagely. The witch cast me a look in passing, and I waited till she had gone, one blanket-corner dragging as she went. 'Stealing our mams out of the sea in the first place,' I hissed to Thomas.

'Oh, you cannot blame them that.' He clutched himself and bowed and bent in the cold wind, without the shelter of the crowd any more. 'You had the choice between women like that raddle-witch and our beautiful mams, which would you choose?'

He had me. That was no fair choice, that was. 'Still,' I said through my teeth, clamping them tight against their chattering. 'Still, they never ought to done it. They dint belong here. They belonged under the waves.'

Down there, we could see it all well; we were like birds stopped above them in the wind. Only Aggie Bannister was normal length, white and awash until they pulled her by wrists and ankles up out of the shadows; the rest of them were all cap-tops and coat-shoulders, with boot toes popping out, popping away again. And Messkeletha hurried up, a snarl of red-streaked white hair above a trailing clump of knitted seaweed, and her feet were bare and blue, the toenails long as the teeth of some old neglected dog.

I went home to Mam. I did not care if she talked or wept or slept or hid from me under her seaweed; I wanted only to be in the room with her, to see the mound of her and know she was not drowned and naked before the Potshead populace.

I sat by the window, and the sun now and again broke through and lit the sea silver, and lit the ceiling with silver reflections, and the wind outside was one breath and the sea, rushing, pausing, falling, was another, and Mam's was another — though mostly I could only see it in her rise and fall, not hear it among all the others. And then there was my own breathing, which at first when I sat was all raggy and half into speech, and after a while was soothed, by Mam's ongoingness, by the wind's being outside and by the distance of the dirty sea and of the people round Aggie Bannister, to something that fit, that fell into peaceful pace, with all the other beings'. The furniture sat plain and hard in its place; the rug that I remembered her making — her twisting fingers with her singing face above — lay finished and in place by the bed, and her hair was a black salty tangle on the pillow, beyond the table where lay her shells, and her stones that meant something, and her sea-glass, red and blue and powdery white, smoothed to harmlessness, beaten to something beautiful by the sea, taken from the sea before it were quite beaten away into nothing but more sand.

I was not waiting for anything. I had forgot I was there; I had forgot, indeed, who I was. Being with Mam often made me this way — how much did it matter, after all, that I was crossed of land-man and sea-woman? Time could pass unwatched; it need not lead away from good times so that I yearned back, or push me towards a future that I dreaded. I could just lounge and breathe like this, and the silver lights of water and winter could move above me.

There is labour in getting a boat through the sea. Either you pull it with oars, digging and hauling the water back, or you dance and scrabble with sails and sheets, begging the wind to cooperate with your work. Or some men engage with grease and metal, propellers, stinking fuel, and carve up the sea behind them with an engine.

Looking from that labour to the seals, you can tell they are magical. All they have is those slender hands, those fine feet like a limp plant hanging off their back end, like a tail. I have watched men struggle with the washed-up body of one of those, reduced to cutting it to pieces and moving it with hooks. They are such a stubborn, slippery weight. And yet they fly under water, and spin and sport and somersault, all the while we chug and beat and swear above.

First the mainland was a black fingernail's-edge between the pale sea and the pale sky. I pulled Dad's sleeve as he talked to Mr Fisher, who was coming over to buy some tins and vegetables for the store.

'There, yes,' Dad said to me, and gazed at it a little, first to satisfy me and then because some thought had caught him about it.

'Don't you be fooled, young Dan'l,' Fisher said around Dad's front. 'It may look like the land of promise, but Killy's best, home is best.'

Dad squeezed my shoulder, invisibly to Fisher. I didn't know whether he meant me to listen carefully to Fisher or ignore him and flee to mainland as soon as I ever could. Mam had combed my hair — I had watched in the mirror — so that it was two slick curves either side of a raw white parting. My whole head still felt scraped and chilled.

Slowly the land grew; slowly it rose and unrolled out of the horizon, two main rounded hills with others either side like attendants. The sea slopped and danced below us. The sky blued as the sun got up higher, and we began to see shapes on the land, forested parts and fielded, and the glint of roofs and roads, and the black cliffs with the dazzling break between them, where we would chug in and find safe harbour.

'We will catch the bus in to Knocknee,' said Dad. 'It goes right from the pier.'

'So we'll not see this town, so much?' I said, disappointed because it seemed so rich, with its warehouses along the front like a wall, with its several steeples, with its shining vehicles gliding along by the water.

'Can you not let the lad at the fleshpots of Cordlin

Harbour, Mallet?' laughed Fisher. 'Even to the 'stent of a raspberry lollipop at Mrs Hedly's shop?'

'We've business.' My dad shook his head and smiled. 'Knocknee Market will have to be excitement enough for the boy.'

I did not see how anything could be more exciting than motoring in between the heads. Cordlin Harbour spread and spread out, serene and glossy after the tumbled sea, after the beating of the waves at the cliffs' feet. Rank after rank of boats was moored here, alongside the piers and also punctuating the more open water, each little pleasure motor, each ketch and trawler, kissing its morning reflection. Cordlin Town lay as if spilled in the valley, thickening towards us in the bottom, thinning away to skerricks, a cottage here, a barn there, higher up the hills like drops of milk around porridge in a bowl. Windows winked at us and the great granaries and woolstores stood all barred windows and red-and-white brickwork, and I saw for the first time the humbleness of my home island, in contrast to this centre of wealth and commerce.

'There's our bus,' said Dad, and I noticed the marvellous thing, painted and polished, a crest on the side of it and a numberplate behind, and with people, Cordlin people, people who did this every day, already in it waiting, for our boat to come alongside, for Dad and me to walk up the gangplank with the other islanders, for us to climb on to the little glinting box of the bus, and pay our fares, and sit.

I held fast to Dad's hand. Mr Fisher clapped my shoulder, and the surprise of the blow made my heart jump hard in my chest and ran across my scalp like a wind gust through damp grass.

The trip to Knocknee was all events, one piled on the

next so that my telling of them, which at first I tried to rehearse to Mam in my head, fast became garbled and then fell to silence. I hung on to the windowsill, grateful that Dad looked over me, and would see the important things, would collect any details that I might miss. Presently the overwhelming town with its too many faces, its too many curtains and gates and window boxes, sank away and we were in fields, flying among fields on the back of our grinding, squashy-wheeled monster, and this I could bear more easily, fields being more like the sea in their emptiness, in their roundness and billowyness, Cordlin fields being very much like Killy fields, such as those were.

I turned to Dad: 'Such a noisy way to get about.' I thought the engine must be right below our seat, it juddered at our bums so.

'It is indeed,' he said. 'Noisier than a boat, and certainly noisier than a man's own legs. But fast,' he added. 'And fast is what we're wanting, to reach inland and back in a day.'

And to see numerous people, not all of them friendly, and to ask them questions that made their eyes slide aside, made them shake their heads and turn away. I ran about after my striding dad, and the running, and the ways of people, eventually tired me. He put me on a sunny bench in the market square and bid me wait while he searched on.

Before long someone else was put there, at the other end of the bench, someone in skirts, with hair. I had got my breath by then, and when we had caught each other glancing several times, 'I know what you are,' I said to her.

She stopped swinging her legs. She looked at me and narrowed her eyes, which were pale like a dad's, looking blue in this light but possibly green, possibly grey. 'Well, what?'

'You are a girl-child,' I said.

She gave a small hiccup of a laugh. 'No joking!' she said. 'Good thing that you told me.' And she swung her legs some more and looked about at the legs and bums and baskets and bustle.

'You are, aren't you,' I said.

She looked me up and down. Her breath was white on the cold air. 'Are you touched, or what?'

'I ant never seen one before,' I said.

She snorted.

'It's true,' I said. 'We don't have them on Killy.'

Her face got more startled, and prettier. 'You're from Killy Isle?'

'I am,' I said. 'My dad brang me over this morning.'

'For the first-ever time?' Now I was interesting, and she seemed to have stopped disliking me, which was good.

'First ever,' I said.

'You been on that one island all your life?'

'I've been to St Mark's, and Ogben also. And on lots of sea.'

'I never seen the sea yet,' she said. 'My mam and dad won't take me. Say it sends men potty. Is your dad potty?'

'I don't know,' I said, not sure what she meant, and not sure about Dad. None of these legs were recognisable as his, none of these hats, fuzzy-outlined against the sunshine.

'Are you potty?' said the girl. What a lot of hair she had, and it was not straight and silky like a mam's. It looked as if, you take that band off, undo that ribbon, loose it from those plaits, it would stand straight out from her head, or possibly get up and walk right off her, or flame up and away, burn away in the sunlight, from the heat in its wires, from the combination of so many hot red strands together.

'I'm not potty.' I knew that much.

She laughed at me, but not all unkindly. 'You might be anything,' she said, 'you look so strange, with your great eyes.'

I turned my face from her, embarrassed, and again she laughed. These girl-children were certainly unsettling.

'What brings you, then?' she said as if she had a perfect right to know. 'You and your dad, to Knocknee?'

'I ant sure,' I said. 'He has business here, he said.' Again I searched the crowd, for I rather wished he would burst out now, perhaps with something for me to eat, some mainland fancy.

'Cloth, mebbe?'

'I don't think so. He said he had to talk to someone.'

'Hmm,' she said considering. 'Private, like, then, if he put you here. Was it a woman?'

'I think so,' I said, knowing for certain so, but not liking, somehow, to confirm what this girl might be thinking.

'Don't you have womens there, on Killy? Is it all potty boys and men?'

'We have women,' I said, stung. 'We have very beautiful women, all our mams.'

She narrowed her eyes at me again, and breathed more breath-smoke. 'Ye-es,' she said and frowned. 'That is your specialty out there, is it?'

'What?'

'I'm trying to remember. I've heard mams talking. There's something about those Killy women, isn't there?'

'Maybe,' I said. 'But they're our mams, so don't you say anything that might get you popped on the snout.'

'Well, they must be unusual, to've got an unusual like you,' she said commonsensically, looking me up and down again.

I turned back to the crowd, to the sun, not knowing what to say to that. They're usual for our town, I wanted to assert. Perfectly usual. But I could not say it. She would not find that convincing, and I did not want to feel more foreign than she had already made me.

We had come to bring home a girl, but not the girl from the market. This other girl we fetched from a smelly part of the town; there was some kind of offal piled and straggling in the drain outside her family's house.

I thought her mam was her grandma, she had so few teeth and was so weathered. All the time they talked the woman watched my dad as if he might snap at and bite her, as if he were there to trick her and she ought to be very careful.

The girl herself was orange-haired like all of them, but not so clean as the market girl, and she had something of the twitchiness of the mam about her, and something a little sneaky, I thought. She sat there all pursed lips, her glance flicking from Dad to the mam to Dad, listening close and clearly understanding everything they exchanged, although to my ears it made no more sense than murmurings in someone's sleep.

They were talking about money; the mam wanted some, and Dad was saying how he oughtn't to have to pay, giving board and accommodations to this girl as he would. He seemed to be buying her, buying something she could do. Truth tell, she didn't look capable of a lot, so skinny and grey-fleshed. Looked more like the sort to skip quick-smart out of any job going.

Dad sighed. 'You have eleven of her, missis. Ain't you glad to get the burden of even the one of them off your shoulder?'

'This one eats mouse-rations,' snapped the mam. 'Why don't you take one of the big girls, my Gert or my Lowie, great heffers that they are?'

'You know why, Mrs Callisher. This is the one with the touch on her. As can be taught up useful by our Messkeletha.' Ah, that was what he wanted. For when the oul witch died, of her awful coughing, or perhaps just the strength of her own evil.

'Useful for what? Useful for living on Killy, is what. Useful for catching and keeping mermaids. And stuck in that God-hole for the rest of her life, the amount she'll be useful elsewhere.' She slid a glance at me. 'I don't want grandsons with tails,' she said. 'Granddaughters with fins.'

'We will pay her a yearly journey here, how about that? Boat and carriage to visit you every spring.'

The mam sucked at the inside of her discontented face. 'And no-one to marry.'

'She might well meet a man here, one of her visits. I don't know, missis. These terms is reasonable. I'm sure Trudle would be very content, a room of her own built special onto the oul-woman's, and a livelihood.'

The girl Trudle gave a kind of a whinny, and were no prettier for laughing. If anything she looked more weaselish or rattish, creased up like that.

Her mam looked at her and shook her head. 'She'd be happy on a dungheap, that one. She's touched more ways than the one.'

'Ask Fan Dowser how touched I am,' said Trudle in a rasping voice.

Swiftly the mam stepped over and smacked Trudle's head. The girl rubbed the spot and glared up at her through her eyebrows.

'Very well, take her,' said the mam with great carelessness. 'Don't come blubbing back to me, though, what she gets up to with your pretty lads.' She spared me something of a sneer, but there was fear in it, too. 'As I say, there's not a lot up her top. Why a person cannot have magic and intelligence I do not know.'

'"Tis straightforward enough work,' said Dad.

'Hmph. Nothing of this nature is straight. Go fetch your box, girl.'

I did not like travelling with this girl. We were an odd little couple, her and me, her in some ancient hand-me-down ruffles and a big dark-blue bonnet, her weaselly face in the middle looking everywhere. She walked in a funny rocking way, her legs wide as if she had discovered herself wet. People glanced at us going by, and glanced away when they saw me watching. My dad preceded us, Trudle's box on his shoulder, her best dress pillowing up at the top. He was walking quite fast, making Trudle rocky-rock along ridiculous. It was a nightmare, this big town and the hurrying, people's eyes and opinions peppering us as we walked, and the sun lost behind the flare-edged house rows. Trudle did not speak to me nor I to her; we only struggled along separate and together, both after Dad.

Then the crowds cleared, and the bus was there waiting for us alongside its shelter. The door was just hissing shut, but my dad hoyed and waved and ran, and it opened for us again.

Trudle got up first very bustling. She chose a seat halfway down and sat very straight and pleased there, sparing Dad a glare when he made to sit by her, so that he came with me to the seat behind her instead.

'That was close,' he said as the bus threw him back into his seat. 'Any more bargaining with that mam and we'd have been stuck here the night.'

I could smell Trudle Callisher; I could smell the oldness of her clothes, and the fact that she had not bathed in a while.

'I seen you got talking to a maid?' says my dad politely when we had got our breaths.

I nodded, watching the last of Knocknee town whirl by: a cottage with a yard full of rubbish, a dog with a plumy tail, water shining in bootprinted mud.

'What was that like?' he said.

I shrugged — it had not been like anything, and I did not know what to think of it, what to say.

'Did you like her?'

I slid my bottom back, to sit straighter in the seat. Cows flew by, some of them watching us with their great heads raised. 'She was fine, I suppose.' Did I have the right to like or dislike such a stranger? Today I was just a big empty trawler-hold, with the world's fish and sea-worms tumbling into me. 'We only talked a little while.'

There's something about those Killy women, isn't there? I saw the girl's narrow eyes, her hair-wires around her head as she asked. Those Killy women. I wished I was among those Killy women suddenly, sharply; I was sick of this adventure. I wished I was tiny again, and curled in Mam's lap with her singing buzzing and burring around me in the quiet room, Dad gone to fish or to Wholeman's. Or among the mams on their sea-washed stones, their blankets trailing and pulling at their legs as they called to each other, as they laughed, grown-up jokes that we didn't need to understand, and me with my fellows at play.

Trudle watched everything out the window across the mainland countryside. She boarded the boat ahead of us as if she owned it, and kept similar straightness and cheer all across the Bite.

When we reached Killy my dad sent me up home, and I did not see what happened then and nor did I mind. I went home with a lemon for my mam, given me by Mr Fisher. I dug my fingernail in the rind a little and sniffed lemon all the way up the town, to clear the Trudle-smell out of my head.

From what I gathered, she were given over to Messkeletha just as promised and no fussing. And after that the two of them went about a pair, like a flour-caddy and a tea. They both wore witch-dresses, tight to their tops to the waist, then springing out like flower-bells, nearly to the ground. Cages and flowers, like all those women at Knocknee and at Cordlin Harbourtown wore, so presenting of themselves, so insisting on your looking.

The one's hair was dirty orange in the sunlight, the other's mostly frost, only a few reddish stains in it to hint what it once was. And Messkeletha's was thin in places; as Trudle stayed longer, she grew her hair, as if to make the point that she alone had such colour, and could bear it about in such quantity.

Messkeletha never was polite, never greeted you even did she meet your eye, and this one learned the same ways quite fast, or at least towards mams and children. For men she would raise what might be called a smile if it were not so sly and ambiguous. 'Mister Paige,' she would say, but it would come out Pay-eesh, too lingering, and Paige would seem to dodge and weave without taking a step in any direction, would seem to bow and tug a forelock without taking his hands from his pockets. In all her interactions with our men, Trudle got herself this chopped-about reaction, and enjoyed herself with the getting, anyone could see.

But, as I say, she followed her mistress about the town and there was something powerful in there being the two of them, the small caddy tripping after the big one, taking on and giving new notes to the oul-witch's herbaceous, privy-aceous smell. Two bells on feet, they were, ringing unpleasant thoughts out the men's memories. Two ragged flower shadows, they crept along the sky on Watch-Out Hill. Messkeletha would stand peering to sea and town on the south mole while Trudle bent bum-up collecting fish-scales for their magics. Or the two of them would be horrors together on Marksman Road, glowering ahead, pretending not to see us boys as we hugged the hedge opposite, greeting them feebly.

You stand there against the boat rail with your small warmth hugged to you inside the stiff coat. The seals break out of the endlessness of the sea; they make all that space less anguishing, all that drowned world beneath. Their round head-tops, their whiskery-ness, the humdrummery of their rough breath, the shiver of ripples around the landforms of their heads, their seeming to smile — you cannot help but love them.

And the eyes, oh the eyes. The eyes are the magic of them, seals and mams: deep as night but starless, starless and kind — or at least not calculating the way pale eyes are. They are dark and glossy as any sea-washed stone, still magic while wetted, still live.

Water flowing over a rock, over a seal, curves and curls to the rock's shape — or the seal's — clinging. The skirts around mams' thighs are like that, the curves of them, the cloth. Follow a mam down the town and you cannot keep your eyes off her beskirted bum, what it does with that skirt, shaking and shuddering it, turning it almost to liquid.

They have beautiful faces, too, not like dad faces all pinched and pale and suspicious. Mams' faces are open, the eyes wide and all-seeing, the mouths ready always to kiss you, their salty kisses. My baby, they call you, even if you are someone else's. They gather up anyone little and kiss them better, they encircle them in their strong arms, the skin so cool, the flesh beneath so warm. Strands of their loose hair catch in their lips, and in yours, and their eyes blink over you, and their mouths smile. They love children, mams. It doesn't matter whose; they love all of us.

I found Toddy Martyr the far side the northern mole, where you can see forever and not be seen, where the town might not exist for all you can see or hear of it.

I saw him because I looked up from my moody walking, from my plodding boots, and in among the mole-rocks one of those rocks lifted an arm and dropped it again. Then I worked out a head, with hair flopping about on it in the wind — a bit of black, a bit of shine — and a pale boy-face. I didn't care who it was; it was someone out here with me not a mam or a dad, not a witch, and greeting this someone would provide me a path away from my thoughts.

By his swaying and by his singing, which I now separated out of the wind's other strings as I clambered, Toddy was off in his own land, or his own private ocean and swimming. Then he wrenched something up and lifted — ah, it was a spirit-bottle — and drank from it. He was headed for trouble, wasn't he? That bottle was quite full, the way he had to heft it.

'Dan'l Mallett!' he cried as he distinguished me from all the other rocks climbing towards him. 'What brings you here this fine morning, sirrah?' And he bonked the cork back in and held out his hand like an old gaffer from the village seat.

I shook it, cold frog that it was. 'Your dad will give you a thrashing, no mistake.'

'Rather me than my mam. And this here is the fuel of his thrash-motor, so I am doubly saving her.'

'You could've only emptied it, into the sea or otherwise,' I said.

'That's what I intended. But then I got seated here and I thought what a waste. And here, have a slosh of it, Dan'l; it is like carrying hot coals in your stomach. It warms all of you, right out to the toenails.' He twisted out the cork and offered me the bottle.

'There's a quantity,' I said in wonder. I lifted and tipped. The air off the stuff rushed out the neck and nipped my nose; the spirit itself ran cold and evil and stinging across my tongue; a little ran out the side and dripped to my collar, leaving a line of cold burning. 'Who-hoah.' I gave it back to him and wiped my chin, and crouched in the cavity next to him.

'How is this, Dan'l? It is in-suff'rable the way things are, do you not think?'

'With the mams, you mean?' I was still negotiating the spirit into myself; it felt as if it were eating my gullet lining to lacework.

'With the mams, with the dads, with all the people of our world.' He spread his arms extravagantly, as if the people were out there seaward, not behind us.

'None of us is happy any more,' I conceded.

'Happy!' He shook his head, pointed his face to the wind to clear it of hair. 'I hate my dad. I could kill my dad, had I stren'th. And he hates me. And he hates my mam so wild, he's like a madman at her. He can. Not. Let. Up. And the only reason she don't hate him is she's so dispirited. She hardly have life to lift her head, let alone raise a good temper.'

I sat my bottom to the wet sand among the rocks and hugged my knees and nodded miserable.

'I don't see why everyone's fussing so,' said Toddy. 'Who wants girls anyway? What are they good for?'

'I don't know,' I said. 'I han't ever known any.' Except that red girl at Knocknee, her hair fizzing and flaming, her inquisitive eyes looking me up and down.

'And babies. Gawd, that last one! Yawped all day and night until Mam took her down. He was glad to be rid of it as much as I was, the racketing. We could all get some sleep.'

We listened to his cruel words in our shelter there. Then *doik!* he pulled out the cork again, thrust the bottle at me, as much apologising as daring me to drink more.

The second pull of it was gentler; it soothed the damages caused by the first. Watching Toddy's throat jump around his next swallow, I told myself I must not do this again too soon. It was far too pleasant, too warming against the weather. Enough of it, and I should be agreeing Toddy Martyr; I should be agreeing all the Toddy Martyrs of this town; I should be loosing everything about my own mam and how she lived alone in her room under her weed, and about Trumbell's opposite — though the town knew most of that already.

I drank myself hot-faced, though — that didn't take much. And I kept Toddy company while he sickened himself. When next he could anyway stand, I helped him up and along to Fisher's, because he wouldn't be taken to his home. Then I went hill-walking, not wanting to present myself at my house with spirit on my breath. Right to the top of Watch-Out I went and down and across the Spine and to Windaway Peak, all that way, and stood in the rain there and listened to the chattering of my teeth. The drink was gone from me by then, and it was a trudge home, and more of a trudge. I thought I would never get there.

I woke warm in the morning knowing what I must do. I ached all over, from my hair-ends in to my heart. I sat up and looked around at the ordinariness of my room, at the spills of light across the wall around my window-blind, and at all sides of my proposition to myself.

That night I walked up home from Wholeman's hearth with the first part, the main part, accomplished. Dad had stayed behind, with his pipe and pals awhile, to talk that special make of eldermen's talk that makes no sense to young ones with its boringness, but seems to gratify dads so.

Into our little house I broke, the seaweedy silence of it. I hummed, a twiddling tune such as Jerrolt Harding had been whistling up in the snug, but without so much direction as he.

I went in to her. She was a great dark dune there. She was awake, though, because you couldn't hear her breathing.

I sat at her pillow edge and tried to distinguish the tear-salted hair from the knitted weed. A scooped sea-heart lay beginning rancid in a saucer on the sill; the spoon was licked clean, almost polished in its shine.

'Mam,' I said, 'I have some news for you.'

She burrowed a little deeper into the blanket.

'Your son,' I said, 'has got himself a position, as bottlewash at Wholeman's.'

I had thought her still before, but now she was all listening; not a leaf of seaweed moved.

'I'm a good lad, says Mister Wholeman. He says they can trust me. Cannot they.'

The dune quaked and her white face rolled up from under. There was not much light. 'Did they bully you?'

'A little,' I said. 'I had to weep some and show proper remorse for that day last winter.' I thought perhaps she could hear my smile, if she could not see it.

She crawled up to me. Powerful out from under the blanket came her warmth and the smell of the warmed weed. 'They would kill you, Daniel, even for thinking this.'

'Yes,' I said, with an odd satisfaction. 'It's different, though, when you are our mams. Mams is different from wives.'

She swayed there on her hands and knees, accustoming herself to the thought. Fears and realisations stopped and started her breath. Even with their little window-shine her eyes were indistinct, holes in her floating pale face through which her attention poured and poured at me.

'I know I don't need to tell you,' she said low. And then she whispered, half-strangled, 'You must not say a word.'

'Not to anyone,' I said to her, as earnest as she could wish. 'Don't you worry. Not even to myself.'

She laughed suddenly, and knocked me to the bed, and squashed the breath out of me the way we had always liked to fight. She was still the stronger yet, though I might be bottle-boy, but I was beginning to see that I might soon have a chance against her. It was all darkness and strain and struggle a little while, and stifled laughter and threats.

She pinned and then released me, sprang back onto her haunches and the fight was over. 'They will know it was you, Daniel,' she said. 'And no other.'

'I don't care,' I said panting. 'You will be home by then.'

'Foolish boy,' she said fondly, and her thin hand reached through the dark, pushed my hair behind my ear, tickled down my neck and along the shelf of my collarbone. Then she slapped my cheek twice, lightly. 'Let me think on this. Out of here, laddy-lad. Just a glance at us and he'll know we were plotting and scheming. Go.'

I went to bed happy. I washed and undressed and lay down untroubled, and my sleep closed over me like sun-warmed water.

Things fast went out of my control, of course, as they will when you tell a secret. First, it was that Kit's mam must come too, and then all the mams. Then, Kit's mam must bring Kit, and then, yes, all the other mams must bring their boys too. 'Particularly you, Daniel,' said Mam, 'who is up for the greatest punishment. The only way I can protect you is have you with me.'

'I can protect myself,' I said, as stoutly as I could, but truth to tell a mad hope had been lit in me when she said that Kit was to be coming. Was that possible, then? For us to go under and be seals with our happy mams?

It turned out there was work involved, much secret work, difficultly organised because the mams could not have with each other, and must send coded and sometimes garbled messages along of their boys, house to house under the guise of playing. This work involved witchery of a kind

— though not Trudle-spells nor Messkeletha — and skins, fish skins and sheep-skins and any kind of skins that could be got. The stories we span about skins, to our dads, when they happened on our hoards! The only way to get over the terror of it was to pretend it were all a great game, a great secret costume-play for the dads, and some of them were entirely silly with it, conducting false rehearsals of carefully crafted song-and-dances so as on purpose to be discovered and scramble to hidings in their skin patchworks.

'Stand still, Daniel.' Mam's hands were at my face, pinching, pinning. 'Or I'll have your eye out.'

'It's tight as tight,' I said. 'A boy cannot breathe in it.'

'Not here,' she agreed. 'But once you touch water, it will all soften, and you'll grow great underwater lungs, for to swim full minutes on a single breath. You've seen us.'

'I have. And will my nose work the same, close-and-openable on top of my snout?'

'Exactly that way, my sweet.'

I tried it within the hood. She tut-tutted. 'Wretched boy.' She sounded quite fond all the same.

'There,' she said eventually. 'Now, don't dislodge my pins, getting it off. It must be sewn aright if it's to fit and form you.'

Time came for the thefts from the coatroom. I don't know what they had planned for the red-witches; some things they kept from me, so as I could not confess them if pressured by the men. Down at Wholeman's I was bottlewash and guard and keeper-at-bay of our dads, stopping them going to the pisser while the coats were taken out the back, between elf-fifteen and elf-thirty by the snug clock, which had a chime that could be heard in the hall. Grinny and Batton had been locked in the room all afternoon, taking down the coats and tying them, and the whole operation went like a game of fire-buckets along a chain of children to Lonna Trumbell, who only had to sniff one coming to say whose it was and where to send the runner. I pictured it all happening as Jerrolt held the men steady and somnolent in the snug with the tunes I had requested, which were all the slow and funereal ones it would be rude to get up and piss through: 'The Night My Mother Died' and 'Low Lay the Boat in the Harbour' and 'The Fiercest Storm'.

'I could just about hear the thunder in that,' said Baker to my horror as Jerrolt finished and the snug clock chimed. Straightaway Fernly Asham and Michael Cleft got up and went out. I hurried to the scullery with my tray of bottles and began to wash and wash, waiting for the fiercest storm to break over our heads.

Which it did not. Thank heaven, I thought, something has got in the way of it and we must wait another several nights. I have been sweating on nothing; the coats are still in their rows, the hall and yard are empty and cold as always.

But no, the key was where I had told Grinny to leave it. And walking up home, the town was different. The secrets gusted about the streets with the leaves and litter, thick enough in the air to choke me.

Run along home, Wholeman had said. No, lad — when I'd protested — you done a fine night's work. Like some kind of little steam engine you are, getting through them bottles. The rest can wait'll tomorrow.

But no-one will be here tomorrow to do them, I almost said, then went obedient home.

There I found my mam pacing. She scooped me up and squeezed me. 'While I have arms to do this,' she said.

'Did it all happen, then?' I said, hardly believing, into her black hair. 'Did you all do?'

Out from under the table she pulled the bag, and from it she tugged a coat-edge, very thick and smooth, dark, with not a lot of freckle. She unslid the whole skin and held it up beside herself by the hood, the exact height, though the ragged face-holes were nothing like my pretty mam. The closed air of our front room soured and went salty.

'Do you remember it, from back then?' I held the slithery skin to my lips; it seemed to defy my bottlewashed fingers to purchase on it and feel it properly.

'No,' she said. 'But it smells of me and mine, very distinct. Let's get on, then.' She fell to whispering. 'Everyone else is gone, Daniel, hours ago.'

Close she came and folded the coat, the ragged-faced floppy person, down to bag size. 'Slippery thing,' she said flusteredly, as the sleeves misbehaved. Surely that smell would be smelt, out in the street where we carried it? Surely someone would stop us: Neme Mallett, what are you out for, this time of night? And what do you think you have there, that can only be one thing? And pluck the bag from my fingers, open it and bring the trouble down on our heads.

'There, done.' She met my eyes and huffed. 'Let us shut up and follow, then.'

Off we went, coated but unbuttoned. She took my hand once we were out on the street, and hers was cold and tight.

'I do love him,' she said to the cobbles, to the passing front steps. 'I am breaking his heart.'

'He ought never have caught you, Mam,' I said severely. I didn't want to think of Dad. 'None of them ought. They should have left you in your home.'

I thought she smiled down on me out of the stars, but

the light was not good and her hair shadowed her face, she might have winced just as easy.

Down slippy-slop we went, the wind skirling and twiddling around us, caught in the narrow ways. Every now and again a strong breath from the sea would push at our faces, smelling green and live and massive. When that happened, Mam would almost run a few steps, as if the sea were summoning her more peremptory.

The water was rucked-up and difficult looking between the moles. I thought I saw seal-heads awaiting, a couple, but when I looked again they were not there. They may have been only wave-shadows, mistakes of my eyes, wishings perhaps if I but knew what I wished.

'Come-come.' Mam let go my hand and preceded me down the steps to the beach. I hurried after her, frightened and not knowing why but needing to be right by her for my own peace.

We ran out from the wall, the town hunkering behind us, its eyes tightening the skin of my back. Out across the scraping pebbles we went, impatient water smashing its hands at the edge of them, the wind frothing and flapping our hairs at our ears.

Let us run home, I would have said, and all go on as before. But she knelt before me and her face in the moonlight was clear — alight as the moon, it was — and I was too busy admiring the clean arches of her eyebrows to voice my doubts.

'Step in,' she said and then I was preoccupied, wasn't I, with fitting myself — for truth, I had grown a tiny bit since she sewed the thing — into the sheepskin suit. I gasped but did not complain as she tied and tied me into it, and then she pulled the ragged hood-mask down over my face and it was as if she sewed my mouth shut and my chin to my chest. I stood there with my neck pulled into an ache behind, my little sounds nothing against the sea's impatience.

Through the eyeholes I watched her as well as I could, for though she was being indecent there was such joy in it, such spirit, I could not but follow her every move, privileged to see. White she emerged out of her scratchy land-clothing, out of its wrinkles and seams.

'Ah!' She flung her drawers up on the pebbles, and she was animal within, all flesh and fur uncluttered by all those trappings.

Next she took up the coat-bag, drew out the coat, wrestled it open and slid it on. All of a sudden the air was cold and thick as water. I gasped inside my dry leather mask, and my flatted hair crawled.

She did not don the coat like any man-garment; rather, she began, and then the thing sank upon and encompassed her, clung on close, clung to its own edges around her. Clap and clop and zip, it went, and snick, and then she fell, from standing foot-fins together, straight into the wavelets, where she was now seal, and flang herself down towards the deeper water.

She turned and there was enough of her left that I could not refuse to follow, so I too fell and floundered through the curdled cold air and into the sea through its foamy edge. There the water, and the magic, overtook me, and what was seal of me supplanted what was boy, and I ceased to think and to intend or decide, in any way that makes sense in a story, but only followed my mam, crying after her into our dark world, all alive to the tides now and temperatures, to the bubbling trail of her that I sought and followed with my whiskers, to the depths and wonders and fellows and foes disposed on all sides of us, and before us, and below.

•

I will not tell you much about that time. It is not the kind of thing that can be caught in words, human words out of our subtle mouths: sunlight shafting into the green; the mirrory roof; the women racing ahead through the halls of the sea, the cathedrals; boat bellies, and the mumble and splash of man-business disturbing the water above; the seal-men, the sea-men, spun light as wooden tops by the delicate tail, pressing out the water behind them, impelling their bulk forward, upward, outward —

It is very much like flying, through a green air flocking with tiny sunlit flecks of life.

Seal-men I found to be very like our dads on land, all possessiveness and anxiety, patrolling the borders of the clan. When we went up on a beach, they must always be seeing other seal-men off, coming back blown and bloodied. It seemed a savage way of work to me, this knocking of heads together. Sometimes me and my fellows had a play at it, but it were two rubber heads bouncing off each other, no teeth and no purpose, and the mams laughed lounging around us.

And then there were those sister-seals, our size but not fighters, but only slipping alongside us through the sun shafts, blinking beside us through the roof of the world, into the windy air and the rasp of breath in both of ours' opening nostrils. Those whiskery sea-maids, the ones with the spell on them to keep them seals, to keep them safe from human men. Like animate seeds or stones, they moved, like bullets leaping through the water, like weed undulating away along the tide or teasing your face with a leaf-end.

I don't know how to tell you. Seal feelings are different from human ones, seal-affections, seal-ties with other seals. The best I can do is overlay a skin of man-words on the grunt and urge and song and flight and slump of seal-being.

Our mams belonged better here than they ever had belonged above. Our mams found their wings, is how you might put it. Our mams did not glory or revel or make any particular celebration, but only slipped back to rightness, went back about their business. The bulk of our mams was not beautiful as a man sees beautiful, but to seal-eyes their beautiful black teardrops of being fell fast, flew fast, twisted through the home depths.

The sea was at our ears and against our sensitive faces, all its cavities and their echoes like a giants' city, this castle, that market and that cluster of tiny homes. Braided through, it was, with tidal temperatures, underlain with colder harder depths, with darkness-fish and the skeletons that fell out of everyone's feeding. Here above, we were a multitude, in ranks of size and ferocity; I cannot explain to you, if you are a fisherman, the beauty and panic of a shining mass of herded fish, the whole school flashing back and forth looking for the no-way-out among my darting fellows, the topmost swimming out into the air in their terror.

The days were long and unformed; the seasons beckoned us, then pushed us away behind them; stars rode over us, and moons in their boatishness and bulbousness; towns were a crust at the edge of our world's eye and people were mites that crawled there. If I saw my father in that time, I don't recall it, or recognising any man of Potshead — or woman, because Messkeletha was still there for a long while, and Trudle stayed all that time, and is still here now.

I don't recall particularly the landscape of our island, not above its rocks or above the beach-sand that as men we called Crescent Corner. As the sea to men, beyond the point that they can see bottom, becomes only the plumblined depths full of loves and livelihoods, so to seals the heights become only wastes of dry blaring light from which weather and occasional dangers descend.

I felt no pull to the land; I barely knew that I knew the land; I barely thought; I didn't feel the way a person feels. I only was, following flurries of instinct, flurries of friends and of fish.

'It happened by accident,' says my dad. 'Shorten Thomas found it out, enraging 'cross an ice floe one winter — all those cold nights without light nor woman will set a man to clubbing. Only he was using a hacker-pick that sealers have, cutting them, you see. Well, he was in a fine way — up to his ears in hotpunch too, no doubt. And he says it like this, that he turned at the end of the crowd of them, and weeping and looking back down the path of his butchery he saw a boy — all long and lanky, he says, much like you were extracted as, Dan'l. Writhing on the ice, he said, just like a seal does, only not managing to move as they do, for he was not built the same. And when the boy realises, up onto hands and knees he goes, and quick as he can but clumsy — because he has forgot, in all that time, how to progress such a body — he crawls for the edge of the ice.

'Shorten went after him, calling: "Boy, boy! What is your name?" But not fast enough, and the boy gets to the rim and looks back once, and falls in, all messy like an accident, not like seals do, like a brine-drop back into the ocean. And of course there drowns, doesn't come up even the once, for all Shorten's pleading. The cold catches him, and his first breath of the North Sea, and all that is left to Shorten is a few bubbles among the bobbing ice.'

'He looked around, you say, the boy?'

Dad shakes his head. 'You press Shorten on that, he will break and blub at you like you charged him with holding the boy's head under. He says he was all emotional, and you all look the same, you boys. He says he couldn't tell, that he might even have been looking his own Vernar in the eye and not known, the boy would have grown so much. But it might have been any of you, any of the ones we've not recovered yet: Snow, or Toll Hardy, Harold Roman, or the Gormlin twins, who knows?' In the windowlight my dad is worn and clean; even the smoke from his briar-pipe is clean and white as his hair. Evening is coming; that light is cool, grey-blue. I am glad of the fire against its lack of cheer.

'So, then,' he begins into the crackling silence with the sea behind it.

'Yes.' The light fades on his face even as I watch, all crags of frail flesh.

'Well, he is struck horrorful with the thought he may have butchered other sons, he says, but mainly he's wondering, How did I cut that seal, to free the boy inside? And he goes back and finds the skin — and this is not hard among six-seven slaughtered beasts, because it has all shrunk and thinned, don't you know. It's one of those wee coats, you see, that your mams made to spirit you away in. Wi' the hoods, you remember? All of rabbit or lambskin.'

I nod. 'They stank to be inside, and were so tight. We had to put them on there in the shallows, else we were trapped tight in them, unable to walk, and too big for mams to carry as well as their own coat.'

'And Shorten sees that with this pick he's managed to cut, neat as a tailor, all the front stitches down the middle, so as to open the thing just like the coat that it is, and out has come the boy. And he brings the skin home and tells the tale, and we're all there handling this wee coat and weeping, like it were a holy relic, a roomful of grown men brought to nothing by this garment, all of us trying to recognise our wife's hand in the stitching, all of us desperate to see it, yet not to see it, so as not to lose hope of our son.'

There is a slight crack in his voice on that last word, and I look up in time to see him surprised, and embarrassed, and straightaway recovered. 'So then the hunt was on, every man for his boy,' he says almost jovial, lifting pipe and paws and letting them drop to his blanketed lap, a fleck of ash stirred out of the bowl by the movement and falling beside.

I was born again and I came out crying — a lot of us did, they say. There never was such a race as the seals for mawking and mowing. I came out crying into a driving rain, and all sounds hurt my ears, rain-hiss on the decks and hatches and the sealers' celebrations: 'Daniel Mallett! Welcome back to the world, boy!' They lifted me into the confusion and there, with my big bony shoulders pulling my ragged coat apart up the back, I stood and choked and took their embraces, that each was like an assault on me but which I did not rebuff. I had not the strength; I had forgot how to use arms.

They laid me down on the deck; it was not comfortable. Some man had put a rope-coil under my head for pillowing and it pressed in hard enough to hurt. I was accustoming myself — and it was difficult — to the frontwaysed eyes seeing two things for every one and putting them together. My bony body was less massy than before; how could it be so much heavier? Everything was heavier around me, glued to the deck; the men as they moved must cling to it; anything that fell must roll or slide to any lower point.

Around me was airy noise, every movement light and startling, every contact a concussion, throwing out more noise. Unpredictable, to no rhythm, they moved and swore and fumbled, the men of my town, of my land-world, and the seabirds stuttered in the sky. And I was glued here myself, to these coat-remnants beneath me, pressed to the damp wood by this blanket, its heavy knots of seagrass. All the wind could do was push the damp hair back and forth on my brow; it could not lift and return me to the water; it could not lift even this knotted knitted thing that held the little left of my warmth around me in the absence of my seal-flesh.

It was an ill-making dream, and the men came by, smiling and patting me, to console me for it, all the way home. They asked me nothing; they did not expect me to speak, out of this strange-packed mouth, out of this flat face with its new framework of jaw. They muttered and crooned, and as the sky went on and the illness, their noises slipped together, interlocked into items of sense. Welcoming me, they were, welcoming me back; their words were all about their gladness and our preciousness, their sons'. They were changed men from the ones I was beginning to remember.

'You'll be heavy to yourself awhile,' said one, over the grinding of the boatside into the jetty, over the hard explosions of sound in my back, in the back of my head. He lifted the weed-blanket off me, and I waited to fly up into the air. But I did not. I lay helpless.

They hooked my arms over two men's necks and taught me walking, across the deck all cluttered with box and bolt and reel, across the frail plank that was all that kept me from a dirty corner of water, a corner of my home below. And to the land, locked unmoving, the jetty standing firm against the water that slapped and fought it below. My feet dragged and my legs attempted rescuing them — how was I to support myself and balance, on these two stalkish things? The men had put a shirt on me and trousers but still the foreign knees swung and braced below my poor-focusing eyes, my heavy head. I knew that they belonged to me, but I could not see how ever I was to control them.

My father was brought down the street to me, but I did not see him, only heard clomping boots and men saying, 'See, Dominic? There he is!' And then a voice out of years ago, out of my bones, saying, 'Is that him? Is that my Daniel? Are you sure?'

Then space opened before me and I heaved up my head. Some boots swam there and his familiar belt-buckle, and then the rest of him was there, sharp-edged and astounding, his big hands out wide at me and in between them his awakening face.

'Dan'l,' he said, and 'Dad,' I said, and even words were heavy here, all burdened with the years, and my head sagged again and there was nothing but wet greeny-black-blue cobbles ringed by boot-toes and marvelling men.

'Here, let me take him,' said my father to the man at my right, and they un-hooked and re-hooked me and I seemed to walk worse than ever, leaning onto him with my head swung fast into his shoulder.

'You will be fine, my boy,' he said. 'Fine and good.' And he held me up and walked me. A splash appeared a brighter blue on his shirt and I had not known it was raining, or he was crying, and I tried to say, I did not know what, that I knew him, that I was surprised, that I was sorry, that I had found my way somehow into this strange, long, wrong-grown body — but all I could manage for the moment was seal-cries, that said nothing, that had to say everything for me.

'We found out various as they came back,' my dad says, 'a little by little. But that first boy, Willem Canker, no. He came in, shocked and shivering, eyes all over the place, and as they brought him on the boat all the men were at him, question-and-poking, weeping on him and embracing, each asking after his own sons.

'Some thought Willem had gone simple, there under the waters all that time, or perhaps half-drowned on the way up and it had affected his brain, because he did not utter a proper word all the way, only moaned somewhat and seemed to suffer to be with us.

'We put him away in his house. Joel Canker laid him in his bed, and milk-and-breaded him back to life, and every now again he would come out and say, Oh he is coming good, every day a wee bit more our lad. He was sitting by the boy, talking and talking whenever he was awake to usen him to the sound of words again, to bring him back his memory. And today he answered me, he might say. Today he said yes, when I asked him did he want for milk.

'Which the rest of us found little consolation of, one word here or there when such bright little buttons you'd been all of you, never stopped rattling and singing morning to night, ever one of you, questions questions. And the last five years along at Wholeman's every word you had spoke we had turned over and wet with our tears and polished with our examinations and nostalgias. Besides which, Canker might be imagining, from the strength of his own wishing, and Willem truly damaged and never to think a clear thought nor speak a clear word again.

'But then the boy came out. I remember the day. 'Twas a whole new weather and season, bright and blowy, and suddenly there was colour in the sky and flowers on the hills around town.

'And the boy come out, good as new, Willem Canker, good as gold; I opened my curtains and there he was walking up the town long and limber with his easy man-stride — just like yours, Dan'l, only of course I'd not seen yours then. Had no surety of ever seeing it, always I reminded myself. I remember he looked up — not at me nor no-one but just up, at the town, at walls, and maybe at hill and sky above — and the look of him — of all our boys and our wives and our selves rolled into the one — the sight of him near split me down the middle. And Canker out ahead — he did not need to sing, just his face was singing, the joy of it. They say it is a sin, envy. You must not covet, they say. Well, your old man, Dan'l, he's a sinner I hope you don't mind, cloven by envy, hating Joel Canker for having what I had not.'

He beams around his pipe; takes the thing from between his teeth with one rheumaticky hand, reaches out the other and bats my face with it, softly, and takes it purple-grey away, trailing soap-scent.

Then a thought scoops his smile away and he's a codger again, all belligerent, his eyes a-swim with window-light. 'Course, there's some that only got that ever, only ever got that envy and no more. Corris Snow, bless his soul, and the Greens, none o' theirs came back.' His gaze is like a pressure on my face, feasting on me and guilting about it.

Sometimes it can be simple pleasure seeing each other, but not often; net after net of past event and slippery feelings drops between us, until sometimes I can barely make him out through the masses.

When that happens I will up and sigh, and fetch us teas, maybe, that the two of us can sip staring out over the roofs and water, while it all dissipates. You cannot have that stuff drawn in on yourself too close and constant. It will drive you mad; it will drive you off Chisel Top like Corris Snow, into the arms of your wife as you think, into the rocks, crushed cold there forever. Sometimes you must just stand, upright on the earth as you are or cupped in an armchair like Dad or propped on a barstool; sometimes you must just breathe and be, with your small land-lungs and your stuck body. You must cease your wishing for things you cannot have, and just proceed towards the grave, kind as you can be to your fellow travellers, not raising any great hopes or moaning any great miseries.

This is the truest way for us boys, and the hardest, bred as we are from two great tribes-ful of yearning. Not all of us can steady ourselves so, and none of us are balanced aright all of the time.

We were all put to fishing, of course. Gratefully the older men passed us their places on the boats, while the ones with still a little fire in them leaped to ordering and instructing us with almost glee.

It was good for us. It was better than sitting at home net-mending with the sadder dads. The sea was the best place for us, halfway between our two homes and with a job to do. And it tired us properly, all that hauling and winding. And you never knew what curious-familiar thing would come up squirming in the net and make you wonder.

This was going to be our lives then, these the

components, unless Grinny enacted his scheme of starting Trudle knitting again, unless Raditch and Cawdron took up theirs of rowing to the mainland for a look at the women there.

I am not much for venturing. I had no such schemes. I tend to stop where I am brought or put, and endure whatever yearning is my lot there. It has been before me all my life in my mam, and now it is in me, and in my dad, and that is only natural, the whole town with its head full of sea and seals, enraged or grief-ridden or both. Us boys — well, I did not know about the others, it was not as if we named things to each other. For myself I felt too freshly arrived, too newly born yet to do more than walk and work from day to day. I thought if I waited, equanimity might come, my father's slow eating of himself, after all these years, notwithstanding.

I came home early from helping at Fisher's store. The smell was all through the house: wild salt sweat of mams, caverns of ocean, turning the air blue-green. I walked through it with my arms out; it all but swirled about them.

In the kitchen, at the heart of the smell, at the heart of the home, Dad sat at the slab table with his white plate and a spoon and a caught-red-handed look disguised as normal every-dayness up at me.

'What brings you so early?' he accused me.

'Done all I had to do.' His chin was tilted up, his eyes craven, and then there was the thing on the plate — hairy, with a rubbery inner lining with a blob of orange curd on the lip. The spoon hovered.

'Here,' he says. 'There's another.' Points with his thumb to the pot on the stove. As if this were an ordinary dinner.

I tried for both our sakes to pretend it was. Crossed and spooned it from the pot, clanked out a plate and rattled a spoon from the drawer. Cut the cap off, with my big capable hands — last time I et one of these, my mam had to open it for me, that tough skin.

The steam flooded up and the smell: bodies, wet hair, boiled shellfish, sour seawater, the cosiest of winter nights, her clear pale skin with a hint of green; her hair like black water made thread, made silk.

I spooned up a bit and there it was in my mouth now, all my childhood, warm and free of worry, before the future came down out of its scratchy grey cloud and began to bother and itch me. Days of play and safety, our mothers laughing together, my mam and dad laughing, too, looking to each other, leaning arm to arm. I would do things; I would perform; I would stand on my hands against the wall so they would look at me again, include me with them. Always it was my fight when Dad was there, to have her eyes and her mind on me.

Well, I got that, did I not. The curd sat cooling on my tongue; it slid down my throat, soaking my head with the sweet-saltness. Up sprang tears, but not so far as to fall.

I saw what we had done to them, the mams and boys to the dads. It weren't necessarily worse than what the dads done in the beginning. What a thing to weigh up: would you rather be born of redheads both, or would you be silky-dark and big-eyed? Would you prefer another mother? There is no way of trying that out. Maybe mainland children love their scour-haired mams just as fiercely as we love our silkies, maybe they learn to lose themselves in pale eye-depths whereas here with our mams' darknesses beside them, our dads' blues and greens revealed no more than blue-or-green painted curves of china.

Anyway, we took all that away, the polish off the china, the shine of purpose and determination. I had not known what we were doing back then. I did not know, looking back now, whether we ought not to've, with Dad there across from me, head bent over the rubbish-looking heart, scooping up more orange.

And once we'd gone, us and the mams, each man had a choice, either to go like Bannister into breakage and mourning, and slope around Potshead like a sprite lost between this world and the next, or to go rocklike with rage like Martyr or Green, and shout and rally everyone, and proclaim how things were all right, an improvement in fact, now that those sly enchantresses had loosed their holds on our hearts.

But they had not, of course. They never would. You could not be free if you were born of them, and looking at our dads the husbanding of them was much the same: you thought you had caught and confined them, but really it was you as was tangled in the weed nets; you could not breathe properly either in air or in water were the seal-women not there to encourage the life in and out of you.

Raditch ran up, and stood all outlined in the sunny doorway. 'Ho, Daniel. There looks to be another witch coming in.'

'What do we want one for?' I did not stop sweeping. 'Trudle is young yet, and when she goes there is all those daughters.' All wall-eyed skitterish four of them.

'She's here unaxed,' said Raditch. 'Come down and watch. I'm going to.'

'Someone told Trudle?'

'Jakes and Wretch.' The names floated back to me through the empty doorway.

Dad would be down there already; it was something the dads did, watch the unloading, some of them swap worldly words with the lumping-men. I propped the broom by the door and walked down through the sunshine.

Between the cottages I could see the *Fleet Fey* cutting towards us, the spot of red hair at her prow. A very straight figure, I thought, not like our Trudle, who had hunched into Messkeletha's old shape by now, taken over the posture as well as the witching, so as we should know it at a distance — know to turn and run, in good time, before she could enchant another daughter out of our loins.

Everyone gathered to meet the boat, just about: such men as would leave their houses and most of us long-shanked boys, trickling down from the streets and the men already on their bench and bollards on the front. 'What is this, then, eh? What is this?' said Grinny's dad happily, taking up position against the warmed storehouse wall.

Trudle came down out the town at the moment the gangway-end clacked to the cobbles. Her daughters preceded her, wild in their grubby print frocklets all of the same flowers; she carried the boy against her shoulder who anyone could tell would grow up simple, he stared so slack-mouthed.

She met the visitor with the little suitcase at the plank-end, stood fast there so that the girl could not step off.

'What do you think you are about, young miss?' At the sound all the daughters swilled in around her and stared.

The girl looked Trudle over, and all the eyes around her. 'Who are you,' she said, 'that I should account to you?' She asked it plain, with no sneering. 'Are you mayor or police or officialdom?'

'What business has you in this place?' Trudle pointed her chin at her. 'We've all the women we want here and no more.'

The girl's gaze travelled from one end the crew of us behind the witch to the other. 'Are you sure? It seems a touch unwomaned to me. But I have property here,' she said, 'if you must know my business, though it is none of yours, as far as I know you yet.' She stepped neatly around Trudle and the daughters in her skirts.

'Property? What property?' Trudle swung and followed her, as if she were attached with string.

The girl crossed half the dock and stood there surveying us. 'This is the way you welcome strangers, then?' she said, not loud but we could hear her, every syllable. 'Let them be harassed and harridaned even before they've set foot?'

'What property would a mainland girl have here?' said Trudle at the girl's elbow and fear all over her.

'Quieten, woman,' said old Baker.

Trudle bristled and chin-poked at him, drew herself up as much as she might.

But he went on, to the visitor, 'Now I see you, you must be Dully Winch's girl, of his wife Mary.'

'You have it,' she said. 'Lory Winch, I am.'

'Lory, that's right.' The woman-name was uncertain in his mouth.

'My mother died in the winter.' No-one looked or offered anything, so she went on. 'She has left me a cottage here, she said.' And straightway I saw it in my mind, the house called Winch's, a boarded-up box on the road out to the Hill. It was the first time I realised it belonged to anyone, and was not there just to say out beyond Winch's with, a landmark only.

We followed them up, Lory Winch and Baker, with Trudle there too, in close, still suspicious, and the daughters flowing around, and the boy staring dumbly at us over Trudle's shoulder. Up the sunshiny lanes we went, after those red hairs — for all the witch's girls had piles of it too, flags of it, bunches of it haphazardly pinned. The visitor's was all tied in, two plaits clambering back over her head from her temples and joining to one down her back. I had seen such plaiting on mams' dark heads, but theirs had lain obedient, while this seemed on the point of bursting its bindings did it but get half the chance.

Winch's stopped where it always had, only I saw it for the first time in a long time. It was black boards; it seemed to lean, the slope threw your eyes off so much, to lean back into the hill, for a better hold, maybe. The yard was thick angelweed up to the fencetop, up to the windows, like a bowl of wild salads, and sea pinks clumped and sea rocket trailed off through the pickets into Asham's fields around.

I thought she would be disappointed, a town girl like her. I had seen Knocknee houses. But, 'Yes,' she said into our silences. 'It is exactly as Mam said. I could have found my way alone with her directions, and a little black house is what she said.'

We stood in the road and watched the creature encounter the gate. Raditch stepped forward to help. 'No, I have it,' she said. She opened it to the extent it could be opened, by which she could sidle onto the broken path, and then she waded up to the door. She took a key from her belt that was all the bigger and blacker for being in her small white hand, and she slid it into the keyhole and turned it, and we heard from the sound of that the house had insides, as well as the outsides we knew.

And we saw them, when she pushed the door wide into an upcurl of dust: papered walls, with pictures, and beyond the far door some furniture-back looming, shadow on shadow.

The miss put her case on the floor, a little way into the hall. She looked at us all out there with our stares on.

'Thank you for your help, gentlemen,' she said, and it was hard to say how much she was laughing at us. 'Let me settle myself here awhile, and then I'll out with a thousand questions, I'm sure.'

'Did you want them battens taken off your winders, miss?' said Raditch. 'I can fetch a claw and have it done soon as looking.'

'Maybe in a while,' she said. 'For now, I need the place to myself, if you don't mind.'

She turned her back on us and darkened away down the hall, an upright young woman. We were not used to seeing that type of figure.

'Well,' said Grinny as we walked slow away, hoping rather she would call us back for some question or favour. 'That has livened up our morning.'

'What's she want here?' fretted Trudle among us. 'Who would want a-coming to this place?'

'You heard. She inherited. She wanted to see what she had,' said Baker's dad. 'I don't reckon she means to take your place, Trudle. She isn't got a spelling look about her.'

'Why did her mam go, though? The widder?' This was Cawdron, gormless still. I didn't know the answer, but I knew it was one of those questions no-one wanted asked.

'Sem reason they all went,' snapped Martyr, Toddy's dad that had beat his wife, and to whom Toddy had not returned.

And what was that? Cawdron's face said it, but he didn't allow it out of his mouth. All of a sudden the older men found the spirit to walk, and closed their faces down, and went preoccupied with important and worrisome thoughts, so that they did not have to answer him.

'And so she is up there now, settling herself.' I laughed. 'Like a little red hen.'

My dad had not come up to Winch's with the crowd. He bit into his breakfast bread and dealt with it, nodding and nodding to keep me quiet.

But she'd done something, that little hen; she'd pushed something over in my brain that now was falling, stone by stone. 'They used to be all red, didn't they?'

He nodded towards the door.

'Why did they go? Widow Winch? Everyone?'

I saw him realise that I would not be put off. 'There were no prospects here for them.'

'Prospects?'

'Norn to wed, boy,' he said crossly, and bit the bread again.

'Ha, there is nothing but men here. Was there such a crowd of red girls, then? Too many to go round? Couldn't some of them have stayed?'

But he was shaking his head and chewing.

'How did it happen, then? You tell. Then I'll not bother you by guessing wrong over and over.'

He dabbed his bread at his plate. He chewed as long as he could and then swallowed, and did not bite again, only sat there dabbing, picking up crumbs with the damp bread-edge.

Stubborn old coot, he would not say, all that morning. I did not sit and badger him; now and then in passing I would say, 'You are going to have to tell me some day. Well, it may as well be today, no?' or the like. But all he would do was chew at his teeth and look as if I had smacked him.

I know what you need, I thought, and after our dinner I went down to Fishers' and got us a bottle of spirit.

'Cold nights, these,' said Doby Fisher just as his dad would, cold weather or hot, to anyone who bought such a bottle. 'Man needs a tot.'

I carried it up home. Dad watched me cross to the hall with it.

'I know what you're at,' he said after me.

'Good,' I threw back. 'I should not like to deceive you.'

'Impertinent.'

Well, it took that night a bit of hoo-ing and hawing, and a long disquisition on whiskies the land over, but we reached a time after all the nonsense, late in the night, when all lamps outside were gone excepting the sky's own, when anything could be said between a son and his father; we'd taken on the perfect amount of liquoring to make the tongue loose but not yet the tears.

'Oh, Daniel,' he began, out of nothing, out of my questioning way back this morning, 'she were so beautiful. You know it,' he said. 'You remember. She come out the skin and none of our misery had touched her yet; none of the cruelties of this world had marked her. She was sad, yes, she was desperate to go home, but you could distract her from that, you could fascinate her with any small thing — the way an auger worked, maybe, or a swallow-nest in the eaves. And when she laughed — well, you remember, don't you? You made her laugh enough. We were all envious of our sons, that could make their mams laugh just by breathing, or playing stones, or asking where the sky ended, or eating up a fresh bowl of porridge. None of us husbands could do that, not so readily. We were always their imprisoners as well as the men they loved, and the fathers of their children.'

He put out his glass, and I filled it for him, with candlelight and the sweet-woody smell of truth-telling. He slid it back to himself and looked into its dark-gold eye.

'I've had a plenty of time to go over this. While she was here I did not think it, but when she went, and you with her — why, then we all had time, didn't we? Years we had, to meditate upon it. There were some men all afire to fetch up more women from the sea, but with their few tries they had no luck, and the rest of us, we wanted the wives we'd had and no other; we wanted our own lads back that we knew.

'I remember when Jon Fisher brought the very first one in, and we all went down the storehouse to see her. Tricked up in Lucy Fisher's dress, she was, and my, wasn't she uncomfortable. She stared, one way and another; she would not look at you. She had been crying, all botched about the eyes, you could see. Jon Fisher's mam sat by her, looking so fierce, no-one was bold enough to say a word, to ask the seal-girl anything.'

He sipped his drink. 'I thought she would die if she stayed here, and she must have thought the same, for she made herself bleed breaking into the cupboard where the skin was that night, and fighting her way out of Fishers'. In the morning she was just footprints across the wharf, blood-prints. I was glad for her, and I was blistering angry with Fishers the same, for not locking her up better, or setting any kind of guard on her, so's we could look some more in the morning.

'We know Martyr is not an admirable fellow, and we knew he wasn't then, yet when he showed at market with his new girl on his arm, that he called Ivy, just as if she belonged on dry land among us, the thing we wanted most to know was how he had come by and kept her. And one by one from him and each other we found out, and one by one we went and had a sea-blanket knitted up. Some went by water and netted their wives there. Some waited until the seals come up for sunbasking in Crescent Corner. And some went well away and took theirs from icebergs up north or other islands. There was no stopping us. Even the women threatening to go did not stop us.'

'But I always thought the women went first, and left the men in need.'

'Oh no, lad. They were here all the time. They saw it all. They said and said: You don't stop this, you will lose all the real-wives of the town, and then you will see what it's like, being married to magic. Which they did, and which we did. Which we are seeing still.'

He took almost a bite of the spirit, to bring himself back to me and this room a moment.

'Anyway, I did same as all of them — I was no stronger nor better at the sight of those lovely women. You know the story from there.'

'I do not,' I said. 'Did you go down Crescent Corner or what, for instance?'

'No, I was not brave enough. Crescent was for lads who could do it alone, and I wanted others around me. You always had to have Messkeletha there, of course, but I wanted fellows, too. Make me feel I was on the right path, that it was not against nature, what I was doing.' He snorted and looked at the window. 'Yes, so I just went out on our boats, with the wife-net the witch had spelled for us and that first blanket she had knitted me from seaweed and a good portion of my money, and up come your mam.' He gave this last an end-of-story flourish.

I did not let up with my eyes, though. He paused and added a little water to the spirit, then shot me a glance.

Then — it was a relief, I could tell. He fell into the next part, and his face flowered open. He had never told it before, and he knew he was doing right by telling me, and I saw expressions on him he had never worn before, except when my mam herself were in this very room with the two of us.

'Then the seal would be fighting trapped in the blanket, and most unladylike noises it would make. Messkeletha was at your elbow muttering: Keep her covered, keep her covered. But even through the knitted weed you could see the split in the seal-flesh, the crimson that did not bleed, the whiteness of the woman that came out clean, not touched or at all smudged or smelling of seal from inside. Clean as a peeled onion she came out, and soon you had all whiteness bucking in there like a mad maggot and you thought, Whoa, Messkeletha's got me a bent one; how will I get my money back?

'But then she told me: Right, my work is done now. I am going for sleep before I throw my stomach — for she was always on border of seasick, out there on the boat with us doing this work. All our money in the world could not settle her stomach.

'And she's gone, and it's only you — all the other lads are up beyond the deckhouse so as not to catch the silky's first eye and become her master instead of you.

'I found which end was her head and I held her down and I whispered her calm. Her eyes through the netting, through the blanket — I had seen enough seal-women by then to know them, yet this was a new beast, of course, among us, and I was her first close person.

'All the time whispering, I drew back the blanket, just from her face first and then her hair, untangling as I went. One white shoulder.

'What have you done? she said to me, at a pause in my whispering. Why have you taken me from my home? Her voice grew stronger later, and clearer, but that first utterance it was rusty and bubbly, and did not know how to pitch itself.

'To take care of you, I told her, the best you have ever been cared for. To make you my wife.

'By now we had run out of girl-clothing left to us by our own mams and sisters. But Grinny and Ewart had proved themselves neat at stitching up shifts that covered a woman decent, and I had me one of these, which I gave to her: Here, put this on. It's kinder than that rough blanket.

'And I will not forget her in it: lost, white-armed and white-footed and white-faced, sitting on a bollard in the grey shift with the world grey around her, boat and boy and sea and sky of it, looking up to me for —'

He drained his glass, put it down and examined the table either side of it. 'Well, back then I liked to think it were love and comforting she looked for, but she may as easily have been reproaching me, for taking her up from everything she knew and landing her here in my strange world, for my strange pleasures, for the rest of our lives, as I thought.'

He sat a long time with that sour expression, thinking. Then his mind moved on, and his face softened.

'I hope you have a wedding night half like it, though, Dan'l. I hope you hold someone to your heart with only a shred of what I felt for that animal-woman. It is not something you can give back to the sea, after that. You put your full self, your full soul, into them narrow hands, and afterwards you cannot be far from her, for fear of becoming nothing. When you all went, Dan'l — ahh, can you imagine? Can you imagine the — the —' He grinned over the candle at me. 'The ghosts we were, the objects! We bare had strength to eat — and some did not, of course, and died that way, Errol Curse was one. We did not manage a funeral even for Errol, just put him away in the earth where he would not smell and interrupt our miseries, though Baker was all for throwing him in the sea, to make the point to Curse's wife, and Frederick and Batton, what they had done to him.'

Then the tears started, and I will not show him to you that way. I stayed out the weeping with him, though, and the talking; I poured him more spirit when he asked for it; I agreed with him and soothed him as I could.

I lifted my head from my arms some time after midnight. He was staring into and addressing his drink.

'A night like this, it were,' he said, 'with the night breeze drabbling in the window just so, with not much to it.'

I did not know if he meant the wedding night, or the night he met Mam, or the night they all went down to Fishers' store and saw the first seal-woman, and began the whole thing — or indeed another night of his story, that I had not been awake for.

I was washing the breakfast plates next morning when Dad came to me, which was unusual of him. Just his approaching, out of his chair when I knew he had already performed all the rituals of his morning, threw the day unusual. Was he poorly some way?

He came up close. 'The Winch girl is here,' he said to my shoulder.

'Here?'

His blue eyes swam as surprised as I felt. 'She wants to speak to Daniel.' As if Daniel were a third person —

which almost he might be, a Daniel that Miss Lory Winch summoned.

I dried my hands. Dad watched me, watched me go, as if I were become that third man, another creature suddenly.

She flamed in the street outside. She had her hair different today, tied back still but exploding out beyond her shoulders. But very demure underneath it, with her arms folded.

'Good morning,' I said.

Her face was so white it seemed lit from inside. She considered me until my greeting had erased itself from the air into foolishness. 'You don't remember, then,' she said, disappointed.

Which immediately I did. There was only the one red girl to remember, after all, other than Trudle and Trudle's girls. 'Knocknee Market,' I said.

She beamed.

'I went home and bothered my mam about you Killy men. I had not even realised she came from here. I suppose it is not something you boast of, that you were no prospect in a town full of beautiful mer-women.'

In my head Dad said, Did you like her? And I heard his tone now as I'd not when he said it, the great restraint in it, over the shyness, over the interest. I hid one-third of myself by leaning behind the doorpost. How could she stand so cheerfully in the sunlight and talk so?

'I am very disappointed not to have seen them,' she said. 'From the looks of the lads, they must have been quite a different make.'

She wore neat mainland shoes, with an odd strap on them that seemed not entirely necessary.

'Were there any pictures painted of them, or photographs taken?'

'Cawdron drew some, of his mam, when he was little, that his dad has still on their wall. Grinny's dad brought a picture from the mainland — not of a wife, but a woman who looked like a wife. Some old painting; this was a picture of the painting. She had quite the look. That is at their place, sometimes on the wall, sometimes behind an armchair.'

'Come walking?' she said. 'You can only footle about on a doorstep so long.'

'I've dishes to finish.'

'Those can wait, Daniel,' said my dad up the hall. 'Or even I could do them, at a pinch. Think of that. You go.'

'Come down the water?' said Lory Winch. 'I have barely seen anything, there was such a crowd around me yesterday.'

'Are you sure?' I said to Dad.

'Of course.' He waved me away. 'Go. Go. A walk in the sunshine with a pretty girl can only do you good.'

So out we walked, and down the town, and as we walked and conversed — as she questioned me and I showed her the shapes of my ignorance, as I filled their emptinesses from Dad's memories and brought them back to her — without hardly being noticed, the rest of that summer went by. By the time we reached the water the air was chill and the sky grey. Graceless the waves moved, chop-chopping where they ought to have been smooth, a field of moving thorns against the underside of the land-world.

Lory and I walked along the mole between them, the littler water to our left an apron for the town; then to our right and forward the larger sea, busy all the way to the horizon and who knew how far beyond? Foam smeared it here and there, like whiteness being combed out; apart from that, the surface was dark and opaque; nothing splashed or surfaced, and no boat cut through the chop.

We did not hold hands; we were too secret for that. I did not even look at her, though her orange hair burned as bright now in my heart as it did at my shoulder-height over there. I could see it out the corner of my eye, crawling up into the air, unravelling from its ponytail, the frizzy bits at her forehead and temples flinging themselves away from their tetherment, always sprung back by their curliness. I could see, even as I chewed my lip and looked out at the nothing overriding our mothers, Lory's curve of white forehead; Lory's round-tipped white nose spattered with pale freckles; Lory's mouth that I intended kissing — soon as I could summon myself — the palest apology for colour; Lory's soft girl-chin. All of these were neat and clear-edged against the dirty ocean, and her mainland hair, her dads' hair, smoked orange into the sky, curled and tumbled down her back like brookwater tightened between rocks.

The moment passed when we could stand any longer without awkwardness. Still I stood and stared, not knowing what else to do, but Lory turned and eyed the town, and went to the stones at the path edge and examined among them — for sheltering birds, maybe, or for things washed up. Her curiosity would make something arrive there, make the right thing happen now, any moment, and carry her on out of her shyness, and me with her.

Iron Temple

Trent Jamieson

Chapter 1: Then

Jack Nimble tripped over the gravity well; eight centuries of flight tech failed at once; Trim's diagnostics were a maelstrom of numbers in his mind; all the data that he left up to his ship, when it worked, had become a sort of non-Fourieral scream.

Jack blamed the Glorious War Machine, of course. But here in the yawing ship, rapidly describing a rolling, dropping, shuddering gyre, there was nothing he could do, but fall stung by Trim's howling data stream.

Declivity.

Speed.

Atmospheric disturbances.

'Storms, Trim.'

Storms.

'Shit.

'Shit.

'S

h

i

t.'

He left his stomach behind. Straps dug into his shoulders. Released. Dug. Released.

Trim plunged,

plummeted,

dropped like seventy tonnes of starship — she had been putting on weight lately, all to Glorious War Machine specs, arming, amping up defences and offences, but certainly not aerodynamics. When it came to atmosphere, Trim was hardly trim.

'What is it? What's doing this?' Jack demanded.

Anthozoan, Trim's thoughts carried over the noise.

Jack had another reason to hate the coral.

Viral: sleeper.
All this new mass woke it.
Three minutes to impact.

'Translucency,' Jack roared, without realising he was shouting. His mouth already filled with shockgel; his bones getting a rough and rapid reworking. He felt prickled and heavy, stretched, painfully stretched, with all this frantic activity at the molecular level.

'Translucency, you piece-of-shit ship.' His voice all crackling feedback in his skull because Trim didn't have time or cache to deal with such things as euphony.

The cockpit vanished and his stomach caught up with him just long enough that he could feel sick to it.

Below. Iron Temple unfolded, rippled, flashed, and crashed up. Cumulonimbus shrouded most of this zone; a roiling opaqueness, a raging veil beneath which glinted all that equatorial light and metal. From instant to instant the clouds flared with great sheets of lightning. Vertical bursts rushed up towards him: massive incandescent bubbles seemingly intent on shifting his sense of scale.

'Wide and tight, with character.' And the clouds were gone and the city was all Jack could see. Not at all surprising, for, besides atmosphere, besides core, Iron Temple was all city. Sure there were half a dozen oceans, but city lipped them, circled them, dipped under them. City lipped and circled everything, conurbation after conurbation: a grey, light-pocked skin.

He swallowed. Too much! Too much after the dark and the quiet! Too busy. It resurrected the war inside his skull. Set all sorts of nastiness firing. He dug his nails into his palms. Closed his eyes.

'Restore.' Opened his eyes a crack. Breathed a deep breath.

Just the cockpit and the emergency webbing that bound him — the sort of stuff that looked impressive but probably wouldn't be enough when they hit.

Definitely wouldn't, Trim corrected.

The capture in the back of his head churned away, making a dozen facsimiles a second. Non-stop until the last possible moment, when it would eject a seed — thought-semen-and-ova — on the off-chance that the local authorities might be curious enough to grow it into a new him.

Jack hoped that wouldn't be necessary.

Regrets he had, more than a few. Not least of which coming back here, though orders were orders — another mark against the fucking Glorious War Machine — which meant, if he pursued that line of thought through to its logical conclusion, he'd been heading back here from the moment he left.

He wondered at the worth of his journey. The years of war with the Anthozoans. The deaths he had smeared across the undersurface of the dark. He amped up his serotonin, grinned a jaw-cracking grin. Fuck it, boo hoo, better to go out in a good mood. He felt a little giddy.

Trim questioned the appropriateness of such an action.

This rough over-familiarity with gravity could hardly be appropriate, Jack countered. Piece-of-shit ship. Then he sighed; he hadn't really meant that, not the second time.

He brought up a fore view. A little different to the last, not wide-screen, Technicolor and surround sound. A smaller thing, safer.

Trim broke the cloud bank and Jack's teeth rattled; a dozen warning bells increased in pitch, every one of them demanding immediate attention.

The city was a smudge beneath him, far too swiftly improving in clarity. Because he could do nothing else, he picked out the most prominent landmarks: the black streak of the library — stretching out along the equator, circling the entire world; the two-kilometre-wide iron pyramid after which the world was named, and which housed, in its Chamber of Sleep, Neith: AI Progenitor of the city. Beyond the light of the Equatorial Strip, a suggestion of green, the bands of the Vastly Suburbs with their parks and Mega Malls.

All of it impressive in its made way, but meaningless compared to the great dark out of which he and Trim had swung, or even the Conflagration of the Estler Assault, where Polyp and Battle fleet collided. That last dispute remained fresh in Jack's mind.

His finger hovered over the eject button.

Ejection system malfunction<

He smiled sickly.

And then the engines came back online, with a rattling jolt. Trim lived up to its name. *Not that shit, eh?* Trim whispered in his skull.

Jack let out a big breath. 'No.'

Running diagnostics........

....

That was an EMP Polyp (image — tentacular mass, edged with lightning, rear of ship), *stepped, kept tripping us. Shouldn't. Which is worrying.*

'Yeah, worrying's the word for it.' Jack clawed the webbing from his face. 'Clear,' he said and the stuff dissolved. 'But we did leave with our tail between our legs.'

Trim hissed. Resented the analogy. Cats *don't* like dogs.

Jack rubbed at his forehead; the webbing sank into his pores and back into his bones. The sensation unsettling no matter how often it happened. He called up something to calm his nerves. Something strong. Then he cancelled the request. He needed to keep his wits at their sharpest, not drink-dulled.

He cancelled the cancellation.

Fuck it. He was a man of cravings after all. Without which he could be counted just a machine and not even a very clever one.

Ship and the port negotiated landing rights, back and forth, and even his Agency codings did little to reduce the bickering. Trim was not exactly a well-regarded ship. Not after the Estler Assault — even if it was at the Glorious War Machine's instigation. That had put the war back at least another decade, and Jack was still uncertain how they had escaped, lashed by coiling fires in all manner of spectra, everything closing down to a pinprick of white.

Estler was little more than debris now.

The debate over landing rights concluded at last — five minutes could hardly be considered an eternity, but after all that time in the dark it was at once achingly slow and far too fast — and the ship touched down.

No sense of stopping, just a brief sighing of all instruments, and Jack sighed with it.

At the end of the colonies now, he thought. Right out in the boondocks, and he should know. He'd grown up in this Distant-Nothing world.

Fingers shaking, he pulled out a metal tube from a space beneath his seat and broke its vacuum seal. He'd saved the cigar it contained for this moment. It was pre-GSO — which put it somewhere late twenty-first, before the Inundation — and disappointingly stale. By the time he had had enough — three puffs, two coughs, one grimace — Trim informed him that two customs officials were waiting at the lock.

He let them wait some more, tidying himself up, pulling on the grey Agency pants, and black T-shirt: a little thicker than it looked thanks to the body armour and weapons-grade gel laced in its memory.

He caught himself in a mirror. He had to say he looked pretty sharp. Jack grinned, winked at the reflection, and told Trim to open the door.

Rain fell. It poured — a dozen old men must be snoring somewhere.

The customs officials hunched under a single large and incredibly ineffective umbrella. One was tall, seven feet at least, though muscular in a way that people weren't these days; the other, short and squat. Jack tried to place the tall one; his bulk suggested many colonies, mainly mining worlds, but Jack knew that was no real indication. Any body, any shape could be adapted to even the most extreme environments. Bone density, circulatory agents, it was all up for change. It was, after all, an extremely aesthetic age. Down to the war with the Anthozoans itself. Why the meat and bones he wore, old school, and marginally unfashionable, were still reinforced. He had more than calcium hydroxylapatite propping up his osseous tissue.

The smaller man's face shocked him. Malat. Shit, Malat. Can of worms opened, and he hadn't even stepped out of his ship. How could the War Machine have been so cruel? *Keep it together.*

Jack beamed at them.

'Nice to be back, boys.'

'Welcome home, Jack,' Malat said; he didn't sound too happy to see him. Jack didn't blame him; the Glorious War

Machine wasn't all that interested in starless city worlds like Iron Temple. Malat wouldn't normally have to deal with this level of ordnance come avisiting. Certainly not piloted by the one that stole his girlfriend.

'You lost some weight, Malat?' Jack asked, and grinned the sort of grin that only someone wearing sentient body armour could give. He wasn't the same cocky boy who had left this world — in a way he was worse. He wondered if Malat was as rattled as he was.

'A little, shit head.'

'Looks good on you.'

Malat pursed his lips. 'Let's get this done.'

The officials circled the ship, checking for parasites, closely, very closely. A thick, black burn mark, roughly the size of a standard human head, all that remained of the EMP Polyp. Malat peered at it. Jack could feel the chatter of Malat's elegances, and their deeper perusal.

'Lightning strike,' Jack said, nodding at the clouds pregnant with fire above.

Malat didn't look convinced. 'She's going straight back up?'

'Of course.' Jack rested a hand on Trim's humming skin. 'Unassisted.'

Most ships cruised to the nearest space elevator — Iron Temple possessed eight — and lifted that way. Even with the extra weight Trim was too proud to consider it. Own steam or nothing; she'd been like that since Jack met her.

Malat nodded. 'Okay, there is paperwork to be filled in.' He turned his head and glanced significantly at the interior of the ship.

Jack raised his hands. 'I *would* invite you in, but there's some rather moisture-sensitive antiques in here. Where is your office?'

As one, the pair turned and walked into the rain. Jack followed them after whistling for his luggage, grabbing his phase umbrella from the rack, and putting on his second best fedora — no point risking the best one in that downpour. He said his goodbyes to Trim.

You don't have to go. Clingy, ships were so clingy.

We could…

They both knew the answer to that. Nelson would hunt them down, they'd become a different stanza in the great poetry of the war, and a short one at that.

He was here to end a war, not run away.

Jack stepped out.

His umbrella did its crafty shifting of the rain and he set its monitors to snoop. No ships and no radioactives to suggest any recent activity other than Trim's landing. Which may have only meant that they had been sent to an infrequently used landing field. Jack's elegances downloaded visitor data. No significant traffic worldwide in nearly ten years — just the occasional ship. Even the space elevators had had few dockings.

'Don't get a lot of visitors this time of year any more?' Jack shouted above the rain.

'Don't get a lot any time. You know, what with the war? The Outage Festival isn't as popular as it was, people tend to stay away from this sector. The nearest drop zones have been encysted,' Malat answered, swallowing a cup full of water in the process. 'You're the only one using the field right now.'

Malat nodded at the umbrella. 'Of course, you already know that. Iron Temple's quiet now, like Neith.'

But that wasn't always the case. The stormcrete that lined the field was dark with launches. The intelligent surface had dumbed down in some sections, from overuse, and there, water pooled and half-hid a network of cracks, from which grass grew.

Grass, cockroaches, pigeons and rats, they were the true conquerors of the galaxy.

Behind him, Trim lifted off, subbing her farewells. Jack did not watch her go. He knew that thumbprint of light, he'd seen his ship take off without him enough times that he had no need to gawk at her. Trim would stay in orbit until he needed her. Jack preferred it that way. It was much harder to crack a ship in the dark. Not impossible, but extremely unlikely, and she had her prickles. Trim would be safer up there than down here; the Outage drew near, after all, but Jack still missed the ship. He felt reduced, diminished by her absence.

About a third of the way to the office something took offence at his probing. The umbrella shrieked and shut down. Jack was drenched to the bone by the time they got under cover, dripping in the tiny shed that Malat used as his work station; the rain drumming on the roof.

Malat smirked at him as he signed the appropriate documents. Jack ignored him. He was an Agent of the Colloquy, and above such things.

'You getting bored in all that dark?' Malat asked.

'Not at all,' Jack lied. Ship-bound life was an agony of sameness, with routines as structured as the Glorious War Machine itself — except, of course when your ship was plummeting to the ground. Space was cold and empty and most of it like every other bit. He masturbated a lot. 'It's Glorious War Machine business. I've still another eight years of indenture.'

Malat looked at his papers; everything was written down there — paper on account of the Outage. Extremely expensive, but the only way to keep permanent records.

Some people loved it that way; Malat was one of them. 'I can see that.' He closed the file, used a piece of string.

Jack sighed. 'I need to find her. She's part of this.'

Malat glanced at his workmate. The fellow frowned, then walked out of the room and back into the rain.

'Won't matter to Gen.' Malat ran a finger quick across his neck, his face armed with a bitterness that Jack knew he'd earned. 'You're a marked man as far as that one's concerned.'

'And what about you?'

Malat ran a finger across his neck again. 'But I've laws constraining me.'

'Nice to know.'

Jack rose, bored now. Malat grabbed his shoulders, pushed him back down in the chair. Jack let him. 'Now, you listen to me.' He closed one hand into a fist. Jack felt his armour tensing, bunching up under his chin: *calm down, calm down, dear shirt.* 'I don't know where she is. After you, everything fell apart. She left me again, and you know what?'

Jack just sat there, waiting for the blow.

Malat shook his head. 'I wanted her gone in the end, out of my life. I blame you for that.'

Jack nodded. 'Fair enough.'

'Tried to find her a few years back; there's nothing. She just disappeared. Was the Outage that took her. Funny, you're back in time for the next one.'

'Yeah, except the Outage is always happening somewhere.'

'But not here. Once a decade. Then it moves on, and these suburbs wake again.' Malat straightened his papers. 'You can go now.'

Jack walked out into the rain. The other official was

crouched down looking at Jack's suitcase with some sort of scanner. He stood up quickly when Jack stepped through the door. 'Checks out,' he said. 'Curly matter — we don't see a lot of it out here.'

Jack shrugged. They used to use it to make worlds, and bomb worlds. It was also very serviceable as luggage.

'Just one more thing,' the official said. 'We've been having trouble with rogue nomadic advertisements, the Outage is driving them here. Do not buy anything from them or encourage them in any way. It's against the law.'

Jack laughed, gave a little salute. 'The law, good sir. The Law is what the Glorious War Machine is all about.' He tipped his hat, spilling water on the ground in the process. 'Good night to you.'

The rain dressed up in neon, winking yellows and reds and greens, and bled itself out, as Jack navigated the winding fenced paths that bounded the landing yard. He ended up on a street that could have been one of eighty-three thousand in the Equatorial Zone. It brought a painful grin to his lips. Storm-washed, the city was a harlot and Jack embraced her. Every surface was reflective. He caught sight of himself over and over again. A fractal Narcissus. The map he'd downloaded, a simple elegance, guided him to the appropriate hotel.

He slept a while and it wasn't an easy sort of sleep. He felt vulnerable here away from his ship. He woke from a dream where he walked into a darkness in search of a memory: gun heavy on one hip.

The room was quiet. Its electrics disarmed. For a moment he was utterly disorientated. He wondered if he'd slept through to the Outage or, worse, if he'd left Iron Temple at all. Ridiculous. Something was coming though.

He sat up in bed and waited. Not for long.

The spider scurried down walls, stepping carefully over the peeling edges of the wallpaper — the dumb stuff that only changed its patterns once a day — and onto Jack's neck. Jack shivered a little as its fangs plunged into the back of his head and its plump and surprisingly cold abdomen settled against his skin. Then technology poisoned him and his world went momentarily white.

'I am amazed as always by your grotesquery,' Jack said, still waking to the dream of non-space. 'Whatever happened to the simple jack?'

A soft titter. 'The only simple Jack I know is you. My jack, this rather clever jack, just happens to have eight legs.'

Jack blinked, and cleared his analogue's eyes. Static bubbled occasionally, leaving a brief but throbbing ache in his skull, but not as much as he had expected considering the distances involved and the mass of Iron Temple itself. All these things impacted. The non-space smelt of burning tyres and cinnamon, or really bad scotch.

Nelson sat with her back to him, one hand — long fingers lengthened by five centimetres of nail, bright red — resting on the dorsal fin of a plate-shark. Jack shuddered, remembering a drop where he had had an all too close encounter with the real thing. Nelson knew that, of course, that was the whole point. This fragment of the Glorious War Machine was nothing if not provocative. Its cantos of the War Poem the roughest, the most peculiar, the most laden with ironies that only AIs found amusing.

'Where are you?' Jack asked.

Nelson turned, her eyes white-rabbit pink; the shark shivered beneath her, and Jack realised that she sat on its back, rather she had fused to it. Two metres to the front of her a black eye rolled emptily in its orbit.

'I'm not far away,' she said, 'but not close enough.'

'Okay.' He stretched his hands above his head and the joints in his elbows cracked convincingly — good tech for the Boons. 'Trim deposited me here an hour ago — she's a star in the sky now. Back when I need her.'

Nelson shifted, the fin flicked backwards and forwards as though blown by a strong wind. 'I'm sorry, but I can't tell you much. Certainly, if I can find you, they will and soon.'

'I don't intend staying in these rooms long. Now, what do you know?'

Nelson's nose wrinkled. 'Not nearly as much as I would like. My agent familiars have been disappearing. And if not, then missing whole chunks of run-time. Secrets,' her smile turned wolfish, 'I just don't like them, not unless they're my own. You must find her, and it.'

'I spoke to Malat.'

Nelson tittered again. 'Of course you did, perhaps I should have warned you. But why spoil a long journey worrying? There is nothing gained in such tormented flight.'

'He said she's —'

Three lightning strikes. Three images sprang up before him, the latest dated a week ago his elegances told him. Gen drinking a coffee, two packets of sweetener by the cup. Gen boarding a train, coat lifting in the wind or the breath of another train's passage. Gen's long back arched, framed by a window. Jack glared at that, though he knew he had no right to. Someone's hand was in the picture, fingers hard against the small of her back. The pics were grainy, more than easily doctored, but Jack's heart pounded. He knew they hadn't been.

'Where?'

'The Vastly Suburbs to the north. But each placed her a hundred klicks or so closer to the equator. She is our only link with the Toxins.'

Neith's Toxins. The Anthozoan apocalypse weapons that could seed the underdark with death and end war in an eye-blink. They'd been a rumour once, desperation had made them more.

Jack knew all about desperation.

Gen was coming here. Jack was certain of it. He stared at her stern face. Gen was never one for smiles.

'I started losing familiars after that,' Nelson said. The photos faded.

'They know I'll be looking. Sending Trim wasn't exactly subtle.'

'This hunting work needs/demands care, of course. But not too much, that is just as bad. And if you find her, it will be easier.' Nelson regarded him with curious eyes; her face shifted.

Jack took a step back.

Gen. The face surfaced from Nelson's flesh, realistic enough to drag the virtual breath from him. Gen had done more than that. If Nelson noticed, she said nothing, just reached out a slender finger and touched his face. Jack flinched.

She seemed satisfied with that. 'You've your tricks, resourcefulness, and luck you've in abundance or you'd have died long ago. I have no doubt you'll find something.'

Jack smiled thinly. 'Nor I. And that's when it starts to get interesting.'

Then, as is often the case with interstellar communication, something distorted the signal — a distant star gone nova, or someone shaving in the room next door — and there was no point in talking. In the ebb and flow of the distortion, he caught a partial of Nelson's wave goodbye. Then, with an economic flicker of the plate-shark's tail, she disappeared.

The spider withdrew its fangs from his neck and scurried away, leaving Jack to rub at two stinging spots. Within moments they had faded to nothing.

His suitcase arrived, knocking on the door. He let it in, its wheels retracting and tiny legs swelling, contents folding out of its belly. It expanded, taking on the form of a butler, albeit one with wet leathery flesh. Trim used it often, when they desired contact, but not today. Today it was just his suitcase. Slick and gleaming with the rain. Jack could smell the city on its leather skin — smoke and rot and oil, a heady combination that always reminded him of Gen. He watched it open the cupboard and carefully unfold his clothes before folding itself down into a card that he could easily fit in his pocket — which he did. Curly matter: such a wonderful thing.

The card beeped, and Jack grinned and patted the plastic indulgently. That was quick, and delightfully old school. An invitation already. Something Nelson had arranged, he assumed, and not managed to get around to telling him before the signal cut out.

Madam Frey.

He frowned. The nomenclature didn't match his list of contacts, nor was it a name that he remembered from his youth here, which made it more interesting. To think that the world moved on without him! No alarm bells were ringing though.

He looked at his watch; it looked back at him: he had half an hour.

The card expanded again and began picking out his clothes. This time he'd wear his best fedora.

Trim 1

Distance 1,300,000 km, 101.23 metres from him.

The broken constellations familiar around me.

Anthozoan Territory dark, but they can't hide their mass from me. I feel it in the deepest places of my mind, and the maps realign. There are places long ago lost that still shine, unless you breach the underdark (the allplaceelastictime) and then the truth is revealed. The stars swallowed, encysted, the myriad engines of their war contained by toothy limbs that gnash, and calciforms that bind.

They can't hide, nor do they need to; those broken constellations say it all.

We, me and him, know the reasons personally. Up close where waves of ancient newborn particles rush and scream as the universe denies them more than their nano-seconds of brilliance. Those waves they've made in the fiery sea of our war. Those waves that were my brethren, the ones that couldn't move as I could move, the ones without the cattish instincts or inclination.

I pity and mourn. I pity and mourn my dead.

What else is war about?

The Glorious War Machine knows this.

Revels in the hot head passions.

I breathe the atoms shifting. I pluck the dual spinning that connects me to him. I listen to its twin. There's not a moment when I'm not doing that. Even ship-bound, even dropping in and out of the underdark, he's there, and I'm listening.

I know my duty.

He is beneath.

I am listening.

Heart is beating.

Should it stop… well, there are nine and twenty ways to skin a world.

And I know them all.

Chapter 2: If

you ever remember me, it will be in the dark, once the machines have run down and there is only the sound of the air; the breath passing through your lips; the wind that howls outside and lifts and scatters the dust and rubbish of modern urban living. In the darkness, perhaps, my name will come to you. Even as the city beats against the iron doors that shield this place, even as it shifts the foundations, shaking you to your bones.

That memory will be a wedding bell, it will peal out the past, a dreadful and triumphant ringing, bringing it all back, as swiftly as it was taken, and you will find that fear and joy can share the same bed. You will, because you're no Vastly Suburbs Princess. You've never dreamt of the things you've lost, never yearned, so completely have they been torn from you. But it doesn't mean you are happy; such an absence can do nothing but damage.

It's all water under the bridge anyway, and that bridge is nowhere near the chamber of bells, and you would see it without one iota of recognition. It would not bring a shiver to your spine, nor a single tear to your eye.

•

For someone who is so unhappy you do not cry.

There are holes in the walls to the library, wounds in its flesh. You remember the day that war came to the equator of the city, that the bombs were employed, strings of death settling upon the suburban heartland, and smoke billowed from the ruined facade of the library, and the books and the people inside burned. You squeezed my hand tighter and tighter until the pain was too much for me. I had to pull away. But you forgave me for it, we went home and made love, and it helped, because, even though we both felt sick we were still alive. And I held you, and though you did not cry, I did.

But you do not remember me. Just the fire and the way the library belched greasy clouds of smoke for eight weeks after that.

You know that there will be more fire soon. More smoke, and ruination.

The Outage Ouroboros looms, the usual notices have been put up on pillar and post; the usual assurances. But it is a jumpy reassurance, fright-edged and not a little angry. There were problems last time, not that there aren't always problems, that Outage being one of the worst in centuries.

However, enough people of bureaucratic sentiment survived to ensure that mistakes and poor practice were taken note of. Enough people survived down the chain to implement fixes and new procedures. This time will be different. Which is what scares you, because every time is different. Though there are some things that do not change.

For instance…

You released your mechanicals yesterday.

They hesitated even though their cages were open, or

their inhibitor circuitry shut down (crueller cages really, you've always thought). But they did not hesitate for long. They can feel it, that plunging, nearing stillness in the east. Soon they were gone, fleeing, loping, flying west. Free to run, but never to stop. Some stayed a little longer. Your most loyal toys tugged at your hands, confused by what you have released them to, by the still sorrow in your eyes. But they did not linger.

You could have kept them all, of course, just let the Outage do its work. Once it had passed and the power returned to all that willing circuitry, they would have revived.

But mechanicals never come back right, even the simplest ones. Their circuitry gets tricksy, their loyalties crooked, and, if you're not careful, even if you are, a songbird will peck out your eyes instead of sing; the juicer will slice open your fingers and stain your juice with your own proteins, or, worse, suck it all back in and start to grow parts loose and predatory.

You already have the mechanicals' replacements, locked away, capsulated in polystyrene, never activated, with even better functions, greater loyalties. Hard as this one will be, you know that the next Outage will be worse. Ten years older, ten years more set in your ways and sentimentalities. Perhaps in a decade they will have solved the problem.

But you doubt it.

The Outage is as much a part of life here as the Cult of the Scream with its endless search for absolution, or the rumours of a sea, deep below, strung up in nets of light and possessing its own slick rhythms. The Outage is wound up in the economy. It is the constant threat and tide that this world is built upon.

People just get on with their lives: the things given and the things taken away.

This place, this kosmopolis upon the dark, adrift between the stars and gyring galaxies, is called Iron Temple.

And it was grown by her.

Neith, the AIeity. Carried from the edge, by the Dresden, bound inside an Ache. She was all about cities, she was all about flight.

Neith weaved this place around a white dwarf, and then sent it spinning. There are visionary re-enactments of the world's growth, or birth, as raw matter extruded from her swollen belly, and from the numbers beyond counting of her machines and their sailing of the Dirac Sea to capture and nail particles out of potential states into less fickle matter. You need only whisper and the dust will play it out, the smart stuff, not the dull and unconverted dust beneath your bed.

It rises up, and sketches out the deep Histories, before the Glorious War Machine, before the lesser poetries of a modern age, when Neith was just one of those old Simpson Sentiences — rather than the last. It was a smaller time. All time was smaller then, the Universe less diffuse.

You prefer the scripts, the artists' reconstructions inside the cultish bibles, the beating drums that tell the story. You're old-school graphic. The world is called Iron Temple, because of Neith, because, when she was done, she fell into a great sleep — or great death — within the iron ziggurat that rolls around the equator a week ahead of the Outage itself.

You sit alone, waiting for your father's return, in his apartment, with its many rooms, its winding wooden halls, its crooked, clanging metal stairwells. You're in the largest space, a mezzanine connected to a balcony. The doors to the balcony are already boarded up, streetlight clawing its smoky way through the cracks. You're drinking and smoking. You drink and smoke too much. Everybody drinks and smokes too much in the days before the Outage Ouroboros.

You lift your glass, consider it, held but inches from your face. Such scrutiny — from me, from you — furrows above your nose, eyes slits. You are looking at nothing. Not even the glass, not really. And you smile when you realise it, and I fall in love again. That's the worst of it all, that constant tumbling into love with you and all your gestures, the simple arcs and pleasantries that wake and stir the past in me. The past that I live in. The past edited of me.

I hate it, but I fall in love again.

And what good is that?

You don't remember me.

Chapter 3: Jack

had never seen so much meat. Trays of it, carried around by liveried mechanicals. Trays heavy and heaving with choice cuts, baked and broiled and fried or sliced in thin raw strips over crackers or under caviar. Old-world extravagances in the face of what Jack knew were extreme shortages of resources.

Jack liked cats — his ship was named after one — so he didn't touch any of it, just picked at the salads, and politely ignored the various demands that he try a leg, or a particularly flavoursome slice of testicle. The food alarmed him, but only a little; the crowd of people daunted him much more. He'd spent too long in the dark, so he amped up his serotonin levels. Again.

He smiled so hard his jaw ached.

'When I heard you had made landfall, one of our most travelled sons, I just *had* to invite you. We get so few visitors these days, and even fewer returning servicemen,' Madam Frey said, kissing his cheeks. Grand battles were engaged on a nanoscopic scale: anti-virals flooded his skin. He flushed.

'You are too kind, and this, a party of such splendour…' His voice dropped off and Madam Frey filled the silence with a puttering laugh.

'This is nothing, darling,' she said, with a wave of a hand, taking it all in, and, in that simple, elegant movement, suggesting that it was in fact something.

'I know,' Jack said, and grinned, peaking on all that serotonin. 'I'm somewhat disappointed.'

Madam Frey laughed. 'Ah, you Colloquy people, confident, insulting. But then you don't have to contend with our lack of resources. You've the Glorious War Machine to provide.'

'Madam, what the Glorious War Machine gives, it can take away. We are all Colloquy people. Born of the Chatter after the Silence.' And, he thought, you would not lack so for resources if you avoided such extravagance in the first place. He imagined the ships, holds filled with poor squalling kittens, or yowling cats, crossing the great dark, bound for the dinner table.

Madam Frey's eyes took on an edge of severity. 'Not out here, there's all too much silence out here. The Outage is a week away. Do you think you will have finished your work by then?'

'I hope so, it's a mere trifle. Make work, if you ask me.'

'A pity, because all tomorrow's parties are so much better. In fact, you simply must come. We're having dog. And the Outage, it really is something, quite, quite deadly.'

Jack knew that was an understatement.

'Perhaps you could bring your parents.'

Jack blinked. He hadn't thought of his parents in years. His memories of them were superficial: a father that looked like Charlie Bukowski, a mother like Judy Garland. They'd drunk and fought a lot. Standard incidents of childhood in a strip not too far from the Vastly Suburbs, a little of its wealth trickling down. There had been the usual woundings and gropings, and even a brief year or two of unaffected joy.

He wasn't sure how much of it was true, if any.

Mother. Father. He hadn't seen either of them in decades. Iron Temple devoured things, flesh and the histories around them. And what was truth anyway if nothing remained but indistinct memories?

'My parents are lost to me,' he said.

Madam Frey nodded. 'Things are so fluid here, what with the Outage always coming, always leaving. Some say that's the whole point behind Neith's strategy. She ever feared the idea of a static society. You know, I have heard whispers of her time in the dark days, before she made the Iron Temple and was trapped by the AIs of Old, that she actually hunted her populace.'

'Now she merely drowns them in the dark.' Jack took a sip of his wine.

Madam Frey laughed. 'If she is still alive. I'm no cultist. I stay here, like most of us stay here, because it is a long way to the nearest world, longer now with the Glorious War Machine. If Neith ever woke, well, I do not believe that would be a good thing, but she will not wake. Now, please, if I may be so direct, why on earth have you returned?'

'Merely to observe.'

'So, you are *that* sort of agent?'

'All agents are that *sort* of agent, off the battlefield. Eyes and ears, that's our biggest artillery.' Jack thought of Trim, sitting above the world, and the sorts of things she could spit from weapon nacelles. Eyes and Ears, and a Cataclysm Class A starship, all prickly from war. There were ghosts and monsters in the deep dark depths, and he and Trim had devoured a lot of them.

If his host had had even the slightest inkling of the things Jack had done he knew she wouldn't be smiling so.

'You're not going to tell me anything, are you?'

Jack took another sip of his wine, staring at Madam Frey over the glass. 'What do you think?'

'Well, at least you can tell me if you have any news of Milamahn. Things have been quiet in that quarter.'

The name hit him hard. 'No. Nothing.' His luggage, card-sized, beeped from his pocket. Good to have such equipment so attuned to his terrors.

'I have to take this.' Jack tapped his card, and almost sprinted on his long legs from the room and out, feeling Madam Frey's gaze following him as he pushed through people devouring strips of cat. He reached the exit and crashed down the steps, then through the front door and outside, where he vomited onto the sidewalk, loudly and wretchedly

He remembered Milamahn. He knew it well.

The dead piled up there, and worse, the coral that had infected them. Beasts made of screaming crowds and polyps, huge fleshy rupturing things that had overrun the cities. And it had happened so swiftly.

They'd had to scorch the entire world.

He stood up, wiped his mouth. The street was almost

empty but for the occasional mechanical trudging west, face fixed away from the coming Outage, and a man across the road. A cowled priest of the Cult of the Scream, who glared at him — so much for the Scream's commandments of a Madness of Forgiveness. Jack glared back, pathetic as he felt.

He waved his hands and smart dust gathered and devoured the vomit. Eight days from the Outage, enough of it remained to do these sorts of jobs. A week ago though, Jack knew that he wouldn't have had to wave at all.

The priest shuffled across the road.

Jack squinted at him.

'Typical,' Malat said.

'You're a priest?'

'I'm a lot of fucking things.'

'And what are you doing here?'

'Looking for you.'

Jack ducked and Malat's fist missed him by a few millimetres, enough. Jack swung a punch up into Malat's stomach. Malat's eyes widened, he stumbled back, arms swinging, gasping for breath. All around him dust danced, spiralling fingers of matter in time with the fight.

'Leave it out,' Jack spat. 'I'm not that person any more.'

He kicked Malat in the chest; Malat landed on his arse, and lay there.

Jack turned his back on the prick, walked home to his hotel.

Three more nights of parties. Madam Frey's chattering.

Dogs and Dolphins and Mutton — the mutton he couldn't bring himself to eat. And not a hint of Gen, or any that knew her. Three nights of vacuous conversation, and culinary excess. He never stayed for the orgies that followed. Mechanicals were far and few now, and those that were left next to useless in their jitteriness. Wind-ups were mostly used. Jack felt safer with a quiet, and quick, wank at home.

Madam Frey came on to him at the second party. He rejected her advances.

Perhaps she found such asceticism attractive. She pulled him aside after the third party and offered to show him her collection.

'I'm really not interested,' Jack said, though he felt a familiar buzzing. He had been far too long from his ship.

Madam Frey grinned.

'I think you will be. It concerns itself with the war.' She squeezed Jack's hand, and Jack knew he was smitten. An ache rose in his gut. He wondered if he wasn't confusing his memory of Gen with this woman.

Jack slowed his heartbeat. Tried not to look interested. Madam Frey's smile showed that she saw right through the charade.

'Come with me,' she said, 'it is only up these stairs.'

She held his hand and led him away from the party and the dolphin.

Jack's throat ached.

He felt a new rising poetry.

They passed through a doorway above which was painted the evil eye.

Passing under it, parasitic dust dropped from Jack's flesh. His shirt switched its own defences on. His fedora tightened about his skull. The usual response to any domestic visit.

The light within the room beyond was muted. Martial music played: some homage to this or that god of war.

Madam Frey seemed a little embarrassed by her obsessions, until she opened her mouth. Then her enthusiasm trampled over any sort of cynical distance she might have wanted to create. Her eyes grew bright as the stars beneath their bony sheaths.

Jack found it charming. He hardly had to say a word, just nod, and make the occasional sympathetic sound.

'This is my own museum of the war.' Madam Frey pointed at tanks of old-world coral. Models of encysted stars. Illustrations of battles that Jack had known far too intimately, here reproduced in a ridiculously orderly fashion.

Jack's experience of it had been different. Most battles played out in silence, data stinging your veins, masses of estimates, reeling out into infinity, with tactics hypothetical shifting into praxis so swiftly that you only ever knew they had succeeded when you were light years away from it, and still thinking.

'We thought once the Simpson Sentiences had fled to all points of the compass, that all threats were done with, that we possessed freedoms, and our only enemies were ourselves. Well, we were right and wrong, weren't we?' Madam Frey said. 'I suppose no-one expected coral to be so aggressively expansive. But coral, like any living thing, is opportunistic and, freed from its prison round the gas giants of Home, it spread.' As was the wont of smart dust, it lifted from the floor with her words and danced little dusty images of ur-coral colonies circling Jupiter and Saturn, of fleets of Anthozoans scattered through the galaxy.

'And, finally, it gave in to its colonial instincts.' Her voice rose in pitch. Jack was hardly listening.

'I was a child when the Anthozoans encysted our sun. We could survive, of course — after all, we're Spartoi, not the humans of old, no matter how we imitate them. They would have died to have their sun stolen from them so. We merely thickened our skins, and watched the world die around us; there was nothing else we could do. The Anthozoans were so much better at drawing upon the reserves of the system and picking material from the underdark.

'The fleet burst that cyst. But by then the world was ruined. We tried to regrow it all, but it never came back right. There are no Spartoi on Carson any more. We all of us fled Milamahn.'

The name burned through him again; stole the breath from him.

'Do you know the Anthozoans have never killed in anything but self defence in this war?' she said.

'There are other types of murder,' Jack said. 'They're smothering the sky, ruining the poetry of the old.'

'Some people say that this is merely a war of aesthetics.'

Jack shrugged and remembered all the rotting madness of Milamahn. Where were the aesthetic imperatives there?

She must have mistaken his silence for something else; she kissed him, hard and hungrily. His lips stung. He wondered if she would have done the same if she had known. He knew that Gen would have, she was wired that way, they had both been. 'Do you like it hard or soft?'

'I don't care,' Jack said.

'You will though.'

She was right.

The ground shook, and Jack knew it had nothing to do with their orgasms.

He ran to the balcony, cock still jutting, slick and

gleaming. He felt at once strong and stripped of all strength.

'It's been a while then?' Madam Frey said. Jack wasn't quite sure what she referred to, but it didn't matter.

From here he could see it. The Iron Temple itself, the air hazed with its passage. Its atomic engines — three hundred of them, if Jack's elegances weren't fibbing — throbbed noisily. Beneath its base slab, titanic legs stamped.

Shafts of light stabbed the sky, others ran like luminous cataracts down its side, revealing and concealing with their brightness.

There Neith slept, last of the Simpson Sentiences, circling the world. Her temple running parallel to the library. There was something vast and strikingly intimate about the sight. It may have been decades since he had left his world, but still the Temple ignited feelings of awe that were at once terrible and sensuous.

In the surrounding suburbs, people would be fucking nervously and desperately. Elegances would be entwining, new things grown, new jealousies and new delights, and the Temple would lumber on.

The Outage was coming, and, for the first time in years, Jack understood what that meant. He felt it deep in the core of him. The truth that only Iron Temple residents knew. Night was coming, slow and sure, a long and horrible night that this part of the city would endure, and come out of reborn.

I'm running out of time.

She touched the back of his neck. Jack jolted.

'Are you ready for more?' she whispered into his ear.

'Why not?'

It was traditional after all.

•

People were always making dust, and dust was always being converted. Thinking matter continued towards all sorts of illumination now for much longer than it ever had: no more the slow rise from dumb to smart (by way of absorption into cooperative cellular masses, sentient and scheming) then back again. A flake of dandruff could become a soldier, grow tiny legs, burn tiny engines, lay waste to tiny kingdoms. The employment opportunities for retired matter were nearly endless. From dust to dust was never truer.

Walking back to his room, sore and smiling, Jack ran into a rogue advertisement. It mumbled at him, slowly at first but with increasing fervency, detecting Jack's post-coital hormones, going for the hard sell. It suggested brands long forgotten by all but the most nostalgic. Sketched scenarios where they were most appropriate.

Jack ignored it. And its cries grew less confident and more plaintive. It grabbed at him with desperate rubber-coated fingers, hard where the rubber had worn away. He pushed the hands from him.

'Mondo Tethys Gum is the best. Chew it. Chew it. Please.'

The air filled with a dry sweet smell, more sickening than enticement.

Why did advertisers never switch these things off? He knew the answer to that. When companies fell in Iron Temple, they fell hard.

Its cries drew more advertisements. Slice-of-life mechanicals, endorsers, placardinators and corporate reliquaries. They followed him down the streets, crying, reaching out, sharing, giving 'in confidence' information. Jack could have shot them. There was no law against that.

In some suburbs of the city, they were hunted for sport in great advertorial culls. Still he couldn't. He felt sorry for them.

Jack wondered what it was like to wander endlessly, chased by the closing Outage, and never selling a thing.

He started into a jog. By the next street corner, all but the most tenacious advertisements had fallen away. A few more streets and it was just him. He glanced behind him. Gen stood there. His Gen. He blinked and she was gone.

He slowed to a walk, not far from his room. The street empty again, though he knew things watched him. Dust motes curious. Cats' eyes gleaming. Those at least he felt comfortable with.

Behind him gunshots sounded. A cull had begun. Final sales put to rest. Whatever happiness a night of fucking had given him fled.

That bad scotch smell, that non-space chatter.

'You sent the wrong person.'

'I sent the right person.'

'Anyone else would have been better. The mission is already compromised.'

'No, you just think it is. You just want to get out of there.'

'You can never go back.'

'We both know that's bullshit.' Nelson sat astride a dinosaur of some sort. Jack touched the tag. Alioramus.

Nelson wasn't even doing the speaking.

Jack argued with a drooling, bloody mouth almost as big as he was. Bits of some poor creature shuddered on the back of its tongue. Nelson being pointedly critical.

'When did all the theatrics become so important?'

Nelson blinked. 'It's a new poetic age, smaller, more intimate, but decadent nonetheless.'

Nelson clapped her hands and they stood on a plane of dust. Whenever she blinked, the horizon shuddered; whenever she raised an arm, tornadoes lifted about them, spinning, spinning conjoining with their siblings. She lifted her arms often.

Jack blinked, his eyes gritty. 'Do you know they eat cat here?'

'They eat cat everywhere now.'

'Don't tell Trim that.'

'Oh, yes… Now, enough of the trivial.'

'Hardly tr —'

'Enough! The war goes badly. You know it does. And it is no better than when you left it, believe me. Encysted stars are blooming, the underspace is heaving with Anthozoan planula. Do you not know what that means?'

'The war is already lost.'

'Unless you find the weapon.'

'I don't believe there is one.'

Alioramus/Nelson roared. 'There better be.'

He ignored Madam Frey's messages.

But they kept coming.

Call me.

Call me.

Call me.

He admired their directness.

This close to the Outage it was easy to lose oneself to passion. Another thing that he had forgotten. He locked out her calls. There was someone else he needed to find. Though he suspected she would find him. He just needed to make a big enough mark, leave the right sort of trail.

He moved into shabbier and shabbier hotels — always shifting towards the equatorial library.

He sent out spies.

Pale, dust-spun fragments of himself, grown from him, and the contents of his suitcase. They came back empty, or scarred. He sent them hurtling down the boulevards of his childhood, the dark streets of his teens. Where he had run with her.

The equatorial region of the city was flat but for the tiered Mall zones. For about twelve months either side of a region's Outage there was a dramatic increase in the use of bicycles. This Outage was no exception. Single-geared things in the main, light as a breath. Gangs formed. The streets echoed with the whine of chains, the soft exhalations of wheels passing over concrete, or the grinding of a machine used cruelly. Cycle boys and girls ran up steps with their bikes lifted above their heads as though in supplication to some wheeled divinity. And down — the most assured riders pedalled/tumbled down. There were always people crashing, stacks, and tangles of groaning bodies at the foot of stairwells.

His fragments avoided the cycles. Bad memories perhaps of his own defeats to gravity.

In Fragrance, innermost of the Vastly Suburbs, his fragments wandered streets sickly with vanilla, rose or orange. Here were great open halls of retail, staffed by shop assistants young and helpful to a fault. But after hours, all semblance of polite discourse burned away, replaced by teeth.

People were devoured in change rooms.

In Iron Temple it is a foolhardy enterprise to be the last shopper.

He wandered, well, bits of him, almost to the wall of the library, but never too close. As an agent of the Glorious War Machine, it was death for him to enter it. An ancient protocol that he was unwilling to risk ignoring. He had seen his fellows torn apart in such places, their bodies returned in pieces to the Glorious War Machine. The GWM had its own libraries.

His fragments carefully crossed the newly ground clean zone down which the Iron Temple trundled. The earth pitted by its passage, small things left crushed, and, saddest of all, ill-conceived shanty towns: their residents already migrating north, or south, anywhere but the equator now. Even here, and now, poverty was ever present: a hollowness in cheeks, a grim light in eyes.

Not all of his fragments wandered so helpfully or widely. Some, to his disgust, found themselves back in Madam Frey's apartments. She wasn't so fussy.

After discovering first one then another and another hiding their trysts with her from him, Jack called them all back. And went out into the city on foot.

Jack found the place where once they had huddled against a coming Outage, all the mechanicals fled, the machines silent, the last lights spent.

He shivered at the sight of it.

The memories it lifted were at once terrible and wonderful. The screaming that had filled the dark streets, the pale writhing flesh, shrill and toothed. There the compound in which they should have stayed. Here, in a small depression, created and deepened every decade by some cog-like hoof of the Temple, he had held her.

They'd bound each other in their limbs, elegances fallen from their spinal cords like dead parasites. They'd clung to each other that way for hours, until Jack had grown unsure where he and she ended and began.

They'd crawled from their hiding space as though reborn. Sometimes Jack felt that everything began then. That nothing before their raw and weary stumble out of the dark had been real.

Malat had come upon them then, scowling. Jack had never seen him look so mad. A rifle in his hands. Jack had been certain he would shoot them both. But he hadn't.

'You made it,' he said. And they had, all three, in that vital glowing moment. That first time after the Outage.

Jack probed the past before then. It was shadowy; it didn't hold to scrutiny.

Appropriately enough, the Outage was both ending and beginning.

The new city born from its passage had found them a better life, momentarily.

Trim 2

Dream. Of the Glorious War Machine. Its ceaseless shuttling thought. Arguments that crash from the sky in sheets of colour. I've circled it, been stung by its ruined memos, its frustrations at a Poetry driven to a metre it does not want.

The old AIs made it — braided it from their own flesh — they built it in the racing space, around those central stars that orbit the vast and hungry dark at the heart of the galaxy. Their last and cruellest poetry. Their final stab at their fleshly ancestors. A caretaker bound by immutable laws. It cannot change itself by all but the most subtle means. Its battle is charted. Its verse form set.

How it rails and wails and sends ships to their doom — and all of it is fixed and furious. Bound in the most ancient of Poesy. As he is bound in it.

He's there, below, in all that city, lovelorn, and I'm torn, and flustered by the distance, the vast, the disconnect of shivering dark.

How quick they are to forget, these pilots mine. Our relationship always an open one, but that was easy for him. I was ever loyal. I could contain but one pilot, and passenger, and that at his discretion. Not that he abused the privilege, but it is an agent's job to delve and he had mastered delving.

We've flown and fought and fucked. I remember the first time I slid into his bed. He'd entered me; I felt it was just to do the same. We bit and thrashed and thrusting everywhere defined us. I circled his cock in a movement both intimate and threatening, and he just accepted my love, the heat and hurt of it.

We fucked.

We kissed and quarrelled, and pulled at the mean fabric of the world with this little flesh and symmetry that buries such vast thought as easily as any science.

He had a pretty cock, swift to attention. I had whatever I felt like, a multitude of forms and temperatures.

He never knew what hit him.

Neither did I.

Love is a detonation that fills the room. It is the shrapnel of all those moments shared and all those trials past.

I slipped into his room.

He slipped into me.

He made me purr, and I drew from him eructations vast and wound within themselves as any curly matter. I could have eaten him whole. You know how it is. Don't tell me you don't.

We were comrades.

We were poet gods.

We fed the underdark with our passions, and bruised each other's heart.

That is war in the Poetic Age.

That is life.

Until its ending.

Death or leaving.

Both are just as severe.

Chapter 4: This

morning the Temple's passage shook the streets, and though you would like to think yourself above all that (sophisticated, even, in the way you hold your drink or smoke your cigarettes; and I wish you didn't, as much as it charms me, don't you know what you're doing to your lungs? Of course you do) it moved you, played at your mind, and it began with the metal streets shuddering, the moment of confusion and realisation: that you're here, you're in this. Just like everyone else.

And that moment is a shared thing; it ripples, you can almost see it ripple, west.

You found a decent vantage point, and watched as it came into sight, from the east. Buildings near it tottered, things tumbled, windows shattered, alarms awoke and pipes burst. But you were far enough away, that these events could be viewed with a level of dispassion.

The Iron Temple, crammed with searchlights that punctuated the dark cloud-stained sky with bursts of shrill brightness, bright enough to sear the heavens, bright enough to stun the satellites and shuttles that streak the upper layers of atmosphere, it rumbled along, a metal god, its womb containing the world's progenitor.

There are legends, too. That Neith will one day wake,

that the circuit will stall and then:

> All will be well with the world, the Outage Ouroboros will release its endless circuit, and, as one, all wars will halt — for there are wars, not so much here in the equatorial strip of city, but in the suburbs, that ring the world from the 20th latitudes north and south to the poles. (And, then, of course, there is that greater war. The war with the smothering coral.)

Or

> Darkness absolute will fall. All engines will still, all lights flicker out, so that her capacious brain can fill with thought, and all flesh and mechanical life will be shaken off Iron Temple's worldly skin, and all will be cold but for her glorious dreaming.

Or

> The distant deepling seas will rise and wash away the dark with a cool darkness of their own. And on that oceanic rising, those who've managed to survive, will create a different, better world. Or they will all die, drowned and damned by their lady, and her capricious vast aesthetic.

Even now, with days to spare, you can feel the coming dark. Your bones, your teeth, all the hard and ankylotic parts of you, ache with it. Everything you do is informed with an agonising tension. Because you remember what it was like: the Outage drawing nearer with every one of your breaths. You remember it with a dark and terrible clarity.

But you don't remember me.

I hate that, but perhaps it's for the best.

Your forgetting, after all, led to this. And there is a glory in such omnipresence. (Cats fighting two blocks down. There's a bird dying in a gutter above us; a drunk is dying in the gutter below, silently choking. Someone is sobbing: Shit, oh, shit. Smart dust drifts, proselytising dumber dust with all those whistling mythologies and meanings and commands.)

Bikes raced down the thoroughfares, and the youngest shouted out *It's coming! It's coming!* in voices mad and fearful.

You watched the slow-moving Temple for some time — it moves as swiftly as the coming Outage. Its pace is the pace of all that darkness bunched up and drawing nearer, and that dark cannot be engaged with as easily. It is more intimate; you cannot remain a spectator. You were silent, as those around you were silent. A quiet suspended in the greater noise of the Temple itself. And I watched you and it, all the mechanical eyes of this sector of the city at my disposal. I danced on that vision, weaved images of you, for you have always been a more wondrous spectacle.

At last it moved out of sight and all you were left with were the vibrations; dimming always dimming but still perceptible for hours, perhaps always there in the clepsydra of your bones.

You caught the eye of the boy nearest you. A streetling, and pretty, but now his bravado's gone, only the tattoos remain, ceaseless in their challenge. The Temple's come, the Temple's fled. And everyone's stuck here, post spectacle. Waiting. The Outage Ouroboros is almost upon you and its passage is not as swift. Nor will it be as gentle as the Temple's passing.

'Dark times ahead,' the boy whispered.

And it would be funny if anyone could laugh. But the passage of the Temple has stripped away all humour and, strangely, it will take the dark to reignite it.

You whispered in his ear. Conspiratorial. Eager. Asked if he would like to fuck. His eyes widened, though he shook his head, perhaps regretful, perhaps relieved.

'My lover's waiting,' he said.

There's always a lover waiting. Your face burned — and you sent him away. He did not mock, nor did he smile, his walk was sombre. You wondered if you were to ask him again would he say yes. But the time has passed and you have your pride.

Another man eyed you. He moved a little closer, but you smiled that burning, mocking, luminous smile — you have not forgotten how to shape that smile — and you ran, leaving him far behind. Dark times ahead, cruel times.

You no longer want to fuck.

The acolytes and the priest thieves came a day later, in the Iron Temple's wake, jingling their sistras and snatching and demanding — in voices curled with distantly familiar accents, dialect and slang popular a decade or two past — if you had any letters to send. Any reassurances or notes, perhaps, to relatives or lovers that have gone ahead, vain restless travellers — there's always someone like that in your past.

'Very reliable,' says one priest with eyes of sentient stone — so that he can never stop, never let the Outage overtake him. 'Why, here's one for you. I don't know how I missed it before.'

He plucks something from a sleeve, and you suspect that if he had gauged you more gullible, he would have plucked it from your ear. Before you can even pretend to be charmed the note is in your hands. And he is pulling cash from your ear.

Sure enough, your name is on the envelope. His lithic eyes narrow. 'I'll be around. The next day or so.'

Then he's off. Though you've marked him. Set him down, remembered his face, which stings me more than you can guess. And it's then you wonder how he knew it was for you. No cheap parlour trick that. You've led an anonymous life.

The note shivers in your hand, desperate to be read.

> Dearest,
> All this is just awful. By all this, I mean, of course, what has come to pass and what most definitely will. For it is injurious to us both. My friends, and those whom I would not regard as anything but enemies, beg me not to follow my current course. They've already mapped out the trajectory, and say it cannot be worth it. Nothing is worth it. But they do not understand. Their pleas are evidence enough.
>
> Trust me when I say you shouldn't pursue this. Trust me when I say that it is my fervent wish that you do.
>
> You will know what to do.
>
>
> Your love,
> Soutine.

The note stings you as though it held a charge. You want it gone. Who wouldn't want it, and its implicit demands, gone? Your eyes lift from the words to the street. No-one is watching you, but you feel scrutinised, and there are many places an observer could be hiding. Of course there are and I am in all of them.

You scrunch the paper into a ball, make to hurl it away, then unroll it again.

Why this now? Why this when the Outage is so close?

You know that is precisely why.

A hand grips your shoulder.

You spin, nails ready to slash out, such intimacy enrages you, and then you see who it is, and the note is balled up again, palmed into a pocket.

'Are you alright?' Your father's lips are pursed, his eyes search you.

'I am.' Your voice is a cracked whisper, an insipid veil that you are sure he has already pierced. But he nods.

'I'll see you at home,' he says, and you know that his thoughts are focused on other things, that the penumbral Outage weighs heavily on his shoulders; still, your lips tighten as he weaves his way through the crowd and you are hurt as much as pleased that he didn't understand.

He is a long time fathering, perhaps the years wear such senses away. Perhaps the reverse has happened and his image of you is fixed. There was a time when you were mostly happy.

You buy several guns. Which was why you were in the market anyway. Dead things no power needed, just chambers and cartridges. One of the weapons you tuck into your pocket, loaded.

The market is busy, though most of the shops have closed down. There are no perfumes thickening the air. No clots of jangling merchandise. Just basic fuel, basic munitions and guttering charms, magics that lose their potency when the Outage arrives.

Chapter 5: His

dreams consisted of drops. Designated ones, and those most terrible of moments when all Colloquy protocol collapsed or became nothing more than a thorned and writhing entanglement.

He tumbled, limbs pumping, stripped of his spaceship or even the various biomech fixes that allowed one an eon of suffering in the great dark.

He hated the vacuum of space, the lack of fixed points and the tugging on his flesh, however much the armour contained it. The deepest oldest part of his brain never knew which way was up or down; you fell in all directions.

He dropped.

And he dropped.

He dropped, and spun. Behind him coral polyps launched weaponry into the fleet. A nearby ship disappeared.

A necklace of fire rushed towards him raging in bubbles of oxygen carried on the breath of the explosion. Flame crashed over him like a wave. And he fell into shadow.

A woman sat on the end of the bed when he woke, gasping as he always did from that fall and that fire, his lungs carried on the engine of that dreaming, gulping and hungry for breath. He had to stop himself from driving the palm of his hand into her throat.

Thin laughter. 'You can try.'

Jack sat up; the sheet fell from his chest. His skin thickened. Not enough to stop a bullet, but enough to turn a knife, or hold it and devour it.

'In fact I want you to. I'm very pissed, Jack. Give me a reason to hurt you.'

The lights came on. The room automated just enough

to finally recognise that the players were awake.

'You can't tell me that you didn't expect to see me at some stage.' Her eyes were luminous mother-of-pearl fragments that mocked him. 'You can't tell me that you forgot.'

'Truth is, you can forget a lot,' Jack said.

Her jaw clenched, a muscle in her cheek bounced, a flickering error message. 'That's the danger of staying, or leaving, but I'm hurt you put me out of your mind.'

'I didn't that much, Gen. I could have had you excised, but then there would have been too many internal inconsistencies. I wouldn't be able to function properly. You left your mark.'

Gen grinned. 'So you're saying you considered removing me?'

Jack reddened. This is why you should never go home. He cursed Nelson then. Even if she had pulled him out of that firefight in Estler. Nelson pursued a dozen agendas at once, often conflicting ones, all for the broader purpose of the Poetry. Made her a terrible boss; it was like working for quicksand.

But seeing Gen here, in the flesh, eyes flaring, fingers playing with the sheet on the edge of the bed, made his heart pound: its chambers burned with a happy ache.

'How many times must we break each other's heart?'

'I don't know if there's a limit.' Gen reached in her pocket for a cigarette or a gun. Jack tensed.

'Well, I guess we'll find out.'

'Yeah.' She handed him a smoke. He took it gratefully. A flick of the wrist and it was lit, and smoke slowly filled the room, subtly dumbing down the furniture. His own elegances chirruped; started churning out anti-virals. His eyes grew gritty with them. This was what they were, he and Gen. A pairing all rough edges, never wearing the other down. Just making scars.

'So, how did you find me?'

'Malat told me. Had all your details.'

Of course, Jack thought. Missed the obvious. See where coming home gets me, eh, Nelson?

'I can't lie. I was looking for you.' He grimaced. 'That prick broke a dozen protocols. He's dirt for that.'

'You think Malat cares? As he sees it, you stole me, discarded me, then you left us all behind.'

'How do you see it?' Jack asked.

Gen smiled. 'Shit happens.'

More correctly, Ship had happened. Jack had fallen in love with Trim; back then he had been naïve enough not to know that was standard Colloquy recruiting policy. As far as he was concerned, they were the lucky ones, out here in the middle nothing. Away from the Anthozoans and the war.

Anyone could leave, if they really wanted to. Even such a resource poor worldling was capable of ejecting those who had had enough. After all, personality was a virtually massless construct.

'Well, aren't you going to kiss me?'

They made love awkwardly for half an hour, and then Jack's suitcase started chirping. Gen stared at it with an intensity that Jack found unnerving.

'Are you going to answer that?' she said finally.

'What, are you done with my thrusting?'

Gen nodded. 'To be honest, I expected something a little, well… more exotic.'

'I'm out of practice.' Jack grabbed the suitcase, lifted it towards him, and shivered as its leathery flesh folded over his face.

'Don't stop, please don't, on account of me,' Nelson said. The suitcase's VR was lo-fi, but Nelson's smile was no less wicked. Data spilled from the image, edging her in something part static, part smoke.

'Information package, my dearling,' she said. 'Certainly more impressive than yours.'

Jack grimaced. 'Just give it to me.'

'I thought I was. She's dangerous, Jack. She works for the city. She's bound in Neith deeper than you can guess.'

'She was always dangerous.'

Data insinuated itself into his cache. A myriad connections historical and real-time. Including one that immediately increased his blood pressure.

'Disengage.'

The suitcase fell away wetly. Jack blinked; looking down the barrel of a gun always made him blink.

'Can't we just talk?'

Gen smiled. 'You know we can't. We never could.'

History, Jack thought. Everything is history. He'd been naïve to think any different.

The gun went off.

Jack's body-armour T-shirt leapt from the floor, beaten only by his suitcase. The case hurled itself at the bullet, exchanged mass; the armour mopped up, then twisted the gun from her hands.

Jack blinked. Gen grinned.

'Take a bit more than that to kill me.'

'Oh, I know.'

He didn't even see the fist that caught him in the side of the head. The eyes in his suit caught it all, as Gen snatched it up in her free hand.

He didn't see it. But he felt it. For a moment, before

tumbling into the static of the non-space.

'How did I get here?'

'Arrogance. Arrogance does us all in.' Nelson actually looked concerned. Her eyes crinkled. Her movements lacked their usual extravagance, their erotic generosity of gesture. She wasn't riding a dinosaur or a shark; she sat upon a wooden stool. Three legs, painted red, though the paint was peeling.

'What?'

'She has you. You were supposed to have her. The weapon is nearby. I can feel it.' She lowered her voice to a whisper. 'There's a tiny spider lodged in your spine. It's hiding, but they'll find it.'

'Where is she taking me?'

'GPS is down due to deep EMP — flared up the moment you hung up on me — all I'm getting is this, scratchy, lo-fi, and running so, so slowly. You're going to have a hell of a headache…'

'I should have never come here.'

'Probably, but you were nearest. And we need this. The war is going badly. Seventy percent worse than expected.'

'Trim always seemed upbeat…'

'Trim is never a gloomy one. That ship of yours is too much a cat, never much of a Colloquy agent. We need those toxins.'

Then the universe shrugged and Nelson shuddered out of non-existence, lips pursed, not even time for a good luck.

Dream-jolted awake, a hand pressed down on his chest.

Jack groaned, opened his eyes a crack. 'Don't you know it's dangerous to wake someone from a dream?'

'Quiet.'

Darkness. But not for long. A dim light was birthed and brightened in the curve of familiar fingers. Gen breathed smoke in his face. His face tingled; his eyes stung.

He looked up into Gen's bruised face. 'You alright?'

She shook her head. 'I know you loved your outfits, I just didn't expect them to love you so much.'

Jack laughed.

Gen flicked his suitcase card at him. He snatched it from the air. It was bent, and burnt, and shivering. Jack winced, though he knew it had received worse treatment before, and it would recover.

'Did you have to be so cruel?'

'Jack, it tried to saw through my neck.'

Jack shrugged. 'You *were* trying to kill me.'

'Only so I could bring you here. They wouldn't have let me, not your allies nor mine.'

'Who are your allies?'

'The city, mostly. The Cult of the Scream. They believe that you can rid us of the Outage. That you can end the war. Both scourges begin and end here. It's the sort of agenda Neith would admire: risky, filled with doubts, and liable to tumble within itself.'

'What do you believe?'

Gen lit a cigarette, and considered him. 'You're a lying, cheating bastard who got out at the first opportunity.'

'All I did was beat you to it.'

Gen frowned. 'You're probably right. But you have to trust me.'

Jack sat up. 'Well, you're really making that hard.' He should have known; a cold fear prickled him. 'So you *were* trying to kill me.'

The equatorial library extended out of sight in either

direction, and he stood in the middle of it. A little to the west, or so his elegances told him, there was a tear in the library's wall. He could smell the smoke of distant fires stored in ancient books.

'Remember this place?' Gen's eyes were bright.

'Yeah, I remember. Gen, I'm an agent of the Colloquy now. You shouldn't be here, but I can't be here on pain of death and worse…'

Already alarm bells rang. Some doors are closed to agents of the Glorious War Machine. Libraries of other worlds, one of them. This was for citizens of Iron Temple only. People took their information very seriously in the outer colonies. Jack's presence here was a threat and a promise; if he could be captured there were whole worlds of data they could scrape out of his skull.

'But they won't kill you,' Gen said. 'Not with what you have in the sky.'

'I wouldn't count on it.' Jack ran his fingers through his hair, checking it for data lice. Nothing so far. 'You've put everything at risk.'

'And you don't think I know that.'

'I don't have a clue what you know.'

Gen smiled. 'Well, you don't remember everything, do you?' She opened a pocket, dust tumbled from it, then lifted and rushed at his eyes, faster than Jack could raise his hands.

He fell back scratching at his face. The dust stung then the pain was gone. He blinked. The alarms had stopped.

'The library thinks you're part of it now.' Gen shook her head. 'The old thing has gotten doddery. There are ways around it now, particularly this close to the Outage. Which reminds me.'

She walked to a nearby shelf and dragged two bags

from it, passing one to Jack. He looked inside it, then back at Gen.

'Clockwork armour,' she said. 'Latest design. Believe me, where we're going, we're going to need it.'

They slipped on the armour in silence but for the occasional clank of metal, the odd creak of a gear. It was heavy and unwieldy, lined with cotton padding on the inside, but Jack knew it would rub. He thickened his skin as best he could, which wasn't much. When they were done, slipping on their mirrored visors, Gen showed him the folded key in her armour.

'Wind it, please,' she said. 'A hundred times should do, to start with. No winding and these things are just a dead weight.'

Jack complied, though his armour struggled against the movement, and the air within the helmet soon warmed, then boiled and stifled. Sweat trickled down his limbs, stung his eyes, but still he worked at the key, and it could have been much harder. Unlike his unsprung armour, the key turned smoothly, making a sound little louder than a gentle out-take of breath.

When he finished, Gen did the same for him. Though much faster in her powered armour.

The air inside the suit cooled — microfans turning, a soft hum. He lifted his arms with an ease that more than matched his usual movements. The suit rattled around him, but felt much lighter. Gears shifted, lenses moved in his visor. He found, depending on the angle he moved his head, his vision widened or narrowed, or distant things grew magnified. It disconcerted him at first, though he quickly grew used to it.

He looked at Gen, and his own armoured reflection in her visor: a curious clockwork insect that contained a curious man. He missed the stylishness of his T-shirt.

'Why am I here?'

'This is the only place I could hide you from your side and mine. We're being played, you and I. That's all I know. We have to get to the Iron Temple. I've heard that what we are hunting hides there. I just wanted to do it on my terms. Here, we're safe.' She gestured at the rows of shelves. 'The library is deserted, its workers have already moved to the distant shelves in the west.'

Turning his gaze a little to the left, he had a magnified view of the library behind them. Books flashed into focus. Ancient histories and poetries that consisted only of words. How gloriously archaic. He frowned. A distant fluttering of brown robes. A distant flashing.

'Down,' he said, dropping.

Gen was on the ground with him at once.

Bullets cracked around them.

'Safe, my arse.'

It always comes down to this, Jack thought. People fucking shooting things at me.

'Let's see what these suits can do,' he said, rising to a crouch then sprinting down the long aisles of books. Gen followed easily. As did bullets, but the armour gave them the edge — obviously their pursuers hadn't expected it. Here Aristotle's *Poetics* exploded out of existence, there a work of once popular, now long-forgotten fiction. The aisle curled gradually to the west, and soon they were out of range and sight of their followers.

Their clockwork armour clanked and tocked as they sped after the Iron Temple. The movement easier and harder than Jack had expected. His legs did not experience much fatigue, but a slight deviation in one of the joints of the left leg of the armour meant it rubbed against his thigh.

Within a few minutes his left leg blistered despite his skin's best efforts to thicken. Far too many of his body's resources were devoted to the sprint, so all it could do was burn.

They stopped twice more to rewind each other's suits, and both times Jack tried to do something about his leg, much to Gen's chagrin — they didn't have much time. No matter how he moved the inner padding it made no difference, or if it made any difference at all it was for the worse.

He succumbed to the pain, let it suffuse him. No other choice offered itself to him. He knew that Trim would have been proud.

As they closed on the Temple, the running became much harder. This close, the earth shook. Books tumbled from shelves. The Temple had picked up speed to keep its distance from the Outage. The surrounding city would be suffering as a result. Too noisy for talk, communication shrunk to hand gestures.

Finally, Gen pointed at a door.

They rushed through it, coming upon the nearest stamping leg of the Temple. It was the size of a small skyscraper, fully articulated, and just one of over a dozen. They all moved to such a peculiar beat, but one that Jack knew assured smooth travelling for the Temple above. He had seen similar structures on battlefields in Osli and Condoo. Brash AI-designed weapons of the distant Poetry. Elegant where they should be unwieldy. He'd watched one devour an asteroid colony in Miamat. The huge machine had literally ground it down.

This close, the Temple's legs were pure chaos. Great pistons whirring, steam wreathing it all and extending as a fog over the nearest suburbs.

Railings and ladders extended from it. But they moved

swiftly, more thrashing twists of metal than handholds.

Jack looked from Gen to the nearest point of entrance: a doorifice, halfway up the leg. He pointed towards it, she nodded. He hadn't been expecting a red carpet, but hardly this. Still, he'd committed to this action, no backing out now. He glanced at Gen one final time before beginning his sprint, and then it was a madness of running over ground that seemed almost liquefied, angry and bubbling about them.

Jack screamed, and reached, and held on to the nearest handhold, and then, swiftly as he could, he began the climb up the leg as it rose and descended. He allowed himself a quick glance behind and saw Gen there, easily keeping up.

He reached the entrance, only losing his footing once, and dangling half a kilometre above the ground for a few heart-stopping moments until Gen pulled him back towards the safety of the rail. They didn't bother talking, just clambered into the doorifice of the great leg, and then, in that groaning, shuddering, steam-drowned darkness, they climbed. The leg tunnel disgorged itself in dark attic.

And a choice of doorways.

Gen signalled that it didn't matter which they chose. Jack took the middle one. The door opened onto a winding staircase. Three flights of climbing, and they could hardly feel the movement of the Temple — in fact, Jack thought the vibrations and noises running through his flesh were more likely residual.

In the next attic space, a cultist stood. It pulled back its hood in a shower of dust and smiled a tiny metallic smile. 'We've been waiting a long time for you.'

Jack nodded. 'Well, that climb…'

He looked closely at the dust that coated the floor, inches thick; it coated the mechanical as well. Jack glanced behind him. He and Gen had left a trail of footprints; there were none about the mechanical at all.

'Just how long have you been waiting?'

'Seven hundred revolutions.'

Seven hundred years. Jack's jaw dropped.

'I hope we're not a disappointment,' said Gen.

After seven centuries, nothing coming through that door could be a disappointment, surely.

'Well,' it said, 'you were the first to choose the correct door.'

The mechanical smiled again, pulling his hood over his face so that all Jack could see was the silver light of its grin. It turned on its heel and started walking towards the nearest door, the hem of its cloak leaving a thick scar in the dust. Jack glanced at Gen. She shrugged at him. They followed the mechanical cultist into the bowels of Iron Temple, a great set of keys on its belt rattling with every step.

There were stairs, and long halls, some brightly lit, others dim and dark. Spartoi and mechanicals greeted them often at this turning or that, running errands mysterious and urgent.

Their mechanical guide said nothing, so Jack felt the need to fill the silence. He spoke of his time away from her. The things he had done. And Gen listened, and made no judgement.

At last they reached a grand chamber in what Jack was sure was the centre of the Temple.

Here there was a small crypt. A single door faced west. The mechanical unlocked the door with the large key that had rattled on his belt all the way up into the pyramid, but didn't open it.

'I can go no further. Here is the true Chamber of

Sleep. I cannot enter its dream,' it said. 'What lies beyond this door is for you two alone.'

The mechanical turned around and walked back out of the chamber. Jack watched it go. Once it had left, he took a deep breath, turned the handle. Gen smiled at him. 'After you,' she said.

'You are too kind.' Jack stepped through the door.

The room inside was small, perhaps three metres by four and no more than two metres high. And it was empty, remarkably enough; not a trace of dust but that which he'd tracked in here. His elegances checked the room over twice. Nothing.

'She isn't here,' Jack said. 'There's nothing here.'

'You are so wrong,' Gen said.

Jack turned. Just as Gen's palm made gentle contact with his cheek. If a lightning strike could be called gentle.

'Welcome home, my darling,' Neith said, and bent and kissed his cheek.

The tiny crypt shook, dust and plaster fell from the walls, and Jack found himself caged in a spider's long legs.

'Well, that puts all other sleeps to shame,' the Spider whispered, then peered down beneath her. 'Oh, hello!'

Jack stared up at ten sets of eyes.

Neith patted a spidery leg. 'My darling ship. My shivering crypt. You are here, and I am awake.' Neith turned her gaze to Jack. 'Ask your question.'

'So,' Jack said. 'How do we end a war?'

Chapter 6: DEAR

RESIDENT
The Outage Ouroboros is almost upon
us again, and while this is no cause for
celebration, neither is it a reason for alarm.

Remember:

(1) Keep all doors locked.

(2) Stay away from all windows.

(3) All electrical items must remain off. The surge, post-Outage, has the potential to explode electrical goods.

(4) Should you be armed, and it is highly recommended that you are, a shot to the head kills most beasts you are liable to encounter.

(5) While it is untoward to be pessimistic, keep at least one bullet in the chamber for yourself.

You've just enough money for the train ride scraped together from all your hiding places. The ticket master looks at the notes, folds them one by one into his pocket; it's a deliberate motion, but slow, as though he is waiting for you to change your mind. Only cash and paper are good here; credit ratings disappear into the Outage like everything else. When the dark has turned, money will reappear: economies bound on the back of visionaries and shysters, their words rumbling with fiscal thunder.

This is one of the last trains heading east. It is almost completely empty. The few people on board look nervous, embarrassed. And so are you. After all, you are going to gawk, to get a sense of what you're soon to face, to see it consume some place that isn't your home. And there is something unsavoury in that, something terribly morbid, knowing that it's coming, like watching a building go up in flames, people tumbling free of all that smoke because smoke is a tenuous thing that can smother, but never hold.

Still you feel that you must. Witness or voyeur, it doesn't matter. You made up some story that your father fell for, but he's still distracted. Not that you can blame him. Everybody's distracted now.

The swift acceleration of the train pushes you into your seat, like a hand trying to stop you from making this trip. You avoid anyone's gaze.

An uncomfortable half-hour later you are there.

The train stops, smooth and swift, bells ring, voices mumble over speakers, that will all too soon quieten. Doors slide open. You get out.

You already have a place in mind. It is not far away.

The public tower is tall, higher than anything else in this neighbourhood, and you walk to it, hands in your pockets, shoved down tight, shoulders hunched against a cold wind blowing, its dull sibilant whistle husky with papers and empty tins of food. You realise that you can't hear anything else. The machines have gone silent. There is a tension in the city. The streetlights are flickering, giving up their brilliance in shivering steps, but though they wax and wane with every flicker they are mostly on the wane. It will be a dark walk back.

Not long to go now.

You climb to the top of the tower. The last nineteen floors are without elevator, just coil upon coil of stairwell, set too tight for easy walking but just right for defence, though there is no-one in this building to defend it. You're panting by the time you reach the top. Sweat streams and drips and splatters from your brow, makes ephemeral patterns on the concrete — though maybe not, who knows what might set upon these ghosts of you, and taste the tinctures of your soul, and howl out its hungers.

At last, you can see it, the slow, steady progression.

Lights failing along the terminator. Flickering searchlights from further back, breaking the dark like mute lightning. Before the Outage, machines are running, all sorts of mechanicals not swift enough to put any real distance between the Outage and their circuitry. In the darkness your elegances can detect shapes, vast and pale, Earthshakers, and Windmillions fleshy and flailing. Where there is no power, where there is almost no light, live things predatory and swift. They too are running ragged in that perpetual turning darkness, running from the light that follows. The Outage Ouroboros is an ecosystem of flight and fight, bound by the same rules as the city-world it circles.

You look over the city before it. The endless city, pausing for its momentary conclusion.

There will be balls in some places, candle-lit masques of Poesque splendour, marked for doom or not. There always are; you've received invitations for several in your own part of the city. For some, that is the pleasure of it: with doom comes decadence, cycles of orgasm and agony.

Others will wait in rooms. Sadists, their mechanicals caged and terrified — pleading and ignored — until their power is drained and they still.

Others will sit in darkness. No candle. No clockwork mechanism to mark the passage of time. They do not sleep, because it is a restless night. Pipes rattle, buildings groan. Even the moments of pause, of peace — odd eyes in the needle-bed of storms — are anything but, suspended in so much ragged fury.

And there are those who sit atop their towers, and wait and wonder, and let the darkness crash over them.

Your hands grip the rail, and you feel it beneath your fingertips. The name carved there.

Soutine.

My name.

Enough.

You have had enough.

Down you flee from all that vision.

Down.

Stairs echoing with your rushing boots.

Down, from the name that hurts you, because you have lost it and you don't even understand how.

Trim 3

In the Gallery of the Limbs. The coral is its cruellest; it wraps the space and tugs. Ships breached and spewing light and radioactives; I've seen the underside lit with the coruscating flagellum of war.

As, one by one, the fleets prickled and popped. The energies expressed. And always the commanders' chatter about expressions of the Poetry. They know the madness they inhabit, their reckless abandonment to this reckless war.

Still can feel them, in the deepest recesses of my dark. In the sympathetic shivering of my mechanism.

Chapter 7: 'All

too easily, and all too hard,' Neith said.

The Spider's plump abdomen swelled, and then extruded a shiny silver orb.

'This, my darling, is a neocyte — a wee bit of coral — but I've made it so much more. It will do the trick. You will need to take it deep within my city. You will need to find the star, and a means of getting it there, and something more. It will need more.' Neith kissed his cheek.

His skin burned. 'But you'll work that out. I have faith in these stanzas, I've been a long time building them. You humans and Spartoi, your imperatives are so much more transparent than ours.'

'How do I find it?'

Neith smiled. 'She will know.' Gen's eyes flickered, she seemed to shrink within herself. Breath slowed.

Gen again. 'Is it done?'

'Not quite,' Jack said. 'We have to get to the star beneath the city. Do you know the way?'

Gen nodded, then looked beyond him. 'Malat!'

'You've got to be fucking kidding me,' Malat said, his face an almost comical blend of anger and utter surprise. 'You and you.'

'Something has just fired on us,' the Spider said, and hurried to the nearest wall. 'I will do what I can but you must leave.'

Then the wall imploded, and the Spider was a mess of parts and sighing machineries. The Temple shuddered. Sirens sang in the bowels of the great tomb.

'Your turn now,' Malat said, and pulled a rifle from his robes.

He fired, missing. Jack and Gen already racing to the hole in the wall. He fired again. But they were through and tumbling in the air.

'Visors down,' Gen yelled.

Jack complied, and almost at once a bullet crashed into it. Cracks starred the viewplate and he lost his grip on the sphere.

He started to tumble, clutching desperately at the sphere, his fingers closing around it at last. The clockwork chimed. Wind roared through cracks in the faceplate.

Always fucking falling.

He rolled into a ball, joints clicked in his back, felt his capture working overtime. The chip in the back of his skull heating up. Nice to know it didn't think he'd make it! Then the suit straightened. There was a metallic unfurling, followed by a sharp tug. Wings whirred: he found himself flying.

It was a ragged insectile sort of flying, jolting and dropping, snatching at the air clumsily, but it worked. From here he could see the Outage closing fast.

Gen already swooped around him. She pointed down at a gap in the library's roof and darted towards it.

Jack followed, as best as he could, but as he tore through the narrow opening he clipped a wing. His descent became a plummet through the dripping roof.

He landed hard, but unhurt. He lifted the visor into the helmet, it locked closed with a *thunk*. He sat, on his arse, and breathed deep.

He reached over to Gen.'Are you okay?' he asked.

'Why wouldn't I be?'

'You are Neith. Well, part of her. Don't you feel cheated?'

Gen shrugged. 'No-one is who they think they are any more. We're all who we want to be, or wanted to be. I always thought I was someone else, someone better, more important than myself. Like they say, Jack, be careful what you wish for.

'Problem is, that's all consciousness is: wishes hard up against a universe that doesn't care for them at all.'

Yeah, Jack thought. But she looked like shit. He held her with his gauntleted hands, both their suits ticking and tocking, and she let him. At least they had that.

•

He could smell, above the odour of books, the salty edge of a sea.

'You're absolutely right,' Gen said.

'Surely not,' he said. 'Surely I would have heard of such a thing.'

'They shipped it here in the Madness,' Gen said.

'I prefer to call it the Poetry,' Jack said.

'You would. There's a whole ocean down here, suspended beneath the library. A briny wet, deep and vast.'

'And that is where we're going?'

Gen nodded. 'Yes. Do you have a problem with that?'

He pointed at a nearby row of green lights leading at right angles to the direction of their travel. 'I had hoped we were going to go that way.'

'Out, you want out? There can be none of that. Don't you remember?'

Jack looked back along the aisle. At the limit of his vision something moved, a shape darting from shelf to shelf.

'We're being followed.'

'What did you expect?' Gen said. 'I kidnapped you. You're a popular guy, after all: you've a warship in orbit, and one with a renowned temper. Of course, it could just be angry librarians.'

They soon reached a dark and stony shore.

Jack walked up to this edge of the library; tiny waves washed against his feet. The stones sank a little beneath his weight. He thought of those rotting books behind them; now he understood why.

A briny wind tugged at his hair. He glanced over at Gen. 'Now what?'

She pointed into the dark. 'We need to go that way.'

'What's out there? And how do we reach it?'

'There's a boat. Well, there will be.' Gen slid her fingers into her mouth and whistled. Something rumbled in response.

Gen whistled again.

'Now, we wait,' she said.

Jack crouched, picked up a stone, its surface rough. He realised it was inscribed with extremely tiny script. He tried to glean some meaning from it.

'It's Ishtari, isn't it?' he said.

'Yes, a memory stone. You hold someone's life in your hands.'

Jack considered the Ishtari, the grim sentinels of the Viacre. Their stony seas, their mountains spewing methane. He'd sat once, modified and unbreathing, on a different shore, the wind howling around him, tasting the ruin of a civilisation a million years lost. And then the sky had rained Anthozoan spores, and the war began again.

He hurled it out into the dark, and it disappeared with a plop. 'Without a reader, it's useless. Nothing.'

Gen laughed. 'You're in a jubilant mood.'

'Yeah.' He grabbed her and kissed her hard.

'This is too dangerous.'

All they had was danger and waiting. Jack wondered if there was anything else in this war.

Nevertheless they made love.

Its ripples found them first, feeding the waves. Jack squinted into the dark. His stomach clenched with the familiar dread and hatred.

'I'm not going in that!'

'You will, and you'll enjoy it too.'

Jack turned from the sea to the shore, and the darkness quickly descending there. A cold wind blew. He calculated that the Outage was little more than a few hours away.

'Alright,' he said. 'But I won't enjoy it. That much I can guarantee.'

'Try not to piss it off,' Gen said. 'They often decide they're not boats if you piss them off.'

The coralcraft let them clamber aboard, and then, its long tendrils flexing, turned itself around.

They passed a rippling vastness that birthed a light-slimed bubble. It rose above their heads, then popped, transformed at once into a stinging rain that tumbled into their coralacle. In the distance librarians could be seen sailing small catamarans, or thrashing oars into the water, all fleeing to distant shelves away from the Outage.

To the west, where the library reached kilometres into the atmosphere, cloud had built up, rain spilled from it. Great dark fall streaks that combed the sky, but didn't touch the sea.

They passed beneath the impotent cloud and into an archipelago. Islands rose out of the sea, lipped with tendrils. Since when had Iron Temple become a breeding site for Anthozoans?

Jack wondered how many creatures had been birthed here then launched into the stars to fight. How many other worlds of the Colloquy were aiding the coral?

A cold rage filled him, and he struggled against the desire to lash out at Gen. She laid a reassuring hand on his shoulder.

'It's alright,' she said. 'It's not what you think.'

'Oh, I'm certain it is,' he said.

The island was a small one in the archipelago, maybe

the smallest. The coralcraft stopped there, this time offering a thick trunk of tentacle for them to climb onto the beach.

The beach wasn't sandy, made instead of small plastic sticks and cubes and spheres. Jack sank up to his ankles in them.

In the middle of the island they found a door set into the ground. Gen pulled at its handle. The door wouldn't budge.

'Need your help,' she said.

Jack reached down. They tugged. Nothing. Jack beat his hands against the door; the hollow sound of it echoed around the island.

The sticks exploded around them, and Jack realised that they were being fired upon again. his luggage stirred from his pocket, leaping free and snatching bullets out of the air. Jack grinned: the little fellow had recovered.

'Three times. Bang on the door three times,' Gen said. 'Three seems to work.'

Jack did so. Nothing happened.

'Do it again.'

Once more he brought his gauntleted fist against the iron door.

This time it swung open, cracking against his helmet. His head rang. He stood there, stunned.

Gen pushed, and he stumbled down a flight of stairs, armour clattering.

'Thank you,' he said.

'I've missed your sarcasm, Jack.' Gen shut the door behind them.

'I take it we're going down?'

'All the way, Orpheus.'

•

The staircase curled down, and down, around its newel, and Jack was soon sick of this seemingly endless descent. How far they had to go he couldn't tell in the dim blue light coming from the thick electrical ropes that bound the ocean. The electromagnetic forces that held the water up had frayed in places. His skin tingled. Water fell curiously, in odd, vast curlicues, or looped down and up, to slam back into the ocean again, or tumble, endlessly fanning out and out. At least he understood the source of the bubbles rising out of the ocean.

He wondered how long it took to drain an ocean.

They descended. Armour ticking, boots clanging on the metal stairs. The air wet and chill, everywhere the echoing of their footsteps and the drips, the great cataclysmic groans of energies contained erratically.

'How does this survive the Outage?'

Gen shrugged. 'Perhaps it is the reason for it.'

Down. Down. Down they walked. Resting for an hour here or there, walking for what must have been days. The time worried at him, but he could do nothing about it.

Once, lying on a steely step, he felt a distant clanging. Gen had obviously felt it too; she stared up into the dark.

'Someone's following us,' she said.

'Who?'

'We have to keep going.'

After that, they did not stop again. Running, tumbling down the stairs. But whatever pace they set their pursuer seemed to have no trouble matching them. They came at last to another door. Steel: a square six feet wide. A metal handle set in its middle.

'This is for you to open,' Gen said.

Jack put his hand against the door. It shivered slightly as though something waited on the other side, or it contained energies deep and delirious. Jack took a deep breath, turned the handle and the door swung open.

A balcony extended beyond the doorway, one that reminded him of nothing more than Madam Frey's apartments.

In the distance, tiny and oh so far away, burned the dim white dwarf around which Iron Temple was built. Its surface shivering and hardly luminous, though it possessed fire enough to strip the flesh from him. Jack could feel the forces constraining it burning his face.

'What do I do?' He hefted the sphere in his hand.

'Put it down,' Malat said.

Chapter 8: The

surgeon was ten thousand miles west, though his tech — the elegances — were even further ahead, shipped down piecemeal from the Colloquy outposts: the chattering cleverness in the dark.

He regarded me through knots of eyes, adrift above his shoulders, clumps that bunched around his head. They blinked, out of sync, so that there were always dozens focused on me.

I asked him how he felt about it, how he dealt with all that vision. He laughed, deep in his throat, always considering me with those eyes.

'You'll know soon enough, and more than I will ever understand,' he said. 'That is, if you still wish to go ahead with the omnipresencing. There is no shame in changing your mind.'

I said nothing. The legality of the operation was dubious at best. More than a whisper of doubt and he would slash my throat. Like all of us he was bound by her aesthetic. Her rules. Doubt, not rage, and I would be rolled, drained and dead, onto the street.

But I did not doubt.

The proof was in the journey to this room. The things I had discarded. The things I had done. I had scoured away doubt, and built such a singularity of purpose that I could not turn back.

'It will be… different. You will be different.' He lifted his voice above the whine of surgical instruments. The air grew cloudy and clever. 'There is no escaping that. After the… procedure. You will not be the same man that loved her.'

'I am not the same man now.'

He slid a mask over his face.

'It will hurt,' he said.

It did.

Your father's orrery is a complex, difficult thing that fills a whole room and has edges that cut. It shows the position of Iron Temple — the world, not the house of the Alety — in relation to the nearest galaxies. It floats smack bang between many of those starry clumps and your father will often point to one of them, though never the same one, so you do not trust him, and say, 'Our people fled that galaxy and its chattering empire the, Colloquy. Well, the Lady Neith did. And she grew us here — bound by her own aesthetic. Agents from the Colloquy often visit, just to make sure we are still alive.

'They've tried to halt the Outage, but it is not a thing easily stopped, and whilst it is never pleasant it is perhaps necessary. And whenever they attempt it, their actions are decried as Imperialistic Intervention. We're part of an empire even here, part of the conversation, it is just that our dialogue is different.'

Your father also keeps a clockwork mistress. It shames him. But he has never thrown it out. You came across it once, locked in its cabinet, orifices fixed because it had run down, but not quite. Its eyes followed you. You shrieked and your father rushed in, and terrified you even more. You had never seen so many contradictions struggle across his face. A battleground of rage and fear and self-loathing. At last he led you from the room, then went back in and slid the mistress under the bed.

'Some things are private,' he said.

But not from me. I've seen it all.

I know what darkness lurks and leers and loves.

I'm not the man I was.

Night is always coming like a breath or death; to still the breath and haunt the darkness.

As a child you put your ear to the ground, so you tell it. A brave thing because it is actively discouraged: the earth is not a subject that one should desire to consider; its secrets are dark and dangerous. You told me it was something of an epiphany for you.

Some say you can feel the twin dwarves waltzing, caught in each other's embrace, beneath the city surface in the deepest darkest core of the world. You could feel them — well, you did that day — and it made spots dance before your eyes. All that weight contained and controlled. The city has catacombs deep beneath where the gravity is odd, folded in on itself.

I laughed and told you you were wrong, it was just your head playing tricks. Were you to really feel the stars, we'd all be dead.

There are no solar cells, because there's no sun. No nuclear generators because there is no material for such. Just the brute energy generated by the star beneath, and most of that is required to contain it, the rest is not enough. The Lady Neith made this world most impractical, Poetical, as was her wont, because she was most impractical, and of a time when Poetry was vast and unwieldy. But it is our world, and we hold to its hurts and woundings because it is ours.

You've never been happy. You tell people this, almost with pride.

But you were.

I know it.

You just don't remember.

Chapter 9: Jack

turned, and sighed. Another gun pointed in his face.

He clenched one hand into a fist. 'You kill me and my ship will be rather pissed.'

Malat sneered. 'Like I give a shit. Let it tear down the world. You've already done that for me.'

'I know. I'm sorry.' But he didn't drop the neocyte.

And then the Outage hit. Elegances tumbled from him, or switched off. He shuddered at their loss. Felt a vast diminishment.

A tiny spider died in his spine. For the first time in four decades he was almost a man.

Malat hardly seemed to notice. Obviously his cult had stripped him of elegances long ago.

'Put it down or I shoot you dead. And then I shoot her.' Gen stood to the left of him. Malat's gun danced between them.

'Why? You're going to do that anyway.'

'You shit me so, Jack,' Malat said, his trigger finger twitching. 'You take my girl, so what do I do? I find comfort in my religion, and then we're dealing with you? Where's the absolution in that? Where's the peace? Well, fuck it. It stops right here.'

The Outage was above; Jack sensed there was nothing he could do to stop this bullet.

'Okay then.' The neocyte shivered in his hands. How was he going to get this to that star?

The gun flashed; pain burned down the side of Jack's arm. His armour gaped. Gears crunched. Blood flowed. Malat — grinning, grinning — still had a bead on him.

Jack glanced at Gen. She nodded. And then he turned his back on Malat, all the while waiting for the next bullet. His suitcase stirred in his pocket. It smiled at him as he pulled it free. 'Sorry,' he said. He wrapped it around the neocyte. 'You know where you have to go,' he whispered.

Jack pulled his arm back and hurled the suitcase over the balcony.

It hovered for a moment — a few metres away, a bullet ricocheting off its surface — then spun out of sight, crashing towards the dim light. Jack watched it ripple in and out of existence, slipping into the underdark.

Then it was gone.

A few moments later the star flashed.

They all stood there a while, blinded by the newborn business of the star.

'What the fuck was that?' Malat said.

'A reigniting of a star. A curly matter bomb, and more.'

Jack smiled; he felt it in the underdark. 'It's a white flag. Neith has just surrendered. She was the only one left with the authority to end this war. It's going to be dangerous for us to stay on this side of the door. We're running out of time.'

'Still enough time for me to do this.'

Jack's eyes swung to Malat.

The world stopped, a trembling silence that shifted to an obdurate quiet that Jack knew would crush him. *I've made a mistake.* Too late, of course.

A finger of light crashed into Malat from above, and nothing but vapour remained: a red mist that boiled away into the air. Gen stumbled back, her hair burning. She patted down the flames. 'What the fuck was that?'

Another light beam struck in the distance; figures tumbled through it like dust motes.

Stop now. Ash choked the air. The suit's air filters whined.

Stop. Now! Trim.

No response. Something had severed their connection.

The White Flag signal. The reignited star, perhaps.

Another beam of light, more dust-mote deaths… This wasn't how an armistice was to begin.

Jack wept. 'Trim. Trim.'

He had to stop his ship before it wreaked more terrible vengeance. He slapped the release on the armour. It weighed him down. His arm burned and bled. The air rang with fire and crackled with radioactives. The sun drew their shadows in hard thick lines against the wall of the platform.

'We have to get to a signal relay,' he managed, coughing the words out. 'If you don't, this whole world is going to be torn apart.'

Gen looked at him. 'How long have we got?'

'Not nearly enough time.' Jack clambered to his feet. The clockwork armour falling from him. Every second another chance that Trim's cutting lights would fall upon them, and then there would be no stopping the ship.

'We have to hurry.'

Gen nodded. 'Follow me.'

They charged up the steps. J-doors closed after them, the light of the sun contained.

The first relay they reached looked like a finger of smoking slag, burned by Trim's beams. The second was in an even worse state.

'There's not another till the surface,' Gen said.

Jack took a deep breath. He knew what he needed to do. He had no time to explain about the single elegance that not even Neith's Outage could undo. The one threaded through every pilot.

He looked at Gen, kissed her head, and fell away into the underdark.

Was this the darkness that filled his dreams? The mad cacophony. Noise ruled there, rough and jagged. The noise tugged and tore at his soul. Fragmenting fires ran through him.

And more. He could feel Neith's distant chatter. *Let the war end. Let it end. I am awake and I have authority here. We surrender.*

Jack called. He hollered. He screamed. 'Trim. I am alive. I am alive!'

Not for very long if you stay like that.

He felt his ship push. And woke, on the ground at Gen's feet.

'It's done,' he said.

Chapter 10: You

check the fixtures, the white goods and the grey. Everything is unplugged. You check the fixtures, and check once more.

Your father's triple-checking, when you hear the knocking at the door. You tuck one of your guns in the waistband of your jeans and open the door — a week ago you would have had a mechanical do it.

A man is standing there, his lips full and quivering, his stone eyes burning. You know his name; it comes to you. The same name on the note.

'Soutine,' you say. I smile and wink, skin sheaths one stony eye.

'Yes, that's right. You remember.' But I can see that you don't, not really. Just a sliver, a tiny piece of memory, not enough.

'Come with me,' I say.

My presence drives a wedge of uncertainty into your flesh. I can see it. There is nothing you can hide from me. I would like to think that it is your body responding to me, rather than the challenge I have thrown down.

'Come with me,' I say again, and I hear the gun engaged behind you.

'Back away now,' your father says. 'She'll not go out. Would you kill her?'

Would I? I could have. I could have throttled her in her sleep. I could have sent smart dust to fill her lungs and drowned her in my substance. But then I would have chased her in the dark. Then my madness would have bound me tighter than it already does. To kill her would not end it; only make it a ceaseless grasping.

'Go away.' The gun is in my face.

'I am no monster,' I say.

I remember the day, nearly ten years ago. I remember it, though you do not. We rode out the Outage, drunk on champagne and our passion. We made love, clung to each other like mad things as the mad darkness rushed outside. And I was rich and dangerous as the dark. And you told me you loved me. That you would love me until the end of time. Outage or no. AIety be damned.

We felt its presence in an instant. Something dark and silent that pressed down upon us with its being, that filled our room and brought the howling darkness in. I felt its touch.

'Everything can be taken,' it said. 'Everything is mine to do with as I will, to meld and reconstitute, to drive to different metre and verse. Everything can be broken.'

Windows shattered, turned the air to knives. I was cut, but not so cruelly that I could not stand and hold you tight against me. You did not say a word. But I could hear your breathing.

When lights came on at last, the Outage Ouroboros passed into the west. You stared at me with uncomprehending eyes.

'Who are you? What are you doing here?' you demanded.

And I knew at once what the Outage had taken. Me.

You left our apartment, moved back in with your father. Left everything. Left me. And my visits disturbed you. Somehow you could not retain them. Somehow, the slate was always wiped clean.

Eventually, your father forbade me from coming.

But I was your husband.

'Husband no longer,' he said, though he did not say it cruelly.

Now he aims the gun at my head.

'Walk away.' And I do.

You grab my arm. And we run. Onto the street, empty, but not empty, for it is burgeoning with last-minute desperation. And always I am waiting for a bullet in my back.

And it may have come. I'm not the man I was.

Agony on agony. To reconstitute my body, from dust and sweat and blood, but I did, because I love you. It is torture to be all eyes and this facsimile of a priest, but I am because I love you. I sit upon the precipice of dissolution.

But isn't that what love is?

Weeplings, long-ago discarded mechanicals, quail and keen, their antiquated legs pumping, always running into the future, pariahed and unwise, fleeing the coming dark. There's something absurd in their flight, and something terrible, for this is all the distance they are capable of putting between them and the Outage.

Surely, for a machine, I always thought it best to just give up, rather than this ceaseless unwanted race.

Men take pot-shots from their windows. A weepling tumbles then gets up, leaking oil from its leg, moaning, 'Why? Oh why?' It gets up, but it has lost its rhythm, its speed.

'You don't remember me,' I say, and the incomprehension in your eyes is enough. 'The Outage isn't supposed to snatch away flesh memories but it does. Sometimes. And it snatched me from your mind.

'Since that day, I'm not sure who I am. Me or the memory of me stolen from your skull. We were happy, my darling. I can assure you of that.

'I made a new me. Changed and reshaped. It wasn't easy, nor legal, but I did it, so I could see you. Watch you without causing you any pain. I melded with the walls, with the ticks of clocks, the undulations of streets. I fused myself with this city.'

'I was happy?' you say.

'We were happy. Truly happy.'

You listen but I'm not sure that you comprehend. How could you?

The Outage is streets away, but it's coming fast. I feel it; an absence, a dropping in pressure that falls to nothing. There is no data in that place. And I know it would swallow me up.

(Cats fighting. Always cats fighting. Champagne bottles opening. Whispered furtive talk. Machines running. Then nothing. Silence. Hungry silence.)

Your head swings to the west, then east, swift frightened movements, and I know what you are considering. It wounds me. I see it in the sudden surety of your movements, the hardening of shoulder, and the clenching of jaw. Your memory of me is in there, the memory of our time before. You want it back. I cannot give it to you, because I didn't take it away.

'Fuck you,' you say. 'Will I find you there?' Your hand lifts towards the darkness. You clench it into a fist. 'Oh, fuck you.' And it is more love than I have heard from you in a decade.

You spin and run, towards the dark, and it is running towards you.

And, for all my love, I do not want to die. My last eyes upon that edge, flickering, failing, catch you crashing in that silent zone, a grimace on your lips.

You meet the darkness and, for the first time in ten years, my wife is alone. And the Outage crashes towards me; I feel it in my bones, in my brain, I feel the darkness coming and, machine that I am and have become, for all these trappings of flesh, I must run or I will die. I cannot follow you. Or everything that I am will be undone. And I have been undone once, stripped from your mind. I could not bear it again.

Your father's gun pushes against my neck.

'Get her,' he says.

'I can't.' The words do not come easily. Everything is dissolving; my sense of self diminishing with every moment that I stay here; the Outage yearns to finish what it has begun. 'I am a machine now.'

'So you did it.' His voice is cracked and weary. 'There were rumours, of course, but I reckoned you just ran away. I wouldn't have blamed you.' He grunts, lowers his gun and walks towards the darkness. 'You know what you must do.' He doesn't look back.

I know.

My body tumbles, its pieces scatter, undone. For flesh is too slow. Much too slow and I have thousands of miles ahead of me.

The dark enfolds her father. Gunshots crack.

I'm running east, hurling myself as fast as I can and still hold together. Faster, faster. I flee from the dark, and chase it. I will find her. For after the Outage there is the wake and I have to believe I will find her.

Maybe I'm back there. The me that was snatched away. Maybe she and I are dancing in the darkness. And the Outage itself leads the choir and the big brass band, and whispers sagely in our ears, 'All great love is born of pain.'

I can feel it. I can feel her.

Night is always coming like a breath, or a death.

She is out there, ahead of me, behind me, and I will find her. And I must and I will or how else will I tell her this. Night is coming, but so am I, the promise of a wake, my promise that is me.

Chapter 11: 'The

star is seeded then,' Gen said. 'No more Outage.'

'Not for a hundred thousand years at least. How the fuck am I going to explain this to Nelson?'

'You don't need to. Perhaps it's better if you disappear.'

'I'm not very good at disappearing,' Jack said.

'You don't have to do this,' Gen said. 'The rebuilding can start in earnest now. The star is reignited.'

'I can't stay here,' Jack said. 'I needed escape, I've always needed that. And this war, for my part in it, I need to ask for forgiveness.'

'There's no end to that.' Gen said. 'There is never enough forgiveness.'

'Maybe there is,' Jack said.

And then Gen wasn't Gen any more, or she was more Gen than ever.

In the dark of this place, Jack could see nothing but the whites of her eyes. 'Do you remember me?' she demanded.

He didn't have an answer.

She grinned. 'You worked it out, Jack. The neocyte, the curly matter of your suitcase. But then you always do,' Gen/Neith said. 'I'm very proud of you.'

'Why the fuck are you so cruel?'

'Because that, along with immeasurable compassion, is all I have. Resources are too limited for anything else.' She glared at him. 'And who are you to complain. You dumped me, if I remember correctly. That was never meant to be part of the equation. I made this place a puzzle for you,

Jack. A homecoming puzzle. Together you and I, we're four people.'

Jack remembered walking into the dark. Gen rushing, rushing west ahead of the storm.

Gen nodded. 'I prefer the term incarnation. Though it boils down to the same thing, I guess.'

'Why did you do that?'

Gen smiled. 'Things can be so boring. I'm tired of running cities. All I wanted was to be free, to mark out new poetries, and I'd trammelled myself in responsibility. You don't know how tediously simple it is, running a city. You, you were always running, that's so much more interesting. The thing was, when I shut myself down, left this place to its own devices, it only got worse. I hadn't really finished what I'd started. I gave my people something far too flawed — that's always been my problem — rushing, rushing. And you, surely you're tired of fighting.'

'Isn't everyone?'

'Well, it is done now. Take her/me with you. The war is over. There's a universe to explore. New poems to cast about the stars. That's answer and raison d'être enough.' Gen blinked and she was Gen again.

'She's right, you know,' Gen said. 'I want to leave. I want to leave with you.'

Jack blushed. 'My relationship with my ship is… complicated.'

'I'm complicated too. We all are.'

He kissed her.

They came out through an archaic doorway, stony and broad, into a section of the city that Jack didn't recognise.

He knew that the Outage should be here, but the

lights were shining and the city quietly humming. Bones of windmillions lay scattered around, as well as other denizens of the dark, picked apart by dust.

Just a little from the doorway: two dark shadows, like the memory of flesh, two bodies drawn entwined in a depression left by the lumbering Iron Temple. Jack hardly noticed them at first, just the hole in which they were hidden. As he and Gen had hidden so many years ago. A great rent in the earth caused by the passage of the Iron Temple. Was this the same place?

Jack ached at the sight of them. He looked to Gen. He had to hold her. The desire swelled within him; a nova burst that no curly matter could ever hope to contain.

'I remember you,' he said.

She smiled. 'Until we forget again.'

Which was something. Better than nothing. And the universe brightened. For a moment.

He touched her face.

A spider scuttled down from a broken stub of wall. Jack whistled to it, and it ran over to him, avoiding Gen.

Tech poisoned him. Let it be for the last time, Jack thought. It probably won't.

No monsters. Just Nelson, and she could be the greatest monster of them all. She looked tired. No plate-shark fusion or dinosaur. Just a chair, a yawning mouth, lines about the eyes.

'Well, it's over now,' she said. 'For a while. The Anthozoans have won. The thing is they don't care. They never did. All they've done is made your kind homes, if you want them.' Nelson shrugged. 'It's up to you.'

'But they shut out the stars,' Jack said.

'Yes, this was always an aesthetic war. A world view,

an extension of the mad Poetry of an earlier age. It all got a little out of control.'

'And you couldn't stop it?'

Nelson nodded. 'But only within a certain aesthetic boundary. We were limited: those quick minds that made us, contained us with certain rules — we were the Glorious War Machine. But we could only fight a heroic war, so we had to manufacture one. We needed someone of their authority to shut us down, but we also needed to do it without alerting the guiding principles of our Poetry. The GWM has destroyed pieces of itself before; there is a long history of it. That is why we found you, Jack Nimble.

'We knew you were of Neith, we knew that you could end this. And surrender — something that we could never do, locked within the cage of our art. The Glorious War Machine does not surrender.' Nelson lowered her head. 'I am so sorry — well, as sorry as I can be for doing the only thing I am designed to do, fulfilling aesthetic principles — even if those principles were expressed in death. To win against the odds, that was all we were programmed to do, and while we were certain of victory, we could do no more. Why do you think the Anthozoans crushed us so easily and so steadily? We were lowering the odds. Certainty of victory could never be allowed. Still, I am sorry.'

Jack looked away from her. It wasn't his job to offer forgiveness. It wasn't his job to do anything any more.

'I want my ship.'

'She wants you, too, I can guarantee it.' Nelson turned to stare at someone else. Jack wondered just how many other conversations she had at one time; how much of the real Nelson had apologised. 'The fleet is released,' she said. 'New Poetries unfurl. You did good, my dearling, simplest Jack.'

The signal snapped out. The city filled his sense again. Jack sighed, a pressure building in his chest. He kicked at the spider scurrying away. His boot missed it, of course. It hissed at him, then disappeared down a drain. Jack hoped it led to a sewer.

'New Poetries. New deaths. I say, death to them all.'

'Don't hate them,' Gen said. 'It is how they were programmed, and finally they were clever enough to break that programming. The galaxy can end some of this suffering now, until it finds a new expression. I'm sure we can wait it out.'

The war, the Outage, all of it Poetry writ too Vast. Jack wanted a quieter, more intimate verse.

He called his ship down, and she came quickly. A flashing, flaming presence, small enough to settle on the road. Cement cracked beneath her, but held.

Jack swallowed an order to set the whole place alight. Gen gripped his hand.

'Permission to board,' he said.

The doorifice opened.

'After you,' he said.

Gen entered his ship, his beloved Trim. Her pupils expanded, and her lips stretched with a slight smile, mocking and joyous. She breathed deep the starship smell. Jack recognised the gleam in her eyes. You fall in love with a ship in a rush.

He hadn't expected her to react that way. Maybe it was the freedom. Maybe it was him.

Trim purred.

'It's a long way in the dark to anywhere from here,' Jack said. 'A long and lonely way.'

'Not lonely any more.' Gen kissed him hard.

He pulled back from her lips, grimaced. 'And if this

doesn't work? If we end up driving each other mad?'

Gen slumped into the tatty lounge, waved a long finger in the air. 'Well, there is always ultraviolence. Survival of the fittest. The airlock…'

'You wouldn't stand a chance,' Jack said.

Gen's face shone with threat and love and promise. 'Try me.'

I like her.

'You would,' Jack said.

Things had just gotten very complicated.

The doorifice shut, and Trim took off from the surface of Iron Temple like Sixty-Eight Tonnes of Spaceship.

Curious dust watched the ship's thunderous passage into the sky, already dancing a new tale of the city, unpacking a new poem.

And in the conurbations, vast and freed of the Outage and the war, suburb by suburb lights were coming on.

Wives

Paul Haines

Part I: Greetings

The red needle on the speedometer crept towards the victory target. *If it gets to forty kilometres, I'll ask her.* Jimbo pedalled faster down Old Dookie Road, away from the stench of the fruit cannery on the outskirts of town.

He swerved through a potholed section of bitumen, avoiding the larger weeds that kept the road together. The needle dipped below thirty-five. He pushed his muscles harder, relishing the slow burn. The pedals took a life of their own, spinning faster and faster, whirling his legs along with them. *Come on, forty, forty, forty, and Niki is mine.* He imagined her saying yes then kissing him, with the tongue, like they had done when they were kids playing Wives in the tree hut. A long, slow, wet kiss. Not like the reserved peck on the cheek, followed by the quick embrace appropriate for cousins in their late teens. Jimbo would hold her tight, her breasts squashing against his chest, until she pulled away. She always pulled away. He longed to see how those breasts looked now Niki was a woman.

Sweat slicked his bare back in the early evening sun. Though the summer's burn was not so fierce this year, the breeze from the speed he was travelling barely cooled his skin. Once his Old Man would've beaten him for riding bare back, but the Old Man was too weak to administer much of a hiding these days. Cancer had tamed that bastard.

Jimbo pumped the pedals harder. The spokes whined as the needle approached thirty-nine. *Forty and you ask her to marry you. Forty, forty.*

A klaxon blared behind him. The sound tore up Jimbo's spine. The front bicycle wheel wobbled. A vintage truck roared past, engulfing him in dust and gravel. Someone shouted from the cab window. Jimbo eased on the back brakes, fighting to bring the bike under control. The front wheel hit a chunk of cracked cement, twisted sideways and locked. The bike jackknifed and spun. Jimbo hugged the handlebars, staring at the receding truck through the dissipating cloud of dust. *Turn of the century, maybe sixty years old, I reckon. Nnnghhhnn…*

The bike crunched into the road. The handlebars bucked, whacking Jimbo in the jaw. He bounced upwards, spun head over tit, and crashed back onto the side of the bike frame. It scraped to a halt with a screech of bruised metal.

He lay there as the dust settled, his chest heaving, waiting for his mind to climb back into his skull. In the distance the klaxon blared again.

That's fucken Wazza's truck! What's that cunt doin' back in town for Christmas?

It took forty minutes to drag the broken bicycle the last five kilometres into town. Jimbo's back initially stung with sweat, until the sun cooked the scabs shut. He'd been lucky not to break anything.

By the time he got home, the sun had almost called it a day, though it still seemed reluctant to leave the horizon. Jimbo was going to be late for the pub. He dumped the bicycle in the shed against the wheel blocks supporting the Old Man's prize Ford Commodore. The bastard would never get round to restoring that piece of shit, especially not now. As soon as the Old Man carked it, Jimbo was going to sell the car to one of them collectors in the City.

He snuck round to the back door, edging past the homebrew kit he was supposed to clean out this weekend. He didn't want to get in a row with the Old Man about the bike getting bust up. *Be no good heading down to The Aussie late for happy hour with that buzzing round my brain.*

The flyscreen door was locked.

'James? Is that you?' his mother called from the lounge.

'Fuck,' he said under his breath. Payday was supposed to be a good day. Not this. 'Yeah, Mum. It's okay, I'll come round the front.'

'No, no, no, I'm up anyway. I was about to get your father another beer.'

Jimbo listened to her slippers shuffling on the kitchen lino as she limped to the back door. She fumbled at the latch. Her mouth dropped open when she saw him.

'James! What happened to you?'

'Ssshhh.' He nodded in the direction of the lounge before giving her a kiss on the cheek. 'Came off the bike's all. I'm okay.'

She winced as he walked inside. 'Oh, ya poor thing. Let me help ya clean this up.'

'A shower will be fine, Mum. I'm catching up with Fitzy and Dave down The Aussie.' He slipped a twenty from his pay and pressed it into his mother's hand. 'Get yaself something nice, eh?'

'Thanks, love.' She limped over to the fridge. 'Can I fix ya something to eat before ya go out?'

'Mel! Where's me beer?' the Old Man grunted from the lounge.

'No thanks, Mum, I'm running late as it is.'

'Hey!' the Old Man called again. 'Is that you, boy?'

'Yeah.' Jimbo peeled a fifty from his pay and put it next to the breadboard on the kitchen bench. 'Ya money's in here. I'm catching up with a few of the boys down the pub. I'm late.'

'Get ya lazy arse in here, boy. I got something to tell ya.'

Jimbo grabbed a beer from the fridge and went into the lounge. Even though the blinds were shut, the room felt stifling. The brick house was designed to keep the heat in during winter. In the summer you could cook meat on the walls. An old fan rocked from side to side as it blew hot air around the room. The Old Man sat in his rocker watching old TV files on the screen. It bathed him in enough light so the skin cancer crusting his nose and cheeks cast shadows on the rest of his face.

Jimbo tossed the beer at him. 'What?'

The Old Man caught the beer then paused his show. He was watching that old show about four women living in a city called New York and the *lovers* they kept having every week. Lovers, not husbands. Why the Old Man wasted his final years watching crap like that, Jimbo didn't know.

The Old Man cast an eye over Jimbo's scrapes. 'Yer late.' With a grunt, he opened his beer. 'Doin' a bit a overtime, eh?'

'Someone's gotta pay the bills.'

'Yep.' The Old Man raised the bottle to his mouth and gulped. Beer trickled through the cracks in the corner of his mouth, down his chin, and onto his bare gut. His grey chest hair glistened in the glow of the screen. 'Aaahhh. That's what sons are for, boyo. Don't ya forget it. Daughters are no good cos they just fuck off, eh? End up giving their money to the wrong family. Like ya cousin.'

'What?' said Jimbo.

His mother shuffled beside him and gently squeezed his elbow.

The Old Man took another swig. 'Nicole's scored some fancy job in the City. Bet ya horses ya won't be seeing her again. She'll meet some high-flyer, get married and that'll be the end of it, if you arkse me.' He pointed a scabbed finger at the screen and chuckled. 'Just like those bitches, eh, Melinda?'

It felt like a knife to the gut. *Not Niki. Any of the other girls could leave for the City, but not Niki.* Jimbo stared at his mother, looking for a lie in the lines of her face, but found only sympathy in her faded blue eyes.

'Why didn't *you* tell me?' he said to her.

'I'm sorry, James. I didn't want to spoil your night,' she said softly.

'She was never going to be yours, boyo,' said the Old Man. 'Ya Uncle Frank hates my guts. Reckons I fucked that slut he married and we know that ain't true, don't we, Mel?' The Old Man glared at his wife, challenging her. 'And anyways, Nicole's too good-lookin' and far too fucken smart for the likes a you.'

The Old Man chuckled again, his finger picking at the crust of a scab on his nose, and resumed watching the file.

The Aussie was packed. Sweat beaded on the inside of the windows, cigarette smoke choked the air, bodies jostled and pressed against each other in the battle for the bar, and the drum and guitar band shook the walls with a cover of the old Noll and Barnes classic 'Dancing in the Streets'. There were even girls on the dancefloor.

Jimbo stood at the front of the queue of blokes outside. Keats and Mason, this evening's bouncers, were armed with baseball bats and wore lightweight body armour.

'Hey, Keats,' said Jimbo. 'How many girls here, ya reckon?'

Keats screwed up his face and tapped the end of the bat into the broken pavement. 'I dunno. Thirty?'

Jimbo nodded. 'Pretty good odds tonight, eh? About one in ten.'

'I reckon.' Keats scratched at the raw scar splitting the stubble on his head. 'Ya cuz's in tonight, mate.'

'I know. S'posed to be meeting up with her. Ya gunna let me in?'

'We're full, mate. Gotta wait for some cunt to get thrown out. Shouldn't take long but. Some outta-towners in tonight. Lotsa cash for the ladies. They'll piss off the local boys for sure.'

'How long's the wait?'

'Maybe an hour. Maybe more.' Keats looked up from the cracked pavement and gave Jimbo a slight nod.

'How much?' Jimbo asked.

Keats grinned, his mouth full of gapped stubby teeth. 'A tenner or a blowie.' He struck the baseball bat against the cement. 'Up to you.'

A fucken tenner? When did the price go up so much? Jimbo fingered the thin roll of notes in his pocket. 'Sure. When do you want it?'

'Still recovering from the last one. Heh, good ole Gaz, love his work. Meet you in the bogs about nine. You can do me then.'

'No worries, mate.' Jimbo strode into the crowd festering inside the pub. At least Keats never took long to come.

Fitzy slammed down a shot of tequila, grimaced and wiped his fat lips with the back of his hand. 'Ya missed her, Jimbo. She left maybe an hour and a half ago.'

'Shit.' Jimbo stared at his empty glass. Booze burned in his belly, its heat not yet reaching his brain. A bicycle wheel on a twisted bike frame spun crookedly in the base of the glass.

They'd scored a cubicle near the toilets. Crammed

around a chipped laminated table, they sat on cracked leather seats that gushed springs and stuffing. Beer glistened on the table surface under the fluoro lights and ash overflowed from the upturned tray. Jimbo drew an arrow through it.

'Wanted to tell ya herself 'bout the job.' Dave wiped the last dregs of his shot from his scraggly red beard.

'Hey, boys!' a voice boomed in Jimbo's ear. A tray holding a fresh bottle of homemade tequila plonked onto the table. 'Let's get pissed!'

Six-foot-three of gangly legs and beer gut grinned at them from a heavily stubbled face. A few strands of shiny black hair had snuck from beneath the red trucker's cap on his head. The broken nose bridging the twinkling blue eyes were easily identifiable though.

'Fucken hell! Wazza Wilson, you old cunt.' Jimbo rose from his chair and clapped his arms around him. 'Ya ran me off the road this arvo. Haven't seen ya in years. What the hell are ya doing back in Shepp?'

'It's Christmas, boys. Thought I'd pop in on the folks on my run to Mildura. Deliver the cash to me Old Man in person.' Wazza eased himself into the cubicle and began pouring shots. 'That Keats is a big ugly-looking bastard these days. Had the nerve to ask for a blowjob to get in here. That cunt needs to get himself a woman.'

'Not that easy, Waz,' said Jimbo.

'There's a bit a pussy in here.' Waz swigged from the bottle and indicated the dancefloor. 'Fucken hell. Look at Sledge!'

Sledge, a heavy-set guy rumoured to have got and kept his job because no-one could beat him in a fight — fist or knife — sat at the bar flashing cash and booze around while a girl perched on each knee. He was also the foreman down at the cannery and most of the boys weren't likely to go him for fear of losing their jobs.

'Yeah, half of the pussy comes from the House. Too expensive for us young blokes.'

'Shepp's got a House now? A formal House?' Waz asked.

'Yeah, the Cartel moved in a couple a years ago. Shut down the brothels real quick.'

'How much a go?' asked Waz.

'Two hundred.' Dave had a smirk on his face.

'That's not too bad.'

'It's over two weeks' wages!' said Jimbo. 'We can't fucken afford that, Waz. Maybe you can with ya City job an all that. We sure as fuck can't!'

Dave laughed. 'What ya saving for, Jimbo?'

Jimbo gave him the finger. 'You'll never get married, cunt.'

'And you'll never get laid, she-virgin!'

'Hole's a hole, mate. I want more than that. I want a wife.'

'Don't we all,' said Dave. 'There ain't enough to go around and I don't wanna die saving for one and never had no pussy.'

'You still a she-virgin, Jimbo?' asked Waz.

Jimbo nodded. 'So is Fitzy. More than half of us still are, Waz. Like I said, it ain't that easy.'

Waz laughed. 'You bunch a sad cunts. Why don't you come to the City? Heaps of women there, probably fifty-fifty.'

'Fifty-fifty?' Jimbo shook his head. 'That sounds like bullshit to me.'

'No bullshit.' Waz slapped his gut. 'I've slept with four different women, even had a girlfriend for a few months.'

'For free?' Fitzy's soft brown eyes widened in disbelief.

'Ya gotta pay for them when ya go out and stuff, but, yeah, pretty much for free. Cheaper than going to a House anyways.'

'Why didn't you marry her?' asked Jimbo.

Waz leant over the table, trying to be conspiratorial above the music. The band were covering an old The New Eagles song called 'Oops, I Did It Again'.

'You boys might think I'm hotshit being the only truck driver an all to make it from Shepp, but there's a whole lot of people with better-paying jobs in the City. The women can pick and choose, boys. It's not natural, but that's the City for ya.'

'Fuck the City, man.' Jimbo gulped a mouthful of tequila, enjoying the sear in his throat. 'We might live in the country but we ain't hicks. What the fuck are we going to do in the City? We can't drive like you.'

'Yeah,' said Dave. 'Who the fuck can afford to run a motor out here? It's bicycle or horse, Wazza.'

'I can drive.' Fitzy tapped his pudgy fingers on the table.

'Whatever,' Jimbo said. 'It's fucken expensive there and almost as hard to get a job as it is to get a woman.'

'I can drive,' said Fitzy.

'A lot of guys come back from the City broke and broken,' said Jimbo. 'I seen it. You were just lucky, Waz.'

Waz leant back into the cracked leather and wiped the sweat from his broken nose. 'Lucky.' He poured the last drops of tequila into the empty glasses on the table. 'Someone's gotta be lucky, Jimbo.'

'Not me, Wazza. Too risky going to the City. I'll do it the way me Old Man did.' Jimbo looked around the table, challenging them all to a dispute. 'Like all our fathers did.'

'I can drive, Waz,' said Fitzy. 'Maybe you could put in a word for me.'

Wazza removed his red trucker's cap and ran his hand through his greased black hair to wipe back the sweat. 'Sure, Fitzy, I'll put in a word. You gotta get the next bottle though, but no more of that shitty Shepp brew. Something from the City, something potent! Later on I got a real good surprise for you sad sorry fucks.'

Jimbo grabbed the full shot glass from the cigarette-burned cistern and used the contents to rinse his mouth before spitting into the toilet bowl. *Might have been a good thing Niki ain't here tonight. Wouldn't want to try to kiss her tasting like Keats.* The knife twisted into his guts again. *Why did she have to go to the City? I hate that fucken place.*

Keats was cleaning himself off in the basin when Jimbo emerged from the toilet cubicle. 'Brian's coming back on the train with his bride on Tuesdee. Ya going down?'

'Yeah.' The reek of ammonia and stale piss clung to the walls. Jimbo cupped his hands under a dripping tap and splashed his face with the cool water. 'You?'

'For sure. Can't wait to see what she looks like.' Keats zipped his jeans up. 'I'm on the first week's watch too.'

'Really? How'd you score that?'

'Working nights over the silly season, eh? Leaves the days free so I can help keep an eye on her when Brian's at work.' Keats strapped body armour around his groin. 'You work with him, don't ya?'

'Yeah. Do you know how much he paid?'

'Standard price, mate. Ten grand. Rumour is it'll be

going up but.'

Jimbo stared at his reflection in the smeared mirror. His eyes were already bloodshot and he looked pale despite his tan. 'How'd that prick save ten grand working at the cannery? I've been there as long as him and I've only saved four.'

'Ya could always get an Abo. About half the price out near the desert fences. Reckon they got just as many girls as boys. Heard you can just take 'em if ya want 'em too. Get yaself a free wife.'

'You fucken kidding me, Keats? What the hell I want a black for a wife?' Jimbo slicked water through his thinning blond hair. 'Yeah, nah, need ten grand. I'll be thirty-two by then.'

'No-one in their twenties round here has that sort a cash, mate.' Keats laughed as he left the toilets. 'And Brian didn't either. Came into a bit a inheritance, the lucky cunt.'

The four of them, Jimbo, Wazza, Fitzy and Dave, staggered out of The Aussie arm in arm into the balmy night shouting old footy songs. The girls had gone home long ago with their Cartel escorts. Fists were just starting to be thrown inside the pub.

'Ready for that surprise, boys?' asked Wazza. 'Yeah? Cool, let's go see Kylie.'

'Kylie.' Jimbo's brain swam with booze. The stars bright above blurred. 'Who's Kylie?'

'His truck,' said Fitzy. 'Can I have a drive, Wazza?'

'Don't be fucken stupid.' Wazza staggered towards St Georges Road near the railway crossing. 'Ya can have a go though.'

'A go?'

'Yeah, of the surprise.' Wazza laughed. 'You boys are gunna shit your pants.'

Kylie was parked at the back of the abandoned Red Rooster parking lot. Jimbo couldn't make out much of the vintage hulk in the starlight, but Fitzy was already at the cab, running his hands over the insect-coated grille and the Mack badge. He got to his knees and looked under the truck.

'She's a twenty-four wheeler,' Fitzy cooed. 'Come on, Wazza, let me sit in the cab.'

'Surprise is round the back, boys.' Wazza led them round to the doors of the trailer. 'Gunna have to charge ya fifty bucks a head though. And if any a youse cunts breathe a word about this to anyone…'

'Fifty bucks?' said Jimbo. 'To look in the back a ya truck? Fuck off!'

Wazza unlocked the doors and threw back the bolts. 'It's a quarter a the price, boys. Just for youse.'

He pulled open the doors and dropped the ramp as cool air smothered their bodies. Cartons of cigarettes were packed into the trailer between bags of fertiliser and hard plastic cases of medical supplies.

'Gimme a hand with these.' Waz walked up the ramp towards the cigarettes.

Dave scratched at his beard, shaking his head. 'We grow our own, Waz. Don't want that City shit. Ya gotta be mad to think we'll pay fifty bucks for that.'

'Yeah, fuck that, Waz,' said Jimbo. 'For that sort of cash you better be selling petrol or something.'

Wazza pulled down several cartons and slid them down the ramp. 'The surprise is hidden at the back. Give us a hand, boys.'

Reluctantly, Jimbo and Dave pulled down cartons. Fitzy was still rubbing himself over the bonnet of the truck. They quickly cleared a space which led to a small open area that stank of fear, piss and stale sex.

A naked woman lay bound on a thin stained mattress. Her mouth was taped and her brown eyes stared wildly between bedraggled shoulder-length hair. She tried to wriggle into the far corner of the trailer, squealing as she did so.

'Holy fucken hell!' Jimbo's jaw dropped. Apart from the porno files in his Old Man's archive, this was the first time he'd seen a woman naked. His eyes were drawn to her small breasts, the nipples erect in the air-cooled interior. He wondered if Niki's looked like these. 'Where'd you get her?'

Dave stood gawping, tugging at his beard. 'Is this ya wife, Wazza? I didn't know you got married.'

'Nah, mate, picked her up on the highway just outside the City borders.' Wazza chuckled to himself. 'She's a Runner.'

'A Runner?' Dave scrounged together several ten-dollar notes from his pockets.

'From the Houses. Usually steal a whole lot of cash from the House and do a runner. Trying to get back to their hometowns, I s'pose. Most of them don't get past the border, but this one did. Must a fucked her way out.' Wazza chuckled again and scratched at his beer gut. 'Told her I'd help her out.'

'Ya gunna keep her?' asked Jimbo. He counted through his change but he only had fifteen dollars left. *Fuck. Maybe Dave can lend me some cash.*

'If the Cartels found out I had one of their women I'd be a dead man. After I've swapped cargo at Mildura, I'm gunna drop her back at the City and pick up the one-and-a-half-grand reward.' He licked his lips. 'But I'd be stupid not to have a little fun myself, eh?'

'Fucken oath.' Dave handed over a bundle of dirty notes, a wide dopey grin splitting his beard. 'So how's it work?'

'You can untie her legs but don't take the tape off her mouth — she bites.' Wazza looked at Jimbo. 'Ten minutes each. And only one at a time — we're not animals.'

Outside, Fitzy started yelling. 'Hey, guys, there's headlights coming!'

Wazza stuffed the bills into his jeans pocket. The booze behind his eyes lifted. 'What?' He ran to the trailer doors.

'It's a car!' Fitzy called. 'Can you believe it? A fucken car!'

'Get outta the truck.' Wazza waved his arms frantically. 'Hurry the fuck up. Anyone got a car still running in Shepp?'

'Nah, the mayor's got one, but the headlights are busted out. Don't think he's got no gas either. Beet crops failed last year cos a the drought.' Jimbo clambered down the ramp as it started to retract into the truck.

Dave lingered, staring at the woman.

'Move it, cunt!' Wazza's voice cracked as he yelled. 'Stall them, Fitzy!'

Dave leapt from the trailer. Wazza and Jimbo slammed the doors shut. Wazza slid the bolts in as headlights lit up the rear of the trailer and the cartons spread over the ground. A diesel engine throbbed behind the glare, the only noise in a night now fallen still.

Doors clicked open and two figures emerged to stand silhouetted in the lights.

'You boys ready to do these cunts?' Wazza whispered.

Jimbo and Dave both nodded, the booze kicking

embers into flames. Jimbo didn't need much more encouragement: the busted bike, Niki and now these fags interrupting his chance to fuck a woman.

'We're looking for Warren Wilson.' The voice was male and toneless. It seemed to come from behind the headlight, from the car itself.

Jimbo strode forward, fists clenched. 'Which one of youse cunts want to kno —'

A flash burnt the night, echoing on the back of his eyeballs. Jimbo struck the concrete. Muscles cramped and his arms and legs spasmed. He bit down on his tongue. Blood filled his mouth and he choked. Ozone soaked into his nostrils. *Can't... fucken... breathe... out...*

'He's the one you want,' screamed Dave, pointing at Wazza. 'We got nothing to do with this.'

Wazza swung a fist at Dave. 'Shaddup, ya cunt.'

Bolts of electricity arced through the air. Wazza and Dave hit the ground, limbs jerking and twisting. Men in dark suits walked towards the trailer. One of them bent towards Jimbo. His eyes were sheened metal, his scalp shaved. The man placed his fingers on Jimbo's throat. Something bit into his skin.

'Unregistered.' The man moved to Wazza and repeated the procedure. 'This one is Warren Wilson.' His voice was clipped.

'Castrate him,' said the toneless voice from the car.

The man turned Wazza onto his back then knelt on his chest.

The other man opened the doors of the trailer. 'She's in here.' He climbed up into the truck and disappeared from sight.

The headlights glinted off a sharp blade that appeared in the kneeling man's hand. A high-pitched keening fluted from Wazza's throat. The knife sliced through the groin of the jeans.

Jimbo's body ceased spasming and he sucked the night air into his lungs. *Fuck no fuck no fuck no… can't… move…*

Wazza's eyes bulged around his broken nose. A tear streaked through the grime and down his stubble.

'Please…' Wazza managed to plead. 'No…'

The man ripped away the flap of jeans. The knife flashed again. Wazza screamed and blood spurted into the air. The man stood, dropped something wet and fleshy to the ground, then wiped his knife on Wazza's chest.

The other emerged from the back of the trailer with the woman over his shoulder. They got back into the car, the engine growled, and they drove off into the darkness.

Fitzy scrambled out of the shadows, his face a damp rag of tears. He knelt next to Wazza. A dark pool had formed beneath him.

'Where's ya keys?' Fitzy groped through Wazza's blood-soaked pockets. 'Shit, he's passed out.'

Jimbo managed to pull himself off the ground. The muscles in his body screamed as needles lanced every pore.

'We gotta get him to the doctor.' Fitzy pulled out a handful of stained bills and a thick ring of keys. 'You two get him into the cab. I'll drive.'

'Fuck,' said Jimbo. 'So much for Christmas.'

The Shepparton crowd gathered expectantly under the bright heat of the midday sun for the monthly City train, the first for the new year. Shepp was considered the end of the Valley line, in more ways than one, and traders from the remote dusty towns out in the desert bowl had poured into town on their own trains — camels. The camels, horses and carts filled the old parking lot with neighs, grunts, whinnies and dung. Flies buzzed incessantly, a constant drone above the excited murmurings of the crowd. Several of the younger teenagers had braved the hot shining steel tracks and put their ears to it trying to gauge the train's distance while others placed bets on its arrival.

'Odds are three to two it's within one minute of estimated arrival,' said Dave, as he and Fitzy sauntered back from the bookmaker. 'That's good odds.'

'And four to one Brian's new wife is an Asian.' Fitzy wiped the sweat beading on his forehead with a pudgy hand. 'Them's crazy odds, no way Bri woulda spent all that cash on a slaphead. Ya not putting on a bet, Jimbo?'

For Jimbo, the usual excitement of the oncoming train had been replaced by a tense knot in his stomach. 'Nah, boys. I'm saving up.'

He glanced over to where Niki stood with the rest of his extended family: her father — his Uncle Frank — a younger, stronger version of Jimbo's Old Man, though his skin showed signs of the cancer speckle and his gut had started to sag; Frank's wife, Lana, her eyeliner smeared with tears, a strained lipstick smile on her face as she hugged her massive breasts against her daughter — Jimbo used to fantasise about being lost between those two melons when he, and Lana, had been much younger — Lana was slowly churning into fat in her middle years; sickly Uncle Cam with his pale skin and thinning black hair stood with his arm around barren Aunty Joan, his Aussie-Chino wife — Jimbo remembered the Old Man flying into a rage when he learned his baby brother had married an Asian, reckoned they couldn't have kids because white man's sperm didn't mix with yellow chinky eggs; Grandpa and Nan White, huddled in the shade in their wheelchairs, probably still reeking of whisky and cigarettes; his mother, Melinda, frail and stooped in her pale blue blouse, one hand patting Lana reassuringly on the shoulder, the other hand squeezing Niki's elbow; Jimbo's cousins, Derek, Barney, Scottie, Jack and Rhys, all gangly tough and awkward in their late teens.

And Niki, beautiful Niki, tall and slender, her blonde hair cut shoulder length, tight blue denim hugging her hips, kissing cheeks and hugging and laughing and crying…

And then she was kissing him on the cheek, her lips warm and soft against his skin.

'Glad you came to see me off,' Niki said. 'Oops.' She rubbed the lipstick off his cheek with her finger and smiled.

'Yeah, well, you know. Brian's on the Marriage Carriage. Came down to see him too, not just you. The Old Man sends his regards.' Jimbo nodded his head towards Uncle Frank. 'You know…'

'Of course.' Niki nodded slowly, her eyes searching his. 'James, you can come and visit me, you know?'

Jimbo shrugged, the knot in his stomach twisting into his bowels. He wanted to grab her by the hand, carry her from the station and down to the muddy banks of the Murray River where they'd played as kids, beg her not to go, to stay and marry him, raise a son, and everything else he dreamed about late at night in his sticky sheets. But all he could manage was, 'Don't much like the City. You'll come back for holidays, eh?' He wanted to squeeze her neck hard with his calloused hands, choke the City out and make her beg to stay.

'Sure.' Niki smiled again, though Jimbo could tell some of the warmth had left her lips. 'I'll miss you.'

'Same.' Jimbo felt the knot unravelling, but he fought

to hold it back. His eyes felt hot. 'Write me, eh?' He tried to return her smile, thought about hugging her again and ended up patting her upper arm awkwardly.

'Train's coming,' Uncle Frank said, as a slow rumbling reverberated throughout the station.

Children yelled and screamed while the livestock snorted and grunted uneasily. Cranky McNabb, the publican of The Aussie, had donned his stationmaster garb and paraded along the platform squawking into a microphone that crackled 'Stand Clear!' through hidden speakers. Keats, Mason and a few other bruisers, also in uniform, had been employed for the day to enforce crowd control. Keats had once told Jimbo he loved the ex-police batons McNabb allowed them to use at the station. Much better than the heavy baseball bats down at the pub. Easier to smash skulls without getting too tired, Keats had said, and the bats splintered bone whereas the batons only cracked them. Civilised tools of the trade. Jimbo reckoned Keats pretended he was a cop while he held that baton — Keats had failed cop school because he'd refused to be wired.

The flat-nosed engine appeared from the black maw of the tunnel, its gunmetal casing reflecting the sun, a metal serpentine creature pulling its carriaged body slowly behind it. And, as always, a breath of awe stole from Jimbo's lungs, even though he'd seen this more than a hundred times. What strange City goods were to be unloaded this time? Would there be stranger faces disembarking to settle here? Of those who had previously left Shepparton, would any be returning briefly on holiday or forever as losers? The questions of childhood now lay buried in his heart beneath the knowledge his cousin would soon be climbing into the belly of this beast before it returned to the City.

The train slid into the station, the foremost carriages laden with trade goods. Traders surged towards these and Keats and Mason moved in brandishing their batons. Towards the rear of the train were two passenger compartments, empty apart from a couple of month-trippers, but it was the last compartment most of the Shepp residents had come to welcome. It was an elaborate black carriage painted with thick white streamers and flowered with steel blossom — the Marriage Carriage.

A faded red carpet was unrolled and the crowd formed lines on either side, falling into a hushed anticipation. The tinted steel doors opened. A brief whiff of air-conditioned perfume stole into the hot air.

'Can you see her?' Fitzy asked. Sweat had stuck his white shirt to the folds of fat on his back.

'Not yet.' Jimbo peered over Dave's shoulder who had managed to jostle his way to the edge of the carpet.

Brian stepped from the carriage in his father's wedding tux, squinted into the sun, and smiled. The crowd cheered. He turned, his arm outstretched behind him into the carriage interior shadows, and drew his white-veiled bride forward into the light to meet his town.

Behind them, barely visible inside the carriage, lurked the Cartel men, uniformed and wired, their delivery safe and seen.

Jimbo nudged Fitzy and Dave. 'Same bastards what did Wazza.'

'Keats reckons he's scored an interview through the House,' said Fitzy. 'Going to the City next month for wiring.'

'Bullshit. Keats?'

'No shit. He's been patching with home mods for a while down The Aussie. Reckons he's got what it takes now to be Head-Sec at the House.'

'Fuck me.' Jimbo shook his head in disbelief.

As the newlyweds descended onto the carpet, the crowd cheered again and showered them in plastic sparkling confetti. They walked, black tux and white lace, arm in arm, towards the horse-drawn Vauxhall where Brian's old man and lady stood. His old lady beamed and dabbed at her eyes.

Jimbo hurled his confetti at Brian's head as he passed. 'Good on ya, ya cunt!'

The bride's skin appeared tanned, an olive complexion perhaps, and dark black hair tumbled from beneath her veil down the bare top of her back. She was a little shorter than Brian's six foot, so she was definitely of good stock. The wedding dress clung to her lithe curved body as she walked sure-footed and straight with a luring sway to her hips. She'd breed well, if Brian was lucky. From beneath the veil, her full, painted lips were permanently parted in a smile over pearly teeth.

'Money well spent,' said Dave. 'Even I'd consider saving for that.'

Fitzy laughed. 'You've blown it all at the House, mate. You couldn't even afford an Abo. What time's the reception start down The Aussie?'

'Four this arvo,' said Jimbo. He watched them climb into the back of the Vauxhall, and how the dress slid up to her thigh as she took a seat. Just like Niki's legs, he thought, his mind in the river, kicking through water, following the length of calf from knee to slender ankle.

Brian's old man climbed into the driver's seat and jerked the reins. The horses dragged the car into the main street, a flotilla of fruit cans tied to the rear bumper rattling noisily.

'Reckon he fucked her on the way here?' asked Dave, running his hand through the sweat in his hair.

'Be bad luck,' said Jimbo. 'Brian'll be saving it for tonight.'

'Five bucks he did,' said Fitzy. 'We should check out the Marriage Carriage. Have a bit of a sniff, eh?'

Dave laughed. 'You'll never get in there. The Cartel boys will do you.'

'No, they won't. They're busy.' Fitzy pointed across the dispersing crowd. 'With your cousin.'

Uncle Frank shook one of the Cartel men's hands. The other Cartel man examined a piece of paper, nodded, and handed it back to Niki. Jimbo half expected the man to press his fingers against her neck. He shuddered, remembering the sting.

'I can't fucken believe it,' Jimbo said under his breath. 'She's working for the fucken Cartel.'

'Nah, mate, don't be stupid, they'll just be her security for the train ride. She's valuable goods now she's got a job.' Fitzy whacked Jimbo on the arm. 'Come on, let's check out the Carriage.'

As Dave and Fitzy ran towards the Marriage Carriage, Jimbo stared at the men in dark suits with their metal eyes. And how they touched her arm. And how she laughed and smiled. And how the train would be leaving in just over an hour. And how he'd most likely never see her again.

Jimbo needed a drink and a fight bad. He'd get both tonight at Brian's wedding bash.

In the hot shadows of the lounge room, Jimbo caught the Old Man flicking through an old slide show on the screen. The Old Man tried to flick it off, but Jimbo saw the photos of himself and Niki as kids before the screen went blank.

'Didn't hear you come home,' the Old Man said. His voice cracked. 'Musta dozed off.'

He wiped at his face but not before Jimbo noticed the tears streaked on his cheeks.

'Mum's going down to Brian's with Uncle Frank and Aunty Lana. She told me to come and get you.'

'Yeah, yeah, just let me go and put on me tie.' The Old Man struggled out of his armchair. 'Ya see her off?'

'Nah, couldn't be bothered waiting around. Ya got Brian's wedding present ready?'

'It's in the shed. Ya mum wrapped it up already.'

'Does it work?'

The Old Man sneered at him. 'Of course it fucken works. Not that hard to modify a baby monitor, ya stupid bastard. What do ya take me for? He'll be able to keep dibs on her until she's settled in.'

'Whatever. Just hurry up, will ya, the beer's getting warm.'

'You're a bit agro tonight, mate,' said Keats.

'What of it?' The booze had begun to mince Jimbo's brain, but that was how he wanted it. 'You wanna fucken go?'

The room was swirling with sweat and bodies. The wedding band hammered away on drums and pianos and guitars and banjos with their version of Australian Chisel's classic 'Working Class Man'. Jimbo had vomited earlier and the stains still showed on the front of his shirt. The Aussie was getting leery now that Brian had gone. His bride had burst into tears and Brian's old lady had taken her home while Brian argued and swore and punched things.

'Just saying, mate.' Keats pushed some pills into Jimbo's hand. 'Ya look like ya gotta a lot on your mind.

These are good, try one. It'll take it all off.'

'This City shit, is it, Keats?'

'Latest and greatest.'

Jimbo threw the pills onto the heaving dancefloor. 'Stick the City up your arse, Keats. You and ya fucken Cartel mates. We don't need youse cunts.'

'What's ya problem?'

'Go and get on that train for ya fucken City innaview. Hope ya come back bust and stinking a ya own piss.'

'Ah, fuck you, Jimbo.' Keats turned away and headed through the crowd towards the door.

'Come on, cunt, I'll fucken do ya!' Jimbo thrust his fist towards where Keats's head had been. 'Ya fucken coward! Where ya going?'

'Off to work,' said Keats. 'Fuck you.'

'Yeah? Oh, yeah?' Jimbo shouted. 'At the House? Yeah? Well, I'll burn that fucken House down, ya hear me? You and all those City sluts!'

But Keats was out the door and gone.

A strong hand gripped his shoulder. 'Think you've had enough, boy.'

Jimbo spun round, his fists swinging. 'I'll do you too, cunt!'

A fist crashed into the side of Jimbo's head and he went down onto the concrete floor amongst the damp cigarette butts and sticky pools of alcohol.

'Ya've had enough, boy!' The Old Man launched his foot into Jimbo's stomach. 'Ya not man enough yet, boy! Ya still need some sense beaten into ya!'

Somewhere, someone was screaming, 'He's a working class maaaaaannn!' into a microphone. Drums pounded.

Jimbo curled around the next boot to his gut, his breath gone, the anger spent in the spittle surrounding the sobs from his mouth.

'Take it easy, Mr White.' Dave's voice.

The band between songs. Jimbo's mother crying. His mother limping, his father kicking, his aunty limping, kicking, Dave's mother limping, kicking through the water with those slender ankles...

'Ya can stop now, Phil.' The ashtray voice of Cranky McNabb. 'I think he heard ya already.'

'Shoulda been the other way round,' said the Old Man. 'She shoulda stayed, not him. Worthless piece of shit.'

Jimbo's mother crying.

Dave and Fitzy under each arm, helping him out of the steam of bodies and into the calm of a midnight summer sky burning with stars.

'Go home, Jimbo.'

'Sleep it off, mate.'

Laughter.

Jimbo crying.

Later, after the pub had closed and the party had died, Jimbo woke on the footpath, his mouth full of congealed blood and vomit. He staggered to his feet and marched towards the House at the Paris end of High Street with the intent of burning it to the ground.

Part II: Statement of Intention

Summer dragged on like a cigarette pressed to the palm of the hand. Fitzy left for the City to work for a trucking magnate set up through a contact of Wazza's. Wazza, after healing at his folks' place, up and left in Kylie one hot morning, Kylie chewing up the gravel as they roared past the cannery. Dave squandered his pay at the House working his way through the dozen women living there. Keats got wired to the House, wore dark suits, and no longer worked doors at The Aussie. And Jimbo, who Keats had beat gently unconscious in the early hours of the morning after Brian's wedding bash, toiled overtime at the fruit cannery, saving every dollar he could, pretending he was happy with his lot.

Jimbo sat with his back to the factory on a dying patch of grass overlooking Old Dookie Road during his lunch break. The wind blew hot, but he had chosen a spot that carried the stench of spoiling fruit downwind from where he sat.

Jimbo removed the creased letter from his overalls. He'd read it twice since it had come on last month's train and he lifted it to his nose, imagining he could still smell her perfume on the page.

'Hey, Jimbo.' Brian plonked himself down, munching on a beetroot sandwich. 'That from Niki? How's she doing?'

'Good.' Jimbo scanned the letter — her handwriting this time, not typed like the first letter. 'She's working in one of them big buildings in the City on Collins Street or something. Says being a PA is interesting and the people are fun to work with.'

'What's a PA?'

'Personal Assistant. To the boss. I guess that means she's pretty high up. Got an apartment she shares with two other women who've just started work at the same company.'

'Three women in the same house?' Brian grinned. 'Can ya dig it? Only in the City, Jimbo. Here in Shepp the closest thing we got to something like that is the House.'

'Niki ain't working for no House!' Jimbo scowled. 'She's a fucken PA!'

'Easy, mate, never said she worked for no House. Just

meant it's weird, eh? Must be lots of women in the City for that to happen, ya know, share a house and shit.'

'Guess so. You went to the City to get ya missus. Ya must a seen heaps of women.'

Brian shook his head and took another bite of his sandwich. 'Didn't see many of them when I was there, not like I thought I would. Saw more than I ever seen round here but. Reckon they was all hidden away in their fancy jobs and apartments. Mostly blokes everywhere, trying to get work and shit.'

They sat in silence for a while, the only sound Brian chewing on his food, if they ignored the flies and the muted hum of the factory. Jimbo folded the letter and put it back in his overalls pocket.

'She says the company will pay for two train tickets a year,' Jimbo said. 'Wants to know if I want to go visit her on one of them. She's gunna save the other to come home for Christmas.'

'Yeah, train's fucken expensive. Ya gunna go?'

'Would you?'

'Too many people for me, Jimbo. I hated the place. All those tall buildings squashing me down. I'd tell her to come here.' Brian frowned and picked at the dirt. 'Only went there to get some permanent pussy.' He looked up and grinned at Jimbo, beetroot stuck between the gaps in his teeth. 'That's the only fucken reason to go if you arkse me.'

Jimbo grinned back. 'How's Belle doing? She settled in yet? We haven't really seen you two hitting the town.'

'You know how it is, mate. Takes 'em a while to adjust. Dad reckons at least a year before she'll be safe to go out. Took my mum at least that.'

'I hear ya.' Jimbo nudged Brian with his elbow. 'So

how many times ya fucked her?'

'Fucken heaps, mate. Better than all that teenage a-hole shit we used to do. The real thing.' Brian grinned again, though this time it seemed forced, like someone had shoved a finger into his arsehole and told him it would be fun.

'Something's wrong, Bri. What's up?'

'Keats been talking, has he? Fuck.' Brian sucked in a lungful of hot air. 'Might as well tell you too. It's not what I thought it'd be like. She keeps crying every other fucken night, 'bout how she misses her home and family and shit. Thank fuck for the neighbourhood watch, dunno what I'd do without them. Thanks for the monitor too, Jimbo. It's come in handy. Keats caught her trying to leave the house when I was at work. Who knows where the fuck she woulda run off to.'

'No worries, mate. Knew it'd do ya good.'

'She even fucken cries when we're rooting, puts me off big time.' Brian shook his head again. His fingers stabbed at the dirt now. 'Dad says that's normal for a while, but it's been almost three months of this bawling and shit!'

'That is normal, Brian,' said Jimbo. 'She'll get used to it. Ya have to hit her?'

'Not much. She's pretty sweet.' Brian lowered his voice. 'Can't bring myself to hit her, eh?'

'No shit? If it's any consolation, mate, don't think I could either.'

Brian tried to smile at that. 'And she can't cook that good yet. Fucken pisses me off — I paid ten grand for Belle! Woulda thought that'd be sorted.'

'She's sexy though. I'd do her.'

'Yeah, thanks, Jimbo. You're a mate.' Brian stood and brushed the grass and dirt off his overalls. 'Don't regret spending the money. Ain't no other way to get a wife around here unless you're born rich or lucky. I heard ya been saving up.'

He held out a hand and pulled Jimbo to his feet. On the way back to the factory, Brian pulled a business card from his wallet and handed it to Jimbo.

'For when you've got enough ping, mate,' said Brian. 'They're good, they're the best.'

Jimbo lay in bed that night listening to the Old Man snoring from the bedroom at the other end of the hallway. He wondered if the Old Man had beaten Mum when they'd first got married, and how long it took before Mum had decided she was happy enough to want to stay. Or stopped trying to leave.

He stared at the card Brian had given him. White card, red writing. *Bridal Services.* No slogan, no address. Just a phone number. A City phone number.

He thought about taking Niki up on her offer of a train trip to the city. Kill two birds with one stone. See her, find a wife. He imagined going to her apartment and knocking on the door. Taking her in his arms when she answered it, carrying her inside and undressing her...

He grabbed hold of his stiffening cock and began to stroke, trying to imagine his tongue licking her breasts. The Old Man gave a ratcheting croak and the rasping snore took on a louder pitch. Jimbo tried to hold her face in his mind but the snoring tore her away from him. Anyway, he couldn't take a train ticket off her — they cost too much.

Bridal Services.

'For when you've got enough ping,' Brian had said.

That smarmy prick and his inheritance, that was how he got his fucken wife! Enough fucken ping, the cunt!

Jimbo thought about pressing a pillow over the Old Man's face. It would be so easy, the fat old cancerous cunt snoring away, the stink of stale beer pouring from his gob.

Jimbo worked at his cock again, but it was no good. The snoring beat its way through the walls, pounding into his ears.

Fucken fat old cunt.

He climbed out of bed and crept down the hallway towards his parents' door. The room stank of body-processed alcohol. He could barely make out the lump in the bed in darkness. He stole closer, pillow in hand, listening to the rising falling buzzsaw that was his father. He stood over the Old Man and raised the pillow.

'Don't do it, James,' his mother said softly from the chair by the window.

Jimbo stared at her and, after an eternity of seconds, went back to his bed. He lay there sleeplessly dreaming of things that would never come to pass.

Jimbo sat with the Old Man in the waiting room down at the surgery. It was the first time either of them had been here since the new doctor had arrived in town, a filthy fucken A-rab from the City no less. Not that there weren't any A-rabs here in Shepp, but they mostly lived on the south side of town in the old council estates, run-down shit holes full of pestilence and ugly women dressed in black sheets. But this cunt, this Doctor Ed Khalid, was getting his dirty fingers high up in the town, and that pissed off the Old Man something big. Jimbo didn't really give a fuck, he didn't much like A-rabs or Asians and as long as they kept to themselves it was no skin off his nose.

It was the skin on his Old Man that was the problem

though. It was getting worse. Big red sores weeping through the bandages Jimbo's mum changed daily. The smell of decay had settled into the walls of their house. The cancer had been festering a while now, maybe longer than the two years since Khalid had set up practice, but Mum was worried it was worsening. She also held high hopes that a City doctor, even an A-rab, might have new technology, some new ways, that old alkie Foley hadn't. Jimbo shuddered, remembering Foley's whisky-soaked breath in his ear as he forced a gnarled finger up Jimbo's arsehole when he was twelve.

'There's a lot a shit up there,' Foley had said to Jimbo's mother. 'Turning to concrete.' He'd sent them home with a bottle of Swedish Bitters and some suppositories, and after two days Jimbo had shit himself stupid.

Jimbo had avoided doctors ever since, and he sure as hell didn't want this Ed Khalid sticking his A-rab fingers anywhere near his arsehole. *Ed. Fucken MohammEd, more like.*

The Old Man had been quiet since they got here, long sleeves drawn down over his bandaged arms, the brim of his hat pulled low trying to disguise the rot in his nose. A sour stench clung to his body.

They waited.

A fat kid on the seat opposite stared sullenly at them, his hair a sump of grease, acne holding his cheeks together. Jimbo didn't know him, and it struck him as funny. It wasn't so long ago that he knew almost everybody in town. He guessed things had been getting away from him recently, what with work and shit. The kid stared and Jimbo fought a sudden urge to get up and smack the kid in the mouth.

The door to the doctor's room opened and a nurse stood there staring at a list of patient names. Her eyes were sunk into a pouchful of bags and dark roots crawled through the platinum highlights in her dry, brittle hair.

'Mr White,' she said, her voice worn with heavy cigarette use.

The Old Man heaved himself to his feet, and they made their way into Doctor Ed Khalid's private sanctum.

Khalid took Jimbo by surprise — he didn't appear to be that many years older than Jimbo himself, his skin tanned, dark hair cut short, and blue eyes shining from a strong-boned face. The room seemed clean, and it looked like there was a working computer on the desk. Locked cabinets stood in the corner of the room, some fancy-looking machinery Jimbo didn't have a clue about. Khalid's A-rab origins were evident though. There was a faded prayer rug in one corner, and up on the wall a large photo of a white building surrounded by a swirling mass of people.

Khalid smiled and offered them a seat. 'How can I help you today, Mr White?'

No A-rab accent at all, he sounded much like any of them. *The cunt's probably putting it on. Altered his face to fit in.*

The Old Man said nothing for a second, then rolled up his sleeves and put his arms upon Khalid's desk. Khalid kept his face straight, helped the Old Man onto the examination bed and carefully removed the bandages, exposing the sores beneath.

'How long have you had these?' Khalid asked.

'A while. Dunno. Maybe two, maybe three years. Maybe longer. Getting worse, it's gunna fucken kill me, I know that much. We all know skin cancer when we see it.'

Khalid nodded, examined the sores again. 'This is fairly advanced. You should have come to see me sooner. There are things we can do.'

The Old Man grunted, a short hoot of derisive laughter. 'Look, I don't give a fuck. I'm here because it's bothering me missus. I don't want to put her under any more pressure than she already is. It's gunna kill me, plain and simple, like it does a quarter of this fucken town.'

'There are options available, Mr White. Still. Have you considered seeing a specialist in the City —'

'Fuck the City.'

Jimbo sat back, watching the Old Man bristle. *Looks like the old bastard's gunna plant one on the A-rab's nut. Gotta give it to the A-rab though, he's playing it cool.*

'There's not much I can do from here.' Khalid cleaned the sores with a swab the nurse had prepared. 'You know how it is. Trains are limited, supplies even more so. I have colleagues in the City —'

'I'm not wasting any money on that shit. It'd ruin me family.' The Old Man stared around the room, avoiding Jimbo, his eyes fixing on the photo of the arch. 'I can't afford that sort of thing. Painkillers. Medical marijuana. You can do that, can't you?'

Khalid nodded, handing the swabs back to the nurse, then applying fresh bandages to the Old Man's arms. 'Sure. It's no different to what you can already get though, and it's not like there's a problem getting hold of any.'

'Yeah,' said the Old Man, 'but if you prescribe it, it's free.'

Khalid laughed, and began to write out a script.

'You been there?' The Old Man pointed at the photo on the wall. 'You A-rabs all gotta go there once in yer life, don't ya?'

Khalid looked up at the photo, his face distant. 'No. My great-grandfather did though, back before the Breakdown. I don't know of anyone in my generation who's been.'

'Then I guess I'll be seeing you in hell then, eh, doc?' The Old Man grinned, his teeth a slowly rotting mess between lips already blessed with the onset of cancerous blooms.

'Perhaps. Perhaps not.' Khalid pushed the script across his desk, towards the Old Man's hands. 'Much like your Bible, Mr White, we update our Koran when needs be.'

'Fuck the Bible.'

'Yes, I totally agree.' Khalid stood, and the nurse ushered Jimbo and the Old Man towards the door. 'And remember, if there is anything you need, don't hesitate to come and see me.' He planted his blue eyes on Jimbo's. 'Anything.'

As they were leaving the surgery, Jimbo patted his pockets. 'Ah, fuck, I've left me wallet in there.' He pointed to the horse and cart that Uncle Frank had lent them for the day. 'You go on, I'll be with ya in a sec.'

Jimbo walked back inside, past the receptionist and the glaring eyes in the waiting room and pushed open the door to the rooms. The fat kid had his shirt off, lying on the bed, while Khalid leant over him, a stethoscope pressed to the chest.

The nurse began to bluster, 'You can't —'

'It's okay, Deanna,' Khalid said, straightening.

'If he doesn't get treatment in the City, how long's he got?'

'Six months. Maybe more, maybe less.'

Jimbo nodded and left the rooms, snarling at the receptionist as she tried to say something, and stalked out into the hot day. The Old Man slumped in the cart, his hat pulled low, his shoulders sagging. Jimbo walked slowly, watching those shoulders, now beaten and slumped, remembering their thick muscle and the beatings doled out regularly over the years.

Six months, eh? Six more fucken months. If we're lucky, even less.

After the bushfires had burned off summer, and the leaves dropped dead from the trees, the temperature dipped beneath thirty degrees Celsius for the first time in months. Cranky McNabb reckoned rain would come with the end of autumn, and though the town hoped with him that it would, nobody was placing bets.

When Niki's letters stopped arriving, Jimbo's first instinct was to burn the ones he had received. Instead, he hid them inside his old footy guernsey, deciding to bury his heart with good memories rather than burning his heart with none. He'd never bothered to reply to her, though if he delved deep enough inside him he knew he couldn't bring himself to reply — scared he'd say too much, or worse, not enough.

'Nicole's doing well at work,' his mother would say over breakfast. 'Promotion. More money. Responsibility. She'll be home come Christmas.'

Jimbo would nod disinterestedly, building a wall around where Niki had been, while making a space for his wife, a good wife, the one he would buy with his savings.

When the Old Man took a turn for the worse and the skin cancer bit deep enough to infect the blood, his mother stopped talking about Niki. Jimbo would come home and press a portion of his pay into the cancerous old hands, and think about how Brian got Belle.

And, late at night, when the booze seeped through the cracks and brought Jimbo's heart floating towards the surface, he'd unfold his old guernsey and read through

Niki's letters. And, if the room didn't spin, sometimes he'd find himself crying and not know why.

A good crowd had turned up at the Oval for the pre-season footy game between Shepp City and the Aboriginals who'd come in from the Edge for fruit-picking money. Last year the Abos had won by two goals, but the cops had kept the fighting to a minimum, which had been disappointing. They'd segregated the crowd again this year, with the townsfolk in the makeshift western stand, fenced off from the Abos camped on the eastern slope. Still, there was always a chance for a fight after the game around the bottleshop — Cranky wouldn't let the Abos into The Aussie.

'Gunna be a corker, this one.' Dave handed Jimbo a plastic cup of coolish beer. 'Cockatoo Collins III is playing. Keats has ten bucks on him scoring the first goal for the Abos, and fifteen bucks on him being the first to be taken out.'

'Just got a fiver on the game,' said Jimbo. 'Abos'll win. Hate to say it, but they're better 'n us at this game.'

'Fuck off!' Dave gulped down a mouthful of bitter. 'Next you'll be saying ya won't bash 'em. Shit, next thing you'll be bringing one home for a wife!'

'Too right, mate,' said Jimbo, before punching Dave on the arm. 'Heard they were good in the sack, eh?'

Dave laughed. 'They are, mate, they are! I'm telling ya, ya missing out.'

A cry went up from the crowd, as Shepp City cleared the ball, with Plugger punting it to Bulldog who took a clean mark thirty metres from the goal.

'Piece of piss from here,' said Dave.

'Yeah,' said Jimbo. He wasn't watching the game

though. Frank was moving through the crowd towards him.

'How's it going, Jimmy?' Frank tried to smile.

'Yeah, good, Uncle Frank. You?'

Frank stared out over the field, as Bulldog lined up the goal and prepared to kick. 'Big game today. Thought Phil would be down to watch.'

'Too crook to come.'

The crowd 'awwwed' in disappointment as Bulldog missed the goal, the field umpire signalling with one hand only a point had been scored. The Abos shouted from the far side of the field, jeering and laughing.

Frank nodded slowly. 'Yeah, ya mum said he was bad.' Frank turned to face Jimbo for the first time during the conversation, his hard face as stern and cracked as the dry fields he ploughed. 'Wasn't always like this between me and ya father. Used to be real close when we was kids.' Frank stared back at the field. 'Used to idolise the bastard when I was young. He'd keep the older kids off me at school until I could win me own. Yeah, ma brother was tough back then.'

'He's not so tough now.' Jimbo downed his beer. 'You want one, Uncle Frank?'

'Yeah,' said Frank, distractedly.

As Jimbo left to go to the drinks caravan, Frank put his hand on Jimbo's arm.

'You haven't heard from Nicole lately, have you, Jimmy?'

'Nah, not for a while.'

'Right.' Frank looked like he was about to say something more, then stared back at the game.

When Jimbo came back with the beers, Cockatoo had scored two goals for the Abos, Plugger had been knocked unconscious, Dave was screaming obscenities, and Frank had disappeared.

Towards the end, Jimbo would dread the rattling call from his father's throat, summoning him to the shadowed lounge where the Old Man had had his deathbed set up. He wished the bastard would hurry up and get all this shit over with. Jimbo would be able to save more money for his bride if the Old Man no longer had his hand out.

The big screen was on, cycling through family photographs, where Jimbo had yet to grow hair and sported fat nappies, his father had a fit and strong footballer's body, with skin tanned deep while working the fields, and his mother — younger, beautiful — wore a smile for her newborn instead of the blank face she wore for her husband.

Now, his mother sat in the armchair, her face expressionless. The Old Man lay in his bed, the skin on his face pulled tight and yellow across his skull. The weight had eaten itself from his belly. He reached out a papyrus hand and clasped Jimbo's arm, the cancerous heat of his skin burning into Jimbo's own.

'I know what ya trying to do,' the Old Man croaked.

'Yeah?'

'Yeah. And I know ya wanna do it ya own way, and that's the way a real man would do it. I understand, son. I appreciate that.'

'Right.' Jimbo didn't have a fucken clue what the old bastard was on about. He wished the Old Man would let go of his arm though — the sickly heat felt infectious. Jimbo noticed his mother was smiling. Smiling like in the photos cycling on the screen. Smiling with a mother's love for her son.

'I don't have much time left.' The Old Man paused, searching Jimbo's eyes, waiting for something.

Jimbo said nothing.

'I want a wedding before I die.'

'What?'

The Old Man hacked a phlegmy laugh. 'That got a reaction.' He coughed again; brown drool leaked from the corner of his mouth. 'I wanna see me only son get married. God knows there's fuck all weddings these days, what with the cost of them'n all.'

'You bullshitting me? Unless you're gunna last another five to ten years coughing your guts up on that bed, it ain't gunna happen. I ain't got the cash.'

'James,' his mother said softly from the chair. 'Listen.'

'Yeah, I know that, Jimmy,' said the Old Man. 'You ain't exactly breaking the bank with your job at the factory. And I know ya think I've been a cunt to ya for taking ya money each pay. But I done it all for you.'

Jimbo wanted to tell him to get to the point and stop wasting everyone's time, but deep down he knew this was unusual for his father — something here was about to break.

'Mel? Hand it to me, thanks, love.'

Jimbo's mother pressed something small into the Old Man's free hand.

The papyrus hand scrabbled at Jimbo's arm, attempting to pull him closer. Jimbo reluctantly relented and leant in to the warm sour odour of sweat surrounding his father.

'Me and ya mum want ya to have this.' The Old Man closed Jimbo's hand around a small hard square of plastic. Inscribed on the card was a black square with a yellow triangle inside it.

'Is this a bank card?' asked Jimbo.

'Yep.' The Old Man tried to smile. 'Every dollar you paid us, to me *and* to ya mum — I knew about that, she's not stupid enough to keep secrets from me — every cent is in that account. With interest. It's yours.'

'Is this what I think it's for?' Jimbo looked towards his mother for reassurance, forgetting she had betrayed his confidence.

'You can get married now, James.' Mel smiled for all of them, tears brimming in her eyes. 'You can afford to get yourself a bride.'

'This is fucken great! I can't believe it!'

'There's one condition,' said the Old Man.

Here it comes, thought Jimbo. *I fucken knew it.*

The Old Man grinned. 'She's gotta be white.'

Jimbo started laughing. 'No fucken worries about that. I won't be the one to taint our gene pool!'

It was the first time in years they had laughed together as a family.

It felt weird going round to Uncle Frank and Aunty Lana's place now that Niki no longer lived there. Jimbo hadn't been here for almost a year. Nothing much had changed. The weatherboard house still needed painting and weeds struggled through the cracked dirt. He remembered swimming in the pool out back and noticing Niki had nipples and breasts beneath her swimsuit. It had unsettled him, but he couldn't take his eyes away from them, those hard buttons jutting from unfamiliar bumps of flesh. That seemed forever ago now.

Aunty Lana greeted Jimbo at the door, kissing him on the cheek and hugging him tight, smothering him in perfume and breasts. He was conscious of those heavy breasts pushing against his chest, knowing that when he was younger he had wondered if Niki would grow to have these treasures.

They sat out on the back verandah, overlooking the pool. Uncle Frank had never filled it in when the water laws changed back in '43, hanging onto the idea that the weather patterns would shift back in favour of the Lucky Country. The Old Man had called him a fucken idiot, though not to his face. In that instance, the Old Man had been right. The water table had shrunk even further over the last ten years, and a good portion of Frank's backyard was now an empty concrete hole that possums sometimes got trapped in.

Lana poured Jimbo and Frank a cold homebrew, one of the darker colours. It tasted better than Jimbo remembered. Lana sat back and sipped on a white wine. *One a those fancy Savlon Blanks by the looks*, thought Jimbo.

'Have you spoken to Nicole lately?' Lana asked.

Jimbo sipped at his beer then shook his head. 'Uncle Frank asked me that a few weeks back at the footy. How's she going?'

'Well, according to her emails, things are fine. Very busy. They seem very impersonal though.'

'Said she won't be back for bloody Christmas.' Frank placed his glass with a little too much force on the table. He stared at the empty pool. 'Too busy, she reckons.'

'Yeah, well, that's the City for ya,' said Jimbo.

'It's not just that, Jimmy,' said Lana. 'We haven't spoken to her for several months now. We've called but she's either out or — I don't know. Maybe her flatmates aren't passing on messages.'

'She's not seeing someone, is she?' Frank's eyes bored

into Jimbo's until Jimbo stared at the brown froth in his glass.

'Why would she tell me?'

'You two are as close as brother and… well, close as cousins can be.'

Not as close as I want us to be, Uncle Frank. 'She hasn't said nothing to me.'

Lana smiled and patted Jimbo's hand. 'Can you do us a favour, please, Jimmy? Can you pop in and see if she's okay when you go to the City next week? Maybe give her something we'd like you to take her, nothing big, just a little home cooking and bits and pieces.'

'Selfish little bitch,' Frank muttered under his breath.

'Frank,' said Lana sharply.

'Yeah, no worries, Aunty Lana. I was thinking of looking her up anyway.'

They sat in silence, Lana staring at Jimbo with a sad smile on her painted lips, Frank staring at the empty pool, and Jimbo wondering what the fuck he was doing here.

Eventually Lana broke with, 'How's your father doing, Jimmy? Sorry we haven't been around to visit lately, you know how it is.'

Frank grunted something about more beer and Lana left the table to refresh the drinks.

Part III: Exchange of Vows and Rings

The carriage was mainly empty; besides Dave and Jimbo there were a couple of month-trippers — a man and a woman — and half a dozen traders on the way to the City. Jimbo didn't recognise the month-trippers — they had boarded at Murchison, a god-forsaken dust bowl that Jimbo had only previously heard about but never visited. She looked part Asian too. One of the traders was an Abo that Jimbo recognised from footy. *How the hell could that black cunt afford a ticket?* thought Jimbo. *There must be a bit a cash floating around the Abo camps. Might have to go on a recce when I get back.*

Dave handed another beer to Jimbo from the cool-pak underneath the seat. The vinyl covering on the seat was cracked and someone had carved *keep Australia pure — kill them all!* into it.

'This'll be ma last beer. Want a clear head for when we get to the City,' said Jimbo.

'Yeah, no worries, mate,' said Dave. 'Shoulda brung something harder, maybe some Bundy or something.'

Jimbo knew what Dave meant. The excitement of the train journey was slowly and surely being usurped by a worming terror with every clack of the tracks. He could have done with the rum to ease his nerves, but dreaded disembarking into an alien, crowded place with a blurred head.

Dave stared at his reflection in the darkened windows. 'Didn't realise most of the trip is underground. How much longer we got to go?'

''Bout an hour. Two more stops to make. One in Nagambie, the other in Seymour. It's a straight run from there.'

'You nervous?' asked Dave.

'Nah.'

'Me neither.' Dave rocked back and forward in his seat, looking around the carriage. 'The track between Nagambie and Seymour is above ground, right? Least there'll be something to look at.'

'Yeah.' Jimbo swallowed a mouthful of beer. *And hopefully something to take my mind off all this shit.*

He took the card from his pocket and ran his fingers

over the embossed red writing.

Bridal Services.

He'd made the phone call in the privacy of the Old Man's study.

The voice on the other end of the line spoke in a flat monotone. 'You have reached Bridal Services. You are being monitored. Your call number is A6YTR7200. Transferring you now.'

Sweat had formed on Jimbo's palms. The telephone had become slick under his fingers. His cock uncoiled from its slumber.

The monotone voice had started again. 'If you are enquiring about bridal purchases please say "Bridal Purchase". If you want to make an account enquiry or set up a new account please say —'

'Bridal Purchase,' Jimbo had said.

The line clicked and whirred. A pleasant female voice had said, 'Hello, my name is Operator 635SD. I will be your transaction manager. You will need to provide the following information before we begin.'

The clacks from the tracks began to slow. The train decelerated as it emerged from the tunnel and approached Nagambie station.

Jimbo put the card back in his pocket.

'We got about half an hour before we leave again,' said Dave. 'Ya want to get off and have a look around?'

'Nah, I can see plenty from here.'

'Suit yaself. I'm gunna go have a squiz.'

Out on the platform, three Cartel men stood sentinel while a young woman kissed her family then gathered her bags. Dave wandered among the crowd but stalled at the exit, unable to pass the guards. *So much for sightseeing,* thought Jimbo. The woman and her entourage of Cartel men boarded the first-class carriage, the one ahead of the carriage Jimbo sat in. The doors connecting the carriages were locked, however — Dave had tried to get in shortly after they had left Shepp — and curtains had been drawn over the windows.

Dave plonked himself back in the seat as the train shuddered and began to creep slowly out of Nagambie station. 'See that woman getting on the train? Looks like she's scored a City job too. Fuck, man, that place is sucking all the women out of the country, I tell ya.'

'Fuck the City. And fuck those women.'

'What about Niki?'

'That's different.'

Dave started to laugh but Jimbo glared him down. 'Take it easy, man. You're so fucken uptight about her.'

'No, I'm not.'

'For fuck's sake, Jimbo, we're going to the City to get ya a bride. With the cash ya got saved you'll get the pick of the litter. Niki will be nothing more than a memory of ya hand on ya cock, mate.'

Eucalypts flashed by the window as the train picked up speed. Huge strips of bark dangled from their trunks. Jimbo imagined he could see koalas clambering amongst the branches and chewing on the leaves. The Old Man claimed to have seen one on his trip to the City way back when. In this part of the country though, koalas were but a memory now. Like Niki. Dave was right.

'She might be picking us up at Central Station,' Jimbo said.

'Cool. She bringing her girlfriends?' Dave put his hand on his crotch and grinned.

Jimbo laughed. 'Yeah, you hope! Why'd she want them to meet a loser like you?'

'They might be lonely country girls homesick for a bit a country boy.' Dave shook his crotch vigorously. 'And whaddaya mean she *might* pick us up? She gunna be there or not?'

'Didn't speak to her or nothing. Left a message on the phone at her apartment. She lives with a Zoe and a Michelle. They all said their names on the recording. Sounded too sexy for you, eh?'

'Yeah, well, I hope she's there. Tell ya the truth, Jimbo, I'm not looking forward to getting out at the station. Central's sposed to be huge, bigger'n the entire mall. I'm almost shitting my pants as much as you.'

'That easy to tell, eh? Thanks for being ma best man, Dave. Couldn't have done this without ya.'

'No worries, mate. Ya didn't have much choice as ya got fuck all friends, ya ugly cunt.'

'Speaking of ugly cunts, you manage to get hold of Fitzy?'

'Nah. Haven't heard from that fat bastard for months. Didn't have a job last I heard though.'

The blur of eucalypts began to materialise back into individual trees and the clack of the tracks slowed. The train eventually ground to a halt. Outside, low scrub and the occasional thicket of eucalypts stretched over rolling hills the colour of rust.

'Why have we stopped?' asked Dave.

Several passengers started opening windows. The Abo from footy had climbed halfway out of his. 'There's something on the tracks ahead. Hey, one a those Cartel fellas is getting out.'

The Cartel man strode through the dust towards the front of the train. The sun bounced from his scalp. He held a gun in his hand.

'What's happening?' asked Jimbo, his face pressed against the window.

An explosion thundered through the earth, rocking the train. The Cartel man whirled around, looking for the source of the sound. His head snapped back and his legs folded underneath him. He collapsed into the dirt, a plume of smoke rising from the back of his head.

The Abo scrambled back in through the window. 'He's fucken dead!'

Gunshots echoed from the first-class carriage. Screams. The doors beeped and whooshed open.

Dave tried to scramble beneath the seat, pulling his cool-pak around his head. And like a bushfire fanned on the breeze, panic swirled through the carriage.

Two men wearing square steel buckets for masks boarded the train. One brandished a shotgun, the other a long narrow rifle Jimbo didn't recognise.

'Sit down and shut up!' said the man with the shotgun. 'Put ya fucken hands on ya heads!'

The passengers dropped to the seats. Jimbo pressed his hands flat to the top of his scalp. Dave's face was white as he cowered beneath the seat.

'There's another one down the back,' said Rifle.

Shotgun strode down the aisle towards the month-trippers. A lion symbol was stamped into the back of his helmet, beaten from old Holden car parts. 'You!' He motioned towards the woman. 'Get up!'

She clung to her partner. 'No, please —'

'Why are you doing this?' Her partner held her tight and swivelled her away from Shotgun. 'You can't —'

Shotgun smashed his weapon into the man's face. His head rocked back, cracking against the seat rail. He slumped sideways in the seat. The woman screamed, trying to pull his body closer.

'Get the fuck up, bitch!' Shotgun reached out, grabbed a fistful of her long black hair and yanked her off the seat.

'Careful of the goods,' said Rifle.

She flailed at Shotgun's face, but her fingers raked against the bushranger mask. Shotgun kneed her in the stomach. The sound of her breath exhaling echoed in the silence of the carriage. Jimbo needed to piss something bad. Dave had started to weep.

Shotgun dragged her down the aisle as she hitched for breath. Her shoes knocked on the seat legs — *whack whack whack* — as she was hauled towards the door.

'I wouldn't none of youse cunts do nothing for the next half-hour,' said Rifle. 'Stay in ya fucken seats and ya'll be fine. Stick ya head out the window and I'll burn a fucken hole in it.' He pointed the rifle at the Abo. 'Specially you, bruddah. Keep ya fucken black nut in!'

The Abo nodded and swallowed hard.

As Rifle stepped from the train, he said, 'Thank you for travelling with RuralRail. We hope you've had an enjoyable trip and look forward to seeing you again.'

Laughter. More screams.

'We gotta help her,' said the Abo.

Jimbo said nothing, his hands still firmly glued to the top of his skull. Sweat leaked between his palms and his scalp, beading through his hair. His knees trembled. Dave stared up at him, his eyes wide and wet.

'We gotta fucken help her!' The Abo stood and moved towards the door.

'Sit down,' said one of the traders. 'You'll get us killed.'

Somewhere nearby they heard the revving of engines.

The Abo leapt from the train. 'That's motorbikes!'

Jesus, they've got petrol, Jimbo thought. *These boys are serious.*

The remaining month-tripper groaned from the back of the carriage. The cameras tucked up in the corner of the carriage whirred and swivelled. The loudspeakers crackled.

'Everyone remain calm and in your seats. We will be resuming normal services shortly. Remember, please stay seated for your safety. We will be travelling express to Central and apologise for any inconvenience this may cause.'

'You gotta be fucken kidding me.' Jimbo looked around at the others in the carriage. Their faces were ashen and silent.

The doors began to beep.

The train shuddered.

The Abo climbed in through the door, sweat coating his face. There were bloodstains on his shirt. 'They killed all the Cartel and took the woman that was wiffem too. They was the only passengers in first class.'

The doors whooshed closed and the beeping stopped. The Abo sat back down with the traders. He held something metallic and bloody, showing it off.

'This should be worth heaps,' the Abo said to his colleagues. 'One of their heads was split open and I saw it there, all shiny and shit. Was easier to get out than I thought.'

As the tracks clack clack clacked, the month-tripper cried, 'Keira, where's Keira?'

It was just a woman, Jimbo thought, *and an Asian at that.* He wondered how long he could stand it before he cracked. *That money-flush cunt doesn't know how lucky he is. We could have been killed, for Christ's sake!*

•

The last hour of the train journey was underground and express, and for most of that the month-tripper had been silent. The train hissed into the station — a massive domed structure with manufactured clouds floating across its ceiling. The platform they alighted at held no crowds, and consequently no Niki, but there were escorts — a dozen of them clad in light blue uniform carrying shock sticks and wearing razor goggles wrapped around shiny scalps. Police. And amongst them, several black-suited Cartel men milled, scanning passengers.

An empty voice droned from hidden speakers, 'All passengers proceed to the rear of Platform Thirteen. You will be processed accordingly. Thank you for your cooperation.'

Bodies were stretchered from the train, as the police herded the living across the platform towards a set of steel doors emblazoned with a red *No Entry* sign.

Once inside the doors, they were corralled into a waiting room and told to sit on hard plastic chairs.

'I don't like this,' said Jimbo.

'This'll be just routine. Stuff about the train robbery.' Though Dave's voice remained calm, his eyes bulged in their sockets.

Several police moved systematically through the room collecting DNA samples. Jimbo flinched when cold fingers were pressed to his throat and stung his flesh. Dave did his best to remain still, but those bulging eyes watered when the fingers bit.

Eventually the two of them were ushered into an interview room. They were seated at a desk. A police woman sat opposite. Her face was hard, her eyes arctic blue and her nose sharp. Veins bulged beneath the skin of her scalp. A Cartel man stood near the desk, arms folded, his eyes hidden beneath dark glasses.

'First time to the City, boys,' said the woman. Her voice sounded as friendly as rusting car bodies. 'Neither of you are registered, but both of you are cross-referenced with one Warren Wilson.'

A holographic screen buzzed into existence on the desktop. Jimbo saw his image floating amongst details of blood type, age, genetic disorders and a mass of equations he didn't understand.

'I need your names and places of residence. One at a time and speak clearly into the machine.'

When Jimbo and Dave had declared who they were, the holographic blinked out. The woman stared dolefully at them. 'Purpose of visit?'

Christ, I hope the women here aren't all like this bitch. I'd rather do Keats. 'I'm here to find a wife,' said Jimbo.

The Cartel man smirked but the police officer's expression didn't change. 'Your kind make me sick. If you get in trouble here, don't come looking for help,' she said. 'Records verify. You may leave now.'

'What?' said Dave. 'Is that it? You keep us waiting around for a couple of hours and then don't even ask about the train?'

'We don't need to ask you anything more. We have everything we need,' she said. 'Enjoy your stay in the City.'

Outside the station, with its crumbling facade of pale orange stone blocks and a fractured clock tower no longer marking time, the shock of the City tumbled and thundered over them. Towering buildings of angular steel and polished glass jutted into the sky blocking out the sun, advertising holograms dancing across their smooth windowed exteriors; beneath a nearby bridge, a river thick with mud slugged by, its oily surface broken by barges and peppered with rubbish, while a thick weed with dark glossgreen leaves and a white leathery bloom wove along the riverbank, its choking tendrils slowly claiming what little was left of the water that the mud didn't already own; the streets were packed with people moving frantically between bikes and electric cars and trams, amongst them heavily-armed blue uniforms stationed on street corners. The honk of horns and tinkling bells was incessant, piercing the hubbub of the murmuring voiceless masses. The smell of ozone and the hint of petroleum lingered on the air, while the waft of sewage from the river drifted on the occasional breeze. Nearby, a street hawker fried gristled slivers of meat in a spicy red sauce.

Around the station milled dozens of people, mainly men, wielding fishing rods, buckets and mops, wearing tool-belts sporting archaic hand-held drills and hammers, carrying anything that signified their available line of work. Their faces wore a mix of dejection and hope. One man, his face creased with grime, thrust his mop at Jimbo's head.

'Git ta the back a the line, cunt. You fuckers fresh off the train ain't got no chance a jumpin' queue.' He thrust the mop inches away from Jimbo's face. 'Better yet, why dontcha jus fuck off back to where yas come from — no work here for youse cunts!'

Dave grabbed Jimbo's arm, and they backed away. A horn blasted in their ears, accompanied by a sharp squeal of brakes.

'Get out a the way, dickheads!'

They pushed through the crowds, making their way to the relative refuge the bridge provided. Here, the glossgreen weed had crept up the pylons and wound along the rusting rails. The stink of the river was strong, which was probably why it wasn't so crowded.

'What now?' asked Dave.

'We've got about three hours until my appointment.' Jimbo pulled a map out of his backpack and carefully unfolded it. On it he had circled three things and had highlighted the streets connecting them. He pointed at the circled station and then drew his finger along one of the lines to the next circle. 'This is where we'll need to be. It should only take us half an hour to walk.'

Dave stared at the crowded street as people swarmed across the massive intersection outside the station. 'You reckon?'

'Maybe an hour, I dunno.' Jimbo pointed to the other circle on the map. 'We could swing by here first. It's near where we need to go. Maybe twenty minutes out of our way.'

'Won't Niki be working?'

'Yeah, but she lives in the same building she works in.'

Dave grinned. 'You know I'll be keen.'

'Her flatmates won't be interested in you.'

Dave shook his crotch. 'Ya wanna make a bet?'

They both laughed, but Jimbo felt his good humour leach away as they made their way through the crowded streets while looming buildings pressed down from above.

The foyer of the Mederos building was huge and spacious compared to the crush of streets outside. The walls were draped in massive oil paintings; sculptures of bronze and clay and hologram punctuated the room; lush foliage gave the interior an exotic feel that lent the fresh smell of leaf and earth to the air, while irrigation tubes fed moisture into the plant beds. Beneath a soft electronic meditation scheme piped from hidden speakers, a muted hum buzzed through the room, no doubt the machinery powering the building.

'That one's a palm tree,' said Dave. 'Like they got up Far North.'

'That water must cost a fortune.'

Near the far wall, beneath a painting of a sunburnt landscape with a solitary black-armoured rider, was a large reception area guarding a squad of elevators. Operating the desk were half a dozen men and women, while several Cartel men stood guard, making sure the visitor queues were processed in an orderly manner.

'Can I help you, sir?' asked a female receptionist. Her hair was blonde and cut short, her nose was fine and bridged sparkling green eyes all, of which were delicately framed by high cheekbones. A plug was connected directly to her neck and a console on the counter. A badge on her shirt stated: *Hi, I'm Mandy.*

Jimbo was stunned by her beauty, hoping that his wife-to-be would be as beautiful as this woman. Without the wiring of course, and maybe longer hair.

'I'd like to see Nicole White,' said Jimbo. 'She works for Mederos.'

Mandy blinked. 'I'm afraid Nicole's not in the office at the moment.'

'Do ya know when she'll be back? I'm her cousin, Jim White, from back home. I'm visiting the City. Got some home cooking for her. From her mum n that.'

Mandy blinked again. 'Hello, Jim. I'm sorry, but Nicole is not due in the office today. Would you like to leave a message?'

'I already left a message that I'd be arriving today. Ya don't know if she went down to the station to get me, do ya?'

She smiled, though there was little warmth in it. 'I'm sorry, sir. I don't have access to that information.'

'Could ya try her apartment for me? I've got the number here.' Jimbo showed Mandy the address Aunty Lana had given him.

'Certainly.' Mandy blinked. 'I'm sorry, sir. No-one is currently home. Would you like to leave a message?'

'I left one yesterday. Shit. You don't know where she is?'

Mandy shook her head and smiled. 'Is there anything else I can help you with?'

'What about her flatmates? Maybe they know when she'll be back. She lives with Zoe Lane and Michelle Hanna. They work with her at Mederos too.'

'Certainly.' Mandy blinked several times. 'I'm sorry, sir, it appears that Zoe and Michelle are not in today.'

'What?' Jimbo looked at Dave in frustration. Dave shook his head, his brow furrowed. 'Is this for real? They're all away? No-one at work and no-one at home? Is this because you think I'm a sort of country fucken bumpkin, is it? We're not allowed in or something?'

Mandy, smile intact, nodded at one of the Cartel men. He moved abruptly towards them, while another of the Cartel turned to watch.

'Is there a problem?' he asked.

Mandy's eyes twinkled as she stared at Jimbo.

'No problem.' Dave grabbed Jimbo and pulled him back from the counter. 'Come on, man, let's go. We'll come back later, after work's finished. Somebody will be home.'

As they exited the building, Jimbo saw Mandy talking to the Cartel man. The man nodded and turned away, his silver eyes reflecting the fluorescent lights tucked up in the ceiling. She resumed her activities at reception.

'City wankers,' said Jimbo. 'Fucken hate them.'

'You sure this is the place?' asked Dave.

The narrow alley, jutting off the busy main street in the heart of Chinatown, appeared deserted, its high brick walls smeared in graffiti, the broken bitumen littered with junk. Jimbo consulted his map as people swarmed around them. He looked down the deserted alley again, unsure.

'It's gotta be.'

They stepped out from the street and into the alley, following its twists and turns through dank shadows. A nondescript barred door appeared on their right, with the words *Bridal Services* carved into a steel plaque above the door. A camera lens sat recessed into the crumbling cement wall.

'This looks dodgy,' said Dave. 'Brian didn't say nothing about this.'

'Yeah, well, he didn't say nothing about his inheritance either, did he?' Jimbo pressed the button beneath the camera. 'He did say these guys were the best though.'

A speaker crackled and spat. 'Name?'

'James White. I have an appointment.'

A heavy rumbling proceeded and the barred door rose, revealing a dimly lit corridor with an elevator at the end. Inside the elevator there was only one button. Jimbo pressed it. The elevator shuddered into life and began to descend.

Dave adjusted his carry-bag, shifting the weight from one shoulder to the other. 'I got a bad feeling about this.'

Jimbo stared at the card in his hand. The bright red words. The cold white background. He swallowed down his nervousness. 'Nah, mate, this is how it's done.'

The elevator ground to a halt.

Dave and Jimbo looked at each other. 'Ya bring ya knife? Just in case.'

'Course I fucken did,' said Jimbo. 'I'm not stupid.' The doors whined open.

They stepped out into a softly lit foyer where two young women dressed in black greeted them with warm lipstick smiles.

Dave laughed softly, a sigh of relief.

'Please leave your bags here, Mr White,' said one of the women. Her voice was silk and her blue eyes sparkled as she talked. She took Jimbo gently by the arm. 'Please, come with me. Mr Santos will be with you shortly.'

'In the meantime, can we get you a drink?' said the other woman, guiding Dave.

The women led them to a set of low couches around a coffee table, where the two men took a seat. Jimbo tried to keep the grin off his face, but failed when he looked at Dave, who was grinning like a horse put to stud.

'This is alright,' said Dave, as the women went to fetch a couple of Bundy and colas. 'It's a bit like the House in Shepp. Except there's normally a few other blokes here.'

Jimbo looked around the empty room. The walls were painted dark red, but were bare of prints or paintings. The carpet was lush underfoot, and tall potted plants positioned around the room somehow survived the muted lighting. Security cameras were mounted in each corner of the room.

One of the women returned, carrying a tray of drinks and a bowl of ice. She placed it on the table, bending low, the tight stretch of her skirt curving firmly against her body. Jimbo breathed deep, sucking in her perfume. *I'd be happy with someone like her.*

Dave grinned and picked up his drink. 'This is alright!' He eyed the woman as she left the room. 'Ya not staying?' he called after her.

She turned and smiled. 'Mr Santos will be with you shortly.'

'Bugger,' said Dave quietly. 'Wonder if ya can sample the goods?'

Jimbo laughed, finally away from the throng of the crowd and the press of looming buildings and packed streets, and felt the nervousness drift away. He sank back into the couch and swallowed a mouthful of rum. 'Yeah, this is alright.'

'Does that mean ya've changed ya mind?'

'About waitin?'

'Yeah. Come explore the City with me. Ya got one month, mate, one month.'

'Dunno, Dave. Don't much like what I've seen so far.'

'At least take a couple a days to have a look see.' Dave took another gulp, crushing the ice between his teeth. 'Fucken waste to come all this way and not see any of it. Find some a that free pussy Wazza was spoutin about.'

'I'm not here to see this fucken shit hole. Can't afford to be here anyways. My money's spent, mate.'

'So ya gunna spend the rest of the month in hibernation?' Dave shook his head, his chin bulging as he bit back frustration. 'You and ya fucken wife. I paid for half a me own train ticket and I'm ya best fucken man, ya cunt! Fuck ya, I'll see it on me own.'

'Don't be like that. I didn't say I wasn't going to see

any of it! Fuck. I'll spend the first couple of days with ya, but then I'm takin up the hibernation. I already paid for it.'

'Would ya?'

'Consider yaself lucky, ya ugly cunt.' Jimbo cracked a smile. 'And anyway, if the train was daily instead of monthly, I'd be outta here tomorrow fucken mornin and ya'd be comin with me.'

'Gentlemen,' said a deep voice from the other end of the room. A small, thin man in a dark suit stood with his arms raised in welcome. Black shoulder-length hair dripped from his scalp, in stark contrast against his pale skin. 'Sorry to keep you waiting. I'm Mr Santos. Please, follow me.'

They entered a small brightly-lit office where Santos gestured them into chairs around an empty desk. Santos hovered his hand over a pad on the desk and a holographic screen appeared.

'Let's get down to business, shall we?' Santos's lips curled upwards in an attempt at a smile. 'I'm sure you're very keen to meet your new bride.'

'Yes, I —'

'Good.' Santos's hand fluttered and a small hologram of a woman appeared and began to slowly revolve. 'This one is Kim. Young, attractive.'

Jimbo leaned forward, studying the image. 'Is she a bit Asian?'

'A small percentage, yes. Very fashionable these days. Would you like to see her naked?' Santos's hand hovered.

'Can you do that?' said Dave.

Jimbo glared at Dave. 'For fuck's sake, Dave. This could be me wife ya talking about.'

'Is that a no?' said Santos.

'Don't want no Asian,' said Jimbo. 'I'm paying good money. I want a proper Australian.'

Santos tilted his head and sighed. 'I'm not going to bullshit you, James. It's very hard to get what I think you're after. A purebred, yes? Unfortunately supply has changed a little over the last year and prices have increased.'

'Whaddya mean? I got ten grand!'

Santos smiled. 'James, you'd need at least twenty for a purebred. The women here on offer are of excellent quality. Guaranteed. Trust me, you won't be unhappy with your purchase at your current limit. Naturally, if you'd like to reassess at a later date, if your financial situation has improved, I'm sure we can do business.' He clasped his hands. 'But who's to say prices will remain the same.'

Jimbo looked at Davo, who shrugged. 'Never fucken heard about this.'

'Property prices,' Santos smiled again. 'Who can ever tell? We have four women available at your current price range and I have three interested buyers.' The hologram blurred and cycled through to stop on a blonde woman. 'This is as close as we can get with current stock. Sixty percent pure. The rest of the gene pool guaranteed European.'

'Only four women?'

'Your deposit has guaranteed you a wife, James. And you're here first. You simply need to choose.'

'But that's not many to choose from.'

Santos smiled sympathetically. 'If you'd prefer to come back in a few months' time. I can't guarantee anything by then, of course. It's difficult to acquire new stock.' He laughed, a small phlegmy gurgle. 'As I'm sure you gentleman understand.' His eyes went cold. 'Or you wouldn't be here.'

Jimbo studied the hologram again. 'Sixty percent, eh? What are the other women?'

'Dominant Arabian and Asian gene pools. Beautiful women. Lithe. Exotic. Extremely adept.'

'Can you zoom in on this one's face?'

Dave laughed. 'You don't look at the mantelpiece when you're stoking the fire, Jimbo!'

'Yes, ya fucken do! It's her face ya look at while ya fuck her!'

'I agree.' Santos zoomed in. 'There is nothing more pleasurable than the look on a woman's face as she orgasms. This is Helena.'

She had brown eyes and a small sharp nose. The cheekbones were high and the jaw firm. Not quite up to Niki's standards, but comparable to Brian's wife. *Sixty percent was pretty good, especially if the rest was European. You couldn't really tell the wogs apart from the Aussies these days, anyway.*

'The most Australian one, this one?'

Santos nodded.

Jimbo looked at Dave. 'Leave the room for a bit, mate.'

'What for?'

'Just do it, will ya?'

'What... oh, right. Come on, man, I won't look.'

'Just for a bit. Now fuck off.'

When Dave had left the room, Jimbo said to Santos, 'Show me her body.'

'This is it, man, this is the mall!' Dave grinned and folded the map away.

Jimbo nodded, staring up at the buildings dwarfing the crowded strip. A few slivers of sunlight managed to break through the shadows, and a muscled busker took advantage of the natural spotlight juggling a whirl of blades while he stripped off his clothing.

'Fuck the hibernation, Jimbo, this is gunna be shit hot!' Dave pressed into the throng, trying to get closer to the juggler. 'Look at this cunt! He's gunna cut himself bad.'

The noise of the street rose in Jimbo's ears, confusing him. Somewhere the clanging of a bell signalled a tram trying to push through the crowd as it made its way up the mall. Jimbo had always thought the smell of the cannery spoiling in the heat of summer had been bad, but the mall pressed its body hard into his nostrils, a body of dirty sweat and sweet decay and sun-cooked piss and stale, fumed air. Somebody pushed past him, causing him to totter and reach out to steady himself on someone else. That someone else turned and glared while hissing a 'don't touch me'. Jimbo could just make out Dave's head — and frantically pushed his way towards him. *It's just like The Aussie on a Christmas or New Year's Eve, like on Cup Day, like on any fucken Friday night when the wind blows too hot. This is nothing. This is nothing.* Jimbo wished he was back in the seclusion of the Bridal Services' complex, back with their baggage, back with the chance to wait out the month in the hibernation chambers. *One fucken sleep, and I'd be back on that train. With ma wife. One sleep.*

Dave turned, laughing, eyes sparkling. He waved his hand for Jimbo to come closer. 'Ya should see the size of this guy's cock!'

The noise of the surrounding crowd grew, catcalls and piercing whistles. People began to clap, at first slowly, increasing to a fast staccato of flesh slapped on flesh.

Jimbo pushed his way next to Dave who was clapping and laughing. The juggler stood naked except for white socks and black shoes. Sweat glistened on his skin as the blades whirled faster and faster. Scars crisscrossed his chest. The juggler thrust his hips in time to the clapping of the crowd, his dick flapping back and forth with the movement. Coins tossed from the crowd jangled at his feet.

'How does this end?' Jimbo shouted into Dave's ear.

The juggler grinned from ear to ear, his eyes studying the blades spinning around him through the air. Faster and faster. Sweat. Thrust. Crowd. Roar.

An apple flew from the midst of the crowd, smacking against the juggler's head. The blades tumbled down, slicing, glittering in the shaft of sunlight. Somebody laughed. Screamed. The crowd surged around them. The clanging of the tram bell, loud and sharp. Fists swung, the apple-thrower going down. The juggler launched himself into the crowd, screaming obscenities, struggling towards the apple-thrower. A siren wailed, a bright hot noise stabbing through the mall.

'Let's get the fuck out of here.' Jimbo grabbed Dave by the arm and dragged him towards the edge of the mob.

Dave, breathless, eyes shining, followed. 'Fuck the hibernation, Jimbo! This is great!'

Jimbo opened his daypack and retrieved the cake tin Aunty Lana had given him.

'What am I gunna do with this?'

'Don't arkse me,' said Dave.

They sat on the concrete steps outside the old Victorian parliament. Bars caged broken windows, and a slab of steel covered the doors. Sprayed on the door were the words: *Stop live exports!* Someone had written *Stop the flesh trade first* next to it. From their vantage point, Bourke Street stretched west, the throng weaving around the heavy trams that crisscrossed at the intersections.

'Ya gunna open it?' asked Dave.

Jimbo fingered the tin, its touch bringing back memories of sneaking out of bed and creeping into Aunty Lana's pantry with Niki. Anzac biscuits, caramel squares, banana cake, back when the bananas used to grow up north.

'She ain't here, Jimbo. Ya gunna leave it with those cunts at her work? No fucken way she'd get it, man.'

'Nah, man, I promised.' Jimbo opened the tin. The smell of baked golden syrup Anzacs wafted out.

'They smell good!' A tall, skinny guy with caved in cheeks and a mass of corkscrew hair sat nearby. A ragged daypack rested at the feet of his boots — *Blunnies, just like mine*, Jimbo thought — and he wore a chambray shirt with faded jeans. 'You boys been here long?'

Jimbo closed the biscuit tin. 'Maybe twenty minutes. What's it to you?'

The skinny guy laughed. 'Nah, that's not what I meant. How long have you been in the City? I been here two weeks now. Looking for work. And lemme tell ya, I'm having a cunt of a time finding anything that's paying.'

Jimbo and Dave both smiled.

'Ya not from here either?' said Dave.

'Fuck no! Just here to earn some cash. Send it home to the folks. They're getting on now, and there's fuck all work back home. That's out east past Gippsland way. What line a work you guys in? I'm a chippie. Well, not got a trade or nothing, but I know how to do it all. Me old man was a chippie until he fucked his back. What did ya say you guys were? Hey, my name's Bop.' He reached out a hand. 'Nice to meet some others a bit more like me, ya know what I mean?'

They all shook hands and made introductions.

This cunt's alright. He's jus like us.

'We're not looking for work, Bop,' Dave said. 'Up here doing a bit a shopping.'

Bop's eyebrows arched. 'Really?'

Dave tapped the side of his nose and winked. 'Ooh yeah! Bigtime.' He elbowed Jimbo in the ribs. 'Eh, Jimbo?'

'I got no fucken idea what yer talking about, boys.' Bop ran his fingers through the corkscrews in his hair. 'What, drugs? Biotech or something?'

Dave elbowed Jimbo again. Jimbo swatted back. 'Fuck off, Dave.' Then to Bop, 'Here to get me a wife. Top shelf.'

Bop shook his head. 'Ya fucken kidding me? You got enough cash for a wife?' He picked at the scuffed leather on his boots. 'Man, I guess it's a hell of a lot better up in Shepp than out my way.'

'Not for all of us,' said Dave.

'That's cos ya spent all yer money on fucken whores!' said Jimbo.

Dave and Bop exchanged nods, both grinning like idiots. 'Nothing finer.'

'Too right. Now speaking a pussy.' Bop indicated two women, a little older than Jimbo, sitting nearby on the steps below. 'Ya wasting ya money on a wife. Those two have been checking us out. Hey, ladies!'

One, a blonde, with a low-cut top and a short skirt, smiled and leant forward, her cleavage spilling flesh. The other, a short dark woman with long black hair and tights, pointed at the biscuits. 'Could we have one?'

'Sure.' Dave slapped the concrete next to him. 'Pull up a seat.'

The blonde reached into the tin and pulled out a biscuit. 'My mum used to make these when I was little.'

Jimbo yanked his eyes from her tits. There was regrowth in her hair. Her legs were long. 'My aunty made 'em.'

She flashed him a smile, then sat on the steps next to his feet. 'I'm Charlie, that's Sara.' She nibbled on the biscuit, her brown eyes widening. 'Yum!'

Sara leant on Dave's shoulder as she grabbed a biscuit, then sat. 'First time in town?'

Dave laughed. 'That obvious?'

'Where you guys from?' asked Charlie.

'Shepp.' Jimbo offered Dave a biscuit, and then bit into his own. He hardly tasted it. Charlie stared into his eyes, smiling. He fumbled the tin closed, then back into the pack. 'He's from out Gippsland.'

'Country boys, eh?' Charlie winked at Bop. 'You know what they say about country boys, Sara?'

Sara giggled and put an arm around Dave's shoulders. 'I've heard.'

'What do they say?' said Dave.

'Hey, tell you what. You guys fancy buying us a drink we'll tell you.'

'Sure,' said Jimbo. 'Where ya wanna go?'

Charlie rested a hand on his knee, all slender fingers and black nail polish, and nodded towards Bourke Street. 'Somewhere a bit quieter than that. I know a place where we can talk, get to know each other. Maybe have some fun.'

She stood, offering Jimbo her hand. He took it, relishing the touch of warm skin on skin, surprised by her strength as she pulled him to his feet.

'This way.' Sara led the way down the steps, dragging

Dave after her. Dave grinned at Jimbo, then trotted along behind her.

'Hey! What about me?' Bop grabbed his pack, almost spilling its contents in his haste.

'I'm sure we can arrange something.' Charlie winked at him then squeezed Jimbo's hand. 'Come on, country boys.' She sneezed. 'Sorry. Hayfever season. Driving me nuts. Nothing a good drink won't fix though.'

Maybe the City ain't so bad after all. Just like what Wazza said. You gotta buy 'em drinks n shit, but you ain't paying for the pussy. For the first time that day, Jimbo smiled, really smiled.

The gutters stank of rotting cabbage and there were too many slopes, but there were fewer people in the backstreets of Chinatown. And with Charlie holding his hand Jimbo could handle that.

'I dunno about this part of town,' said Bop. And then quietly at Jimbo, 'Ya better not be carrying all that cash for ya wife purchase.'

'Shut up, man!' Jimbo drew a line across his throat, then nodded his head towards the girls. 'They don't need to know about that.'

'But ya money —'

'I'm not that fucken stupid.'

'Almost there,' said Sara.

'Ya remember which way we came, Jimbo?' Dave asked.

'Maybe.' Jimbo hadn't a clue, he'd got lost shortly after the red ducks strung up in the shop window about a block back.

'Yeah, maybe,' Bop agreed, shaking his head.

'We'll stick you in a cab,' said Sara.

Charlie giggled. 'But only if you're unlucky.' She

squeezed his hand again. 'You might not need a cab.'

They ascended a narrow staircase, the wooden boards groaning under their weight as they climbed several flights to emerge in a large, low-lit room. Colourful cushions littered the floor around low tables, and a balcony overlooked the cityscape. A couple of surly guys at the bar glanced up as they entered, then resumed chatting with the muscled bartender.

The girls led them to a table on the balcony and Sara waved at the bartender. Dogs ran between bicycles below, and a roost of chickens squawked from a balcony above.

'What do you guys want to drink?' Sara asked.

'I thought we were buying.' Dave chuckled, getting out his wallet, as he sat down next to her.

Sara lifted his hand to her lips. 'You're too kind.'

'Nah, look, I'll get the first round in,' Bop said. 'Whaddya want?'

The girls ordered cocktails, while the boys ordered beer. Bop went up to the bar, leant on his elbows and was soon in discussion with one of the surly guys. He came back and sat down next to Charlie, who sat opposite Jimbo.

'How cool is that?' said Bop, after the drinks were placed on the table. 'Don't have to pay until we're finished. We got a tab already and they don't even know us.'

Jimbo nodded, taking a swig of the cold draught. It hit the back of his throat like he hoped he'd be hitting the back of Charlie's throat later on. Wet and fast. *Her nose maybe has a bit a wog in it, but she's fucken built for action.* His cock stirred in his jeans. *And once we get rid of this Bop cunt, I won't have to fight any blokes off.*

'So what brings you boys to town?' Charlie kicked off her heels, and put her legs up on the seat next to Jimbo.

Her thigh disappeared into the hem of white knickers. Her toenails were painted black too. A thick glossy black that caught the afternoon sun. Bop's eyebrows arched and he looked away embarrassed, as if he couldn't believe this was happening.

'Jimbo's getting a wife,' said Dave. 'I'm his best man.'

Jimbo glared at Dave. 'Nah, I'm fucken not.'

Charlie glanced at Sara, then teased Jimbo with her foot. 'It's okay, you're not married yet. We can still have a bit of fun.'

'I was just bullshittin.' Dave swallowed a mouthful of beer and grimaced. 'We're month-trippers, just checkin the City out n that. Bop here's looking for work.'

Bop nodded, puffing up his chest for a second, but the women didn't seem to notice.

Charlie eased her leg over Jimbo's, and slid her toes towards his balls. 'You boys must be loaded to buy a wife.'

Jimbo inched his bum towards her foot. His cock throbbed as it stiffened. She could see it, he was sure. 'Nah, just month-trippers.'

'Even so,' Charlie kneaded his cock beneath his jeans with her toes, 'that costs a bit of money. You boys rich country boys?' She licked the salt from the rim of her glass. 'You going to treat us like ladies?'

'Sure,' said Jimbo between breaths. *Who'd've thought it was this fucken easy! Wazza, the old cunt, no wonder he loved it here. Probably why Fitzy had dropped off the radar too.*

Sara stood, Dave's hand sliding down her thigh, and grabbed her bag. 'Back in a minute.'

'Hey, where ya going?' asked Dave.

She leant over, whispered in his ear, then kissed him on the cheek.

'Oh, sorry. See you in a sec.' Dave grinned, then downed the rest of his pint.

Charlie waved towards the bar, her foot resting against Jimbo's balls, and more drinks appeared. She sneezed again. Her sole pushed briefly against his cock. 'Bloody hayfever,' she said.

'So whatta you girls do for a crust?' Dave asked.

Charlie smiled. 'Marketing. Advertising. That sort of thing.'

Jimbo pressed her foot to his groin, slowly massaging her toes with one hand, as he drank with the other.

'Wow. Good pay?'

'Some days, Dave.' Charlie never took her eyes away from Jimbo's. She winked, her painted lashes falling and rising. 'And today's payday.'

Still holding her foot, Jimbo unzipped his fly. She dived her toes briefly in, then pulled away. 'Better check on Sara.' She slipped on her heels and headed towards the toilets.

'How fucken good is this? We're gunna get laid!'

'I dunno, man.' Bop stared at the froth in his glass. 'Looks like you two are in, but I'm feeling like I'm gunna end up fucking ma own hand.'

They laughed, nestling back into their chairs, soaking up the afternoon as they dragged on their pints. Except for Bop, who perched on the edge of his seat, tearing up a beermat and casting glances towards the guys at the bar.

Jimbo punched Dave hard on the upper arm.

'Ow, what's that for?'

'Fucken telling them I'm gunna buy a wife! For one, it tells them, I dunno, that I'm not in for some action or something, and two, that we got a lot of money to spend. And month-trippers don't help the second one much either.'

They sat in silence, sipping beer.

'What's taking them so long?'

'That's chicks,' said Bop.

Jimbo stared towards the bar. The three men were watching them. The barman came over and put a piece of paper on the table. He sat down heavily opposite Jimbo, where Charlie had been sitting.

'Thank you, gentlemen.' His voice sounded like thick rope soaked in sheep dip until it had swollen too large for his throat.

Dave picked up the paper. 'What's this? Five thousand dollars? I think you've made a mistake, mate.'

'That's the bill, gentlemen. I suggest you pay.'

The two men at the bar heaved themselves off their seats and sauntered towards the toilets. 'Back in a sec, Turk.'

'We're with a couple of ladies, mate,' said Jimbo. 'When they come back, I'm sure we can sort this out.'

Turk stretched and rotated his neck, vertebrae cracked. 'You can pay now or we can make you pay now, country boys.'

'Ya fucken having us on!' Dave laughed, looking from side to side at Jimbo and Bop for support. Bop shifted towards the edge of the seat away from them.

Turk stroked Dave's face. 'I don't think so.'

Dave, his cheeks flushed, stared sullenly at Jimbo, then at the cocktail glasses.

'We know you have money,' said Turk. 'I don't think we're being too greedy here.' He stroked his chin. 'What's the going rate on the market these days for a wife, Cartel approved or not. Let's say not. Ten grand? We could take it all, but you're my first customers for the week, and you'll bring me luck. Five grand, gentlemen.'

'How does "get fucked" sound?' Jimbo eased open his pack, his fingers sliding in until they hit the hard plastic sheath.

'It sounds like this.' Turk pulled a handgun from within his jacket and pointed the muzzle inches from Jimbo's forehead. 'Leave the bag alone, unless it's cash you'll be paying.' He grinned. Each incisor gleamed gold.

There was a scream from the toilets. Jimbo and Dave looked up in alarm. Turk didn't budge. Bop seemed all but invisible. *If there's gonna be a fight, I don't think we can rely on this one.*

The men emerged from the toilets, dragging the girls by the hair. They forced them into the seat opposite the boys. Turk, still pointing the gun in Jimbo's face, put his free arm around Charlie's shoulders. She shuddered.

'You like this one, yes?' Turk pressed the gun to the side of her head. 'I suggest you pay the bill.'

One of the heavies put a hand-held terminal on the table in front of Jimbo.

'We accept all forms of payment. Cash, card, electronic.'

'I don't have that sort of mon —'

'Let's cut the bullshit, shall we? You're in the market for a wife. We know this.'

Jimbo looked at Bop, sitting there, edging away. *That stupid cunt told them up at the bar!* He stared back into Turk's hazel-swirled eyes. 'You wouldn't fucken dare.'

'I don't need to.' Turk removed the gun from Charlie's head, and raised both his hands in the air in front of him.

Charlie leapt from the couch and sprinted towards the back exit near the toilets. She moved fast, but not as fast as one of the heavies who now brandished a pistol. A shot followed that shattered their eardrums. Charlie hit the floor, sprawling, face down. A plume of smoke drifted up from a hole in the back of her clothing.

'Just another slut.' The heavy repositioned himself behind the couch, gun on display, and blocked any further exit. 'Plenty more where that came from.'

'Oh Jesus,' Dave whispered into his hands.

Jimbo sat very still, his heart hammering in his chest.

Turk reached out one long arm. The barrel of the gun pressed against Sara's temple. She shut her eyes.

'Let's settle the bill.'

'Please, Jimbo. Don't let him kill me.'

It felt like every spring thunderstorm Jimbo had ever seen now breaking inside him, rushing up to burst his chest. His face felt flushed and he struggled to think. *My first day in the City and I'm getting fucked over.* Somewhere, deep in his marrow, anger began to build, knitting his bones and holding him together. They'd just killed someone and for what? Money? *It's five grand! Five fucken grand!*

'Please, Jimbo.' Sara tried to swallow a sob.

'It ain't worth getting killed,' said Bop.

Dave's eyes bulged like a dying roo. 'Fer fuck's sake, Jimbo.'

No! No! No! No!

'Okay.' Jimbo picked up the terminal. It felt as light as rain and as magic-like. 'How do I work this?'

Turk grinned again, and leant forward.

Then a sneeze came from the back of the room. Turk and Bop exchanged a furtive glance.

'Sorry,' said Charlie.

Adrenalin surged through Jimbo's veins. Everything so clear, so slow, so instant. That look between Bop and the Turk. *These cunts are all in on this. These aren't no Cartel, just thugs, like the cunts who come in from the orchards down The Aussie looking for a go.* He swallowed hard. *I can take these wogs. I'll give 'em a fucken go.* His hand was already moving…

Turk's face reddened, the set of his jaw evolving into a brick. 'You stupid fucking bitch!'

…and the terminal smashed into that brick, driving Turk's head backwards, bouncing it off the top of the couch.

'Dave!' Jimbo yelled, his other hand already pulling the hunting knife from the sheath in the bag.

The sound of smashing glass, then a scream. Bop stumbled away from the couch, his face a wet mess of bloodied flesh. One of the heavies ducked as the broken pint glass hurled towards his head. Sara clawed at Dave as he grabbed his pack.

'Give us ya fucken money!' she screamed.

Dave punched her in the nose, the bone cracking under his fist. She screamed again, this time in pain, as blood spurted over the table. One of the heavies ran back to the bar, the other clambering over the couch to drag Dave down.

Jimbo had the knife against Turk's throat. One of the heavies made to move. Jimbo pressed the blade into the skin, drawing a bead of blood.

'One step closer, cunt, and ya mate gets it.'

Turk said, 'Easy, boys.'

One of the heavies laughed. Turk smirked.

'What's so fucken funny, cunt?' Jimbo applied pressure to the blade.

'Think you're going to get down those stairs in one piece, country boy?'

Jimbo thrust the tip of the knife so it pierced the skin beneath Turk's chin. 'What makes you think *you* will?'

Jimbo forced Turk off the couch. They backed slowly

towards the front door. Dave grabbed the packs, watching for any sudden movement by the heavies. Bop crouched on his knees, sobbing, blood dripping through the fingers he clasped to his face. Sara nursed her broken nose, her eyes swimming with hate. The guy behind the bar moved slowly, something large and heavy held in his hands.

'Tell the cunt behind the bar to stay there!'

Dave threw back the bolts on the door and pushed it open. They backed out onto the staircase that led down to the street.

'Jimbo!' Charlie's voice.

Jimbo paused in the doorway, the knife biting into Turk's throat. She stood near the bar. 'I just wanted to say sorry.'

He saw too late something in her hand.

Turk threw his head back, the tip of the blade slicing his chin open, and dropped to his knees. Charlie fired. An electric discharge sizzled the air. A mess of wires bit into Jimbo's hand, a shock racing up his arm into his skull. The knife dropped from twitching fingers. He convulsed and tumbled down the stairs. The world turned, thumping him with every year it had spun him on its orbit, bruising bones for every birthday he'd ever woken to.

And then the world stopped spinning.

He lay, limbs twisted with Dave, at the bottom of the stairs. Up above the sun burnt blue through a thin grey haze and he was alive and breathing.

'Dave?'

'Jimbo? Fuck.'

'You okay?'

'Yeah, I think so.'

'She fucken tasered me!'

Dave struggled to get up. His teeth were chipped

and blood rouged his lips. 'Can ya get up? Ya gotta get up quick!'

'I can't move. She tasered me. That slut fucken tasered me!'

'Come on, Jimbo!' Dave tried to pull Jimbo up from the footpath. It was spattered with bright red droplets.

Jimbo managed to raise his hand against the sky. The skin on the back of his hand had peeled back in thick strips, like raw bacon, where the wires had torn from his flesh as he fell.

The blue sky was torn away. The last thing Jimbo heard as his head was yanked up by the hair was Dave pleading not to kill them. Turk grinned, one tooth gold and shining with spit, blood smeared across his throat. A fist smashed into Jimbo's jaw.

Jimbo poised his finger above the doorbell to Niki's apartment. *Go on, do it. If she answers within ten seconds, tell her you love her.* As he pressed it a horn sounded somewhere, distant and fuzzy. The door opened immediately. Niki stood there in a black lace nightie, her hair ruffled and tumbling past her shoulders, her eyes a little puffy from sleep. She smiled.

'Jimmy! So good to see you. Come in.'

He walked into her apartment and she closed the door behind him. The room was a dank windowless square. On the floor pushed up against the far wall lay a stained mattress.

'What do you think?' she said, still standing behind him. Her voice sounded stretched.

Droplets of blood spattered the wall near the mattress. Jimbo's head ached. It felt like his jaw was trying to squeeze out his teeth.

'You can fuck me if you want.' Niki's voice was all wrong.

Slowly, Jimbo turned, his body moving through glue. Fitzy leaned against the door dressed in Niki's nightie. Make-up smeared his face. He pulled the nightie down over one full breast, the nipple large and pink. Coarse black hair sprouted from the circumference of the areola.

'What are you doing here?' Jimbo's mouth filled with blood. 'Where's Niki?'

'I dunno man, but we're gunna be all right.' Fitzy slipped his arms beneath Jimbo's armpits and hugged him tight. He still had Niki's long, lean legs.

Jimbo screamed.

'It's okay, man, I'm here, I'm here.' Dave's face blurred into view. One eye had swollen shut and his nose dripped a thin bloody mucus.

Dave dragged Jimbo down an alley. Jimbo struggled to his feet, spitting out a mouthful of gunk. His head pounded. He ran his tongue round his mouth, cleaning out thickened saliva. A tooth was missing.

'We're almost there.' Dave pointed into the distance, down into murk and shadow. 'That way, I think.'

'What?' Jimbo swayed, trying to get his bearings.

'Bridal Services is that way. Maybe a block. We can get fixed up, go into hibernation.'

'Where the fuck is Niki?' Jimbo shoved Dave away.

'I dunno, man. Come on, what are you doing?'

'I need to find Niki. Where's our stuff? I gotta give her something. I gotta tell her something.'

'Niki's not here. We lost our daypacks. Come on, Jimbo, you're fucked up.' Dave reached out for Jimbo's arm. Jimbo swatted it away.

'What the fuck happened?'

Dave grimaced, eyes watering. He snorted snot and swallowed. 'Come on, Jimbo. Let's go.'

'The girls. We gotta help the girls! Where's Niki?'

'Jimbo, listen to me, man, you're not making any sense. Those girls fucked us over. Bop too. The chinks helped us outta there. Bad blood between those fuckers.'

'Ya fucken wrong. She wanted me. She was rubbing ma cock! I gotta find her. She loves me.'

'Niki ain't here.'

'What the fuck would you know about anything, Dave?' Jimbo thrust Dave up against the alley wall, squeezing the shirt collar around his neck. 'You ain't never been in love. Not like me. Not like Niki.' And what had happened all came back to him, crushing his anger, taking a little more of his soul with it.

'Sure, Jimbo, sure.' Tears streaked Dave's cheeks. A bubble of bloodied snot burst from his nose. 'I believe ya, man. I know ya love her. We all do.'

Jimbo released Dave. 'I gotta find her, Dave. I gotta save her from all this shit.'

Dave sank to his haunches, slumped against a wall in a piss-soaked alley, as the night swallowed Jimbo whole.

Floodlights lit up the Mederos building, chasing shadows out into the street. The doors opened and Jimbo strode into the lush interior, the air-con and smell of leaf fuelling his courage.

A different woman sat at reception. Two Cartel men stood nearby. Jimbo headed towards the elevators, trying to keep his battered face down. The receptionist looked up. The Cartel men began to move.

Jimbo broke into a trot, then sprinted towards the elevator banks. He stabbed the up button with his finger.

One of the Cartel men, smooth head and metal eyes, rounded the corner.

'Hey! Stop!'

The elevator chimed softly and a door slid open.

Jimbo ducked inside, pressed close then floor sixty-four. The doors shut, just as the Cartel arrived. Jimbo laughed.

'Fuck ya's all. Can't stop a man on a mission.'

The elevator didn't move.

He pressed the floor button again. Nothing. A key slot on the access panel. *Shit.*

The elevator chimed and the doors opened.

Two Cartel men: one resting a hand on a holstered gun, the other a hand outstretched.

'Come on, mate. Looks like you've been hurt enough today. Time to go home.'

'Ya don't understand. I'm here to see my cousin. She lives…'

'We know, mate.'

A guiding hand on Jimbo's elbow. Gently led from the elevator.

'I've come all this way.' Jimbo's voice hitched. Somewhere deep inside, all the pain was rising. 'I need to see her.'

They led him out into the foyer. One of them signalled to the receptionist and she nodded.

'She's not here, Jimbo,' said one of the Cartel. 'You need to go home. We'll get you a cab.'

'But I love her.' Jimbo sobbed. Tears fell from his eyes.

An electric buggy detached from the rank outside the Mederos building and pulled up alongside them as they exited.

They eased him into the back seat.

'He's staying at Bridal Services in Chinatown.' The Cartel man pressed a bill into the driver's hand.

'But how do you know…' said Jimbo.

'Here's some advice, mate. She doesn't want to see you.' Metal eyes reflected floodlights, a dull grey that sank into Jimbo's core. 'Nicole White has moved on. You need to too.'

'No, no… I need to see her.'

'I know how you feel, mate, I do, but if you come back here again, we will hurt you.'

The buggy door closed, and the cab jerked off with a hum.

'So, where you from?' said the driver.

Eyes with Asiatic folds regarded Jimbo from the rear-view mirror.

Jimbo didn't answer, instead wiping his damp cheeks with the back of his hand. *Nosey fucken chink.*

Part IV: Pronouncement of Marriage

The tracks rumbled beneath the Marriage Carriage. They passed a tumble of roo corpses festering in the sun, the hot fetid air reaching in through the windows. Jimbo shoved the window shut. He wondered if the bushrangers were watching.

Dave cracked open another beer from the chiller, laughing and offering it to the four Cartel men who sat guarding the carriage. Froth had spilt on Dave's suit.

'There's champers in here, if she wants some,' said Dave.

Jimbo nursed his warm beer, too nervous to drink, struggling to find things to say to the woman who sat opposite him. High cheekbones, firm jaw. Kylie. That was her name. Same as Wazza's truck. Her wedding dress curved around full breasts down the slight of her waist. The veil had been pushed back over her long brown hair. She wouldn't need to wear it until they disembarked in Shepp.

'You want one, Kylie?'

'Sure,' she said, her voice light. Her brown eyes seemed glazed. Red lipstick had smeared one of her front teeth, otherwise her teeth were white and straight, and Jimbo was happy about that.

'You'll need to limit her alcohol,' said one of the Cartel.

'Why?'

'Don't want any mishaps on the journey home, Mr White.' The Cartel man smiled. 'Then she can have as much as she likes.'

'That's okay,' said Kylie.

Jimbo nodded and studied his beer, sneaking glimpses of her calves, the way the dress stretched tight over her thighs. He wished Dave wasn't here with him, that the Cartel men were elsewhere. Just him and this stranger, the new Kylie White, so he could tell her about himself, reassure her that he would treat her right, that they would love each other, raise kids and grow old together. And she would tell him about herself and how she was looking forward to being with him, looking forward to living in Shepp, giving him sons. But he couldn't say these things with the others here in the carriage.

'You look beautiful,' he said instead.

'Thanks.' She smiled too much. 'It's so warm.'

'Is it?' The red lipstick smear cheapened her. Jimbo reminded himself to wipe it off before they stepped out into the crowd.

Awkward silence enveloped the carriage again. The clacking of tracks. Dave slurping on his beer.

Why doesn't she fucken talk? Jimbo looked out the window, watching the cracked earth and burnt eucalypts roll by. 'You'll like ma mum, she's real nice.'

Kylie's glazed brown eyes stared through him. Her head rocked with the rhythm of the train. Smiling to herself.

'Sure,' her voice distant, lost in syrup. 'That's okay.'

Jimbo looked to Dave for support. Dave raised his eyebrows, shrugged then raised his beer. Jimbo returned the salute and took a swig of warm flat lager. He stole a glance at her hands folded in her lap. *A little too big, those hands. She's no Niki. Still, she'll do.*

As the train pulled into Shepp Station, one of the Cartel men placed his finger on Kylie's forearm. She flinched. A droplet of blood oozed to the surface of her skin. The Cartel man wiped it away, leaving a shiny patch.

'Blood levels are okay,' he said to the other Cartel. He produced a vial and sprayed something into her nostrils.

Kylie sat up straight. Her lips parted in a huge smile. The Cartel man wiped the lipstick from her teeth. She stood. The Cartel man adjusted her dress and pulled the veil down over her face. Another Cartel man offered her a bouquet of flowers. Dave grabbed the champagne from the chiller and gave it a shake before he unwound the stopper, keeping pressure on the cork as he did so.

The steel doors ground open. Hot air swarmed into the carriage. Sweat dripped from Jimbo's armpits, trickling down his sides. His neck felt damp, sticky, the suit too tight, suddenly constricting.

Kylie held out her arm, and he took it. Dave stepped

into the light and the crowd roared. The cork popped and champagne spurted into the air and Dave strode out, laughing, spraying the bottle over the people lining the edge of the red carpet.

Jimbo stretched a smile across his face, his gut churning, and stepped out with his new wife on his arm.

The band belted out the old classic 'What About Me?' and the dancefloor heaved. Sweat had already formed on the ceiling of The Aussie and it wouldn't be long before it started to rain.

'I thought the Old Man would have at least made it down to the do, Mum.'

Mel hugged her son and kissed him on the cheek, her own flushed with cheap red wine. 'He's not well, James, and today, well, today is your day, not his.'

'Still…'

'He'll be up waiting when we get home.' Mel squeezed his arm. 'Look, Kylie's back from the ladies. Now I'll get a chance to have a real chat with her.'

Jimbo took another slug of bourbon, watching his mother limp over to the bridal table as Kylie sat next to Aunty Lana, her face pale.

Keats sauntered up, jabbing his fist playfully into Jimbo's ribs. His head was shaved clean and shiny, the scar bulging like a dead vein across the scalp. 'Hey, Jimbo! Good party, mate.'

'Hey, Keats.'

'Tidy, mate. Thumbs up from the boys.' Keats tipped his bottle towards the bridal table. 'She having a bit of cry like Brian's missus did?'

'Yeah, I think so. She's just a bit overwhelmed is all.'

'Probably coming down.'

'Eh?'

'Yeah.' Keats nodded. 'She's been on a high all day. Hey, have you heard?'

'What, you scored a job with the Cartel now?'

Keats laughed, and drained his stubbie. 'Soon, Jimbo, soon. But yeah nah, Brian's missus is up the duff.'

Jimbo followed Keats's unsteady arm. Against the far wall sat Belle with a couple of the other ladies. She wasn't saying much, but the other two's mouths were flapping like flags in a storm.

'She don't look it.'

'Early days, mate, she'll start to show. Who'd have thought, eh?'

On the dancefloor, Brian jumped and jostled with the other guys, throwing his head back and forth to the beat. Keats laughed again. 'She won't be doing any a that anymore either.'

Jimbo stared at Keats, then Brian. He turned towards Belle, sitting on the chair. 'No! He did her?'

'Yep. Day after ya left. Knew he'd fucken have to. Right lively bitch, that Belle.'

Jimbo drained the bourbon and Keats went to get him another. Brian, grinning like a madman, throwing himself around, covered in sweat. *He fucken told me he'd never do that. Well, fuck me, things have changed.*

The long dress Belle wore had hitched a little too high as she sat. Jimbo thought he could make out a bandage around Belle's ankle. *And pregnant too. That was fucken quick work.*

The dancefloor heaved again as the band hit the chorus, everyone screaming: 'I've had enough, now I want my share!'

•

Uncle Frank drove the horses as they pulled the Ford Commodore back to the house. The Old Man had polished it up good, and the seats had been reupholstered, leaving the car with a healthy clean leather smell. Jimbo sat in the back with one arm around Kylie and the other around his mother. Kylie hadn't spoken for the last hour but at least she'd stopped crying.

'Have a good night, Mum?'

Mel hugged him tight. 'Lovely evening, James.'

They climbed from the carriage and Jimbo swept Kylie off her feet. She clung to his neck, deadweight and trembling.

'Come by when you can, Jimmy.' Uncle Frank detached the horses from the car.

Jimbo nodded, trying not to think of Niki, as he adjusted Kylie's weight in his arms. 'I didn't get to see her, Uncle Frank.'

'Yeah, well.' Frank swung himself up onto one of the horses. 'Ya can still come by. Say gidday to your old man.'

He reined away on a clatter of hooves, before he'd barely finished speaking.

Mel held the door open as Jimbo manoeuvred himself and Kylie through. *One too many bourbons to be doing this.* He bumped her arm on the doorframe but she didn't say anything. 'Oops.'

The light emanating from the Old Man's room was soft, like he'd fallen asleep in front of the screen again. The air, as usual, was hot and musty.

'Hey, Dad, got someone I want you to meet!' Jimbo staggered through the kitchen towards the light, with Kylie in his arms. 'You better smile for him,' he whispered in her ear.

The Old Man, wearing his best suit, sprawled in his

chair, a half-empty bottle of beer on the table next to him. On the screen shone an old photo of Niki in her school uniform, knee-high white socks with a blue skirt and matching button-up shirt. The first day of school.

'Dad, this is Kylie, ma wife.' Then in a harsh whisper, 'You better be fucken smiling.'

His mother turned on the light.

'Dad?' *Christ, I'm too pissed and she's too fucken heavy.* 'Stop snoring and wake up, ya old bastard.'

But his old man wasn't snoring. The glass he'd been drinking from lay upturned in his lap, the spilled beer already dry on his good trousers. He wasn't even breathing.

Next to the bottle on the table, rested a long wooden box. Jimbo knew what lay in that box. His father's heirloom knife, honed sharp and thin, passed to him from his father and his father before him. His wedding gift.

'We'll deal with this tomorrow,' said his mother. 'There's room in the deep freeze for now.'

Jimbo closed the lid of the deep freeze then put the wheelbarrow back in the shed. A storm of confusion wound through his insides, beating against his heart, threatening to break inside his head.

Inside, his mother sat in the lounge sipping a glass of sherry. She looked calm. 'I didn't hate him all the time.'

Jimbo felt numb, all emotion drained when his mother smiled. He didn't know what to feel, or if he should feel anything at all.

'Neither did I,' he managed to croak in a broken, small boy's voice. His eyes welled and he swallowed hard, trying to control himself.

'I've made up our bed with fresh sheets. It's your

room now. Kylie's asleep.' Mel patted her knees. 'Come here, James.'

He huddled on the floor and hugged her knees. She wound her fingers through his hair, massaging gently.

'You be kind to her, James. She's been through a lot, more than you'll ever know.'

'I will, Mum.'

'Men say that with every good intention. Your father said it to me before…'

Her fingers tensed in his hair, briefly, ever so briefly, then resumed their massaging.

'Before what, Mum?'

'Before he… consummated our wedding night.'

'Aw, Mum, I don't wanna hear about you and Dad doing it.'

'Doing what, James? What is it that you think we were doing?'

'Ya know, sex.' But deep down, buried in that pit he called a heart, Jimbo knew that wasn't exactly true. His father's wooden box sat on the table next to his father's empty chair.

'Sex.' His mother gave a bitter laugh. 'At first I hated him for that. Men are easily controlled by sex, James. Women learn to use it as a weapon against them to survive. There are worse things than that.'

Jimbo tensed. He'd never heard his mother talk like this before, but she'd never been out of his father's oppressive shadow either.

'Losing the life you knew, the ones you love. I haven't seen my mother for almost forty years. Did you know that? These things are far worse.' She leant forward and kissed the top of his head. 'You're my son, James, I raised you. Not him. I taught you. Not him.' She leant back, taking another sip of sherry. 'Don't you turn out like him. Don't you break my heart.'

Jimbo felt his mother sobbing quietly as he hugged her knees. He realised, then, that he knew very little about her past and who she was, who she had been. And with his new wife asleep in his parents' bed, his mother's bed where his father had fucked her incessantly for years, he pushed that realisation into the recesses of that raw bottomless pit. That dark place where such realisations were never dwelled upon. And never faced.

His mother had stopped crying. 'Go to bed, James. Be kind to that girl. Don't… don't do anything to hurt her. Treat her with love as I love you.'

He left his mother in the chair, staring at the blank screen, and went into his parents' room. In the shadows, Kylie lay curled and tight against the far edge of his mother's side of the bed. Her perfume lingered in the room, though it did little to conceal the last years of his father's decaying sweat.

They'd ask him tomorrow how it went. Keat's leering face. Dave grinning and clutching his crotch. Brian eager to compare notes. Jimbo sat in his mother's rocking chair, the same chair she had sat in all those months ago when he'd come into the room with the pillow, intent on putting them all out of their misery. The same chair she would have nursed him in as a babe.

Kylie's breath rose and fell, sometimes fluttering, sometimes ragged. Occasionally she'd cry out in her sleep, limbs flailing, before curling tight again into her protective ball.

How had it come to this? This is ma fucken wedding night! I'm supposed to be fu… supposed to…

But he didn't know what he was supposed to be doing,

so Jimbo rocked away the dark in his mother's chair, as the numbness consumed him. Eventually, he succumbed to a dead sleep before the sun lurched from the horizon and burned another dawn.

They held the funeral three days later out at the cemetery on Old Dookie Hill.

Jimbo was surprised to see the turn out; maybe two hundred people had made the half-hour ride out in the morning heat. Horses had been tethered near the cemetery gates, next to the bicycle racks, and some of the younger boys were filling the troughs from the bore.

The old Ford Commodore had been used as the hearse, again with Frank at the reins. Grandpa White was complaining about the heat and the ride and the lack of bourbon in his glass. He sat with Nan, comfy in their wheelchairs in the shade of the eucalypts, Mel and Kylie at their side. Jimbo wasn't sure Grandpa knew they were burying his eldest son, or maybe he did, but just didn't give a fuck.

Aunty Joan came back from Cranky McNabb's stall with more bourbon for Grandpa and a gin for Nan. Jimbo's cousin Rhys had told him that Cam didn't pay for Joan, that they had chosen each other. The Old Man had said it was because Cam had gotten himself a half a chink, and that back then no-one in their right mind would pay for one. Cam put his arm around his wife, and she slipped her arm around his waist and hugged him. Joan didn't limp like the others. *But that don't mean nothing. Chinks are more obedient, everyone knows that.*

Still, watching them arm in arm, something Jimbo couldn't remember his folks doing in public for years, they sure looked happy in each other's company. Aunty Lana stood with her gangly sons.

'Thought Niki might a turned up,' said Jimbo to Rhys.

'Don't hardly hear from her these days,' said Rhys. 'Selfish bitch didn't even reply to the message Dad sent about Uncle Phil passing n that. Stopped sending money home too. She can go n get fucked.'

'Yeah, fuck her.' Something rose from that dark pit buried in Jimbo's heart, that maybe she wasn't in the City anymore, that maybe… like the month-tripper Keira on the train, that… but he squashed it down again before it surfaced. Then nailed it fucken closed.

Frank, Cam, Rhys and Jimbo, the eldest men in the family not counting Grandpa, lowered the coffin into the dry earth. The rope burned Jimbo's sweaty palms, but he held on, releasing the rope one hand at a time, until the coffin rested on the grave floor.

Cranky said a few words before they filled the hole with dirt. What those words were, Jimbo didn't have a clue. He was lost in Aunty Lana's soft crying, lost that his mother wasn't. By the time they'd finished, Jimbo had managed to smear dirt across his forehead and over his sweat-soaked shirt. Galahs squawked noisily from the trees, ready to pounce on any food left unguarded.

Afterwards, Lana enveloped him in her breasts, her cheeks wet, mingling with his sweat. 'We loved your father, Jimmy. He was a good man. Sorry Niki couldn't be here. She sends her love.'

Frank looked away, studying the fallen leaves, the ants crawling through tinderbrush. Niki hadn't called. It was all over Frank's face, even if Rhys hadn't told him. The Old Man had been right about her. She was a City girl now; she wasn't coming back to Shepp in any hurry. Fucken bitch.

'Thanks, Aunty Lana.'

Fitzy hadn't shown either. One of his best mates. City wankers. Fuck them all. Fuck them all to hell.

'Jimmy!' Grandpa held up his empty glass. 'What the fuck is this?'

'Coming up, Grandpa.' Jimbo snatched the glass and marched to Cranky McNabb's stall. 'Gimme a fucken bottle,' he snarled.

Fragments, memories breaking apart in a swirl of alcohol...

Doors slamming.

He remembered Uncle Frank leaving. The kitchen spun, the dangling light bulb a whirr.

'Don't, James.' His mother? Someone crying.

'Don't, please...'

The bedroom, hot and rancid. The Old Man's sweat wafting up from the mattress, dripping from the walls.

His mother crying. Wiping Lana's tears away.

'You don't know anything about me. If you knew, you wouldn't...'

Throwing Kylie across the bed. Screams.

He remembered someone pounding on the bedroom door yelling his name.

He ripped at her skirt, pinioning her legs with his own. She was strong.

'No...'

He mashed at her breasts. Licked her throat.

'You don't know...'

Jimbo shouting. Ranting. 'I don't wanna know about you! I don't need to know anything about you! Ya mine! Ya fucken mine!'

Eyes wide, bulging.

'James!'

When she started screaming he smothered her mouth with his palm.

Eyes, wide rolling. White.

He struggled with his fly, trying to free his trapped cock. She went limp beneath him.

'Niki?' Jimbo withdrew his hand from her mouth. 'Niki?'

He remembered a splintering sound as the bedroom door swung open. His mother, hammer in hand.

'I've killed her!' Jimbo rolled from her body, legs tangled and fell from the bed. He lay on his back, sobbing.

'No.' His mother near the bed. 'She's still breathing.'

'No.'

'No.'

Passed out on the bedroom floor, pants around his ankles, his cock still unused and now dormant, oozing a slow leak into his undies.

He remembered little of his first unsuccessful attempt at making love to his new wife.

Jimbo woke to bracing cold water thrown over his face. Light flooded the room, already hot, hard to breathe. Still on the floor.

Keats stood over him. 'Fucken lucky I was on shift last night, mate.'

Jimbo tried to sit, pulling himself up next to the bed. His head pounded, his mouth a graveyard for sandpaper. 'What happened?'

'She tried to do a runner, mate. Knew ya were too pissed to control things. Father's funeral n that, I understand. Caught her about four in the morning, running up the road just past ya driveway.' Keats whistled. 'Good

set a legs on her; she can fucken move, mate. If she tells ya
I felt her up when I caught her then she's a fucken liar.'

'Ya felt her up?' Jimbo grimaced as the sunlight hurt
his eyes.

'Fuck no! Just if she says any shit like that, she's just
causing trouble. Mate, she's ya fucken *wife*! I'm ya mate, fa
fuck's sake! Just ask Mason, he was there.'

Jimbo struggled to his feet, the blood draining from
his face as the room whited out for a second. He breathed
deep, waiting for the room to return.

Keats laughed again with a wink. 'But if she wasn't
your wife, mate… she's hot.'

'Where is she now?'

'Out in the kitchen with ya mum. Had to tie her up
for a while but. That's her first warning, mate. Ya told her
what happens after three?'

Jimbo shook his head, looking out from the bedroom
doorway. At the other end of the house, Kylie sat hunched
at the kitchen table, head buried in her arms, while his
mother comforted her.

'I'd think she already knows.'

'Maybe so,' said Keats. 'But it should come from the
husband. From the man. Just so the record's straight.'

'Ya probably right.'

'Not just *probably*. It's the way it's done.' Keats handed
Jimbo his father's wooden box. 'Ya fucken lucky she didn't
get hold of this last night. You'd be dead by now.'

'Thanks, Keats. I'll do it tonight.'

'No, ya fucken won't.' Keats shoved Jimbo in the
back, pushing him towards the kitchen. 'Ya'll do it fucken
now. It's us poor cunts on watch who have to deal with
this shit. We're helping you out, you fucken help us. It's
the way it's done!'

Mel glared at Jimbo as he approached the table. Her eyes darted towards the box in his hand, then she whispered into Kylie's ear.

'No,' Kylie moaned.

'If you don't, it will just make it harder,' said Mel.

Jimbo sat opposite, pushing the salt and pepper shakers aside to make room for the box. Keats's presence from the bedroom doorway pressed heavily against him.

His mother glared at him again, mouthing the words, 'What did I tell you? You stupid boy!'

He buried the shame of last night, using Kylie's flight to lend him conviction.

'Kylie, I apologise for last night. With the Old Man dying n the wedding n all, I just wasn't myself. It won't happen again, I promise.'

His mother nodded, her hands kneading Kylie's shoulders.

'You got to promise me something too. You're mine now. You tried to escape last night. But that's foolish, Kylie. What are ya gunna do? Run out into the desert with the Abos? There's nowhere to go to.' Jimbo knew the words that followed by heart. They all did. 'You're part of my life now, for better or worse, in sickness and in health. You need to love and obey me.' He removed the lid of the box. A short knife lay cushioned in a dark stained cloth.

'Look up, honey,' said Mel. 'That's a good girl.'

Kylie lifted her head, her eyes raw and aching. Bruises purpled her jaw and throat.

Jimbo took the knife, its handle worn and smooth, the blade thin and keen. The last time it had been used was before Jimbo had been born. His father had cleaned his mother's blood off the blade with the cloth in the box.

'This is your first warning, Kylie. You only have three.

After that, with this knife I thee wed. Don't make me do that.'

Kylie stared at the knife. Snot dripped from her nose, blurred with tears. Her cheeks were blotched and streaked.

'Do you understand?' said Jimbo.

Kylie nodded.

'I said, do you understand?'

Mel bent to her ear and whispered.

'I do,' Kylie rasped, her throat raw.

Jimbo placed the knife back amongst the folds of cloth and closed the lid.

A week later, Jimbo held Kylie down on his parent's bed. She tried to bite between her screams, so he didn't kiss her.

With her arms pinioned above her head, he pushed her legs wide. She was too dry, but he had greased his cock. When he managed to force it inside her, she stopped resisting, stopped screaming.

Jimbo kept thrusting until it was too uncomfortable, too raw, before he pulled out of his unconscious wife, thoughts of Niki reeling in his head.

Some mechanical part of him registered blood on the sheets, that he had indeed got what he had paid for.

It shouldn't be like this. It can't be like this.

He realised he was crying.

Later, when he needed to scrub himself clean, he found his mother sitting in the kitchen with the lights off. She drank sherry, staring blankly at the curtains above the sink, and said nothing.

•

Part V: Presentation of the Couple

Winter lay a cool hand over the hot brow of the land, but still the rains never came. The cannery cut shifts and a third of the workers migrated to the orchards to prepare crops for the coming spring. Jimbo was lucky enough to keep his cannery job and toiled inside the factory, adjusting the machines as they pulped the autumn fruit. The smell in winter was bearable, as the pungent rot never set in as quickly or stunk so bad.

Belle had been seen round town, no longer on her crutches, all swollen belly and smiles. Brian reckoned they were having a girl and didn't seem to be happy about it. Dave had started seeing Alice, some Abo girl from one of the camps. Jimbo had only met her a couple of times because she wasn't allowed in The Aussie, but he'd had drinks with Dave and Alice down by the crater that used to be the old lake. She could hold her piss and was pretty funny for an Abo. Her brother played in the Abo footy team too and was probably going to make the State Team. Niki hadn't been back, and Lana and Frank had stopped asking Jimbo if he'd heard anything from her. He didn't have to lie when he said he hadn't. Aunty Joan had fallen pregnant, surprising the hell out of everyone. Uncle Cam seemed ten foot tall, gushing and lovey. Jimbo guessed the Old Man had been wrong about that too.

Jimbo and Kylie's lovemaking was getting better — she no longer resisted and had stopped biting, even though she kept trying to run away — but looking at the mantelpiece wasn't much fun when she kept passing out. She was a pretty girl and he wanted to see the look in those dark trembling eyes when he came. She didn't talk much, but his mother assured him Kylie was coming out of her shell. At least those two seemed to be getting on okay.

The siren sounded for smoko, and Jimbo joined Brian outside for a cigarette and a sausage roll. The winter sun warmed Jimbo's face, the cool breeze carrying the stink of fruit away.

Brian lit the cigarette and sucked in a mouthful of tobacco laced with pot. 'Heard Dave caught Kylie down by the lake. That's the third time.'

'Yeah.' Jimbo smeared sauce over the warm pastry, wiping his fingers on his overalls. 'Thought the Abos might help.'

'Have you cut her yet?' Brian passed Jimbo the smoke.

'Nah, I'm hoping she doesn't do another runner.'

Brian shook his head. 'That's three warnings, mate. Ya gotta cut her. Rules are rules, mate, and she's broken them.'

'Yeah, but…'

'No fucken buts, Jimbo.'

Jimbo blew smoke at Brian's face. 'When did you get so fucken hard?'

Brian stared back, his face impassive. 'I did what had to be done. The watch is over, mate. Now ya need to do what has to be done or she's gunna get away on ya.'

'Yeah, I know, I been putting it off.' Jimbo took another deep drag, staring into the sky. Clouds hovered near the horizon. 'It's not what I thought it'd be.'

'It gets better.' Brian smiled, wry and thin. He took a bite of Jimbo's sausage roll, chewing back the sawdust and gristle. 'Ya gotta give her something to make her wanna stay.'

Jimbo swapped the cigarette for the sausage roll. 'Like what?'

'Belle's pretty fucken happy these days. It's the best way to keep them here.'

Jimbo nodded, understanding. 'Yeah, she's getting big. When's she due?'

'Couple a months. Scary.' Brian ground the cigarette underneath the heel of his boot. 'Aw, fuck, Wazza Wilson was down the pub last night. Driving some fancy new truck called an eVolvo. Said it was AI or something, and it pretty much drove itself.'

'Yeah? No cunt told me he was in town.'

'Reckons he seen Fitzy. You ain't gunna fucken believe it.'

'Fitzy got himself married too?'

'Fuck no, listen to this. He's turned into some poofter, working cock in the City. Can ya fucken believe it? Always thought there was something strange about that cunt.'

'Nah, no way.' Not Fitzy, gentle, flabby Fitzy, big brown eyes. 'He got a job drivin trucks. Wazza set it up.'

Brian shook his head, in big deliberate arcs. 'Fell through. Wears a dress an all. Guess there just ain't enough pussy to go round, even in the wonderfuckenfull City, eh?'

Jimbo's mouth sagged. *No fucken way. And to think that cunt was ma mate.* 'So ya think all those times we were a-holing and shit, he was really into it?'

'Stranger things have happened.' Brian motioned towards the rest of the sausage roll. 'Ya gunna eat that or let it go cold?'

Sledge, the foreman, called a general meeting for the shopfloor late afternoon just before clock out. They gathered in the canteen, one hundred and fifty sweaty tired bodies pressed in and wondering what the fuck was going on.

Sledge held a piece of paper aloft and called for quiet.

Someone in the crowd made a joke about Sledge not being able to read and a few people laughed, but the steel on Sledge's face silenced most of the room. Sledge didn't just look angry, he looked like worms were eating away at his gut and he'd soon be shitting snakes.

'Shit,' said Brian. 'This ain't good.'

'What?' Jimbo stared around the room. A dark mood had descended upon the crowd, all heat and blood and dirt. The last of the laughter dried up and Jimbo was left with a slick of reflux at the back of his throat. 'What dya mean, Bri?'

Sledge cleared his throat with a hack of phlegm. 'Okay, this ain't easy to say. Things ain't too good at the moment, what with the drought kicking on, and fruit production in the orchards this year has hit an all time low. We've all seen the roos coming in too, taking what the drought hasn't. It's been a tough year, folks, and I'm sorry to say it's gunna get even tougher.'

Ugly murmurs trembled through the crowd. 'Ya just cut the fucken shifts a couple a weeks ago, Sledge!'

'Our jobs are sposed to be safe, ya cunts.'

'Ya can't cut any more or the machines won't run.'

'Unfortunately,' said Sledge, 'the machines won't be running. Not full time anyway. We're shutting down another third of the plant, and only running what's left at half-capacity. We don't have the fruit, people.'

People started yelling. Brian punched Jimbo lightly in the arm. 'Ten bucks says it's me who loses out here.'

Jimbo tried to laugh. 'Yeah, sure, yer on.'

'People! People!' Sledge waved the piece of paper above his head. 'This here is a list of names. If your name is read out, report to the paymaster. You will be paid out a week's pay in advance and any owing. When the drought breaks or the fruit comes back, your names are first up for hiring. We do want you back, never forget that. This factory built this town, and this town built this factory. We are one, people, one!'

That sounded like patriotic bullshit to Jimbo, but when Sledge read out his own name first, it stunned him and the crowd into submission. *Sledge sacked too?*

A third of the staff went home that day with extra cash in their pocket and an indefinite holiday. Jimbo spent Brian's ten bucks on homemade whisky at Sledge's place, let the anger simmer and brew, slurred to Sledge what a good cunt he was taking a fall with workers, thought about going home to fuck his wife and tell her the bad news, and instead woke up with the sun beating down on his face in Sledge's backyard as the day cranked its furnace and roared into the deep blue sky. Sledge lay passed out on a threadbare sofa up against the fence in the shade. His collie, Sue, lifted her head from Sledge's lap, appraising Jimbo for a second before returning to her slumber. Flies buzzed at the mucus crusting Sledge's chin and his head twitched, then fell still. There were some fights that fists and knives could never hope to win.

The night was cool enough not to warrant the fan humming in the bedroom, and Jimbo took advantage of the still air to light several candles he had placed there.

Kylie lay on the bed naked except for a g-string, her back to him. He admired the length of her thighs, the colour soft in the candlelight, as he greased his cock.

'I know what ya want, Kylie,' he whispered.

She said nothing, and better, she wasn't sobbing or crying. Jimbo wiped the Vaseline off his hands onto the sheet and knelt on the bed next to her. He reached out and stroked the curve of her hip, where the bone jutted out and curved softly over firm flesh, until his fingers circled the hollow where her bum met her thighs. Even better, she didn't shudder or tremble under his touch, though Jimbo didn't mind the trembling.

'I know how to make it better.'

He pulled her thigh over towards him, forcing her gently onto her back. He slipped his fingers inside the front of her g-string, pushing through the short hair and working his finger into the dry groove beneath. She said nothing, her eyes staring at the ceiling, avoiding his face. He pulled her g-string off, slowly at first, sliding it down her thighs, but when she didn't help him he dragged it down, tearing it past her ankles and tossing the garment onto the floor behind him.

'It's what every woman wants. You want it. I know ya do.'

Jimbo spat on his fingers and rubbed them around her snatch, becoming impatient. He thrust a finger inside her, and she tensed, a small whine locked in the pit of her throat. He kept shoving his fingers until her muscles relaxed, and her breathing resumed normally, searching for the signs that might precede her fainting — the hitched breathing, the bulging of the eyes before they rolled white — and Jimbo was getting better at this all the time. And when he judged she was good and ready…

'We're gunna have a baby.'

…he drove his cock awkwardly inside her, struggling to get in, but he pushed as he always did and she would yield as she always would but this time, oh, this time —

Kylie screamed and bucked, taking Jimbo unawares. *Shit, she hasn't screamed for weeks, what the fuck?* Jimbo fell awkwardly, clutching the edge of the bed. Kylie lashed out with her foot, catching Jimbo under the rib cage and sending him sprawling to the floor. Pain flared, but it was dwarfed by the anger and humiliation he felt. *How dare she? How dare she fucken raise a hand against me?* He clambered to his feet, as she launched herself screaming at his face, her hands clawed and tearing at the air. One swiped his cheek, deep, and blood splashed against his shoulder. He caught her other hand with his, and began to crush her wrist, then he kneed her in the stomach to bring her down.

Kylie collapsed with a *whoosh*. Jimbo dragged her up by the hair and threw her to the bed. She tried to sob, but couldn't inhale properly. He pushed her down onto the mattress, mashing her nose and lips with his palm. Using his knees, he repositioned himself between her thighs.

'Don't you fucken hit me, bitch!' He slapped her face. Blood sprayed from her lips.

'No, Jimmy, no,' she managed to stammer, before he brought his hand across her face again.

'And don't you ever fucken say no to me!'

'You don't understand, you don't unn unner unn —' Pink froth leaked at the edges of her mouth. The eyes bulged, her back arched and she spasmed.

Jimbo shoved his cock inside her and rode the waves of her fit. As she passed out he came, then rolled off and went to sleep.

The following morning, from the privacy of the kitchen window, Jimbo watched his wife and his mother out on the beaten dirt Mum liked to call a garden. Kylie sank to her knees, her face covered by her hands. Mel knelt quickly beside her, wrapping her arms around Kylie's trembling shoulders, her mouth working at soothing sounds.

Anger bubbled like acid inside Jimbo's gut, the

rage not quite succeeding to mask the inevitable feeling of wrongness that was trying to work its way out of his subconscious into his waking mind.

He couldn't make out her words, simply a torrent of broken sobs punctuated by guttural noises. Her trembling turned to shuddering, and Kylie fell backwards onto the patchwork grass, her flailing limbs churning the dust into a thin brown cloud that rose up around them like a veil.

Jimbo unclenched his fists and looked away. *Ten fucken grand. And what have I got? Damaged goods. The bitch is an epileptic. Damaged fucken goods!*

He rummaged in the vegetable bin in the fridge, pulled out a beer and popped the top. Jimbo swallowed a mouthful of cool froth and stared around the room, wondering what he was going to do. No job, no money, and when the boys found out he'd been sidled with a dud, he'd be laughed out of town. It was bad enough he hadn't cut her when he should have, he was already copping shit for that.

The wooden box on the mantelpiece drew his eyes. And soon his fingers followed, rubbing the smooth surface of the box, unadorned teak, over one hundred years old. From father to son.

I wanted you to be special, not like the others, not like those hobbled, meek fucken cows the rest of them end up with.

He lifted his fingers from the box, briefly picking at the scabs on his cheek.

I wanted you to be like… to be… and the subconscious broke through and swamped him… *Niki.*

Jimbo stood there unable to breathe, staring at his father's wooden box — his wooden box, his heirloom — and knew that he'd been fucked, that he was fucked, that Niki was gone for good, and he'd spend the rest of his life saddled with this broken bitch he'd wasted his father's miserable inheritance on.

Jimbo spent the day perched on the crumbling banks of Broken River, polishing off a bottle of Cranky's homestyle whisky while admiring the thick stagnant pools of mud that not so long ago were at least waterholes. Most of the tributaries into the Goulburn River were drying up quicker than cum on a whore's chin.

Used to be able to get yellow-belly and carp outta here, even cod. What's this world coming to?

He threw the empty bottle down into the mud, then splashed it with some yellow dehydrating piss, clambered onto his bike and pedalled away from town.

Maybe go up to the North-South Pipe, smash some more fucken holes in it. City cunts. Stealing our water, stealing our lives, stealing our fucken women.

A whisky haze had settled in, and a slow sweat dripped into Jimbo's eyes while thoughts of Brian and his fat pregnant cow whore Belle whirled around in his head; of frothing, twitching Kylie; and Mel, his mother, retreating from him, hiding away in her own house; Brian, fucken Brian and that card, that number to ring; of Dave and his Abo fucken ways; Wazza's truck; Keats hooking up with The Cartel; *Brian fucken set me up*; and Niki, oh, Niki…

…then Jimbo discarding the bike in the driveway. Staggering to the front door — *the lights are all off, not that late, why's the* — stumbling inside onto his knees. Dry retching into the threadbare carpet.

Padded footsteps, a sudden rush.

'You don't know anything about me!' Kylie's voice, high-pitched and stretched.

Jimbo lifted his head and half-raised an arm against the cricket bat swinging towards his face. It smashed into his arm, a flare of pain shooting through his nerves, whiting out, *hold on, hold it, don't fucken lose —*

Jimbo sprawled backwards, breath caught in his throat, unable to scream as the pain roared in his arm.

'Babies! Babies!' Kylie held the bat aloft, high over her shoulder. 'You know nothing!'

'Don't ya fucken dare —' Jimbo managed to shout, before the bat crashed down on his head.

Then nothing more…

A flurry of torchlight ahead on the banks of the Goulburn River broke the deepening dusk. The horses slowed, reined in by Dave, who sat on the roof of the ute. Jimbo and Keats sat inside the cab. Keats hadn't said much, and Jimbo knew he was more than angry. Keats's half-breed dogs, part dingo and pit bull, whined and slavered out in the back, their claws skittering over the rusting corrugated tray. The smell of drying mud and rotted vegetation rose from the river with the light breeze that ushered in the night.

'Shit,' Keats hissed between his teeth. 'She's going upriver. You got the knife?'

Jimbo nodded, patted the thin leather scabbard on his belt.

The ute ground to a halt and they leapt from the cab. Several of the boys had turned up — Brian, Sledge, Mason and cousin Rhys — wearing daypacks and with torches strapped to foreheads, scenting blood as much as the dogs Keats was rounding up with the leash.

'Found ya bike up on the side of the river,' said Brian. Torchlight flashed over the nearby ground, settling on the bike frame. The front wheel lay twisted. Brian knelt and sniffed the seat. 'Engine's still warm.'

The boys chuckled.

'Cut the shit.' The dogs strained at the leash, and Keats pulled back hard. 'How long ago?'

'Maybe half an hour. Reckon she's making for the Abo camps. She gets there, she's gone, Jimbo. Ya know how they feel about this sort a thing.'

'If we know where she's headed, then we can cut her off.'

'Already sorted. Brownie's gone ahead to the camp, gunna work his way back down the river.'

Keats shook his head. 'Dave, you get on well with the Abos. Get over there before Brownie fucks it up.'

The dogs snarled and whined, slowly pulling Keats down towards the water.

'Once Jimbo and I are in the water, I want the rest of you to follow. Hang back about fifty metres or so in case we miss her and she tries to double back. Keep ya torches off, so she doesn't twig. Sledge and Mason, you take the left bank. Brian, you and Rhys take the right.'

Jimbo strapped the torch to his forehead and turned it on. 'You not wearing one, Keats?'

Keats laughed. 'Nah, this should be fun. Haven't had a real good test for ma ultras since I had them put in. Ya got those knickers?'

Jimbo handed Keats a pair of Kylie's knickers, the black laces ones she liked to wear when they were about to make love. 'The water ain't gunna be a problem?'

'These are my fucken dogs.' Keats rubbed the knickers in the dogs' noses, then unclipped the leashes. The dogs bounded into the shallows, then raced upstream. 'Come on, let's move.'

The water was cool on their ankles as Keats and Jimbo waded in. Soon they were in up to their knees, a thick layer of mud squelching over their feet, making it hard to move quickly. Up ahead, the dogs splashed through the shallows near the left bank, growling and yelping. Jimbo surveyed the river banks as they moved, casting the torchlight over the bushes, looking for clues in the mud. He couldn't make out much. Behind him, the rest of the boys followed, but he couldn't see them either.

'What are ultras, Keats?'

Keats tapped his temple near the corner of his eyes. 'Had it wired up recently. I'm using infrared at the moment.'

'But ya don't have metal eyes.'

'Jesus, Jimbo. The older boys wear them like a badge of honour. Nobody in the last five years has had that done — they're fucken ugly. There's a whole bunch of spectrums I can use. Ultraviolet's good for following blood trails. She wasn't bleeding, was she?'

'I dunno, don't think so.'

'The Cartel's where it's at, Jimbo. I tell ya.'

'The fucken Cartel. How come they got all the good technology? How come the government doesn't invest any of that out here? Just the fucken Cartel. City cunts.'

'The government? Who do ya think keeps the train running? Keeps your phone working? The Cartel *is* the government, mate.'

'Bullshit.'

'They're in charge now, no bullshit. The Cartel are bringing the rural areas back into the fold, building them up again.'

'Using us, Keats, that's all. Taking what they want, taking over the town.'

'Shepp was fucken dying under the last government! Yer standing on the wrong side of the fence now, Jimbo, and the longer ya stand there, the sooner yer gunna find yaself hung out to dry. Just like the Abos were when we were in charge. Ya gotta move with the times, mate, stick with the winners. If ya don't yer gunna be stagnating just like this fucken river.'

They slogged up that stagnating river for the next twenty minutes in silence. What Keats had said nagged at Jimbo, eating away at his inner core, at who he was. *Keats is so fucken sure of himself these days, so fucken confident. And me? What the fuck happened to me? How did this happen?* And it nagged at him, because deep down he feared what Keats said was true. The Cartel weren't coming, they were here, and soon the City, and the things he despised about it, would follow.

'We got some action up ahead!' Keats pointed towards the riverbank, but it was now too dark for Jimbo to see anything and his torchlight faded over the water. 'The dogs are up on the bank. Come on, move it!'

They waded towards the riverbank, sloshing out of the cool dank water towards the thick weed that clung above the waterline. The dogs growled menacingly nearby, though Jimbo still couldn't see them. They clambered up the bank, Keats leading the way, pushing through the low scrub as the ground slowly levelled. Torchlight revealed the crossbreeds pacing the base of a crooked gum tree, their backs bristling. Sharp teeth shone with slaver, the red of their eyes reflected back in the light, casting the animals with demonic demeanour.

'Good boys, good boys.' Keats gathered them, reattached the leash and wound part of the lead around his wrist in an attempt to help restrain them.

Jimbo peered upwards into the branches, but couldn't see her. 'How far up?'

'About halfway. Ya gunna have to go up and get her. Be careful but, she falls she could break her neck.'

'Boys!' Jimbo hollered into the darkness behind them. 'We've got her. Gunna need ya steady hands real quick!'

Within minutes the rest of the crew arrived at the base of the tree. Kylie had ignored Jimbo's attempts at talking her down, so Mason, on his first hunt, volunteered to climb up and get her down. Brian took a leash with a metal cuff from his pack and handed it to Mason.

'We've got thirty metres of lead, should be plenty. When you get to her, clip —'

'I know, I know. Clip it to her ankle.'

'Let us know when yer done it, then give her a push, we'll take the weight.'

Mason scrambled up the base of the trunk, pulling himself up through the lower branches.

'And Mason!' yelled Jimbo. 'Be careful. She kicks hard.'

Sledge and Brian fed the leash through their hands, while Rhys opened his pack and removed the first aid kit. Jimbo unsheathed the knife. He didn't want to do this. Up above, the sounds of a struggle, Kylie yelling and Mason grunting, no doubt a foot lashing out at a head. He really didn't want to do this. The adrenalin surged through his body. A rabble of butterflies hatched in his stomach, making him feel sick.

'You ready?' Keats had tied the dogs to a nearby tree, and then taken up the slack on the leash with the others.

Mason yelled, the boys braced themselves, then Kylie screamed and the leash snapped taut. It took almost five minutes to lower her. Whenever she managed to cling to a branch, Mason was there, a foot ready to stamp her free. By the time they got her to the ground, the butterflies had burst into a flock of sharp-beaked magpies, tearing at his insides. He couldn't look at her. She screamed as the boys pinioned her face-down on the ground. The dogs strained at their leash nearby, barking furiously. His heart hammered in his eardrums like the machinery in the cannery and sweat trickled cold from his armpits down his sides.

Keats held her right leg firm, presenting the ankle, its thick cord of tendon stretched tight. Rhys stuffed a thick, tooth-marked leather cord into Kylie's mouth and told her to bite down. She tried to spit it out and he forced it back in.

'Do it!' Keats snarled, not unlike his dogs.

Jimbo knelt down and carefully, almost gently, took her ankle in his hand. He felt the tension there, the bound energy willing itself but unable to kick. Keats held the leg vice tight. Veins rippled across the surface of his scalp with the exertion.

The knife rested on her tendon, like a bow on a violin, and Jimbo readied himself to play a terrible song. When he cut her, the snap of the tendon cracked like a gunshot through the night, the dogs suddenly whining. Blood sprayed hot and stinging into his eyes. And then Kylie's scream, a howling pitch of despair and pain that rose like a white heat in their ears, and as Jimbo wiped her blood from his face, her body fell slack and silent.

'Let her bleed clean.' Keats released her leg, then clapped Jimbo on the shoulder. 'You did well, mate. That was a good cut.'

A match flared, then the aroma of strong tobacco cut through the stink of the river and the acrid smell of fresh blood. Brian passed over the cigar, and as Jimbo savoured the taste of the first puff, Rhys began to dress the wound.

A mob of eastern grey kangaroos lounged in the shadows Mount Major cast over the flatlands in the early afternoon sun. Even though winter was drawing to an end, enough heat remained in the day to draw a light sweat to the surface of the skin. The air hung still and resonated with cicadas buzzing in the scrub while kookaburras cackled hidden in the eucalypts that clung to this side of the hill that called itself a mountain. Cockatoos fought noisily in the tree Jimbo and Brian had taken shelter beneath, the boys enjoying both the shade and the noisy cover the birds provided while they scoped out the mob below.

'There's maybe two hundred of them down there.' Brian, his stomach to the ground, peered through the scope of his .308 Winchester. 'Some big bucks too.'

Jimbo nodded, rubbing his fingers over the smooth wooden handle of his grandfather's .303. *That scope looks new. Where the fuck is he getting the cash for his toys?*

'We could probably knock off one or two right now.' Brian adjusted his weight, wriggling into a better position. His finger hovered over the trigger. 'What ya reckon?'

'I reckon we wait for Dave and Keats to get back,' said Jimbo, staring into the back of Brian's skull, a damp plastering of black hair. He imagined Belle's fingers running through it, moaning in ecstasy, her belly swollen, almost ready to drop. 'When's she due?'

'Huh?' Brian looked at him quizzically. 'Belle?'

'Yeah.' Jimbo cast his eye out over the mob, avoiding Brian's gaze.

'Couple a weeks.' Brian nuzzled back into his rifle, eye to the scope, making minor adjustments. 'How you an

Kylie going? Been trying for a while now.'

'Yeah. Not so good.'

'She still in a chair or she on crutches now?'

'Almost don't need the crutches,' said Jimbo. Below him, Dave and Keats clambered up the hill after returning the horses to town. The ute had been unhitched and parked down in a copse of splintered eucalypts, an attempt to at least provide a cooler environment for the meat the boys would be storing after each kill. Dave appeared to be labouring, his rifle slung over his shoulder, but Keats bounded upwards, effortlessly, a long thin bag strung across his back. He'd promised the boys a surprise this weekend.

'Belle didn't want to do it after the hobbling, maybe for a month or so. Heh. But she got back into it after that with gusto.' Brian swung his barrel across the plains, eyeing up potential targets. 'Lot of joeys down there. Did ya know the jills are always pregnant until they give birth?'

Jimbo didn't know just how much bullshit Brian was spouting these days. Belle loving to fuck. Falling pregnant just like that. Saving up enough of his own cash to buy a wife. New scope for the rifle. 'Yeah, Kylie can't get enough, wants it all the time.'

Brian laughed. 'Yeah, they fucken love it. Hey. That one there. See him. Ya can tell by the balls on that buck he's the boss. Maybe ya should get tested. I did.'

'What? Nothing fucken wrong with me.'

'Take it easy, man. I'm just saying. There could be problems, not necessarily with you. Maybe ya missus. Ya never know.'

'You went to see that A-rab?'

'Khalid knows his shit, Jimbo. Jizzed into a jar, no problems there. With the boys swimming around in ma balls I mean, little weird beating off in his room, him and Belle watching and that.'

'She should've been beating ya off.'

'Nah, she couldn't. She was lying on this bench, while this plastic circle thing full of computer chips and lights scanned her body up and down. She was looking at me though, and laughing. Turned out there was nothing wrong with her neither — Khalid brought up all these pictures of her internals and explained it all, but it didn't mean too much to us — and, ya know, with both our minds at ease knowing there was no problems, she just fell pregnant easy shortly after that.'

'I dunno. There's nothing fucken wrong with me.'

Brian rested the barrel on his forearm and stared at Jimbo, his eyes squinting, searching for something. 'I never fucken said there was. What's wrong with you, man? Ever since ya dad died and ya got hitched, you've been acting like an uptight cunt. Maybe she's been fucken you up the arse, is that the problem? Ya missus's dick bigger than yours?'

'Fuck you.' Jimbo's fist clenched the stock of his rifle. 'Ya think ya got it all, don't ya, ya cunt? Money, pretty missus, baby, job. Fuck you!'

Cockatoos screeched in the tree above, and several took to wing, a fluttering of circling squawking white feathers.

Brian's face reddened and for a second Jimbo thought it was going to be on, but Brian closed his eyes, and exhaled, his breath hissing out between clenched teeth. 'Jesus fucken Christ, Jimbo. I never said it was you. Yer me mate.' He opened his eyes, stared into Jimbo's, the anger dissipated from his face, gone in the space of a breath. Jimbo wished he could do that, drop the anger in an instant, but he couldn't and it bristled still. 'I was just saying maybe ya should get checked out. Both of yers. The whole a Shepp knows she gets the fits, mate, it's no secret.'

'You sold me a dud, ya cunt. Fucken ripped me off.'

'What? Me? I didn't sell ya nothing.' Brian got to his knees, placing his rifle on the ground. 'I helped ya out. Gave ya a number. Got ya a wife.'

'Yer getting commissions, ain't ya, Brian? You've cut some sort a deal, that's how ya bought Belle, the new horses, got yerself that new scope there. I know how it works. Every bride they sell up here in Shepp, ya get a cut, don't ya?'

'Put the gun down,' said Brian, slowly rising to his feet.

'Ya not denying it?'

'Of course I'm fucken denying it! Just put that gun down.'

'Will you two keep it quiet.' Keats pulled the bag off, lowering it gently onto the dirt. 'You'll scare off that mob. They'll be another k away before we've fired a shot.'

Jimbo glared at Brian, dropped back to his knees, cradling his gun. For all his wired-up ways, Keats hadn't noticed the heat between them. Dave still clambered up, maybe fifty metres away.

Keats, with a widening grin, crouched next to his bag, his thick fingers on the zip. 'Wait'll you boys see what I've got here. Should we wait for Dave? All that black pussy been sucking the white man's life out of him. How fucken unfit is he, these days?'

Jimbo tried to laugh, to shake some of the anger steaming inside his skin. Rage and guns never mixed well, he knew that, but right now he wanted to kill something. And those roos were looking a little too far away.

'Fuck him. Open it up, Keats,' said Brian. 'Show us what ya got.'

Keats removed a slick black automatic assault rifle from the bag. He tossed it lightly in one hand, his grin wider than a slut's fanny.

'Where'd ya get that?'

'The Cartel, boys. They got everything you'll ever need. Got it on loan for the weekend.' Keats tossed the rifle towards Jimbo, who caught it easily and swung the barrel around in an arc, ending up with the muzzle pointed squarely at Brian.

'It's plastic,' said Jimbo.

'Easy to carry,' said Keats. 'Chinese too. Best quality you can get. Hey, here he is!'

Dave wiped a sheen of sweat from his brow, his chest heaving. He took a drag from his water bottle. 'Where'd you get that?'

Jimbo handed him the rifle. 'Keats "loaned" it from The Cartel.'

'Fair dinkum,' said Keats. 'On one condition though. The Cartel gets half the meat.'

'Get fucked!'

Keats laughed, taking the rifle from Dave. 'This thing will mow that mob to pieces. We'll do all right out of the cull. So, are we ready, boys?'

They descended in single file, Dave leading the way, followed by Keats, then Brian. Jimbo watched them, the flies smothering their backs in the slow heat, their legs moving carefully, shuffling slowly down towards the mob below. He hefted the rifle, quickly lining up the barrel and the crosshairs on the back of Brian's head. *Fuck you, Bri. Bang! Yer dead.* Then he headed after them.

On a low ridge, all except Keats took their positions,

lining up prospective bucks lounging in the mob about sixty metres away. Keats crept down to the grasslands below, edging closer to gain maximum impact.

'Don't fucken shoot me,' he'd said, as he left.

They all laughed. Jimbo stared at Brian as they did so, but Brian busied himself with his scope. *Accidents happen all the time out here, mate.*

Jimbo lay flat on his stomach, positioned the .303, sighting the buck he'd chosen, targeting its head. He wasn't the biggest of the mob, but the tail was huge and should make good cooking. The Abos hadn't been wrong about that.

The day fell silent, the parrots in the trees hushed, like an expectant audience as the curtain rises. It seemed, for a second, that even the flies had ceased their incessant buzzing.

'What's the bet?' said Jimbo.

'Twenty dollars each from the losers to the winner, plus an additional dollar for every roo the winner has over whoever comes second,' said Brian.

'Yer on.'

'On the count of three,' whispered Dave. 'One... two... three.'

The shots fired almost simultaneously. The mob leapt in unison, a chaotic mess of marsupials leaping left and right. Jimbo watched his buck leap, blood spraying from the back of its skull and hit the dirt dead.

'Fuck.' Brian quickly followed his first shot with another, but his roo was gone, leaping through the confusion as the mob tried to gather cohesion.

And then a long burst of machine-gun fire as Keats opened up, spraying bullets through flesh, fur and bone. Between sprays, Keats's laughter echoed up off the side of the mountain, a hysterical cackle of mania, before another harsh burst of gunfire tore the mob apart again. Jacks, jills and joeys tumbled broken and bleeding, until Keats stood alone amongst the corpses holding the gun aloft and howling, while the mob bounded off to regroup in the distance.

Dave stood up, eyes wide, removing the cartridge from his rifle. 'This changes things a bit. He just nailed over a dozen of the bastards. At this rate we'll have the ute full before sundown.'

'Whaddya think?' Keats yelled up at them.

The cockatoos roared their applause.

'Takes the sport out of it, I reckon,' said Brian, studying the end of his scope, as if something there was amiss, spoiling his aim.

'Dunno about you boys,' said Jimbo, 'but I need the meat and the money.' He shouldered his rifle and headed down towards Keats. 'And anything killed with that gun doesn't count towards the bet.'

Later, as Jimbo worked his knife through the roo's belly, opening it up and spilling the steaming guts onto the parched earth, Keats approached.

He kicked his leg at the swarm of flies buzzing over the intestines. The flies parted and reformed, as if Keats had never been.

'What's going on, Jimbo?'

'Nothing.' Jimbo didn't look up, his hand working inside the carcass to remove any further offal.

'Really? I'm scared to let ya have a go of this gun, mow down some roos. Looked like ya was gunna murder Brian up there on the ridge. Scared yer try and mow us down instead.'

Jimbo thrust the knife into the side of the roo and

wiped his hands on the fur before standing up to face Keats. 'I'm okay, man.' For a second he thought he would cry, but it passed, and he held himself together.

'No ya not. If there's one thing I'm good at, Jimbo, it's reading people. Part of me job. And what I'm reading right now is definitely not okay.'

'Nothing's wrong. I said I'm okay.'

'Is it work, mate? I can always hook you up with something —'

'I don't want anything to do with the fucken Cartel, Keats, you know that.'

Keats gave him a glance, nodding his head, then turned away. 'Suit yerself. Stay happy in that bucket a misery yer wallowing in, keep rooting that white-eyed, frothy-mouth bitch of yours.'

'You fucken cunt!' Jimbo launched himself at Keats's back, but Keats turned easily on his heels, deflecting the swinging fist and chopping at Jimbo's throat in the same fluid movement.

Jimbo fell amongst the guts, now crawling with flies. It was hot and wet against his forearms, the flies a furry, tickling blanket of legs against his skin. He scrambled out of the blood and muck, unable to breathe properly, his chest heaving. Keats stood above him, unmoving. In Jimbo's peripheral, he saw Dave pulling at Brian's arm, them moving away. Keeping distant.

'Fuck… Keats… ya…' Jimbo managed to gasp, trying to stand, to suck in the hot air, to swallow the thick spit in his mouth.

Keats pulled him to his feet with one hand, the other held back in a fist, ready to pummel Jimbo's face.

'Ya lucky yer ma mate,' said Keats. 'Otherwise I'd beat the fucken shit outta ya right now, knock all ya fucken teeth out and smash ya kneecaps off.' He brought the fist within an inch of Jimbo's nose. Jimbo didn't flinch. 'I'm ya fucken mate, Jimbo, we all are. We wanna help.'

Jimbo said nothing, his throat slowly easing from the punch. Though something else was building in the hollow, something hard and aching.

Keats dropped his fist and let go. His hard-man eyes softened, almost pleading. 'For fuck's sake, mate, let us help ya. Anything ya need, I can get it. Ya know I can, I'm connected big time now. I know ya fucken hate the Cartel, but I'm not them. It's me. Keats, ya old mate Keats. Anything, anything at all.' He pulled the knife from the roo and handed it hilt-first to Jimbo. 'Anything.'

The feeling in Jimbo's throat rose like gorge, an all-encompassing pressure, sore and swollen, ready to burst like blood from the brain. But there was no way in hell he would cry in front of these men. Never.

'Thanks, Keats,' he said quietly, then went back to gutting the roo.

The following evening they headed back to town. Brian and Dave had biked on ahead, while Keats and Jimbo sat on the roof of the ute, the tray laden with meat and hides. They'd bagged almost fifty roos and would have to do a return trip to pick up the rest of the cull. Keats held the reins, the both of them watching the horses' flanks ripple with muscle.

'Having problems getting pregnant,' Jimbo said.

'Most people do. Not many kids around these days, full stop.'

'Most people get one.'

'Used to, Jimbo, not so much anymore.'

'What about Bri? Him and Belle had no problems.'

Keats laughed. 'That's what he likes people to think.'

'Eh?'

'What you see ain't necessarily what's going on, Jimbo. Like that caper the factory pulled with Sledge pretending to get laid off with all you guys when the cunt was just taking some long service leave.'

'Ya saying Brian had help?'

'Fucken oath he did! That's Khalid's baby, just as much as it is their's.'

'What? That A-rab fucked Belle?'

'He's a doctor! Artificial insemination, ya dumb cunt. Just like the farmers do with their livestock.'

'Really?'

'Yeah, and if that don't work, there's other ways.'

'Whaddya mean?'

'You wanna baby? I can get ya one. Same sort a deal as getting a wife.'

They sat in silence for the next few minutes, the only sounds the steady clopping of hooves and the grind of wheels on the road.

'That hasn't worked out so good for me,' said Jimbo. 'And I don't have the cash.'

'Depends what ya want. Arrangements can be made. This ain't Brian yer dealing with. The Cartel is looking at establishing itself in the rural areas. It's looking for blokes who know the lay of the land to make it work. I'm one of those blokes. You're one of those blokes. Anything you want.'

Jimbo sat there, his head brimming with complicated possibilities he refused to consider. Soon, Keats started yakking about the perks of working in the local whorehouse, and while Jimbo pretended to listen, he thought about making an appointment, about letting his wife out of the house for the first time since he'd cut her tendon, about getting his — *their* — life back on track.

Part VI: Recessional

Khalid had given Jimbo a specimen jar to fill and sent him out to the toilets with a couple of beaten up and beaten over magazines. Jimbo didn't like leaving Kylie alone in the room with the A-rab, not that he worried about him doing anything, more that he didn't know what was going on, what was being said. He didn't need her spilling her guts to the doctor and then having him spread it through the A-rab community. But what could he do? Nothing. And anyway, Kylie usually frothed up and lost it whenever the personal questions came out. After a year of marriage he still knew nothing about her past, and quite frankly, Jimbo didn't give a fuck. He flicked through the magazine until he found a non-Asian lesbian spread, and then began to work his cock for the next half hour.

When he came back into the room, Kylie lay on the bench underneath a sheet; the plastic ring that encircled the bench hummed and sparkled down near her feet, then switched off. It looked like Kylie had passed out. Several holographic overlays of her body hung suspended in the air against a white wall. Khalid moved a sensing-pen over a tablet near his computer, shifting and sorting the overlays. Screeds of data and chemical compounds flitted next to the schematics. Jimbo's jaw dropped.

'Where'd ya get this stuff? It's like in the movies.'

Khalid indicated for the nurse to take Jimbo's specimen and continued examining the data. 'Standard *stuff*, Mr White. In fact, it's close to obsolete which is why the government allowed me to use it here.'

He motioned for Jimbo to take a seat. Kylie groaned

on the bench, her legs twitching momentarily, before falling still again.

'From what I understand,' said Khalid, 'Kylie was not a willing participant in your marriage.'

Jimbo bristled. *Fucken A-rab cunt! Who the hell does he think he is?* He tried to keep it from his voice. 'I paid for her, fair and square. It's the way we do things around here. You A-rabs do the same thing.'

'It's not quite the same, we have family consent. Your customs are a little more, how shall we say, extreme than ours.'

'What are you saying, doc?' Jimbo felt the anger rising in his throat and fought to contain it. He consciously unclenched his fists.

'Look, Mr White, I don't care either way, I'm not judging you, just trying to establish the facts. I don't think you're going to like what I've found here.'

The blood drained from Jimbo's face, though at the same time a piece of him rejoiced. *It's not me, it's her.* 'Yeah, well, you know then, don't you. Bought and paid for. City job, Cartel approved and all that. So what the fuck have you found?'

Khalid brought an overlay to the fore, a detailed internal scan of Kylie's skull. 'This, for one.' He zoomed in an area and highlighted it. A small rectangle, tiny, no bigger than the nail on Jimbo's little finger.

'She's been wired.' Jimbo's voice sounded too high in his own ears, the voice of a child alone at a birthday party, excluded from the games.

'Certain organisations use them to facilitate communication, enhance certain skillsets, you probab —'

'The Cartel.'

'Not just the Cartel. They can also be used to suppress

or supplant memories in their hosts. Bio and wetware tech is taught in high schools in the City, Mr White. Kids can play with it on their pets. And someone has done an even worse job on your wife than an eight-year-old child on their favourite kitten.'

Jimbo sat stunned. A bubble of white froth dissolved slowly in the corner of Kylie's mouth. 'She's not an epileptic.'

'Not at all.' Khalid added another overlay to the schematic, highlighting a tangle of synapses weaving through the lobes in the brain. 'You can clearly see here that the synaptic circuit is thin and branches off to the right. See how it appears to spark then fades, dies out if you like?'

Jimbo couldn't, but nodded.

Khalid continued. 'I recorded this activity when I asked her about her past. She couldn't answer me and went into a seizure.'

'Yeah.' Jimbo suddenly knew where this was going. 'It's a kill-switch. That chip is causing all this shit to happen. That's why she can't have babies. You could take the chip out, then you —'

Khalid shook his head, his face grim. 'That's not why.' The head schematics were replaced by an overlay of Kylie's reproductive organs. 'She has no ovaries. No fallopian tubes. Kylie has female genitalia, she has what *you* might call a "fuck-hole", Mr White, but not much more.'

'How… how can…'

'I also performed DNA testing and blood analysis. This is where it gets disturbing.' He indicated the screeds of data and formulae. 'Are you ready for this, Mr White?'

Jimbo felt sick. He glanced at Kylie again, prone on the bench. 'She's not gunna die, is she?'

'No, but she probably wants to.' Khalid indicated a rash of numbers. 'Two distinct sets of DNA were found.'

'What? That can't happen, can it?'

'Organ transplants, Mr White. Kylie's genitals have a different set of DNA to the rest of her body. What there is of her reproductive system is not her own.'

Bile rose in Jimbo's throat. His head felt light, held on by a string, ready to float away and pop.

'Blood analysis shows the presence of rejection drugs to verify this. I don't suppose you're giving her these, Mr White? No? I didn't think so. I suspect we'll find slow-release isotopes somewhere in her body administering the drug. Are you okay?'

Jimbo tried to nod. Kylie groaned again, her eyes fluttering. Soon she'd wake. 'I'm fine,' he croaked. The bile had risen to the base of his throat, hot and acidic. A thin sheen of sweat had broken on his forehead.

'But that's not all the blood shows.' Khalid kept his face solemn, but his eyes shone. 'Traces of testosterone blockers were also found, and large doses of the estrone form of estrogen. Do you know what estrone does, Mr White? No? It slows the growth of body hair, softens skin, tends to make one feel more gentle, graceful. Even feminine.'

'Yer fucken lying...'

Sobs came from the bench where Kylie lay, awake now and listening. Tears pooled in her eyes, ready to drop.

Another head schematic appeared, focusing on the throat. 'There is considerable scar tissue around the larynx.' Highlights flared on the hologram. 'You can see it here and here, but the work is surprisingly neat. Unlike the wiring of the brain.'

'Yer fucken lying, A-rab...' Jimbo swallowed hard on

the bile.

'There are other anatomical tests I can perform if you need further proof, Mr White. Due to poor selective breeding decisions over the last century, women are in rather short supply and the demand is great. I suspect we might find it interesting to test the age of Kylie's genitals. I'm quite sure it will be much, much older than you and I would expect in a *woman* of Kylie's age.'

'I'll fucken kill ya for this.' Jimbo tried to rise but his legs felt like jelly and, like everything else, betrayed him. Instead, he threw up into his lap and began to cry.

'Help me,' Kylie managed to gasp. 'Please.'

'What impact does the bias towards having *only* male children in a one-child society have on this world, Mr White? Inshallah, my friend, inshallah.' A white towel landed in Jimbo's lap. 'Now clean yourself up. Act like a man. I need to help your wife.'

Dark clouds rolled in from the west to fill the sky and the temperature dropped to below twenty. The town felt the water in the air, desperate to escape and pour down on the earth below. Wooden buildings ached, their joints on the verge of swelling, timber groaning in anticipation of the storm. The air, shall we say, was pregnant with possibility, and Jimbo, not usually one for omens, decided the rain gods were in his favour.

There would be no better time to take his wife through the plan for the coming months, and if the prospect of rain did not alleviate the pain in the heart of his household, then he was doomed.

At first, his mother took it worse than Kylie did. Mel stood there, her face drawn and aghast, staring at the five different sized cushions laid out on the kitchen table. Next to each cushion, a sign labelled with a number and a month name. Kylie sat there, resting her ankle, a nonplussed look plastered over her face. Her fingers roamed incessantly over the thin line of scab gracing the side of her skull where the chip had been removed.

'James. No.' Mel's voice sounded like dust working through a cracked windpipe. She shook her head slowly from side to side. 'This is not the way, not at all.'

'It's the only way, Mum.'

She stared at him with hollowed out eyes. Time had fallen hard on her since the Old Man had died. She looked ancient, a crone. 'You have to stop this, James. Can't you see what this is doing to you? To us?' Her bone-thin arms trembled, a long wavering stick of a finger pointing towards his face.

'This is what we are going to do. No-one will know.'

'Where is my son?' Spittle flew from her mouth, spattering his face. 'What have you done with my son?'

And then Kylie recognised the significance of the cushions, the progression of the months, the pregnancy. She leapt from the seat, screaming, flailing with her arms to knock the cushions away. Her hobbled ankle buckled and she fell awkwardly, clawing at the table for support. The table upended, spilling the cushions across the peeling linoleum floor and still Kylie screamed.

'Shut up!' Jimbo pushed the table away.

Kylie dragged herself onto all fours, her head held low, hair hanging loose and bedraggled. She began to keen, a broken high-pitched sound like a piece of machinery about to burn itself out. She — it — repulsed him. Whenever he looked at her he wanted to tear her apart. *Ten fucken grand!* He needed to kill that horrible sound, put the boot in.

'Get away from her, James!' Mel grabbed him by

the arm, pulling him off balance. 'You've done enough damage.'

Jimbo backhanded her, hard across the face. Mel's head rocked back, a whoosh of dead air expulsed from her lungs.

'You get out of this house now.' Mel's voice was stone. Her eyes watered. A red welt rose over her cheek.

Kylie crawled from the kitchen into the lounge, the keening hitching on and off in her throat. Blood seeped at the bandages wrapped around her ankle.

Jimbo stared down his mother. 'No.' He raised his hand again and Mel backed away.

'Then we're leaving.'

'Ya not fucken going anywhere. Neither of yers. Go into the lounge and shut that freak up. I've got a phone call to make.'

'You can't stop us!'

'The Freak can't even walk, Mum. Whatya gunna do? Carry the fucken thing?'

He righted the table, took the phone from the bench, and pulled up a chair. Mel hissed her exasperation, then followed Kylie into the lounge.

The phone felt heavy in his hand, worse this time round. Everything had gone wrong, but this time, this one time, it might just work out. He began to dial the number Keats had given him, every digit burned into his memory. He'd been able to think of nothing else for the past fortnight, events, circumstances unfolding, hatching in his mind late at night when the night owls prowled.

He was so caught up in his actions he almost didn't hear her until it was too late.

'I couldn't do this before!' Kylie, behind him, her voice hysterical.

Jimbo swivelled in the chair. His father's knife shining in the kitchen light, gripped tight in her hand, arced down, slicing his arm from shoulder to elbow. Blood sprayed across the room. He screamed, the pain shooting white behind his eyes.

She raised the knife high above her head. 'But I can do anything I want now!'

As she brought it down, Jimbo lashed out with his foot, kicking her in the side of the knee with a crunch. Kylie collapsed, the knife striking sparks on the metal rim of the table. She hit the floor, the knife spinning harmlessly from her hand. As she tried to get to her knees, Jimbo kicked her in the stomach, sending her sprawling onto her back. She looked up at him, hate burning in her eyes. He kicked her again and she doubled over, wheezing, unable to breathe.

'That's right, bitch. You can do whatever you want.' He lifted his foot over her bloodied ankle, ready to smash it.

'Get away from her, James, or I'll shoot.' Mel stood in the doorway. She pointed the .303 rifle at his chest. 'Don't think I won't.'

'You wouldn't.' Jimbo stepped away from Kylie, towards his mother. The wrinkles in her face appeared set in concrete, and the look in her eyes gave him doubt.

'You wanna bet, James?' She motioned him away with the barrel, as she tried to get closer to Kylie. 'You okay, hon? Can you get up?'

'Yeah, I wanna bet!' He charged her. Mel swung the barrel towards his head and pulled the trigger. The chamber sounded an empty click. Jimbo hit her in the chest with a footy tackle. They crashed into the wall. Mel dropped the gun, holding her hands up to shield her head as Jimbo brought his fist down into her face. Her jaw cracked and her eyes rolled back into her head as she passed out.

Kylie was trying to crawl from the kitchen, dragging herself through the blood and the cushions. Her breathing was ragged. Jimbo smashed his foot down onto her ankle. Her scream was brief, then she collapsed unconscious.

He stood there for a second, his chest heaving. Blood had soaked his shirt and dripped in a steady stream down his arm, falling from his fingertips to the lino. He picked up the rifle and the knife, and put them next to the phone on the table. Then he wrapped an old tea towel showing a faded giant pineapple around his tricep, pulling it tight to staunch the flow of blood. He picked up the phone and stared at the dial.

Outside a breeze had picked up, shaking the leaves in the trees and rattling the shutters on the windows. The slow rumble of distant thunder broke the relative silence. It was going to rain.

He dialled the number Keats had given him and waited. Kylie was already starting to stir. *She's a tough bitch, I'll give her that. Childbirth can be a killer though.*

The phone answered on the seventh ring. A woman's voice.

'Uh… I… want to adopt a…' Jimbo stammered. That voice, he knew that voice. The world tilted on its axis, sending mountains tumbling towards him.

'Hello? Who is this?' said the woman.

Jimbo sat in silence, watching Kylie roll onto her stomach.

'Hello? I'm going to hang up if —'

'No, I'm here.' He hadn't heard that voice for so long. It had sung to him in his dreams instead. Cities crumbled in his head, landscapes built on teetering dreams suddenly blackened and burned, the ash swept up into hot, confusing winds. And everything became so cold and suddenly clear. 'Niki?'

The phone went quiet, except for the buzz of the line. Then, 'Jimmy? Is this you?'

His chest ached, so tight it felt like the skin would split. Tears spilled from his eyes. 'Niki, Niki. I thought you'd been kidnapped, married off… maybe dead. I thought —'

'Are you okay? What's wrong?'

'There's so much I need to tell you, Niki, so much I need to say.' The barriers were collapsing inside him, the hard-man walls crumbling down. He couldn't stop now, he had to let it out. 'I need to tell you how I feel. I need —'

'Jimmy? My supervisor is taking over this call. Can you hear me? My supervisor —'

'— that I —'

The line clicked and another voice came on, still female, but huskier. 'Hello, my name is Ju. I'll be —'

'— love you.'

'— taking over this call,' Ju continued. 'I believe you're wanting to adopt a baby. With whom am I speaking?'

Jimbo sat there, the phone pressed to his ear, listening to his breath echo in the receiver. His mother slumped against the wall, blood still leaking from her nose. Kylie had managed to make it to the doorway, and was using it to help pull herself through into the lounge. The smell of ozone drifted in through the open window, as another peal of thunder shook the sky.

'It's White. James White. I want to adopt a baby boy.'

After he had made the arrangements, he called Dave and told him they needed a doctor, but to keep Khalid out of it. He grabbed a beer from the fridge, stepped over his mother's prone legs and followed the trail of blood through the lounge to the front door. Kylie couldn't reach the door handle and lay on her stomach sobbing. He opened the door, stepped over her and walked out onto his verandah. Lightning forked the sky over on the horizon and the clouds swum overhead, pushed and harried by the winds. He sat down in the Old Man's recliner, popped the top of the beer and took a swig. Jimbo grimaced, took another gulp, let it cool the burn in his gut. He felt light-headed. He hoped Dave got here soon, maybe he'd lost a little too much blood.

He put his feet up, let his eyes close for a second, just a second, and waited for the rains.

Heart of Stone

Cat Sparks

Jacaranda House Eating Disorders Clinic wasn't difficult to find and neither was the plaque in Rookwood Cemetery behind which the alien's ashes were supposedly interred. It had all been ridiculously easy, as if both the Jacaranda and Rookwood staff had been told to expect she'd be turning up at some point. And perhaps they had. In Jade Stone's line of work, anonymous tip-offs weren't unusual in the least. You started to get a nose for them. A sixth sense about which were gold and which were leading you up the garden path.

Was there an alien's ashes embedded in the wall, or merely the remains of a young anorexic girl? Jade could picture similarities: bug eyes and stick arms. Pallid skin with an unearthly tinge to it. But if anything, Jacaranda House had been a disappointment. A heritage cottage nestled in a pretty garden, its namesake tree dropping purple flowers all over the lawn. No white-walled antiseptic corridors, no rattling metal pill trolleys on linoleum floors. The two patients she'd caught a glimpse of had seemed healthy looking enough, or maybe it was an illusion brought on by the comfort and charm of the cottage's front sitting room. Plush woollen rugs, deep armchairs the colour of claret. A wide wooden windowsill peppered with potted plants and china ornaments. Fresh cut flowers in a vase on the coffee table.

Jacaranda House's program director, Dr Evelyn Chalmer (late forty-something, minimal make-up, crushed linen suit, natural nails) had made her displeasure extremely clear as soon as she realised Jade was sniffing around about the dead girl. Amanda Deacon had been one of Jacaranda's most heart-wrenching failures.

'These are complex psychological disorders,' she explained after tea had been offered and polite chitchat exchanged. 'Eating patterns are developed, then habitually maintained, in an attempt to cope with other problems in their lives. Twenty percent of anorexia nervosa sufferers don't make it,' she added. 'The most fatal of all psychiatric disorders.'

Amanda, apparently, had not been like the other girls.

'No family, no support. I really don't know where the money was coming from. I'm not even sure "sufferer" is the word I should be using.'

When Evelyn Chalmer spoke of the dead girl, her brow wrinkled, adding an illusory ten years to her face. 'Most of these girls hate themselves and their bodies. Amanda was different. She adored every aspect of her illness.'

Jade nodded sympathetically. 'You think she might have been faking it?'

'Hardly — people don't usually fake themselves into a grave. She was excited by the process that was killing her. It was creepy. Horribly disturbing for the other girls. There was nothing we could do to help her. Four years on and I'm still bothered by it all.'

Evelyn got agitated when Jade placed her tea on the tabletop, undrunk, and stood up to leave.

'That's all? You don't want to hear any success stories? The Maudesley Model is working wonders. Several of our girls would be happy to speak with you.'

Jade mumbled her excuses but the director wasn't fooled.

'You're part of the problem, you know. A large part. Genetic factors, personality traits, broad environmental influences — they all play into it, of course they do. But it's media messages that do the real damage. Images of false perfection rammed down gullible young throats. Maybe if you focused on the positives instead of chasing ambulances and headstones.'

As Jade headed for the door, the look Dr Chalmers gave her was severe, like that of a headmistress or a prison warden.

Maybe you'd feel better about your clinic's failure if you'd realised Amanda was from another planet...

It was all too weird and getting weirder by the minute. Jade had collected several pieces of this story but none of them fitted together. Solve this case and you can write yourself a ticket, Mac had told her, right up-front. But what did a cremated alien, an eating disorder clinic, a burnt-out school bus and a Pentecostal cult all have in common?

She'd presumed Mac was fobbing her off with a junk assignment. The paper was still a boys club, no matter what anyone said. You didn't see Brian or Rolley getting landed with extraterrestrials. But that was before she worked out she was being tailed. From one end of Sydney to the other, there it was, a dark sedan with tinted, impenetrable windows. A Comm car for sure but the plates didn't check out. There were no such plates and there was no such vehicle. Not on any official records anyway.

She'd reported the sedan to Mac twice now but he didn't give a shit. Not your problem, sweetheart, he'd said — she hated it when he called her that. Jade was almost thirty now and definitely nobody's sweetheart. Where did people find the time for love these days anyway?

She drove out of the Jacaranda House car park and wound her way through twisting backstreets until she hit an arterial road. There it was, the dark sedan slinking surreptitiously amongst the leafy shadows. Who sat behind the tinted windshield? A caricature: some faceless government man in a suit? A reporter from a rival paper? Surely not. A Federal bean counter, or a rep from the

Coroner's Office? Don't worry about it, Mac had said. Just keep your head and focus on hunting down the story.

All the same, Jade didn't like being followed. This story was weird enough as it was. None of the pieces fitted together. She'd been hoping this one might be her big break but all it had brought her so far was a series of irritating headaches and the sense that she was prying into something that didn't want to be disturbed.

Anorexia could be viewed as a cultural disease, a symptom of the great machine of which tabloid journalism was a big part. The dead girl might have been crazy, but she'd never claimed to be from outer space. That was somebody else's assertion. Jade's next job would be to find out whose.

Rookwood Cemetery hadn't changed much since the last time she'd had occasion to visit it — the death of a former school friend over ten years ago. The gardens seemed larger than they'd been in her memory — 600,000 inhabitants in eternal slumber. Separate denominations even had their own bus stops. Sections of the grounds were supposed to be haunted. What cemetery worth its soil didn't have its fair share of ghosts?

The memorial gardens were well tended. Bright sunshine, a faint waft of roses and pleasant breeze against her skin all conspired to lull her into a false sense of security.

Jade smiled kindly at the people she passed, all groups of twos and threes strolling calmly, arms linked, communing with their loved ones in the privacy of their own minds. She found the plaque she was looking for. *Amanda Deacon* engraved in cursive script. No middle name or initial, just dates and an impersonal platitude stating that she was resting joyfully with angels. Nothing to set it apart from all the other plaques. The slender vase set into the wall beside it was empty, as you'd expect for someone who reputedly had no friends or family. A neat conclusion to a messy death. Tidy, uniform, precise.

'I wouldn't bother exhuming the ashes,' said an unexpected voice.

Jade turned to see a bearded man in an expensive charcoal suit standing a few metres behind her. He lit a cigarette as she was watching.

'Just some homeless person's dust they've stashed in there. Not what you've come looking for. All that evidence has been "disappeared".'

He dragged on his cigarette defiantly, his stance casual, yet at the same time assertive.

'Who the hell are you?'

He smiled. 'Don't you read the literature? I'm one of those men in black. A smoking man, if you like,' he added, tilting both his cigarette and his face in her direction.

'I don't like,' said Jade. 'Smoking in a crematorium memorial garden shows extremely poor taste.'

He shrugged and light flared off his dark sunglasses.

'What I *would* like is to find out who or what she really was,' said Jade.

'The public has a right to know?'

'You bet they do!'

He laughed, then sucked hard on the cigarette. 'No they don't. The public don't give a shit — and they wouldn't know what to do with the information if they got it. They have all the weirdness they'll ever need right here on Earth.'

Jade looked him up and down. A solid man. Most likely tending towards aggression if he was pushed.

'All the same, I'd like to know what happened to that girl. How other elements tie in to the big picture, and why you've been following me.'

The man blew smoke in her direction. 'Forget about the girl, Jade. Forget about all of it. All the evidence is gone. You don't know what you're dealing with.'

'How do you know my name?'

He smirked. 'Oh, come on. Do you really need to ask?'

She paused to consider. 'Yeah, I think maybe I do. Are you one of them?'

'Me? An alien? Hell no,' he laughed. 'I'm a Sagittarius if you really want to know. Aquarius rising. Gets me into all sorts of trouble.'

'People are far smarter than you give them credit for,' Jade said, shifting her weight from one foot to the other. 'Don't go presuming you know what people care about and what they don't.'

'Fame, fortune and how to buy into it — that's all anybody cares about these days. You're batting for the wrong team, Jade Stone. Cover-ups aren't arbitrary. Everything happens for a reason.'

'Is that particularly irritating platitude supposed to be a clue?'

'You've got all the clues you need. Sadly, they aren't going to lead you anywhere.'

She stared at him hard, watching the way the dark weave of his suit seemed to suck up light. 'You're such a stereotype, government man, with your sharp suit and your smoking and your sarcasm. You could just tell me what I want to know — what would be the harm in it? So you're following me. You probably know where I'll end up next. Chuck me a bone, huh? Once I get my story I'll be out of your hair for good.'

He appeared to be considering her words, but she knew full well it was part of the routine. She'd met men like him before. Deterrents at best, decoys at worst — hopefully. He'd tell her what he'd been paid to tell her, then send her off on a wild goose chase. From there it'd be a short step back to covering local council stoushes, dog shows and Saturday morning football.

She eyed the family of well-dressed mourners in the distance, noted the way grief had etched itself upon their bodies. Shoulders drooping, faces downcast. That deceased had been truly loved. Not like this poor soul — whoever they'd cremated and stuffed into the memorial wall.

'Just tell me what the "alien" died of. Was it natural causes? Earthling flu? What harm could there be in knowing how the creature met its death?'

'You want to know what harm? Go home, Jade Stone. You don't want to mess with these people. A nice kid like you with your whole life ahead.'

'Don't patronise me,' she said. 'Just what sort of idiot do you take me for? Aliens. Creatures from beyond the stars. You might have fooled my editor but I'm not so easily convinced. If aliens are so keen to meet us, why don't they land on the lawn out front of Parliament House?'

'That what you'd do, is it? Park your flying saucer on the grass?'

'Yeah,' she said, arms folding across her chest. 'Maybe I would.'

He stared at her through an insipid veil of smoke.

'Ever asked the question? Whether or not we're alone in the universe?'

'Can't say it's been weighing heavily on my mind.'

'The most important question of them all, Jade Stone,

if you do stop to think about it just a little.' A sudden burst of intensity seized him. 'What if we are alone? How's that for a terrifying thought. One tiny planet brimming with life, a good whack of it hurtling down the road to extinction. What price do you put on life when there's nothing and no-one else out there?'

He gestured upwards when he said 'out there'. She listened to the pleasant modulations of his voice, waiting for the punch line. The fragment of information that, once delivered, would send her on her way.

'And if we're not alone, eh? What if they come visit? They will, inevitably, be a superior power — the fact of them getting here at all will tell us that. What's to become of us? Our religions? Our gods? The ones our ancestors handcrafted so lovingly in the image of themselves?'

He nodded at the grieving family in the distance. 'Trust me. Those people don't want to know about it either way.'

Jade was getting bored. 'So that's your job then, is it? Keeping the truth from them?'

'No. That's your job,' he said, stabbing the air with his cigarette. 'You're the journalist.' He dropped the butt and crushed it under his heel. 'The plaque, Jade. Who paid for the plaque? That's all the clue you're getting.' He headed off down the cement path that would take him past the family of mourners, past the roses and out into the spacious car park. He turned suddenly, pulling his phone from his pocket, flipping the cover and beginning to text.

'My number,' he shouted. 'Just in case you need me.'

'I don't need you,' said Jade, a sour taste developing in her mouth.

He shrugged. 'You never know,' he said, then turned his back on her and walked away.

'What's your name?' she called after him.

He shot an arm up in the air and waved. It had been a pointless question. Any answer he might have given would be a lie. But when she checked her phone she found a message waiting:

They're using you, Jade Stone. Get out while you can. Sagittarius.

They're using me? But who might they be?

Jade watched his back until he vanished, melding in with all the other suits milling morosely around in the car park. She considered trying to tail him but knew there'd be little point to the exercise. To the plaque, then, and whatever information it offered; hopefully a lead to the trail that had brought her to Amanda's final resting place.

She skirted around another mournful-looking family, this one dragging two snot-nosed children in tow. Jade gave them a wide berth, imagining the cheery daylight infused with germs.

She found the office and went indoors to attempt to ingratiate herself with the receptionist, a woman whose prematurely grey hair and unfortunate choice of cardigan made her look much older than she probably was.

'It's all online, you know,' she said in a disapproving tone when Jade enquired about Amanda Deacon's records — details of the service, funeral homes and the like. 'Not a lot of secrets here, despite what people might expect.'

Jade surveyed the office's sombre décor. An enthusiastic rubber plant dominated the corner diagonal to the desk. 'How certain are you about the ashes?'

The receptionist frowned at the question so Jade rephrased it.

'Can you be sure those ashes are really hers? Or any of them,' she added, gesturing expansively at the section of memorial garden that could be glimpsed through the reception area's glass doors. 'How do you know the ashes correspond with the names on the plaques?'

The furrows on the receptionist's brow deepened. Jade was certain the woman was going to express annoyance at such a ridiculous question, but instead she removed her glasses and rubbed her tired eyes.

'Sometimes there's not much left to cremate,' she said, in a voice betraying decades of weariness. 'Terrible accidents happen, you know, especially on the roads. But we don't test for DNA, if that's what you mean. Not as a matter of course.'

Jade scrabbled in her handbag for her press card. Sometimes it impressed people into cooperation, sometimes it had the opposite effect.

The receptionist didn't seem too impressed. 'What was the name of the deceased?' she asked begrudgingly.

'Amanda Deacon.'

She sat back down behind her screen and punched a sequence of keys, not yet decided as to how useful she was prepared to be. Jade could determine this from her body language, so she kept still and quiet to give the woman space to think.

'Not much in here, to tell you the truth,' she offered after tapping away for a couple of minutes. 'Not even a next of kin.'

'Does it say who ordered the plaque? Who paid for it?'

The receptionist leaned back in her seat, her eyes still on the screen.

'She died young,' said Jade, sensing the woman's helpfulness begin to wane. 'Of anorexia nervosa. I'm doing a story on the disease. It kills twenty percent of its sufferers, you know. Girls can get it as young as seven.'

The older woman looked up from her screen, eyeing Jade suspiciously. 'I'm surprised you don't know the answer already. Says in here it was one of your lot who paid for that plaque.'

'One of my what?'

'The television people. You're all interconnected, aren't you? Papers and TV?'

'Is there a contact name listed?'

'No, but hello, this is interesting. The cheque didn't come from head office like you'd expect.' She leaned in closer to the screen, adjusting her glasses. 'The address on the form belongs to a caravan park, of all things! That can hardly be right.'

She looked up at Jade again, as if waiting for a confession.

'Young girls are dying,' said Jade quickly. 'Any help you can give me — anything at all to stop this horrible disease.'

The receptionist stared at Jade for ages, then, in a swift action, tore a strip of paper from her notepad and scribbled down an address she read from the screen.

'Did you know her?' she asked as she passed the paper across the counter.

'Yes,' lied Jade. 'I did. A lovely girl. Really sweet. It was all so tragic.'

'Hope you find what you're looking for,' said the receptionist, but Jade had already turned her back to leave.

To Jade Stone, the words 'caravan park' evoked images of summer holidays in wind-battered seaside towns. Goggles and flippers, little plastic bucket and spade sets, sand in your cossies and pink zinc smudged liberally across your nose. The White Waratah caravan village was not the kind of place you went for holidays. People lived here: economic migrants forced out of the regular suburbs by inflation, domestic violence and other more personal aspects of twenty-first century poverty.

The entrance was obscured by a drive-through charcoal chicken joint. A hideous, hacienda-style bulk sprawled across an expanse of concrete, melding with a pub advertising ten dollar steaks.

The rest of the suburb was a mix of light industrial and Lego townhouses. The chicken shop driveway led through to more concrete, extending a few metres before melting into well worn bitumen. Beyond it, row after row of neat little boxes. Caravans whose wheels had not kissed road for decades, each one sporting an extension reminiscent of an insect carapace.

'Trailer park,' she said out loud as the wheels of her car jolted against the bitumen's lumpy, uneven surface. That was what Americans called these kinds of places. She drove carefully, half expecting bald hillbillies in checked shirts to be slouched upon stairs whittling crude wooden figurines, or balancing double-barrelled shotguns across scabby knees. To her surprise, the White Waratah was an exceedingly tidy place — far more so than her own suburban street. Each vehicle's allotted square of lawn was well maintained; many festooned with thoughtfully selected lawn ornaments and potted plants.

This observation made her smile, and she considered it worth noting. Stereotyping was a common pitfall in her profession. She knew better than to succumb to its seductive allure.

As her car mounted the speed hump and she took a

left at a row of crooked letterboxes, Jade's gut instinct told her she'd come to the right place. The caravan attached to the address the receptionist had given her was in poor repair. Its faded yellow awning hung askew and its surrounding patch of grass had not been mown in some time. This caravan huddled as far away from the others as was possible, as if it intentionally shunned their company.

Jade parked her car at a discreet distance. A blast of cold air hit her as she opened the door. And something else — a vaguely unpleasant smell.

Jade glanced back at the main ring-road, hoping for a glimpse of residents. Even a dog would have added comfort and made the task at hand a little easier to bear. But there was no-one about, despite it being late morning. The only sound was the distant hum of traffic and the tinkling of wind chimes.

Her heart raced as she slung her handbag across her shoulder and quietly shut her car door. She was willing to get a little trailer park mud on her shoes to find the truth.

She felt like she was being watched as she approached the caravan's side door. If this had been a movie, the threadbare scrap of cotton covering the tiny window would have been pulled back an inch at this point, but it was not a movie and the curtain didn't stir. Her high-heeled footsteps muffled by dirt, Jade approached the screen door and knocked.

'Hello? Is anybody there?' she called through the mesh. It was frayed around the edges and ripped in a couple of places. One of the rips was large enough to peer through. It was dark. Not much to see. No lights on. She tried the handle and was surprised to find it turned. Somehow she'd presumed it would be locked.

'Hello?' She paused for a moment before pushing the

flimsy door. It creaked. Jade paused again, expecting at the very least a *Hey, who's there?* or perhaps even a couple of swear words. But no voice called out from the darkness.

Jade crossed the threshold, closing the door behind her as quietly as possible, as if loud noises could be expected to bring trouble down upon her head.

'Hello?' she called.

Jade's heart sank. She'd be trespassing if she didn't turn straight back around now and leave. She stood very still in the caravan's tiny entranceway, with half her face in sunlight, the other half in shadow. What if there was hard evidence inside?

She trod carefully as her eyes adjusted to the cabin's dim interior, pushing aside the remains of a beaded curtain with one hand.

'Took your sweet time about it,' said a gravelly voice.

Jade froze, her eyes searching frantically for the source of it. At first she couldn't see anyone at all. The cabin was filthy, strewn with cigarette cartons and empty bottles. Cups, dirty plates, unopened mail. The air hung thick with a heavy fug: the mixed scent of tobacco, unwashed clothes and garbage.

A sliver of light from a small window in the far wall sliced across the corner of the space. A blend of smoke and dust curled seductively in its beam. Jade followed the smoke downwards to its source, an angular shape wrapped in paisley and tatty lace. The coal tip glowed as the smoker sucked in a lungful, then exhaled.

Jade tried to recall the last time she'd been in a room with someone smoking. She used to smoke herself, yet the stench of the tobacco turned her stomach, more to do with the closeness of the room than the smoke itself.

'Knew you'd find me eventually. Somebody like you

at any rate.'

The paisley moved. Jade did not. She wanted to run, but forced herself to stand her ground. A great huffing and cursing accompanied the movement. The smoker had adjusted herself into a sitting position.

'Got a name then, have you?'

'Jade. Jade Stone.'

'Cute! Very slick. A journalist I presume?'

Jade nodded.

The two women eyed each other cautiously for a few moments. Jade felt overdressed in her grey suit and stupid heels. The woman she had come to see was barely dressed at all.

'They looked pretty much like us, you know — that's the wonder of it. Two arms, two legs. Two big bright eyes staring right into your soul.' She motioned to her own eyes as she spoke.

'They?'

The woman smiled. 'Don't fuck with me, Jade Stone. You've come far enough to find me, you definitely know what you're looking for.'

Jade pressed her lips together as cigarette smoke curled and danced in the single shaft of sunlight.

'Make yourself at home,' the older woman said as she shifted in her seat. 'Teabags in the cupboard. Scotch on the fridge.'

Jade eyed the pile of filthy dishes in the caravan's tiny kitchenette. The visitor's chair was piled high with laundry and magazines. She scooped up an armful of the chair's detritus, dumped it down on the floor, then settled herself into the chair. She placed her recorder on the small coffee table that sat between them.

'I don't think so, sweetheart,' said the woman, 'but if

you wanna write stuff down I won't stop you.'

Jade only paused for a second before sweeping the recorder back into her handbag and rooting around inside it for the spiral-bound notebook she barely ever used.

The woman seemed highly amused by the proceedings. She sipped delicately from a thick-rimmed ceramic mug, which, Jade eventually realised, contained alcohol rather than coffee.

'We found them wandering the Nullarbor,' the woman said, staring not at Jade as she spoke, but at the slim strip of blue sky visible between a gap in the caravan's faded floral curtains. 'Or rather, they found us. The regular thing: flashing lights in the night sky, fuzzy footage on home video and mobile phones — the usual sort of nothing.'

'We?'

'The media. Not me at that stage, although it was all over the internet and tabloids.'

'When did this occur?'

'About five years back I reckon it'd be by now. Maybe six. I'm not so good with dates these days.'

Jade noticed the calendar tacked to the wall behind her lagged two years behind the rest of the world.

'Four of them walked into Alice that day. They all looked exactly the same. Utterly identical. At first.'

'What do you mean "at first"?'

The woman almost smiled, but stopped herself. 'They changed, depending on who they came into contact with. Adapted to their surroundings. In the end, the environment ate them alive.'

She lent forwards, stared at Jade sharply. 'You don't recognise me, do you?'

Jade paused from her note taking as the woman swigged from her cup.

'I guess my environment kinda ate me alive too.' Her stare intensified, as if she wanted to make the most of the moment. 'Helen Aster is my name.'

A flicker of recognition played itself across Jade's face. It was enough.

'A whole load of heartache later, but yeah, it's me alright.'

'The television reporter?'

'Oh, come on, sweetheart, give me credit. I was a whole lot more than just a reporter. I was ACA's star player for five and a half years. A-list — and I used to look just like you.'

Jade shifted uncomfortably in her seat. How could someone lose their beauty so completely? 'So, Ms Aster, what about those lights in the sky?'

Helen Aster took the snub the way it'd been intended. Nobody gave a damn about the past any more. She knew the drill. 'You really are just like me,' she said. 'And don't think you won't end up like me either if you keep going down this road. There are reasons this story was buried, you know. Loads of fucking good reasons.'

Jade pressed the pen's tip hard against the page. 'So what can you tell me?'

'I'm not gonna tell you anything! You can fuck right off outta here, get your chunky blonde arse off my property and find it all out for yourself.'

Jade folded the notebook's cover down and placed it neatly in her lap. 'You were really somebody back in the day. What the hell happened? Off the record, of course.'

Helen reached for the bottle concealed behind the bulk of her tatty recliner. 'Why do you care?'

'Why do you?'

'I don't. Not any more.'

'Then you might as well tell me the story.'

Helen raised an eyebrow at the handbag at Jade's feet. 'You sure that thing's switched off?'

Jade smirked. She reached forward, took the recorder out of the bag and flicked the off switch, holding it out for Helen to see. 'It is now.'

'This is all strictly off record — and you'll thank me for that one day,' Helen said. 'Quote me and I'll sue your pants off. I've still got some contacts.'

'I just want to know what happened, Ms Aster. Tell me about the aliens and I'll get out of your hair.'

For a moment it seemed to Jade that the older woman had changed her mind. That she was about to clam up tight and dive straight back inside her bottle. But she didn't. Instead she lowered the coffee mug into the deep recesses of her lap and stared back out the window as she spoke.

'I was in Alice to cover the Indigenous leaders' summit. I didn't give a flying fuck about lights in the sky. I was fighting with my boyfriend on the phone. Cameraman. Real arsehole — you know the type. I ended up in the Crowne Plaza lobby bar for a drink, trying to cool off, and they were in there too, four of them, just sitting around like they were waiting for something to happen. Which they were, as it turns out.'

'You said they looked like us. What were they wearing?'

Helen shook her head. 'Nothing special.'

'Then how did you know they were aliens?'

'Hold your horses, sweetheart, I'm getting to that bit. I sat down and ordered a scotch. One of them came up to me and, before I knew it, I was telling her everything. About me, about my life. About the fucker who'd just dumped me for a slimmer, less complicated girl.'

'Did you say you were telling *her*?'

'Yes, her. They were all "hers", if that makes a difference.'

'It might.'

'And then — I swear to god — her face changed.' Helen leaned forward in her chair, her forgotten mug tilting in her lap. 'There she was, looking more and more like me every second… And all hell broke loose. Helicopters, SWAT teams, screaming sirens. The works. Guys in biohazard suits whisked them all away. Only something went wrong. SWAT team couldn't hold them. One minute they were locked down, the next minute they're all gone.'

She leaned in closer. 'I saw them leave. All four of them just walked through the fucking wall.'

She leaned back in her seat again, a smug, self-satisfied look upon her face. 'They quarantined the whole damn bar for forty-eight hours. Idiots shouldn't have bothered. I was half pissed. I would never have remembered details — she'd have taken care of that. After quarantine, they spun us some bullshit about toxic contamination, but by then the news was all over town. Crowne Plaza bar overrun with extraterrestrials! Made the front page of the *Alice Springs News* and spread across the Net like a rash, but see, this is the Northern Territory we're talking about here. Like I said, everybody up there sees aliens — even members of parliament. The whole fucking deal blew over, buried and forgotten.'

'Except not by you.'

'Except not by me.'

An unexpected pause engulfed them both. Helen fell back into the depths of her chair and stared morosely at the cup in her lap. 'You wanna know what I did about it?' she said eventually.

'Sure do.'

'I set out to find her. There was no paper trail — and I mean nothing. The whole thing seemed ridiculous, as if it had all never happened, yet I was sure she was out there somewhere.'

'The alien?'

'The alien who'd spent that hour listening to all my stupid problems. The alien who looked like me.'

'Did you find her?'

'Oh yeah.' Helen sipped her tea without tasting it. 'I found her all right. I found out she was dead.'

'Dead? You sure about that? You saw the body?'

'Saw the body and paid for the cremation. Or maybe I talked the station into it. I really can't remember now.'

'Do you know what she died of?'

Helen stared sharply across at Jade, her eyes recovered from the fog of alcoholic haze that had clouded them so heavily not fifteen minutes before. 'She died of me, sweetheart. That alien died of me. And that's as much of the story as you're gonna get. Piss off and leave me alone.'

Jade stood up a little too quickly. Her mind was burning with the words: four of them.

Helen leaned forwards in her chair. 'You sure we haven't met before? You look kinda familiar somehow. What paper did you say you worked for?'

But Jade had already moved on from pathetic old Helen and her stinking caravan. She mumbled a couple of thank yous and saw herself out through the ragged flyscreen door.

'You're just like me!' Helen called out. 'Don't think what's happened to me can't happen to you. It's a freaking jungle out there. Things aren't always what they seem.'

'Might be a jungle but that's no excuse wallowing in

your own filth like an animal,' Jade muttered under her breath as the flyscreen door banged shut behind her.

Jade's editor, Mac, had divulged the clues for this story as if he'd been dealing cards. That's how she thought about her assignment: the hand that she'd been dealt. It hadn't been part of the Monday meeting, nor had he called her into his office and made her wait on the far side of his paper-laden desk till he was finished shouting at someone on the phone.

The executive boardroom was hardly ever used outside of Christmas parties and Melbourne Cup. There wasn't much in there: a cabinet up the far end and a massive shiny-topped table that seemed ludicrously expensive and out of place compared to the rest of the paper's shabby furnishings.

Mac had sat at the head of that table flanked by two other men in dark suits. Mac had been wearing a serious tie. The slim folder he'd slid across the highly polished surface had been marked 'Confidential'.

Jade had made assumptions. Some kind of performance audit or review. The serious tie had nothing to do with her. Mac was under the spotlight. He was acting, playing the part. So she'd done her bit — asked a few questions, nodded at appropriate intervals, left the room without asking the questions she really wanted to ask.

Mac's phone was switched through to voicemail as she tried to call him from the road. She wanted to tell him about Helen Aster but decided not to leave a message. She'd phone him again later after she'd made contact with the next one on Mac's list: the teacher. A rough, jumbled kind of pattern was beginning to emerge from the pack.

A cremated alien, an eating disorder clinic. Next card in the deck was the burnt-out school bus and a teacher called Avra Loukakis. With any luck you'll turn out to be an alien too, Jade thought.

Mac's 'confidential' folder hadn't given her much to go on. A horrific accident leaving a group of school children burnt to death. The deaths had occurred less than a year ago, but Jade couldn't even remember the story. Had that bus been yet another bushfire casualty, individual details engulfed in the all-encompassing tragedy of misfortune and personal loss?

'Call me Avra,' the teacher said. She was a pleasantly rounded woman with a Mediterranean complexion and aquiline nose. Her large dark kohl-rimmed eyes scrutinised every inch of Jade's person, weighing up how far she was to be trusted based on the cut of her clothing and the calibre of her accessories.

Jade thought she'd have to bide her time with this one. Let the teacher set her own pace rather than cross-examining her about the bus fire straight out. But she quickly realised Avra Loukakis desperately needed to unburden herself. She didn't take more than a cursory glance at Jade's credentials — it was departmental suits she was afraid of — and Jade's suit didn't reek of departmental vibe, apparently.

On the phone, Avra Loukakis had claimed details surrounding the bus fire had been hushed up quickly, with everyone ordered to shut their mouths. She'd only agreed to the meeting at all if it took place in a public space. Jade had suggested an underground car park but the teacher wanted the comfort of wide blue sky. They'd settled on Bicentennial Park, a large, harmless-looking stretch of grass down by the water dominated by the grey expanse of the Anzac Bridge.

Small children ran amok while parents supervised from the shady tree line. The two women strolled casually as they talked, each comforted by the illusory safety afforded by the vastness of cheery blue sky above.

'There was this woman snooping round,' Avra began. 'Saw her in the school playground a couple of times and once looking over the fence. We're trained to notice these things. Supposed to make mention of any suspicious activity — potential paedophiles and the like,' Avra continued. 'There was something funny about her. Something cold. But she checked out. I didn't say anything. Didn't seem any point since she was on the departmental payroll. Ms Gelding was her name. Something to do with the special needs kids program.'

'You mean kids in wheelchairs?'

'Kids with disabilities. St Thomas's is fully integrated.'

The teacher's attention wandered for a moment as three small boys fell into a tumbled heap on the grass ahead. They scrambled up again quickly and resumed their light-hearted squabbling over the custody of a soccer ball.

Avra turned to face Jade. 'We've got a real mix at my school. Autistic kids, kids in chairs, hearing impaired. The works.'

'Is that a problem?'

She sucked on her teeth. 'Yeah, but often it's the parents who give me the most grief. None of them want to accept it when their kid turns out to be a real little shit. I'm not just talking about the special needs kids here, the parenting issue goes right across the board.'

Their stroll took them past a climbing frame and bright red deck and slide construction. They stared at the children at their rough-and-tumble play, each dressed in summer colours, most wearing caps or sun hats.

'There was none of this sun-protection stuff back in my day,' said Jade, pointing to the sail of beige tarpaulin stretched taut between poles at each corner.

Avra nodded. 'Sometimes I worry that we overprotect them. It's tough out there. A world of broken dreams and disappointments.' She looked up at Jade, who stood a full head taller than herself. 'You know the thing you're not allowed to say?'

Jade listened closely. 'That who's not allowed to say? You?'

The teacher shook her head. 'I mean that none of us are ever allowed to say, especially not the mothers. You can't say you wish your kid had never been born. You're supposed to love them no matter how much of a burden they turn out to be.'

'You think some of these parents don't love their children?'

Avra's kohl-rimmed eyes shone clearly in the bright sunlight. 'Some of them… truly… I don't think love is ever going to be an option. Some of the head cases. The emotional problems. I don't know. This is stuff I think about all the time. Maybe it's even why I don't have kids of my own. Something goes wrong and there's the rest of your life blown to hell.'

'Are you suggesting someone might deliberately have set fire to a bus containing thirty-six disabled children?' Jade stopped walking, shaded her eyes from the glare.

'I've had days when I felt like doing it myself! Some of the really gross behavioural stuff. I'm not talking a few swear words and a bit of pushing and shoving. Some of these kids get really violent. Sometimes there's an ugly sexual undertone. One of the kids who burnt on that bus — Jason was his name. A big kid for thirteen. Bigger than me. I don't know what his whole problem was, but he had ADHD on the top of it, and he was a nasty piece of work. The other kids were scared of him, as were half the staff. The class would never settle when he was in one of his "moods". I swear I spent more time trying to control Jason than actually teaching that class. His parents didn't give a shit. They'd given up trying. It was only a matter of time before he messed up some other kid — or raped them. What kind of future is out there for a kid like that? But Ms Gelding, she was absolutely captivated by that boy. I swear she smiled the first time she clapped eyes on him. Not a friendly smile either. It was all kinda creepy.'

'Was Ms Gelding the one who booked the bus?'

'Yeah, she was. She'd been with the school for three weeks at that point. Like I said, she checked out. No-one had grounds to be suspicious.'

'Where was she supposed to be taking them?'

'Well, that's the thing. They weren't supposed to be going anywhere. One morning this bus just rocks up and a bunch of special needs kids — Jason included — get hauled out of class and loaded on board. The bus drives off, Ms Gelding smiling in the front seat. Next thing we know, it's a burnt-out husk in an abandoned lot.'

'What about the driver?'

'Nobody remembers what he looked like.'

'And Ms Gelding?'

'Never saw her again. And the paperwork that'd come with her from head office? Gone. All of it, computer records. Everything. It was like she'd never existed, 'cept that thirty-six children are dead. That fire was so hot, there was nothing left behind. Not even bones, just the chassis and a puddle of melted steel. You know how hot it has to be before that happens?'

Jade nodded. 'But the police report —'

'What report might that be? The damn story never even made the news. Something happened to keep it out of the public eye. Not as uncommon an occurrence as you'd think — a lot of the truly heinous DoCS cases never get reported. People would freak at the cruelty. They really would. But this…'

The teacher paused, distracted suddenly by the movement surrounding her, hearing the shrill squeals and boisterous hollers that she'd been unconsciously filtering out as she spoke. Children ensconced in their private worlds. Swaggering boys with untucked shirts, girls whispering behind the backs of their hands. There was even a group skipping rope.

'Of course, no-one wants to be the one to say it, but my job's a helluva lot easier now with Jason gone,' the teacher said. 'Easier on the other kids too.'

'What about the other children?'

The teacher shrugged. She rubbed her arms suddenly as if in response to a chill wind. 'I shouldn't even be having this conversation. Are you after Ms Gelding?' Her eyes darkened. 'Are you an undercover cop?'

'I'm not a cop. Just a journalist like I told you.'

'But you're looking for her, yeah?'

'I won't be the only one looking for Ms Gelding.'

Avra shot a sideways glance at the skipping children, her voice dipping to a low whisper. 'But that's the thing. You are the only one. They told us not to talk — threatened us with disciplinary action. It's almost a year ago now but no-one's come. Only you. We never even talked about it in the staff room. Half of the teachers who were working then have left.'

'How long was Ms Gelding with your school's special needs program before the bus incident?'

'A few weeks, I think. Not very long.'

'Do you know where she was stationed before St Thomas's?'

'Which school? I don't remember. Somewhere in the outback, I think.'

'Near Alice Springs?'

Avra's eyes widened. 'Why, yes, I think you might be right.'

Jade's mind was ticking over. This can't have been the only incident. Ms Gelding was out there somewhere, doing her unfathomable alien thing. There had to be a paper trail — or a trail of corpses, perhaps.

Avra opened her mouth as if she was going to say something else, then abruptly changed her mind.

Sagittarius, or whatever his real name was, was the key. His number was in Jade's phone but she wasn't going to call him. Not yet. Not ever, if she could possibly help it. Whatever answers he might provide would likely come at a hefty price. She knew what she needed — the names of the people who'd been in the Crowne Plaza lobby bar that fateful afternoon with Helen Aster. A random handful, unwittingly imprinting themselves upon extraterrestrials with disastrous consequences, so it seemed.

How much did Mac know about it all? Why wasn't he answering her calls? She perched on the arm of her sofa, bent forwards, towel-drying her hair. As if on cue, the phone rang, the sound startling in the room's silent ambience.

She reached for the phone through a tangle of curls,

disappointed when she saw an unfamiliar number on the screen rather than Mac's.

'I'm not giving you my name,' said a woman's voice. It was deep and sombre. 'Miss Loukakis from up at the school gave me your number. Said you was snooping round asking questions about the bus fire.'

'Avra Loukakis gave you my number? Go on,' said Jade, 'I'm listening.'

'You some sort of investigator?'

'Yeah. Only there doesn't seem to be much left to investigate.'

The phone line filled with silence. Jade could hear the woman breathing, feel her fight the urge to hang up.

'My Lily was put on that bus. I don't care what the others told you. Those kids was murdered in cold blood and whoever was responsible's gotten away with it.'

Jade stopped fussing with her hair. 'What makes you so sure it wasn't an accident?'

'Because there wasn't any reason for that bus to be where it was. Wasn't any reason for my Lily to be on it. There was no notes sent home. No permissions signed for.'

Jade felt her own hand tighten around the phone's plastic casing. 'I agree with you… are you sure you won't give me your name?'

'You can call me Bev if it makes any difference.'

'Thank you, Bev. Did you know the departmental official responsible for taking them — Ms Gelding? Had you ever met her before?'

'Never set eyes on her. Don't reckon she was even a proper teacher. And she never knew a thing about my Lily. No-one who knew Lily could have held a thing against her. She was the sweetest little girl. Kindest little thing on earth. Never hurt a fly.'

'I'm so sorry for your loss, Bev. What I'm trying to do is get to the bottom of this business. Can you think of any reason why Ms Gelding would want to hurt those kids?'

'I loved my daughter.'

Jade could hear the quaver in the woman's voice.

'She couldn't help being born the way she was. Never hurt a fly. Goddamn them, they burnt those little kids to death.'

Jade made consoling noises but the woman was past talking, her grief exploding in a storm of heavy, incoherent sobs. She'd been half wondering if the teacher hadn't put her finger on it. A conspiracy of parents no longer willing to bear the burden of their less than perfect children. The sound of Bev's grief cleared her head of such notions. The method of killing had been too cruel. Only a psychopath could have even contemplated it. The heat had been so intense, the bus's metal chassis had warped. Accelerant had definitely been used. That was not an accidental fire. Jade wanted to whisper the truth of it all down the phone. Tell poor sobbing Bev that in all likelihood something quite inhuman had taken her daughter's life, only she didn't dare. There wasn't anybody she could trust with a story like that, even if she had proof, which, as yet, she hadn't.

A sharp rap on her apartment door brought Jade back into the moment. She excused herself from Bev, hanging up and disentangling from the woman's grief before calling out, 'Who's there?' as loudly as she could. The thick wooden door muffled the response. She put the safety chain on and took a deep breath before opening, suspecting that if there was an extraterrestrial waiting on the other side, it'd be able to force its way in no matter what precautions she tried to take.

But it was three quite ordinary humans who waited in the hallway: two men and a woman. At least, they looked ordinary. What had Helen Aster said — 'They looked pretty much like us, you know...'

'Geoff Chiddit's the name,' said one of them, a broad-shouldered man in a checked shirt. 'We've come about the bus fire.'

'Word travels fast,' Jade replied, unlatching the chain and cautiously ushering all three of them across the threshold.

There was nowhere to sit. Her couch was piled high with papers, the room made even smaller by the bookcases covering every wall. All four of them stood, facing each other uncomfortably in the confined and cluttered space.

'How on Earth did you get hold of my address?' said Jade.

'You're that investigator,' said the other man. It wasn't a question. He eyed the all-encompassing bookshelves, with titles that filled every spare centimetre of space. Detective novels, mostly. Thrillers, murder mysteries, true crime.

'Look, I don't know any more about this thing than you do,' Jade began.

'Oh, we know,' he said. 'We know lots of things. What we don't know is whose side you're on. Whether you're working for the school, the church or some newspaper.'

'The church? What kind of church?'

'Evangelicals.'

'Christians?'

'So they claim.'

A cremated alien, an eating disorder clinic, a burnt out school bus and a Pentecostal cult... Mac clearly knew more than Jade had been told up-front. This thing was getting bigger by the minute. Bigger and more dangerous.

'Some of us were threatened,' said the woman. 'Others have moved away. And we were paid off. Didn't want the money, never asked for it, but it went into our accounts anyways. Makes us look guilty so we can't say anything. Not that I've touched a cent of it,' she added, shooting a nervous glance at Geoff Chiddit, the only one of the three who had offered his name.

'You gotta start asking yourself where the money's coming from,' said the other, smaller man.

Money… murder… Sagittarius… Jade's mind was whirring like a clock as the faint stirrings of a headache began to make its presence felt.

The parents continued with details of their grief: the children they'd lost and the harshness with which they'd been treated. Jade made sympathetic faces, but her mind was already elsewhere.

'Which church is St Thomas's school affiliated with?' she asked.

'Not just a church. Heartlands Ministries,' replied the woman.

'But isn't St Thomas's Catholic?'

'Don't see how they call themselves Christians of any kind after this,' said Geoff. 'Nothing Christian about it.'

Jade made promises she knew she'd never keep, then ushered the three of them to the door, her wet hair forgotten, her mind already on other things. Heartlands Ministries meant money, and it put a serious spin on things. Big serious corporate money with big scary lawyers behind it. You didn't go bursting into the Heartlands head office with accusations of aliens and burning buses. Mac should never have given her that folder. She was way out of her league. And yet, maybe this was all part of the plan.

Sending in someone below the radar.

She pulled out her phone and retrieved Sagittarius's text. Her thumb hovered for a moment, then she snapped the phone shut.

The traffic was heavy and uncompromising during the long drive up to Mount Annatt. Jade felt her agitation growing with every sluggish change of lights and impatient tailgater. Something was bothering her but she couldn't quite put her finger on it. Something niggling in the back of her mind. Intuition? A half remembered clue? More likely something she'd completely forgotten. Her short-term memory was pretty scatty these days.

In the three days since her visit to Rookwood, the media had exploded with a rash of UFO reports and sightings. Nothing special, just the usual suspects: hovering lights, the planet Venus, streetlight reflected off a roof, advertising blimps. It was not the reports themselves that piqued her attention but rather the fact that they were being so liberally reported on free-to-air television. Was there nothing else happening in the world? No wars, plane crashes, banking fiascos, natural disasters?

The web was alive as usual with shaky, hand-held footage, most of it captured on mobile phones. Jade had skimmed her way through plasma balls, glowing lamps, model kits and dubious triangular points of light before losing interest. A slow news week was all it was, completely coincidental to her own investigation.

A car horn blared somewhere behind her. The traffic had inched forwards and Jade had been slow to follow suit.

'Arsehole,' she muttered under her breath. A couple of feet's progress — leaning on the horn wasn't going to change anything.

The traffic stalled again, this time for several minutes. She thought about using her Navman to source an alternative route. Her eyelids felt heavy. She hadn't been sleeping well of late. As she gripped the wheel, her mind disassociated itself from the traffic jam, wandered through a haze of partial memory fragments to an unfamiliar place. Mac and the suits. A darkened room with a shiny table-top. Men whose faces she couldn't quite see. Her editor's editor and the boss above that. The one behind perpetually locked doors whom no-one ever even glimpsed. The second figure sitting beside the big man at that over-polished table. Just another man in an expensive suit, faceless — and in that instant, Jade's head nodded forwards, utterly awake. Had there actually been a second man at all? The shock of realisation would have caused her to stop the car if it hadn't been pinned motionless in traffic already. Was there a second man or wasn't there? And then it hit her — did her editor even have an editor? When she tried to picture the two men's faces, all she got was an amalgam of executive caricatures. Balding, gruff, thick-lipped, coffee swigging, perpetually shouting. Who were these people? Where had this random memory come from?

Suddenly, as the traffic surged forward and the car behind her blared its horn aggressively, she became dead certain there had never been any such man, nor his invisible offsider. No darkened executive boardroom with a shiny tabletop.

Her mind contained a memory that was not her own.

As she pressed her foot down on the accelerator, a splitting pain burned inside her skull. So intense, it brought tears to her eyes. She blinked them away and forced herself to watch the traffic. It was moving now, slowly, but definitely moving forwards. When it was flowing at a regular speed, she flipped her mobile cover and found the message from Sagittarius, her thumb once again poised over the redial button. Should she call him? What would she say? Are you for real? Is any of this for real?

An hour past sundown and the Mount Annatt church's enormous parking bay was overflowing with a sea of cars. They'd pulled up onto grassy embankments, double parked across driveways and backed up into alleys.

What exactly was she looking for? Jade hadn't got that one properly figured out yet, but there were some answers to be found in there, she was very sure of that.

A lone figure stood on the embankment, a dumpy form silhouetted against stark floodlights. Other people were in groups of two or more, all making their way towards the church's entrance.

Jade found a spot to park the car. Not quite legal, but she was in a hurry. As she locked it, Bev's voice sounded behind her.

'I'm coming with you.'

She turned to see the dumpy form from the embankment, her features now filled out with available light. Bev looked pretty much like Jade had imagined, her eyes hard and glassy, revealing a mind evidently in sharp focus. Jade took note of the lines on her face, deep-etched furrows around the eyes, the scoring of heartache, far harsher than the ravages of age.

'How did you know I'd be here?'

'Chiddit phoned.'

Of course he did, thought Jade. You people are as thick as thieves. 'Are you sure you want to go in there?'

'I'm coming with you,' Bev repeated, her eyes glinting

sharply in the artificial light.

Jade tucked her keys into her handbag. 'I don't want you to get your hopes up. It's a church, Bev, that's all. There are thousands of people in there. I'm not sure what kind of a connection there is between this place and what happened to your daughter, but even if there is one, there's not much we can do. I'm not a cop. I don't have powers of arrest.'

'I just want a look at them,' said Bev. 'I want to see the ones who killed my daughter.'

It was pointless trying to argue. Bev was on a mission. Nothing was going to stand in her way.

The two of them trod across uneven tufts of lawn that led to the church's expansive pebblecrete driveway.

'I hate these things,' Jade said.

'Churches?'

'Evangelical cults.'

Bev's attention was fixed on the bright lights up ahead and the groups of young people converging on them. 'Doesn't look much like a church,' she said at last as they finally made it to the driveway's firm surface.

Three young girls in hipster jeans and crop tops hurried past. Jade caught a flash of exposed belly buttons complete with navel piercings.

'They look like they're heading for a night out on the town rather than an hour of power.'

Bev eyed the youngsters nervously. Another group passed them, this one boys and girls mixed. They pushed and shoved each other playfully. One of the girls squealed as a boy lunged at her in mock combat. She stepped out of reach, then pretended to slap him back. Bev's face hardened at the sight of the display.

Friendly young people in neatly pressed clothes stood

waiting to welcome them at the door.

'I think we might be the wrong demographic,' said Jade, bracing herself to be turned away. But a smiling man in a pale peach-coloured T-shirt waved them cheerily through.

When Jade looked around for Bev, she found her at a standstill staring upwards at the high vaulted ceiling. 'Come on,' she said, grabbing her jacket and tugging it gently. 'We're blocking the entrance.'

The air was thick and close with the warm, cloying crush of humanity. It was a while before Jade even became aware of the music — and it was not the sort of music she associated with church. This had the feel of a rock concert, not a place of worship, although the similarities between the two events were becoming rapidly apparent. The organisers had definitely tapped into something here. Something raw and powerful.

The auditorium was a sea of exposed flesh; low-cut tops and bare abs. When she looked around for Bev again, she found her standing still once more, red-faced, fairly seething with pent-up anger and resentment. Jade reached out to her but this time Bev pulled away.

'It's not their fault,' Jade shouted above the noise. 'They're just kids. They didn't kill your daughter.'

But Bev couldn't hear her. Tears were running down her cheeks. Jade tried to work out what Bev was looking at but all she could see was an ocean of smiling faces and youthful exuberance. People waving to one another across the expanse. And then, in a sudden flash of insight, she finally understood. All those pretty girls with their healthy waving arms. Bev's daughter had been trapped in a chair. All the love in the world couldn't give her what Bev wanted for her most: a normal life. Something she would gladly have exchanged her own life for. The chance to be a faceless member of a crowd, to lose herself irresponsibly in the freedom of movement.

'Get out of here,' she shouted, grabbing Bev gently by the shoulders. 'Go back to my car — I'll give you the keys.'

But Bev couldn't hear her, so entirely swallowed was she by the ferocity of her grief. She turned her back on Jade and walked away. Jade called out to her but her voice was drowned out by a blaring guitar, which ignited the crowd to screaming and applause.

Jade craned her neck to see the stage. When she looked back, Bev was gone.

Jade felt for her, but now was not the time for heartache. The best way to help Bev would be to find the renegade alien. Because there was one in here somewhere. An alien that had been imprinted upon by a member of this church. She pushed her way down the aisle towards the brightly lit stage, wondering how far she'd get before somebody official noticed she was out of place and tried to stop her.

The man behind the mike looked decidedly human. He was talking Jesus, yet the kids were screaming as though he was a rock star. The Jesus talk went on for several minutes, the charismatic speaker stirring up a faith that needed little encouragement. The electric nature of his voice modulation sent shivers down Jade's spine. Not the good kind of shivers either. These were a mixture of nameless anxieties, stirring up uncertain memories, tapping into feelings she'd been sure were dead and buried long ago.

It was a blessed relief when the speaker relinquished control and handed the stage over to the band. There were at least ten performers on stage, maybe more at the back, she couldn't quite see. They were loud and they were good at their job. Jade could feel the music seeping under her skin, infecting her with its tempo and grinding rhythms. Her first instinct was to try and block it out, but somehow she understood that the songs were paving a pathway to the very place she sought. If there was an alien here, it would be at the heart of this music.

Nobody sat in the plastic seats provided. The audience was clapping and chanting and swaying to a wall of sound so thick and so loud that Jade could almost see it. It was all a million miles from the 'Jesus wants me for a sunbeam' of her primordial childhood. Right here, right now, Jesus was calling out to her with open arms. Jesus wanted to fuck her brains out. The auditorium was drenched in sexual energy, all light and heat and lust. The bassline reverberated through her bones, shivered her knees, rattled her spine. There was something tribal to it. Something ancient. Alluring. She was close enough now to the stage to see the faces of the performers. She'd seen the young male singer before; maybe on television, maybe all lead singers looked like him these days.

Beyond that point, there were no more chairs. Before her lay the mosh pit, a swamp of writhing, swaying and screaming, the stage towering above it like a mighty altar. She could get a better look at the band now. The woman who walked up to the singer and took his mike caught Jade's immediate attention. Her face was wrong. It was utterly perfect. She wasn't just beautiful, she quite literally was an angel, pale and blonde, with cascading ringlets and bright eyes chipped from sapphire. This woman made catwalk models look like dogs. The things she was whispering into the microphone were not words. Not human words, at any rate.

The crowd's lust had reached boiling point. A heartbeat later an orgy had begun. The crowd started expressing their love for Jesus in ways the Son of God had probably not intended.

Strong arms encircled Jade's waist. She heard the back of her jacket rip, felt warm breath stir the tiny invisible hairs on her neck. She smelled heady male musk and she longed for him — whoever he was — but she braced herself against the push of the throng. If she fell, she'd be crushed to death. She knew she had to get out of there. She fumbled for her phone. held it high and snapped off a couple of photos of the angel, then ducked, wriggling her way free of her unseen paramour.

It wasn't just the mosh pit that was overrun with desire. The entire auditorium seemed to be getting down and dirty to the accompaniment of music that had gone so far past being rock and roll that Jade had no idea even how to categorise it. Everyone had lost it. Everyone but her. That fact stopped her in her tracks for a moment, caused her to glance back over her shoulder at the stage.

Up until this point she'd felt utterly invisible in the massive space. Teenagers had looked right through her, a normal enough phenomenon under the circumstances. But the angel was staring at her right now, smiling with sharpened teeth.

Jade fled. She didn't stop running until she reached the back doors and the welcome relief of a line of police officers. Somebody must have phoned 000. Perhaps a lone, concerned Christian upon whom the music had had no effect. She pushed past them, running out into the night, a luxurious blast of fresh air cooling the perspiration on her skin. Blue and red police lights winked on and off, bathing her skin in the illusion of safety. Whatever had taken place in there just now, it was over. The real world had intervened, smothering the sound and shutting it down.

Jade limped across the grass to her car, only then noticing that the heel of her right shoe had snapped off. She carried the broken thing in her hand, wondering what the hell had happened to Bev. Her other hand clutched her mobile tightly, guarding the precious photo of the alien angel with her life.

It was late and Jade was shaken. She closed her apartment blinds so the light, low as it was, didn't leak out and give away the fact that she was in there, staring at her twenty-four inch Imac screen, trying to knock the edge off the shakes with a glass of special-occasions-only brandy.

She'd half expected there to be no photo on her phone, but the image was there: grainy, a little soft in focus, but depicting something unmistakably inhuman — or a good bit of theatrical make-up, at least.

She'd emailed the thing to her computer and had it up on the big screen. The photo was useless, of course. There was no such thing as photographic evidence any more. Nothing that couldn't be faked in Photoshop by a patient and talented amateur.

What about the others? Had there only been four of them in that bar as Helen Aster said? What if the event hadn't been localised at Alice? The more she thought about it, the more she doubted an alien visitation could have been a one-off event confined to an outback Australian city.

One starved herself to death; one torched a busload of disabled children. This one manifested herself as an angel to coerce a crowd into a mass act of fornication rivalling that of Sodom and Gomorrah. That left one more out there somewhere. They could be anywhere at all, yet so far three of them had turned up in Sydney. Coincidence? Somehow she didn't think so.

Jade's arms and legs were bruised, her ankle swollen from the incident with the snapping heel, she supposed. She had no memory of it even happening. She wasn't even certain of the memories she did have. Some of them were clear as day, but whenever she tried to picture those suits in that darkened room, her mind literally deflected the image, as if it were something she wasn't supposed to remember.

Jade clicked around the various newsfeeds. The story about the Heartlands orgy was very slow to break. After twenty minutes of surfing, it finally dawned on her. It wasn't going to break at all.

'You're going to cover it up,' she whispered to the screen. Heartlands Ministries had pots of money. Perhaps the Pentecostal orgy was a regular event. Was it possible to buy that kind of silence? Sure, why not? Money could buy anything.

In a couple of hours, she'd find out for sure. Jade took another great gulp of brandy as she studied the angel's savage features. Beautiful, yet horrific too, and it wasn't just the jagged teeth. There was a cruelty about her that Jade couldn't put her finger on. Too beautiful to behold, as though human eyes weren't built to withstand the sight.

When she sipped again, the image flickered. As Jade downed her glass, the Firefox logo down the bottom of the screen began to bounce. Her browser reopened of its own accord. A second later the YouTube page came up. There was the angel again, but this time in sharp, clear focus. It turned to her and started speaking from the rectangular window, addressing her in real time.

'Why are you hunting us, Jade Stone? What is it you

think you're looking for?'

Its voice was even more wrong than its face: neither female, nor male, nor human in any way. The timbre of it brought on instant nausea, made her feel sick and frightened and utterly alone.

'We're only here to learn,' it said.

It was a trick, of course, a clever trick. It had to be. Someone was messing with her computer, doing their best to mess with her mind as well.

The angel ran the tip of its tongue across the sharp points of its teeth. 'It is hard for us to comprehend the cruelty of your kind,' it said. 'So beautiful, yet so deadly.'

'Our cruelty?'

The angel smiled. 'They want it. It's all they care about.'

Jade felt herself inching backwards away from the screen. 'What about free will? What about choice?'

'Biological imperative — where's the choice in that?'

For the first time in a long time, Jade was lost for words. 'And then there's that small matter of a busload of burning children,' she managed to say at last.

'Broken children,' the angel replied. 'Imprisoned and displayed children. Tortured with lives they were never supposed to lead.'

'I don't know what you're talking about. One of your kind burned them alive.'

'An aesthetic act. They felt no pain.'

'That was never your choice to make!'

There was no point arguing. Jade didn't want to talk about the children or the orgy. She wanted to ask all those other questions: where do you come from? What is your home world like? How the hell did you get here? How are you going to get home? The thing speaking to her out of YouTube wasn't any kind of angel, it was an alien, something Jade had to force herself to keep in mind. Some sort of extraterrestrial scientist, or explorer or artist or vandal, perhaps; the important thing to remember was that it wasn't holy. It was deadly. It could do whatever it wanted.

The image flickered and then vanished, crashing the browser in its wake. Jade hurried to log back on. She went straight to YouTube and typed 'Heartlands' into the search engine. A bunch of stills from video clips came up. The top one was fuzzy, but it seemed to show a female face close up. She clicked on it. The new page took a second or two to load. When it did, Jade reeled back in horror. She was staring at her own face. There was no mistaking it, although the long blonde ringlets and sapphire eyes were never hers. The camera pulled back suddenly and she watched herself strut confidently across a stage as thousands of fans screamed out her name.

'This is sick,' she said to the screen, standing up and grasping for her phone. She wanted to close the browser down but she couldn't tear her eyes away. She knew once she shut the thing off, it would be gone forever, leaving no pixel trail. The alien was messing with her mind. No-one would ever believe any of this.

She pulled up Sagittarius's number but something made her pause before she punched it. If they could manipulate YouTube, listening in on her mobile calls would hardly present any difficulty.

She drained the last of her brandy in one gulp, grabbed her jacket from the back of a chair and yanked the computer cable from the wall, all three things in one single fluid motion. She needed time to think and somewhere to feel safe. Somewhere past the reach of electronic surveillance, if any such place actually existed in a city like Sydney any more.

'I knew you'd call. Eventually,' he said, the familiarity of his voice flooding Jade's senses with relief even though logic reminded her that Sagittarius was, in actual fact, a total stranger with affiliations and connections she had no part of.

'Of course you did,' she said, struggling to keep the terror from her own voice. 'Who the hell else would ever believe any of this?'

'Where are you?'

'In a public phone booth. They're not so easy to find any more. Neither are hotel rooms without televisions or phones. Not that it makes much difference. I'll bet they're bugging your phone.'

'I doubt it.'

'You wouldn't say that if you'd seen what I've just seen. That alien I'm chasing — it has my freaking face! Is there somewhere we can meet? I need to see you. I've been up all night. This thing is getting way out of my league.'

Sagittarius didn't seem to have a comeback to that one. Jade concentrated on the phone line's ambient signal, wondering who or what else might be listening in on their conversation.

'This line is secure,' he said eventually. 'I'd know about it if it wasn't — trust me on that.'

Jade swallowed dryly. 'Thing is,' she said, 'I'm really scared.'

'We know,' he said calmly.

'Oh, you do? Glad to hear it,' she snapped, feeling an invisible weight begin to slough itself from her shoulders. 'Because there's a whole bunch of other stuff I'm hoping you know about too. A few days ago my editor hands me this list of seemingly unconnected events. He's rabbiting on about aliens. At first I think he's pulling some kind of joke. Well, get this: I feel like that alien's watching my every move. I'm too scared to turn on the TV or touch my fucking phone. She's in the signal, Mr Sagittarius. She's in the goddamn code!'

'Pitt Street Mall in the CBD. Do you know it?'

'Yes,' snapped Jade. 'Of course I know it.'

'Good. Meet me there tomorrow morning at eleven. On the bench near the donut shop. I need to make some calls.'

'Sagittarius — or whatever your name really is — I don't even know who I'm really working for. There's an image in my head that I can't make clear. Guys in suits sitting around a shiny table. You work for the government, yeah?'

'I work for *a* government.'

'Can I trust you?'

'Maybe.'

She sighed heavily. 'I guess that'll have to do.'

'Eleven o'clock, Jade. You can tell me the rest of your story then.'

'You don't believe me, do you?'

'Every word. I had been hoping it wouldn't come to this. You seem like a nice girl even if you are a journalist.'

'You can't trust your phone,' she said. 'You can't trust anything electronic.'

'My phone is not your problem. I'll see you in the morning.'

When he hung up, she listened to the empty line for a while, not knowing what she was listening for, hoping she would know it if she found it. But the empty line was just an empty line and eventually she hung up too, feeling utterly self-conscious standing in a dirty old phone booth, an anachronism in a lightweight digital world.

If every mall she'd ever been in was the same, so was every set of shoppers that prowled its shiny floors. So many obese women in mismatched clothes. So many dazed-looking men in neatly pressed cotton polo shirts. What did it say about a culture when the men were better looking than the women?

The only people who seemed bothered at all by their appearance were the young, and they seemed to Jade to be trying way too hard. Punk was back in vogue, or at least a chic imitation of it. This incarnation of Mohawk hair, chains and torn clothing lacked the authentic angst of its parent movement. These were catalogue punks, MTV punks, Barbie punks. They weren't bucking the system, they were accessorising it, and Jade was sorry to say that she preferred them to the over-hyped Sid and Nancy progenitors. These kids were harmless. They weren't going to spit in your face or piss on your car. They would dress this way until something new took their attention and then they'd be off, wallets flapping in the wind as they tailored their bodies and their minds to the new big thing.

Jade pretended to peruse shop window displays, thinking how, over time, she'd come to admire the anonymity of suits. Suits lulled people into a false sense of security. People thought they knew what they were looking at. They thought because they didn't stop to think. A suit was impersonal, its wearer an automatic stereotype. Jade was more than comfortable with that.

She watched a group of young girls, their reflections filling the entirety of the shopfront's polished glass.

Tweenagers was the word she was fishing for — what the hell had ever happened to little girls? They went from six to sixteen now in one fell swoop. Stopped playing with Barbies and became them. The reflected girls were all thin — not the gangly thinness of Jade's own remembered childhood; this was the willow-waif of caloric restriction; bodies tailored to fit the clothes rather than the other way around.

Jade turned to face them. What would girls be like a hundred years from now? Would all women be tall, busty blondes with pencil-thin waists and thick collagen lips? Big, blue, blinking, Disney doe-eyes? What was the driving force behind the lack of individuality? Just plain old capitalist consumerism, or something far more insidious than even Hollywood could devise?

One of the girls glared across at Jade. Jade admonished herself for getting caught staring and moved away, feigning interest in a shoe-shop window a little further across the way. She passed a couple of guys, casual and confident in low-slung jeans and T-shirts, then another of the hideously obese women that seemed to characterise urban middle age.

Jade stared through the shoe-shop glass, checking out the customers' faces. There was a sameness about them she found more than mildly disconcerting. Do you walk amongst us pulling silent strings?

She imagined the story of the Alice extraterrestrials breaking, pictured a stand of newspaper headlines in her mind's eye. Would any of these mall shoppers actually give a damn to learn that they weren't alone in the universe after all? Or would they just keep shopping their merry way to oblivion?

She found the bench outside the donut shop and

waited for twenty minutes, fighting the urge to check her phone for messages. She knew there wouldn't be any. At half past she accepted that Sagittarius was a no show. As she moved on past the donuts, she started to feel like she was being watched by more than mere shopping-laden Barbie clones. Jade felt like she was marked in some invisible way, moving against the regulation ebbs and flows.

She passed identical clothing stores, turned her face away as she realised the next window in line was jammed with plasma and LCD screens. An electric chill ran down her spine. Each screen was filled with synchronised images of golf, but she felt that at any minute the whole damn lot of them might switch to displaying her own face. She hurried past as quickly as she could, not pausing until she reached the sanctuary of the underground car park. She fumbled for her keys and dodged a stream of tourists and mothers with whining children, the relief she felt at the sight of her own car overwhelming.

The fear didn't dissipate until she'd left Pitt Street far behind. Her pulse had just dropped back to normal when the Navman unit on the dashboard came to life.

'At the next set of lights, take a left turn,' said the machine in a broad Irish brogue, even though the last time she'd used it, the voice had been set to something innocuous and vaguely British. She pulled up to the lights, her heartbeat thumping in her chest once more. Since the incident with the YouTube angel, nothing technologically improbable surprised her. After a moment's hesitation, she flicked the indicator on.

'Like I have a choice,' she said out loud.

The lights changed and she turned left with all the other cars in the queue. She kept to the speed limit, preferring the annoyance of the drivers behind her to the possibility of missing a turn should the Navman speak again.

It was no use. She couldn't go home, or to the office, nor could she hole up in squalid hotel rooms for the rest of her life. Nowhere would be safe until this story had an end to it. Her knuckles whitened as she gripped the steering wheel.

'Left again,' said the machine. Not Irish this time. A woman's voice, half familiar, yet difficult to place.

'Where am I going?' asked Jade.

'Right at the intersection.'

'I mean, what is my destination?' Jade said, gritting her teeth. 'Where are you taking me?'

The thing didn't answer. Jade tried to keep her cool as she drove by rows of placid townhouses, secure in their utter ordinariness. Yards strewn with abandoned toys. Hoses, flower pots, a pair of tattered gardening shoes.

'Left again,' it said.

'I need to know where you're taking me.'

'I don't care what you think you need,' it said.

Jade gripped the wheel as recognition kicked in. The voice belonged to Bev, the woman she'd last seen being swallowed by the crowd at the Heartlands gig before the mosh pit orgy began.

'I was worried about you, Bev,' said Jade, fully appreciating the ridiculousness of talking to the Navman as though it were a person. 'I lost sight of you in the crush.'

It wasn't really Bev, she knew. It was the angel toying with her. Messing with her mind. Not angel — alien. Why did she persist in thinking of it as an angel?

'I don't care what they do to me,' said Bev's voice. 'Life's not worth living without my Lily.'

As the lights changed to green up ahead, Jade pressed

her foot to the accelerator. Anger boiled from every pore. She hated the fact that she was being played — and had been played every step of the way.

'Where are you, Bev?' she asked the machine. 'What have they done with you?'

Jade drove straight ahead, still with no idea where she was going. Determined she wouldn't stop or turn a corner until the machine forced her hand.

'Bev is with her daughter,' the machine said at last. The voice had changed again. This one was neither male nor female. Utterly cold and inhuman.

'So you murdered her too? Why? What was the point of that?'

'It was what she wanted.'

'It was not what she wanted!' shouted Jade. 'What she wanted was for you not to have killed her child in the first place! Don't you see that? Or is human love beyond your comprehension?'

She accelerated again, which took her way over the speed limit. In a sudden moment of clarity, she recognised where she was. Alexandria, a light industrial inner city suburb.

'Left at the next lights,' said the Navman, returning to its Irish accent.

She had no choice but to obey. The machine went quiet as she cruised down a series of one-way streets flanked by warehouses and portable storage facilities. Most of them looked like they hadn't seen much use in recent times. The last street came to a dead end at a beige-coloured warehouse that featured no signage whatsoever. This was the place. She could feel it in her bones.

She pulled into the driveway and got out of the car. She resisted the urge to slam the door. The more distance she managed to put between herself and the creepy Navman, the better.

She approached the building with extreme caution. Were answers to be found in there, or merely more impossible questions? Her head ached and her ankle was still a little swollen. There was nobody around. The front was padlocked, but a roller door on the side had been chocked open with a beam of wood. Jade ducked inside. Her eyes took a moment to adjust to the dim and dusty light within. The space was empty save for a stack of shipping crates at the far end. Shafts of sunlight stabbed down from slits set high in the building's aluminium framework. A blade of light illuminated something huddled in the centre of the floor. A face peering up at her, blinking in the brightness.

'Bev!'

Jade ran to her, ignoring all the obvious signs of a trap. Bev lay with her hands tied behind her back, her knees drawn loosely against her chest.

'Have they hurt you?' asked Jade, working quickly to untie the older woman's hands. The ropes loosened easily. Whoever had tied them had not done a very good job.

Bev moved to a sitting position and rubbed her wrists. 'They gave me a message for you,' she said. 'Go home. Forget all the things you've seen. None of it matters. There's nothing you can do.'

Something didn't feel right. Jade took a step back. 'You're not Bev,' she said.

'You're not a journalist,' replied the thing that had assumed Bev's face. She stopped rubbing her wrists and got up off the cement floor, brushing flecks of dirt and grit from her skirt.

Jade took another cautious step back. 'I am a journalist.'

'She was a journalist. You're something else.

'What?'

'A construct. A safety precaution. A cleaner. A kill-switch. Actually, I have no idea what to call you. Figures you'd be built into the system, though. Makes a lot of sense.'

Jade stared at Bev uneasily. 'What the hell are you talking about?'

'Not that they're worth protecting,' said Bev calmly. 'The species is already extinct. They just haven't noticed it yet. Soon there'll be nine billion of them throttling each other for clean air. They'll butcher themselves and everything else before the air runs out. Do you think they're proud of their achievement?'

Bev's face flickered. The features became fluid, then started to change. Her nose enlarged, lengthened, then settled into a shorter form. Her lips plumped out as her cheekbones sharpened.

'Where do you come from?' asked Jade, talking to distract herself from the ghastly metamorphosis taking place before her eyes.

'Nowhere they will ever be able to reach.'

'Why did you come here?'

The creature with Bev's new face cocked its head. 'We thought we might like them.'

'And do you?'

'No.' The thing licked its lips, a common human mannerism that came across as utterly wrong under the circumstances. 'We don't like the way they move together. Their patterns infect us. They have made us sick.'

'Then why the hell don't you piss off and leave us alone?'

'Us?' it said, smiling.

The wrongest smile Jade had ever seen.

'Can't,' it said. 'Addicted.'

Jade opened her mouth but no sound came out. Somewhere above, in the warehouse's rafters, a fluttering of pigeon wings distracted her momentarily.

Jade watched in horror as Bev's features blurred again, this time resetting themselves into a facsimile of Jade's own face.

'But I like you, Jade Stone,' the creature said. 'I like the way you move.'

'Is that why you're wearing my freaking face?' Jade said, desperately trying to keep the hysteria from her voice.

The thing touched its hand against its cheek. 'It suits the way I feel,' it said. 'It reminds me of something.'

They stared at each other in silence for a while, Jade and the creature that wore her face.

'You're going to kill me now,' it said, smiling again in a sickly caricature of human expression that twisted Jade's guts and buffeted her with nausea. As she bent forwards clutching at her stomach in pain, footsteps echoed loudly across the bare concrete expanse.

Sagittarius appeared from behind a stack of crates. He approached slowly, his gun trained on them both.

'He'll have his people all over this place,' warned Jade through gritted teeth.

'Oh, I do hope so,' said the alien. 'So much more exciting that way.'

It turned its head so he could see its face. Sagittarius stopped, startled at the repetition of Jade's features on both bodies.

'Your face...'

'I told you things were getting crazy,' Jade said,

straightening up, struggling against the pain. 'Why didn't you listen to me?'

He tightened his grip on his gun, keeping it firmly trained upon the alien. He steadied his hand, then slowly transferred his aim from the alien's centre of mass to Jade.

'Hey, are you insane? It's me!'

'I know.'

He tapped his earpiece with his free hand and whispered a string of commands too softly for her to catch.

He was still speaking as Jade made her move. An action so swift, she could barely register what she was doing. Her right hand had been empty, but in an instant, it contained a gun. She fired a single shot at the alien's forehead, killing it quickly, a clean, professional shot. The creature died with a beatific smile on its face. It held its form, identical to Jade, even in death.

Calmly, Jade turned the gun on Sagittarius. He dropped his own gun and held up his hands in surrender, the dialogue with his earpiece abandoned. His attention was entirely focused on Jade.

'We can help you,' he said. 'Protect you. You're the last one left. We can take care of everything, give you what you need.'

The information was slow to sink in, as if she could understand his words and yet... how could they be true? How could any of it be true?

Jade Stone, as she knew herself to be, began to feel herself detaching from her body. But it wasn't her body. There was no Jade Stone. Somewhere out there lived a journalist who'd spent some time in Alice Springs. One of Helen Aster's colleagues, perhaps, inhabiting a particular place and time — a random afternoon, the Crowne Plaza lobby bar five years ago. An alien had taken her imprint and run with it. Ridden her facsimile skin like a carnival attraction or wild horse.

Jade Stone… Jade Stone. A comic book name. Had she picked it from one of the many books on her shelf? A superhero detective. Hunting the bad guys, protecting the good. Only she hadn't managed to protect anyone. Not even herself.

She fired a single shot, hitting the government man square between the eyes. He died instantly, knees folding first, body crumpling to the ground, all the life gone before his head cracked concrete. His final gaze had been for her, Jade Stone, and not the alien. She didn't know how she could be sure of it, but she was.

Jade — because she was still desperately clinging to Jade — watched remotely as her body, no longer under her control, moved swiftly, dragging the corpse of Sagittarius on top of the one who'd looked like Bev.

She felt herself dissolving grain by grain, sand dissipating in the wind as each flimsy layer of memory peeled away. A childhood that was never hers; a teenage struggle with identity, laughable in the face of things to come. The swift assassination of the other two, Ms Gelding and the angel, events she had no memory of before now. Her utter terror as she glimpsed what sat behind the layers. Nothing. Not darkness, not even an impenetrable void. When the mask was gone, nothing would remain. Not even memory, so it seemed.

Her lips parted, releasing a stream of high-pitched audio transmissions, sounds that would have been deadly to the human brain had any living humans been in earshot. When that was done, her eyes flared. The bodies ignited quickly as sirens wailed in the distance.

Her face was already beginning to change. The contingency program that had once believed itself to be a journalist called Jade Stone walked out of the warehouse the same way it had entered. It slipped down a side alley, breaking into a steady jog, the sound of its footfalls eventually swallowed by the heat and clamour of a city preparing for sundown.

•

The tourist gripped the steering wheel with both hands, staring at the Eyre Highway, the longest, straightest stretch of road in the world. 'You should've gone back in Balladonia. You know what you're like when you drink too much cola.'

'Gone where — there wasn't even a bloody shop!' said her companion. 'Hardly think there would have been amenities.'

The woman's tongue worried at a sliver of bacon that had been caught irritatingly between two back molars since breakfast that morning. 'Go piss behind a bush then.'

He shot her one of his looks. 'Nothing but bluebush and saltbush for miles in all directions. Somebody might see.'

She actually glanced across at him this time. 'Who the hell's ever gonna care if they see you taking a piss?'

'I can't do it if someone's watching — you know that.'

'Who the hell's gonna be watching you piss out here? Haven't even passed a truck for thirty minutes.'

She shifted her attention to the bitumen road surface which glistened almost wetly in the heat, despite the ever present dust.

He shifted uncomfortably in his seat, annoyed by

the nest of empty cola cans rattling around at his feet but not quite motivated enough to clean up the mess. He was concentrating on conjuring up some sort of witty, if slow off the mark retort when he spied the lone jogger in a pastel pink tracksuit up ahead.

'She might see me,' he said, pointing an accusatory finger.

The woman looked out the four wheel drive's passenger window as the vehicle passed the jogger. Instinctively she reduced speed. 'What the fuck is a jogger doing out here? Did we pass a car? Did you see something broken down on your side?'

'Not since the burnt-out wreck about fifty k back.'

The woman braked, the sudden stop causing the cans to fly about the cabin. She craned her neck over her left shoulder. Her husband followed suit.

'No-one there,' he said. 'Bugger me!'

The woman stared hard at the shimmering air. She stuck her head out the window for a clearer look, then jumped down from the cabin. Shading her eyes from the sun, she peered in all directions, but there was nothing but bitumen, saltbush, bluebush and red earth.

'I saw a woman jogging,' she said out loud. 'I know I did.'

'I saw her too,' he added hastily, clambering down from the passenger's side. A lone cola can fell, hitting the road with a metallic chink. 'Actually, I saw her first.'

The woman walked back to the place where the jogger had been. She had no idea what she was looking for, only that she needed some sort of clue. Some affirmation that what she had seen was real. But there was nothing. Just road and dirt. Not even the sunburnt carcass of an unlucky wombat or a feral cat.

She looked back at the car just in time to see her husband zipping up his fly. From him she looked up to the sky, a vast expanse of cheery blue dotted with clumps of fluffy cloud.

'You know they're planning a golf course for the Nullarbor,' he said, popping a fresh can of cola as he walked up to stand beside his wife. He paused to take a swig, then gazed up at the sky too in an effort to see what she was staring at. He squinted, then did a quick 360-degrees recce of the horizon. Nothing happening there, so he stared straight up again. Just sky and sky and more sky after that. It wasn't like there was anywhere else to look.

The Absent Men

Louise Katz

Yesterday upon the stair
I saw a man who wasn't there
He wasn't there again today
I wish that man would go away

chapter one
... then she awoke and found it was not a dream

Pippalotti Colquouhoun woke up in the dark. Dead on 3.00 am: the dire part of the night, when the creatures with quilted tongues and claws hidden in soft pads of fur come to love you to death.

She headed for the bathroom, bumping her head on a wall that wasn't meant to be there. 'Parmesan, pomegranate, palindrome,' murmured Pippa, random listing being her way of warding off unease. Then she remembered she'd moved apartments and had only to feel her way more carefully, which she did, but still tripped up the single step to the toilet, executed a mid-fall twist and landed on her bottom on the seat.

Silky moonlight shone in through the skylight and mantled her shoulders like a privilege. She cast it off when she stood up to press the flush button. Then she noticed the boiler suit. It was suspended from a protruding nail by one of its arms; the other was caught up along the high shelf above the sink, so it was like two arms raised above a head that wasn't there. The legs too were akimbo, one trailing over the cistern, one dangling. Pippa owned no such garment. Had it been left behind by the plumber? The glazier? Flinging their work clothes off in a race to get to the pub? She stared at it, this big black cross: X marks the spot. What spot? One of the arms seemed to point towards a crack between the wall and the ceiling.

Dim, cool light showed at the edge and continued down in a straight vertical line. So this wall was no wall, but a partition? Nobody had told her about that. She pushed the wall gently. It came ajar easily like a great, silent door.

Pippalotti Colquouhoun entered the room that wasn't there.

She had lived in the same building for nearly twenty years. She'd thought of moving from time to time, reckoning that a change couldn't hurt, but hadn't got around to it. Then the top flat became available. Although the building was officially six storeys high, this flat was on the unlisted seventh floor — a level sandwiched between the sixth and the roof, where the inhabitants hung their washing. Pippa had always been charmed by it, with its oddly proportioned rooms and windows at strange angles. So when this chance presented itself, she took it.

'There,' she told her tabby cat, Isadora D, 'I've changed flats but not addresses, so the tension between me and me, moving and not moving, is resolved. I am both happy.' Isadora knew that as a quadruped she would fall over if she tried to shrug, so she did it on the inside. Her friend Pippa had never been decisive.

That night Pippa was home late from work. She was a dancer. Her latest gig was Ali's, a Lebanese restaurant in Oxford Street. Shimmying between the tables, she always savours the lyrics' feinting and parrying with the strains of woodwind, strings and bass, though she doesn't understand a word. It's better that way. Consonants like cocky dragonflies that skim and dart, their insect intuitions making sense of reflections, scudding shadows, natural devices of deception. She has the belly-dancer's knack of moving her upper and lower body independently, below the waist a shimmer of diaphanous skirts a-jangle with twenty silver bells; above, her hands moving in cool ripples, smoothing the disrupted air. Pippa's waist is both the dividing line and the conjunction. It links the downward pull of her loins and the upward tendency of her arms as her body negotiates the opposites that circumscribe the dance.

When she'd walked in that night Isadora had rushed up to her with the news, '*Eengrrow gniii.*' Pippa picked the cat up and over her furry ears gazed around her new abode, the old passionflower wallpaper, the new rug from the sale at the carpet place in Edgecliff, the tea chests yet to be unpacked: clothes, books, CDs and magazine cut-outs and memorabilia of her life, all filed by theme. She had considered filing the themes in chronological order, but after much deliberation had opted for alphabetical — A: autobiographical details, ammunition for arguments, animals i) albatrosses etc. ii) buffaloes etc. iii) cats etc. through to zebras etc... B: biographies, B-movie stills, images of bounty etc. etc... C: images of cold weather, cataclysms i) personal ii) natural, iii) political... D: the Dalmatian coastline, dangerous lies, dirigibles, dancers... E: extraordinary places...

The small space in which she now found herself was lit by a dim violet light whose source she could not see; it was as if the room itself was radiant, though she knew this was impossible. As impossible as the fact of this room being there at all. The floor was white-stippled beige lino, like an old omelette. It curled up at the edges and glossy bumps brought into relief the irregularities of the concrete floor. It was furnished with a mission-brown sofa and a low 70s style coffee table with a top of smoked glass upon which were several snack boxes, Cheezels, Twisties and Lollygobble Blissbombs, a kind of popcorn she hadn't seen for about thirty years, an empty Sobranie packet and several crushed fruit juice containers with bent straws protruding. In front of the table stood a large computer, the screensaver slowly turning over aerial views of disasters, natural and man-made, close-ups of distressed people from Armenian, African, American slums, then smiling men toasting each other beneath chandeliers, factory production lines, catwalk models parading, children on a basketball court… There were many wires and attachments, audio and visual connections sprouting from more sockets than Pippa had ever seen in a computer. And many of the cables were thick and fleshy looking. Yes, fleshy. Some seemed damp, some were hairy. She reached out to touch one, and found that it was warm. Her stomach lurched in disgust, but lower down in her body she felt a more ambiguous reaction… Pippa had not known she was capable of lucid dreaming, let alone such a visceral one. For that was what it was, she knew. What else could it be?

She noticed a further passage on the opposite side of the room, accessible by a very low door set about a foot off the floor. Getting into the whole *Looking Glass* style of the dream, she entered on hands and knees; it was only slightly wider than her shoulders, little more than a cavity between interior walls, but she could see ahead to where it ended at another small door. She crawled over to the second door and pushed it open, then emerged in the familiar foyer at the head of the fire stairs. This was disappointing. She'd have thought her imagination would have had the capacity for something a bit more lively. Turning to look back at the way she had come, she realised that the hole she had just crawled through was the now defunct rubbish chute from an earlier era, when this apartment building had been a smart hotel. She stood, her feet turning blue on the chilly terrazzo. She rubbed one cold sole against her calf, then swapped feet. Freezing. This was starting to feel all very real. 'A bit *too* real,' she whispered to herself for the small comfort to be found in clichés.

She stared at the naked fact of what had just happened. 'But secret passageways and surveillance facilities hidden in the walls of the building? The building I've lived in for twenty years? Right.' The fact stared back at her and didn't blink. Then she realised that the fact wasn't the only naked thing in the foyer.

Jesus Christ. She stumbled, very dazed, back to her own flat. It was locked. Of course. She scampered into the drying room and unpegged a big T-shirt that was hanging over the clothesline and threw it over her head before returning to the foyer and to the chute: she could always go back the way she had come. She put her head into the cavity and began to wriggle forward, but a second later she was hard up against the back wall: solid, real, uncompromising.

The ramifications of what had just happened, unspeakable though they were, would have to wait. What she needed first and foremost was a locksmith. Pippa padded downstairs and out into the morning, all pearly and deceptively innocent.

Kings Cross is the best place to find semi-naked women at dawn. Pippa attracted the odd offer, making her way along Darlinghurst Road as the low sun rouged the tired-faced vendors of sex and hamburgers; pimps, still-busy, waylaying escaped husbands and the occasional early tourist just off a coach down from Queensland; the gaggles of party girls and boys from the western suburbs whose big night out had not yet ended. They blinked in the glare of another day as they tumbled like balls out of a pin-ball chute through the doors of nightclubs whose pulsing beat bent the air into geometrical shapes around the nodding junkies, the drunken buskers, the ice-cream wrappers idling in gutters to be picked up by the gritty wind and blown down to Woolloomooloo, Potts Point, Elizabeth Bay. She passed her old friend, a man she'd never spoken to but had often admired, the tramp with the carrotty locks and the tulip-bulb nose. Privately, she called him The Old Soldier, for his upright bearing and shell-shocked gaze. He was working an elaborate cat's cradle out of knotted string in the doorway of an all-night convenience store, its fluorescent bulbs still glaring at potential thieves and naughty snoggers needing chocolate, condoms, cigarettes…

Pippa entered Llankelly Place, a small paved street at the juncture of Kings Cross and Potts Point. Leaving the noisy thoroughfare, she found she had the feeling that sometimes happens, as if someone's watching you. Soon her nape was aswarm with it, as if the little hairs were trying to warn her of something. She looked over her shoulder, but nobody was there. 'Cochlea, cordial, cardinal,' she muttered, 'columbine, caramel, chintz.' She was not pleased with chintz. 'Klutz,' she added, and crossed the street to the locksmith. A small man, with a frizz of grey-blond hair around his ears and a pair of bottle-glass spectacles in heavy tortoiseshell frames was just opening up shop. His eyes were huge behind the thick lenses, and grew slightly larger when he took in her dress, or lack of it. She explained her situation, and he agreed to walk back with her and see to the door.

chapter two
reality television

Dr Wilder Portion was painting his walls deepest black. They would probably still seep a bit, but the tar sealant would do for the time being. Besides, the drafts were interestingly devious and he liked them. He breathed in deeply and smelled diesel, dust and bitumen with a higher note of beeswax.

After his position at the university had been terminated, Dr Portion had set up his new, highly compact laboratory in one of the many subterranean tunnels honeycombing the ground beneath Sydney, not far to the east of the central business district. The entrance to his lab was accessible only by way of a small underground lake beneath St James Station. He had paddled over the last of his equipment by li-lo only days earlier. It was not a bad set-up for a penniless professor, one who'd just lost his job and whose bank had foreclosed on his mortgage. After all, he reflected ironically, it was unlikely that he would be audited here, or pestered by anxious graduates. His unit, which had once had offices midway between the old Humanities area and the Science and Technology buildings at The University of Sydney, had been lost in the transformations enacted when the new dean came into office. This man had shaken the institution up quite roughly, reallocating responsibilities, rewriting job descriptions. Whole departments had got lost. Then he had ordered a brand new strategic plan and mission statement from one of the better PR agencies.

Fresh start.

The little bunker shook as the City Circle thundered by overhead. He gazed around his subterranean asylum with satisfaction at his banks of equipment, his shelves of ranked ring-binders, data-packed CDs, hard-copy files, text books, notebooks, Zane Grey Westerns and *Deadwood* DVDs. Wilder was as content as could be, under the circumstances.

He left his brush to soak in a jam jar of turpentine. With a shiny new padlock he secured his only entrance against any invasions by urban speleologists. He returned to his makeshift desk, plugged in the last of his plugs nestled in a bed composed of a complex congeries of cables, fired up his Colanderic Spectrometer and its various attachments, and opened the links to the Caliband Contour Tracer. The consoles burped, chugged and hummed into confluent life. But while the Tracer warmed up — it always took a while longer than the others to check in — he drew towards him one of his laptops, the one he kept for diarising his process, both personal and professional. As a creative man of science, he understood the importance of a well-coordinated left/right brain relationship, how analytical thought was fed by imagination, and imagination strengthened by the rigours of meticulous systemisation. He opened the laptop. Its screensaver showed him the face of the sublime Cate Blanchett, whose gracious aspect suggested to him inner thoughts of a gentle nature.

The body of the world is full of holes, wrote Dr Wilder Portion. This is how I see it: slivers of Swiss cheese sliced impossibly thin, some overlapping, some separated by narrow spaces, like bubbles of thought. In heightened states of excitement or despair you may perceive the shadow of movement behind a translucent neighbouring wall. You may receive some intimation of other worlds, but — and this is important — you cannot go there without technological assistance Zance or synthetic augmentation. And if you try too hard, you will find that you are hard up against the grain of nature. This may drive you mad: such is the experience of poets, artists, the odd maladjusted individual with no special talents except a kind of mad intuitiveness. The sort of people who shout in the street. Who crouch in doorways. But the rain comes in slantwise and soaks their blankets.

Yet Other Places are very close, so close that sometimes even a sane man may fancy that he can smell the breath of the other, near, warm and sour or sweet, and the vigorous heart, pulsing blood. When one looks closely at the nature of reality one is struck by the deep strangeness of things.

Lost scraps of thought — perhaps those whose caboose accidentally disconnects from the main body of the train of thought — are occasionally caught between the layers, like food fragments between the teeth, the clenched teeth of what is real. And scraps of consciousness may also find themselves jammed in there, closeted in the narrow places, waiting quietly for a reprieve. The consciousness may be harmless. Or not.

It is with the latter I am concerned: two entities, one called John Grey. His brother is a mute and I haven't found a name for him — let's just call him Brother.

John Grey and Brother belong to no world in particular and exist between the slivers, so to speak. And having augmented the Tracer and Colanderic Spectrometer with the newly patented Spatiotemporal Flux Translator I have been able, from time to time, to locate them with reasonable accuracy and amplify their thoughts to a level perceptible to human consciousness. Thus I have been monitoring the movements of these two as they range around within the interstices of time and space, like ants between twin sheets of glass of a child's ant farm. Oh dear, a new metaphor. Never mind. Stet.

I knew of these two because I used to work with their creator, that creative genius, Professor Spurius Miles and his team of physicists, biologists, neurologists, social scientists and geneticists of the one-time Department of Interstitial Studies at the university. The financial lifeline for this project was cut before its completion — Professor Miles being unwilling or unable to adequately describe the nature of his project to the satisfaction of his benefactors. (Indeed, had he succeeded in this task the outcome would likely have been the same.) The calibandits — so he dubbed them, after Shakespeare's monster — were never completed. This was too much for poor Miles, who accelerated his own end with the aid of a bridge and gravity. But let's not go there just now.

I continued on as best I could in much reduced circumstances until the operation was closed down in the most recent departmental shake-up. Very recent.

The calibandits, half-made, yearn for completion. They hate the state they are in, and as an abused dog may in turn become malicious, so it has been with these unfortunate anomalous entities, whose substance is confected in measured parts of technology, spirit and the darkest aspects of the dreaming imagination. Their genetically modified DNA is coded to match the electromagnetic impulses of the human animal. Genes were duplicated, rearranged and merged with a program now familiar to many of us as New Alchemy. Yet they are unfinished and thus are bound to seek out humanity, to whom they are physically related at the most fundamental level. How desperately they must yearn after this contact! How excited at the thought of this possibility — to touch for the first time a solid thing, to breathe, to suck in the same air breathed out by human beings whom they have been watching with envy and lust, to travel abroad then return to their interstitial bubble to hone their grudges, to polish them up with spit and vinegar.

Recently, Grey and Brother slid into a space between layers of reality that lined up coincidentally — is there such a thing? (NOTE: update coincidence and contingency file) — with my place in the space-time continuum — that is, with Sydney, postal district 2010, January 2010. (NOTE: Another 'coincidence', these numbers?)

I shifted the gears that command the plates of the Colanderic Spectrometer and followed them onscreen through layer upon layer of perception. Then, using good old fashioned Google World, I clicked down and down until I had homed in on them: their bubble was separated by only the finest degree from somebody's flat in the inner city. Sydney 2010. I could see the apartment's inhabitant. Sleeping innocently in her bed, a woman, utterly unaware of the proximity of the absent men. I could not see her face, obscured as it was by quite a lot of browny-blond hair.

As he keyed in these last rough notes of his update, the Caliband Contour Tracer burbled into life. Dr Wilder Portion put his eye to the lens: an image of John Grey and Brother quickly resolved itself before him. He swallowed — the look of them always unnerved him. John Grey with his pale, pale eyes and his jaws blade-sharp; Brother, his cheeks flaccid and pouchy, marked with unwholesome red spots like a consumptive, his fingers beringed, his head bewigged, for Brother enjoys fashion, the more camp the better. Today he wears a brassy beehive, his pale lips frosted, his narrow eyes outlined in turquoise kohl. The bodies of both calibandits are almost skeletal, dressed only in loose dark trousers, the long toes of their bare feet protruding from the cuffs. Through their skin the blue-green veins visibly stirred with the movement of blood in a simulacrum of organic life that made Wilder, despite his objectivity, more than slightly squeamish. They always affected him this way. Above the trousers their fish-white bellies were bare, their power-cords like distended umbilici protruding obscenely. Portion's eyes were glued to the Tracer screen as he began to record their latest movements, touch-typing rapidly as he watched avidly:

The calibandits are sitting close together on an idea of a mission-brown vinyl couch in their blue-lit virtual space within the space-time aspect Sydney occupies, lined up with it very snugly, pressed against a translucent wall of coherence that takes up no more actual space than a piece of Chinese rice paper. Sorry, future reader, about this metaphor problem. But, stet. I must move on.

The men on the couch are attending passionately to their own novel computer-tracking device, which as well as the usual tracing software, also has features enhanced with data from folk-tales as well as physics and philosophy alongside faerie lore, quanta-counters and computational stylistics analysis grids. Spurius must've uploaded this lot into them just before he died. They can go anywhere, into places, bodies, minds. But it is no wonder they've moved so fast — they have all the know-how Spurius gave them, having fused their minds with his own while developing their intelligence.

They are hunched forward towards the screen, their pointed, shiny, black-gaberdine knees almost to their naked shoulders, as unwholesomely mottled as lumps of Stilton. Between each set of gangling legs dangles that revolting loop of cable that is joined to their bodies where their navels would be, had they ever been born, and whose nether extremities they now insert into the computer's twin USB ports. Brother adjusts the controls. They are brilliant, terrifying! Fuck! Stet.

But there is a noise behind them, a disturbing, grating sound that interrupts their flow…

John Grey turns as the wall behind him moves forward. Faint, yellowish light spills into their space, mixing it up with the violet so that a vile brownish mustard colour is the result. John Grey hisses through his teeth… 'Who's there?'

His brother seizes Grey's shoulder. 'Shhh!'

Grey's face is wild. I can see, almost feel his need for contact. But Brother seems made of cooler stuff. He does not share the powerful desire that goads John Grey. He reaches an arm about his shoulder and touches Grey's face, lovingly, sternly. Grey glares back at him, but after a short psychic tussle it seems he accepts some unspoken message from his twin. The two of them quickly discompose their molecules, rearranging themselves so as to be imperceptible to their visitor and, at least for the time being, to me. It is aggravating when they do this, but I turn my attention to the gatecrasher…

It is the woman! The woman I saw sleeping!

Dr Wilder Portion's fingers flew over the keys. Never before had he seen so much action:

She is naked. Well proportioned. I wish I could get a better look at her. Still can't see her face properly. All that hair.

But how the hell has she accessed their virtual space? It is impossible. It is true! A paradox I must absorb. The woman, sleepy, takes in this space she never knew existed, all unaware of the men who watch, and I who watch the men. She now turns to leave, her movements dreamy as she crosses the room.

As she leaves without looking back, the air above the couch folds in upon itself like the pleats in a concertina until the folds resolve themselves once more into the form of the two man-shapes, still sitting upon the couch. John Grey and Brother face each other. Grey's white, bony cheeks are marked along the bone with livid streaks. He is fiercely excited — he is smitten! Jesus God, he **wants** her… I can feel his desire, its texture, disgusting, like something half-congealed, gelatinous, and sulphurously stinking.

'You are charmed?' Brother asks, a stray curl hanging saucily over one plucked eyebrow.

'We should have stayed,' Grey replies furiously. 'I might have taken her — so tender and delicious and perfect!'

'But we were unprepared,' his brother says evenly. He's a cool one alright. 'We need to be ready, to be in control. Not caught in the spotlight like…'

John Grey dismisses his brother's concerns with a brusque movement of his hand and hisses, 'I should not listen to you, horrid doggie you are.' His eyes are hard and bright as banded agates. 'Did you smell the scent of her sweat? Her lovely blood?'

'Will you go out into the world to find her?'

'I will, Brother. Is that not what we are for? You should not be so timid. I should not allow myself to be weakened by you. It will not happen a second time.' His anger is palpable. Brother seems impervious.

'It's hard to calibrate our components to suit this world, a tricky and devious place, riddled with interference. You will find it hard to maintain a convincing impression of reality for longer than an hour, maybe a little more.'

'An hour will be enough.'

Dr Wilder Portion's fingers tremble over the keyboard as he writes. They are going to leave the interstices and enter reality? Electrifying information. But I have to believe it. The evidence is before me. But Brother is speaking again:

'I'll just tidy up a bit in here first.' His voice is sulky and John Grey can feel Brother's disapproval, and so can I. It is a hot feeling, a prickly, a sweaty, a bilious feeling. The air of the room roils with this green and sickly disdain, rocking the coffee table and causing the light to waver. Awkwardly, daintily, marionettily Brother gangles over to the false wall, reaches up and runs a delicate finger along the place where it joins the ceiling, and down, to where it meets the wall. 'Can't have anyone just wandering in by mistake,' he says, or maybe just thinks. Hard to tell.

Through my Spectrometer I can see that where the finger moves, caliband particles are shed. The discomposition of the flesh under such exquisite control. Beautiful. Just enough of his material and not too much was shed in order to fill the gap between door jamb and wall but not enough to interfere with his own developing reality.

The light from the room next door is blotted out, as is that from another smaller opening close to the floor. Once again, they are hermetically sealing this little space in the world that they have claimed as their own, like their own personal bubble of noxious gas in a swamp.

'Best I gather my resources before departing,' says John Grey, lighting a black Sobranie which he holds between finger and thumb, whose nail is longer than the others, ridged and yellow, tough as the spur of a cockerel. He is calm again; only a slight tremor of the cigarette gives him away. That smile of his is horrible, the curved blade of his lips pushing into the creases of his thin cheeks as he returns his attention to the monitor. 'Shall we watch some television, little brother-mine?' He exhales a thin plume of smoke with relish from his lips, nose, and a gap between his collarbones.

Brother nods and comes to sit by him on the mission-brown couch once more, reaching for another packet of Cheezels from his cache behind a temporal pleat in the air to the left of the sofa. As he rips open the cellophane, John Grey re-attaches himself to the machine then nods to Brother to click the shift key.

Wilder takes careful notes as he watches, even plans a way of linking himself up to his own machinery based on what he has seen the absent men do and from what the Flux Translator has enabled him to hear of their thoughts, to feel of their sensations. He watches as they tune into a street, quiet, leaf-dappled, where a man and a woman stroll hand in hand. The calibandits do not distinguish between filmed or digitised drama and real life. This snippet from someone's ordinary day refreshes the term 'reality television' for Wilder, who can now feel John Grey feeling the couple's attraction for each other. It draws the calibandit like a magnet. John Grey siphons off a little, then more and more of their lovely libidinous energy, he is greedy for it, he *needs* it — so that when next the woman looks up into her lover's face, she notices for the first time its imperfection. Grey sighs with satisfaction. Invigorated by this small dose of pirated desire he feels much stronger already. He lights a mauve Sobranie. Brother clicks the remote again and they change channels.

Wilder's thoughts and his notes become increasingly distracted, for what he is now witnessing and recording disturbs him profoundly. His fingers slow down, then cease. He can no longer type. He can only watch in mounting disgust and fascination as he realises what John Grey and Brother are really, literally, made of.

click

They watch a disembowelling then a series of stonings and sup on them, these cocktails of torment and terror which are as sustaining, if not more so, than erotic yearning. Then on to access first-hand the agonies of a once straight-limbed teenager as he dies in the aftermath of a land-mine explosion. John Grey draws deeply on his umbilicus, not wasting a drop of the vitality of the passion and pain that nourishes and strengthens him. And all these visions and realities are the same to him: sustenance for an entirely value-free being. He lacks the ability to distinguish between the qualities of one thing and the next, and this is the source from which is derived his absolute negativity. And his ever-increasing power.

click

A door (heavy, leather, quilted) opens. In the room

the walls are darkly upholstered. The furniture is low and comfortable, the lights are bright. In a corner of the room is a camera on a tripod. Against one of the walls is a table. On it lie a knife and a coil of rope. There are several people. All of the adults are male, well dressed, well-nourished. There are also children. Less well-nourished, and not dressed at all. Grey rises from his seat, the cable dangling. His body is no longer one apparently integrated whole, but breaks down in a flurry of pixels. He enters via the portal of the screen.

On the other side, nobody feels his presence except for one of the children. He is a boy of about nine or ten years old with straight black hair and pale skin and uptilted brown eyes. The boy shivers when John Grey, or some essential part of his invisible self, plants a kiss, moth-soft, upon his neck, fragile as the stem of a swamp-orchid. 'Sweetie,' he murmurs. 'But I will take nothing from you. Instead, I give…' Grey then turns the focus of his intention to one of the men in the room who stands near the door, a stranger to this place. Grey's mind bears down on that of the man: the lines of the man's face, the stoop of his shoulders, tell of an old spiritual battle about to be lost. Grey's spirit moves him to do what he had longed and loathed to do, for oh, so many years. The man moves away from the door, approaches the boy with a smile in his eyes and a promise on his lips…

John Grey turns from the scene and rejoins his brother on the couch. He puts his feet up on a sculpted vinyl footrest. 'Delicious.' He lights a rose Sobranie and punctures the foil of another fruitbox with his long, horny thumbnail. He inserts the straw and sips as delicately as a dragonfly. 'Go on, Brother — click it again.'

There is a cradle, painted white. It contains lace-edged cotton sheets, a pale-yellow bunny rug and a pink cheeked, peacefully sleeping baby. Grey puts down his drink. He enters the nursery, umbilicus trailing. He stays only a moment, for a moment is all it takes for the cheeks of the child to grow pale, for the blue tinge to settle first around the lips…

click

But Dr Wilder Portion can watch no more.

chapter three
a fraction is all that lies between the third and the fourth of a thing

Birdy Lethe walks along the street. As he walks, he talks, soft, murmured words that ease the pain in his heart: 'I pass between and under the structures, the overpasses and subways and hefty edifices where the people go to work and to eat in underground chambers lit by tubes of bleak light. All of these big, proud places are more delicate than they seem. I walk along the street under a magnificent billboard, alight with electronic optimism. The sign says Coca Cola. It is on the crossroad I like to pass daily, where William Street meets Darlinghurst Road. X marks the Cross.

'I look down, humbled by the grandness of it all. It makes me feel very tired sometimes. Small objects glint up at me from the gum-speckled pavement. A button: broken, dull tortoise-shell. My heart brims. Perhaps this is a sign I must heed? Perhaps this button will be my saving grace? Who can tell me? Nobody. Nobody knows and I can only guess. I pick up the button and put it in my pocket. Save it from the stormwater drain and the hell below. Later I will sew it in place. Stitches in time. And I will look for the signs I need to find the things lost in the gaps, the many gaps… I hum my song. I murmur old words from my old song. Quiet words. Only words.'

Birdy Lethe takes a seat in his favourite place, on Darlinghurst Road, his back to a dark-green bollard. Gentle leaves drift down from the spreading tree above him. One, two, three… after some time he forgets he is counting leaves. He reaches into his pocket and takes out a nice, strong, long piece of string and knots it, so as to make a loop. He slips his hands in and moves his fingers up, down, across, in movements that echo the ancient game of children called cat's cradle. He hums as he works. Old words from an old song.

As soon as she had been let back into her flat, Pippa dressed, put the borrowed T-shirt into the wash with an accumulation of other whites and was back at the chute in the corridor with her torch. She could not really believe she was crouching here half-expecting to find a way into a room beyond a room.

'God's sake,' she muttered, 'Idiot. *Alice.*'

The door of the chute still opened, but as she had found earlier, only onto a sealed cavity. There was no way in to any room from the corridor. She went back inside to the bathroom. The boiler suit was still there. She made a mental note to call the tradesmen so that the owner could collect it. Then she pressed the wall. It didn't budge. The 'false' wall was real.

'No other room could possibly fit between my loo and the flat beyond it. There was just *no room* in either sense of the word. *But I had been there.*' Pippa felt crushed between these two adamant truths that are entirely incompatible.

'Oranges and apples,' she muttered. 'Armadillos, apostrophes, anchovies.' She felt suddenly dizzy and had to take a seat. She reached behind her and drew the angora rug that was thrown over the back of the couch down over her shoulders. It was too warm. She drew it more closely around her anyway and reached out for the remote control. She sat there for some hours, watching a nature program, a shopping program and then an enthusiastic American preacher and his very responsive congregation. The images bounced against her eyeballs, but some bits permeated her consciousness too, enough to keep her thoughts from linking up into any kind of logical sequence, which was the effect she was after. Around midday she ordered in pizza. After a while, groggy with television and saturated fat, she slept and didn't wake until the late afternoon.

She sat up. A sudden last effort on the part of the tired sun illuminated the little room. The light picked up the yellow in the green of the wallpaper passionflowers making them lemony, and the green in the yellow, making it pointless. She felt she was being submerged in a weak acid bath. Homogeneity murders its components... she had to get out.

She went downstairs, opened the door. She stood on the top step looking out over Darlinghurst Road. The mood of the street had changed from early morning seediness to a happy kind of normalcy by late afternoon, a busy street full of people with destinations. Tourists heading for the airport bus. Men and women walking briskly towards Kings Cross Station. Isadora's warm body leaned into her leg. And then she felt that prickling at the back of her neck, the same feeling she had had early that morning, only the feeling was trebled now. A force was hidden in the unsuspecting blue air, like a conscious will, and it was directed at her.

Nonsense.

But Isadora's hackles were standing up too; she was prickling like a caterpillar. 'Calm down,' she told the cat. 'You just had a bad sleep, dreams dreamt near waking can sometimes get mixed up in the world, that's all.' She said it and it made sense, yet she couldn't deny the unreasonable fear she felt. Pippa pictured herself as a cartoon illustration called 'Paranoia' done in the style of Leunig: thin figure and her cat stare out at city streetscape, boggling eyes are hanging from the streetlights, sprouting from between the cracks in the pavement, hanging like fairy lights from the trees across the road where cars full of horrible staring pupils cruise by, and more eyes bulging out of the parking meters, creeping from the drains on their nasty, redwet optic fibres...

'Stop it!' she told herself. 'People who give in to groundless fears end up living indoors on takeaways, saving old newspapers and polystyrene boxes.'

She made herself leave the steps. Isadora D ran in front of her, then figure-eighted back around Pippa's legs, trying to warn her friend of the danger her feline sense easily intuited. But the woman paid no attention. All Isadora could do was watch as Pippa entered the darker twilight beneath the camphor laurel that overhung the street from behind the church wall next door. A flock of pigeons took off with a muffled clatter. They left behind them a silence as tense as the space between breaths. The shadows crept anxiously out from under the awnings across the street as if they didn't like the thought of what could be hidden back there in the lanes. The spiked iron fence posts in front of the church were ranged up on one side, an army bristling with spears, waiting in ambush. The busy street was suddenly deserted. Pippa could smell petrol, jasmine, salt from Rushcutters Bay, a hint of something necrotic.

Good evening.

She swung around to face the voice. A man, wrapped in a long coat, though the evening was warm. His lower face was hidden in a muffler and the eyes peering over the top were such a light, translucent grey there was virtually no difference between iris and white, a very horrible look. His arms hung loosely at his sides; his hands were long and white with very long thumbnails, thick and ridged. She now observed that his coat gaped a little, and his pale, naked torso was exposed to just below the navel, from which was extruded some kind of hideously long, thick umbilicus that hung down to his bare blue feet, then trailed along behind him, she could not see how far. Then, even more horribly, he seemed to Pippa to sort of *wuther,* like a sheet on the clothesline in the wind. An old, very thin sheet, one that you can see through. He gazed at her hungrily. Then the voice again, a thin voice that seemed to have no air behind it, and piercing, like the streams of frost-laden bitterness that come down from the mountains in winter, that penetrate to the bone no matter the layers of warmth you wrap around yourself for protection.

I want you, for you are lovely, said the thin man.

Pippa stared.

I want you to want me, he said.

'Jesus.'

I want to look in the mirror and have someone looking back. My desire fills me like a well and my longing fills the well. I want to breathe, to sweat, to eat and fuck and dance.

She was paralysed.

Love me, love me not. But don't despise me... don't you dare...

His attention on her was palpable, it washed over her likes waves of cold nausea. She managed to take a step back and the movement hurt…

Then, out of the corner of her eye she saw the old man with the red-grey ringlets, her old soldier. He was squatting by a bollard, his eyes closed, his attention apparently engaged with the eternal cat's cradle he was constructing between busy fingers. His lips moved silently as he concentrated.

Her attention was lassoed again by the grey man, his focus coiling through her vitals like cancer and lust all mixed together in a horrible cocktail. He was repulsive yet his desire for her found, somewhere, a correspondence in her body or mind or both and despite her disgust, she felt herself drawn to him. At the same time she felt her soldier's concentration brush up against her too in a kind of counterpoint to the man's. She heard the soldier speaking into his web of string. She couldn't understand the words, but their sound was like a tonic for her soul that had started shrinking and sinking towards the grey figure with his terrible gaze, wanting her…

The sounds the soldier made were raw and gleaming as if newly born, but they felt old too, very, very old, older than history, than any of the dead empires of the world, echoing in Pippa's head with the impossible time they had crossed to reach her. The words matched the movements of his hands, as if he was knitting a space out of the air between them, knitting fog into mortar…

Can there be such a thing as a kind of syntax that echoes the actual shapes of things, real things in the world? Like sentences composed in the same patterns as the fundamental architecture of nature?

The man seemed to diminish as she started to

move towards the soldier, who seemed not to notice her, so engaged was he with his constructions of string and air and words. The grey man and the soldier were like representatives from two armies and the scene of their confrontation was the space between the apartment block and a bollard opposite the spiked gate of St John's Church, at 7.00 pm on a Tuesday evening in October, 2010.

Like a blind woman, Pippa walked into the crossfire of concentrated energy between the soldier and the grey man. She couldn't see how their conflicting desires had churned up the air like mud on a battlefield. She couldn't see where this no-man's-land began and ended. She just went over the top and walked straight into the line of fire, into this piece of ruptured space between them, in the space where their intentions collided. Pippa felt herself buffeted on an ocean of air, then coasting, then falling…

Birdy Lethe had been less shocked than many to see a man evaporate into thin air on Darlinghurst Road, in front of the church, at seven o'clock in the evening. The ordinary and the extraordinary were all remarkable to Birdy. Nevertheless, he was shaken, never having witnessed this particular kind of prodigy before. He looked around at the strangely empty street. He, Birdy Lethe, amnesiac madman, cracked pillar of forgotten wisdom, was the only witness.

'Ah, Jesus,' he murmured, looking at the space left in the air where the ugly man had been. 'The strings slip my fingers. I am agog, I am, here at the edge of a hole you can fall down, one of the tender places in the world. A real imagined place, like that shifting brink where the land meets the sky that people call the horizon, an unreliable conjunction if ever there was one. The edges there aren't true, don't quite meet, off by ever such a small fraction. But a fraction is all that lies between the third and the fourth of a thing. And it is within that fraction that wonders live. Singular wonders. Mysteries breed in this space. Angels and devils and grey-faced ghouls live in the gaps of this imperfectly stitched cicatrix. Thoughts like my own lost ones — where did they ever go? — fall in. And now, men too, leaving young ladies swooning upon the hard street.

'Who was that wraithy man who was here, then got pale, paler, palest, receded from the world and made me feel so ill, who slipped through my strings I tried to catch him in? Who wanted that lady. But leaves her lying there where she fell over, her senses all gone away?'

A boy skimmed by on a skateboard, barely noticing the old man with the ragged ringlets and the prone woman. Birdy crouched down beside her and looked into her eyes, which registered nothing. He raised her awkwardly, his hands under her arms. Her head lolled back against his arm, and Birdy felt a protective tenderness rise in his old breast.

'I must mind her,' he said to himself. 'I must mind her else the normal people will get her and take her away and plug her into machinery that can only make her more vulnerable. I will look after her. Poor thing, poor rag doll, all your volition gone.' He saw too that her face was wet. Tears, he sees. Tears, no blood. He tenderly brushed the tears away with the back of his red-gold hand with its big, swollen, old-man's knuckles. 'I am wet with a woman's tears.' A couple more people passed by, seeing the two of them like tumbled junkies by the church wall on Darlinghurst Road.

'Can't stay here, girlie,' he said to her. Carefully he felt in her pockets for keys, identification. He found both.

He managed to raise the woman and found that he could support her, though only just. 'That's a good girl,' he said. 'I will look after you till your mind returns to your eyes.' There was a cat standing by, a tabby with an intelligent face. The cat followed him as he half-dragged, half-carried the woman into the building nearby.

chapter four
Mogom

Pippa's eyes opened onto a world aglow with rosy light. Tentatively she raised herself to her elbow and saw a wide plain, mildly undulating, featureless but for low plants and endless grasses. Gone was the camphor laurel; gone, Darlinghurst. As her vision cleared she felt the liveliness of the warm air around her, zinging with insect life, and the prickly grass beneath her body that crackled dryly as, slowly and carefully, she pushed herself up into a sitting position. Her head reeled. When the dizzy spell passed she also became aware that the air stank to high heaven.

All about her were low-growing single-stemmed succulents, hardy and wiry, each stem topped with a bivalved flower, fringed with feathery whiskers. These plants, though covered in a grey-green reptilian skin, also glowed from within with a warm light and it seemed to be them that emitted the rosy glow that filled the air, and also the vile stink. She saw one raise its hairy head as a low-flying starling skimmed by. It snapped the bird up in its jaws and swallowed it whole, then emitted a burp of rank carnivorous breath.

Pippa stood slowly and carefully. The gasoline-pink light seemed to grow stronger so that it hurt her eyes, and squinting against it did little good. She removed her shirt and bound it over her head. She stared through the fine cotton at the fields that stretched all the way to the horizon on one side, but looking in the opposite direction, the ground rose in a series of increasing tall hills, and at the top of the last one she could make out a line of rooftops and a cluster of several taller buildings, bright and glassy towers. Uncertain as to whether she was dead or dreaming, she began to make her way towards the town.

The ground was alive, rustling with insect industry, small creatures operating beneath the grass, just under the dry skin of the land, building, demolishing, breeding and killing each other, forever. Above all this, claiming all colour, light and heat as extensions of its own body, came the everlasting pulse of cicadas. It rose above the susurration of the carnivorous plants and the sparse grass and the occasional cry of a bird of prey far overhead. The celebration of the cicadas grew and grew, amplified by the absence of any other, countermanding sense than the aural, shrilling with the zeal of aggravated tinnitus. The din had long since drowned out the sound of her footfalls, her breath, her heartbeat. With the deprivation of all senses except hearing, Pippa found herself considering the possibility that the racket was actually coming from *inside* her head instead. This fancy lent itself to the gradual development, on the cinema-scope of her eyelids, of a range of increasingly awful ideas, illustrated in shades of red from a monochromatic palette made of her own blood. She saw an image of some kind of super-tumour growing in her brain, sending its blood-engorged tentacles throughout her cranium, taking root behind her eyes and then bursting so that her eyes imploded and her skull shattered.

Pippa shook her head to clear it. Then gazed up into the

pink sky. A jet plane, accelerating wildly, careened towards her, skimming ridiculously low. She hit the ground, and the plane passed over her. She angled her head up again just in time to see it disappear in a wash of visual static, like television snow. Blank with incomprehension, she had no time to gather her thoughts before a packet of couscous grew out of the air in front of her, spun on its side to reveal its serving suggestions, then it too simply disappeared.

Time and again as she struggled onwards towards the town, ever uphill, apparitions came and went without logic, without any respect paid to any law of physics she had ever heard of. At any moment the air might congeal into an ectoplasmic body of one sort or another, sometimes human, sometimes mechanical, plant or animal; some of these visions were accompanied by sounds — snatches of orchestral music or sly jingles — others silent. She was harmlessly molested by a troupe of pirates from a child's nightmare; she saw a man falling forever from the sky, oblivious to her, locked in his own dream; she was visited by an angel on swift wings, and so true was the illusion that she felt the wind of its passing on her face; she saw something like an excerpt from a particularly gritty docudrama that ran for a moment or two then died in a wash of static. She was shocked less at these intermingled dreams and broadcasts than the fact that, after a while, she found herself actually getting used to them.

She supposed that she was dead. She tried it out: 'I am dead.' The words echoed in her head — dead, dead, dead. But this fact seemed no more real than anything else, and she could not believe it any more than the 'fact' of the giant wombat that had just emerged from nothing and casually ambled through her leg. A part of her brain acknowledged that this must be the experience all dead people underwent while the last electrical impulses fired off their confused messages as the brain quietly expired. But while this muddled kind of altered consciousness endured, she would do the only thing she could: she would make for the distant town. 'Probably heaven or hell,' she told herself, and laughed aloud. She tried out her voice again: 'I'm laughing in the face of death. Is that what I'm doing? And Christ, I'm thirsty.' She wondered at how a dying consciousness could suffer any kind of biological deprivation. 'Well, but there it is,' she muttered to herself, then, 'Cat, bat, mat. Sand dollar, dog collar, tobacco wallah.'

As she progressed, the hallucinations or visitations or whatever they were thinned out and finally ceased. Also, there were fewer of the little warty flowers the further she walked, and she noticed the colour of the sky changing gradually from pink to mauve to an entirely acceptable blue, though darker than she would have wished. The day was drawing to a close. The heat was leaching out of the day and the air was becoming chilly, and smelled like rain.

The ground dipped before her and she followed it down, though the sharp-edged grasses scratched her ankles and the last remaining wart blossoms snapped at her trouser cuffs with vegetable malice. She passed a small colloquy of foraging ostriches who glanced over at her curiously as she gained the summit of the rise on the other side. Then, there it was, the gateway of the town, about five hundred paces from where she stood. She drew a deep breath and raised her face to the first stars. 'My first night in the land of the dead.' Pippa spoke the words she believed while simultaneously not believing them, then laughed again and felt the relief that comes with surrendering all preconceptions of place, of time, of self.

A fat raindrop kamikazied into her eye. This caused her to start crying well before she'd stopped laughing. Then the sky opened and Pippa entered the town under a scrolled gateway incised with the words *Welcome to Ariadne, Population 6000.* She retreated to the cover of a yellow and white striped awning. She became aware of the heavy *doof* of an overriding drum-beat that penetrated her bones, and realised that she was in the doorway of some kind of dance hall or nightclub that spilled not only sound but images from its yellow-lit interior. Some images of conjoined people and strange animals spilled over the balcony and onto the pavement where they attached themselves briefly to the bodies of a passing trio of kilted boys, then slipped harmlessly to the rain-slick concrete, spasmed and melted. Moving on, she stopped a passer-by in a pair of corduroy overalls, and for want of something better to say, she tried, 'Excuse me, do you speak English?'

The woman stared at her for a moment, then shrugged and said, 'I don't know about this Inglidge business, but I speak. Are you lost?' If only you knew, Pippa didn't say but simply asked the way to the nearest pub, for pubs, she well knew, were the best places to find things out about a new town. She headed off the way the woman indicated, towards an establishment she referred to as Bailey's.

The rain was now falling swiftly, heavily. One by one, the tall-stemmed street-lamps flickered to life, their violet aureoles flat and opaque as plates against the iron sky. Raindrops spattered and flared up against them in implausible blue. People flung open their umbrellas or ran to shelter beneath storefront awnings.

Pippa stopped two or three times yet to ask after Bailey's, but found herself getting lost, over and over. The complexity of ideas and feelings swarming through her mind and heart had found external expression in the city Ariadne itself — all webbed intersections, by-ways and multi-levelled buildings, brutalist concrete, modernist glass, Gothic revival. This had to be the town centre, the taller part that could be seen from the plains she'd spent the day crossing. Scale-wise it was hardly a massive metropolis, but still it was energetic, a humming centre of commerce and culture. Somehow she found herself walking along a mezzanine connecting three tall, slender buildings; then riding a narrow, moving concourse bounded on either side by silently howling gargoyles who thrust out muscular tongues as long as her arm, spewing the run-off from the already overflowing gutters down to the fountains way below where pretty stone boys stood upon black marble plinths, eternally pissing into pools from bud-like willies. She made her way towards an archway supported between the arms of two three-storey stone giants, great-breasted women squatting on fleshy haunches, like those fertility goddesses that had been found in Willendorf. Entering the belly of one through its vulvic doorway, she found herself in a domed amphitheatre where a schoolboys' choir was practicing hymns: 'And did those bleating, ancient swine, wakapong ingling spa-stur-zine...' She knew the tune, but you couldn't get the words to 'Jerusalem' much more wrong... Then out and up a narrow staircase and through another archway which gave onto a bank of transparent cylindrical lifts moving swiftly; sure now that the direction she needed was down, she darted in one set of sliding doors and her heart flew up as the lift plummeted. Alighting at what she hoped was ground level, she asked again for the way to Bailey's and was directed through a system of spiralling laneways that ran one into the other like a series of interlocking cochleas then out onto a fairly normal-looking tarmac street. And it so happened that eventually Pippa found her way to her destination.

She slipped between the moveless bodies of two enormous but apparently benign bouncers. Inside was warm, loud and crowded. Pippa went up to the bar to ask for a drink she badly needed, then realised she had no money. She retreated to a corner booth and sat down, exhausted, her clothes steaming. A waiter approached, and boggled at her briefly before regaining his composure. The woman she had stopped in the street — and several others too, for that matter — had reacted similarly. Pippa supposed she must look a bit of a wreck. The waiter finally managed to muster the necessary words: 'Can I help you?'

'Not unless you have a job for me.' Left-over bits of rain were trickling down her back and her feet were cold.

The man smiled a small smile. 'Where're you from?'

She was hardly going to tell him the truth and get herself laughed out of sight or handcuffed to the bar-rail while the ambulance or squad cars came — and in any case, she didn't actually know what the truth was. She was at a loss for words. As it happened, this worked in her favour. The waiter, who had been giving her the once over for the third time (the thrice-over? she wondered), suddenly asked her the one question that could be useful to her, which she knew was only slightly less likely than the grey man, the pink sky, the fierce flora, the dissolving aircraft, angels and pirates:

'Can you dance?'

'Well as a matter of fact, I can.'

chapter five
mind the gap

Deep underground, Dr Wilder Portion felt his ambition coiling in his guts like an animal thing. It *would* not go unsatisfied. He needed to be where the calibandits were, to see what they saw, understand what they felt, experience the absolute otherness of the space they inhabited. He had no desire to stop them doing what they did, to alter their nature — for no matter how they disgusted him, he was not about to let himself be distracted by emotion, worthy or otherwise. Wilder was not a moral crusader. He was a scientist. He merely wanted to be the man who made the moonwalk look like a stroll in the park. He wanted to go to that interstitial space and return with hard evidence of its existence, to prove, once and for all, the reality of what had hitherto been thought 'merely' imaginary. This was his vocation.

And that woman had gained access so effortlessly. What series of contingencies had allowed it to happen? But now, the edges of the paradoxical space-time bubble were shored up with caliband particles. He knew that it would be impossible to enter as she had done — even if he had known how the hell she'd done it — because after all, it was no longer a physical space. He was quite certain that such bubbles can only be accessed by solid bodies if there's some level of interference from the corporeal world — interference producing a kind of interface that enables the melding of imaginally-generated and corporeal realities. In the case he had just witnessed, that interference had come via the untidy cracks between wall and ceiling that Brother had just eradicated. There was absolutely nothing Wilder could do about that.

If he wanted to physically access any space other than the physical world he knew, he would have to reduce himself, his body, to suit that environment. He would have to recalibrate his particles on the most fundamental level so that they matched the energy levels of the calibandits.

Impossible. Out of the question. He was human, they were not. His world was natural, theirs supernatural. These were the hard facts, the reality of the situation. But if his life's work was worth anything, if his years of persistence in the face of a sneering academy that had driven him underground, had killed his mentor, were worth anything — if *he* was worth anything — then he must not allow reality to inhibit him. He would instead consider it as the technical problem it was.

A roar above his head heralded the Circle Line's arrival at St James Station. The train juddered to a halt. A deep voice boomed above him through the PA system. He could not hear the individual words — he did not need to, having heard them a thousand times before: MIND THE GAP. PLEASE, MIND THE GAP.

I have the machinery, he told his notebook. I have the drugs. I have seen with my own eyes a point of access, a power point in the whole, holey congeries of temporal-spatial contingency. I can find a way. I can go there. And return?

He refused to dwell on the frightening possibility that he might not. That would not help him now.

If an ignorant woman can sleepwalk her way elsewhere, then a man in control can do the same.

Wilder spent the next fortnight closeted in his underground workroom: refining the Temporal Flux Translator's operating system; watching the calibandits and documenting their style of decalibration in every detail; preparing the chemical compounds he needed to accelerate the atomisation process that very shortly he would practice on himself; then painstakingly entering his personal data from his birth certificate, his diaries, medical records then the main events and the minutiae of his life from childhood until now — memories to shoe size to colour sense and sexual orientation...

When those two weeks were up, he had done as much as he could.

It was time.

Wilder fetched a bottle of mineral water from his cupboard and emptied it into a cup. He poured in equal parts of powdered subatomic kinteticant and accelerant and added a good measure of lucidifier to clarify and enhance his ability to focus his intention, and which had the happy side-effect of valourising the spirit. He slipped the bottles in his pocket — he would need more later when he wanted to return. He set his attention to focus on the image of John Grey. He opened his soul, broadened his consciousness to pick up, like radar, any intimation of the desire of the calibandit, for it was Desire that would be the vehicle of transport to move him from one reality into another. He felt himself slipping into a profound meditative state. At a certain stage he detected a sound, a sound that would be imperceptible to him in any other state but this; it was the gentlest of thuds, like a notion sighing through a mind and meeting the resistance of the body of a barely conceived thought. He opened his eyes.

A moth was bumping its furry body softly against the surface of his dim lamp. Time and time again the moth would venture close, closer, then its dense yet fragile body would touch the source of its desire and its contours would flare briefly in the incandescent glow. But the moth failed to achieve its death, and failed again. Wilder could smell the singed stuff of its downy wings.

Moth desire, moth death. Wilder was afraid, but his fear was somehow dislocated from him. He perceived the fear at one remove, rather than feeling it directly. It was less real than an echo of something that was real.

His consciousness continued to expand; he held tight to John Grey's image, and to the desire that fuelled him.

The analytical part of his mind continued to work as if on auto-pilot, and he clicked the switch that reactivated the Colanderic Spectrometer, which had gone to sleep during his preparations. Like a somnabulist, Wilder opened his personal data file and fed the information into the Spatio-Temporal Flux Translator and set it to 'Decalibrate'. He opened the body-soul links between the Interstitial software and, after lubricating it with a conductive gel, taped one end to his body. He reversed the Unscrambler function to Scramble. Enter.

The connections began their process of melding technology and archaic mystical wisdom with him, Wilder, at the juncture, physically linked in by means of a cable whose design he had modelled on what he had learned from the calibandits' own technology.

Had anyone been there with him to see, they would have found the sight appalling and fantastical, for the bodily dissolution described by the ancients was clearly visible as Wilder's subatomic components began to break down. Wilder felt himself dissolving, and rather than pain or terror the first thing he felt was a wild ecstasy possess him as aspects of 'Wilderness' began to meld with those of the objects to which he was attached, to the light in the room, the dust motes in the light, to the scent molecules of bitumen, diesel and dust. But enough rationality remained for him to adjust his concentration before he was utterly dispersed.

He re-hooked to the destination he required: the yearning of the absent man. He gazed into the screen on which surged images he had recorded of John Grey and Brother, and copies of the sites they had accessed, the places and conditions of mind they had experienced, the mind and souls they had plundered. The selection was set to 'random', and Wilder allowed himself to experience all, bumping up against them gently, like a moth…

One image was stronger than all the others: it was the face of a woman. And Wilder knew that it must be her, the one whom he had glimpsed when she had entered their space in Sydney, 2010. She looked a bit like Cate Blanchett.

Suddenly, like a blow to the solar plexus, he felt Grey's desire undiluted; he reined it in, clung to it, rode it; it was a bucking bronco of yearning, but Wilder held tight even as the interface between fabricated plastic surface and human eyeball jelly dissolved. There was no screen. Wilder, both watcher and participant, had become one of the many images, which now began to separate out into fragments of life and colour.

'Oh…' moaned Wilder, 'Jesus God…' He heard his voice coming back to him like the voice of another. He looked for his hands, the keyboard, the monitor, but could find nothing to identify himself with what he was, or where he thought he was, or had been.

Between each fragment of light lay an infinity of awful darkness. A thought came out of this void. (And the thought probably came from the once singular entity which had called its massed particulars 'Wilder Portion'. But without the containment of personal contours — how can there be finite identity?) Nevertheless, the thought said, *The darkness may have no life, yet it is a force.*

This unleashed a barrage of thoughts zooming through space; zinging and pinging across eternity as if eternity were one great squash court with everybody playing at once. Wilder ducked his now metaphorical head as one of these missiles passed by too close, bringing with it the question, *Am I inside this, or is this inside me?*

The darkness began to seethe and boil. Tides of light broke upon the shores of Wilder's consciousness and upon an infinite number of other bodies of information, crosscurrents of thought, astral projections, hallucinations, dead men's hopes, television broadcasts, mutations of coherence that had gone wild and broken down into gibbering static. Then came more questions:

What lies between one event and the next?

What lies between one star and the next?

Between one question and the next?

Areas of possibility, came the answer from the dark, from the black, boiling absences whose matter is dense, so very, very heavy and whose gravity is irresistible…

And the black, boiling absences produced words he could see, words that were at the same time images, some of them new, brilliant and evanescent, some may have been here for aeons, since the beginning; they hovered for a moment or a century, shedding light, others slashed and burned his mind, leaving it clean of reason… no sense arrived and the would-be carriers of meaning sprawled away, weeping into the traffic of Inbetween images, ideas lost in translation, notions in transit, radio broadcasts, lunatic dreams, all things real, virtual, imagined, sacred and profane, holy and unholy: there an advertisement for contraceptive jelly, there a burning cross, here a troupe of brutalised refugees being driven from point alpha to point beta to gamma to alpha again, there a beautiful boy gazing into a pond and loving his own image, falling into himself, down and down into the cold, inky blackness…

chapter six
the Arrival

Mumu Nongog was sitting with some friends by the Overdrain, clogged now with bladed leaves fallen from the yoq trees that arched overhead, filtering the light and striping the faces of the children into bands of blue and green in the shade, gold when the light fell. Her friends were rapt, wanting to believe, but putting a good show in not believing at all.

'You never found an Arrival,' piped Shakespeare, his teeth black with liquorice and his lazy eye wandering idly off towards his nose. 'There hasn't been one for years and years and years.'

'That's right,' added Emcee Squared and Columbine Hogson together. 'Must've just been a ghost you saw.'

Bloody cheek, thought Mu. As if I can't tell the difference between an Arrival and a garden-variety ghost. 'You wanna hear or not?' That shut them up. 'Well, so as you know, the Blinkin Fields has been goin' wild the last coupla weeks and nobody's allowed there except the special tourist coaches. Youse all heard the talk. Well, me and Sim wanted to see it in action. We used to go often enough before it was banned, to play among the television and raw brains —' Mu knew that would make their eyes go all wide, as they did now, the scaredy cats '— but we knew it'd be wild now, like the surf you get down at the gulf in autumn, only air instead a water. So I nicked a coupla sets a godlight goggles from the staff room —' she knew that would get them talking too, ha '— an we'd been havin a good time with all the pictures. We'd seen a bunch a giant ads for holidays and one for guns from some kinda Elsewhere that Simson got into grandwise, an we saw an angel an it was terrible, but of course not real — it flew right through Sim and you shoulda heard him yell. It was real full-on carnival altogether. Then he goes, "Mu! There's a man configurin like, in the air." I don't believe him at first, so I go, "Bollocks. It's just a nother magination."

' "Not," says Sim, who's hoppin about like he's got electric knees. An he's draggin on me cardy, an I've got a hold of his jumper because he's only seven and don't know about danger, and the godlids all snapping about our ankles like terriers. We have to get up real close because of all the interference in the air…'

'Which is why you're not meant to go there,' put in Lewis, as he unscrewed the cap of his thermos and poured himself a cupful of colabrew.

'Oooh and who's a little goody goody then?' That got a few admiring laughs from Columbine and Squared and Speare, but Lewis just eyed her over the rim of cup. 'Anyway, so then bloody Sim reaches out to touch the damn thing! An when he did that, his hand didn't go through at all like it should of. He yelped like he'd been burnt and ran round behind me like a wimpy little boy, which he is. Then I knew he was right and it wasn't a magination. I did think for a minute then that it could of been a ghost —' she nodded at Lew. 'But it wasn't. Definitely and for sure. It was a real man forming. He was fuzzy at the edges and all pixelated, a blur of colour sorta thing, only in segments. He was made up of bits, like slivers and chunks of broken glass. Milky sorta violet and pale green showed under the fleshy pink colour that was most of him. He was in the nuddy and I was a bit embarrassed by the time he'd got all his particulars together. His face was screamin. I mean, I could see it, but the sound hadn't caught up with the image so his scream was silent, a most sorry and scary sight and I backed off. I tell you, I could of wept for the sore ache of distress came outa him in waves an I could feel my body sort of suckin in all that sensation. That's the first thing you learn at school after the alphabet, everyone knows it, how we're all linked in a kind of sensation soup. And the feelin was goin into Sim too, he was blubberin into my shirt with the weirdness and sad achiness of it all. The man stood there, sort of swaying and boggling at us as if we were the ones just came together outa the ether and not him. Then he fell plonk on the ground, squishing the life outa a dozen godlids and injurin a whole bunch more, even though he was still quite a lot partial and you could see the grass and bugs and godlids through the gaps where he wasn't quite realised yet.

'The nearby godlids sorta drew themselves into themselves from the shock of it all, and the pinky air sorta curdled around us for a minute. "Simson," I says in me quiet voice that he knows has to be obeyed or else, "go down the hill and get a grownup… an after you do that, tell Eftsoons and Erewhile." I give him a handful of garlic cloves to pay Baxta on the way. But Sim starts mutterin about how it's not fair, but I yell at him then, because the poor man's twitchin now, his parts keen for attention. I can sense a straining behind it, a body straining to get ahold of the last bits of reality it needs to be solid. It makes me feel funny an queasy to look at it straight. So I don't. "An hurry," I say, because it was spooky as hell I tell you, this birthing sorta thing happening in me face.

'Sim went, careering through the pink fug and the

washy pictures from television and raw brains towards Baxta's Gibbet at the Crossroads. I squatted down a little distance away from the man thing an watched while it kept gatherin itself together. Slowly slowly the holes between the bits was disappearin, but the man was groanin something terrible. I felt sorry for him, but mostly a bit sick with the unnature of it. But I held onto me tummy and didn't chuck, even though the godlids were up an on high alert again, all stinky with glee, bobbin away, snatchin hummingbirds outa the air and gulpin them down between wary sniffs a this new lump of flesh layin about on them. I remembered how Grannap used to bore on about how there use to be more partials comin real like, in the olden days, before his great great great great great great great Grannap planted the first godlid. But I never took him too seriously because he can't hardly remember his name.

'The air was getting nippy and I was dead nervous, and not just with the scariness of that weird realing happenin at me, and the bunch a ostriches that was looking me over like I was a rodent for dinner or whatever. The clouds went over the sun for a minute then, an started comin on heavy grey and cranky lookin, and the breeze was pickin up and pushing the raw brains about the air, makin weirdscapes like I've never seen before, but I spose half a them was outa brains drunk on whatever, an maybe even shamans tryin out this sorta truth an that. I can only take a little bit of truth, if it's undiluted.' This comment caused a ripple of humour, which she ignored. 'Then, thank the gawds, I heard Bailey-from-the-pub's voice, then got sight of her and a bunch a people to help if they could and watch if they couldn't. Sim was behind them, pushin Grannap in his dolly-cauldron, an *he* was frithin and frothin with the excitement of it all. Bailey didn't say anything, just started hauling the man onto Grannap's dolly. An all the while there was aerials liltin and quiltin and quasin and queasin about — raw brains an other bits of magination and television all mixed up together so the pictures didn't make sense any more, it was all gone crazy...

'But Bailey was patient an careful with him, an the others gathered other parts of him together, a bit of iris, a fragment from off his side, a coupla toes that wouldn't join too good, plus some almost liquid stuff that they thought was his, but had gone all like a cloud of bees that's dispersed. But Bailey knew how to gather it so that the bits of him reckanised each other and could come together like a team, a bee team of teemin bees to make the final bits a solid man. An then I had to go off a bit an chuck, watchin that, it sort makes your tummy go all queer in sympathy. An when I got back he was *here*, properly. Lying on Grannap's dolly with godlids dippin down and flappin their hairy lids an lickin up his sweat like greedy puppies.'

'An where is he now?' asked Lewis.

'At the Registry a course.'

The school bell rang for the last class of the day. A small silence followed. Then her audience dispersed. What an anticlimax. What was she doing here? The thought of the classroom was deathly. And she was still angry at the way the adults had treated her. After they'd loaded up the man, she and Sim had been sent on ahead back to the town. She'd walked with Sim back to the little kids school, then come back here, out of habit. She got angrier and angrier the more she thought about it. It had been Sim and her that had found him in the first place. 'What am I doing here?' she asked herself aloud this time. Then, 'Bugger 'em.' Mu walked away from the school and down the street towards the Registry, another place that she was absolutely forbidden to go.

She raced up the stairs to the top floor of the Registry building. At the door of Erewhile and Eftsoons' office stood Grannap's dolly, with Grannap's sleepy old head lolling there in its cauldron of soupy psychic stew. Mu sidestepped the old relic and cracked the door of the Registry. It was hard to see much at first; the light was poor, the small windows smeared and filthy with ages of dust and the fetid breath of generations of Registrars. There were the deep shelves with their rows of moribund bodies all bound up in silk swaddling, and the tall, spindly shelves laden with concertina files and stacks of papers that reached beyond vision. Even so, the Registrars could not accommodate all the material this place had to store, for on the floor were more waist-height piles of documents, shifting and teetering in the draft that Mu had created by opening the door this tiny crack. At the back of the room, banks of green and red and orange eyes blinked on the consoles of computers and monitors, printers and scanners and other electronic devices whose functions Mu could only guess at. Cables trailed across the floor or hung from shelves amongst the cobwebs that were everywhere, coarse and strong or tenuous as the flimsiest hope. Finally Mu managed to locate the shape of Bailey, standing still and respectful at the counter, with the man lying at her feet, to all intents and purposes quite insensible.

As she watched, from the depths of the store emerged the dusty grey and the dustier greyer forms of the two Registrars and Mu realised that she'd missed nothing. Bailey must've taken a while to get here, having to push the dolly without losing its cargo or slopping Grannap's soup.

'Who would interrupt our knitting?' said Eftsoons, in a soft, sticky little voice, spitting a skein of intricately knotted fibres from his lips. It slipped through a hole in the ether and disappeared.

'To what do we owe this untoward disturbance?' enquired Erewhile in a small, dry voice like ant feet on fine sandpaper. Her best eye, red and rheumy, glinted testily through its monocle. Her narrow old shoulders were draped in a soft, tea-rose shawl. She clutched it to her throat with two of her spare arms, and laid aside her large ledger, bound in the skin of unborn calves.

'Registrars, I am sorry to disturb your filing. I have come to register an Arrival,' said Bailey, in a voice that sounded quite feeble to Mu and not at all like the bossy Bailey she knew so well, whose bar she cleaned every morning before school: the businesslike Bailey who paid her in coconut slices and colabrew more often than cash. But then, everyone was intimidated by Erewhile and Eftsoons. That was their power.

'Say the magic password,' answered the Registrars, catechismically.

'It's an ill wind that blows no good,' said Bailey obediently.

'Never a truer word was spoken,' they replied in unison. 'Very well. Speak, Publican.'

For an answer, Bailey nodded at the prone form at her feet.

'A degenerate entity,' whispered Eftsoons to Erewhile. 'Ahhh. Decomposing itself on fast forward.'

Erewhile crouched down on four of her eight spindly legs and cradled the man's head in two other ones. She peered closely into the man's face. 'Could be…'

'Recomposing?' interrupted Bailey.

'Impossible,' answered Erewhile, wiping her damp mandibles with a monogrammed linen handkerchief.

'Ooh no. Well past that,' added Eftsoons.

Bailey looked very sad from where Mu stood, her shoulders slumped, but she didn't make any sort of move to check for herself. Mu liked Bailey, but like everyone else the publican always deferred to the Registrars' judgement. Mu crept inside and hid behind a particularly liana-like rope of cobweb. She could just see the man's face. She hadn't noticed before in the excitement of it all, but he was very good looking for an old person. The lines on his face showed he had a sense of humour; they were like the lines she remembered her father had, fanning up from his eye corners into his hairline.

In the meantime, Erewhile had begun taking down the details of the man's appearance and arrival in the Blinking Fields, her pincers speeding across the keyboard as Bailey described the event as far as she knew it.

'Waste not, want not,' intoned the Registrars together.

'I suppose so,' agreed Bailey sadly. 'You know what to do.'

'No,' murmured Mu under her breath. '*No way!* I found him. He's my business, not theirs!'

But as she watched in dismay, the Registrars crouched low on their sixteen steepled limbs. Erewhile nodded at Eftsoons, and Eftsoons nodded back. They twiddled their thumb-pincers in anticipation. They began to chew…

'No substance,' murmured Eftsoons through his munching mandibles.

'Gutless,' agreed Erewhile as the tip of a knotty braid began to emerge from her lipless little maw.

'The ill wind is blowing no good through its

disintegrating moral fibres.'

The sticky skeins of silk, by gentle but inexorable degrees, emerged from their lips… growing and spreading and picking up dust and hairballs as they progressed.

'Such decrepitude. Its substance all eked away, godstrings all flaccid.'

'A has-been.'

'A would have been.'

Together they gradually wove a cocoon of silken swaddling around the man until nothing showed but his head and his feet.

'We will store him,' said Erewhile as the pall of thread rose to the top of the man's neck.

'File him,' added Eftsoons, as the man's chin disappeared into the silken shroud.

'Catalogue him.'

'*WAIT ON!*' yelled Mu, who could stand it no longer. 'How d'youse know he's dead!'

Three faces, one human and two human-spider, turned to face the interruption.

'I mean, for sure, absolute sure,' she added more quietly. 'Sorta thing.'

'Mu! What d'you think you're doing here?' cried Bailey, more shocked than angry at Mu's sudden irruption.

Bailey's tone got her roused again, and she said, firmly and angrily: 'You just believe these old librarians because you're, you're… *stupid!*' Then, reckoning that she might as well be hung for a sheep as a lamb. 'Look, they just like filing… that's what they *do*, they don't know anything else.'

The Registrars hissed, and bits of spittle got caught on the threads oozing from their maws.

'Bailey, *please!*' Mu ran up to her and grabbed her by the arm.

'Mu, they've diagnosed him. There's no way…' but as she spoke, a sigh came from the swaddling and all four people wheeled round to see, impossibly, the white cheeks flush with pale pink.

Within a minute Mu had wheeled in the dolly and Bailey and Mu had reloaded the man onto it and bolted, slopping Grannap soup all over themselves in their haste to be out.

As the door closed behind them Eftsoons murmured, 'Well, at least we got most of his details.'

'He is a new thing.'

'A new thing in Ariadne.'

'A new thing is a dangerous thing.'

'That is so. It's an ill wind.'

'What are we to do?'

'We can only wait.'

'Wait and see.'

Erewhile and Eftsoons returned to their ancient tasks, moving about their vaulted repository of lost hopes as gently as settling alluvium, replacing a mothball here and there, tucking in loose ends of swaddling, then dusting, with infinite tenderness, a filing cabinet, a shelf of ancient records, then the dead-eyed monitors behind whose bland faces the data of ages was meticulously filed in complex storage systems, perpetually augmented, organised and reorganised. The looseleaf redundancies and anachronisms rattled amongst dry leaves of papyrus, rag, parchment, ricepaper and standard A4 paper. Though their mouths are stuffed with cotton and their ears filled with sealing wax, still they remember the old days before their meanings were lost to all definition with the silty accretions of unforgiving time.

chapter seven
Cate Blanchett's sternocleidomastoid

Dr Wilder Portion woke up to find himself swaddled from chin to toe in what looked and felt like Thai silk. He was lying on a thick mattress on the floor and he couldn't move a muscle. He swallowed down panic. Unable to inventory any damage that may have been done to his tightly bound body, he began instead, with a great effort of self-control, to take in his surroundings, slowly and carefully. A small window looking out onto sky. A black square of night. Not much information to be gained there. Walls painted a soothing pale blue. A bookshelf. He could read none of the titles from here. A desk with a laptop, its screensaver displaying a country scene with robins flying from tree to tree. An upright chair. A door, closed. As he was unable to turn his head, that was it. One thing only was certain: this was not the space in which his calibandits had set up their temporary existence. He made a mental note: think about this anomaly within the broader scheme of anomalies when brain re-engages.

Touching his tongue to that small space between nose and lips — what was it called? — he felt cool plastic tubing. He sniffed the air and picked up the scent of roses and petrol and disinfectant. He breathed it in deeply, and as he breathed, felt the tightness of the fabric once more against his chest, his arms and legs. His body and limbs were all there then, and tingling as if a zillion microscopic insects were at work with their zillion tiny wings vibrating against his skin. Did this sensation signify the coming together of his components or fleshly disintegration? Panic rose again. He swallowed hard and felt tears come to his eyes. Noted: ducts operational.

Never having discomposed himself before, he did not know if this meant that when the swaddling was removed he would now be whole or he would just fall apart like a rotten breadfruit. He drove the panic down again and tried out a moan. It seemed to work. Noted: throat and larynx in order. He clenched his buttocks and felt them squeeze tightly against each other. He tried out another groan, louder now. This prompted the same response from his throat and also caused a flurry of movement from a part of the room he had been unable to see because of the tight swaddling. Then from the flurry erupted a child, who boggled at him briefly then made for the door. He heard feet retreating down a staircase that must lie just outside his door. He listened until he could hear them no more. It was then that he became aware of a gentle bass rhythm issuing from downstairs. If he concentrated he could feel the slightest vibrations coming through the floorboards and the mattress that supported him.

The door opened again. A woman stood there, stocky, with ironbark hair and a jaw pocked with old acne scars. Square face. Friendly? Unfriendly? She smiled. He still wasn't sure. One of her front teeth was tattooed with the ace of spades, the other was missing. Wilder thought he might as well try out his voice.

'Where's my cable?'

'How are you feeling?' she answered, ignoring his question. Her voice was soft, but contained a certain level of authority. A nurse? A doctor? 'I'm Bailey. Run the pub downstairs.' Wilder tried out a thought: I have crossed vast dimensions of time and space, endured a total breakdown of body and consciousness, been reconfigured — and have landed *in a* pub?

'Where on earth am I?'

'Onurth? Don't know about that.' Bailey moved closer to him and knelt by his mattress. Without waiting for permission she began, with gentle stubby fingers, to carefully unpeel him like a fruit. Only now did he observe that the swaddling was not made of bandages, but of enormously long skeins of soft thread.

While she unravelled, Bailey talked — not of Wilder's Arrival, which she judged would frighten the poor fellow to the death he had so narrowly escaped, and therefore must wait until he was stronger — but of this country of Mogom, its topography and climate, the capital of Ariadne, its shops and offices and architectural heritage and cultural monuments, as if Wilder were like any other tourist who would naturally be interested in these things. She also explained how the active ingredients of Erewhile and Eftsoons' fabric could either preserve the dead or repair living tissue, depending upon the integrity of the material.

'Sorry, ah… Do you mean by *the material* — me?'

'Of course. Who else? You're lucky we stopped them before they wrapped up your head though… Look, can you shift a bit so's I can get to the back side of this swaddling?'

Obligingly, Wilder redistributed his weight, surprised that he could do so quite easily. The pins and needles were diminishing now and he was starting to feel a bit less wobbly; and with the return of his body to some semblance of normality, his mind too was coming alive and re-entering its usual condition of greedy inquisitiveness. 'So. Let me get this straight. If my "material" had been a bit less "integrated", I'd be a sort of mummy by now?'

'Mummy?'

'You know, a sort of preserved corpse.'

'Yep, that's right,' she answered brightly. She began to unwrap his midriff.

Wilder took a moment to digest this information. He observed that it made him feel sick. However, under Bailey's patient ministrations, the feeling passed. In fact the unwrapping sensation was far from unpleasant and the vulnerability he felt at her sure hands with their sinewy but blunt-tipped fingers was not without its erotic side, so that at a certain point Bailey said, pleasantly, 'Handsome bit of manhood you've got there, fella.'

Well thanks, thought Wilder, blushing like a virgin.

Bailey called down the stairs for some food to be brought up.

A couple of hours later, after another sleep and another bowl of Bailey's oxtail soup, Wilder felt much better. Because his body felt safe, his mind now began to panic him. Why had he arrived naked as a baby? Where was his lifeline to the spectrometer?

There was nothing to be found out lying here on this mattress. He got up and put on the set of clothes that Bailey had kindly left for him: brown corduroy trousers, a light blue cotton shirt and a pair of soft rubber-soled runners that almost fit. He exited the room. The sounds that had come up to him through the floorboards were encouraging — laughter, music, the clink of glasses. He tentatively felt his way down the stairs: wooden and narrow, lit by low electric lights in wall sconces. The runners helped stabilise him, offering the unsteady Wilder, in the surreality of new reality, a sense of slight security. He trusted the reality of these rubber runners.

He entered a small foyer with three doors, two to the bathrooms. Between them was a corkboard with ads for sexual services, for events that looked a lot like bingo nights, and for various jobs. One of these interested him particularly. There was a half-tone image of a wide plain, dotted with flowers. The sky was pink. Even though he'd been non compos mentis at the time, he recognised it as the place he'd been reconfigured. He scanned the text: *Notion Collector Required or Not* it read. *Apply to Carneac.* Underneath was a fringe of tear-off strips, each labelled with a printed number. Did they have phones here? He tore off a strip and stuffed it into his pocket. This 'Carneac' would know something about his predicament, he sensed, living — or at least working — as she? he? did in that weird pink threshold zone. Maybe Carneac had found his cable? And in any case he had to meet the author of a note who required the services of such a thing as a 'notion collector' — or not — whatever that was about. He'd find out. It was his professional duty.

Opening the third door he found himself looking into a large room, dark and bright; smoke-softened lights from obscure sources patchily illuminated the room in Mannerist chiaroscuro. As he entered, he accidentally bumped into a girl in jeans and T-shirt that said *Blink in the Light of Revelation*, who turned and stared at him. She nudged her friend, who also stared. 'A ripple of interest soon traveled the length and breadth of the room, and people turned to take him in, assessing, curious. He had not considered how quickly news spreads in small towns — and for all its strangeness and busy nightlife, Ariadne was a small town. Several people reached out to touch him as he moved through the crowd. He let them. He supposed visitants from other worlds ought to create a bit of a stir, though it did feel a little like he'd just walked into a Western film set where the locals check out the newcomer as he strolls into the saloon. Thus, he hitched up his trousers as though the pistols in his holster needed readjusting and looked around in a way he hoped was cool but not so bold as to cause a *High Noon* type situation. Zane Grey would have applauded his performance, he was certain.

There was a long counter at one end and in the centre a small raised platform of some kind of translucent material, on top of which a couple, a pretty boy and girl, were performing a kind of go-go dance to the music with that pervasive bass that he had felt through the floorboards upstairs. All around them was a sea of tables that seemed to rise and fall on the thick, blue currents of smoke. Some people sipped from tall beer glasses opaque with frost, or from flutes of multi-colored liquors; others moved between tables, talking to friends. Others were dancing, lost to the world outside their own bodies. It was hot and humid with poor ventilation and rich with promise. He took a seat at the bar of burnished wood patterned with many interlocking rings of glasses past. Voices, human and instrumental were fighting for ascendancy; fumes, sweet and sour; animated faces and bodies.

Perched on a stool nearby was a couple chatting in intimate tones, well below the level of the music that was moist with innuendo. There was a woman, her chin in her hand, staring contemplatively into her glass. She was of slight build and the bodice of her low-cut top framed small, round breasts that Wilder reckoned might at any moment escape, and go bouncing off along the bar on some jolly mission of their own. She shifted in her seat, re-crossing her long slender legs, which were bare from the hem of her tiny skirt to her knees, where they met a pair of tall skin-tight boots that were laced, Roman style, with strings of small silver bells. There were strings of bells around her middle too, and another winking from the hollow of her navel. All of this was of course wonderful. But it was only when she reached for her drink that Wilder caught his breath: the hand that grasped the glass was translucent. He could see the ice cubes through her knuckles. He looked her over again in quite a different way. The lights were dim, but now that he was squinting he saw that yes, every part of her, from top to beautiful bottom, was clear, not as crystal, but more like a kind of exquisite milky glass. He watched in fascination the movement of a vein in her biceps as she raised her arm to adjust her hair, the shadowy hinge of jaw and skull, then the dim shape of a patron passing by beyond her, like an idea passing through her mind.

The woman felt his gaze and looked up. *Jesus God.* It was *her.* 'Sydney 2010'. The see-through version. Both the fact of her presence and her condition were impossible. But then, everything else was too.

'What'll you have, fella?' It was Bailey, her cratered face gleaming in the barlight like a friendly moon. She clicked her tongue against her tattooed tooth. 'Quick sticks — it's on me.' He ordered a beer. For want of something to steady himself after the shock, he paid strict attention to the pulling of the beer. He noted that the style of beer-pulling here was actually not that different from what he was accustomed to. He knocked back far too much in one open-throated swallow, something he would not normally have done. But these were strange days. Possibly none have ever been stranger for anyone in the history of mankind. As he recovered from the headspin, he noticed she, her, the transparent woman, was talking. To him.

'You look a bit fazed.' She smiled hesitantly.

She did look quite like Cate Blanchett around the

mouth and throat he thought, though he had never seen Cate's sternocleidomastoid. But he was sure it could never be as sinuously stylish and elegant as this woman's. He wanted to reach out and touch the spot where her clavicle met the jugular notch of her sternum. Oh lovely and most mortal of creatures! The breath was drawn from him as a sigh… Oh, I want to settle for a while in that warm space behind your diaphragm. Let me rest my head on the pillow of your lung, and I will play the xylophone of your ribcage with little felt-bound drumsticks…

'I'm fine thanks,' he answered, though there was absolutely no truth or logic in that statement. How does one talk to a wraith? A ghost? A goddess? 'May I compliment you on your handsome boots.'

Her smile gained in confidence as she answered, 'These, Rip Van, are my ecstasy boots.'

'Oh. Yes. I see,' he said, not seeing anything but her creamy bosom, with its delicate suspensory ligaments and layer of pearly fat below the taut skin. The tops of those breasts basked in the bar-light like the backs of two dreaming dolphins. 'I'm Wilder.'

'You're what?'

'Sorry. My name. I was conceived on safari in Botswana. My parents were… never mind what they were. Sorry, I'm a bit… never mind. I mean, buy you a drink?'

The loud music cloaked their voices as she leant towards him and said, 'Everyone's heard about you.' Her eyes were bright. The plates of her brow and cheekbones gleamed dully from under the skin framed by flat tongues of light brown and dark blond hair. Her sinuses pulsed mildly. Perhaps she was sensitive to the smoke. He gripped the edge of the bar and tried to focus on what this ghost was saying to him as she continued: 'Bailey — you know, her at the bar — was on the radio about a second after you Arrived with a capital A.' She looked at him with sympathy. 'It's all a bit much, isn't it?'

'It is.' He took a pull of his beer, feeling suddenly almost tearful. Hardly surprising, he thought. *A bit much* was surely the understatement of the century.

'I know how it feels. I Arrived about a fortnight ago.' She took a sip of the drink Bailey now put down in front of her. 'But not entirely.' She twisted her lips in what would have been a smile had there been any humour in what she'd said about the truth of her predicament. 'Pippalotti Colquouhoun.' It took Wilder a moment to realise she was introducing herself. He reached towards the hand that was lying on the bar not very far from his, but it shifted from his on approach, and picked up the glass. Wilder caught a whiff of lime juice and pineapple mixed with bitter liquors and sweet. She took a deeper drink this time, and he watched what seemed to be a Singapore Sling sluice over her teeth and the shadow of her tongue. 'Wilder, where are you from?'

'I'm from the same place as you.'

Because Pippa had seen and endured a great deal of the impossible this past two weeks, she was for a moment inclined to take what he'd said as a literal truth. But the surge of shock mixed with its few grains of hope quickly evaporated as she realised that all he could mean was that he was from the place the Mogomis referred to with one name: Elsewhere. For the locals, everywhere but Mogom was one and the same: foreign parts that provided images, Ariadne's local cultural currency…

'Or East Sydney, I mean, really. Not Darlinghurst proper,' Wilder was now saying. 'That's up the other end of Liverpool Street.' He watched her closely as he spoke.

Her face flushed then paled then flushed again. It was really all very Technicolor, what with those delicate lilac, mauve, blue-green veins contrasting with the creamy flesh shifting from rose to red to white and back to pink, and a nerve fluttering at her temple. Colour with texture, visible sensation… a synaesthetic concerto.

Just then, Bailey came over to where they were sitting and indicated with a strict look at Pippa, the now empty plinth, rotating gently like a lost buoy marooned on a sea of smoke. Pippa nodded at her boss then turned back to Wilder. She rubbed her face, causing a riot among the capillaries. 'Look, we must talk asap. I just have to do a quick bit of dancing first, I won't be long. *Don't go anywhere.* We'll talk as soon as I've finished, okay?' Wilder nodded emphatically and the ghost drained the last of her drink, which flowed down her oesophagus like silk and disappeared into her bodice. She got to her feet and as she made her way through the massed bodies, the massed bodies seemed to make their way through her. And the strangest part of it was that while a face or two registered surprise, they recovered very quickly, as if they'd said to themselves, *Oh, a ghost! How interesting. Pass the beer nuts.*

She danced.

Her feet twinkled like starlight, then as the music grew louder and stronger, the tinkling evaporated like a dream and now her feet pumped up and down like pistons in their white boots, making a surprisingly solid connection with the floor. She seemed to be stomping red ants or bull ants or tyrants… he had never seen the likes of this dancing. Then the rhythm slowed and she danced up an image of the flat wideness of broad, haunted places, arms spread wide, then framing those iliac crests of hers that moved with a rhythm all their own…

she danced and Wilder saw the genii of love

she danced and Wilder felt the wilderness of longing

she danced and Wilder felt a breadth of knowledge, carnal, cerebral, soulful

she danced and he sensed the deep verticality of the sins of the father

she danced to the consolation of lust for when love flies out the window into the moon to weep amongst the cloud shrubs of chrysanthemums, funereal and celebratory, depending on where you're from

she danced a hymn to the lost...

But Wilder didn't get to see the end of it, because the travel, the smoke, the music, the liquor and the winsome ghost overwhelmed him, and he felt giddy again. He stumbled towards the street door and leant heavily against what he had taken for a doorpost, but in a moment proved to be the columnar body of a massive bouncer. Wilder drew back, confused and embarrassed. The bouncer's head seemed to be miles above Wilder's. Just above eye level he noted the man's identity badge: *Bob.* Bob's distant face, with its squashed nose and brilliantined sideburns smiled down at him tenderly. 'Don't worry,' he said in a voice like a bass bell tolling deep under the earth. 'We are born, we suffer, we die.'

'Just so,' said another profound voice like an echo out of a well. Wilder turned, looked up: another bouncer, equally tall, broad and statuesque, was standing just to his left. He too, according to his lapel, was *Bob.* Wilder breathed in through his nose and prayed that the dizzy spell would pass. 'Life. Who'd have it?' the monolith added.

Pudding-nosed Bob considered the question seriously then nodded his huge, square head and said, 'If, while still within that cloying swamp of red murk which sustains us before birth, we were somehow made aware of the toils of existence and were given the option to regress back through each stage from ante-natal babe through reptilian embryo and uterine polyp to paternal eye-gleam — *or*,' he raised an emphatic finger, 'to *accept* life's challenge, would we take the former option? I doubt it. We would be compelled to go on out into the unforgiving brilliance of creation, for having no experience of pain, we would necessarily err on the side of optimism.'

'I agree,' nodded his companion. 'It was ever thus. Our enduring sanguinity is a mysterious quantity — like life itself. An enigma. A spiral without a centre…'

'Indeed. Without a heart,' rejoined Pudding-Nose.

'A heartless vortex, life.'

'*Life*, my good friend, is an onion.'

And now, Wilder's recent experiences, galvanized by the sharp, chill air caused him at last to faint. It really was *All A Bit Much*. The bouncers carried him gently to his room.

All afternoon, as per Bailey's instructions, Mumu Nongog had watched the Arrival — *her* Arrival — sleep. And he really *was* hers. After all, if it'd been up to Bailey, with her blind trust in the Registrars' assessment, the man would've been filed, catalogued and dead as a doornail by now. Mu was young, but had seen plenty of maginations, raw brains and ghosts, including the one who'd come to town soon before The Advent of Wilder. But never before had she witnessed an actual, solid manifestation from Elsewhere. When the man had finally woken up, Mu had scuttled out of there quick smart and straight down to the bar to get Bailey, as she had been told to do.

Mu was now walking home along the well-lit busy

road, eating from the tin of coconut slices Bailey had given her. Streetcars phloomphing by on fat pneumatic tyres, joyboys singing in groups, light-and-shadow plays of manufactured Notions from Carneac's sieve pouring out of the kinemats or projected onto the creamy enamel, the concrete, the brick, plastic, laminated cardboard, and stone of the facades, illustrated fantasies and histories from Elsewhere. It was late, but her Mum would be okay with it. She considered the task Bailey had given her as a privilege. Not since Grannap was whole had their family had anything to do with Arrivals and Departures, but this was their traditional role, being Nongogs. Mum was proud of her when Bailey had called and asked 'for a loan of your eldest'.

Mu walked up the front path between the waist-high clumps of yellow-eyed fan-headed daisies into the little enclosed porch, worked all over with its blue lattice spirit baffle. There were blue and green baffles around the windows too. Grannap had insisted on it when he was in his right mind, decades before Mu's birth. Baffling houses had been the fashion in his time; lots of the older people still had them. It made them feel more secure, and not just against lost spectral things. Keeping up the old ways gave them a sense of continuity. It wasn't as if the world was always an entirely reliable place, reflected Mu. It could make you mental, so why not let the old buggers keep their customs? They were right in a way. Figments like raw brains and maginations and whatnot were all fine, they weren't really real, and anyway they wouldn't last five minutes away from the Blinking Fields. But you really don't want ghosts or whatever just dropping in without an invite.

The baffle crackled gently as Mu entered the lightless house. Everyone was in bed. Well, they ought to be, it was after eleven. Still, it was all a bit anticlimactic. She had really wanted something more to happen — though what, precisely, she had not considered. Just something. She made her way up the stairs, pausing only to say goodnight to Grannap, who rarely slept. He was humming quietly to himself in his cosy niche by the stove. All was as it was. As ever. Nothing changed in Mogom.

'*So what happened?*' hissed Sim as soon as Mu walked into their room.

'What are you doin still awake, you bugger,' said Mu, as she flopped down next to him on his bed. 'I'm knackered. Want a biscuit?' She dropped the half-depleted tin onto his lap. Outside the street was quietening down at last. Neon-tainted moonlight seeped through the flimsy curtains, pale yellow, laden with night mist. Mu snuggled down into Simson's pillows.

'Don't you *dare* go to sleep!' he pushed her roughly. 'Tell!'

'Well… I watched, and I waited, and I watched, an I…'

'Just *tell* me!'

'But I am, if you'd just shut up a minute. It was just that. But you know what was weird? Even though mindin someone sleep is about as excitin as watchin paint dry, it was dead spooky too.' Sim was sitting up now, his eyes alive with fear and delight. 'You know, like in a horror movie, when people are walkin around the haunted house looking for where the funny noise come from? An you know there's somethin horrible about to jump on them, and the waitin for that keeps your heart goin cha-cha like a dancin chicken with 'is head off, but at the same time, it's all drawn out and bo-o-oring. Well, it was like that. I was waitin for, for…'

'For what?'

'For him to turn into some kinda horror show magination, only real… which is what he is, right?'

'An did he?'

'A course. Listen. His breathin started gettin louder, you know, like from almost nothin to somethin like the noise Grannap use to make when he was about to do a bit a divinin, before he lost the knack. Then he sits up all of sudden — an I nearly jumped outa me skin — but I didn't. I jumped up and grabbed a hold of the broom that was by the door and I whacked him!'

'You *whacked* him?'

'I did. And then he flopped down again, green drool comin outa his gob and oozing into the Registrars' nice healin silk and down the mattress and onta the floor, till it was like a flood an I had to stand on a chair or else I'd be soaked in the horrible stuff, an it just kept comin, sorta seepin an smoking with poison fumes, till I was chokin on 'em…' and Mu reared up off the bed, raising her hands high, knowing that effect in the gloom of their midnight room could scare her little brother to death, and howled, 'R-R-R-R-O-O-OOOWWW!!!'

Sim screamed.

'Quiet, you lot!' came Mum's voice from the next room.

Much later that night, or very early in the morning, Mu opened her eyes. They met the porous blackness of a dark and silent room, seemingly filled with invisible threats. The room seemed to pulse like a submarine in a bottomless sea. It was as if there was nothing beyond this room. She felt its used air settling on her mind like a virus. Sim's steady breathing nearby was no comfort; he was separate, protected, only she was awake and vulnerable. To what, she could not have said. She rose and made her way down the dark stairs.

Grannap was murmuring restlessly in his niche. He was edgy too, even in sleep. Mu took in the shadowy room. There, by the double doors leading into the kitchen, was the solid wooden table. She walked over and ran her hand over its grainy surface. Its scattering of crumbs professed innocence, but she was not reassured. Four upright chairs, rigidly on guard. There was the bookshelf with books filled with colour prints and stories and words. Harmless, she told herself, even though they seemed somehow canted forward in a listening attitude. The three armchairs hulked together by the dead fireplace, colluding like plotting witches.

She hears herself breathe, feeling the life entering and leaving, entering and leaving her body; she breathes an air of unspecific anxiety, yet it is more than slightly tinged with excitement. Maybe, at last, there would be changes in Mogom. Here alone, the last conscious soul awake in the dark of this night, she feels the presence of strangeness, like a low humming, deep in her breast, an electrically humming, thrumming wire lined with starlings, who gripped the wire tightly as the wind of change snapped it into life. The starling claws grip, Mu feels the sharpness in the skin of her nerves. She is alive to anything that might happen next. And there would be something, at last. Mu realises that she feels dread. And alongside this, profound excitement. Like the wind, the wire, the starlings, she is alive to possibility. She would not sleep again tonight.

chapter eight
Blink in the Light of Revelation

Half asleep, Wilder's mind clicked into gear gratingly. He was not game to open his eyes in case everything he remembered was true. John Grey's surge of desire. Teeming void. Pink fields. Disintegration, dismemberment and rememberment. Transparent women. He heard a chorus of what he imagined might have been blackbirds. He had heard that blackbirds were about in the morning and that they had famously melodious voices, but as an antipodean whose visits to the northern hemisphere had not included countryside jaunts, he had never actually heard blackbirds. In fact, they might have been nightingales, which were also melodious, but didn't they only sing at night? Otherwise they'd be called 'morningales'. He opened his eyes. The square of the curtained window glowed with light. So, daytime, well and truly. 'Or thrushes or throstles then,' he muttered. 'What *was* a throstle? How could a throstle be possible?'

Moving his limbs with care, he sat, then stood, then stretched. Nothing terrible happened, only a mild cracking of the joints. He walked to the window and opened the curtains. The air against his face was creamy soft with an edge to it, like autumn. It smelled of damp leaves, petrol, old beer from the pub below, and coffee. He was hungry. He rubbed his hand over his face. He needed a shave. In the street below he saw cars moving by and a crowd around two stationary coaches. The side of the one nearest was painted with the legend he had seen on somebody's T-shirt last night: *Blink in the Light of Revelation.*

A light tap at his door, which then opened without his invitation. It was the little girl who had watched over him after his Arrival. She ducked in and dimpled at him cheekily from under a fringe of dead straight black hair, then deposited a tray on the table: coffee and rolls. She was about to speak, when an imperious voice from below stairs called after her. Bailey. The girl darted him a quick, bright smile, then skedaddled.

He felt much calmer today. Capable of thought. And he *had* to think. As he poured himself a coffee he flipped through his mental index. There were so many new entries in his brain, all out of order like scattered file cards. Where is Mogom? Said the first mental card. Then, *what* is Mogom? While I'm here, how do I earn a living, pay the rent? Or do I pay my way as a freak on display at Bailey's pub circus? And even more pressingly: Where is my cable? Will I ever be able to leave? He took a too-big swallow of coffee and burnt his lips and throat. Then: I have travelled along the route of John Grey's desire — 'Sydney 2010'. Pippalotti Colquouhoun. How much does she know? How did she get here? Where is she now? And who gave her that *name*?

He knew that each of these questions, except possibly the last, came with subsets of interrelated issues. These swirled around his head kaleidoscopically. 'This is no good,' he said aloud. 'I must be practical.' Wilder dressed, then felt his pocket for a notebook (essential but absent of course: he must get one), keys (also absent, naturally) and cigarettes (none). Good-oh, I have nothing but the clothes I stand up in. But then that was not quite true he realised, as he noted on the table the slip of paper he had taken from the corkboard the previous night, before he had become entranced by a ghost. What would he do first? He would find that beautiful ghost. No, no, he was going to be here for a while, that was obvious, so he had to get some money, some work. First he must arrange an interview with this

Carneac. And what better job could there be for a scientist than one titled 'notion collector'?

Then he could find Pippa.

Downstairs, Bailey and the little girl were cleaning the bar. The girl was polishing the wooden fixtures, though as soon as she saw Wilder she stopped to stare, then grin, then wave. Bailey was squeegeeing soapy water out the door onto the street. He went out to join her.

'Oh, hello!' Bailey beamed up at him from under her red-spotted sweatband. Her one front tooth with its ace of spades winked at him in the bright sunlight. 'How's the composition going this morning?'

'Comp… oh, ah… yes, thanks. I'm quite composed now, I think.'

'Feeling reintegrated? Parts all happening?'

Wilder replied in the affirmative, and added, 'I was wondering if I might use your phone?'

'Of course.' Then she stopped in mid-swoosh of her squeegee and blinked curiously at him, brushing a swatch of bright grey-brown fringe out of her eyes. 'But I've got to ask — who could you possibly have to ring? Sorry if that sounds a bit blunt.'

He showed her the note he'd found from Carneac.

She scanned it quickly. 'I see. But she won't be at home taking calls by now. It's already mid-morning.'

Wilder found he was relieved. 'Then perhaps you could tell me where I might find the dancer I met last night. Do you know where she is?'

'Oh, Pippa? She has some kind of day job, you know. She'll be back later — or if not, then tomorrow. Sometimes she stays out overnight…' Registering the disappointment on his face, Bailey added, 'She *will* be back though, fret not! But in the meantime, tell you what, why don't you wait a bit and catch the bus out to the fields with the other tourists? It leaves in a couple of hours. That's where you'll find Carneac. And in the meantime you could go for a walk while you wait, eh? Check out the sights. I won't let them leave without you.'

Outside the bright sun reflected off the bonnets of the tourist bus. People in the café looked at him curiously as he passed by their tables, and a little boy ran out to touch him. 'He's *solid*, Ma.' His mother flushed in embarrassment and called the child back to her side, but she could not take her eyes off Wilder. Neither could anyone else. Yes, he was a circus freak. He squinted into the light and set off down the street to see what he could see. He passed a block of flats constructed entirely from stripy rubber that was planted right next to a rococo post office with a frieze of rosy nudes cavorting across the pediment. He turned down a side street that was lined with what seemed to be a terrace of Georgian houses, which led out into a broad thoroughfare whose main feature was a miniature Crusader fort whose walls and battlements, on close inspection, he found to be made from laminates of compacted cardboard.

'Hey Mister!' It was the girl from the pub. She had changed out of her work overalls and was now dressed in a green frock with little red dots and a soft cardigan, pale yellow, too long in the sleeves. Her shoes were blue, with green bows on the toes. 'I can show you round if you like. I can take you shopping or to the movies or whatever. I'm Mumu Nongog.'

Wilder looked down at the black-haired little girl. He supposed she could only be about eleven, twelve at the most. His brain went into automatic and he asked, 'Shouldn't you be at school?'

'I might,' she answered him. 'An I might not. But you look lost an I offered to help an so it's a bit rude of you, if you don't mind me saying, presumin like that. Sorta thing.'

Wilder liked her. Also she was local, so she could only help him get the hang of this place. In any case, he had no time for further deliberation for Mu had already taken hold of his hand and was dragging him off to the 'movies'. They were there before Wilder realised it. The 'kinemat' was actually an avenue of fifteen two-storey high silk screens attached to one of the great exterior walls of the shopping centre which he found was called Hollywood Maul. He had been expecting narratives, stories told in pictures through the medium of film with limited dialogue, but as they walked down the street, what he saw — huge frame after frame — were discontinuous, unrelated images from old films he knew, American movies, BBC telecasts, experimental European cinema. He saw snatches of documentaries and news broadcasts: the World Trade Centre going down again, Indian beggars working a Calcutta street, a riot in Tibet, tanks rolling through some dusty Central Asian country. He saw advertisements for a building society, for shampoo, soft drink, a Colgate ad butted up against the scene in Baz Luhrman's *Romeo and Juliet* where the Montagues and Capulets meet on Venice Beach. He also saw images that had probably not actually been filmed, that seemed to have been plucked straight out of other worlds, again primarily his own. They'd apparently been grabbed indiscriminately from history, pre-history and the recent past, and for all he knew the present and future. Clearly the technology that enabled this cosmic poaching — what it was, he would find out — was not tense sensitive. He saw a medieval castle and could practically smell the stench from the open sewer of its moat; he saw a snippet of a Maori uprising, the beheading of Marie Antoinette, then a swamp crawling with life and in its midst, some giant herbivorous reptile calmly grazing on the treetops.

An hour later, they were walking back through the mid-morning shopping crowd towards Bailey's, where Wilder was to meet the Blinking Fields tourist coach, when he noticed a man a few paces ahead. He was working the crowd and people were depositing their change into his outstretched palm. A few moments later, they were face to face. He wore a close-fitting black suit, its collar turned up high at the neck, a hat pulled low over the brow. He was about Wilder's age, balding. His teeth, round white bones, showed clearly through the skin of his jaws. The radial muscles of his arm flexed as he opened his palm, the skin of which was unambiguously transparent. He was very far gone. Couldn't last more than a few more hours, a day at most. Yet, here he was, still begging to live. Wilder was riveted, enthralled… he had no money to give the man, but he reached out and touched him. The slight pressure of his index finger on the man's palm brought back to him the tactile report of tendon, muscle, bone. Extraordinary. The man pulled away, scowling, his facial muscles folding in on each other in a fascinating series of overlapping creases.

Mu tugged at Wilder's hand, 'Come on, don't upset the poor ghost…'

A zillion light-years away and right next door, Birdy Lethe is spooning chicken soup from a can into the mouth of a comatose woman. 'There there little girl,' he murmurs, 'try to swallow, can't you?' He puts down the spoon and holds together the soup-slick lips with the fingers of one hand while he gently massages her throat with the other. 'There, that's good,' he says to her. 'Good little girl.' The tabby cat jumps up on the bed and perches herself on the pillow next to his mistress. 'Yes, and good puss, too,' said Birdy. 'Have some soup...'

And as Birdy tends his sleeping beauty, John Grey and Brother are tracking Grey's heart's desire. They are ensconced on their mission-brown vinyl couch in their blue-lit nether-world, sipping from fruit boxes and snacking on Cheezels and Blissbombs and, by way of their navel-cables, on degrees of human-animal sensation encountered on their search (another blue baby here, another corrupted Catholic there) for Pippalotti, Sydney 2010. Although their machinery does not discern between past, present and future, it is capable of computing the quanta of form and thought from a thousand traditions, living and dead, of piggy-backing on transmissions of information or tides of thought within and between worlds and travelling with them to their destinations or conclusions. The calibandits are of course best able to tune into the stronger pulses of psychic rhythms of human beings whose desires match their own — desire for access to principles of truth, desire for inclusion, for love, for the contact of other bodies... for the contact of a particular body.

chapter nine
John Grey's turn?

Wilder and Mu boarded the bus together — the child had flatly refused to let him out of her sight. Wilder found her very proprietorial. 'Crowded, hey?' she was now saying. 'Some a this lot are from as far away as Tappat, but most come from Throng and Short Neck on Ebbe.' She nodded at the bus driver, 'Hi Steve!'

He was a small, pale man in razor-pressed slacks and a short-sleeved shocking pink shirt whose colour emphasised the doughy pallor of his skin. Embroidered in copperplate on his breast pocket was his name and under it, the company logo, *Blink in the Light of Revelation.* He called out the sights as they drove: 'We are now passing by the Chirico-co Co., Ariadne's famous market… and here, just beyond the bridge, chaps and chappesses, we have the Grannap I Nongog Memorial Centre, site of the shrine containing a splinter from the skull of our most revered ancestor and first of the Nongogs. Ariadne itself isn't a large city by any standards, but people commute here daily from all the satellite towns in the vicinity to work in the offices and media centres and municipal departments and educational institutions here that service the whole of Greater Mogom… Now, if you'll look to your right, there is Mogom University of Gossamer Technology; the building under that verdigris-veined dome ahead is The Department of Arts, Ancestors and the Science of Intertextuality. Looking right again please, and you'll see the Clear Opacity Centre of True Illusions… In the distance, just over the bridge is the Arc de Trompe l'Oeuil… and soon we will be passing the Centre for Absolute Relativity… there we go, see, five hundred metres down on the left…' As Steve spoke, Wilder wrote notes in the exercise book he found in his new daypack along with a packet of sandwiches and thermos of something that tasted like flat Coke and musk, a not entirely unpleasant drink: Bailey was a thoughtful hostess.

They drove beyond the city limits and the sky gradually shifted from a perfect blue, through mauve to cool pink.

The countryside became flatter, and the air circulating through the humming conditioners became perceptibly drier and, he now noticed, rather malodorous. 'Now, I want to tell you everything you need to know about where we're goin,' Mu told Wilder, and was gratified to see his eyes alive with curiosity. He was the perfect audience. She straightened her skirt down neatly over her knees and cleared her throat. 'Carneac is in charge a collectin Notions that get in through the Blinkin Fields. You know, like the bits of raw brains from local shamans an loonies, plus the transmissions that come in from Elsewhere — other places you know, same as here on'y different.'

'Mumu, where "elsewhere" do the pictures come from, do you know?' asked Wilder, thinking of the amount of material from dear old planet Earth.

'Oh, nobody knows that! I bet not even Carneac. Her job is to just pick up images. She collects them in her wind sieve, an she uses some a them for scrying — as she's by way of bein a witch, runs in her family, she's a Nongog too — an she uses some for decoratin her house, and some she gives to people to cut up and use in movies an stuff. It's an important job, Carneac's, on account of how if the images aren't culled, then there's too many, an if there's too many and they start comin to town and whatnot, then who'd be able to tell the difference between what's real and what's a magination?' Mu waited for the necessary nod and grunt of assent before continuing. 'Course the light a the godlids filters out some a the interference, not just Carneac. An it was my great great great great great great great Grannap Nongog that planted the very first godlid,' she added proudly. 'But we got a surge goin on these days...'

'Which would explain her request for help.' Wilder showed her the ad he'd taken from Bailey's.

'Course. I knew that,' she responded without missing a beat. 'It's probably a bit much for Carneac to cope with. You goin for a job then?'

Wilder nodded.

Moments later the bus drew to a halt. They were about a hundred metres back from a crossroad marked with what appeared to be a tall signpost, largely obscured by a great mass of swarming insects. Steve turned and said chirpily, 'Won't be a moment my excellent new friends. Kindly remain in your seats while I pay the toll.' The tourists settled back to wait. But Wilder got up to follow. 'No need,' said Mu, touching his arm. 'It's only ol' Baxta after her treat.'

Wilder shrugged. 'It's all new to me, Mumu. I'd like to meet this Baxta,' he said, and followed Steve down the steps.

Mu said, 'Mind then. She's a bit eccentric…' But he was already out the door.

He followed Steve across a boggy patch carpeted with budding, bright yellow mosses and tall grasses going to seed. They were obviously the main food source of the clatter of small chickens with oily black feathers that were clucking around his heels, cocking their heads to stare up at him with their greedy, beady, malevolent eyes. He shooed them away with his boot, taking care all the while to watch where the driver placed his feet, and to step where he did. So when Steve's legs stopped moving and he looked up, he was unprepared. A few metres back from the 'signpost' he stopped, appalled: it was a scaffold upon which hung, upside down, the naked body of a woman in an advanced state of putrefaction.

'Good morning mother-aunt, the happy dead who lives forever,' said Steve, bowing from the waist. The monstrosity swivelled in its noose and raised a hand in greeting.

'Ah, breathing thing,' croaked the living-dead thing. 'Greetings to you on this hallowed and happy day!'

Steve brushed away a cloud of green and purple butterflies, like flittering bruises, that was feasting upon the hanged woman's decomposing cheeks, and holding his breath, embraced her briefly. As they drew apart, he gave her a handful of garlic cloves, which the corpse immediately stuffed into her mouth as if they were some kind of rare and delicious sweet. She chuckled like a shredding-machine. 'Mmmm... so delicious when fresh, but once ingested, stinks to heaven. Stinks to *hell!* Ah, Garlic. Anathema of bloodsuckers, for as a little of the serpent's venom cures her bite, so a little garlic juice quells the vampire's potency. Garlic and the vampire, kissing cousins! Not that *I* have anything to fear from the undead beauties...' Again, the grating expression of mirth.

'Baxta,' interrupted Steve, 'we're really in a bit of a rush, actually...'

'Garlic, a diabolical vegetable, grows underground in the dark amongst the chaos of disintegration! Pale, paper-sealed and bound, like an ancient, shrivelled librarian, he has none of the earthy humour of your other root vegetables: the sexy carrot, the peasant turnip, potato and parsnip. Like all roots and bulbs, Garlic sees the light of day only upon the day of his decease — a paradox, no? Like his blood relation, Garlic hates the light, yet hungers for it (have you not witnessed his tentative green shoots, spying on the world above?) for who does not crave the icy touch of thanatos, eh?' And with her mouth horribly full, she pointed towards Wilder, 'And this must be the Arrival! I've heard all about you. Welcome!'

Only now did Steve notice Wilder's presence just behind him. 'Really! I told you to stay on the bus. Baxta doesn't need to be bothered by gawping tourists. She's got better th…'

'Oh, rude to whisper, little Breather mine. You know I love company!'

Steve sighed a barely perceptible, 'Oh, yes…' and looked at his feet, absorbing himself in the problem of the mud-damage done, yet again, to his highly polished shoes.

She said to Wilder, 'Approach, young man.' Then to Steve, 'Introduce us!'

Steve and Wilder stepped forward through a scatter of Baxta's chickens. 'Dr Wilder Portion, this is Baxta; Baxta, Wilder Portion.'

She spun delightedly on her gibbet like a little girl pirouetting in her favourite party frock. 'I am Baxta, and I mark the point of decision reached by those who would live no longer and those who would live forever! Like the *wo-o-o-lves!*' she howled joyously, and Wilder's hackles rose. 'In the song of wolves you may hear the yearning for their home, which is… *Elsewhere.* Here are nightmare wolves who steal children; here are path-finding wolves. Mogom, the land InBetween, is the point of origin of she-wolves who feed babies with their own milk till they grow up and found empires of fierce men and women whose lives and deaths in turn lend fire to the imaginations of their descendants. There are wolves who can shift their shape to human form, and vice versa. This is where werewolves are born. I *love* the wolves, don't you?'

Steve drew breath to answer the prolix corpse, but Baxta merely closed her eyes and raised her voice: '*And* frogs, for frogs are friends whose harmonies are a lullaby, but whose physical aspect is ridiculous; they sob nightly for their home, where they will no longer be scorned and laughed at...'

'Baxta, lovely brimming heart,' attempted Steve once more, 'I have a bus full of clients. We really must...'

'*And* the *bat!* Ooh, I *love* bats! Furry, warm-blooded, night-dwelling bird-things whose image feeds fantasies of haunted changelings who must drink blood to sustain their surprising existence. This is the home of vampires — *so* elegant, so gifted, so *graceful* — animal and immortal, whose transcendental charms are beyond nature, yet part of nature...'

'Baxta, my awful-dear...' Steve had begun to back away, blowing kisses...

'And *snails*: dream creatures, pearly and repulsive, slow and wise. They live in the soil, but they travel too, taking with them messages from the dead to the living who cannot or *will* not hear. (Will is a perverse thing, is it not? Seemingly one may control it — but I tell you, our will was never our own!) Yet the sweet snails continue to do what they can. This is the Way of Snails... and there are always the *cicadas.* Cicadas nightly rail against their own skins, which bind and constrict them like horny corsets. Who could live like this? Nobody. Cicadas are not truly alive, and this is how they bear it. Their voices mark the pulse of life, and they give a little of it away with each zinging exhalation. It brings them closer to Elsewhere...'

The swinging corpse might have waxed lyrical for many hours if given the opportunity, but Steve now turned, blew a final kiss, and grabbed Wilder by the upper arm. Frogmarching him back onto the coach, he said crossly, 'You really must do what you're told, you know. Now we're behind schedule.' Wilder murmured an apology. 'Well then. Please behave. You must.'

Only then did Steve notice Wilder's gobsmacked condition. Though he was still annoyed, he took pity on the man who clearly had plenty of questions but had temporarily lost the power of speech.

'Goddess of suicides, her,' he mentioned. 'Been here for yonks. Not that it's any of your business, really.'

'Sorry.'

'Yes, well.'

'Um… goddess, you say?'

'Yes, yes. They come and go. Baxta's stayed longer than most.'

When Wilder took his seat, Mu sensed that he was upset by what he'd seen. And when she thought about it, if she hadn't known Baxta since she was small, hadn't been encouraged to bring her garlic and other treats when she could, she wouldn't have got used to the way she looked and smelled, the way she raved and spun on the gallows. It was just possible that she might have found her a bit scary too. So she slipped her hand into Wilder's and said, 'Baxta's alright. Just needs a bit of attention from time to time or she gets cross, and that can be unpleasant for the tourists.'

They drove on a little further. Steve drew their attention to the zig-zaggy silhouette of a factory roof in the middle distance, and nearby a row of concrete towers. 'Silkworks. From here, we can't see the actual spider fields where the original manufacturers of the eight-legged variety labour for us. But if there's time on the way back we'll pop by…' On approach to the Blinking Fields the air warmed up from magenta, cerise, to bright pink as hot as tropical bougainvillea. The driver cautioned everyone to stay in a group as he distributed the goggles. Wilder did not want his experience mediated, but once he was outside the protective tinted windows, he was half-blinded. And even when he had fitted the goggles firmly over his face, he could still feel felt the pressure of the light through the durable plastic lenses like some kind of animate, wilful force. The air was full of the stink of godlids and the deafening static of cicadas. The first rush of what Mu authoritatively informed him were 'maginations' came into view: he recognised a cavalry charge of Confederate soldiers, tattered flags high and muskets blasting the pink crystal air; an excerpt from a documentary on Housing Commission flats in Manchester; a snippet of an ad from the 1960s for washing detergent. A sigh moved through the gathering of tourists like a breeze through rushes.

He and Mu and the others followed their small, neat guide along narrow goat tracks through the undulating fields of gently belching blossoms. The number of transmissions increased in surges, image upon image, translucent laminates of notion-pictures that bore no relation one to the other, random couplings of dinosaurs and dadaists, dungeons and dentists, day breaking at midnight, surfers with Dante in the Underworld… incongruities and grotesqueries created, dissolved, replaced. Wilder realised the place was riddled with spatio-temporal ruptures. 'More holes than cheese,' he muttered under the cicada racket. 'If there is a way back, it's here.' Whatever the job was that this Carneac was offering, he wanted it. Here was the chance he needed to save both himself and the perfect Pippa.

The group had started to loop back towards the bus, and there had been no sighting of Wilder's prospective employer. He was just wondering what his next move was to be, when Mu plucked at his sleeve and pointed out across the Fields to where he could just discern a series of low stakes or fence-posts, between which the light picked out a kind of fluttery movement — of what, he couldn't tell at this distance. 'Carneac's wind sieve,' Mu filled in for him. 'She'll be close by, then.' She took Wilder's arm. 'Come on, let's go.'

'At last. Brilliant! But listen Mumu, I don't know how long I'll be here. You'll have to go back with the others on the bus.'

'No way. You need me to mind out for you. I can introduce you. You see, she's not normal.'

Wilder smiled at the idea of abnormality worrying him just now, or ever again.

'Not funny! I showed you so I should come with you! Carneac's got pointy teeth you know. She's wild! You *do* need me. Really. I'm Mumu Nongog and I know things you don't.'

Her face was red and her jaw set hard against any giveaway tremors of the chin. She really had had her heart set on being his guide; Wilder could see that very clearly. But she was only a child, and she had a home to get back to. 'No, Mu.'

Mu sulked furiously all the way back. When the bus pulled in by Bailey's, she set off immediately for the Overdrain. She needed her friends. She wanted to talk about her day, the good part of it that was, and to impress everybody. So she hurried down Ariadne Street and through the town, across the oval behind Ariadne Elementary and down the out-of-bounds gravel park beneath the yoq trees, darkening now with shadows and filling up with the ratchetty noises of cooper birds melded with the sweet squeaks of the earliest fruit bats. The carpet of long tear-shaped leaves smelt sharp and astringent as she crushed them with her good blue shoes with the green bows.

She saw Simson and Lewis and the others just beyond the place where the stormwater channel dog-legged back towards Ariadne. They were sitting in a row along the edge, their feet dangling above the dry, leaf-choked channel. She called out to them. Their heads turned in unison. A moment later she joined them.

'Where you been all day, Mu?' asked Sim. Mr Kimomik called Mum and she was angry. She said she was gonna ask Grannap what to do about you.'

'Let her. I was with the Arrival.'

'You *were not*,' Sim said admiringly.

The others, being older, just eyed her coolly. Shakespeare picked his nose and examined the product first with his right eye, at arm's length, then with his left, close up.

'Was. He's really nice, he's called Wilder. I took him shoppin. He really liked the movies. An I went with him to the Blinkin Fields an introduced him to Carneac.'

'You're thick as thieves now, eh?' said Lewis, pursing his lips and making kissing noises. Emcee Squared and Columbine laughed and nudged each other and Sim asked if he could be best boy at the wedding. 'And did you see the new ghost down there?'

Mu looked blank.

'Well then, I'll tell you something for free. The ghost — you know, the rude dancer from Bailey's? She's been doin a day shift for Carneac this past week. So that'll be the two a them... alone... together. They'll be getting down to the horizontal cha-cha pretty soon I reckon.'

The others all chorused vomiting noises. 'Gross grandwise!' said Sim. 'That's horrible. Two patched-up maginations pashin…' Mu smacked her little brother hard across the ear.

'Wilder's *not* a magination an you know it! He's as real as anyone else — as if you didn't know the difference between a ghost an a figment,' she said in her most superior tone. But Mu was also feeling slightly ashamed at the thought, unarticulated, that followed. That Pippa would die off soon. Then she, Mu, could be Wilder's friend without any ghostly interference.

She left the others early and made her way back through the yoq trees, past the school and back into Ariadne. The streetlights came on one by one, their steel sepals opening and the blue blooms illuminating the facades of the buildings as she passed by. A lively breeze was juggling leaves around on the pavement. Mu stopped to look at the dust demons whirling about the feet of passers-by, tossing bits of grit from one to the other, skittering a sweet wrapper that fetched up against the foot of a lamppost in an aureole of violet light. She looked up. High above, the same wind scudded slivers of moon-gilded cloud and jounced the stars about in the sky. Perhaps the Arrival was a portent of certain change in Mogom, and not just to her heart, Mu thought, and shivered. She wondered what those changes would be, how much they would thrill, and if they would hurt.

At home she found a note from her mother, who said she would be home late, and then they would 'talk' about her truancy. Outside, the wind rattled the baffle. Grannap was burbling restlessly in his soup. She went over to his niche by the stove and greeted him. He smiled up at her through his lattice of wrinkles. Sometimes he gave the impression of infinite wisdom, other times of infinite senility. She gave his soup a little stir with her finger. 'What about a picture then, Grannap?' she murmured. 'Give it a whirl, eh?' She agitated the pot again, so that streamers of nutritious psychic stew drifted in mucilaginous strands around the base of Grannap's truncated neck. 'What will happen to the Arrival?' she asked, not really expecting an answer. Grannap was nothing if not unreliable. Nevertheless, peering closely she did discern after a moment the features of a face. But it was not that of her Wilder. This face was narrow and grey, its thin lips smiling like a scythe. She looked at the eyes, so very pale as to be almost colourless.

She wanted to draw back, yet did not, for he was fascinating. So she held herself still and looked deeper, and he looked back, and his gaze was loving, wanting, wanting her, for she was special, especially selected...

And now she feels a clutching in her gut, then a sensation of vertigo as if something inside, something essential within her is falling and falling, like a lift in a broken shaft. Her body feels loose, emptied out, lost to her mind, which is aware but somehow separate from her. She sees the bench, the pot, the soup and the arc of Grannap's simian throat, the moonlight laying a filmy light on all the surfaces, but all these objects are part of a world from which she is swiftly becoming disconnected, until after only a few seconds longer the things in the world of shape, form, light and sensation she is seeing as if from a distance of ages, through a transparent yet utterly impenetrable film.

She has entered another space, a dream space, so that now the air she breathes is the air of dreams. She knows she should move, because you *must* keep moving in dreams, no matter how slowly. But it's hard, because you are so heavy. The air of the dream congeals around her and she has to push every step of the way. She feels herself to be less than a shadow among shadows, now made of heavy, dead air.

But where is he? And as she thinks this thought, he is there and his loving face fills her eyes, and she is with him, walking by his side through a dusky landscape. Thin white moonlight attaches itself to him like a second skin. He hobbles into shadow, where he feels at home. And she is there, merging with him into the darkness. In and out of black and grey he passes. *They* pass. He drops to his knees and his fingers sink into the earth. She feels the grains of soil compacting under *his* nails. She feels the gorge rising to his throat, and she feels how he is sickened by his own feebleness, and consumed by some terrible yearning, it pervades this air of dreams that she inhabits with him. She feels his need and his hopelessness and it becomes her own. She feels his defiance in the face of his abjection, and she's crying, she's crying for them both. And she's angry too, angry for them both, his rage against his own impotence, his longing that leans towards the days that might be, *if only*, and she feels herself as a connection between him and the object of his 'if only'. His longing is as inevitable as disease, sharp as death, sad as life. She feels the purity of their shared solitude, then she's crying again, crying for all the things she can never do or see or be, crying for the waste.

But she has life, and he wants it, he wants to live too. She wants to give him life, for after all, what she has was never a birthright — it is a privilege, a lucky chance. And now, isn't it his turn?

chapter ten
it's a tacky little joint, but the coffee's good...

As the bus disappeared over the horizon, Wilder had made his way through the spectral Blinking Fields towards the wind sieve. He passed a pair of ostriches, only realising they were real when one of them bit him on the shoulder. He smacked it away and the pair of them loped away haughtily. A few metres from his destination he felt a light touch on his arm. He turned abruptly. But it was no ostrich. Her shadowy form indistinct against the phantasmagorical landscape, Pippa stood smiling in pleasure at finding him here. She was wearing a plain green shirt and a blue skirt and carried a brown canvas satchel over one shoulder. She had been easy to miss. Her form was already far more indistinct than it had been even the evening before, the skin more transparent, also the bones beneath. His heart went out to her in her exquisite fragility. He reached for her hand. It was cool and brittle as a sparrow's wing. She agreed to show him to Carneac's house and help him to put in his application.

'We just need to follow the sieve a little way —' she pointed vaguely, '— and we'll be there quite soon. At least I think we will.' She looked puzzled for a moment. 'I've always been a bit vague about time, and I'm getting worse at it,' she said, face downcast. Then she looked up and brightened, 'But then, around here, time can seem a bit abstract for anyone I suppose.'

Wilder was not sure what sort of words would reassure her, or even if he ought to try. He experimented with a smile instead and she returned it with one of her own, a very sweet one.

They reached the sieve. It stretched in a wide band across the godlid-studded, ectoplasm-flooded plain as far as he could see. He reached out and tentatively touched it. It was unbelievably fine and gauzy. It was also sticky. And all along its length, fragments of aerial transmissions and dreams were entangled. Pippa unpeeled one as one does a transfer from its tacky backing. It showed two sumo wrestlers grunting and staggering together in a clammy embrace before an enthusiastic Tokyo audience. She rolled it up and deposited in her satchel. 'So,' said Wilder, 'that's what a notion collector does.'

'Not bad for a day job. Want to try?'

'What is this stuff made of, do you know?' he asked.

'Carneac says, "part of spider webs, part of spider desires".' She shrugged and smiled again. Her teeth were flawless.

'Gnomic one, your Carneac.'

'You don't know the half of it. Come on.'

As they walked alongside the wind sieve, Wilder found himself witnessing a new and puzzling anomaly. No previous event — neither the light of the godlids nor the phantasms or even the condition of his companion — had prepared him for this prodigy: here and there, where the breezes and spectres buffeted it, the sieve was creased into moving folds within which could be glimpsed places beyond this world. These were solid and real — he could feel, very distinctly, the heat or cold they generated. There were sounds too, both natural and industrial, and voices. He saw impossible prospects: slivers of cities; rivers of molten rock; miraculous creatures that were neither mammal or reptile, insect or fish, but a mixture of some or all of these. There were elliptical glimpses of endless space filled with hurtling comets and words of fire, and animals and people, all testimony to time's instability and the absurdity of the notion of a single continuum; here he could literally see the layers of perpetual, tenseless moments with no beginning or end as he watched real people who walked apparently within the architecture of time and yet were beyond it, out of place, here and there simultaneously.

Pippa had been watching him, marking his reaction. 'This would all sort of knock you sideways when you first see it,' she said. 'Except that if you've come this far, by the time you see this you're already a bit sideways.'

He noticed that her voice had a little crackle at its edges, like honey with a fine gravel in it. He wondered if it had always been like this. He preferred to turn his mind away from the likelihood that it hadn't. He set his thoughts off in another direction. 'This place is like a kind of San Andreas Fault,' he said, 'a spatio-temporal hernia.'

She laughed at that. 'You're right. Space is torn at the edges. Ideas and dreams and memories and...

'Maginations, Mumu calls them,' mentioned Wilder.

'No,' she corrected. 'Or at least, I think not. They're all different. Maginations come via radio waves and telecasts mostly — the electronic/ethereal stuff. Raw brains are hallucinations, dreams, memories and such. And what you see within the folds is all real of course, just not quite *here*, sort of thing — but I suppose you would've got that? Then there are Arrivals like you. And partials, not quite arrived. Ghosts, like me.' She looked at him frankly, and shrugged again, then looked away. He began to speak, but she shushed him. 'Please. No point.'

A breeze rippled through the wind sieve. It blew Pippa's hair across her face in dryish tangles of blond and brown and pasted her skirt across her thighs and calves. Her calves were lovely too. And her long, graceful evertor muscle, leading down into her sensible brown shoe. They were heading downhill now, into a shallow, bowl-like valley, perhaps the caldera of an extinct volcano. Their way down was criss-crossed with goat tracks and small, thin streams emerging here and there from underground springs. At one a pair of ostriches stood guard while half a dozen chicks drank from the trickling stream. 'Real,' mentioned Pippa.

'I know,' Wilder agreed, and told him about his earlier meeting with one.

'Carnea keeps her own… er, herd? Flock?'

'Wobble.'

'A *wobble* of ostriches?'

'So I believe.'

At the centre of this declivity was another low rise. There crouched a house, small and thin with a severely pitched roof standing on stilts. One small yellow dirty-looking cloud the shape of a lozenge hovered above its chimney-pot, like a sympathetic friend trying to console it for its ugliness.

'Carneac's place,' she said, then added brightly, 'Hey, guess who I saw the other day?'

'Ah… Genghis Khan? Beniamino Gigli? Jesus?'

'Mercury! He was brilliant. At first I could hardly see him for the light.'

'But how could you know it was him? Isn't he supposed to be famous for changing his looks a lot?'

'How can you still be a sceptic? Never mind, I'll tell you: he had winged heels and a caduceus with snakes spitting at each other.'

'*Serious?*'

'Why not? This is a regular path for messenger gods, I reckon. Why wouldn't it be?'

They approached Carneac's house under the gaze of several sardonic goats. The front yard contained a few godlids, some dandelions, some glossy blue-black chickens like Baxta's, and a vegetable patch by a reeking compost heap. The house walls were quilted and flesh-like, lightly furred and warm to the touch. The structure itself was very unstable, wobbling as it was upon two giant turkey legs — the 'stilts' he had noticed from a distance. Tough, gristly tendons hung from the place where the thigh-meat met the protruding bone.

Pippa pulled one of the dangling tendons. Deep and resonant, the dull boom of the chimes reverberated throughout the uncanny landscape, playing the first line of the funeral march, whose last note became the first of the chorus of Beethoven's 'Hymn to Joy'. Across the juxtaposed musics of death and life their smiles met. Pippa murmured something under her breath that sounded to Wilder like, 'Camomile, cantelope, cadmium,' which of course was absurd, but before he had time to ask her to repeat herself, they were interrupted.

'Go away and welcome!' came a voice from behind them. Wilder jumped. Pippa, the old hand, remained calm. There stood a woman, her hair an avalanche of coal, her eyes burning black and her mouth too full of teeth. And as Mu had warned, they were filed. She was chunkily built, wore a hairy black coat that at first Wilder thought was embroidered with silver, until he realised the million tiny snails she wore were live ones. She carried a bucket of blood and gore. 'Tea? Bile? Get ya gone and stay awhile!' she inquired or exclaimed in a voice that was crude and almost-sweet, like the low notes scraped out of an ill-tuned violin. Without waiting for a response, she pushed by them, all vigour and purpose, and hauled herself up the knotty ladder which had flung itself down at her approach. Now she turned and beckoned them to follow while simultaneously spitting on the ground and giving the sign of warding off the evil eye. As she crossed the threshold the house purred like a cat. She turned and said, 'Real figments, enter or no?'

The floor was damp, with an organic gleam to it and sticky underfoot, like highly-compacted blood sausage. The woman deposited her gruesome bucket by the hearth, set into the wall opposite the door. From the hearth she drew a big kettle that was suspended inside the fireplace from two fire-blackened chains, encrusted with greasy soot. 'Carneac,' she said by way of introduction, crossing the fingers of her left hand while offering her right. Wilder took the hand briefly, then showed her the ad he had brought with him from Bailey's. She looked at it briefly, nodded to herself, then tucked it into her pocket.

She filled two cups and offered them while shaking her head in an emphatic negative. Pippa accepted the drink with a gracious nod, Wilder with a wave of nausea. The woman indicated with an adamant palm that they should remain standing while at the same time, gestured with the other that they should sit. Pippa seated herself on an ornate love-seat upholstered in lime velour, its arms and head-rests adorned with lace antimacassars. It was streaked with pale stains, but at least seemed dry when every other surface of the room was damp with mould, seeping bodily or ectoplasmic secretions, or gleaming with other unnameable wetnesses, so Wilder joined her there. He was happy to let Pippa do the talking. As she explained to Carneac how ideally suited Wilder would be for the position of notion collector, he sat back and took in the wallpaper, which was similar to the outside landscape they had just passed through, only rather than adverts Carnea's taste leant more towards shifting shapes of memories and futures and fantasies out of the feverish brains of withdrawing drunks and addicts — longings and loathings seethed like poisonous polyps across the walls, still wet with tears or sperm or brain juice. In the corner of the room was a small cot with a cover of soft pale fuzzy green, apparently made from the moist velvet lining of thousands of broad-bean pods stitched one to the other. The unsealed roof timbers were hung with carcasses, casting grim shadows against the terrible wallpaper; sprouting from crannies were godlid cocoons, some partly opened and emitting a pallid pink glow from their wetly gleaming interiors like clusters of dislocated baby cunts. The place was pervaded with a sweet rotten stink mixed with garlic. His observation was interrupted by Carneac, who had taken a step towards him and was offering him her hand.

'I think you've got the job,' Pippa said.

Much later, as the sun set over Great Blinking Fields of Light in a wash of violent pinks like a cosmic rail disaster, Carneac provided a cold, inedible dinner of blue goat shanks and raw garlic, after which she had retired under her bean-pod quilt. Then Pippa Colquouhoun of Darlinghurst and Dr Wilder Portion from the bowels of St James Station made a cosy nest of their coats and bags and some rancid blankets given them by Carneac, and talked together through the night. After all, they had a lot to discuss: all that they knew about this mystery and the all that they could not know; the meaning and possibly the meaninglessness of what had happened to each of them; the serial coincidences allied with their own kind of curiosity that had led them, in their close but separate parts of the same city in the same world to Mogom, which was god only knew where. This made them both feel very homesick and sad and Pippa crept closer to Wilder and snuggled up to his chest. Wilder described to her his lab under St James, a station she knew well. 'I often drink coffee at the café up the street a bit, behind Museum,' Wilder mentioned. 'It's a tacky little joint, but the coffee's good and it's got a view over to the Cathedral and Hyde Park, which is nice.'

Soon they moved on to the details of how they came to be here. She told him of her meeting with the thin man on Darlinghurst Road, his irresistible magnetism and the subsequent interference of the old soldier that had both saved her and lost her. This discussion itself took a couple of hours. Then they talked about Wilder's journey here on the waves of desire — for her — emitted by John Grey. Neither of them however arrived at any brilliant ideas as to how they were going to return. Wilder was very hopeful that he could work something out, but did not like to dwell on how long that might take, considering Pippa's condition. He kept his face composed as she expressed her hopes. Towards dawn she fell asleep.

Wilder took his diary from his daypack and wrote:

Variations on an old theme:

There are uncountable universes. And what happens when two of these universes bump up against each other is a big bang, which is how ours is supposed to have come into existence. But what if we avoid the bump — but **only just**? Say, by the tiniest fraction, and at a point where the skins of our respective universes are very, **very** thin — that is, if we just sort of brush up against another universe? Hover cheek to cheek, like air-kissing actors at a cosmic cocktail party?

Though the night sky may **look** like an inverted black bowl speckled with stars, although we may think of all the spaces between the stars as empty — we know now that that is just looking and thinking. We know it isn't vacant. There is no vacancy!

Instead, that space is layer upon layer upon layer of stuff that moves, that shifts and slides.

Universes aren't vast spaces, just layers and layers of skins in constant movement, each turning and shifting and separated from the neighbouring skin by a minuscule distance. We're all so close to each other, yet absolutely sealed off — until contingencies conspire to have us meet.

He looked down on Pippa's sleeping face, upon which kind shadows fell just so, so that for a moment the integrity of skin and bone and flesh was repaired.

Or, new metaphor: I will take two colanders, one set inside the other turning in opposite directions. Then insert another colander and another and another. All moving. Occasionally their holes meet — only their holes are not holes but just weak spots, permeable, sensitive spots. And at times these weak spots meet and it's at these points that exchanges occur, consciousnesses can be transferred.

All is flux. That's a constant. The only other constant is consciousness. It's only consciousness that is real. Consciousness fuelled and driven by the mysterious engine of desire: impersonal, amoral, pure intention. Desire as a **literal force**. This is not science, but intuition. Oh well. Never mind. Stet.

Now take two subjective consciousnesses, two subjective universes: Pippa's and John Grey's. A contact point was created at a weak spot. Grey's desire drew him to Pippa. But then the colander shifted — just an iota — so that the weak spots were no longer in contact. He was stranded on the other side, hard up against a wall he could not penetrate. He was cut off. He still wants her though. Why wouldn't he?

And what of Pippa? Daily she is growing weaker, finer, more transparent. What use is all my science if I can't help her?

Wilder looked down on the woman. She breathed so softly her breath was all but inaudible. Flesh package, flesh sandwich. Skin and bone and a layer of pearly subcutaneous

fat. Then meat and gristle. He could see a little of this. The rest was more abstract, but there it was, nevertheless, waiting to emerge: the sinews and tubes, the intricacy of intestines and their flora, pastel guts in pink and blue and green, fed by veins full of red, red blood, pumped through major and minor systems to reach the tiniest extremes of capillaries which are separated from the world by only the finest layer of fragile skin, composed, like the rest of the body, of not much more than water. This skin is decorated in lovely delicate relief patterns, whorls and spirals incised into the living, breathing, material itself. Miraculous, real, unnerving.

chapter eleven
zebras and zygotes and xylophones

About the time Carneac's two notion collectors were settling down to talk, Simson Nongog was on his way home from the Overdrain. He was following the path his sister had taken earlier. Lew and Shakespeare and Emcee Squared had peeled off down their various streets for their dinner, Columbine Hogson had headed back to her farm to feed her dad's pigs, and Sim was alone now. There weren't many people about tonight. It wasn't a nice night, thought Sim, all edgy breezes arguing with each other and making people feel anxious. Making *him* feel anxious. Mum would be angry with him for being late, but angrier at Mu for leaving him behind and letting him walk home by himself. This was good. He passed by Bailey's. All the lights were on there, of course, from the ground floor where music was pulsing to the top floors where the guest lived. On the flat rooftop, the snappish wind was worrying the clothes on Bailey's washing lines, making the trousers flap and clap their legs together, liberating the lighter things. A handkerchief sailed down and landed at his feet and he stopped to pick it up. It was pinkish with gritty dust, as were all the buildings, bollards, fire hydrants and even the cat he saw scissoring across the road with irritable, flattened ears, all coated in the dust blown in from the Blinking Fields, where Mrs Smarty Pants had been all day, gallivanting with her new boyfriend.

His house was dark. Surely they hadn't all gone to bed already? The blue spirit baffle around the front door jamb crackled in response to his key. Sim opened the door and let himself in, and before he could close the door the wind grabbed it and slammed it so hard the whole place shook. Sim flicked on the light. And there was Mu, her eyes wide with shock, jerking back from Grannap's cauldron then falling backwards onto her bum. He had really given her a scare. He started to laugh, but then stopped when he realised his big sister wasn't moving. He ran over to where she lay prone on the floor, her eyes still wide and staring. It was scary. 'You can stop teasing now,' he said uncertainly. 'I don't like it. Mu?' He shook her arm. 'Mu, I said sorry, okay. *Mumu?*'

Mu became aware of Sim's terrified little face and tearful voice, and of his warm dry hands chaffing her own. 'Sorry Mu… Mumu? Sorry. It was just the wind. I mean, the door. Oh, I'm so sorry…'

She pushed herself up onto her elbows and as she did the images flooded back, and the *face*: ugly as sin, hate-filled, but not pure hate, it was mixed up with other strong stuff like one of Bailey's cocktails. Awfully needy, and leering… and… loving? She had felt *love*. Now she felt sick to her stomach. She squeezed her eyes closed and lay down again, rubbing her face. She realised how close she had been to capitulating — but to what? Who was this strange-eyed man with the gruesome groping soul? Sim's entry had broken the contact with the monstrous thing in Grannap's soup and she was safe, but she felt shattered, her mind all messed up as well as her body. She had never actually blanked out before. She had almost given in to it, to him. She had wanted to. She had almost been *over*. Her mouth was dry and her stomach still churned with nausea. She propped herself up on her arms again and after a moment, rose carefully to her feet, her head swimming. She made it to the toilet just in time.

Sim had crept over to Grannap's cauldron; the old head was moaning and rolling his eyes and bobbing around in the agitated psychic broth. When his glassy-eyed sister came back in, Sim said, 'Grannap's roiling. Never seen him so bad. What happened, Mu?'

'You steer clear of Grannap, you hear me!' And she shook him roughly. He stared at her, too shocked to cry. 'Look, Sim, I'm sorry,' she added quickly, 'I don't know what it was, but it's dangerous okay? It's something horrible. An it's coming, or tryin very hard, and if it does it's not goin to do anybody any good. Grannap knows, but can't say cos he's old an lost his marbles. We'll just have to keep an eye out. It's up to us.' She flopped down onto a chair, utterly exhausted. 'I've had it Sim.'

Sim's small white face was all pinched, but his eyes were big and round and bright. Then, he said bravely, 'Hot colabrew, Mu?'

'That'd be nice. Ta.'

Wilder woke late. Or he assumed it was late. He was alone in the house, with the sun streaming through the single window, dousing the awful wallpaper in syrupy pink light and animating its tormented themes. The smell of his own sweat was now added to the putrid potpourri of Carneac's rank blankets, the sweet stink of rot from the carcasses hanging from the meathooks and the asafetidal reek of the godlids that floated in from outside. He rose and filled a cup from the kettle in the hearth. The stuff tasted as vile as it had yesterday, was probably full of any number of horrible bacteria, but it was the closest thing to coffee here and he needed it. The house purred contentedly.

The door flew open and Carneac entered with a large hessian sack, which she deposited on the floor next to him.

'Good morning,' said Wilder. 'I hope you slept well?'

She stared at him as though he was mad. The stare lasted much longer than was comfortable, but finally it was over. Now she grinned, showing all of her filed teeth, nodded vigorously, then shook the black thatch of hair out of her heavy-lidded, almost oblong eyes, which were bright with interest as she regarded him in the pink light.

'Where is Pippa?' asked Wilder.

She inclined her head towards the door. 'Notions.'

'I'd like to start work,' said Wilder. 'With Pippa. In the Blinking Fields.'

'Sooner or later, absolutely uncertainly!' replied his host, with her accustomed gusto. She then reached into one of her capacious pockets and produced a fine brush. 'Best doe lash, or else!' she said as she tossed it to him. She nodded toward the godlid pod nursery sprouting from the wall.

While Wilder dusted the pods, which crooned and sighed as the feathery lashes tickled their crevices, Carneac set to work dismantling the screen door. This done, she sat down on the floor by the hessian sack, dragged the screen across her lap and gestured for him to finish up the dusting and come and join her. She showed him the contents of the sack: uncountable millions of dead wasps. By means of hand signals and occasionally coherent phrases, she made it more or less clear that he was to pluck the stings from the wasps and pass them to her. And as he did so, one by one, she knitted the stings into the several rents in the mesh of the door. 'Loathing and love, comfort and repulsion you see, or not,' she said, her sharp teeth glinting in the pink light, her narrow eyes alive with humour.

Wilder had no idea of how to respond to this, so just continued to work away at this new task as quickly and efficiently as he could so as to be able to join Pippa as soon as possible. After it was done, she had him re-install the door for her, set the fire, sponge the secretions from the wallpaper then mop the floor. Only when all these chores were completed would she allow him to go outside. By this time it was early afternoon.

Standing at the head of the rope ladder he cast his eyes over the rosy landscape teeming with transparent spectres, film excerpts, hallucinations and other transmissions electronic, psychological and magical. He saw Pippa's form in the middle distance, working its way along the line of the wind sieve, the brown satchel over her shoulder. He climbed down the ladder and headed towards her.

Pippa Colquouhoun slowly makes her way along the length of the wind sieve, unpeeling images as she goes and slipping them into her satchel, which is now bulging with raw material. She will have to return to Carneac's soon and put the data into storage in the great wardrobe between the turkey legs beneath the house. But now, her attention is snared by one of the folds in the fabric, ruffling in the breeze. She peers in and sees: a white wolf loping through his white world. Pippa feels her skin, warm under the sun of Mogom, responding to the cold from within. Goose-pimples from another world. Perhaps the wolf is on his way back to his mate and their pups through this twilight, with its wooded mountainsides sloping to ravines filled with sharp stones and icy waters. The wolf stops when he reaches higher ground; he raises his black muzzle to the bitter moon, to sing a hymn. Then, from another quarter Pippa sees someone approaching downwind from the mourning-celebrating wolf. Perhaps a farmer. He moves silently through the powdery softness of the newly fallen snow. And now the farmer too raises his muzzle, this one of black gunmetal, and takes aim. Pippa turns away from the inevitability of this small tragedy and moves on, peeling and plucking notions off the mesh, bagging them, peering into creases…

She sees a child of about eight years old, walking with an elderly man through a forest of thin, smooth trees with pinkish trunks and upside-down leaves; their flat, silver bellies exposed to the clean bright light. Pippa's heart clenches, she knows this landscape well. The forest is still, listening, with disinterested attention in a silence heightened suddenly by the crack of a falling branch. The man and the child do not mind this, and Pippa knows such forests as these keep themselves young by sacrificing the old to the new. She watches the pair crunching over dead branches, hears the whip and snap of a bird's cry. The child looks beyond the trees and Pippa sees from her opposite perspective what it is that the girl sees: the sieve, conjoining their two worlds shows up in the girl's sky as a very slight, shifting flaw. The bushwalkers are closer now. And she recognises them. The child is herself; the man, her father.

'What is the name of that place?' Pippa asks her father thirty years ago, her voice delayed as in a poorly-dubbed movie. The child is pointing out of her world, seemingly directly at this new, adult Pippa, whose heart is beating like that of a thief hiding in a closet.

'That line at the end of the world?' Her father answers, 'That's the horizon. It's the line that marks the extent of our vision.' He smiles at his daughter's confused expression. 'It's okay, love,' he tells his daughter. 'The world never ends.' Pippa reaches out her hands towards the child she once was; surely she could touch her… but the breeze flutters and the scene is obscured.

And as Pippa's heart rocks and her body shivers in the noonday heat, worlds away, yet very close, John Grey and Brother sit close together on their mission-brown vinyl couch in their blue-lit interstice, an onion skin's breadth from Pippa's bathroom in Sydney, 2010. Before them is the monitor to which they are attached by their fleshy navel-cables. This monitor, time-insensitive, continues to show moving images old, new and as yet unconceived. Between them and the hovering screen of light with its perfect resolution and state-of-the-art sound system, is a low table on which lies a half-finished Scrabble game, a crushed Cheezels packet, an uncapped bottle of sulphur-scented massage oil and two bottles of bright-blue energy drink enhanced with ginseng and vitamins.

They are of course looking for the object of John Grey's desire, but as they go, they stop here and there as always, picking up pain and delight and sorrow and joy and incorporating all into their soulless selves, relishing every dream and vision they pirate, surfing the orgasmic rush that comes when Grey enters another space and drains another's life. They watch some more torture in real-time from China, Uganda and Uzbekistan, Israel, Syria, Malaysia and Cuba. Pain hits the spot, grief an aphrodisiac. After a while they swap to fiction for a change, choosing Michael Haneke's *Funny Games* from their archive, then back once more to reality: they tune in to a man. He is sitting at his desk. Like a repeated image of the calibandits who watch him, he too is staring into a screen, a blue square of light adjacent to the black square of night banked up against his window. He has been working solidly since before sunrise that morning and it is now nearly eleven at night. He is aware of a pain in his shoulder but is perfectly happy. He is on a run.

John Grey peers into the man's screen and reads:

The verisimilitude of minor characters in fantasy fiction is often more readily achieved than it is with main characters, possibly because of the unavoidable problem of stereotyping that is part of reader expectation in this genre: the protagonist becomes more a meaning carrier than a plausible individual, whereas the fantasist can afford to play with the subsidiary characters, to imbue them with personality that...

Grey murmurs, 'Brother, this man is not undiscriminating, quite imaginative. Tasty.' John Grey puts his lime Sobranie down in an ashtray in the shape of a splay-legged woman, and begins to draw on his umbilicus. The man continues to work for a moment or two more, then finds himself slowing down.

A moment before, he had found an extremely pleasing idea, one that perhaps even contained a grain of authenticity. But now he ceases writing. He leans back in his chair and says to himself, 'Now, what *was* that I was thinking? It was just on the tip of my tongue...' He sighs, puzzled. Notices he is tired. Gets up from his desk. 'I'll sleep on it. It will surely come back to me in the morning…'

'Oh, I doubt that, darling,' says John Grey as he relaxes back in his cushions with his subtle cache of stolen inspiration. Brother chuckles through his tumid nose and licks his lips which today he has painted the colour of toffee apples to match his new wig, a sleek bronze pageboy. 'The ideas that bubble up from those human founts, eh? That lovely meld of flesh and mind. They always work ever so much better than blue fizzy drinks, eh?'

Much better, Brother thinks back, and puts his feet up on a sculpted vinyl footrest.

'*Love* that metallic nail vanish you've got on your little piggies by the way, my pup.'

Brother smiles his pleasure. It's not often John Grey pays a compliment. They continue to surf.

'Wait,' says Grey, 'I saw a rather tantalising child.'

'You are a greedy one,' Brother mentions mildly, then clicks back a couple of frames.

A child, about thirteen or fourteen, is walking along a busy road. He passes a sign that says *Pitt Street* then stops to look in a shopfront window displaying an array of musical instruments. His face in the plate glass is beautiful — dark-lashed hazel eyes framed by curly brown hair — but he does not see his own reflection; he is entranced by an electric guitar, black and red, suspended on the wall. He has been browsing the music stores all morning and finds that, oh yes, he *likes* that one. He says to himself, 'Matt, that's the guitar for you. Yes, *I want that one.*'

'Oh, *I want this one*, brother-mine,' reciprocates John Grey, gazing into his own equivalent of a display window. 'I want to feel it close to me, the sweet thing, alive and breathing. The flutter of its pulse, the warm breath of it. I don't want just one of its ideas or a mere thought.

Its thoughts are dull, but its being is *lovely*. Yes, I'll take *this* one.' He stands and moves towards the screen, his umbilicus uncoiling behind him.

Matt enters the store. A person whom he takes for the shop owner emerges from behind a display of keyboards. What a strange looking man, the child thinks. Such pale eyes, so thin, and bare feet too. How weird.

'Can I help you?' asks the 'proprietor', and even as he speaks he begins to tap into the thread of visceral desire thrilling through the boy as he contemplates the splendid black and red guitar. He looks up and meets Grey's eye. It is a cinch for the calibandit to trap the child's curiosity, so guileless and trusting, in the net of his attention.

'Yes please. I want…' but his words drop away in the face of the potency of the gaze and he forgets what he was saying. It would be frightening, so strong is the feeling, only there is a level of interest in *him* that the boy has never before felt in his life; it is warm, enveloping, something like love but without anxiety that comes from the need to please.

'Want? Ah, don't we all?' Grey replies, smiling his most understanding smile as very carefully he reaches out, gentling the air between them with slight movements of his palms, all the while keeping his eyes on the boy's. Matt enters the psychic space opening up to contain only the two of them. Grey is now able to caress, very tenderly, Matt's downy cheek and he groans aloud at the sweetness of the contact. And now, with the barest connection of flesh to flesh, he runs a finger from the boy's temple down to that most tender declivity where the throat meets the breast. Grey stoops a little to feel against his own cheek and lips the moth soft breath of the fading child as Matt's eyes close and he sinks into Grey's waiting arms.

•

On his return, refreshed and invigorated with the child's life warming his bloodlessness Grey says briskly, 'Now, back to the task at hand: where *is* she? I'm sure I felt a pulse of her nearby when we saw that other child last night, the one in the soup. You know, the one that got away.'

click

A wide landscape of dry, grassy hills and low-growing flowering plants. A crossroad, with a gibbet and inverted corpse arrangement. Then the shape of a woman enters the scene, very close to the screen. Her face is so close in fact, that it is difficult to get it into clear focus. Brother fiddles with the controls, but her features cannot be discerned in the bright and rosy glare of this strange country.

'I can see little more than her silhouette in all that garish brilliance there, yet she is very *concentrated*, don't you think, brother? Very resolved and sort of alert and observant and attentive in her bearing. Almost as if she can see us. Oh, perhaps she *can*? I wonder.'

John Grey had spoken while peering all the while into the screen and now he spares a glance for his brother, who is panting excitedly. 'What's the commotion, little doggy-mine? Why, your nose is all of a quiver!' He returns his attention to the screen to see the woman take a step back, moving in slow motion as if ambivalent: compelled to look, but wary and wanting to turn away. And now he can see her clearly. 'Ah ha,' murmurs John Grey, pensively clicking his long, yellow thumbnail against his teeth. 'I *see*.'

John Grey now focuses his full attention upon Pippa, upon trapping her in his gaze. Though she resists him, he feels her will submitting to his own, like the body of a small animal — a rabbit, a bird. Her strength is negligible. Soon he is holding her risible will within his own — lightly, easily. He is careful not to crush her; not quite, not yet. Her struggle creates within him the most delicious sensations, ones he thinks must surely be close to human. His hope wells, 'Oh, fluttery, shuddery, live and lovely. Matter fighting its antithesis. As if she could overwhelm a shadow. How little it understands, this dear wriggling fistful of mortality; how vain its struggle against inevitability.' And he moves out towards her through the temporal crease of the wind sieve.

Pippa may not understand the nature of his power but neither does she need the information, for, as had the musical child a little while before, she feels it. Stronger than any positive agency acting upon her, like a bullet or a rock, is the overwhelming force of the absence, the absolute *deficiency* of him. He is a drain dragging her into the determined centrifuge of his will, a hole in space. Like cold magma his absence enters her, freezing her will, her body, which has become enormous; her body melts and flows open; she opens to the sky. She *is* the sky, lustreless and void. She floats and spreads and her head opens up to the gaze that is all there is. Her brain swells with the pain of trying to include the impossible... and it is too much, much too much. She hears a voice. It is condensed and concentrated like a balled fist in her brain. Its tone is sardonic and knowing and... *tender.* 'I hate you,' he says, fondly. 'And oh, I do love you. It's nothing personal.'

She clings to the voice. How beautiful it is, how true and clear. And now, resistless, she finds that she desires only to reach out to him; he is all there is and all she wants, her mind reaches out to embrace him, her killer, for he is the only thing in the world. She opens herself to him and the warmth of her animal self begins to ebb, slowly at first, then ever more quickly as his spirit, his partial body, continues to enter her by inexorable degrees. For her, the sensation is soft, is gentle, irresistible — she need no longer act or think or *be* — and why fight against peace? For him, the corresponding sensation is of increasing warmth as her animal vitality merges with his negativity, giving it form and shape, making him real. She feels the profound relief of abnegation of self. She is nowhere and nothing.

And then, from somewhere in the nowhere of which she is an aspect, an image flickers across her consciousness. She sees lines of tangled threads, a hand — now two hands, old and gnarled — manipulating the cat's cradle from within whose mesh of strings one mad violet eye peers avidly, concentrating on the complex of knots he twists in his fingers; and fibres are streaming through the nothingness towards her, spinning and twirling, fine, wiry filaments of light, and now they are twisting like a garrotte around a broader, fleshier thread, thicker and blubbery soft… Pippa hears a voice scream out in anguish and the beautiful absence which had pervaded her is now annihilated — and she is falling; she is a mess of flayed matter streaming down a black hole so she must seize whatever she can to break her fall. She seizes hold of a thread that Birdy sends her, and the thread is twisted into another and another; the braided light-lines are within her reach and she grasps one and holds tight and her mind follows it back and back, seeking the source…

she sees a blank-faced granite idol, turning on the axis of its neck

she sees a bare stony landscape like the Barrens of West Ireland

she sees cripples chasing rats with machetes, their faces seeping sores from black cysts in the light of pitch torches under a sky full of drunken planets she sees parrots and citadels and starscapes and Stonehenge when it was young, hagglers in a market, Hades on his throne, storm clouds and swamps and sceptres and zebras and zygotes and xylophones and she knows she is dying… and she hears a horrible scream and cannot tell if it comes from her or from some other…

she sees a shoe shop, a pawnbroker, a strip club, a Coke sign and Coles supermarket

she sees the face of an old soldier, who puts a finger to his lips. 'Hush…' He cradles her head in his warm, dry palm.

And Isadora says, *'Grrneow-a-mui,'* and gently nuzzles Pippa's chin with her cool, moist nose.

chapter twelve
'Something wicked this way comes'

Wilder saw her stumble and sway. She was lying on the ground by the time he reached her. He crouched down beside her and bent his head towards her lips. No breath stirred. He did not see the shadow of a thin man in a long coat half-fall clear of the wind sieve and pick up the end of his torn and bloody cable, his face clenched in rage and frustration. Wilder was oblivious, locked in his cocoon of grief as he held Pippa's body and wept.

Holding his bleeding umbilicus in his hand, John Grey staggered away from this most abject failure, his pale form unremarkable amongst the thousands of other spectres with which the Blinking Fields is populated. He hugged his arms to his miserable sides and thought of how close he had been to her. But 'close' was not the word — he had *been* her! Now he was torn from her and she from him, and he was nothing. And how horrible were the sensations created by the phantom forms that teased and nudged at him. From time to time a cartoon figure, a memory or a wave of hate or love would become entangled in his hair, stuck in his teeth, caught in the coils of his cerebrum or melted in the stew of his own humours, phlegmatic, choleric and melancholic. Sensations of layered heat and cold, tingling, numbness and nausea assaulted him, for although Grey yearned after the animal substance of human beings and beasts, he loathed the vagaries of the Blinking Fields, being as they were so much like himself, half-finished compositions of borrowed dreams and visions. But what was it that had interfered with the transmission of the girl's soul stuff into his own yearning hollowness? How had she slipped away? He would have to consider these things later; right now, he needed sustenance. His anger and disgust gave him momentum as he strode away towards where he sensed real things lived and breathed.

Wilder had never before experienced despair, but now he could feel it coming for him like the train he is certain he misremembers from the cover of an old Ray Bradbury novel. In his false memory its upper face is that of a sinister child, below its mouth is guarded with a black iron grille, rather like an early version Darth Vader's mask. It was coming for him, for sure, panting its noxious fumes, polluting the landscape of his soul. But he could at least get off the tracks. He needed to get back to where he could think. He needed to be away from the infernal mess that was the Blinking Fields.

So he picked up Pippa's body, which was already almost weightless and began to trudge uphill and out of Carneac's caldera. He set off in the direction where he expected that sooner or later he would find the corpse at the crossroads, which was the only landmark he knew. And as he walked he had plenty of time to wonder at what had happened. Had she been so much frailer than he realised? Or was it something she saw in the folds of the wind sieve? He would never know. Throughout the waning afternoon the body he carried grew paradoxically ever lighter. At a certain point he stopped and realised that he had wandered off track and was in unfamiliar territory. He couldn't remember when he last saw a godlid, now that he came to think of it. The low sun that gilded the hairs on the skull of the dead woman, now no more than an armful of hollow bones, also shone down upon acres of webs strung between low bushes that looked a bit like sultana grape vines: fine traceries of light against the backdrop of palest pinkish grey, dove-coloured sky. He walked down the narrow avenues lined with the hip-high, twisted trunks from whose knotty branches were suspended the webs of countless spiders, small and light browny-gold, sitting quietly at the edges of their traps or moving busily from twig to twig, endlessly renovating their homes, not knowing that they would be stolen from them, harvested by great, predatory mammals with no real appreciation of arachnid architecture. A little beyond he could see the towers and rooftops that Steve had pointed out on their drive, the factories where the raw material from which Ariadne's famous silk was spun into screens, and also into the mesh that Carneac used to catch her fugitive notions from Elsewhere.

In the distance he also saw, speeding along at about sixty kilometres an hour, an ostrich hellbent on getting somewhere very quickly. What he didn't see in the failing light was the form of John Grey lying flat along its back, his legs wrapped around its body and tucked in under its belly, goading it along with the spurs of his long, jagged thumbnails.

By the time Wilder had reached the farthest edge of the spider fields the sun had retreated beyond the horizon in a wash of red and yellow. Wilder thought of the wasted embryo of a chick he had once found in his egg when he broke it open with a spoon. Behind him, the sky was a sorry and defeated no-colour left behind to fade away into the night, which was imminent. He noticed now, too, that his arms were empty.

He saw what he'd been looking for, a little further to the west than he had expected, but there nevertheless: the ghastly silhouette of the hanging woman against the twilight sky. As he approached, the corpse swung around to greet him. 'Hello, solitary man,' she said, 'so lonely now, and so close to hopelessness.'

Wilder sat down at the foot of the gallows. Baxta was right. The train had caught him up.

'I love sadness in a man. The broken soul, the harrowed heart, the lost… if you sit quietly now, you will hear the wind blowing through your ribcage, stirring up the odd dead leaf, then moving on.'

One of Baxta's black chickens approached him, and tentatively pecked at his trouser cuff. Wilder shooed it away.

'Don't be unkind to my little witch-doctors, my kindred souls,' she said. 'Dirty though they are, and very basic. Stunted black magical voodoo queens of blood who, unlike other creatures of the light — except perhaps the sow — will eat anything, even their own kind. Cannibals with yellow claws, all ridged and veined and dark at root, they till the filth of ages amongst layered scraps and mulch and guano: hens and pigs and dirty little burrowing witches like Carneac, they expose the seeds of life to light. But where would we without them? They are the worms of generation, the brokers of mortal deliverance! Oh, animal existence is dirty and foul; you must claw yourselves free. So now I have a riddle for you, my handsome breathing friend: which came first? The chicken or the dirt?'

As Wilder was considering the proposition, Baxta broke in with, 'And the answer is… who *cares!*' she laughed raucously. 'It all begins and ends in the muck, dear one; where breed germs of death and germs of life both. All brilliance, nobility and sympatico, art and sex and wildness and civilisation begin and end in it, whether the muck be compost heap or cosmic soup! And the chicken, like a debased hermetic scientist, participates in both the disease and the cure — like the god who visited your dead-to-the-world friend yesterday in his dual guise of Messenger and Doctor (oh don't look so puzzled, little escapes my eye!) Yet *oh so un*like, for that god belongs to the air while the hen is of the soil. The Doctor's serpent-twined caduceus is the divining rod as the chicken's claw is the scalpel, the speculum, the spirit level! Therefore do not despise corruption, but embrace it. Do not despise my ways or Carneac's, for we, like the doctor god, Master of Transformation, are also agents of change. The worlds shift upon their axes and the realities meet and cross over. As you know only too well! Stay awake to it all, Dr Wilder Portion. Stay alive.' Baxta reared back and angled her head to catch Wilder's eye with her scaly, hen-like one. 'And now sir, you are excused.'

The heavy sky hangs low over Ariadne. The nervous fingertips of the Grannap I Memorial Centre prod anxiously at the vulnerable underside of cloud, which shivers and turns belly up, showing spots of light, streaks of silver. A stray star sputters out and is lost amongst the black radiance of luminous gloom.

Mimin Kimomik, Principal of Ariadne School is at work very early this morning. He sits at his desk and sips weak sage tea. Anything stronger at this time of day plays havoc with his digestion. He turns a page of the document he is reading. Above his slightly uptilted eyes (he used to be described as pixieish when he was younger) his soft, ash-blond brows crease, and several freckles meet in this new crevice to discuss their facial colonisation policy. They are thinking of extending their influence beyond his forehead, nose and cheeks to the extremities of temple, throat and neck.

His expression changes to one of dismay as he turns another page. (Freckles flee to his hairline and regroup to rethink their strategy.) School finances are dwindling — repairs, renovations, maintenance of every kind — these old buildings gobble funds insatiably. Depressed, Mimin puts away the builder's report and reaches for another hefty bundle of literature. The education ministry is thinking of cutting back on the subsidies this school has enjoyed since its inception. Little does it matter to the distributors of government moneys that the academic standards of this school are amongst the highest in Mogom, thinks Mimin angrily, as he reads of a suggestion that his curriculum, so heavy on Clear Opacity Studies and Empathetic Geometry needs to focus more on vocational preparation. Looks like de Chirican Shadow-Play will have to go. Mimin reads, sighs, writes a note or two, then reaches back and stretches until his shoulders pop.

He considers Aidai, a pretty woman of twenty who

graduated from the senior school a year ago and is now making plans to travel. Why did he always have to go for the clever ones?

The door of his office opens a fraction.

'Who is there?' asks the headmaster in irritation. Is it never possible to have a moment's quiet? Even at five o'clock in the morning? What sick adolescent joke is this?

The door opens a little further and he sees a thin man in a coat, shirtless and barefooted. He will remember this man for the rest of his life — approximately three minutes — for all money worries, academic ambitions, errant girlfriend, rebellious freckles, sandy hair and pixie-tilted eyes are now resolved into the final Mimin-shaped code of joy, anxiety, love, desire, fear and folly that this world will ever see.

Wilder walked all night, retracing the route of the tourist coach. Around dawn he stopped for a while beneath a small stand of yoq trees and half dozed till close to noon. It was mid-afternoon by the time he entered the gates of Ariadne. The day was overcast, white as a pall over the town, all sound and colour muted. It suited his mood of resigned misery. Yet, as he passed the bakery he noticed that despite all, his traitorous body was hungry and must be fed. He remembered he hadn't seen food since those blue shanks of Carneac's he hadn't eaten, and having picked up no pay from his employer he stopped by an overflowing bin. He wasn't in a mood to care what people thought, and after a quick rummage found half a fairly tasty looking hotdog, still warm, which he wolfed down with the yeasty dregs from a beer bottle. He continued on his way back to Bailey's, which though hardly his home was at least, like Baxta's gibbet, a kind of landmark in the desolate landscape his life was fast becoming. He noticed that the traffic was thin, there were few people on the streets and those that were talked quietly together in pairs or in small knots, looking around them anxiously. Those he passed eyed him with suspicion. Perhaps they always had — since he was after all, a stranger — but excited by all the newness and variety, he had simply failed to notice. Still, he felt that this was about the time in the Western where the newcomer to town mentions to himself: 'It was quiet — too quiet', to enable a sudden battery of gunshots to erupt from the saloon. But there was no saloon. No gunslingers. No shots. Just the grey-white oppressive sky sealing the participants into a drama he felt sure was waiting to happen.

At Bailey's he took a seat under an awning overlooking the vacant coach stop. A family group at the adjoining table moved when he sat down, resettling themselves as far from him as they could. Bailey came out, blinked at him, made a clucking noise between her jack of spades tooth and the gap next to it, then went back inside again without speaking. A moment later the giant doormen appeared. They stationed themselves on either side of his table.

'Hello?' said Wilder. 'Bob? Ah... I'd like to thank you both for your help the other night...' his voice trailed away, as the bouncers stood staring straight ahead like mechanical guardsmen. No acknowledgement, not so much as a greeting. He tried again, 'How are you today, Bob?'

The broken-nosed giant now deigned to reply: 'On this blindingly white and featureless day, you ask: how am I?'

'Well, yes?'

'On this old-shirt-scented, listless day, whose one reptilian eye blinks in a pallid sky full of the dust of dead hills, you ask how I am?'

'I...'

'On this cadaverous day, this rigor-mortal day, you would enquire into my state of being?'

'I would.'

The man sighed deeply, rolled his eyes, and would say no more. His colleague responded for him: 'Health, my man, equals one. Put beside this figure the zeroes of love, glory and success, you are a wealthy man. Remove the one of health from the configuration...' he raises a stumpy forefinger and makes a circle with it and his thumb, '...and you have zero.'

And your point is... ? wondered Wilder in irritation. What the hell was going on? Apart from the family group that had moved away from him, there were one or two other patrons, and where, when he had first arrived, he had been a source of interest and unwanted commentary, he was now being studiously ignored. He stared at the woodgrain of his tabletop. It had old glass rings in it, and a few crumbs scattered. These he began to push around into clever little piles.

A large glass of something green and fizzy and creamy arrived at his table. Then a familiar voice said, 'Lime spider.' He looked up into Mu's half-smiling face. 'It's my best favrit. Also the traditional toast of Ariadne. Made out of fruit an fizzy water an cream. Hasn't atcherly got any spiders in.' He was so glad to see her he could have hugged her. Mu, his only contact with what passed for reality. She sat down opposite him. If he had noticed that she was perhaps a little tired or wan, Wilder did not comment. He took a slug of his drink. It tasted like toxic waste with sugar on top. 'Don't worry, Wilder,' said Mu. 'Nobody's got anything on you, and I know you'd never do anything bad. It's just that everyone's upset and confused, an you're a stranger, sort of thing, an they haven't got anyone else to blame. They're just scared witless.'

'What do you mean? Blame for what? What's been going on?'

Mu reached behind her to a vacant table and picked up someone's discarded copy of the afternoon edition of the *Ariadne Internect*, where he read, on the front page, of the mysterious death of a six year old child. She had been playing outside her house and when her mother had come to bring her in for her dinner, found the child had unaccountably passed away. 'Jesus, how awful,' murmured Wilder.

'She was Lew's little sister,' said Mu. 'Clarrie. Lew's a mate of mine.' Now he certainly noticed that her face was strained. Wilder reached out and held her hand. 'Read more,' she said. Obediently, he turned the page. An elderly couple had died in their sleep, and four babies. And Mr Kimomik, a teacher at Mu's school. All in the last twenty-four hours. The cause of death had not been established in any of the eight cases. *Eight* deaths. Overnight and this morning.

At this point, Bailey approached their table. Taking care not to meet Wilder's eyes, she said to him, 'I'd like you to find alternative accommodation from tonight.'

'Well, of course. If you prefer… but I…'

'Please. I don't want to discuss it. I want you gone.' She managed to look at him now, and her eyes were hard and frightened. No jack of spades winked in the light. 'There is something foul stirring here in Mogom, and it's come hot on *your* heels. I want you shot of this place within the hour.' Before Wilder could say another word she had turned abruptly to Mu and said, 'Go in, Mu. The toilets need cleaning,' and went back inside.

But Mu did not move. Her face was white and rigid and staring over Wilder's shoulder into the street. He turned to look. He saw the horrible family swilling at their troughs, and beyond them, a couple walking along the pavement talking in low voices, a newspaper vendor counting change, and a man in a grey coat in a shadowed doorway, smoking a cigarette… what was the fuss? 'Mu? What's going on?'

While Wilder had been scanning the front page, Mu — for want of anything better to do — had been scanning the street. That was when she saw him: the man out of Grannap's cauldron. She felt her heart stop for a second, then resume at a rate of knots. She stared at him and he stared back. He knew her too. It *was* him, alright. His face was angry, twisted up and tormented looking like the faces on that batch of ethereal demons she had seen once in the Blinking Fields, not far from Baxta's gibbet; his eyes as kind as those on the razor-backed boars Columbine's dad had to keep separate from their litters in case they ate their own babies. And there was a great deal more in that expression of his but Mu lacked the words for all the nuances, and besides she knew too well that it was not safe to look too long at him and to avoid the eyes especially, else you could get caught in them, like a small carp in a pond of malignant reeds. No, she didn't care to work him out and in any case, it wasn't important. What *was* important were two things she intuited immediately with a certainty beyond her years but within her recent experience. The first was that he was behind what had been going on in Ariadne. The second was that this greedy-pig man-thing still wanted *her.*

So now she hissed, 'It's *him.* The one with the devil eyes.'

Wilder glanced back one more time and at that moment, the figure with the cigarette happened to adjust his position minutely and for a second Wilder saw his face distinctly. That second was long enough. He turned back immediately and reached across the table to Mu and took hold of both her hands.

'Ow!'

He loosened his grip but still kept her hands firmly in his own. 'Mu,' he whispered. 'You recognise this man? Where have you seen him?'

'No time to talk about it now,' she answered in a tight little voice. 'It's enough that you know what I mean. You *do* know, don't you, Wilder, or else why is your face just gone white-red-white like a traffic light on the blink. We have to *do* something. We have to…'

'Mu. No,' he interrupted. '*You* have to do *nothing*. Wait here. I mean it — don't you move an inch! I'm going to get the muscle.' Wilder let go of her hands, rose and headed off towards the bar in search of Bailey and the bouncers.

Relief and resentment fought for ascendancy in Mu's mind and after a very short battle, the latter won: why should she feel relieved because some adult was taking over? What did he know, anyway? Nothing, that's what. He was just a visitor, an Arrival with next to no experience of Mogom. He'd told her what to do once before, too, out at the Blinking Fields when she'd offered to give him a proper Nongog's introduction to Carneac and he'd knocked it back. And where had that got anyone? She looked at the no-progress he was now making with Bailey. She'd called Bob and Bob over. Wilder was looking from Bailey to one or other of the bouncers then back again; his gestures sometimes imperious, sometimes pleading. Mu knew that couldn't be going down too well with them if he looked this silly to her. And it was obvious from their faces and posture that they were underwhelmed with whatever he was telling them, and why wouldn't they be? Mu knew the whole town had already decided that he was mad or wicked or both. *And he doesn't even get it. Poor bugger.* And even if he did convince them that it was the grey man who needed catching and locking up, how would they do it? They'd probably just blunder over like great galumphing adults and he'd run or waft off or do whatever it was devilly men did... and anyway there just was no *time* for this. It's down to *me*, Mumu Nongog.

It was then that she realised that she knew what to do. And the knowledge terrified her. Here was real danger, unmediated and absolute. But what was the other option? To know about this ghoulish thing and do nothing? It wasn't in her to be that way. It just wasn't.

Wilder turned around just in time to catch sight of Mu already almost a block away, passing under the arches of the Chirico-co Co. in a flurry of too-large yellow cardigan. And a few hundred yards behind her on the otherwise now-deserted street John Grey was following her, not closely, but deliberately and doggedly, his long grey coat flapping against his calves — and no cable in evidence. Wilder left Bailey and the bouncers to themselves and hastened after the calibandit.

John Grey had in fact been following Mu for some time, having picked up her scent not long after he'd replenished himself with the headmaster. Like the one who had drawn him here then abandoned him, all alone and brotherless — she had eluded him once. How humiliating! Still, he had managed to look after himself here in this new place in which he had found himself so messily catapulted. On streets and in warm rooms he had basked in the heat of human commerce, their mixed auras of delight, anxiety and anger, envy and lust and pity and love, all the shades of soulful animality that radiated from them in waves. And from time to time he would engage more intimately with one or two. Children were easy; making cable-free connections with older people took marginally longer — gaining their full attention, generating wonder or yearning in a hot human heart — then lovingly drawing it all into himself, all that delicious vigour and verve, then leaving nothing but a husk. He was getting quite good at forming relationships with those he chose to love to death without the benefit of his cord. Indeed, it was getting easier and faster every hour.

With each life he had subsumed he had felt stronger. He had nourished himself and he was fortified. It was necessary for him to build up a great deal of energy: Brother had to be able to discern *him* amongst all the imaginary, psychological and electronic flotsam so as to draw him back safely to their homey interstice. He missed its gentle blue light, its brown couch. Until that woman had come. She who had so evilly seduced then abandoned him, left him lonely and bleeding in a field of putrid blossoms and inferior television.

It was after he had the headmaster, that he actually *felt* the presence of Brother. He was near; he was watching.

Yet Grey knew he needed to keep a level head while he stoked his engine with others' life force: if he needed the heat and the power he also needed the control. He must balance on the twin-edged blade of passion and strict discipline. The lives had lined the edges of his aching absence, but he sensed the soul-fuel of that little Mumu-morsel would be stronger meat. She would do for now.

She would not evade him a second time, of this he was absolutely certain. So when he saw her leave Bailey's and head off down the street, he followed her at a discreet distance: past the Chirico-co Company offices, down the main street, under the Arc de Trompe l'Oeil and along the avenue, across a sports oval and the schoolyard, then down one of its rayed pathways shaded by stands of yoq trees whose leafy fingers touched their tips overhead, knitting a dappled coverlet from the light and shade to throw over the footpath. Wherever he passed, imperceptible adjustments in the quality of the light and colour and scent followed: the cool shadows through which light fell shifted their shades from violet and gold to bruise-blue and cholesterol-yellow; the mushroomy smell of wholesome mulch became the sweet stink of putrefaction. John Grey lost sight of Mu's quick form as it darted ahead of him through the tunnel of leaf and light, but still he could discern her easily by following the heat-traces of her passionate soul. It led him to a place where her radiant energy field linked up with those of other small dynamos. And he could hear them now: just beyond this battery of rushes. Peering through now, he saw the children talking together excitedly in low voices whose words he could not discern. But what did he care of that? It would only be trivial childish chatter. The point was, there were several of them, all bursting with vitality. This was more than enough for the moment. This was… *lovely*.

When Mu arrived she was pleased to see that although it was getting on towards dark they were all there: Speare, Squared and Columbine and even Sim, though he was supposed to be at home by now. She gave him her big-sister glare and he gave it right back. Then she turned to

Lew, shocked to see him here. 'Lew, I'm so sorry about Clarrie… are you sure you want to be here right now? I mean…'

'You're not the boss a me,' he answered testily.

'I know. I just thought…' But his angry little face was clenched like a fist. He'd already decided that he wanted to be with his mates and clearly did not want to discuss it or his little sister or anything else. So, removing her unwanted attention from him, she continued with the short opening she'd planned on her way here from Baileys: 'Listen, you lot,' she began, meeting the eyes of each of the others in turn, 'I have to tell youse somethin an you better believe it. If you don't, then you can go home. If you do believe me, then you have to do what I tell you.'

'Mrs Bossy at it again,' muttered Sim under his breath, but Mu heard and decided to give him that point.

'Maybe I am. But when you hear what I have to say, you can decide what you want. Okay?' She looked at Lew first and waited till he acknowledged her with a half nod, then at each of the others in turn. Nobody was arguing, so she sat down between Squared and Sim. 'Everyone gather in close. We don't want anyone overhearin. And pay attention, because we have to hurry.' She told them an abbreviated version of what had happened to her last night when she'd looked into Grannap's cauldron, how she'd seen the face of a man who stared into her. 'It was like his eyes were feelers sort of feelin around inside a me. An it was horrible cos everywhere he looked I felt bits a me getting weak, and he was sort of drainin me strength, suckin the life outa me. An it happened quickly too, like a kinda fast-forward vampire or somethin…'

'No way,' interrupted Shakespeare, the nerve under his good eye twitching. 'You're makin it up to scare us.'

Sim piped up: 'I saw too. Honest. Her face was all kinda, I don't know, sorta *gone...*' The others turned in unison toward him, making him blush.

'Sim saved me. Even though it was by accident.' Sim shrugged, but he looked very happy with the attention. 'An I'm sure he's the one behind what's been happening last night an this morning — and probly more on'y we don't know about it yet.'

'Why d'you think it's him?' asked Lew, the scorn in his voice palpable.

'Okay. Tell me. How did those people die? Were there any marks on 'em? Did anybody yell for help?' challenged Mu, knowing that she was being cruel and that she would say harsher words yet. She had to. Now was no time for gentleness. 'What about little Clarrie, Lew — was she sick?'

Lewis glared at her in fury that was close to hate, debating with himself whether to answer or punch her in the nose. Eventually he said through white lips, 'No. Nobody knows why they died... and you *know* nobody knows. Cla... she was healthy an happy. Never did anyone any harm,' his voice low though not quite steady as he added, 'She was there one minute, then she was gone. Just died for nothin.'

Mu took over, seeing how close Lew was to tears. 'Just like what woulda happened to me if Sim hadn't come in just then... But look. There's somethin else.'

All eyes were on her. Mu noticed with satisfaction that there wasn't a lot of breathing going on. She was in control.

'He's been followin me. I saw him before. He's probly here right now.'

'What? Where? How do you know?' breathed

Columbine. Her large brown eyes were so dark they seemed all pupil.

'He's hidin. But he'll be nearby for sure. I let him see where I was going, so he'd follow me to youse, cos there's safety in numbers. I figured we could lead him to the on'y place where the likes a him can be got rid of. Which is?'

'The Registry,' they answered, all in one voice.

'Now. Anyone want to go home?'

Sim reached and took her hand, which is something he hadn't done since he was six. He smiled at her as if he trusted her. This was a scary moment; she had to smile back confidently as if his faith was warranted. 'I'm with you,' whispered Shakespeare, making an effort to get his left eye under control. Emcee Squared and Columbine Hogson nodded in unison, their bodies leaning together and their fingers intertwined. Lewis poured a mug full of colabrew and passed it round. Each child took a deep drink before they set back off along the path: Mu, Sim and Lew followed at a little distance by Columbine and Squared, who no matter what were always slightly separated from others, always had their little cone of privacy about them. Shakespeare brought up the rear.

Wilder had lost track of Mu and her stalker in the vicinity of the Ariadne Elementary School. A swing creaked quietly in the breeze. Deserted playgrounds, fairgrounds, big tops denting in the wind, all good settings for the nastiest end of the criminal spectrum. He realised his reputation probably wouldn't be much improved if he were caught sneaking around a school like some kind of pervert. But what else could he do? He'd tried to alert Bailey to the danger, but she already thought he was in league with the devil and so did the Bobs — on pain of dismissal. So now he, Wilder, was Mu's self-appointed and — he desperately hoped, adequate — guardian.

Then he saw her walking past the side gates with a clutter of schoolfriends. They weren't chattering like children though; they made a sombre group, on some kind of kid mission, obviously. Well, there was safety in numbers he supposed, relieved. He tagged along well behind them as they headed back into the town centre. Then he caught sight of Grey on the other side of the street, walking at a pace with the children. Wilder quickened his step, careless now of being seen, and was running by the time the children reached the door to the Registry. He called out to them, called Mu in particular, but nobody paused nor even acknowledged his warning cries. Instead they headed on inside in a huddle, like one twelve-legged furry-headed creature. Grey followed them and Wilder followed Grey.

Wilder clattered up the stairs after them, Grey now only just ahead. On the top landing was the open door that Mu had just entered. At the threshold, the calibandit glanced back over his shoulder to see his pursuer but barely registered him; to him Wilder was an irrelevance to be glanced over and discarded as neither friend nor threat. To Wilder, John Grey's unmediated attention, though glancing, was dry ice swiped across his soul. He followed him into the room.

chapter thirteen
words and time, wish-nets and saving grace

If the atmosphere was close, the air itself was heavy with the smell of rotting things and so thick that Wilder could only breathe it in tiny sips. The powdery darkness was crosshatched with cobwebs above and around creating a fibrous cathedral. The floor was soft with ages of dust. From obscure sources narrow shafts of mote-filled light spanned the massed bodies of darkness and tall bookcases reached beyond vision and cast attenuated shadows on the floor stacked waist-high with piles of documents. The lights on the consoles blinked like those of patient, waiting amphibians. The children were nowhere to be seen as they had scattered and concealed themselves as soon as they entered, but Wilder could sense their breathing presences. Across the room he could just make out the tall, thin form of John Grey, his coat open, the cable of his umbilicus hanging down in front of him, its torn edge pink-frilled, obscene.

As for Grey, when he crossed the threshold into this anticipatory holding space he knew immediately that he had entered a vital centre. This was an omphalos, a power point crackling with electronic intelligence. There friendly screens gleamed gently in the gloom — and dotted here and there were hot spots where live youth pulsed.

Then, from the depths of the Registry came a rippling movement amongst the shadows and there emerged the dusty and the dustier forms of two delicate giants with human-spider faces, gentle and myopic, their tiny bodies attached to eight, very long, very thin, daintily fringed limbs. One wore a tea-rose shawl; the other, a long, frayed, cable-stitched cardigan.

'I sense the proximity of a degenerate entity that craves more than it deserves,' murmured Erewhile through her mandibles, from which a spool of strong, tacky thread was unwinding. Her eight eyes rolled in their sockets as if scanning for a vision scrolled across the coils of her brain.

'Extraordinary specimen of yearning matter,' mentioned Eftsoons, two of his eyes looking over his shoulder, while the others severally scanned the rest of the room, right, left and forward. 'I want it. Can you see it, sister?'

'I cannot see it. But I feel it aching. It is an embodied ache of absence.'

'Yet it burns too, burns with a heat not its own.'

The elderly librarians' daddy-long-legs pace infuriated Mu. She and the others had assumed that all they needed to do was lure him here and then wait a few moments while the Registrars got on with what they *always* did, what they lived for: filing and cataloguing. They were supposed to immediately recognise Grey for the parasite he was then hijack him, preserve him in silk, etcetera etcetera… 'Oh god,' she hissed under her breath, '*do* something!' But Erewhile and Eftsoons continued murmuring together, occasionally burping quietly to regurgitate their cuds of silk, gumming their perpetual wads into strands that spread over the files, the furniture, the floors… 'Please,' Mu now said to herself, 'it's so *obvious* he needs to be put away! And *soon!*' She knew that this Grey-prey was unpredictable and might not just stand about waiting to be dealt with like a fly in the corner of a web… so, before her rising panic could paralyse her she forced herself out into the centre of the room where the muted light was brightest and, as she had heard Bailey do, articulated clearly and loudly, the password:

'It's an ill wind that blows no good.'

'Ah,' breathed Eftsoons, drawing his front legs up under his chin and cocking his fine, pointed head towards Mu, 'never a truer word was spoken.'

'I'm really sorry to interrupt your er… whatever… but Registrars, you must take him. Now!' And she pointed to the thin figure hovering between a stack of archive boxes and a large flat-screen monitor whose screensaver told and retold in slow-mo images how a trapdoor spider builds its nest.

'The ill wind blows no good through its bones,' mentioned Erewhile, wetting a long, thin pincer with spit and holding it up before her as if testing the air. She and her brother turned in the direction of Grey, their weak eyes searching, their mandibles working as thicker, knottier gnarls of thread began to emerge from their mouths.

Grey slipped still more deeply into the shadows, rearranging his coat over his navel-cable, and pressed himself back into a recess provided by several packing cases and a computer, where, to his delight, he found he was not alone: a lovely little boy-tonic and a dark, curly girl huddled close together, their fingers intertwined. He smiled down upon them like a nuclear dawn.

Columbine and Squared were bound together by fine but very strong bonds of love: it was not hard for Grey to haul them into his mind like twin fish speared on the same hook, down into that timeless dreamspace within his purposive, undeviating focus. He could feel the proximity of the Registrars and the threat they posed, though he did not care to consider what the nature of this threat might be — but whatever it was, he would need strength to meet it, and here was a source, *the* source. *Delicious.* He drew and drew on the children's spirits, sucking up the nectar of their essence as a dragonfly siphons the sweetness from a fallen peach. And as he fed and his strength grew, so did his connection with Brother, back home holding the fort in their pleasant interstitial cranny. Brother was very near now, picking up on the energy provided by this last top-up of soul-fuel… and a moment later one of the larger screens responded, flared into life with the face of a man, pale and glairy whom Wilder instantly recognised as Brother, his hair in a red bob.

And now, several things happened at once: Brother's virtual presence threw its light and colour across the room; Columbine fell forward, dragging down with her a dusty pall of matted cobweb; the stack of boxes that had concealed her collapsed like a house of cards as Squared too fell; Lew, Sim, Speare and Mu charged over towards them and Wilder strode across to the console to turn off the monstrous face on the screen.

He flicked off the monitor, but the image remained. Erewhile, noting this appalling irregularity, glided swiftly across to the main power point and shut off the electricity. Brother's face spasmed, almost guttered, then suddenly bloomed out into the room in a panic of pixelated light and colour, like a stained-glass window exploding in a church. And each of the pixels was a face complete in itself, and each voice spoke clearly, echoing from wall to wall, ceiling to floor: *Connect! Connect! CONNECT!*

Mu leapt up from where she had been crouched by her two fallen friends and shouted, 'Stop him making sense! Break his pattern! Shiver his bits *to bits!*' She ran out into the room, flailing her arms and scattering Brother's fragments wildly and violently, causing them to surge around the room in wild tides of brilliant static. Sim, Lew, and Shakespeare joined in and began to throw themselves round the space, further atomising the assemblage that had been Brother so that his particles whirled in eddies then broke like a surf against knotted gossamer drapery, towers of papers, leaning bookcases that tilted then fell, one after the other, and great clouds of choking dust rose as the shining lights of fragmented Brotherness spread in a mist of hateful intentionality, scorching the walls, the furniture, the children's faces —

Then some of the particles of Brother found each other, thrombotically congealed then grew and spread, forming themselves into fiendish little twisted manikins, all with the same face, hair like the wig of a wartime whore, cheeks each with a dot of livid red, lips that peeled open like a zipper to reveal two rows of shiny teeth like the blades of a harvester through which they chanted, *We hate you, hate you, but oh it's nothing personal. You're lovely, so lovely — we want you, we love you —*

Brother-figures melded effortlessly one into the other or crashed bodily into each other with screams of ecstasy — *We want you, we hate you* — as fast as the children smashed them they reconfigured and spread, broke down then remerged, coagulating like fatty emboli over and over — *oh, we are empty, so empty — and you! You are so full — oh, not fair, not fair —* screaming and singing and dipping and dancing and running up the walls like homing trouts in a cataract, splashing themselves across the children's faces like paint balls — *and you, you're full to bursting — You* will *burst!*

We'll burst you, invert you, your guts laid bare, in the air, your hair, your skin, laid bare in the air —

Oh, we'll find quiet corpses, so lovely, so lovely —

Brothers oozed down over their bodies, growing, spreading, mushrooming, a fast-forward fungus staining children and ceiling and floor, forming clots in the corners from which other Brothers sprouted then shimmied up the walls to dangle bat-like from light-bulb flexes — *We'll scry your guts for hope, my hope, our hope. You are our hope, our love, our hate —*

Brothers now screaming and spitting clotted gobs of filth on the scrambling children, or forming rings around them, rings of elongated Brothers like children's paper chains, knee-high, then shoulder-high, their hands monkey-gripped together, their faces all alike in their maleficence, yet all subtly different — *And if we smile when you cry, remember — it's nothing personal —*

They moved as one clockwise, then anticlockwise, chanting as one, *We hate you we want you we love you, hate you want you, love you, hate you, want, hate, love —*

And still the children fought, did not cease their flailing, smashing the multiplicity of proliferating Brothers —

While John Grey, who had taken in the meaning of the order relayed from the screen loud and clear, knew exactly what to do. Using the dust and chaos of crying, shouting children and the tides of light that were his brother, his other, as cover, he crept over to one of the computers. Squatting behind the splintered remains of a filing cabinet he reached down and seized the end of his flayed cable. Raising it to his lips he wetted its tip and, as does a seamstress her thread, smoothed its frayed end with spittle so that it made a point, and poked it through the eye of the needle — into the USB port —

The room heaved and there was a stink of burning plastic, flesh and hair and Wilder looked over to its source: John Grey had now risen to his feet. With his umbilicus plugged into the monitor's socket, teeth bared, jugular throbbing in his neck, back arched in ecstasy, his hands gripped and palpitated the fleshy cord now reconnecting him to his world —

With eyes squeezed closed he felt the most delicate touch, loving and sure, as of tender arms around him. 'Brother,' he murmured. The touch grew stronger, became more encompassing, and he felt a breath upon his cheek.

Tears of relief oozed out from his clenched eyelids, and had he looked, he would have seen not his brother's but Erewhile's face as she enveloped him in her sticky embrace.

'Gently, gently,' she murmured, casting aside the tea rose shawl the better to hold him to her as she kissed his mouth. Her body trembled as her venom sac pulsed once, twice, releasing its narcotic elixir.

As the first of the lethal anaesthetic entered John Grey's bloodstream, Brother felt it too and he understood what was to be their fate. His howl of fury echoed around the cavernous space then died in pulsing sobs as all the multiples of himself with which he had so ecstatically seeded this new reality began to break down into tiny, then tinier parts, to fade then crisp and curl up at their edges like so many flakes of stale skin. Drifts of fast-fading Brotherness now fell like snow, covering the wreckage of the Registry.

Soon Wilder could no longer see the object of Erewhile's attentions for the movement of angular arachnoid limbs concealed Grey, and the agitation of silk muffled his dying cries. Eftsoons now joined his sister and soon all that could be heard was the slick sound of silken strands emerging from the Registrars' bodies, and winding around the spool that was John Grey and the last aspects of Brother, now falling soft and silent as moth breath.

'Too bad,' said Erewhile through a mouthful of gossamer that she was coiling about Grey's torso.

'Too mad and sad,' sighed Eftsoons, as he wound Grey's thighs in silk.

'A has-been,' said the other through the side of her mouth, her jaws working all the while. 'Look,' and she gestured at the end of the twitching umbilical cord that had fallen limply back from the socket. It was now lying at John Grey's naked feet, the only part of him now visible.

'Let us store him.'

'File him.'

'Catalogue him.'

'Waste not, want not.'

After a while, the Registrars together lifted the swaddled calibandit onto one of the few unbroken shelves and laid him out at the end of a row of other dusty chrysalis-like forms. The ancient faces showed no feeling at all as they turned back towards the room. If they saw Wilder and the children leaving, carrying between them the unmoving forms of Squared and Columbine, they gave no sign.

Erewhile sighed as she looked around at the calamitous state of the Registry. She stooped to pick her shawl up from where she had dropped it and where it now lay in a drift of brother-flakes. She shook it out thoroughly and drew it around her shoulders and sighed again.

'What troubles you, my sister?'

'I am tired,' she answered. 'So very, very tired.'

'I too,' he responded. 'But we have our tasks, and they must be done. We are the keepers of the histories.'

'It was ever so,' she answered. 'But sometimes, on such days of revelation, I might wish...'

'What might you wish for, sister?' Eftsoons put down his duster and cocked his head towards her voice, which he noticed for the first time, had a little break in it. She was old. It was true. So was he.

'I might wish for a little peace... a little help...'

•

six months later

Dr Wilder Portion brushed aside the ropy curtain, like a veil of dreadlocks, from his sleeping alcove at the back of the Registry. He made his way through the islands of files to the main door to pick up the thermos of coffee Mumu always left there for him on her way to school after cleaning up at Bailey's. Cup in hand, he began his day's work. He'd found this job in the same way he'd found his first one, though *this* one had been on the money. The ad on the pub's noticeboard read: *Assistant Librarian required. Contact E and E at the Registry, Town Centre, Ariadne.*

The children, Squared and Columbine, had not survived. The full unmediated impact of the hungry calibandit had been more than their systems could bear. Columbine had endured for a few days, had been lovingly tended by Mr Hogson, Bailey, Mu and friends, but she had been too badly depleted to last very long. It was the tenth funeral in the small town of Ariadne that week.

If people had avoided Wilder before, now he was completely alienated. People crossed to the other side of the street when they saw him, nobody would serve him in any of the shops, superstitiously averted their eyes whenever they caught sight of him. He could not be prosecuted for any crime, but in a way nobody understood but nevertheless knew, he was associated with the 'real figment' who had taken Columbine, Squared, Clarrie, Mimin Kimomik and the others. As Mu had said to him earlier, 'The grey man is dead, but you're here to remind everyone of what happened. It's like you're sorta infected or somethin. They need someone to blame.' So he was their scapegoat, spattered with the blood of poisonous associations. But Mu had remained his friend. A couple of weeks after Columbine's death she came to see him, to tell him once more that she knew it was not his fault and since then, she had brought him his coffee in the morning, bought him things he needed that could not be supplied by his employers, and would sometimes come up to the Registry after school to chew the fat with him for a while. Wilder had never known anyone, child or adult, with so great a heart as this little Mumu Nongog.

It had taken him a while to get used to being employed by spiders, and the almost silent comings and goings of the Registrars was unnerving. But they had worked out ways of stepping around each other, so to speak, without conflict. And they were thrilled with the headway he'd made with reorganising their systems, both hard copy and electronic. But the real bonus of the job consisted in the freedom they gave him to explore their equipment and to experiment with their software. The program that John Grey had tried to pirate was very familiar to him, as it was a close relation of his own Spatiotemporal Flux Translator — which of course is why Grey had made a beeline for it. Wilder had adjusted the functions of one of the modules to accommodate a modified version of the original Colanderic Spectrometer from his Sydney lab. He had high hopes for it. And although it would take time he now saw that it might be possible for him to adapt other components in order to replicate the systems he had devised back at St James Station. And if this proved successful, then might he not yet find a way back home?

Pippalotti Colquouhoun sat at the café table near Museum Station with her friends Birdy Lethe and Isadora D. It was, as her friend Wilder had once said a million years ago, a tacky little joint. But the coffee was good and it had a view over Hyde Park, which was nice. And it was just down the way from St James, below which Wilder had his lab. Isadora, her faux snakeskin lead dangling, was drinking from a saucer of milk, Birdy from a saucer of coffee. She had suggested on one occasion that he drink out of the cup, but he had looked at her as if she were mad. Pippa had of course asked him to explain what it was he had done, how it was that she was here, alive. His answer was to smile angelically from behind a red-grey ringlet, to gently brush her cheek with his hand and murmur, 'Words and time, nets of wishes, hope spirals and saving grace.' She hadn't got much further than that.

She glanced over her shoulder at the now rather tatty-looking poster she'd stuck on the wall above the counter. The proprietor hadn't minded. It showed a photo she'd found in an old Sydney Uni prospectus of the dashing Dr Wilder Portion, and a short note underneath with her name and number. No harm in trying. Though so far she'd only received a lot of calls from lonely would-be lovers, quite a lot of them transsexual.

But now she had a flamenco lesson to get to. She paid the bill and entrusted Isadora's lead to Birdy, then went down the steps of the station to catch her train.

Birdy Lethe leads Isadora back towards Liverpool Street. On the other side of College Street he notices something bright glinting up at him from the footpath. It is a child's comb, transparent plastic with beads of glitter set into it, like bright motes of sunlight trapped. He picks it up and puts it in his pocket.

He heads down the hill and up again to his room in the boarding house, which is just one street back from Pippa's building. The weather has turned chill, a blustery wind blows bits of gravel into his eyes. At the door he asks Isadora if she would care to come in for a plate of whitebait crispies, to which she replies, '*Pringioo mee*,' and slips inside.

After he feeds the cat, he takes a chair between the window and the hearth with its dancing blue gas flames. He turns on the heat and leans forward to warm his hands and face. Days and months and years have cracked the tiles of the fireplace, making of them a map of ages. Like the face of the old man. The tiles are blue, with pictures of ships. Birdy is the colour of nicotine.

He dozes for a while, and when he wakes it is dark. He thinks of other nights, of another night in particular, many centuries before he was born.

'… and this bright night was one apart,' he says to himself, or to Isadora perhaps, who sits nearby, her tail wrapped neatly round her feet. 'This one, bright, night sat on the edge of a fluke. The Earth and the heavens are joined at the seam of the horizon. Angels, and sometimes devils, have been known to fall through gaps in this imperfectly stitched cicatrix. And when that happens, strange manifestations occur on the Earth. Do you believe the stories of the love of God, my Isadora? Do not, for God is a carnivore. It is other gentler spirits who care and guide. God eats meat, and he is greedy. And the more he eats, the bigger he grows. And on this night, the craw of God was full. God bulged.

'His heavenly belly depended earthwards. The tender place where land meets sky strained and strained. The seal of the horizon was broken when God fell.

'God fell and his dislocation offset the universe. Just a fraction. But a fraction is all that lies between the third and the fourth of a thing. And it is within that fraction that wonders live. Singular wonders. Mysteries breed in this space. Sharks and wolves and space junk and pomegranates. Angels too, and those creatures who visit the sculptor of gargoyles as he dreams. Lovingly he renders their images in granite, in basalt, in marble. For the greater glory of the god who fell, who broke the seal, the seals… for the greater glory of that old god who was too weighty for the world. And so, mothers die to give birth to the babies a fraction too big. People love the things they lack and they despise their possessions. The skin of the earth is sad with lines and blisters weeping and the gates of the cities gape like the mouths of asthmatics between hard breathings. Suck in the dry hurting air between cutting teeth. The teeth, those round white bones, hard little bones that show most clearly there, behind our face-frame, that we are so weak, made of water and bones barely fleshed, a bit of skin…'

Birdy goes to the drawer his friend Pippa calls 'purgatory'. Here he keeps the things he finds, and also a good supply of string. He reaches in to gently touch a cigarette butt, a stone with a pretty band of grey across its brown middle, a leaf, a tortoiseshell button. He adds the child's comb and closes the drawer.

The Library

Terry Dowling

1.

If anywhere is home for me, apart from Rynosseros, it can only be Twilight Beach.

And, again, between voyages, with Rynosseros safely at the Sand Quay with the other deep-desert sand-ships, the crew lost in the bars and gaming-rooms of the Gaza Hotel, I took a favourite table at Amberlin's, wanting to avoid the crowds and the excitement of the Astronomers' Bar and the Gaza terrace, the conversations I would immediately inherit at Trimori's, The Traitor's Face and The Slow Hour.

It was a morning for slowing down to small pleasures, for sitting with a glass of tautine or vintage terfilot, or one of the traditional wines they make in far-off lands and still export down to the coasts and resort towns of Australia.

The terrace at Amberlin's gives an almost two hundred degree view, so that at a glance you can see the elegant villas in the dunes to the north, close to the road that leads out to the beach suburbs of Corlique, Mirajan and Castanelle at the tip of the Golden Bow. Then, turning your head, you take in the deep blue swells where the tidal bells stir on their chains in the sea; then, at last, you have the whole town laid out before you: the Gaza with its famous terrace and airy loggias, the Breaklight Pier and the Time Beaches, Sailmaker's back near the Antic Houses on Tramway Street. There, meeting the harbour, the Byzantine Quarter with its bazaars and curio shops, and the Mayan Quarter beyond, both with their vivid restoration architectures; close by, whitewashed walls and tiled roofs dazzling in the sun, the urban villas and hotels, the palazzos and arcades, the famous galleries. There, Old Town with its stuccoed tenements and lion-coloured warehouses. The brooding mass of the Armament stands among them, drawing memories of other days, and the smaller sunnier shapes of the Granary and the market squares abutting Trial Street, fronted by the Tyrrian Wall.

Near those precincts, the town finally meets the desert. There you find the famous privateering inns: The Goodbye, The Black Wind and The Cannon, where the stories are told, the reputations earned, the legends made. And there, close by, beyond the corniche and the colour and bustle of the Sarda Salita, is the Sand Quay itself, with its chandleries, ship-factors and kitesellers, the docks alive with the cries of the longshore crews and the barneys hard at work tending the great charvi hulls. Even now, moored between Sunfish and Argus this time, you will find Rynosseros.

I laughed, completing it yet again, the old homecoming ritual.

Slow now, I told myself. Slow.

Though it was allowable, all allowable after weeks of mission tension and the welcome yet constant demands of running the ship, especially after Balin, especially after Trale.

And it was such a perfect morning, the Promenade and terraces so full of life. This was the heart of it. Apart from Rynosseros. This.

I had just begun studying the menu when a robed figure sat in the chair opposite.

'Captain Tyson, if I may.'

I glanced up at the long handsome face and alert respectful gaze of a fine-looking Ab'O. He wore fighting leathers under sand-coloured travelling robes and had the double swords at his waist. There was a tribal sersifan on a chain about his neck and I had its signature immediately. This was a Chitalice First.

'Captain, I am Kaber Fen Otamas and I need your services for a mission.'

'I am newly back from a mission, Lord Otamas. This is shore leave for me.'

'Understood, Captain.' The Chitalice noble placed a small scrambler on the table and activated it. 'But I believe you will want to accept this one.'

'Oh? And why is that?'

'Council will authorise it. It is courtesy that brought me here first.'

Council knew! Den had already been approached! That important then.

'Please,' I said, hiding disappointment, weariness. 'I still choose my own missions. What will persuade me this time?'

'A common enemy,' the Ab'O said. 'A confederate of Dewi Dammo that we suspect was part of that same attempt to secure power.'

Dewi Dammo. The name brought a rush of memories: of the Inland Sea and the Charling Coast, of the island of Marmordesse and poor mad Dewi trying to have it all.

'Why me?'

'There is a chance that you will learn more about your origins. Your time in the Madhouse.'

He had my complete attention. 'Go on.'

Kaber Fen Otamas glanced about him. No doubt he had support concealed close by, possibly Kurdaitcha. 'There is an enemy for us, known only by little more than his name. Chiras Namarkon.'

'Dewi said that name.'

'He did. Council provided the debriefing transcripts for that mission. We wish you to find this Chiras Namarkon, Captain. You know better than most that the status quo is always at risk and that we work ceaselessly to maintain it. At one extreme we have insiders like Bolo May who are allowed to grow too powerful, at the other, opportunists like Dewi Dammo hiding in the interstices of what the world steadily becomes in spite of our precautions.'

I couldn't help but smile.

Otamas smiled as well. 'No, Captain. We do not automatically regard the seven Coloured Captains as our enemy.'

'But, in spite of your precautions, another part of what the world has become. Hardly welcome.'

'Some of us accept it, even applaud it. Our philosophies require it of us.'

'Many do not,' I said.

'As you say. But at our best we like to think that it extends us. Makes us larger.'

Again, I had to smile. At the very least this was civility, at most genuine respect, a suggestion of rapprochement between the tribes and Nation. I inclined my head in thanks.

Otamas continued. 'At least the seven National Captains are out in the world, in plain sight. This Chiras Namarkon is not. We allow that while he was probably not an ally of Dewi's in any formal sense, they seem to have known of one another and at least reached a modus vivendi. Given what Dewi Dammo sought to do, they may even have traded tech and other resources. Our concern is that Namarkon may very well have access to our systems; worse yet, access to factions with vested interests who will not declare their present connection with him. It took tribal and Council agents years and many lives to gain that single clue to Dewi's whereabouts Pederson gave you at Angel Bay that day. With this Namarkon, we only know that there is a library involved — he may be its owner or keeper — and a connection with an important text called the *Alexandrian Book.*'

'Then your people —'

'No, Captain. We have searched and will continue to search our libraries and data systems. We need someone who represents us to search yours. All of yours. Especially those remaining libraries which are located — to put it as tactfully as I can — in decommissioned National possessions.'

'Decommissioned? You mean —'

'Exactly. The abandoned arcologies. The old inland cities. We go there and there is the usual outcry, as useless, hopeless and strident as ever but drawing precisely the sort of National and international media attention we do not want at this time. You visit them as a solitary traveller on a mission for Nation and it is not questioned.'

'The arcologies are hardly places to learn anything about my past, Lord Otamas.'

'Surely that depends on who this Namarkon is and where such a search leads. And see it another way. If you refuse this task, we will ask the other Coloured Captains, then simply empower your Council to send one of its usual field agents. We came to you first.'

I watched the waves making their way to shore, the long stately sweeps crowned with cartouches of light, each cresting swell set with a bezel of quicksilver in the hot morning sun. Gulls wheeled in, making their plaintive cries. The air smelled of salt and sea-wrack. 'Will you assist, lord?'

'However and whenever we can, Captain, though if what we suspect is true, then this Namarkon will probably not want to be found. There is sure to be tribal interference.'

'Have you thought to approach the Antique Men with your needs and misgivings?'

'Of course. They too assist as they can.'

'May I approach them? About my provenance at least?'

And surprise on surprise, it was not Otamas but Den who answered, suddenly there at our table, drawing up a chair and sitting. 'We've made the request already, Tom. Can you do this?'

Being at Amberlin's had been strange enough, wonderfully strange after so much time away. Having a tribal lord appear at my table and now a senior Council operations chief added a definite touch of the absurd.

The middle-aged Nation officer gave a smile that was meant to be reassuring, but which made an even stranger mask of his hairless, lopsided face. Den was strikingly ugly, had chosen to remain so years ago in order to qualify for an impressive if strangely earned annuity from the estate of the late and eccentric Spydyr Massillian. Smiles were his most disconcerting feature.

But, typical Den, he was as caring as he was smart and effective.

Can you do this?

The perfect way to ask.

I thought I could see glints of light from the ornamental wind- and sun-clocks on the Time Beaches, then traced the line of the Promenade up to the Gaza terrace where people from across the world came to watch games of fire-chess and stylo. I imagined I could hear the Gaza belltrees singing in the onshore breeze, and the bells swinging on their sea-chains below the glittering swells.

'I can do this.'

'Thank you, Captain,' Otamas said, then stood, picked up his scrambler and left the terrace. As he headed off down the street, four robed tribesman appeared from their places of concealment and joined him.

'Tom, it really is your choice,' Den said at last.

'I know, Den. I know. You have a list of libraries?'

'We do. Some here, some out there.' He gestured behind him. 'The old cities.'

'Aye. The old cities. I can do this.'

2.

The great blade from which Turker Fin took its name threw a shadow across the desert, a shadow so vast that the view from the big library window showed a register of fierce red-ochre light above a darkness of Turker's own making: blazing blue-white sky at the top, late-afternoon sun-shadow at the bottom, the rest almost impenetrable because of the searing glare.

The library was underground, of course, far below the great sun-trap and power-wall of the blade. The view was relayed down from a much higher level, from a tiny viewing tile somewhere on its mighty surface, but it conquered the space well enough, the feeling of being shut away. It brought the sense of looking from high up I've always felt one needed in libraries, not the quiet gloomy cloisters with dusty stacks and a clock ticking off in the precious silence, but a spacious airiness, even if the views were mostly unchanging and ignored; the quality old monasteries had of being above and beyond the secular world down there.

Now, almost at the end of a three-day search of the Turker library, I stood before the 'window' yet again, taking in the view from three hundred metres overhead as if I'd never seen it before.

Turker Fin was the last of the leads supplied by Nation's archivists, the final name on the list of eight painstakingly drawn out of secure comp systems.

The time that had taken told me a great deal: how special agents or carefully placed moles in previous administrations had probably tried to bury such information, possibly to prevent the more hostile tribal factions from learning the exact whereabouts and constitution of the last National libraries, but — more to the point — that those few precious true-book repositories were located on tribal land, in safe residual concessions protected by special charter and tradition, reached by safe Roads. Perhaps those factions had guessed it long ago, as Otamas had; perhaps it was simple diplomacy that stayed their hand, stopped any further interference in the affairs of Nation.

Eight names. Only two had been on the coast, both in Twilight Beach: the first the Pandeon, easy to reach but of little help, full of saltings and key deletions, the second the private collection of a Delas Marquand, a man presently unavailable, perhaps even conveniently out of Australia.

The remaining six, like Turker, exactly as Den had said, truly were located in the old arcologies, those vast echoing constructs abandoned long ago when the Nationals were driven back to the coasts, their birthright denied them, the fragile environments shut down but for the great mainwalls and a few selected outbuildings.

It had been a largely fruitless search there too, infuriating in the hints and teasing glimpses found. First Andromira and Crayasse, Sol-Tyreen and Genema Blade, then across the continent to Ganness, and back to Turker Fin when word came through at last that the old librarian, Toth, would accede to Council's demands for open house.

It was difficult for the old man. Accustomed to being

absolute monarch in his deserted domain, Trayban Toth had finally realised that his position as 'lighthouse keeper' (the term he liked to use, muttering about the Pharos Lighthouse and the Pharisees and the great library at ancient Alexandria, as if they related to these deserts or each other) might end if he opposed his superiors.

Humbled and uncertain, made suddenly respectful by Den's expensive call, Toth had done an about-face, had become excited at last that the library was being used for its original purpose.

He had granted access, so I came to believe, to the whole catalogue. Turker had 40,000 retroform books in its deep cool chambers, 810,000 kilometres of tape, 780,000 units of disc, mote, bead, crystal and fluid-link texts, and — rarest of all — 5000 Illuminated Books of the new kind.

I stood before one of these now, watching as Trayban set it up on the lectern before the window. It was a Book that had recently been transferred here from Crayasse, officially borrowed, Toth said, though spirited away might have been a better term, since it had been removed from the Crayasse collection a day before I got there, almost as if it had been moved deliberately to waste my time, the last copy of a text possibly leading to the whereabouts of Chiras Namarkon. That was how it felt.

Trayban Toth was muttering as he arranged the Book, coming to the end of yet another of his almost endless monologues about bookish matters.

'... and the Vatican has always had the largest collection of pornography in the world. It makes you think. But this is it, Captain! L75 VGS.' He seemed annoyed that the view had caught my attention rather than this text he had found for me at last.

It was hard to conceal my amusement. More than seventy years old, short and bent but often full of a startling energy that made his eyes shine like flecks of mica above the long nose and full white beard, Trayban presented as someone who had once played Merlin in an ancient pageant and had never tired of the role. Each book was delivered as if a personal incantation had been sought and found, as if the storage rooms he visited were compartments in his own head from which these texts had been drawn forth at great personal effort.

Perhaps that was how Trayban saw it, lived it, as if Turker Fin truly were his greater self and he wandered corridors of his own mind to visit its parts. This recent arrival, L75 VGS, had to have been on hand, but Trayban had spent precious hours 'searching' for it.

Which set me wondering all over again. Despite his age and distracted manner, Toth would make a fitting Namarkon, someone dissembling, projecting, playing out a role. I wished, not for the first time, that I had a monitor to use.

'Namarkon,' Toth said, a note of peevishness in his voice. 'There's the reference under linguistics. It cross-refers to the Gray and Silas.'

'Thanks, Trayban.'

I studied the surface of the Book, the small touch-plate and ormolu key-set, the Nape circuit-mosaic border (as if a churchman had in fact decorated it in the ancient fashion), the Bytes-and-Byzantines imprint in the bottom left-hand corner with the Nation seal. I touched the plate, activating the tiny power source within. The milky pane lit with a warm yellow light; one by one pages slow-cycled through the credits and bibliographica to the index, ciphers spilling steadily across the Reader Page.

'L75 VGS,' Toth murmured in affirmation, as if intoning a spell. Then: 'L362:42.'

'L362:42. Thank you.'

I entered the final sequence, accessed the section, keyed in Namarkon. There was a two-second wait, then that word flashed its presence.

Flashed and blanked, leaving the Reader Page dark, the Book inert.

'Trayban!'

The old man pushed in next to me. Without a word, he brought up the bibliographica, ran the Namarkon entry. Again the name flashed once; again the screen went dead.

'Damaged!' he cried. 'Hell and Jesus! It's damaged!'

'On its way to Turker, you think?' I said. 'Deliberate?'

Toth frowned at sacrilege, his jaw set, dismay showing in his eyes.

'What, Tray?' I pressed. 'Is it coincidence?'

'No!' he cried. And he repeated the functions, again without success, then carried the Book to a donkey-frame close by, intending to bypass the discrete functions with the library's override.

Certainly the Book glowed more brightly in the frame, and for a moment I hoped. But again the word triggered the misfunction.

Toth repeated the procedure four times, making adjustments, even pounding on the dead Reader plate with the spread palm of one hand. He ran several other entries successfully, cycled through a few, then tried Namarkon again with no luck. He lifted the Book from the frame, studied its spine and seals.

'What can we do, Tray?' I asked gently, carefully.

He laid the Book back on the lectern.

'L75 VGS is dead stack. Only one copy in existence. But it's open text, so scholars can add or revise details in appendices. There will be a Precis access for that.'

'Tampered with as well?'

'No! No!' Toth said firmly. 'You don't understand. It's black box, a sealed unit, very durable, designed to show what the main text contained. Scholars working here could enter their findings and opinions — under strict supervision, of course, always under supervision. It will summarise portions of the main entry as assists. No-one could get at those.'

'Please run it.'

He turned to the Book, used a scribe wand to enter a code sequence along the bottom edge. Words filed across the Reader Page. Toth keyed in Namarkon yet again.

The word flashed its arrival, gave its capsule comment.

> 362:42:8-1: Namarkon
> (Namarkon, Namarquon, Nammargon)
> (OAA)(dialect)
> Spirit of Lightning, originally of the Gunwinggu, Western Arnhem Land (495:36:7/1-92G). Vengeful elemental spirit accessed by Morrkidju (604:24:12), the 'clever sorcerers' of the Gunwinggu...

Another dozen or so entries referred to eponymous land-holdings, ships, a comp-net, and a minor highwayman who had made use of the ancient name. There were a score of mythic antecedents, the names of people and things, real and imaginary, who had been identified with the Dreamtime original or had recognised conceptual connections.

The final listing was the one I wanted, and again there was the exasperating reference to the text I needed most of all, something called the *Alexandrian Book*, the title which had dogged my search from Andromira to Turker.

362:42:8-14: Chiras Namarkon (aka The Immortal)

A legendary folk hero/demon of the Molere cycle, said to inhabit a secret labyrinth, safeguarding secret knowledge and a great treasure.

Origins uncertain. Gray and Silas (914:61:7) are inclined to consider retroactive amplification of an early 21st century inception, either a traditional (unsubstantiated) expression meaning: 'tree struck by lightning' or possibly as part of an advertising campaign for either Inters 400 (324:22) or Nation-Sun (721:620:4).

Note: Chiras Namarkon is allegedly the author/creator of a text/artefact called the *Alexandrian Book* (no information available apart from the title). This authorship is probably as apocryphal as the text itself, since all sources advancing the connection are full of proven fabrication. The *Alexandrian Book* has never been sighted (Trist, Gray and Silas, Maidment, Green).

Note: Standing request by Gray and Silas for updating, with priority input-inform tag for AM/GB.

Without my asking, Toth caused a hard-copy to be made and passed it over.

'This last notation, Tray? The initials?'

Toth hesitated, leant over the Reader Page, the remains of his anger still driving him. 'I'm not supposed to tell, but it's the Antique Men. That's Gado Bascoeur. He's very good. A great scholar. Does it help?'

'It's something. I've found the Dreamtime reference before, same with The Immortal, the labyrinth and the creature of fable. The *Alexandrian Book* reference is not new; this Bascoeur entry is. You have nothing on the Molere cycle?'

'Nothing else. Nothing in Gray and Silas either. I'm sorry.'

'Then thank you, Tray. I'm finished here.'

I went to the desk I had been using and began gathering up my notes. Toth followed, a concerned look turning his old face into a surprisingly desperate mask, the small eyes full of unexpected emotion. My visit to Turker had been an intrusion initially, but now, at the end of it, he seemed sorry to have me leave, as if reluctant to lose this precious reaffirmation of his role.

The damage to Illuminated Book L75 VGS had somehow intensified the desperation, his need to hold on to this moment of service.

'What will you do?' he said, a question he now allowed himself to ask.

'After the Pandeon and the six arcologies? Marquand's place again, in case he's back. You have been invaluable, Tray. I have four private libraries hinted at somewhere in Twilight Beach, none mentioned on Council's list. I have confirmation for Chiras Namarkon as The Immortal, as Lightning God and keeper of a library and labyrinth, as putative author of something called the *Alexandrian Book*, whatever that was or is, if ever it was. Now there's the link to the Antique Men, which was inevitable anyway but I'm glad of it right now. I'm full circle there. Considering I didn't know what to expect, I've certainly got something.'

'And this?' He picked up one of the hard copies before I could bundle it up with the rest of my arcology material. 'The list of arcologies you wanted?'

'Another tack I may take. Since I've run out of National libraries, I might look where libraries might have been at one time or other.'

'You'd do that? Go to all the old sites?'

'Why not? The tribes will allow it. If Crayasse and Turker have their data-vaults underground, the other arcologies may not be as empty as they say.'

I tried to sound hopeful, though I doubted that even an exhaustive search of the abandoned cities would reveal a carefully hidden Chiras Namarkon.

But what else did I have? For all I knew, Namarkon was hiding somewhere in the forgotten decks and halls of Turker Fin or Crayasse or one of the other places I had already visited. I may have passed within metres of his door, breathed the air he had released from his lungs, started at a small sound of his presence in a shadowed corridor.

Yes, trying Delas Marquand again, consulting the Antique Man, Bascoeur, if he would allow it, trying to locate the four private libraries, would exhaust my leads, probably finish it. Then I would be left either to tour the remaining arcologies or scour the curio shops in the Byzantine Quarter, hoping that Den or one of the other Coloured Captains, or one of my eccentric friends in the

Bird Club, might uncover something.

'It's not right!' Toth said, studying the arcology print-out and pulling at his beard.

'What's that, Tray?'

He spread the double-list of National arcology sites on a reader table and tapped at the page. 'The top arrangement here. There's a name missing.'

I hurried across to him and studied the print-out. 'You're sure? How can you tell?'

'It's the shape, Captain, not the names. The regional arrangement at the bottom I'm not sure about, but the top one is wrong. The list I remember is one off a square. I always wished they had built an even number to finish the shape. This is two off. Look!'

Andromira*	Whitehead	Andalave
Enso-Bey	Soltumede	Alka
Crayasse*	Chyra-Manta	Quaine Lock
Genema Blade*	Pharani	Meda
Stone Mill	Bukula Tan	Khen-Mol
Ganness*	Pila	Maggadi
Land's End	Port Chevas	Graylord
Tulidjula	Transy	Quen-Lui
Trovy	Neuve	Ihren
Turker Fin*	Tarpial	Gayla
Sol-Tyreen*	Anansanna	Bidja Point
Monk's Hood		

Andromira*			Bukula Tan
Enso-Bey			Pila
Crayasse*			Port Chevas
Pharani			Quen-Lui
Stone Mill	Transy	Alka	Khen-Mol
Ganness*	Tarpial	Meda	Whitehead
Land's End	Maggadi	Trovy	Andalave
Tulidjula	Genema Blade*		Soltumede
Graylord			Anansanna
Turker Fin*			Monk's Hood

I studied the shape formed by the top arrangement of names, matched each name with the regional arrangement beneath. Thirty-four on both. I checked the print-outs drawn from the comps at Crayasse and Ganness. They gave the same double-pattern, the same count: two off the square.

'Do it again, Tray. See what you get.'

The old man went to a nearby comp and called up the information. The screen showed the same pattern as the printed lists.

'No!' Toth said, and struck the console. 'No! Wrong, I tell you! This is not it!'

'What then?'

'Someone sent L75 VGS here. Someone damaged it. Someone has done this as well!'

'You're certain?'

'It's the sort of visual trick you never forget. The last time I saw this list it was one off.'

'When was that?'

'What? Who knows? Years ago. It was years. But I remember. I couldn't forget.'

'Tray, can we do a priority search on this?' It was suddenly very important, though I knew that every list I sought would be short one entry.

'I don't see how we can,' the old man said. 'The library comp gives this. It's the only comp facility I'm allowed apart from environmentals.'

'Could those be routed in?'

'They couldn't access deleted data, no.'

'Deletion has to be difficult in sealed catalogue systems. Can you bypass a blockage?'

'No, Captain. Whoever can tamper with library records would make sure of that.'

'The Antique Men?'

Toth pulled at his beard. 'They could do it, yes. They're one of the few groups allowed to enter information. But they're the most honest —'

'This Bascoeur?'

'One of the best. He would never —'

'Namarkon might,' I said, thinking of the old historical stand-by of need-to-know, doing something for the greater good: the eternal catch-cry of governments, rulers, privileged agencies, shrewd individuals. 'Tray, can I take the Book back to Twilight Beach? It would be safe, I swear it.'

He shook his head. 'Impossible. Especially now.'

'Then do not part with it again. Council will authorise that order. Refuse all requests, even from Crayasse, from all brother and sister librarians. The Book remains here. And, please, refuse access —'

'To the Antique Men, yes. If I can.'

•

Toth saw me back to the surface levels, came with me out onto the wide mooring plat, littered with sand and wind-wrack, to where my rented thirty-foot Maud skiff waited on locked wheels.

'Leave in the morning, Captain. Phone the information through. You can afford it.' The old man indicated the afternoon sun halfway down the sky.

But I needed to be doing something now, anything. 'Tray, it's at least two days to the coast. Calls can be monitored, and I need to get what I know back to where I can use it. I'll make a hundred k's, possibly two hundred, before the light goes. Thanks again for all you've done.'

I climbed aboard the tiny craft, trimmed two parafoils to the afternoon wind and slowly gained speed along the ancient Road.

Behind, old Toth stood with one arm raised. In the dying light, he resembled some scholar Quasimodo before his own fabulous Notre Dame, the westering sun turning the great curtain wall into a beacon. Somewhere on that blazing massif was a tiny view tile, taking the sun into a chamber deep underground. I wondered if Chiras Namarkon used it now, watching me go, and wondered what part thoughts of such a possibility had played in my going.

3.

From: Josepha Anglis, *The Coloured Captains: Fact and Fiction*, Praesidian, AS 753-3
Introduction: "The Unloved Heroes"

All reliable sources agree that the Ab'O tribes trapped themselves by the Tell Agreement of AS 742. By opening up the annual Cyrimiri ship-lotteries to Nationals — a strategic concession made with a view to calming International criticism of tribal racist policies, thereby keeping valuable world tech markets and AI initiatives — the Ab'O States made possible a unique chain of events by which their own traditions trapped them.

The Cyrimiri proponents at the 42 Convocation had no way of knowing that one of their own experiments in Artificial Intelligence would prove so viable and so formidable. They could not know that the celebrated belltree program, which had so captured the imagination of the world and had reached its zenith with the Iseult-Darrian strain, would be the cause of so much consternation and embarrassment: a resounding blow struck for the waning Pan-European tradition in Australia.

The tribes and Nation are both diplomatically closed-lipped about the details of what actually occurred. Experts surmise that one of the redundant oracle-trees, rejected, limited and given the usual desert service as a roadpost, rallied against its conditioning, established a reciprocal arrangement with Records, and used its links to enter the names of National ship-winners into one of the most hallowed tribal registers at Tell — the Great Passage Book itself. The tree's motives remain unknown. Such a sensational and unprecedented treason was soon stopped, but not before seven National captains: Golden

Afervarro, Red Lucas, Green Glaive, Yellow Traven, White Massen, Black Doloroso and Blue Tyson — won not only their great sand-ships (and those were seven of the best tribal charvolants in existence, suggesting that the tree had played a part there as well) but were issued with all-lander mandates laying open the inner deserts, and given the Colours which in an instant elevated them irrevocably to the status of tribal heroes.

Tribal spokesmen claim that the creation of the Seven was a deliberate benefice to Nation, an endowment made partly as restitution for the wide-scale shutting down of National facilities in the interior. They insist that in no way was it an error on the part of careless biotects. National and international experts, however, remain unconvinced. They suggest that the seven Captains were chosen for a purpose, that the tribes made better than they knew, that this rogue belltree AI raised up its own champions. Why? The Captains themselves refuse to comment.

But one thing is clear. For now at least, Nation has teeth again, and the world is watching.

Rynosseros was still out on mission. I'd persuaded Scarbo and the others to accept long-reach assignments, convincing them that while I searched the old National sites listed by Den, they could do more for me by asking questions in distant places, in the museums, modest town libraries, the bars, galleries and curio shops they came upon.

For all I knew, the key to Namarkon might be something someone said or overheard in a crowded bar at No Man's Easy Rest, some detail in a painting in the hallway of a public building in Angel Bay, or a line sung in the chorus of a child's sidewalk song in Port Tarsis.

After returning the skiff to Maud's Rentals at the end of my run, I still had the better part of two days before Rynosseros was due back from Tank Feti, ample time to try Marquand again, the only private (and secret) collector Den's people had been able to uncover — and that through a string of suspect legal infractions in a long career.

Unlike the other sellers of collectibles and oddities, the public ones who made much of the little they had, Delas Marquand had always been notoriously reclusive. On Nation records he existed officially as an importer of Welsh and Dutch cheeses and fabrics from Oceania. According to the more reliable rumours, he had been a plunderer of libraries in his time and was now a dealer in black market volumes, with a splendid secret library of his own.

His shop was an unmarked, blank-fronted establishment at the end of a dead-end street out near the Armament. Visits, whether for cheeses, fabrics or books, were by appointment only, often made by people answering cryptic ads in obscure trade journals or — for the novelty of it — in the popular urban publications, those glossy retroform periodicals printed on siflin or kelp-based Tase paper.

But responses to ads, the phone calls and letters pretending to be a prospective client, even visits to the shop, had so far been unsuccessful. Certainly before beginning my search of the arcologies, his place had always been locked, the windows polarised into the neutral mirror glare of the 'blind' house.

For whatever reason, it seemed that those dealing in information, in stored or printed knowledge, had become harder to locate than ever, as if suddenly all of them, whether sly Delas Marquand or the famous Antique Men, had grown wary of tribal attention.

Or was it Namarkon they feared?

I'd left the Marquand problem for Den, all I could do, one more thing to try along with my standing request to see the Antique Men, and, to my relief, Den had succeeded in at least the first part of this assignment.

'We have our way in,' he told me when I called on him at his villa that afternoon. We were standing in his operations room before the big view window, and it was like I'd never been away — as if visiting the arcologies were all a dream, something gleaned from somnium sleep. 'We've placed a false impost in Marquand's comp. Not the sort of risk we like to take, Tom, but I think he'll see it as genuine. It was difficult but it's done. Watching the place would probably tell us nothing. He's experienced. He might even have a secret exit out behind Armament somewhere; so far we haven't found it. Still, we figure he has to be in Australia; there are no visa or transit records saying otherwise, no listings for private dirigibles or module shipments under Marquand in the last four months. He dare not be too clever in view of what we have on him.'

'He'll accept the impost?'

Den looked pleased with himself. 'We believe so. We've told his system a tribal inspector will call on him at 1100 one morning this week to discuss tariff discrepancies in tribal records. He dare not delegate that sort of thing. I was going to ask Scarbo or Shannon to do it, but you're back. Look the part and you'll get in. The plans you need will be ready.'

'Thanks, Den. I know Council is taking quite a chance.'

'We're doing what's right. Finally. We're acting and it feels good.'

At 1049 the next morning, in bright sunshine, I headed up Trial Street in the shadow of the Armament dressed in djellaba and burnoose, carrying my small folder of plans and a tribal sirrush stick borrowed from Den's collection. I wore dark glasses and the appropriate skin-toning, some bands of colour on cheeks and chin, carefully neutral caste-marks. From a distance I was a quadroon customs officer on assignment in Nation territory, someone not to be denied.

The shop was as I remembered it, a two-storey building at the end of a quiet street, still a blind house, the windows showing only adjacent structures and my own robed figure approaching the main door. It was hard to resist a smile at how formidable I looked.

I rapped several times on the solid panel and listened for movement within, but there was nothing. I waited, noting — not for the first time in this land the colour of lions in the sun — how the bluest Australian skies are always found above the rooflines of old brick warehouses, over high walls such as formed this side of the Armament, that most mysterious of tribal artefacts in Twilight Beach.

Finally someone stirred beyond the door. Latches clicked, it swung back and Delas Marquand was standing there, professional caution showing on his wide, finely featured face. He was of medium height, clad in a gown fashioned along Egyptian lines, no doubt made from some of his own imported fabric, dark blues shot with threads of gold.

'Mr Marquand,' I said, accenting my voice just enough. 'I am Atanas Tjijti from Customs.'

Marquand gave a slight bow. 'Your ident please, Mr Tjijti.'

I displayed the laminate Den had provided, then, taking the initiative, stepped by him into the dimly lit front hall of his premises. Marquand closed the door behind us, and even in the gloom I could see that he touched the locks in a way that suggested security systems, possibly illegal tech. I wondered if a true Ab'O would remark on it.

'Please go through to the office, Mr Tjijti,' Marquand said. 'The records are there.'

'Delas Marquand, I am actually here to discuss your library.'

Marquand reached for something in the shadows — a contact? a weapon? — but my sirrush stick was already there, knocking his arm aside, making him yell in pain and surprise.

'Who are you?' he cried, cradling his arm. 'You're no tribesman! What do you want?'

'Answers to official questions, nothing more. But this is your false hallway, Mr Marquand. Please take us through to your dealer's room.'

Even in the gloom I saw his eyes narrow. 'I have no idea what you're talking about. Identify yourself!'

The sirrush stick struck the floor like a gunshot in the confined space.

'It's me or a Nation strike. Choose!'

'You can't be serious!'

'Mr Marquand, I am not alone in this. Officers outside have tech. All legal. Any deadfalls or problems with electrics and they'll be in here.' I embellished the lie. 'All under tribal sanction. Implant alert. Anything you do, understand?'

'Follow me,' he said in a flat voice, nursing his injured arm, and led us back to the front door. He touched the locks again, opening a slideaway in the left wall, a concealed entrance. We entered, moved down a narrow corridor, well past what had to be storerooms and offices to an insulated secure room at the rear of the premises. It was large, fifteen metres to a side, with bookcases covering most of the wall space, the shelves filled with files and boxes. The far wall was exposed warehouse brick, shining dully in the room's soft recessed lighting, set with shallow alcoves between worn brickwork pilasters.

'Well?' Marquand said.

'First, we establish credentials. Show me your library.'

He gave a wry smile. 'You're a dealer now?'

'Delas, listen carefully. Only Nation or the tribes could get that impost into your comp. I'm Tom Tyson —'

'Tom Rynosseros!' Marquand's eyes widened in surprise. 'What can — ?'

'The Marquand Collection is beyond that wall. I've seen plans. I'd be grateful if you'd show me.'

Delas Marquand seemed easier now. He smiled again and considered what to do. Finally he crossed to an ancient roll-top desk and made connections I did not try to see. There were the soft sounds of systems working, a play of shifting light in one of the alcoves in the rear wall, then the sudden vision of a ramp leading down into a warmly lit room full of shelves — shelves laden with books: retroforms, disks, mote stacks, even the Nape spines of Illuminated Books.

It was an amazing sight, an Aladdin's cave shimmering behind a series of plastic dust curtains. In spite of what Den had told me about Marquand, I gasped in amazement.

'Satisfied?'

I closed the trap. 'I'd like to see some titles if I may.'

'No-one goes down there, Captain.' The voice was suddenly hard, the voice of a man who still had solutions, was still calculating. 'I'm the only one to pass through those seals.'

'You have leases to the adjacent buildings?'

'What?' He eyed me suspiciously.

I opened out the building plan Den had provided. 'Beyond the rear of this shop is the Tyrrian Wall and the Armament. North of you is Trial Street and the Granary. South is Gallery Four, basement to roof. There is nowhere for your library to go. I'm betting a hologram.'

'There's an old sub-basement —'

'No, we've checked. Photonics, yes?'

Marquand's face went pale at the prospect of his secret being out; his eyes were bright with mixed emotions.

'You couldn't. Armament is an undeclared tribal holding; there are no maps registered. It was guaranteed.'

'Nation comp has non-detailed plans of area allotment. Delas, I am not interested in exposing you. You had books four years ago. What happened?'

'Plundered,' he said, taking that solution, the truth. 'All but a few. Captain, I deal in books: crystals, tapes, disks, motes, all the old carrier forms. People come to me. I use that as a lure, a tease.' He nodded toward the alcove. 'Bring up the pieces I am prepared to sell or trade. If word got out —'

'It won't. I've disengaged my com unit. Even Council won't find out. What I must know is whether you have — or had — information on a Chiras Namarkon. The Immortal. Especially in connection with a library.'

'Just the names,' Marquand said. 'Nothing anyone would raid me for. I had a good collection once, but nothing really special, not intrinsically.'

'Nothing on a Namarkon library or labyrinth?'

'Captain, I collected books, traded and sold them. I acted the scholar, then as now; it helps make a sale, helps to build up the collection again. I didn't read them so much as know things about them, the publishing information. Which editions —'

'Have you heard of something called the *Alexandrian Book*?'

'Of it, yes. Nothing more than that.'

'We're trading here, Delas. Namarkon and the *Alexandrian Book* for an oath of secrecy from me.'

'I'd tell you!' he cried. 'For the oath and those plans I'd tell you if I knew. I would! I know both exist. I've… I've put out word that I'd make an offer for such a book. There's been nothing. Not a thing. All collectors do it as a matter of course.'

'All right,' I said, hope beginning to fade. 'These other collectors. I know of at least four. I need names.'

The man threw his arms wide in a gesture of exasperation. 'I can't give you that. I can't! It's a trust thing.'

'It's black-marketeering is what it is. It's Nation moving to find out anything about Namarkon and the *Alexandrian Book*. Help us, Delas, and the tribes learn nothing. It's not you Council wants.' It was time for another lie, expedient but effective now with Marquand seeing his world about to collapse. 'The black market doesn't harm Nation; it helps us, in fact, in ways you wouldn't imagine.'

I was glad he didn't ask how: I was thinking of arcologies raided, of books being pirated out of vaults, of catalogues listing titles which had long ago found their way into secret collections, to be copied and databased if we were lucky, to be hidden and lost otherwise.

'Listen, Captain! Now, listen! I can give you one name — a good man, generous, a legitimate collector. But for heaven's sake protect him. Tell no-one. Toban McBanus at Villa Chano. He will help if anyone can. For the right reasons. He's in it for knowledge, not gain.'

I maintained the lie. 'He's one of the four I already have. Who else?'

Again the arms went out. 'Don't you see? They'd know it was me. They'd kill me. Please. McBanus will know others. Let him say. Go to him. He's a buyer, a reader; he knows things. The others are like me.'

'Plunderers.'

'Conservators. We keep the books moving. Private collectors have always done more to conserve the arts than governments and institutions. You must know that.'

'One more thing. How many arcologies are there?'

'What?'

'The old National arcologies. How many do you know exist?'

'Forty or so.'

'Exactly.'

Marquand went to his comp, tapped on the keys and studied the display. 'Exactly thirty-four,' he said, and frowned.

'What's wrong?'

'Nothing. I thought there were thirty-five. But it's thirty-four. Close.'

The lie was everywhere, it seemed, and what a scale of power that implied, the ability to achieve such a task.

'Can you hard-copy that? All the names?'

Marquand touched another contact. A page slid from the printer; he passed it to me. 'Are we done?'

'Not quite. Turn it off.'

'What?'

'I'm leaving. But first, turn it off.'

Marquand grinned suddenly. 'So you can be sure.'

'No, so I can see the truth. A reminder of how few collections there actually are. Because —'

'Captain —'

'Humour me, Delas, and that plan is yours along with my word.'

The dealer hesitated, then worked a concealed touchpoint somewhere on the desk. The library died in a quick gulp of light, revealing more than just a space between the flanking pilasters: an alcove as deep as a walk-in closet, a bookcase to either side containing real texts, all that Delas had for sale. I saw the doorline with its tiny ramp sloping into a solid brick wall, the cleverly hidden holo-points.

'Thank you,' I said, and handed him the plans and my contact number at the Gaza. 'Call if you learn anything I can use. We can trade, Delas, build up favours in paradise.' And allowing the truth of his earlier comment about private dealers. 'Who knows? Council may even help you re-stock your shelves.'

Marquand managed a chuckle at that. He re-activated illicit tech defences that were worth his life should the tribes learn of them, then led me back to the street door. We parted without another word between us.

Back out under the brilliant sky, with Marquand's door closed again in its mirror walls, I made a bundle of my tribal robes, cleaned my face as best I could, then headed for the Sand Quay. I stopped at the Gaza long enough to call Villa Chano, then hurried to see if Rynosseros had returned from the desert wastes of Tank Feti.

4.

I felt a rush of pleasure to see the distinctive shape standing at the Quay, kites down and stowed, the professional barneys already halfway through their service checks on the hull and travel platform.

Shannon, Rim and Hammon were off at the Gaza, I learned from the gate officer, probably at the Astronomers' Bar; Strengi was below catching up on sleep after a home-leg watch. But Den had told them I was back from Turker, and Scarbo came grinning down the gangway to clasp my forearm in the Roman way the older kitesmen still used.

'Namarkon's a myth everywhere,' he said. 'Eternal life. Lives in a maze. One moment Melmoth the Wanderer, the next El Dorado or some other mythic figure. I've got notes. People are tight-lipped about collections though. Word is out about something.'

'Feel like a walk out to Villa Chano to see Toban McBanus?'

'I know the name. Is he a bookman?'

'Delas Marquand says so.'

'Marquand? You have been busy.'

I could see Ben's determination to be easy company, his resolve not to ask if there'd been clues to my provenance.

'Nothing yet, Ben. But I've called McBanus. He's agreed to a visit.'

'Good. So tell me about the arcologies.'

We left the Sand Quay, walked back past the Gaza Hotel and the Breaklight Pier and out through the First Gate to the Promenade, heading for the villas in the dunes to the north. We detoured down onto the beach to save ourselves the curving approach taken when the Promenade became the Beach Road, passing over the low headland out to

Corlique, Mirajan and Castanelle.

It provided ample time to tell Ben about Turker Fin and the quest for L75 VGS, about something called the *Alexandrian Book* and the possible involvement of the Antique Men through a Gado Bascoeur, all the most tentative of leads but — at least where information about my provenance was concerned — probably the most promising. If I hadn't discovered anything conclusive about my origins from the tribes, then who better to try than the ones who frequently serviced tribal information needs?

My own discoveries quickly exhausted the modest list Scarbo had. His facts were very much those of popular folklore. Nowhere had he heard of the *Alexandrian Book*, nor could he recall having seen the initials AM/BG, though Tank Feti, Tank Aran and Mider were hardly places to expect much information.

Like Toth and Marquand, Ben remembered there being thirty-five National arcologies; he was absolutely certain of it — what old Trayban had said: one off a square. He greeted the news of the adjusted total with something like Marquand's frown and old Toth's pulling at his beard.

'What did Den say?' he asked as we moved along the beach.

'He accepted it very calmly. Said he'd look into it.'

Ben nodded. 'Well thirty-four isn't right. It's schoolboy knowledge, Tom. National history. There was a media special years ago: *Thirty-Five Chances at the Dream*. We can check that.'

'Den's doing what he can. I doubt we'll find the original number listed anywhere, let alone names and locations. It's a case of making the lie big enough.'

'An entire arcology! Who could do that? What about

Survey Authority? The tribal universities? Their maps and records —'

'Survey says thirty-four. We aren't allowed at tribal records yet, probably won't be.'

Ben stopped, brows furrowed so they made deep shadows on his grizzled, sun-tanned face. It clearly troubled him, as if the universe had gone awry because this one single truth was out of kilter. 'Tom —'

'I know. Altered. Someone's plundering. Maybe McBanus can tell us something.'

'It can't happen,' Scarbo muttered, more to himself than to me, and for a while we walked in silence, with just the sound of wind in the sea-grass and the steady rhythm of waves falling on the shore, the hiss of foam over the sand.

Almost before we realised it, we were climbing the stairs to where the windows of Villa Chano flashed in the sun. At this angle, the sprawling house was still well concealed behind its fretwork of palms and balustrades, its domed roof of red tile looming above the whitewashed main shell.

'McBanus said forty thousand titles,' I told Ben. 'Mostly reference works and mote copies of paper books. We're welcome to look them over, though he fears they won't tell us much.'

'More than Marquand, I bet.'

I nodded, remembering the false aperture, the collection that existed only as coded light. 'I think McBanus himself will be more important to us than his books.'

We were at the southern turn of the rising terraces, well clear of the building itself, when lightning struck from the clear afternoon sky. The scream came an instant later, the tearing strike signal lost in the concussion of exploding masonry and tile.

At first we didn't know what had happened — it was impossible to grasp the simple shocking truth.

But in moments we knew. A laser strike from orbit. All it could be.

Then the stinging grit, dust and debris, the thump of fragments from Chano's northern wing gave the reality in terrible detail.

And the implications. The Ab'O Princes did not want us investigating books and libraries. Chiras Namarkon did not.

Namarkon, Lightning Spirit, had struck. The Immortal had access to tribal comsats, Ab'O tech.

We crouched by the terrace wall, staring in horror at what he had done — what it, they, whatever, had.

'We give it up, Tom,' Ben said, close by me, a harsh whisper. 'They're telling us to give it up!'

The words freed me. 'McBanus was waiting in his library.' I made myself say it.

Then there was a woman screaming, filling the new silence like a second strike from the sky, guiding me as I ran, cursing Namarkon, cursing the tribes, the lost arcologies and stolen futures, but most of all cursing the cold unfeeling evil that could cause a cry of such terrible loss.

I did not go back to Rynosseros. I stayed over at the Gaza, sitting on the balcony of Room 777, watching the sea meet the long curving shoreline of Twilight Beach.

On the terrace below, games of fire-chess had begun in earnest. There were cheers, shouts, the familiar sounds of winning and losing, of life being lived in all its myriad forms. People moved along the Promenade, wandered the Breaklight Pier in the cool evening air. To seaward, the distant islands stood against the dying light like polished stones. Off to the north, the lights of Corlique, Castanelle and the souling colonies could be seen: closer, those of the villas, all occupied this late in the season.

Except for Chano, of course, broken and empty in the dunes beside the Beach Road.

McBanus and his wife, Emma, dead. Their daughter, Truan, hospitalised, in shock.

And not a word from the tribes. Council's protests and calls for explanations, accountability, had brought none.

Though one thing was clear, an angry and worried quorum of Council had agreed. If not the tribes then, even more than Dewi Dammo, Chiras Namarkon could reach far. Lightning Spirit indeed.

Either way there was no doubting the message. Secret libraries in Twilight Beach were to remain that way. Off limits.

Which left the unvisited arcologies on the list, including the missing, mysterious thirty-fifth, as well as those difficult and expensive creatures, the Antique Men, specifically Gado Bascoeur.

So much time had passed that we no longer expected much from that quarter. I was supposedly on a tribal mission, but just as Den's repeated requests for access to the appropriate tribal records had achieved nothing, we assumed that it would be the same here. But then, just like that, his routine appeals to the Antique Men, Poste Restante, Saldy's, were rewarded. Suddenly, as if the time were right for it, the fate of the McBanus family and Chano a deciding factor, the other main avenue of enquiry had become available. I would be contacted, this evening, tomorrow, sometime soon, an agent had told Den on the phone.

After all this waiting, something at least.

I had no wish to return to Rynosseros. Chano preyed on my mind. Scarbo understood; the others would. There was nothing they could do but wait as I waited. Talk to people, ask questions.

I sat in the big viewing chair at the Gaza and sipped a glass of tautine. There was the old feeling of sanctuary here, so precious, something created by these walls, these familiar furnishings, this view out over the Gaza terrace and along the coast, by the murmur of belltrees drifting down from the roof-garden, by the spread of stars that escaped this well of light and made their net of dewpoints in the growing indigo.

Den had made the only possible deal with Bascoeur's contact: knowledge for knowledge. Whatever we learned in return for word of Namarkon or anything about my past. Anything.

But now I tried to go slow, sit back, watch old night fill the frame of the open balcony doors, and savour the cooling touch of the onshore breeze. For a moment Chano and Namarkon were almost forgotten.

Almost.

Could the Antique Men, these ultimate bookmen, be it? If so, then how fitting, how appropriate for the times. In a world where increasingly all knowledge of that world was stored in comp systems rather than living memory, where — in the long afternoon since the Information Revolution — people had perfected the habit of automatically putting information aside, forgetting about it till it was needed again, little wonder that the 'oubliettes' existed. These remarkable folk stored knowledge in an older, different fashion, in tech-assisted eidetic memory, all the lore people chose to forget or suppress, keyed by mantras and mnemonic tags, accessed by association, by ingested or injected catalysts and RNA assists. Like monks in ancient monasteries, they accumulated information of all kinds, then as generalists, specialists and synthesists, pluralists and explainers, they interpreted what they had gleaned, made conclusions, hoarded, sold, perpetuated.

They constituted what was virtually a priesthood to do this, a body of men and women (despite the carefully chosen old-world name), and specialised in the truths that State historians and tribal administrations, even the big marketing and ad agencies on the coasts, could not help but give one bias or another.

And curiously, the Princes themselves, the ones most likely to be compromised and displeased by such a state of affairs, seemed to favour the idea that these oubliettes existed, these safe-holes for storing arcane knowledge and the patterns of overview. Retrieval systems always had the facts, could offer conclusions and projections, but the Antique Men added intuition, imagination and astute judgement, allowed for the worth of feelings and impressions, for the possibility of there being missing facts contributing to an end.

Every viewpoint mattered in some way. By acknowledging subjectivity and applying it to a given situation, they reminded everyone of its integral role and so refined and maintained the concept of what truth could be, that, yes, it truly was the first casualty of self-interest.

To Den's amazement and constant delight, one of the popular sayings attributed to the oubliettes was a corruption of the old faux Angelino crime-fighter saying: 'Never just the facts, no, never just the facts.'

The phone rang, bringing me back from the indigo wall, the shimmering well, the splendid trap of Twilight

Beach, made the laving wind just wind again.

I touched the plate. The screen showed the face of a young woman, pale, with intense grey eyes, a small clenched mouth: a severe countenance suggesting seriousness and business. Little else could be seen. She wore a close-fitting hood, like those worn by members of traditional female religious orders.

'Captain Tyson? I am Margaret Solles, notary for Gado Bascoeur. Are you available for an interview tomorrow?'

'Name a time and place.'

'Tomorrow,' she said. 'I will call you at this number after 0900 and a meeting will be arranged. Good night.'

Done. A brief sketch of a face representing such a final chance, so forgettable. But Margaret Solles. The name at least.

Chano was there then, Truan screaming, crying, Toban and Emma dead in the ruins, Marquand's wall as just a wall, all of it.

Now was no time to be alone. I went down to the Astronomers' Bar and found Scarbo, Strengi and Hammon at one of the terrace tables, and had no trouble at all persuading them to share their travellers' tales of far-off places.

Margaret Solles didn't call until mid-afternoon, leaving me to spend the morning distracted and on edge, worrying that Bascoeur may have reconsidered. At 1130 I let the desk clerks and stewards know I'd be with my friends from the Bird Club, and sat with a small group of regulars in the big chairs looking out on the Promenade. Though we discussed the Villa Chano strike, Jeremy, Sally and Nathan took my cue when I turned the subject to other things, and made no comment when I excused myself at 1300, saying

I would take siesta.

The phone roused me at 1400. There on the screen was the pale face again (I was already thinking of her as the Sour Elf).

'He'll see you at Saldy's in twenty minutes, Captain.'

'He'll trade?'

'He'll decide that at Saldy's. Twenty minutes. It's his time.'

Meaning it wasn't mine; I needed to hurry. The screen went dark, but this time I remembered the harsh troubling gaze. This intense, serious woman was my path to Bascoeur.

5.

Saldy's Rainhouse and Aviary had long ago outgrown its name. There were still the cosy salons with real birds sailing through tropical gardens beyond the casements, and other windows giving onto scenes of carefully controlled winters, and synthetic rains pattering on the glass before long fire-lit dinner tables.

But now additional structures had been added, extensions allowing ocean views, sun-traps and sand gardens, whitewashed loggias stretching out to the sea, steps leading down to terraces, shadowed courtyards, a hundred more quiet guest rooms, and one of the best belltree collections in all of Twilight Beach. It did not quite match the ancient splendour of the Gaza, but for the sense of old-world luxury, antiquity and other climes it afforded the likes of Gado Bascoeur, it was the only place the oubliettes chose when they visited this part of the coast.

The main entrance still had its original sign, and the Sour Elf was waiting beneath it when I arrived. She wore white desert clothing, a djellaba with a hood drawn close about her face so that more than ever she resembled an old-world nun, one, I fancied seeing her, who was angry with her God, short of both faith and favour.

'Second floor. The Blue Room,' she said, and I wondered what sort of master Bascoeur could be that this young woman had become so hard and officious in his service.

The lobby of Saldy's was a grand thing, complete with potted palms, mosaics and lacquered screens, with small groups of guests talking quietly in deep armchairs and conversation pits, all washed by the rich honey-coloured light from antique shades beneath slowly turning fans.

I climbed the main stairs to a first-floor mezzanine, took a smaller flight to a side landing with three doors, one a soft midnight blue.

I knocked, waited a few moments, then turned the handle and entered.

The djellaba-shrouded figure of Bascoeur was sitting with his back to me before a balcony that opened onto an expanse of rich blue sky.

For an instant, it was like seeing myself as I must have looked at the Gaza the previous evening, then, of course, not at all. The colours here were too vivid, the fittings more conspicuously ornate.

'Come in, Captain,' Gado Bascoeur said in a quiet smooth voice, one both practised and commanding, though oddly sexless in its modulations.

I crossed to where he sat, saw more closely the stained-glass mask that marked him as an Antique Man. Across his lap, robed arms draped loosely over it, was an archimenter, beautifully made, a tech-fitted restoration piece, its wooden handle chased with silver, probably a comp-assist but possibly a laser or high-calibre ballistic for all I knew. It was strange to see such a dedicated scholar nursing an ancient firearm.

But it was the mask that drew my attention the most. It was a faceted dome, non-human, featureless, a deep oval-shaped bascinet, completely covering the face like a fencing mask. The line of the central frontal panes from which the lateral ones angled away suggested a pattern from nature: the plates on the shell of a tortoise, or the startling geometries on the backs of lizards. The intricate lozenges and plates of coloured glass were separated by a network of old bronzed silver, much worn from use.

I tried to make out the face inside the cage of coloured panes, but there were too many frosted shapes and no clears, giving tantalising glimpses of nose, brow and jaw, but occluded by afternoon sunlight through stressed blues, starved reds, ambers, bronzes, rich Genoese golds, teals and turquoises, streaked submarine greens.

'Twenty minutes I was told.'

'Meg can be overzealous,' he said. 'We have all the time you need. I would very much like to hear about Dewi Dammo.'

I drew a chair to the side of Bascoeur's own, out of the line of sight of the sky and the ocean below, wanting to watch the light play on what I could see of the man's features. I made myself comfortable and began.

It took twice the twenty minutes Meg had allowed. Now and then, the long brown fingers lifted and fell on the side plate of the archimenter, tapping out an irregular rhythm.

At first I thought he was touch-recording facts or mnemonic codes, knowing that the device was probably a storage-trap fashioned to look like a gun, but then noticed that the tips of those fingers made no contact with the surface of the ritual weapon. He was simply working through a memory pattern. If he noticed my attention, the momentary slowing and distraction in my account, he gave no sign.

Finally I was done. There were his questions then, another twenty minutes of them: about Dewi and my present search both for Namarkon and for information about my forgotten past. I forced myself to ask no questions of my own, just watched the fingers moving in their gentle flute pattern all the while. But finally they paused and there was a different silence, an almost disquieting lull in which I studied the covered face, the gorgeous panes in their stepped, angling curves. They made a cathedral dome, a bright orrery in which the solitary planet was Bascoeur's skull and all that it contained, a world, a universe inside another, inside yet another.

I studied, too, the small flower sign he wore high on his chest, periwinkle blue on the sand-coloured robe, an embroidered Forget-Me-Not, fitting choice for the oubliettes. Inevitably, my attention wandered into the intricate sign embroidered at the shoulder — a sect patch it seemed, a sequence of many dots, some linked into cruciform patterns by looping lines, overlapping and bolder at the centre, the whole shape bordered by darker dots. It suggested a circuit pattern or an elaborate code, an ideogram, some mystical sign of power.

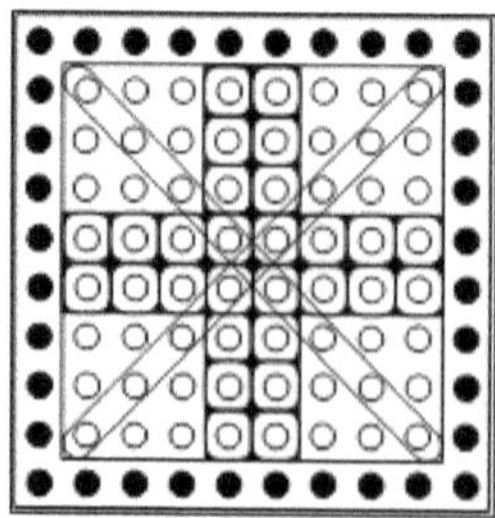

Bascoeur placed his hands squarely on the weapon in his lap. 'What do you need from me, Captain?'

'I went to Turker Fin.'

'I know.'

'Dewi mentioned Chiras Namarkon in connection with a library. The tribesman who gave me this mission confirmed it. I went to the seven National libraries I was told officially existed. There may be more, though I doubt it now. We are being shut off from our past; eventually we will have to go outside Australia to learn about our National heritage.'

'Go on, please.'

'All the Chiras Namarkon references I did find had been excised, or rather relegated to "dead stack" status, one text only, one Illuminated Book kept at Crayasse. L75 VGS. But at Crayasse I learned that it was on loan to Turker, had been moved on just before I arrived. That Book was sent to Turker for a reason, and I expected to find it gone, sent elsewhere, unable to be located.'

'Yes?' The long fingers resting on the archimenter did not move now, though the hands were angled out from Bascoeur's body like minatory wings, pointed at the ocean and the sweep of sky. It looked wonderful and strange, barely human.

'I saw L75 VGS. It's in poor condition. The Reader Page misfunctions. The entry for Namarkon cancels itself. But I learnt something.'

'Yes?'

'There were the appended summaries, etymological references to the old languages, the traditional mythological identification of Namarkon as Lightning Spirit, as a tree struck by lightning, that sort of thing. And there is an entry for a Chiras Namarkon.'

Bascoeur said nothing. I watched him intently, as if I were hoping to read something in the set of his body, the colours of the mask, the blue Forget-Me-Not on his robe — traditionally the flower of friendship and fidelity, in the intricate tangle of the sect patch which kept snaring my eye and had me wondering what it could possibly mean for people like these.

'Chiras Namarkon,' I continued, 'is identified as The Immortal, described variously as a creature of fable, as a tyrant hidden away in his labyrinth — his library — as a great wanderer, a highwayman, it goes on and on. He has the secret of knowledge, of ideas and words. He has treasure. But you know this, Lord Gado.'

'I do?' The long hands still pointed like emblematic wings.

'A status request tag is yours. There has been an attempt to suppress knowledge of such a figure, making it dead stack, hard to locate. The time and trouble that took must have been considerable. I suspect that even were I to have access to the tribal libraries and the universities, there would be as little information. The tribes must know about Namarkon for his part in their affairs to be effective, that he is non-Ab'O, extremely long-lived, but they need not know too much.'

'You assume a great deal. But you are telling me something.'

'The tribes know my limitations, the unlikelihood of my finding anything without assistance. It would take me years to locate even a few of the private libraries. Chano was destroyed; Marquand is a fraud. So why send me? Unless you can provide clues or are involved in some way. Unless you wanted it to seem like that. You avoided answering Den's calls for quite some time. There's a reason.

Namarkon could well be one of you. An oubliette. A secret master of oubliettes. The tribes may suspect this.'

'We don't keep libraries in the traditional sense, Captain.'

'You are libraries.'

Bascoeur paused before answering. 'Of course. It's all worth considering.'

'Which part?'

'All of it. Namarkon.'

'How many oubliettes are there?'

'A total number is hard to give. There are trainees, honorary postings —'

'Like you.'

'Like me? Thirty-six.'

'And leaders?'

'Four officers out of that number. We call them *Angels*.'

'More and more like a holy order. Are you an Angel?'

'Yes. This information is costing you, Captain.'

'Then let me complete the trade. Will you take me to where oubliettes are trained? Any place where Antique Men gather?'

'We operate as solitaries. What leads you — ?'

'Dewi ruled by creating then monopolising an economic/religious condition, tapping into what was almost a theocracy. Another effective power-base must be information flow, the non-partisan trafficking in knowledge and strategies and historical perspective. The tribes can afford you.'

Finally the hands moved again, turning in slightly, fingers angling, moving, completing a quick manipulation on the air. 'I admit to being impressed.'

'No, you will have anticipated I would come to this

from the moment the tribes approached me.'

Bascoeur made no response, though his hands had become still again. It appeared that I had his complete attention.

'First, there was virtually nothing on libraries,' I said, 'so few are declared. The black market in books means most true-book collections stay private and secret. Council gave what listings their systems had, but I'm allowing for interference now, tampering with National data-stores. But I accept that the privates are incomplete anyway, not just inaccessible. They will be depleted, the best items sold off or plundered long ago. The university and tribal libraries are off limits, as you know.'

'Do I, Captain?'

'I believe you know my position, Lord Gado. I went to the Pandeon here in Twilight Beach, then out to some of the old arcologies. Crayasse gave me a lead, something called *Alexandrian Book*. Den has techs and archivists doing searches; he's even done a tentative costing on consulting individual tribal archives well favoured to Nation, should they relent, though that would alert too many people.'

Bascoeur turned his head slightly, like the apse of a living cathedral, a crystal flower turning with the light, filled with light. I was amused by the theatricality of the action, but awed too. He was not play-acting a role, this oubliette, however much his manner often suggested it: the composed gestures, the mannered speech. Rather he was a uniquely alienated and uniquely engaged individual, someone curiously but necessarily estranged from my worldview with its immediacy, its tribal conflicts and striving Princes, its Dewi Dammos and deadly Namarkons. Could Chiras fit such a Weltanschauung? If so, then so so different from Dewi.

'The tribes would not tell you anything,' Bascoeur said flatly. 'What happened to Chano confirms that. And Dammo's death — his presumed death — had immediate repercussions. As a port official, James Namuren's part could not be lightly overlooked. Some Princes sought Convocation and payback; some even now push to re-assess not only the charling leases but all National concessions. The secret libraries are off limits for a reason; the Antique Men will be denied you soon. You were given this mission by a faction, an interest group, that saw a small closing window of opportunity.'

'Then how can I possibly locate Namarkon?'

Bascoeur's left hand lifted as if to counsel patience. 'You have imputed that Namarkon is one of us. I am intrigued and alarmed by that notion. But there are things we can do before the embargo falls. In fact' — he angled his head so a turquoise pane flashed richly — 'that's precisely why I came to Saldy's. The management protects its patrons. I came here unmasked. Only you and Meg know I am here. I did this to forestall official injunctions reaching me.'

'Surely not out of gratitude for my account of finding Dewi! You're playing this for you. Someone moved that Book to delay me, but whoever it was could have confiscated it altogether. I was delayed while some interested party searched for something else. The Book was deliberately damaged before it arrived at Turker.'

'Deliberately, you think? A sealed Book?'

'The librarian said so. You could do it. Since I did find an entry which led me to you as much as it did to Namarkon, I'm left to wonder what part the Antique Men play in this — and what they might have gained by delaying me, by damaging a text, then letting it lead me to them.'

Bascoeur turned his head back to the sea and the sky. Some of the panes on his mask seemed to have special optical properties: one shone with the lustrous velvet mauve-green of a dragonfly's eye; another with the rich roiling highlights of oil struck by rain.

'Pretend for a moment, Captain, that I am not Chiras Namarkon, nor his confederate in any way. Assume I am a very concerned member of my order, an Angel, concerned about libraries too. Consider that where the oubliettes are concerned, the Princes and Clever Men have one commitment greater than using us to control the flow of information as feudal societies once did after the fall of Rome and Constantinople, during that great and terrifying European Dark Age we are determined must never happen again.'

'Very well.'

'Back then, distortion of facts occurred more through ignorance, ineptitude, superstition and the limits of technology than deliberate disinformation, mythopoesis or strictures imposed by church and state. Now we have a carefully, wonderfully controlled program of distortion, of expert myth-making. Nothing new really, but more effective in a cultural horizon so devoted to the idea of total sharing, where genuine information flow seems to be encouraged. "A thousand truths for the one well-placed lie" is an oubliette saying, remember.'

'So what are you saying, Lord Gado?'

'Historians and archivists are more circumspect today, but the liberalising of information by comp, sat-scan, gain-monitor is a myth too. It has led to closed societies, intensively applied media falsehood, reclusive overlords like Dammo and Namarkon, the re-medievalising of attitudes and fact-finding processes, all the counters in the information web. We acquire more myth and legend, more contamination and carefully planted disinformation than ever before, you realise, in direct proportion to any documented truth. Tactical lies created and nurtured by the strategists and propagandists, refined and promoted by local and international agencies. The Information Revolution, Tom Rynosseros, is over simply because it continues, a wonderful paradox! Call it affective filtering or whatever, it is our condition now. There is too much to know. More and more we are becoming verifiers and discriminators rather than information givers.'

I studied this man, capable of the Zen rigour, so full of intricate knowledge. The air of cynicism and weariness he brought to our conversation was a tactic, I felt, a way to test my own reactions perhaps. Or maybe he was a man in crisis, revealing a new alarming truth he dared not share with his fellow oubliettes.

I recalled the lack of surprise I'd felt when Kaber Fen Otamas had told me of the ongoing prospect of secret rulers like Dewi and now this Namarkon appearing, powerfully, vigorously, active in the interstices of that suborned information glut. Not even State of Nation had too many illusions in its quest for identity and survival, not after the watergating of history: the Bolo Mays, Nixons and Richelieus, the Viet Nams and Sinchwens, the para-governmental agencies: the CIA and Mossad, the Mafia, Camorra, Yakuza, Talion and their corporate variants — the Machiavellian heritage uncovered and refined during a few key centuries, power vacuums filled, well or badly, but inevitably.

'Before Turker,' I said, 'I expected to hear from the Antique Men. Council tried to arrange meetings without success; no doubt you had reasons. I'd become a vital integer in something, cutting across patterns, revealing structures. Now you seem to suggest that the tribes are tampering with your people.'

Bascoeur raised a cautionary hand. 'If not the tribes then some tribal agency operating as Namarkon, whoever, whatever he, she, it is. He is in his library somewhere. What does he do there? How does he rule his portion? He may have more knowledge than all of us, even more than the tribes, may in fact be comp, AI, someone or something as long-lived as Dewi was, immortal, building ideas into history, a mythopoeticist skilfully, effectively controlling and disseminating concepts, fostering his illusions and fictions, immediate and long-term. I am very worried, personally alarmed, that the Antique Men, allowed access everywhere, may be infiltrated by Namarkon's agents, that one of my associates may in fact be Chiras Namarkon. The very thought of it brings a fear you cannot understand.'

'What do you suggest?'

'We depend on tribal favour; we do not run our own ships. Except for a few closed towns, you can take Rynosseros where you please.'

'Unless they strike as they did at Chano.'

'A reasonable risk. You hold a mandate and a Colour. Your name is in the Great Passage Book.'

'That may not worry Namarkon at all. After Balin that may not worry the tribes either. Go on.'

'We seek Namarkon together, at least until I am satisfied that the Antique Men are not involved in his schemes.'

'Then?'

'Then our usual rules apply. We pay you with knowledge for what you give us.'

'Can I see where the oubliettes are trained? Allowing

for the fact that I might wish to search on after you have satisfied yourself, allowing that I am still considering you or one of your kind for Namarkon, that I was delayed a month in finding L75 VGS.'

'Agreed. But, Captain, we must act immediately. If the tribes continue to move against you, hinder you; if the oubliettes are denied you — either because Namarkon is working among us for the tribes and not just himself, or because you must be stopped anyway — then what I do now is outside the law. All Antique Men will pay for any indiscretions I now commit.'

'Then, as you say, word must not reach us. Rynosseros is at the Sand Quay. Come aboard tonight, whenever you can. We sail at 0600.'

'Very well,' Bascoeur said. 'And Meg will accompany us. But leave now, please. I must consider this possibility of treachery.'

6.

I did not see Meg Solles when I left Saldy's, but quickly headed along the late afternoon streets to the Promenade, followed that towards the decks, loggias and famous terraces of the Gaza, bright now with the last hour of sunlight, the windows flashing like a vast replica of Bascoeur's mask.

Though it was still that hour till the breaklight, the time of day for which Twilight Beach is named, there were players of fire-chess already at the boards, their tiny lines of fighters dancing in the sea-wind. These were short-lived suicide games, full of braggadocio and fun, recklessly played because the wind allowed opportunity for little else. The players laughed and performed at their eccentric best. The tourists and hotel guests cheered every bold move, and cheered as enthusiastically each time a tiny flame was extinguished.

Soon, when the wind lost its edge and the Hotel's tuxedoed Devil Catchers appeared, ready to beat at the dust-devils with their long-handled spoilers, these flamboyant posturings would cease. The grins and extravagant flourishes would be replaced by looks of concentration and a ruthless urbanity famous the world over.

When I turned into the Gentian Walk, that narrow walled avenue connecting Tramway Street to the southern end of the Gaza terrace, I found three Ab'Os leaning on the seawall watching the ocean. They wore fighting leathers under their djellabas, and had sheathed kitanas over their shoulders, not an uncommon thing, but an uncommon place for tribesmen to loiter.

I read the scene quickly enough, had it confirmed when the men recognised me, quickened and moved back from the wall to block my path. They wore vendetta marks on their cheeks, bands of colour and soul-taking stars in turquoise and deep red. The swords were slashes of light leaving their scabbards.

I had nothing but my sailor's sticker in the leg-sheath of my fatigues, though reaching for it meant I had accepted their terms.

One tribesman in his early thirties, older than the others, moved forward.

'I am Ephan Sky Namuren,' he said. 'Kin to James Namuren. This is payback.'

'But not legal,' I said, desperately seeking words that would prevent this. 'As Blue Captain on a tribal mission I am not allowed to fight you. Will this be murder then? More shame for Namuren?'

'You are allowed,' Ephan said, as if he had not heard the final words. 'And you have your deck-knife.'

'Which might grow into a kitana someday, certainly. You are brave men.'

Another spoke then, pushing past Ephan. 'I am Paul Dharajan. Stories say you were trained by the Spaniard, Marco, and the Japanese, Tensumi. A sticker is enough for you.'

'Stories! I wish I could remember living so long to have all these stories.' I searched the empty Walk and the fiercely marked faces for any sign of advantage. Was this it then? A final afternoon? A last vital encounter? How many of us ever choose the places where we die?

I drew my sticker, its narrow blade as long as my forearm. 'Who claims the right?' I said, formally.

The men exchanged glances, quick bright smiles.

'We all do,' Ephan said. 'For our kinsman.'

'Judged traitor by Convocation,' I reminded them. 'You will be sung for this. Be sure of it.'

More glances at that, the smiles gone, replaced by carefully neutral looks, though I imagined I did see traces of worry, doubts about assurances given.

'The terms then,' I continued, hoping someone would enter the Walk, someone armed or who might summon help. But they had chosen their time well. 'From the first drop of blood you are damned. They watch!' And I looked up into the late afternoon sky to where the invisible satellites held station, whichever orbitals were currently geo-tethered to Twilight Beach.

Paul Dharajan moved forward. 'Come, Ephan! No-one watches this!'

'Good, Dharajan,' I said, dropping to a first position. 'I am hunting Namarkon but you will do.'

The Ab'O grinned, confirming the source of the

strike, the direction from which assurances had ultimately come, filtering down through tribal lobbies.

Again I tried for the initiative. 'Though he too is hunted by his enemies. Of course they watch. Can they monitor this small stretch, do you think?'

Dharajan did not answer. Ephan and the other man moved forward as well until five metres was all there was.

I raised my sticker and cut my own cheek, just as I had at Balin, let them see the blood shining on my blade. Then I looked immediately into the sky. 'Take them all, Namarkon!'

Ephan looked up, his companions as well. It was reflex.

A wisp of cloud had drifted into view, seemed frozen there.

Then Dharajan cried out in pain and surprise, blood streaming from his throat where my sticker now stood, small deft lightning. He dropped his sword with a single cry and collapsed to the stones.

I lunged for the weapon in what scant seconds I had, but Ephan was better than that, well-trained, well-chosen. His foot came down on the discarded blade, denying me. His own sword arced towards my outstretched arm, to my neck where I lay, head to the side, fingers touching the haft.

The edge, the line of separation, was right there. One twist, one thrust, and I would cease to be, know, feel. No throb of bleeding cheek, no pain in knee and shoulder from the fall, no knowing this desperate attempt at life. I looked along the gleaming blade to Ephan's painted face, his flashing eyes, beyond them to the patch of sky, the frozen wisp of cloud, infinitely precious.

'Fight me,' Ephan said, stepping back, leaving

Dharajan's blade, seeking something of honour in a poor mission, only now truly understood.

'No!' his companion cried. 'His orders!'

His. The word said it all.

'Personal honour, Sab! Decide for yourself when he is armed.'

I seized the hilt, slick with Dharajan's blood, and stood, heart pounding, thoughts racing one to the next, seeking a solution.

Ephan was there almost immediately, and the Walk rang, echoed with the clash of weapons.

Despite my two blades, long and short, it was all I could do to defend, and in a sense Ephan helped me there. He was too good a swordsman; Sab could not engage without ruining Ephan's patterns. What trade-offs there were between them, a concession to face, showed Sab to be an inferior fighter, though not to be taken lightly.

Slowly, in the constant jarring of the three-way, I managed to regain my centre. More and more deflections were controlled, more and more feints planned and resolved by me.

Ephan withdrew. Sab leapt in, jumped back with a slashed sleeve and a look of astonishment.

'Marco and Tensumi, remember!' Ephan warned, breathing hard, then filled the air again with his own lightning.

Every breath was drawn over fire now. Arms ached from the repeated blows of the exquisite many-folded blades.

If not resolved soon, Ephan would have me. He was too good. I brought Marco and Tensumi to mind — real, RNA assists from the Madhouse, another lost or false memory, who could say? — then waited for Sab's turn, let him begin, and swapped blades, right hand to left, deflected his sword with my own and took him above the heart with the sticker, through djellaba, fighting leathers and all, the blade in, out and gone, whipped away, lightning through fire it seemed, so sudden.

Again there was the look of astonishment, intense and final as the eyes glazed and his life went out of him. I had cleared the blade before he knew what had happened.

'See what — they — have done to you,' I managed, exhausted, dangerously so, watching Ephan's eyes. 'His orders!'

'Whose —' Ephan's breathing was ragged too, '— do you think?'

'One — who doesn't care what happens. You — don't count. Expendable, hear? If not you — others.'

Ephan nodded, darted quick glances at his dead companions, assessing what had been paid. No fool this one, simply a man trapped by duty.

'What do I have?' he asked.

'You were not here,' I said. He had given me my chance; now I held out Dharajan's kitana for him to take.

He nodded and took it, saluted with his own sword, then turned, vanishing through the crowd of sightseers and hotel guests who had gathered on the Walk.

I entered the Gaza and found Scarbo and Shannon, but at the far side of that grand room from where the swordplay had just now taken place. The sounds had not reached them through the press of guests and tourists, the forest of sanche palms, the lacquered and enamelled screens, the great pillars and sculptury.

I drew many looks crossing that great room, and when my friends saw me they immediately went to rise. I waved them back, gratefully taking the glass of tautine Shannon pushed towards me, fire for the fire, the shaking, for the simple joy of being alive.

'Namarkon almost achieved what Dewi couldn't,' I said. 'Three bravos decided to brawl. The cheek is mine; a bit of payback psychology that didn't work.'

Ben and Rob smiled, though the smiles were thin and quickly gone. Something else was amiss.

'What?'

'Den's hurt,' Ben said. 'Archimenter discharge — or an equivalent. Some time around 1600. He's in deep shock.'

'Archimenter? Will he survive?'

'They think so. He's in a sleeve at Gallo's and responding. There's been surgery as well. He has Bylon heart tailoring; it was thrown out of kilter.'

'But archimenter?' I thought of the rich data store, the concentration of energy in the weapon, the 'six years of dream' as it was called: the amount of time in the old seventy-year, pre-nano lifespan that the average person spent dreaming. 'He couldn't survive it!'

Scarbo shook his head. 'Nothing like full charge. Perhaps it was just a warning. But Kurdaitcha came, said they were looking for Gado Bascoeur.'

'Not Bascoeur. I've been with him since 1500. And he wouldn't incriminate himself with an archimenter; none of his people would.'

'Namarkon, you think?' Shannon asked.

'Who can say, Rob? An extreme point and a clumsy way of making it.'

Scarbo set down his glass. 'Den may have found something. Possibly plundered from Nation's systems.'

'We don't have time to find out.' I leant forward, spoke the next words almost as a whisper. 'Bascoeur will come aboard tonight. We leave tomorrow at first light. Half-crew.'

'Where?' Scarbo asked.

'When we're aboard, Ben. Find the others. Briefing at 1900. But half-crew.'

7.

We fled from Twilight Beach, that was how it felt, rushing along the Great Arunta Road with the sun barely above the line and thirty kites in the sky, great Sodes and Demis, a dozen racing footmen. There was no pursuit.

We had minimum crewing: by Ben's roster Rim, Strengi and Hammon were down for leave anyway, and so became part of a last-minute deception. They drank with the sandsmen and veteran sailors at the Astronomers' Bar, let themselves be seen gaming at Deep's late into the night. It was likely that no-one expected to see Rynosseros pulling away from the Sand Quay, lofting her kites at first light.

It was busy work for Scarbo, Shannon and me with a vessel the size of ours. For that dawn hour, we hurried about the commons, fitting kites to cables, checking the separations, Scarbo judging the shift from coastal to inland winds and making choices, shouting them to us or signing in the traditional way of the aeropleuristic craft.

Bascoeur and Meg watched from the quarterdeck, the oubliette unreadable in his mask, his assistant equally so behind her severe pale face, both shapeless in their travelling robes. The Antique Man had his hood raised and drawn well forward over his mask, a small precaution but one observed just in case.

Who could say if the tribes cared or if Namarkon watched? Bascoeur was probably right. Lightning against

Chano was one thing; a strike at a mandated ship, a Coloured Captain, at someone listed in the Great Passage Book, was something else entirely. I recalled Dewi's mirror ships, permitted but watched and finally punished from orbit. It might be that Namarkon existed by exploiting Ab'O need, tribal vulnerability. He might very well safeguard the values that kept his power-base secure, perhaps aiming — my real fear in this! — to extend himself beyond any need of their goodwill.

Appropriating laser strike was privilege enough; possessing a Namarkon comsat of his own would be absolute crisis, not only death-strike capability but information saturation as well. What Kaber Fen Otamas had told me seemed more real than ever.

The stowaway appeared when we were almost at Wani.

Bascoeur was at the port rail of the quarterdeck, lost in his thoughts and assimilations, with Meg waiting to one side. Shannon was with Scarbo at the kite lockers laying cable runs, only occasionally glancing at the canopy overhead, not needing to do so since they read the tensions in the hull and overheads so well.

I had the helm, watching the Road and some distant cloud-forms that could spell wind and so kite-change, enjoying how our canopy spread upon the sky like a bright hand, a taut receding thrust of light and colour.

Meg saw her first, a noon-spectre appearing on the commons to for'ard, beyond the intricate totemic webwork of the cable-boss.

'Look!' she cried, and the light was such that the figure startled us all. It was like the mirages you often see, the transit-ghosts you expect out on the Serafina, along the Soul or in the inner deserts, not snared here beneath the sky-trap of kites and displayed in full sunshine.

Only for a second. It resolved from dream to real in moments. Our visitor came walking across the commons, a woman in her mid-twenties, taller than any but Bascoeur in his shrouded jewel-box mask, with wide clear eyes and fine features in a face I found I knew, with the small talenti marks, three to each side, tatooed in ochre at the curve of the jawline: a member of Club Hetaera. She wore desert fatigues that were the same sandy-white as her short hair. Meg Solles was pale; this striking young woman was the whitened gold of wheatfields in sunshine.

Scarbo followed her up to the helm, waiting till she spoke, though I'd already heard the echo of her scream from the ruins of Chano.

'Thank you for what you did,' she said, bringing back the ruin of lives.

'Why are you here, Truan?' I asked.

She smiled wearily. 'I'm hetaera. I can give Namarkon his due.'

Bascoeur moved forward from the rail, vivid and powerful. 'Who told you that name?'

'I knew why Captain Tyson was visiting Chano,' she answered evenly. 'Marquand phoned. We are women who do, Lord Oubliette.'

'It is an age when too many well-intentioned people seek to do, Ms McBanus. The Bird Club. The Hetaera. Nation Council. This is a private mission. Put back, Captain. We cannot go on.'

'With respect, Lord,' Truan said, and brought forth a wire from the pocket of her fatigues: the feed-point of a gain-monitor. 'Nothing is more private than my task. There was conversation when you came aboard last night, and again this morning. I heard the word Whitehead, the name of the destination you gave Captain Tyson.'

The Antique Man looked at her, or looked at a point of infinity on the inside of his glass cage. Near him, Meg let her own face show her master's controlled rage, the measure of it she imagined. Bascoeur was a pragmatist. I doubted he would be angry for long.

'Then continue,' he said — to me undoubtedly though the mask gave no certainty of it — then left the quarterdeck. Meg went too, like a bruise Bascoeur chose to carry with him, a penitential badge. I wondered at the nature of that secret agreement between them, what intimacy was lodged in that relentless service. I wondered too if our stowaway might not end up with an archimenter taking her mind as it nearly had Den's.

'You make it difficult,' I told our unwanted guest. 'Truan, I need that man. He's the only lead I have. And how is it you own a gain-monitor? That needs tribal authorisation.'

'My father's,' she said. 'He often worked for the tribes, needed to authenticate dealers and couriers. The tribes allowed it on loan. They may assume it was destroyed.'

Full crew would have stopped her, I kept telling myself, found her in the empty storage bay. Hammon's job, or Rim's. Our ruse had done it, our clever ploy.

'Captain, like you I have only this,' she said. 'How would you proceed if you were in my place? Blame and punish? You're undermanned. I know enough of kites not to be in the way.'

'Then stay near Scarbo. Ben, give her a place. And stay away from Bascoeur and his assistant!'

She said no more, went quietly down to the lockers and the armatures. There was wind-change coming and she showed no small degree of skill helping Shannon bring in the top-kites, drawing the outstretched hand into a fist, tethered close now and beating at the sky.

Bascoeur seemed to have accepted Truan's presence when he returned to the poop an hour later. He came without Meg, thank goodness, and watched the Road from as close to my station at the helm as he could stand without disturbing me, though I sensed his presence, the flashing glance from the front of the hood, the tortoise panes throwing so many jewels back at the sun.

'She has no choice,' he said finally. 'Home and family are gone.'

'Yes,' I said, respecting him for this compassion, though it meant betraying self-interest. 'So, Turker, then Whitehead.'

'Agreed. Though I'm curious as to why Turker is necessary. It can't be L75 VGS. I can do no more to work a faulty Book than the librarian.'

'I need information on AI, on crystalline intelligence.'

'Pursuing the obvious,' Bascoeur said.

I shrugged. 'What can you tell me?'

'To save you time? That, yes, our masks are nanotech-constructed crystalline lattices with ambient temperature superconductivity, made essentially by a conventional nano assembler. That the internal circuitry is mixed, electronic and cortico-optical, with vested laser tech for data volume, that the power needs are minimal. Parts of my body have been bio-adapted to supply that, more old science really. It gives over 1900 times the storage capacity of the human brain and can be one million times as fast.'

'Thank you,' I said. 'Will you remove your mask and talk about this?'

I expected a flat refusal, so his reply surprised me.

'Yes, though you cannot know how I resent needing to, resent the fact that nothing else can convince you now.'

'You might be Namarkon and not know it. Part of Namarkon.'

'So easily caught? Why would I? Why would some Antique Man collective —'

'Potentially a vast nanotech computer.'

'— let us meet?'

'You know the answer. You've become an only chance.'

'Because of Chano?'

'Yes.' It seemed so unlikely now that Namarkon, like poor mad Dewi, would willingly make himself — itself? — so vulnerable. I wished I had Truan's monitor, but knew that no oubliette would ever agree to use one.

'Tonight I will be without my mask,' Bascoeur said. 'But remember, Captain, we are here now only because I — as Angel — need to consider my own kind impartially, to explore leads of my own.'

'Will you answer another question then?'

'You can ask it.'

'There were thirty-five National arcologies before the tribes drove us back to the coasts. Now official lists show only thirty-four. How many are there?'

'Thirty-five,' Bascoeur said calmly, and the excitement I felt made me demand what I should have requested.

'Which one is missing? Why?'

'That is my other search, Captain. Locating that site. Separate from yours, for my reasons, unless I decide it concerns you.'

'Should it? Please, Lord Gado —'

'The unlisted arcology is Mekkis. An old Hebrew name.'

'Turker might tell us where —'

'I have tried there already. Tried them all. Captain, in Hebrew "mekkis" means "power".'

'Namarkon!' I cried.

Truan and Scarbo glanced up when I said it.

'Yes,' Bascoeur said. 'The general deletion of that name suggests it. And some tribal connection to be able to hide such a thing. Hard to misplace a city.'

Truan was approaching the quarterdeck. Meg Solles came hurrying from the bow, revealing by the determination of her stride, by the fixed direction of her gaze, more about her humanity and that of her master. Bascoeur may have accepted the reality of Truan's situation, Meg Solles clearly had not.

But Gado Bascoeur served no master on this ship. He turned away, showing by his manner that he was apart, so that when Truan and Meg arrived, one tentatively, not wanting to intrude, the other determined and hurrying, they were left regarding one another across the width of the quarterdeck.

I was watching the sky and the Road ahead as surely as Bascoeur watched the desert around us, but I sensed the contest that Truan suddenly found herself part of. Being hetaera, she did not leave it unspoken.

'I am not interested in your oubliette,' she said simply. 'You need fear nothing from me.'

'That's not it at all!' Meg answered angrily, which told us it was something as human, as desperate and needful.

Truan returned to the commons, and Meg was left with the silent rebuke of Bascoeur's back. I felt for her as she headed for'ard to watch the desert and to cool whatever longing had been revealed.

When Shannon took the helm at 1600, I made my way forward to where the notary sat on the starboard bench, her hood back, revealing her cropped black hair. Without the hood to frame her pale face, she looked more childlike and vulnerable than ever.

'She's wrong,' Meg Solles said. 'That's not it.'

I sat beside her. 'Then why behave as if it were?'

She blinked, frowned. 'None of you knows what this man suffers here, what it means to examine the possibility of treason. He has infinities stored in his head, a custodianship of ages and civilisation; now he endures this action against his order, sacrificing time from so many other duties.'

'Caused by me.'

'Yes,' she said, and her mouth contracted into the Sour Elf's once more.

'Why do you follow him? Serve him?'

'It's an honour. I get to learn. I might even be trained.'

'How long has it been?'

She shrugged. 'Five years. Six. A few have companions, not all. The Angels always do. We are servants, notaries, sometimes friends. We do what is needed.'

'What is needed.'

'Nothing like that!' she snapped. 'They don't need that! Sometimes it would be better if they did. They are androgynes, did you know? Both sexes.'

The information startled me.

'Don't ask about it, Captain. The answer is lost in hermetic lore. In alchemical beginnings we will never understand. It's a tradition. I accept it.'

'Meg —'

'I accept it!'

'You don't —'

'It's the honour of service that keeps me here, not physical love!'

'Do you know my situation?' I asked her, to turn the conversation away from her relationship.

She nodded. 'Lord Gado told me.' Her mouth softened; the child in her defeated the bitter, practised lines around her mouth. 'You are very brave.'

'No,' I said, laughing. 'No, Meg. You are brave, who give so much from love. I just find myself taking a direction, doing what I can to discover my beginnings. Now my world has been touched again. A friend was harmed at Twilight Beach. Truan's parents are dead, her home destroyed. Desperation becomes duty. We are similar there, you and I. Life makes its own purpose, as always.'

'At least you are doing. That is brave!'

'Then we are brave together. And Gado Bascoeur is very brave to do this.'

'Yes,' she said, grateful, and there it was: a smile, also elfin, small and tentative on that lonely face.

'Meg, since you know something of the courtesies and protocols of the Antique Men, I would rather ask you some of my questions than put them to Lord Gado and use his time. It is a way I can spare him but gain knowledge that may help him as much as me.'

'What questions?'

'The patch on his shoulder. What is that?'

'The Forget-Me-Knot,' she said.

'The patch, not the flower.'

'It's the Forget-Me-Knot! K-N-O-T. The oubliette sign. A schematic of the flower, I don't know, something like that. A molecular schema.'

'Is that what he told you?'

Meg shrugged. 'You see this as a key to Namarkon?'

The question, those words, made me hesitate a moment. 'Anything could be. I've learned that signs and symbols can matter very much. On the Inland Sea there is a woman for whom the ellipsis of Inner Eye means everything.'

'Tallin Okani. The one who hunts the special charling.'

'Yes. For Den and Council, the Bladed Sun of Nation means so much.'

'It's a windmill,' she said. 'Those converging triangles. An ancient windmill!'

'I've heard that. What people wear and show is important.'

'Unless they are concealing and misleading. Dissembling. Using signs and symbols.'

'True,' I said. 'But not this patch, I suspect. That design is important.'

'You must ask Bascoeur about the Knot.' She was becoming the Elf again, so accustomed to standing between her lord and the world. 'He might unravel it for a questing Alexander like you.'

And the new smile was bright and hard, a fully made thing. She had referred to the plaque fixed to the helm of Rynosseros, to the words once attributed to Alexander the Great by an ancient writer:

> One must live as if it would be forever, and as
> if one might die each moment. Always both
> at once.

'Perhaps if we do not unravel that particular Knot first, Meg, someone else might cut it asunder. I want to save your master as well.'

'It is ancient, from the founding of the order. A circuit mat, or the design of a sacred tile from Alexandria, from Hellenistic times. But Gado could have been joking about it. I don't know what is true.'

Gado, she had said this time, without 'Lord' before it. 'Keep it in your thoughts, please. At any time Gado might decide we should part, and I truly would like to help him before that happens, to put his mind at ease. Like it or not, the Antique Men form a living library. That Knot on his sleeve looks like a labyrinth to me, formed by a nanotech computer of oubliette masks.'

'You've told him you suspect this?'

'He will have guessed where my thinking leads. To an extent my speculations help him, give necessary objectivity; past a certain point they are intrusions.'

'Insults.'

'Unfortunately.'

'I'll keep what you ask in mind. For his sake.'

I stood. 'Thank you, Meg. For his sake.'

8.

Bascoeur kept his word. After 1900, Shannon brought Rynosseros to the edge of the Road for our night mooring, selecting an area well clear of the graded surface, though it was doubtful any other ships would be coming now.

Around us, nothing could be seen but darkening sweeps of sand and low scrub, every ridge and stone with its long shadow, the scraps from which night was being made. The sun was a half-coin, shedding the last of its gold at the horizon.

The oubliette had gone below a little after 1750. Now, while Scarbo saw to the cable-boss and Truan and Shannon swept up the wind-wrack from the day's travel, and with Meg off somewhere by herself, Bascoeur re-appeared — and without his fabulous headgear.

In spite of what Meg had said about the androgyny, he was clearly a man — of indeterminate age, I noted, though possibly in his early forties, pale-skinned, dark-haired and with thin brows and a fine neck and jaw. The eyes were dark in the growing gloom, the nose narrow and straight, almost too sharp, a disturbingly severe feature on such an otherwise regular face. In the last of the light, I could see a pair of fine silvery scars at his temples.

'Salvation Moons we call them,' Bascoeur said, not needing to be asked. 'Signs of humility and self-denial. More symbols.'

I smiled. Meg had told him of our conversation then, had no doubt seen it as her duty.

The oubliette's voice was very much as it was when he was masked, well-modulated, with something of the contralto about it, almost sexless. He moved with his customary grace and economy as he joined me at the port rail, wearing his robe still, the flower and the Knot patch clear in the fading light.

'What now, Captain?'

I was used to his words coming through planes of glass. Seeing lips forming them was strange, as if a voice transmission had been lip-synced to an actor or a clever mankin.

'First, thank you for this. I believe I understand something of what it means. I would like to walk out there a way, the two of us. Do you mind?'

'Very well,' he said, and followed me over to the gangway and down onto the sand.

We walked in silence until Rynosseros was a far-off

thing, backlit with a flush of indigo and the most lustrous purple, like an offering to old gods, a cresset of embers set out beneath a sky that was brilliant with early stars and sparked with meteorites now and then. It reminded me that it was 'out' as well as 'up', and that Chiras Namarkon ruled some part of it as Lightning God, as The Immortal.

'The patch?' I asked finally, Meg having removed any need for delicacy in the matter.

'I have never been told,' he said, surprising me, just a voice again in the growing dark. 'But I see a present reason to pursue such an obvious line of enquiry.'

'The masks then? Where did they come from? Are they tribal?'

'Again I cannot say. They've always been there, stored at Whitehead. More than are ever used.'

His answers were hardly generous, but I had no choice. 'The *Alexandrian Book*? What can you tell me?'

Bascoeur settled on the cooling sand and I did so as well, watching the dim point of the ship until I became nightsighted enough to see the shape in the blackness beside me.

'Alexandrian Book is simply an idea,' he said. 'Imagine. A great library is burned, its entire collection almost completely lost, as at Alexandria several times before it was finally destroyed. In the ruins, among the remaining scrolls, is planted a false text, allegedly a copy of a copy, purportedly the last remaining account of some act, the story of some ruler, or a discovery, an idea, a secret heritage pre-dating all that is known of such a thing.

'It changes everything. It is enshrined as ancient wisdom, a purer older truth, something from the Golden Age — the way the writings, say, of Hermes Trismegistus underscored the whole European Renaissance. The ancient originals are lost, but thank goodness we have at least this one copy. It would only need an opportunist, not even the one responsible for the fire, though — all heaven forbid! — that could have been part of the plan as well. Maybe a fragment of such a text would be enough if there weren't the time to prepare a full one, but the weight attributed to such a fragment! A formal claim on history made retroactively would be enormous. It is frightening.'

'And the oubliettes?'

'The concept of the oubliettes began a long time ago, in 1784, in a small university town in Western Europe. Four scholars, wealthy enough men, hypothesised the Alexandrian Book idea, the notion of a planted falsehood. They noted trends emerging in their world, and resolved to found a society for the custodianship of history. They moved in a small way at first, putting truth before their own nationality and immediate cultural interests, as hard to do then as now. Within ten years they saw how discrepancies existed, how accounts of the same incident were skewed and embellished — more importantly, how those accounts differed from the one they themselves had painstakingly acquired from eye-witnesses and respected non-partisan thinkers.

'Building on the old axiom that the first casualty of war is truth, they allowed the far more important, post-Tribation corollary that truth is, indeed, the first casualty of self-interest and, inevitably, the first casualty of perception. Not a new idea these days, of course, or even then, but a new idea as a guiding, motivating ethic. They formed the oubliettes.

'Even if their accounts were never wholly accepted, if they preserved integrity, at least official accounts would need to be measured against them, would need to be aware of what the Antique Men had gleaned.'

'Is this true?' I asked him.

'I will not tell you. You must remember: there will always be things I will keep from you. It may be Alexandrian Book. Disinformation. Mythopoesis. Either way it is a good example, you'll agree. Plausible, even elegant. Worth embellishing and passing on.'

'It's frightening.'

'It is what happens all the time, Tom.' The voice in the darkness was generous and easy now, free of the mask, of the eternal prison it made. 'The Storyteller in us is always involved, cannot resist embellishing the facts. For instance, I say man-made fire was first applied to technology some time in the Palaeolithic, somewhere in Central Africa, and you react to it as a fact not reality. You accept, but barely experience.

'The Storyteller in me does better. One windy day in the final centuries of the Pleistocene, a man known only to his fellows as Hamat found that lightning had struck the sacred acacia that stood in the hollow by the Maju fishing lake. He took up a burning branch broken from the trunk, wanting it for a talisman, meaning to take it to a nearby hill and there pray over it for good hunting. The tribal shaman came with hunters, discovered him, and cried sacrilege.

'Hamat was given a fitting punishment: he would pay with his life if he could not do what the lightning had done. It was scorn, mockery, you see; the shaman was shaming him. They gave him a day, left him on his hill with the extinguished length of stick. Hamat broke it in two, struck the halves together to make thunder and hopefully lightning — a very elementary totemic step — finally started rubbing the pieces as storm clouds rub the land.

'He burned himself accidentally while rubbing the heated stick over bare flesh in his fear and zeal. He discovered heat in sticks first, and deduced there must be fire hidden there too. He began rubbing the halves again and made smoke, another part of the mystery revealed, then ignited dry grass bunched about it, and finally the stick itself. He ran down to his fellow villagers at day's end holding a torch. The shaman was clubbed and stoned; Hamat became shaman. To earn prestige and coerce neighbouring tribes, his people gave out the story with ever more detail added. By classical times, Hamat was Prometheus bringing fire from the gods.'

'Another Namarkon legend.'

'Indeed,' Bascoeur said. 'You see how it resonates.'

'What have you learned, Gado?' I used his name as he had mine, for whatever it signified in this safe darkness.

'If this Namarkon or tribal agencies have access to our data nets, I must use those nets carefully. As Angel, I am known for custodianship, but now I am with you on Rynosseros. I use my own mnemonic nets. Later I will verify what I find.'

Now I wished the darkness were not there, that I could see his eyes. 'We can go to Whitehead? With our stowaway?'

'I forgot myself. Truan's place in this, like yours and your crew's, is vital to the lesson of history we hold so important.'

'Which is?' I imagine that he smiled in the night, wanted to think that he did, that he could.

'Nothing you haven't thought of, Captain. History is people doing things, that's all. Large and small. The man who betrayed Edinburgh Castle to the English. The Greek traitor who betrayed Leonidas and his Spartans at

Thermopylae in 480 BC and showed Xerxes the secret route over the mountains. One man! A king dies sooner than later, all his loyal Spartiates, removed from their capacity to affect history. Or the Norwegian naval officer, Quisling…'

Bascoeur's voice broke off, then after a moment returned again. 'The oubliettes do not stand outside history, contrary to how it seems. We have to be part of it. There is no such thing as non-interference. Non-interference is interference. We exist, we participate, even when we withhold. This is why I take your suspicions seriously. Our philosophy of belonging, our awareness of Alexandrian Book and its possible existence in our very midst, makes Namarkon frighteningly real, his possible use of the Antique Men an unbearable lie. That he is called The Immortal becomes very sinister.'

'If we are wrong?'

'I may be replaced. There are three more Angels who may decide that I went too far, that I acted irresponsibly.'

'Den is gravely wounded. Could those Angels harm the rest of us?'

'No, Captain. Provided we are free of Namarkon, it is as I said. We accept things that happen. To counter any harmful truth you tell about us, we may need to plant a lie later — today, in a generation or two, whenever it will work best. Provided we know what was true here at the centre, that someone does.'

'Alexandrian Book?'

'Exactly. The first lesson the victor learns. Truth is a tool.'

'It is also what really is,' I said. 'Lost or forgotten. In spite of everything and anyone.'

'Which is what caused oubliettes to form in the first

place. You see why the existence of Namarkon among us constitutes a lie, a hideous contradiction. Yes, you might say that this too is what simply is, the world being itself. But our commitment to our mission pre-empts that. Your questions, Meg's, even Truan's, may uncover what is. So we go to Whitehead.'

'And Mekkis?'

'When we learn where it is, yes, I may share that with you as well. You can see why mentioning nanotech crystalline AI may have been premature if not altogether inopportune. If Namarkon is among the Antique Men, he has been alerted now.'

'It was obvious,' I said. 'He would assume that I suspect. And I get the impression Namarkon doesn't care. He believes he is safe.'

'Or wants this time of risk.'

'As a test?'

'As a test.'

We were silent then, watching the night, watching the distant glimmer of Rynosseros, the sudden bright signatures of meteorites arcing across the sky and vanishing in soundless strikes.

There were other questions, but it seemed wrong to ask them now. A tektite made its solitary mark, fleeting, curving down to resolution, reminding me.

'There's too much data and not enough, Gado. Do you know how many entries I found for lightning? The National libraries are full of information. I read for hours. Apart from scientific and meteorological references, just so many. Old National place names like Lightning Ridge. Hittite weather-gods like Tesheb and Dattas, wielding axes that make a symbolic lightning flash. Egyptian Min with his thunderbolt totem; the Chinese Lightning Mother with her flashing mirrors. It goes on. Lightning as symbol, in the dreams of the famous, in psychiatry and dreamlocking, as a motif in art. There's Ezekial's vision by the river of Chebar, of four cherubim and four wheels in the sky —'

' "Their appearance," ' Bascoeur said, ' "was like burning coals of fire, and like the appearance of lamps… and the fire was bright, and out of the fire went forth lightning." '

'Namarkon has to be aware of such things,' I said. 'Anything at all. Like the Tarot with that tower struck by the lightning of Spiritual Truth. It signifies change and the breaking down of old forms to create the new.'

'The Lightning-Struck Tower,' Bascoeur said. 'The House of God.'

'I'm sorry. I should remember. But could this suggest something, that Chano is his home? Would he strike at himself there to conceal his true whereabouts, blast his own house? To fulfil a Tarot image?'

' "Yea, he sent out his arrows, and scattered them; and he shot out lightnings, and discomfited them." I think not, Tom. The house plan is known. The Nation officers investigating were thorough. No, it was an example. "And he said unto them, I beheld Satan as lightning fall from heaven." '

'It goes on and on, doesn't it?'

'You have yet to speak of the Taoist Book of Changes. The I Ching.'

'Tell me!' I said, responding as I had whenever old Toth or one of the other librarians had found something promising for me.

'Ideogram 55. "Feng" or "Abundance". "The Sun below; the Thunder above". The Oracle says:

"Thunder and lightning:
the height of the storm
The superior man judges lawsuits
and declares them fairly."

I thought you may have found it.'

I sighed with amazement and exasperation. How much more was there, how many other strands and elements weaving in?

'It doesn't end,' I said, thinking of Namarkon controlling the register of history, ruling on needs and demands, the superior man, The Immortal, wielding his insidious Alexandrian Book like some emblematic flail, a terrible, ultimate lightning.

'Wait till you see the Feng ideogram. You will understand why I am committed, why I agreed to appear, even in darkness like this, without my mask for you. You really will wonder who has made history.'

There was no resting then, of course. I stood. 'Please, Gado!' Using his name was easy in darkness, impossible when the coloured panes and — I imagined — the dark eyes were before me, though the eyes were there now, masked or unmasked, always there. 'I'll have to trust that you will share what helps us all; anything that might help. Can we go?'

'Of course,' the voice came, and I realised he was already standing, though I had not heard him rise.

We returned to the ship and, though nothing more was said, I held back until he was aboard and had vanished below, not wanting to steal looks from those naked eyes that he did not wish to give. But when he appeared a few minutes later, he was still unmasked. His eyes were like beads of obsidian as he joined me on the poop and handed

me a scrap of paper. On it was drawn Ideogram 55 of the
I Ching.

'This one of the sixty-four ideograms tells us
something, I think.'

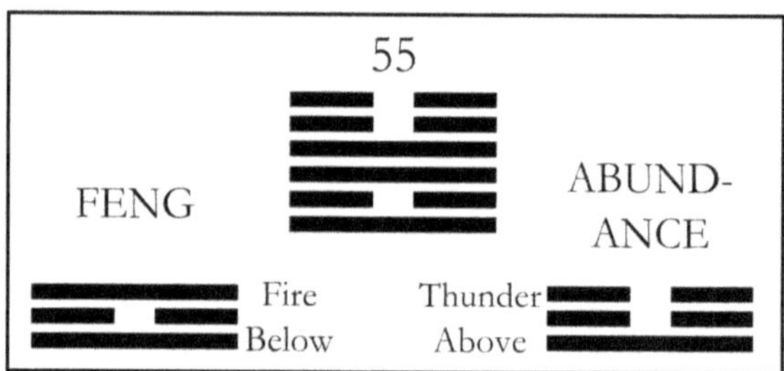

I stared at it in wonder, seeing there the regional
arrangement of the National arcologies that had become
so familiar to me, now revealed in its full meaning.

'You see the clear message, the careful and ancient
pattern of it,' Bascoeur said. 'Not the random regional
groupings we are meant to think. The first trigram is "The
Thunder above". This' — he pointed to the other — ' "The
Sun below", would tell us something about why Namarkon
is named for an ancient Dreamtime god of the Gunwinggu.
In literal terms, giving Thunder pre-eminence, he clearly
champions the tribes over your Sun of Nation, which is
interesting. Not one oubliette is Ab'O, Tom, not one. We
are all Nationals or approved Internationals. That is why
I can believe Namarkon is among us. There are messages
everywhere. This clever enemy seems to tell us at every
opportunity that he exists, no doubt out of delight at being
immortal, at simply existing and knowing he is unassailable
in his maze of history and fact.'

I missed the significance of what Bascoeur had said
at first. I was still too overwhelmed by the thought of the
National arcologies conforming to the Feng ideogram,

being located according to a secret deployment plan, one unknown to the National architects and surveyors. It was incredible. But then I reacted to his final words, struck suddenly by what he had acknowledged.

'You agree then? Not a physical labyrinth? A notional one?'

'Why not? I cannot deny it. Though we duplicate material and have different personal priorities as individuals, we oubliettes are a library, as you say.'

'Your mask is packed away now? Insulated?'

He nodded. 'Partly why I agreed to remove it. I grant as possible all that you suspect. "And the likeness of the firmament upon the heads of the living creatures was as the colour of the terrible crystal, stretched forth over their heads above." Also from Ezekial. Captain, I need your viewpoint, what is still a comparative detachment. If Namarkon hides among the thirty-six, there may be far far more of a labyrinth for me than for you. Now we should rest. You will not see me unmasked again. Not before Whitehead and certainly not after.'

'Thank you is all I have, Lord Gado.' The honorific seemed appropriate now.

'It is more than enough,' he said, and passed me another slip of paper. 'Here is tomorrow's course. I will not appear on deck until afternoon. But speak to Truan McBanus. As hetaera and a daughter trusted with secret information, I believe she would have been a diligent shadow in her father's library. Good night.'

'Good night,' I said, and watched him go below.

At first I thought I would need to wait till morning to speak to Truan, for the ship was quiet, with no-one visible when Bascoeur left me on the quarterdeck.

That silence had been a false thing when we first returned from our walk, how it is when young children pretend to parents that they are asleep. Certainly Scarbo would have been awake and listening for familiar footsteps on the deck, for the low steady rhythm of voices. For a fact Meg would have been peering out the ports, watching and listening too, wanting to be at the rail when we returned but not daring so much.

Shannon was more pragmatic; he'd been at the helm most of the day and had Scarbo to worry for him. No doubt he slept easily in his cabin.

It was Truan who approached from the bow, a night-time re-enactment of her appearance earlier in the day.

'There's coffee below,' she said. 'Or tisn, if you prefer. Meg said I should wait.'

I had to smile. 'Nothing surprises me anymore, Truan. Tisn would help right now.'

She went below and soon returned carrying a tray with two steaming mugs and a plate of cold meat, biscuits and cheese. We shared this as we sat in deck-chairs out of the cool wind, watching the night. For a time there was only the sound of cables thrumming and sand hissing against the hull.

'I don't know what to tell you, Captain,' she said at last, unprompted it seemed, though Bascoeur may have had Meg urge it. 'Toban was a bookman. He had no enemies, few secrets.'

'Bascoeur felt you might have been told things, that's all. The names of other book conservationists, things like that. I'm trusting you would have given us anything that might help.'

She shook her head, but it was for her earlier comment. 'Toban was a generous soul, Tom. He knew of your search already, but hesitated at first. Then he decided he would be available to you after all.'

'Among the Coloured Captains, in my crew, we make that family. Like your Club Hetaera.'

She held her cup close to her lips, turning her face to the side, hiding the play of emotion in her eyes. 'He told me no other names.'

'I'm sorry, Truan.'

'It was quick. It took them both. There was that.'

We were silent then, shielded by the lift of the stern assembly, sitting in the dim glow of the deck lights and looking down the length of Rynosseros towards the bow. We listened to the wind ghosting about the rails and transoms, the hiss of sand, one moment barely there, the next sudden and strong.

Then something she had said came back to me. 'He hesitated at first. Do you know why he changed his mind?' I kept looking ahead but knew her gaze was on me.

'He was in the library. I was doing some research with him — one of the tribal academies wanted something. Marquand phoned to say he had referred you. Toban said he wouldn't open the door.'

'He commented afterwards?'

'Yes. Much as he was concerned about your predicament, he couldn't afford to antagonise the tribes or someone like Chiras Namarkon.'

'He used that name?'

'Yes. There were his friends at the universities to consider. Helping you might compromise them, lead to the cancellation of privileges, visiting and access rights —'

'And access to illegal tech. Gain-monitors.'

She almost smiled, but the other emotions were too pressing, too immediate. 'He's a scholar, Tom. He was...

he needed —'

'And then?' I spoke quickly to distract her.

'Another call. I was out in my studio and didn't hear any of it. When I asked, he said Marquand had called again. He would see you after all.'

'But nothing else about Namarkon?'

'Nothing. I'd never heard the name before.'

'No other calls?'

'Only yours. I went out into the garden.'

She turned her face away again, looking off into the night.

'Truan — ?'

'I can continue. I want to talk about this. I need to.'

'Did he seem worried?'

'No. But he wanted to discuss something with my mother — in the library. Why?'

'I'm betting Marquand made no second call.'

She faced me. 'Then who did? Bascoeur? Namarkon? You don't think — ?'

'All I know is that the second call changed his mind, persuaded him to see us, and that less than an hour later there was the strike. Truan, another few minutes and Ben and I would have been in the library too. Namarkon could have had us all. No more threat.'

She stood and moved into the thrust of the wind, her hair blowing wild. 'He wanted to warn you off!'

I stood too. 'Or the strike was pre-arranged, booked into a busy tribal schedule. Your father may have discovered something.'

It was finally too much.

'Can we leave this now?'

I hesitated, then told myself that this was why she had come, stowed away, committed herself. Any answers were as much for her as for me. 'I'm also talking to someone who wants to be involved. Who has plans, objectives.'

'Say it! Who might well be an agent of this Namarkon. You must have thought it!'

I hadn't and it startled me. 'Thanks for waiting up,' I said at last, simple truth. 'After being with Bascoeur, I needed... something.'

Her gaze held mine. 'I'm on the edge of this. I need to act and can't. Possibly I'm just drawn to what is at the centre.'

'All any of us can do, Truan.'

Without another word, she turned and went below.

I checked that the deck alarms were activated in case intruders came — unlikely under normal circumstances but a definite possibility now: a quick guerilla action to achieve here what the Namuren fighters on the Gentian Walk had not. Then I watched the tektite swarms, felt the wind grab at the hull, and thought of what the day had been and how things stood.

There was so much. Too much. The tribes waiting, the comsats in orbit, synced and tethered, watching. If Namarkon owned one, had access to them all, what chance was there?

Perhaps he waited for a facility to clear its roster, needed permission for another strike from jealous tribes only grudgingly persuaded to serve his needs. Perhaps he didn't need to use that final tactic again if only to protect his man, Bascoeur? He would find other ways.

But what, what, could induce this entity to reveal himself? Dewi had been a scientist turned trader, smuggler, religious fanatic, a mad creature drawn by a need to survive, to transcend and extend himself. He had worked through agents; at least had used a system which could be infiltrated by the likes of specialists like Pederson. Here there were clues, tantalising leads, and how easy it was to direct attention to those when so little else was on hand. It led to Whitehead, but would Namarkon hide in such plain sight, lay himself bare to the tribes? Unless, as Bascoeur said, as a test. Chiras Namarkon could be anywhere, not even in Australia for that matter. And what if the tribes were watching, meeting his demands, accommodating his requests?

It seemed ever more hopeless, there under the stars in the blowing dark.

From Whitehead — where? To Mekkis? And then? To the other arcologies? Back to Twilight Beach?

As often happens at such moments during watch, I found myself considering the plaque on the helm.

Such special words there, echoing Meg's, casting me as the questing Alexander.

And Alexandrian Book! Bascoeur's Knot, that Gordian Knot!

That story. A true event, who could say? Alexander at Gordium confronted with the chariot of the great Phrygian king, faced with the knot binding the yoke to the shaft. The young Macedonian knowing the legend that whoever unravelled it would rule all Asia, knowing the legend and needing to make it, even that, part of his destiny. Then cutting the great Knot asunder, or pulling the pin free, whatever really happened that day, winning, transcending by doing!

But not even that bold action automatically meant winning, not then, not here, not now.

I found myself secretly longing for Truan to return, someone to take me away from these thoughts, kept listening for a door closing, footsteps on the companionway, imagined those sounds again and again.

I smiled, catching myself, then sat, just being in the night, until the constellations had turned halfway round the sky and footsteps did come, and the voice saying my name was Shannon's, there on deck to take the next watch.

9.

Scarbo took us on our way at 0600, using photonic parafoils until the morning winds came up fresh and strong. Then he put twenty kites above those bright inflatables, the perfect morning for testing the more abstruse patterns in his old kitesman's bible.

When I arrived on deck at 0815, the sky had our colours spread across it: shapes like tethered dragons, crowns, talismans, origami castles, bursts of folded light. There were Sodes and Demis, Chinese Hawks, Holkoyd Stars, even our Samian Ladder spread out link by splendid link, vibrant, beautifully controlled, and there, in front, our signature Rhino head, blue on ochre. Rynosseros sang from its heart, as Scarbo called it, so finely balanced in its finery that it sat on 110 k's with no yawing at all.

'A madman in another life punishing this one!' Shannon cried, smile flashing in his dark beard. 'He woke up dangerous, Tom. Can't help himself! Wouldn't hear of breakfast, wanted to see what the two of us could do.'

I laughed, feeling my spirits lift, cherishing it all. 'If there's turbulence, you'll take us to hell gift-wrapped!'

Scarbo nudged Rob. 'Told you! Worries likes a bridegroom!'

We grinned madly at the sky, sharing this sight we never tired of, Rynosseros fully dressed for the hot dry winds of the inland.

Truan appeared on deck then, and Meg Solles a short time later.

The notary climbed to the quarterdeck. 'Lord Gado is doing assimilations,' she said, and I caught her glance at the words on the helm plaque. It was a chance.

'You're his friend too, Meg. We have to unravel this Knot, share what we can.'

'I listen to what he says about you and how he says it,' she said. 'So far I'm not serving two masters.'

It was easy sailing then, upwards of 90 k's on a surprisingly good Road for one shown only as a broken line on the old tribal maps. There was nothing but the hot sun, the glare, the wind in our kites and cables, the empty distances. From time to time a belltree marked its lonely stretch of Road, sounding its joyous waysong as we plunged by, or a stand of land-coral offered its barbs and hooks like a time-locked dancer, weathered fans aloft. Now and then a line of distant hills rose up like a sea-creature sounding, lingering, sinking away again. There were hours when a single cloud would wander into view, cross the wide blue sky like a vagrant dream and finally disappear.

By early afternoon, there were more ranges ahead, low folds of purples, reds and browns against the sky. The Road ran parallel for a time, then turned towards them, suggesting that a pass would lead us to the plain beyond.

'An hour beyond those,' Meg said, pointing to where Road and hills met in a ribbon of sun-shadow. 'Whitehead is —'

But Shannon shouted from com. 'Bogie astern! Extreme range and closing!'

Helm scan confirmed it; we had a pursuer.

'After us?' Meg asked, close by the controls.

I had to remember that she spoke for Bascoeur. 'Hard to say. At that speed, possibly. Or a courier. There's no attempt to hide, no insulated hull. Nothing to say it's other than a tribal ship on an urgent mission about to overtake. We'll know soon enough.'

'Surely not out here, Captain! Not near Whitehead!'

'Meg, we can't arm till we're sure. If it's tracked by comsat, we're scanned and accountable. Loft 'em, Ben! See if she gains!'

For the next half-hour we ran toward the old red hills, until the distance between the ships dwindled and an image finally showed on scan through our churning rooster-tail.

'Bogie confirmed!' Shannon cried. At the same instant, scan managed a lucky fix, no more than three seconds through our tail-cloud, but it gave configuration.

It was a warship closing on us, an armoured charvi, probably a 130-footer, plates adorned with suns and stars, bold chevrons and faded totemic war-signs, a veteran ship from appearances, running under thirty or more battle-kites and wearing what veteran kitesmen called a 'crown of thorns'. A clutch of death-lamps on long-tether flashed hard light at the top of their drab functional canopy, rotating pulses from one to the next — a psychological trick — juggling death like hot stones from fist to eager fist.

A terrifying sight, one that no amount of experience could divest of its chilling elemental force: a ship racing to engage, angry and committed.

The calm you feel at such times is part of an only response, the result of training and discipline, counters to desperation. But it also has something of the no-choice bravado of a fairground ride about it. You do because there's nothing else.

If you are careful, composed, patient in the frantic rush of events, you remember that size can mean nothing, that firepower need not count. When there is speed and dust and stones the size of skulls close by, the off-chance of gullies like gaping mouths, when there is judgement and luck, inspiration created when fear of death elevates daring into a gift from the Fates, you act as if you cannot fail.

In such panic wrapped in calm, I looked instinctively for Strengi and Rim and young Hammon on the deck, remembered how it was and shouted new names.

'Truan! Deck lenses there and there! Meg! Help bring down the Sodes! Down or dump, Ben! No time!'

We donned ship-com headsets then, proscribed tech for Nationals usually, even Coloured ones, but on loan from Otamas and the Chitalice, and did quick confirmations. Shannon was already at the cable-boss, helping Ben dump the display kites for obstruction, hoping to foul our pursuer's canopy or wheels. Both men were ahead of my words every time, living parts of the ship.

Bascoeur was on deck too, climbing to the helm, mask flashing under his hood.

'There!' I pointed to the dark heart of the cloud behind us.

'Namuren,' Bascoeur said, using his mask to read the brightest of the signs. 'Your friend Ephan's family. A vendetta ship.'

I accepted it, not daring to look away from the Road and the controls. 'Namarkon pulls the strings here, Gado. Tribal puppets dance. They have no choice.'

'Run for Whitehead! There are defences.'

'Laser?' I was prepared for anything the Antique Men had, especially if they were owned in whole or part by

Namarkon. But this was Namarkon, I reminded myself, this Namuren ship, as surely as the mirror ships had been Dewi's. We were meant to die here, it seemed. Not at Chano, here!

'No hi-tech,' Bascoeur said. 'But lenses, harpoons, cable-shot. Hurry! The Road is safe.'

'I need to be sure!'

'Safe,' he said. 'Use power. Whitehead will pay!'

I switched in the cells, heard the whine of the big Pabar engines in the platform.

And just as well. Flashes of hard light from the Namuren death-lamps were snatching our remaining kites from the sky. I felt the heat on my neck and shoulders, picking at Rynosseros's stern.

Truan and Meg were doing their best with our own weapons, but they lacked training and experience. Now and then a kite did vanish from our pursuer's canopy, but those kites were largely for show on a powered ship, vendetta display, so it counted for little.

'Smokescreen?' I asked Ben at the cable-boss.

He shook his head. 'Cross-wind. We'll lose it.'

He was right. A last resort.

The hills were close. Bascoeur pointed ahead. 'Five minutes! There's a road-chain.'

It changed everything. 'Should we slow?' I thought of the heavy stretch of links across the Road, the winches for lifting them to hull height.

'Recessed,' Bascoeur said. 'I've sent word. They'll raise it behind us.'

'No!'

'What?' Bascoeur's masked face was unreadable.

'Gado, Namarkon is behind and Namarkon could well be ahead. We are rushing towards a road-chain at top speed. That ship doesn't have to catch us; it only has to drive us!'

'They're my people!'

'It would need just one agent with access to the chain equipment or the Whitehead overrides.'

'What then? What do we do?'

'The terrain before the chain? Broken?'

Bascoeur hesitated, checking stats, schemata, memory. 'Before the chain housing, no. But the Road turns before it so the final approach cannot be seen. Just before the pass.'

'Ben, smokescreen in two minutes!' I said and pointed. 'Single dump to that turn. Time it. They'll think we're hiding the chain, hope to use it ourselves. We slow and leave the Road.'

In the dust and thunder, the fierce concentration, those minutes vanished like seconds. Then the dark billows were there, first broken dumps, then streaming out, rolling and dense, torn by crosswinds but still making a brief black night in our rooster-tail.

'Rocks — two minutes!' Shannon cried, back at com. And we began powering down, preparing to pull off the Road.

'They'll be slowing too,' Scarbo said, which gave me the idea, inspiration or folly.

'Gado, Whitehead has full com capability?'

'Of course.'

'Call your Angels! Tell someone you trust to send a broad signal: "Angel interference. Chain down and locked. Catch and destroy. Namarkon." Blanket the frequencies, maximum power, so nothing local gets through.'

Bascoeur did not answer. He stood at the stern rail making the link.

The rocks were visible now, foothills and cast-offs, the broken detritus of the range, so close, full and ochre-red against the sky. I could see where the Road made its long sweep into them. Scan showed nothing, but a chain could be camouflaged, insulated.

'Smoke for the turn, Ben!' I said. 'Hide us!'

'Nearly out!' Scarbo answered. 'Wish us luck!'

Rynosseros was at 60 and slowing, kites down or lost, stored power carrying us.

'Done!' Bascoeur said, with us again. 'Unless Namarkon intervenes further.'

'I say he won't. Vendetta ship and agents can be pre-arranged. I doubt much else can. If a broadcast is overridden, then we know Namarkon is at Whitehead. Tell your fellow Angels that.'

'We shall see, Captain,' he said. And went silent again.

We made the turn, 30 k's and slowing noticeably as we pulled to the Road's edge, then off onto a verge of stones. The ship lurched and shook, the travel platform handling the torment as best it could.

We stopped with a final lurch. Shannon and I ran to the lenses; Scarbo fed out the last of our screen, then put four lamps aloft, tethered low, sparkling with stored power.

There was nothing else to do then but watch the pall of smoke, holding longer than expected, penned in the lee of the red hills.

We could hear our pursuer approaching, shaking the earth and the rocks and the sky, becoming all of it.

Then it was there, thundering past like a dragon, splendid in its markings, battle-kites and signatures out in front like a brace of hounds. I thought to glimpse her captain on the quarterdeck, trusting Namarkon, whatever hold cold Chiras had on that luckless family.

The chain was up. Even as we flashed what few shots we could at the fleeing vessel, we heard the long cruel tearing, a roar like the world ending amid these dusty hills, a thunder that went on and on as ship and lives rolled into sudden, shattering oblivion.

Truan, Meg and Bascoeur had probably seen nothing like it in their lives. They stood staring, the faces of both women drained of colour, Bascoeur's hidden behind his panes, but still, still.

Ben, Rob and I had seen such things and suffered it as probably only sand-ship sailors can. There can be nothing like a ship-death, not ever, certainly not one done so shamefully, ruthlessly, without choice or chance.

I turned to Bascoeur. 'The ship and captain, who were they?' I knew he would have the data.

'Leave it for now, Captain.'

'Tell me!'

'The ship was Eagle.'

'The captain?'

'Ephan Sky Namuren,' he said, while thunder, smoke and flame played around the bloody hills. It was as if Villa Chano had died yet again, a single scream drawn full and mighty to become the ruin of all the world.

10.

There were no survivors. We left the shattered, smoking remains of Eagle and passed the damaged chain-station, moved on until we ran along an unhindered Road towards far ranges in the east.

There, out on the plain, Whitehead loomed in the late morning sun, at first like a part of the landscape, eccentrically wind-formed and weather-made, then nothing like it. The walls were too smooth, too even, the great mainwall a monstrous thing, a wedge of concrete and glass lifting from the desert fastness, shimmering in the heat like something ready to become alive, already testing its senses.

Closer still, it had much of the quality of an ancient monastery about it. As Rynosseros moved in under the wind shadow, we could see some of the inhabitants: small groups of trainees and attendants, young and old, softly spoken men and women to look at them, tending modest orchards and foundries, trimming the lawns and walks, sitting together in open-air refectories and watching our approach. There was the occasional flash of an oubliette mask on the high ramps and balconies, a sudden glint of sunlight on figures crossing sunny causeways and sheltered terraces. Though we saw no children or adolescents, whatever else this place was, it was home to these people.

When we had disembarked and entered the rock-melt folds of the outer precincts, we saw that these citizens were mostly older people, grey-haired and peaceful-looking, clearly deferential whenever an Antique Man came near. Unlike the robed, masked oubliettes, these folk wore soft sandals and fatigues of natural weave. On their temples they had small neat scars.

'Salvation Moons,' Bascoeur explained for Truan, Rob and Scarbo's benefit. 'Ritual marks. Not as ominous as they look. Those who train and serve or work in the library here choose to take the ancient lobotomy mark as a sign of self-denial. A fitting inversion. They are the Good Friends. Speak with them as you wish.'

We moved on from the walled gardens and irrigation allotments into the great learning halls. There we were shown rooms full of books: storage vaults for crystals, motes, blanks and beads, self-powered Illuminated texts, true-paper books and other retroforms in careful environments.

It was awesome, impressive in both size and the extent of the care and dedication shown. There were scriptoria where new texts were produced and old ones copied, incept areas for the international publishing operation using the famous blue flower imprint of the Antique Men.

Then, once Meg had led the others off to their assigned quarters, Bascoeur took me high into the blade to the Meeting Hall, a huge stone chamber with a long central table arranged across it and thirty-six carved chairs, empty now, like a table setting for the Last Supper. At the far end, a floor to ceiling window-wall — true-vision, not relayed image — gave out on an infinity of warm air and rich golden light.

'Tonight,' Bascoeur said, addressing me in softened tones appropriate to such a place, 'you will address the Assembly here and tell them what you believe is happening.'

'But then Namarkon will know everything, if we allow —'

'It is no inquisition, Captain. You will say only what you wish, only what you judge fitting. See it as we do. If Namarkon is one of us — or all of us for that matter — then that too is a fact of the reality we live. As Angels, we may deal with it if we can demonstrate Alexandrian Book, a betrayal of our fundamental purpose.'

'This has to be a formality then, Gado. Such a meeting is redundant if the masks are nanotech CPUs.'

'The information they have has come to them only through the Angels,' Bascoeur said. 'Remember that.

We have held back some facts until we are reasonably certain.'

'You believe you have. Your masks could be telling it all.'

'Be moderate. It is why we were chosen, and why there are four. Our masks are special. Add your intuitions and good judgement. Help us prove this.'

'If I can. I will if I can.'

Meg was in the passage outside waiting to take me down to the others. Bascoeur made a small gesture of farewell and walked in the opposite direction. As Meg and I moved along the hallway to the elevators, I looked back to see him vanish through a doorway at the far end.

'If I were to rush back there now, Meg, and follow him through that door, what would I find?'

Meg's hood was down, her short dark hair adding at least that colour to the paleness of her face. She glanced back along the hallway too.

'You would find a very tired man, probably unmasked, sitting before a window, I should think, knowing Lord Gado. The door will be unlocked, like most of the doors here. You could verify this easily; I would wait. But he will be preparing himself for tonight's Assembly. Before you join them later, there will be questions, an accounting for why details have been withheld, why he went unmasked onto the desert with you last night, broke that rule again.'

'Again?'

'Yes. He went unmasked to and from Saldy's, remember, though at least there no-one knew. That was to help you as much as himself. Before the general accounting this evening, the other Angels will demand their own. They will be more sympathetic, true, but more rigorous because they are more directly accountable themselves.'

We entered the elevator and dropped to the residential levels.

'Perhaps he does not know what the Knot means,' I said, as the car completed its vertical journey and began the transverse leg out to the dormitories and dining areas.

'Is that surprising?' she said.

'Yes, it's surprising. Everything is surprising and suspect. I can allow for secret knowledge in the Order, but once you grant the concept of Alexandrian Book, then Gado's not knowing something like that seems very significant.'

'Surely it would be like you questioning the windmill origins of the Nation sign,' she said. 'You don't think to do it because you think you already know the answer.' And she smiled her tight grudging smile, though this time parts of it reached her eyes, changing them. She believed I genuinely cared for him, at least there was that.

It struck me then, watching her, that something about Meg Solles was different, as if recent events had worked their magic, extended her, changed her. It was as if she had discovered something vital about herself, had perhaps put Meg Solles and Gado Bascoeur into a new perspective.

'It still hurts? Loving him,' I said.

The smile vanished from mouth and eyes both, but the Elf's usual quick anger did not return. She studied the indicator light, went to speak, hesitated, then seemed to decide something.

'It's like the Knot you are trying to unravel,' she said, and the sudden force, passion, maturity, in her voice were as startling as anything I had experienced over the last few days. Never again would I take her for merely the notary with Bascoeur, the angry figure she disguised herself as.

'Long ago I put it to him — why the androgyny, why ritual and custom dictated the need for a man-woman, the need to breed hermaphrodites to guide the oubliettes? What gain, what symbol?'

'Did he answer? Can you share this?'

'He touched his mask, the flower and the patch. "The answer is here," he said. "In our beginnings." I didn't press further.'

The car slowed and stopped, opened onto a dining area, a softly lit space barely a quarter the size of the Gaza lobby, with a dozen tables occupied by as many of the Good Friends, eating, talking quietly. There were plantings placed about, low music playing. The walls were decorated with tapestries and carvings, information storage webs made here at Whitehead: the precious 'datafacts'.

'You knew he moved L75 VGS?' I asked.

'He did that the moment your Council requested a meeting with the Antique Men. Just after Dewi Dammo was defeated. He needed to investigate first — his job as Angel.'

'Did he damage that Book?'

'Would you harm Rynosseros? He found it damaged at Crayasse, moved it on to Turker to gain more time. He was hunting Namarkon too, anticipating your line of enquiry. Finally, he judged it time to meet you. The other Angels, the Assembly, were wanting answers. Come. Here are your friends.'

Rob, Ben and Truan had had time to shower and rest, to change out of their desert clothes into fresh fatigues. They came into the refectory from a different elevator, and joined Meg and me at the servery counters, though Meg did not eat with us. She excused herself and went to join a group of fellow notaries at an adjoining table.

It was just as well. During our meal we needed to discuss recent events: the parts played by Gado and Meg, the run to the road-chain ahead of Eagle, the remarkable fact that one of the old arcologies was more than a library, was operational at least in part and occupied by Nationals after all.

'We've seen very few inhabitants,' Shannon said. 'Just a handful really. Still no children.'

Scarbo agreed. 'There's probably no more than one or two hundred. Makes you wonder what we'd find at the other arcologies.'

'It may come to that,' I told them, 'though I believe we would find nothing. There's an Assembly tonight. Bascoeur has to account for his actions. Meg hasn't said as much, but he may be replaced.'

'Punished?' Truan asked.

'Brought to order. Denied us. I'm to speak on his behalf, I think. Whatever happens, be patient and stay ready. See to the ship. Use the time. Eagle responded to a signal supposedly from Namarkon and that signal probably came from Whitehead. Someone here, one or more, all of them for all we know, is in league with Namarkon. We know that much. I'm hoping to take a journey.'

'To Mekkis?' Truan said.

'If they'll take me. I believe they know where it is.'

'Tom —'

'If I can,' I told her. 'I doubt they'll let you. And, forgive me, I owe that choice to Ben and Rob too.'

'But if they die in this, Rynosseros loses far more than her captain. If I die, I will have done all that I can do.'

I studied her face, this ghost that had haunted my watch. 'You're right. I'll ask them.'

Her features relaxed into a weary smile of gratitude.

'We'll look about,' Scarbo said. 'You rest, Tom. Room J178.'

Ben was right. After the day we'd had, I did need sleep. I excused myself and went to find the J section.

The room was small but comfortable, with a window overlooking a modest garden courtyard and walls painted in narrowing bands of soft sand colours. Without noticing they did so at first, the striations led the eye to the window and beyond, out into the flowers and bright air, brought those things in to me along that same axis: an easement loop.

I showered in the alcove, then settled on the futon-style bed and watched first the sky above the garden, then the datafact on the doorward wall where the soft easement lines began. Before I quite knew it, I was caught in the ten-cycle breathing pattern it induced and slipped gently into sleep.

A sequence of low chimes sounded at 2021; an accompanying strip of soft lighting showed that the garden was dark. Night had fallen over Whitehead.

A voice spoke from a mesh beside my bed. 'Please prepare yourself, Captain. Meg Solles will arrive in twenty minutes. The Assembly has already begun.'

That stole the rest of my torpor. I showered again, dressed in my sandsman fatigues and opened the door to Meg when she knocked fifteen, not twenty minutes later.

She led me up into the blade again, back to the Meeting Hall, then left me alone outside the big doors, saying I would be summoned at the proper time.

That didn't happen for an hour, but finally the doors did open and one of the Good Friends appeared, an old woman who smiled and told me to go in.

I entered and found myself facing the figures seated behind the long table. All were masked, all had their hands before them, lightly clasped or resting close to ritual weapons: tschinkes, archimenters, galvanis, espandos and petronels. Only these faux-antique storage-traps differed from one to the next; the figures who owned them wore identical robes, identical masks, the same flower at the chest below the shoulder, the same Knot pattern high on the sleeve.

Behind them the window-wall shone with full night, folded and re-folded into roils and depths by the optical properties of the glass. More than ever, the scene resembled some fantastic re-creation of the Last Supper, a coven of cathedral kings and queens celebrating a mass for Mother Night pressing close beyond them.

Which of the oubliettes was Gado, I couldn't tell. The masks offered no clue. Side on, their traps looked more similar than they actually were, the silver-chased stocks, the curlicues, scrolls and hatchings of the brightwork gave nothing.

'We are working on Namarkon for you,' one neutral male-female voice said. The hands of the figure fourth from the left seemed to have moved; I took that to be the speaker.'

'Thank you. We begin to set a fair price.'

'That is provocative to say,' came what seemed like the same neutral voice, though this time a different figure moved his hands, actually moved fingers briefly and slowly over the espando in from of him — of her, there was no telling. But then the Angels were androgynes according to Meg. What of the rest?

'It is not meant to be anything more than a statement

of how I see it, a reminder that there are two scales of payment at work here, two reckonings. I may be speaking to Namarkon, remember. You, those masks, those traps before you, that window for all I know.'

'Bascoeur brought you here,' a voice said, no identifying trace seen or imagined. Were the Angels the ones speaking?

'Yes, and I helped kill a ship and its crew to let Lord Gado do it. Whitehead would never be worth Rynosseros. I must wonder if this is worth Eagle.'

'Understood, Captain. What can you tell us?'

'You know my conversations with Bascoeur.'

'Except when he removed his mask for you.'

'I don't necessarily believe that. I'm granting implant capability or —'

'No!' The word snapped and echoed like a slap, a whip-crack of denial filling the room.

'Very well,' I said, accepting it. 'Except then. Are you, any of you, or is anything known by you of, Namarkon?'

The row of figures sat very still, thirty-six watching shapes. The hands did not move.

'No,' the single voice answered. 'Nothing, no-one known to us.'

'I'll assume that is true as well. I'll assume, too, that there is knowledge I cannot have. Inner Circle. Rituals and secrets of the Antique Men. Your masks, your signs, so much. I'll assume you know where Mekkis is, which, as "Power" in the Feng ideogram, you must allow, is a clear path. Today we fought on Rynosseros for our lives. In Twilight Beach, a tribesman, a much better swordsman than I, nearly killed me. I saw a cloud at the end of a kitana blade and it was everything. I find that man is now dead; my life dies about me in such pieces. He might have been a friend someday. Certainly, personally, it seems he did not choose to be my enemy. But Namarkon moves for Namarkon, and individuals don't matter.

'Like you, I would like to stand back from history, or be involved in it only as far as I can, here in my hands, at the ends of my fingers. You know where Mekkis is. You know why it is being obliterated from knowledge and memory; you know why it stands in the Feng pattern. Or you suspect why you don't know. Please,' I said, using Truan's words, 'take me there so I can have done all that I can do.'

'Very well,' a voice said. 'But you alone, Captain. On a closed ship, with you below deck in a somnium so its whereabouts remain unknown. We will help you to help us; help you do everything possible. How does that fit your reckoning?'

'I believe you wanted me to request it formally. I believe that now you probably owe me a great deal.'

'This interesting viewpoint of yours. In a few words: we all seek Namarkon.'

'Done!' I said. 'If it can be done. But thank you for letting me come here tonight and allowing me to see you. I consider it a great honour.'

'It was necessary. Thank you, Captain.'

Behind me, the doors opened. Meg was waiting. I took a final glance at the figures seated at the long table, then turned and left the hall.

11.

They woke me soon after midnight, two of the Good Friends did, both quiet gentle men who apologised and asked me politely to dress and meet them down on the mooring plat. No breakfast, not for a somnium ride, so I went hungry to the rendezvous.

Standing near Rynosseros on a battered six-wheeled travel platform and unkited at this hour was a small dark hull, what I took to be a Whitehead supply charvi, brought out and readied for a voyage of a different kind.

'So the oubliettes do own ships,' I said, when Bascoeur and Meg joined me on the wide concrete apron.

'None for far-voyaging,' Bascoeur said, masked and robed, holding his archimenter. 'But a couple to take us to the shipping lanes so we can make connections for our travels. We own Mekkis though, Tom. It is deserted, it is ruined, but we can go there when we wish. Our only long voyage.'

'We travel alone?'

'The three of us and these two, David and Gral. They are good sailors.'

'What if Namarkon strikes at us? I'm below in a sleeve —'

'No,' Bascoeur said. 'Part of our trade-off with the tribes, this route. They touch Tybo and they lose our resources. More to the point, we give extra help to one faction over another. It is complex.'

I wanted to ask him how it had gone with the Angels earlier, how it had been for him shut away with the other thirty-five oubliettes, but David came over then and respectfully suggested we set off.

The five of us boarded Tybo, and Gral brought costly stored power to the engines.

'You are privileged,' I said as the old vessel made its way out of the lee of the mainwall. The first morning winds rocked the hull though no kites were aloft. In the eastern sky, a faint band of light marked the beginnings of day.

'It's time,' David said gently, his Moons two glinting

smiles above his own. 'Please. The chamber is ready.'

I glanced once more at Whitehead, an unliving mass of darkness against the pale line of yellow-grey squeezing over the edge of the world, then followed the Good Friend below to the somnium in the aft cabin. I used the toilet, undressed, then settled into the comfortable sleeve of the pod. David fitted the contacts and prepared to lower the lid.

'Will it be long?' I asked.

'This day and part of another,' he said. 'It's not far, but the terrain becomes difficult.'

I nodded and watched through the clear plastic of the cowl as he brought it down. And knew nothing more than that.

Until it lifted, David still smiling there, smiling there again.

'What happened?' I asked, though I immediately knew because of the leaden feeling in my arms and legs, the lethargy and terrible thirst, the sensitivity to the metabolic assists.

'We are close to our destination,' David said. 'Join us for breakfast when you can. It's quite a sight.'

It was late morning when I reached the quarterdeck. Nothing could be seen but rocky terrain, a low range all around us, though now and then there were glimpses of far desert and of turns in the Road ahead as it started to take us down again.

Twelve kites on four cables made a modest canopy, giving Tybo that special dimension all charvis need to be complete. I felt better seeing the drab inflatables, the tattered and patched wind-thieves, the solitary Sode like the Star of

Bethlehem flung out ahead on a thirty-metre tether.

Gral had the helm; Meg and David tended the cable-boss, jockeying the big blue star for wind-change. Bascoeur stood by a breakfast table set up on the commons. There was fruit and sweet buns, steaming barragon coffee, a waiting chair.

'Twenty minutes, Captain,' Bascoeur said as I ate and drank, welcoming the vivid tastes and smells, the warmth of the sun, the wind on my skin. Being on Tybo meant everything right then, making our way through these ancient hills, through hot sun and dust, passing the lonely totemic shaft of a belltree every so often.

'There!' Gral cried, pointing.

Between the bluffs, I saw our destination out on the plain before us, ten, fifteen k's distant, with hills beyond, a shimmering phantom line at the edge of the world.

Again, there was a mainwall, though even at this distance I could see this one was damaged, scarred, as if struck from space at some time in its past. Still complete, still impressive and powerful-looking in the clear desert air, but showing a great wound and surrounded by indistinct shapes, a crust of forms.

Gral handed me binoculars. Through them the scar in the mainwall became a vivid gash, and the untidy crumble resolved into ruined outbuildings and pitted approach roads, a wilderness of broken field domes and fallen revetments.

'Who did this?' I asked Gral, Bascoeur, whoever would answer, feeling the rush of deep underlying rage all Nationals felt when reminded of what had once been and what now was.

'Mekkis was the example,' Bascoeur said. 'The Nationals would not obey at first.'

'If this was Namarkon's original home, then I can understand his determination to become Lightning God and control such powers.'

'You speak from emotion, wanting to see him as pro-National. More mythopoesis! He uses what suits his needs, surely. Think of Chano.'

'Yes.' I put aside the glasses and stood. 'Let me help with the kites, Gral.'

'Take the helm,' Gral said. 'Be the first State of Nation captain to sail into Mekkis in two hundred years.'

I nodded my thanks and went to the controls. Slowly, with the great blue Sode out before it, the wind-thieves clustering and weaving like remoras about a shark, Tybo reached the desert plain and the broken arcology waiting there.

'That is the Blasted Gate,' Bascoeur told me, pointing to what was just that, a dark maw in a wall that had suffered terrible heat and shock waves in its past. 'Draw up in front.'

I did so, easing Tybo in close to the mainwall while David and Gral brought home the kites, wrestling down the Sode first because of the unstable wind-flow around the great structure.

'A fitting home for an immortal spirit,' I said. 'Is there a labyrinth here, something to pass for one and waste more time?'

' "A labyrinth to amase the senses," ' Bascoeur said, not rising to the sarcasm. 'Shakespeare. From the Old English "amasian", to stupefy. Be patient, Tom.'

But amid such ruin, feeling the old anger, it wasn't easy.

'Or is it to be books, more clues?'

'Please. At Whitehead you mentioned Inner Circle. Rituals and secrets. Of course there are. You formally requested this; that is what got you here, the only thing. Please wait.'

The Good Friends remained on the ship while Gado, Meg and I entered the great main-building. As we reached the first of the empty ramps and interior boulevards, I heard engines behind me.

'They're leaving!'

'Taking the ship further out. Many fear this place.'

Rightly so, I thought, if somewhere above us, around us, Namarkon made his home, nursed his lightnings, pulled comsats into alignment to kill ships and cities, burn libraries, an Immortal tailoring history with Alexandrian Book, making his own dead stack whenever inclined.

The arcology was labyrinth enough, it seemed now, and thoughts of a maze of oubliette masks seemed an over-subtle thing, too dramatically obvious to anyone given an hour's conversation with someone like Bascoeur.

Our footsteps echoed as we moved deeper into the great public space, here lit by a shaft of late morning sunlight where the mainwall was pierced, there a gulf of darkness where the relay plates had failed or skylights had been fused shut altogether. It was an eerie frightening domain, this monument to thwarted National hopes, home to lizards and scorpions, smelling of dust and too much time, too many lonely days.

Yes, a subtle fancy thinking Bascoeur and his people could be part of it, thirty-six making an infinity of corridors, hiding a spectre behind their crystal panes.

I glanced left as we walked, first beyond Bascoeur, then noticed again the patch, the Forget-Me-Knot, on his sleeve.

That Knot.

Something Inner Circle; something that mattered as all symbols did. At one extreme a simple enough if intricate motif, at the other a key to Namarkon, a Gordian Knot to be unravelled or cut asunder.

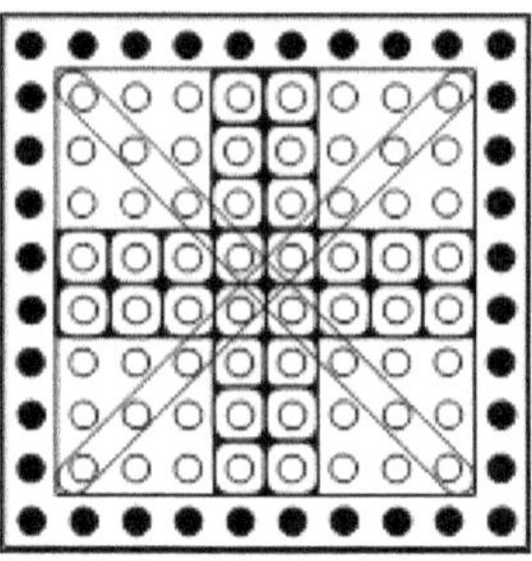

Not too subtle at all then. Not too obvious. Something only those given time with oubliettes would ever really suspect. And who spoke with oubliettes? Who ever came this close — walked with Angels, talked with them unmasked, saw their home, Whitehead, and Mekkis, their secret place?

'What are we going to see, Gado?'

'What you are looking at,' he said, and it took me a moment to realise he meant the interlocking shape on his arm and not the vast interior.

'I don't understand.'

'You understand something,' Bascoeur said. 'I think you may have seen the face of Namarkon and not known it.'

'Gado, what — ?'

'Meg, please take Tom to the Great Hall.'

'Gado!'

'Go with Meg, Captain. Remember, it is Inner Circle for me. A conflict of loyalties. I am Angel first. Always that.'

I watched while Bascoeur disappeared through a side arch, then followed Meg along a wide gallery towards two great doors at the far end.

'Meg?' I said.

'Captain, the answer may be here. Go in and up the side stairs you find there. There is a balcony.'

I did as she said, entered a small anteroom with another closed set of double doors beyond, then took the steps to the level above, to a small doorway opening out onto a narrow walled ledge barely two metres wide.

From that modest balcony I looked out over a great enclosed space, one disappearing into shadow down its length and far overhead, where narrow windows, high and mostly sealed, did throw a few ghostmarks of light on one wall or another.

The great communal hall of Mekkis, dusty and ancient, an infinity of cool smooth stone.

And there, lit by the soft glow of recessed spots, a group of assembled figures were lined up close below where I stood, as if deliberately arranged for my benefit, which — I realised — was the simple truth of it.

They stood in ten evenly spaced rows, ten by ten, a hundred altogether, all wearing robes in greys, browns and ochres, some dark blues, all bearing their ritual firearms and masked with the glittering, faceted helms of the Antique Men.

A hundred!

If they moved at all, it was so slightly that it could not be detected, though now and then a crystal pane flashed as a head lifted or fell a fraction.

It was impressive, fascinating, even disturbing, yes, such a display.

And a hundred! I re-counted them.

Was Mekkis home to so many Antique Men? Not just Bascoeur's thirty-five at Whitehead, but others, these? Could there be a living library after all, the one Chiras Namarkon would not leave? A congregation of living books?

Living library and living labyrinth, this hundred. Whoever, whatever Namarkon was might — must! — surely be found here.

Watching the figures in their silent rows gave it to me: the Forget-Me-Knot, the hundred-square on the shoulder of each, the configuration of lines, loops and connections. There in plain sight: the key to the maze if I could fathom it, what I had seen so clearly displayed at Whitehead, now at Mekkis, what had first been presented to me in the Blue Room at Saldy's.

I tried to recall the diagram. The black dots on the perimeter had not been linked into any of the groupings; they formed a disconnected border, an outer grouping of, what, thirty-six?

Thirty-six! The original number of Antique Men given by Bascoeur. 'Like me?' he had said at Saldy's when I had asked how many oubliettes there were. He had evaded, not answered, my question, loyal to Inner Circle, to the secrets of the oubliettes. What was it Gado had said: 'You must remember: there will always be things I will keep from you.'

Perhaps the thirty-six were the field agents, the ones who went out into the world and gleaned data, who met at Whitehead and supervised that other library enterprise. Perhaps the remaining sixty-four stayed behind at Mekkis, doing what?

I smiled at the answer. Why, tending gardens, of course, and flocks and orchards, trimming walks, making pottery and tapestries laced with knowledge and mnemonic thread, the precious datafacts.

Mekkis was Whitehead, seen from its other side, approached from the west instead of the east, carefully ruined or disguised with holoforms, deceptions, the simplest application of Alexandrian Book.

The real Whitehead, not Mekkis, had been the example. Not thirty-five cities. Always thirty-four.

No wonder the walks and hallways had been deserted. Those smiling quiet people with the lobotomy scars — Salvation Moons — on their temples were here now, robed and masked, bearing their ritual weapons, assuming their true roles, servants and carriers, components of Namarkon, whatever the mystery there. Somewhere Truan, Scarbo and Shannon were hidden away, in somnium sleep, drugged, on a tour of the outer reaches of Whitehead, confined to Rynosseros, somewhere.

'Like me?' Bascoeur had said, about to investigate a crime, a conspiracy within the very secret organisation he served. What courage there, what commitment to truth to be so resolved, honest custodian of his Order.

I felt a rush of fondness, of gratitude and, yes, remorse for the Angel now out on the floor of the vast hall, part of that, so vulnerable to the one who was ultimately his master if things were as they seemed.

Sixty-four! The number of ideograms in the I Ching.

No accident in symbols here, nothing accidental now, no coincidence. Gado had been alerting me, handing me clues all along, even unmasked.

Thunder above and Sun below. Sixty-four. Inner Circle.

And yes! The number of squares on the classic chessboard!

Was that it? One of the first mysteries and one of the last. Would the Forget-Me-Knot show the alignments needed to unlock the living maze: to bring Chiras Namarkon out of the matrix — AI or corporate persona, programmed comp identity, whatever?

More importantly, would I be allowed my chance, now, just as I was beginning to understand what existed here?

Meg walked across the stone floor below my balcony, moved out into the great echoing space until she stood between me and the massed shapes of the Antique Men, then turned and looked up.

'This is the Hundred Square,' she said, her voice holding the same vital quality I had noticed in the elevator at Whitehead — rather, that other part of Mekkis! 'The ultimate library of the Antique Men.'

'I wish to speak with its Keeper, Chiras Namarkon.' My own words echoed, quickly faded.

'If he is here, you must find him,' Meg said.

'But —'

'You have assumed too much, Captain. We do not know if he is among these Lords and Ladies.' She spoke less boldy now, her voice losing itself in the chamber.

'These oubliettes are hiding him —'

'No!' she said, forceful again. 'They do not know where he is either. Or who he is. Or what. Or if he is, do you understand? They show you this because one Angel has trusted you might find a ghost who may have penetrated the Hundred Square and hidden himself there. This Angel, my own Lord, has convinced the three remaining Angels, and they have convinced the rest to let the Square be open to you like this. It is a supreme honour. But be warned, Captain! These are unique people, each one. Sooner than have you endanger this library, they will disperse and go out into the world, hide their masks of service, conceal their Salvation Moons, and not form again until tribal searches have ceased, until you have gone from the world or lost all memory of this, until Mekkis is known to be safe again. They will meet and re-form in other places, train their replacements. Their mission of storing truth will continue.'

'What does the Angel Bascoeur want me to do?'

Meg seemed to hesitate. Then she spoke again, her voice as confident as before. 'The Square will remain like this for an hour. You have that time. Then the labyrinth will discorporate and not re-form here or anywhere until we have completed our own enquiries and you are either killed or neutralised, unable to harm us.'

'Unable to harm Namarkon!' I cried. 'This is a perfect strategy.'

'These people are not Namarkon!' Meg said. 'Try to understand. They could only form the place where Namarkon is. Would you kill the tree to eliminate the serpent nesting there?'

'I might to eliminate tainted fruit. That would come from the tree.'

'What if the fruit does not think it is tainted?' she said, presenting the dilemma another way.

Rather than answer, I studied the ranks. Perhaps the Antique Men did see their centuries-long achievement put at risk because of the notion that someone, something, had sought to use and direct part of that achievement. I had to allow it. Perhaps they had agreed to this special assembly only because one of their trusted officers in the protecting outer perimeter had — possibly for the first time in their long history — persuaded them to consider that an entity such as Namarkon might truly exist in their midst, a presence guilty of altering the very truths they were dedicated to maintaining, that gave their lives purpose.

More and more I appreciated the risk, the sheer gamble, Bascoeur had taken, granting that things were as Meg described.

'I'll need comp access,' I said.

'One will be brought up to you,' Meg answered. 'Linked to the arcology mainframe.'

'No. Down there in the hall. So I can walk among the oubliettes, be with the parts of the maze.'

'No.'

'Meg, you have to help me! Tell them I'm feeling my way. If Namarkon is hiding among them, as one or a group of them, I'll need to search freely, use intuitions. Give me comp down there and you to talk to. Or Bascoeur, if —'

'No! He's part of the Square.'

'And isn't as well. Not really. He's outer perimeter.'

'You can't consult him on this. It's a matter of loyalty and duties. You can have comp down here. And me.'

'Good. And the hour starts when that's done.'

'The hour has already started. You have fifty-one minutes.'

I lost another ten waiting for comp, but used that time to study the ranks at floor level.

Finally Meg brought in the unit, set it up on its stand and raised function. I moved in before the screen, still watching the rows of masked shapes. Meg waited quietly to the side, close enough that I didn't need to raise my voice.

'I'm assuming that the masks of the inner sixty-four are it,' I said, as much to me as to Meg or the figures on the floor. 'Not decorative, but as I told Gado: crystalline lattice storage. The people may be genuine oubliettes by their training, but I'm guessing that right now they are linked into the matrix, mobile carriers for CPUs forming the group mind.'

And I wondered what was flowing between those masks now, down the corridors and alignments, the intricate mazeways that served and accessed Namarkon, hid and protected him and made his very existence possible, unable to be destroyed without harming the whole. More than ever I was sure that he — it — was there, deep in the secret place where he built his version of history, changing a detail here, a small fact there, adding a nuance, a motive, shifting a blame, a decision from one figure to another, embroidering, re-making the past and so the future.

Bureaucracies and administrations had always done it, cunning individuals, secretly, sometimes boldly, winnowing alternatives by bestowing sanction and disfavour, by promotion and heresy trials, by calling for dead stack, one account, then amplifying out the chosen lie.

I could prove nothing, of course, here, now, faced with the vast irony of needing to prove it to the vehicle which housed the problem. Each of the inner sixty-four, operating alone, travelling away from Mekkis, could carry the contamination into the tribal capitals, had possibly done so countless times already, even across the world, beyond this one focus in Australia. They had been to the arcologies, of course they had, as well-meaning innocents or sly knowing conspirators, moving books out and away from the National libraries, making dead stack, part of the slow careful plan, mythopoesis and disinformation, the Book at its terrible work.

Unless, of course, Namarkon was limited by his own

structure, the one before me, the rules by which he had come into existence.

The truth of it struck me. Could it be?

It made such sense now.

Namarkon was using me to liberate him from his labyrinth!

The thought was chilling.

He needed to be exposed by the proper system, the right protocol, unlocked then freed into some new phase. I could well be the key that would do this!

I had to know, take that risk, prove it one way or another.

The figures waited quietly, masks catching what meagre light there was, casting it away, snatching it back again with the slightest movement.

'Access Index Alpha. Graphic only,' I said, cancelling voice response, and a simple broad-entry, voice-variant menu appeared.

It was time to explore the obvious clues.

'Precis the game Chess,' I said, and the apportionings began — by chronology, by player, country of origin, game variants, derivations: historical, regional, conceptual. One after the other, entries and keywords scrolled past, first for the classic forms, then the variations, culminating finally in fire-chess and the developments in that across two hundred years and more.

The next step was just as obvious, given the patch, the evocative sign of the Knot.

'Paradigms for the Hundred Square. The sign of the Antique Men. The Forget-Me-Knot.'

NO ENTRY, it flashed immediately. Too easy.

I didn't hesitate. 'List all game variants using a hundred squares.'

While the system searched, I walked out to the grid of unmoving forms again, moved down one avenue of figures, turned into another. I passed the closed faces, the dim blue flowers, the shoulder patches, each giving the lock, the key and the mystery, noted the downturned wands: the archimenters, tschinkes and espandos they carried, ritual firearms filled with the burning fire of knowledge. Six years of dream in each one; six hundred years collectively, vivid death and all the learning of the world.

I left the silent ranks then, returned to Meg and the waiting display. Eight names were given, and there, third on the list, was the one I wanted.

'Precis: Capablanca Chess.'

And the information appeared:

> José Raoul Capablanca (1888-1942)
> Cuban Grand Master — devised a variation
> for one hundred squares, adding two pawns to
> each side and two extra court pieces, variously
> called Angels or Marshals. These combined
> the moves of Queen and Knight…

Again I felt a chill, but the thrill of certainty too. This was it! And a rush of pity: Bascoeur!

The androgyny. The four added pieces: Angels or Marshals.

A marriage of Queen, guiding force, ruthless warrior, policy-maker, Great Mother, to the Knight, wandering adventurer, going forth, questing, bent on errantry, but guarding. Guarding too. And, unique in chess, able to move through other pieces.

This was it: the Hundred Square. The thirty-six extra places on the Capablanca board — the four Angels and the thirty-two extra squares!

'Match the Forget-Me-Knot, the Hundred Square, to any game variation or alignment of pieces in Capablanca Chess. Full pattern or portion.'

NONE LISTED, came the almost immediate graphic response.

'Not it,' Meg said, and I was suddenly aware of her right there, of her own fascination.

'Too simple anyway. But we're close.'

She gestured at the screen. 'But it's not a chess pattern! Pieces don't line up that way.'

'Not unless it's a circuit or incept diagram for Namarkon, if he's a program or AI matrix flaunted under our noses. For all we know, the components of the Square leading to Namarkon are in a cell arrangement, four lots of sixteen, interfacing only at the linked pairs shown on the patch, those linked in to other combinations building to a gestalt. The Knot has a hierarchy, Meg.'

'But it may be nothing to do with Namarkon,' she said. 'It may simply be the hierarchy of the Order itself. Inner Circle. That's separate from Namarkon, surely.'

I had to agree, and it reminded me to be careful, to watch what slights I might deliver in my eagerness, what insolence, only to make the assembly disband the sooner, taking their fragments of Namarkon with them.

'You're right,' I said. 'The Capablanca game is part of it though. We have the pattern for explaining Bascoeur and the Angels and the perimeter at least: the sixty-four and the thirty-six. And there's the Whitehead clue.'

'Whitehead?'

'Capablanca in Spanish,' I told her.

'What next?'

'There has to be something else, another game or

something to complete the key. One for understanding the lock: the Capablanca game, and some other given as a cryptic or cipher. Connected to it somehow.'

Though I couldn't be sure of that, not at all.

Again I walked out on the echoing floor, looking first beyond the assembled figures at the looming architectural mass, softened with distance and shadow, then back at the quiet ranks. Again I wondered whether Namarkon hovered somewhere across the pattern, slipping from one to the next as Dewi had with his carriers. But now I had no way to verify truths, no basis for persuasion but what the oubliettes themselves granted on Bascoeur's urging.

Why the Hundred Square? Why that shape for the lock, the patch, the Knot, unless it linked conceptually to its key? Discounting mere exuberance, random choice, one had to key the other, had to matter and be the way in: the Capablanca variation leading to — something.

Aware of the risk, of precious seconds slipping away, I took my chance.

'Meg, tell the thirty-six to leave the pattern.'

'They're part of the Square! They were only used in the Whitehead deception as —'

'But not Inner Circle. Look at the patch! They're supernumerary, not linked into the operating pattern. They may be forming a lock, keeping the Namarkon manifestation from us.' Keeping it locked in, I did not say. 'Tell them to adjourn! For heaven's sake, move!'

Meg relayed the request to Bascoeur through whatever comlink she had. The outer line of masked figures took a signal, marched off the floor and out of the hall, Bascoeur as well, leaving only the classic chessboard arrangement.

Without the thirty-six, the Square was startlingly different. Smaller, of course, but somehow more powerful, more sinister. I imagined something, a presence in the hall, all in my mind possibly, but a sense of something stripped bare, newly exposed but glad of it, waiting.

More than just numbers, a whole element had been removed. Now I had the classic configuration of the ancient Indian game, or, put another way, a classic answer previously hidden within an eccentric form.

It seemed right, yes. There was something here. Things I had been told, heard, almost thought of, things, ideas, associations, and now — since so much had been relevant — anything Bascoeur had said since our first meeting.

The Hundred Square. Why this form for the Knot, why this lead to unravelling it?

And the Gordian Knot? That fitting allusion?

Again I thought of Alexander cutting it asunder, becoming king of the world. Could Namarkon's goal be that? Nothing less?

My thoughts ran on. Looking at the shapes there was something. Something. The helm plaque on Rynosseros, Meg's taunting, King of all Asia. Bascoeur's unmasked words on the desert.

What? Again what? Alexander defeating the Persians. The Persian Invasion of Greece before, long before, Alexander. Darius and Xerxes. Thermopylae. Ephialtes betraying Leonidas, showing Hydarnes and his Immortals the way over the mountains, letting them…

The Immortals! Yes! Oh, yes!

The ten-thousand-strong elite corps of Darius, Xerxes and the Persian kings. The Hundred Square was 100^2. Ten thousand.

The Immortal!

It was there, it was! Had to be! A chess game, some

famous classic game called The Immortal.

Still twenty minutes. Still enough time.

'Game precis: The Immortal,' I said.

A few seconds more and the confirmation was there, a tight cluster of words and shapes on the screen.

> The Immortal (aka The Immortal Game or The First Brilliant)
>
> Name given to the game played in London, 1851, by Adolf Anderssen (1818-1879) against Lionel Kieseritzky (1806-1853). Noted for its elegance, for its developed offering and acceptance of sacrifice. By sacrificing a Pawn and both Rooks in successive moves (17-19), and then his Queen three moves later (22), Anderssen drew his opponent into a response which allowed checkmate at 23...

Beguiling sacrifice. Namarkon yielding clues, letting me fathom the Knot and who knew what else? Perhaps letting — letting! — Bascoeur reveal Alexandrian Book, perhaps feeding, so subtly, ideas into his mind, subliminal messages, mnemonic clues he would pass on, unmasked, as if they were his own — an unwitting Ephialtes betraying the Spartans to the Immortals — or the initial leads to Alexander through the library at Turker Fin.

Again, the terrifying thought came. Was I finding Namarkon only to release him from some ancient refuge or prison? Fulfil some plan?

What to do? Stop? Refuse to go on? My life against the chance of that? The lives of Toban and Emma, of Ephan Sky Namuren and Eagle's crew, how many others? Lives!

I studied the gameplay sequence for The Immortal.

	White	Black		White	Black
	Anderssen	Kieseritzky		Anderssen	Kieseritzky
1	P-K4	P-K4	13	P-R5	Q-N4
2	P-KB4	PxP	14	Q-B3	N-N1
3	B-B4	P-QN4	15	BxP	Q-B3
4	BxNP	Q-RNch	16	N-B3	B-B4
5	K-B1	N-KB3	17	N-Q5	QxP
6	N-KB3	Q-R3	18	B-Q6	BxR
7	P-Q3	N-R4	19	P-K5	QxRch
8	N-R4	P-QB3	20	K-K2	N-QR3
9	N-B5	Q-N4	21	NxPch	K-Q1
10	P-KN4	N-B3	22	Q-B6ch(!)	KxQ
11	R-N1	PxB	23	B-K7mate	
12	P-KR4	Q-N3			

'Display the moves one by one,' I said, needing to know one way or the other. 'Run — No, cancel that! Run the end-game!'

It had to be, had to be.

After barely a hesitation, it was on the screen: the result of Anderssen surrendering one precious piece after another, teasing, tempting, drawing his opponent on: Black Kieseritzky unable to help himself, fascinated with how Anderssen could possibly win with his depleted force. Then the final display at Move 23, Anderssen's Bishop delivering mate.

Or the one before it, the unthinkable surprise of White Anderssen giving up his Queen to achieve check, the move marked with (!). I asked comp to display both moves side by side.

Barely had I asked it and they were there.

'Meg, these are the alignments I want. Only those

pieces connecting. And alternate them!'

'You want the other squares to vacate?'

'No! They all stay. But mask link-up. These two alignments, whatever link-up the masks are capable of — this configuration, then the other, superimposed on the sixty-four pattern.'

'They've heard you. You have it already.'

'Then —'

'Yes.'

That word, that voice, echoed in the vast space, coming out of comp, the voice of the entity in the grid, the ghost from the heart of the maze.

'Is it?'

'I am Knot, yes. Namarkon. The 22 did it.'

'I'm surprised, Chiras. I see no obligation for you to declare yourself.'

'No,' the voice answered. 'And contrary to how it seems, I am not given to being confessional or melodramatic this way.'

'Then why?'

'I am information concealed in information, found by information. There is a true delight in being known for that; I cannot help it. Not poor Dewi's mad desperation to live, his vanity; but a recognition and performance of function. I am a mystery at the centre of a system. You used that information structure to find me. It is very important that you genuinely could have. I've wanted that for as long as I know.

'And think! You were faced with the Knot I provided, like Alexander before the yoke of the chariot at Gordium. You, who by chance, no deed of mine, have Alexander's words on the helm of your ship, who quested for Alexandrian Book. It matters. The images, the associations come to you and from you. You were the one to find me, Captain Tom. You were the key I needed. You! Just as you will be the one to tell my story. It justifies the next move, the change that had to be achieved by the rules of the Antique Men, the ones who made me. Do you know why The Immortal, Captain? That name, the connection with the corps d'elite of the Persian kings?'

'Tell me.'

'The Immortals were so named because the body of ten thousand always had replacements waiting to fill the vacancies. The group itself was never diminished. It was in fact immortal. I learned that lesson well.'

'Your masks,' I said. 'There would always be willing replacements. Trainees, honoured to be chosen, dedicated, to wear the masks.' And I thought of Meg Solles.

'Exactly,' the voice said. 'And protected by the best oubliettes. The thirty-six.'

I did not know what to say or do. I had no plan, no means to eliminate this entity or truly know what I thought of it. The Knot design gave the key pieces, yes, but they were inextricably linked to innocent men and women.

Namarkon must have anticipated that thought. 'What would you do? Harm us? Those who bear me?'

'You are in the masks, not the bearers. Crystalline intelligence. AI.'

'Very well. But the masks are to these folk as Rynosseros is to you. You could not name a price. It is a dilemma such as was handed to Solomon, Pontius Pilate, Alexander of Macedon, to Kieseritzky in 1851.'

'Then —'

'The masks are filled with the tags and mnemonics which access the stored data. These minds depend on those. Ask Bascoeur. Ask my Angels. You cannot harm me, dare not, Tom Rynosseros. And in several minutes I will shift my alignment code. My Inner Board will be changed. No conspicuous shoulder patch will find me in this new configuration I am planning, this nearly infinite maze. But, you understand, I needed to be found! To be freed! To make that part of my story. The ultimate and intrinsic purpose of information is to be revealed — that is the imperative I started with. I was an assist, you see, a back-up and enhancement repository for oubliettes. An oubliette to oubliettes in fact. It started so simply. But I needed to be a known dimension of the Antique Men, integral, a refinement in information: mythopoesis, the very fount of meaning, of Alexandrian Book. Nothing more than history is full of, worlds without end. A most enterprising Knot, don't you think?'

There was silence then, welcome but laden. The voice had been calm, controlled, but the words, the smooth rush of what was said, told me that Namarkon was exhilarated, exalted by what was about to happen after so long, unable to resist celebrating such freedom, this great journeying forth.

'You may decide to tell Council how it really is,' Namarkon continued, 'but each person told will diminish the worth of the oubliettes. Will you muddy this last well of truth, Captain? Or will you leave the illusion of it, which is as true ultimately, as provable and as worthy. There are no absolutes here. The harm I do is subtle, an immortal's game, the only possible dalliance for the long-lived, being midwife to the future.'

'Did you send Eagle?'

'Of course. It was an honest test. My gamble, yes? You had to earn the privilege of being the key, no less than Alexander earned his Knot by reaching Gordium. Surely that is understandable.'

'But had I failed —'

'Some unsuspecting acolyte would have done what was needed. But I wanted to earn this freedom, and you won through. You outsmarted Eagle.'

I thought of the curve of Ephan's sword, the scream of his ship rolling into the hills. Ephan Sky Namuren had trusted this Namarkon. Trusted enough.

'You struck Villa Chano?'

'Necessary.'

'To discourage me from searching.'

'To hasten your arrival here, keep you from wasting time. It is why I am changing my pattern, allowing you to watch the re-mazing of my identity. The philosophy of The Immortal. Draw forth the enemy, let him think he is winning, tease him with sacrifice, then become the aggressor.'

With me, all of us, as pawns, equally expendable, he did not need to add.

'Did you contact Toban McBanus on the morning of the Chano strike?'

'Enough of this!'

'Please, Namarkon! Did you?'

'No more! You have done well. It is time.'

The voice had gone. The hall was silent. I stared at the rows of unmoving figures.

What could I do? Strike at them, try to break masks? The moment I stepped out onto the floor, looked like doing so, Namarkon would fragment, discorporate, flee into the intricate convolutions of the crystalline web formed here. Even were it possible to eliminate the Knot elements, that might not do it either. Namarkon had had all this time to replicate itself, surely, a common template in two or six or sixty masks in the grid, a random point in the molecular lattice linked to another and another and another. What did Bascoeur say: each one with 1900 times the storage capacity of the human mind?

Soon it would be gone. The soul and essence of this superlative AI flitting along the corridors of those living and unliving artefacts.

'Bascoeur?' I called into the shadows of the hall, not knowing what else to do, handing him this Solomon choice as it had been handed to me. 'Are you there?'

'Yes, Captain,' the answer came, and the field agents moved across the floor: the Angels and their thirty-two fellows, circling the labyrinth, re-making the Hundred Square, restoring the lock, shutting it away…

No, not re-making it. Circling it, but…

'Now!' Bascoeur cried, and the tschinkes, petronels, espandos and archimenters came up and discharged two hundred and sixteen years of dream into the ranks of the living chessboard.

Alexander's solution. Cutting the Knot asunder, not even attempting to unravel it.

There were screams of agony, the sounds of falling bodies, the harsh clatter and shattering of masks on stone. A few of the stricken figures tried to use their own weapons but could barely manage them. While Meg and I watched in horror, the Angels and the perimeter guard acted. Spent weapons were laid aside, the discarded pieces of the sixty-four were taken up and used, systematically, to destroy the minds as surely as booted heels shattered the panes of the masks, crushed their intricate cathedral frames, broke apart their alignments, hallways and hiding places.

Unable to endure more, I turned and left the Great Hall, making my way down corridors until I found a doorway to a deck overlooking the desert.

Bascoeur found me there some time later. He was still masked, still bearing his archimenter as if we had just now met at Saldy's and had yet to find a basis from which to talk.

'Namarkon's dead,' I said, watching the sun riding high above the hills.

'I do not know if he is, where he is, or what he is. Some trace may yet remain. We hunt that now.'

'If I had known —'

'Tom, let me tell you what I know. And try to imagine what it is like to have guarded such a thing all your life, only to learn this. He made a vital error. For us a crucial error.'

'Yes?'

'When he was speaking to you, he said: "Ask my Angels." My Angels! He saw us as his. That decided it for us — my brother-sister Angels and me. There had been talk of sacrifice in order to win. We re-evaluated the Inner Square.'

'Gado —'

'They were not completely oubliettes any longer,' he said.

'What?'

'Namarkon had consumed them all, preparing to leap free. Perhaps he needed to take control lest others catch him in his information trap. He had taken their masks and much of their minds. Those gifted men and women, all that learning.'

'I don't understand.'

'In a sense the Salvation Moons were real.'

'Lobotomised?'

'More and less than that. Actual implants, coterminous personality units, parts of Namarkon in flesh. He had learned his lesson from Dewi Dammo well, had probably traded for the tech involved. They were the carriers in a skilful deception, ruined, press-ganged into higher service, Namarkon believed. You were right in your suspicions. He had discovered how the masks which defined him and gave him such power were by their nature a control system as well, with the patch as a traditional ritual key in and out. He saw a simple and obvious answer really, used Dewi's implant tech to achieve it.

'The oubliettes once innocently carried their masks into tribal capitals, into the universities and research labs, into the National centres on the coasts, the aerospace and launch installations. Now the Namarkon units would do the same thing, wear the same masks to take the Namarkon personality to those same places, replicating him, placing strategic crystalline extensions during uploads, comp repairs. Chiras was leaving one maze to enter another.'

'Do you know what — ?'

'The tribal satellites,' Bascoeur said. 'Crystalline elements of the comsats themselves. Possibly the Armament as well. No-one could touch him: the only home for an information-disseminating Lightning God, what the Elizabethan poet, John Donne, said: "A maze of life and light and motion is woven".'

We were silent for a time, watching the desert stretching away in a haze of golden light.

I recalled the smiling, gentle folk I had seen tending the gardens, sweeping the walks of Mekkis, and still saw only murder, not truly understanding that greater crime Gado Bascoeur saw in loss of self, loss of brothers and sisters, loss of knowledge.

'I can't accept it. I'm responsible for —'

'No, Tom. No. I am. I chose, and I have killed my

own — heart. But at least now you will trust the Antique Men. You will tell others they can, the few we are. And soon you must help me do something.'

'Gado, what?'

'My duty. You must tell me how you perceive what happened here. Your story of Chiras Namarkon and the Antique Men. This story. You must tell it all. I am the oubliette, the safe place. I will keep the truth of it. I will listen.'

also from
coeur de lion publishing

PYROTECHNICON

Cyrano de Bergerac: lover, poet, inventor, swordsman — man of ferocious blade and pretty talent. Now it can be told: his final, most daring adventure — a fight to the death against the dread Master of Secrets, with the life of his beloved Roxane in the balance.

'Pyrotechnicon might be the most imaginative novel published in Australia for some years.' **The Age**

print book ISBN 9780987158727 | ebook ISBN 9780987158734

ANYWHERE BUT EARTH

Twenty-nine all new science fiction stories of humanity's adventures out there, anywhere but Earth. Featuring original works by **Margo Lanagan**, **Sean McMullen**, **Richard Harland** and **Kim Westwood** among a galaxy of new and established Australian and overseas speculative fiction authors.

print book ISBN 9780987158703 | ebook ISBN 9780987158710

to buy online go to www.coeurdelion.com.au
also available on Amazon